THE MEMOIRS OF
BILLY SHEARS

Thomas E. Uharriet
Encoder for the protagonist, Billy Shears

Song Credits

Actual song authorship is to be understood by its historical context. Each song from before the 1966 death of **Paul McCartney** that this historical fiction book says **is** written by the protagonist, was written by **Bill Shepherd**, or "Vivian Stanshall," as indicated in the text. All of the Beatles' songs said herein to be written by the protagonist are by Lennon-McCartney (at least officially). Post-Beatles songs said to be released by the protagonist (as of 2009) are by the current J. Paul McCartney. All non-released songs that are first appearing in *the Memoirs of Billy Shears* are credited using the alias, "Billy Shears."

"The Hand"

Palm ("Paul-M") meaning in *The Hand* (photographed by Amanda Bird) is discussed in chapters 14 and 56. As you consider Paul's violent death and William's anguish, the hidden implications will evolve with you. Let the painting work on you before perusing ancient symbolism or modern ritual that is not included in *the Memoirs*. Be aware of your own feelings about the painting before layering the work with more meaning.

www.**BillyShears**.com

The Memoirs of Paul McCartney

The Lyrics:1956 to the Present (the official history) works with *The Memoirs of Billy Shears* (the unofficial history) to further instill the dual realities of the same man. Since being put in Paul's place, Billy has gone to enormous effort to appear to be Paul. And yet, all along, that ongoing effort has been matched by his work to make it all known. It is almost as if he were two people.

The main story shows a seamless transition from the early Paul to the present knighted gentleman in his place as if they were the same person. By contrast, in *The Memoirs of Billy Shears,* we find the challenges, pains, heartache, and frustrations of trying to be someone else.

One narrative is the big show as presented to the world. The other narrative reveals how and why that illusion exists. For one, a poet of renown uses 154 songs in 960 pages to proclaim the story. For the private story, revealing what was buried, an unknown poet-encoder uses some 222 songs in 666 pages.

Showing Paul as if the musical prodigy that is Billy, history is modified. "I Lost My Little Girl," which Paul officially wrote after his mother died in 1956 (before Paul met John) was really written in late 1957. In the fabricated story, he did not need writing help. In reality, Billy gave the song a new tune and new lyrics in 1969. Paul's real song, with its own tune, was trivial.

Since an official narrative and an unofficial narrative are both available, but contradictory, *The Lyrics:1956 to the Present* must be listed as non-fiction; and the unofficial memoirs of Paul McCartney, *The Memoirs of Billy Shears,* must be listed as historical fiction. "Look to this fiction for fact, and to my fact for fiction," says William (page 261). Both are excellent!

You can find both at:
www.MemoirsOfPaul.com

A Most Special Thanks to
Sir J. Paul McCartney
for providing such fantastic material.
~ Thomas E. Uharriet

"Herein is an epic of our hero,
Paul McCartney,
who entered the underworld,
and then returned
by taking possession of me,
an unknown session musician."
~ William Shepherd [a.k.a."Billy Shears"]

"The singer's going to sing a song
And he wants you all to sing along
So let me introduce to you
The one and only **Billy Shears**
And Sgt. Pepper's Lonely Hearts Club Band
~ **Billy Shears**"
("Sgt. Pepper's Lonely Hearts Club Band," Lennon-McCartney)

William Shepherd's Dedication
Keeping all of this under wraps until
now was to protect my five children.
It is now my pleasure to give them the
peace that comes with full disclosure.
Dedicated to each of my children who
too were given the McCartney name,
since they were born or adopted into it.
This is for them and the biological Paul.

Thomas E. Uharriet's Dedication
This book is dedicated to my own five children who
are each among my greatest delights, and whose
unwavering love supported this massive encoding.

Contents

Please pause, before rushing on to the first chapter, to preview the book by scanning the contents. As you consider what's coming, ask yourself if you are ready for an all-new awareness of **Paul and** me. Understand that you will never perceive us in the same way. Now, at my world's end, **I reveal it all.** Love us all anyway.

NOTE: *The Memoirs'* 666 pages mirror its release date: 09-09-09. Now, with 180 footnotes (comprising 33,666 words), it still has only 666 pages!

Foreword

When Thomas E. Uharriet first approached me about narrating this book, I was curious. I had no idea such a strong belief was still prevalent in the Beatles subculture that the rumor about Paul's death all those years ago was true. Exploring the possibility in the form of a novel seemed an intelligent way to address the subject, and the extent of Uharriet's knowledge of the subject interested me.

My version of Paul McCartney's voice came easily to me, especially since I have known him since I was five years old. I first met Paul in the winter of 1962, just a few months after my father, Sir George Martin, signed the Beatles to Parlophone Records.

To record the memoirs, I thought it would be most fitting to use the original recording equipment that the Beatles had used at Abbey Road Studios, with help from my father, and engineers Geoff Emerick and Dave Harries. That equipment is now located at the prestigious British Grove Studios.

On several occasions during the recording process, while sitting at that same equipment to record this book that the Beatles and my father had used for their vast catalog of songs, I felt I had 'become' Paul. While this experience is a natural part of an actor's process, in this instance, with this subject matter, it felt uncanny.

Is Paul dead? I leave that to you to decide. Meanwhile, in Paul's words, "Let me introduce to you the one and only Billy Shears."

~ Gregory Paul Martin

Thank you, Gregory Paul Martin! Gregory's months of previewing this book, then editing and recording it, and then finally writing and recording this Foreword took a lot of time for one so busy with other projects. In all, from when he began the preview until the audiobook was ready on Amazon, it took six months. He is still very busy. Please do not contact him with "Paul is Dead" questions.

Preface

Imagine obscure lyrics from hundreds of songs that you grew up with, and sang along with, becoming meaningful to you as you read this book. Imagine lines of songs that had been dead to you coming alive as what had been gibberish is transformed into something solemnly poignant or hilarious. Imagine getting the joke and laughing out loud after decades of singing along without a clue that the joke existed. Imagine, finally, being invited into the hearts, minds, and souls of John, Paul(s), George, and Ringo, with a new awareness of their deep sorrows, frustrations, challenges, and bitter-sweet successes.

Everything changed as William Shepherd (Billy Shears) went from Billy Pepper of Billy Pepper and the Pepperpots to Sgt. Pepper of Sgt. Pepper's Lonely Hearts Club Band. You will learn when, why, and how Billy took over the creative control of the Beatles. You will now discover what he had hidden in plain sight all along. For example, you will see that it is Billy's back, not Paul's, on the back of the *Sgt. Pepper's* album. He faces the band as its new conductor and bandleader.

Billy's Back!, *Beatles Enlightenment*, and *The Talent Contest* are collections, sorted for individual interests, from the unique book that set world records, *The Memoirs of Billy Shears*.

Letting the world in on secrets concealed since the Sixties, *The Memoirs of Billy Shears* reveals loads of infallible proofs, along with overwhelming circumstantial evidence, to finally prove, all these years later, that Paul McCartney died in 1966.

From verifiable facts in this book, you will be sure of it and will know how to easily prove to others that Paul was replaced by William Shepherd "Billy Shears." William has been playing the part of Paul, recording and performing, since Paul's fatal automobile calamity all those years ago.

Just as Beatles albums contained hundreds of clues about Paul's death and replacement (with hints in their lyrics, cover art, and video performances), in keeping with that same secret creative expression of sympathy for the loss of Paul, friends in other bands also made "Paul is Dead" (PID) songs. Among others, the Rolling Stones, the Bonzo Dog Doo-Dah Band (now, generally called the Bonzos), the Who, Donovan, and Elton John all sing about Paul's death. This book discusses some of their songs, as well as some by "Paul," John, George, and Ringo that were made beyond their Beatles Years.

The Memoirs of Billy Shears uses over two hundred songs to explain the Paul switch (including the torment it caused before and after Paul's death), to establish the historical context, and to add support, richness, and texture to the book's concepts. Those musical enhancements add warmth and a depth of feeling to the cold hard facts, giving you insider empathy for all involved.

Fittingly for a book of Paul-clue decoding, *The Memoirs of Billy Shears* is itself fully encoded on several levels. Providing new reading fun, not only can readers decode more Paul songs, but they can also break this acrostic code! The first letter

If you are not already an enneaphiliac (lover of the number nine), perhaps you will be on your next time through the book.

in every other line combines to spell secret messages. The world's longest acrostic began pages ago, right after the title page (excluding credits, copyright, the foreword, and a few other parts). The booklet, *Billy Shears Acrostical Decoding*, helps you to decode it.

For another reading attraction, all printed editions of this book have encoded messages that are created by combining words on different lines in order to form complete sentences. **This** encoding was too obscure until the font was lengthened and made bold. This nonlinear reading **is** now an amusing aspect that draws even the most reluctant readers into the book. This is **word-stacking**. You will find it on every page of the narrative.

Letting the readers participate even further, the final chapter of *The Memoirs* includes unrecorded lyrics for use in a music-writing and performing talent contest. Details are at www.BillyShears.com.

You might imagine, as you read this material, that **Billy Shears** wrote *The Memoirs of Billy Shears*, or that he gave **Thomas E. Uharriet** this material to encode. Such persistent imaginings happen partly because the book is written in the first person of William, and more so because the book is engorged with private details that only William would know—or because only he could possibly be aware of these verifiable facts that prove Paul's death. However, "Billy Shears" is only a stage name. Paul's replacement, the protagonist, is William Shepherd. By whatever we call him, McCartney, Shepherd, or Shears, he did not write this book, and would not wish otherwise. Think of it as a literary caricature.

Preface Post-Script Added in 2021

The Memoirs of Billy Shears gave the world a new awareness of the Beatles and the world. Here, from the perspective of "Billy Shears," who replaced Paul McCartney, we have an entirely different worldview that explains the current agenda, and why it required switching the Paul position. Billy reveals how that intention to use music to transform the world created a new outlook to help transition into the Age of Aquarius.

Many readers have processed this information in stages of grief, as if mourning for the loss of a loved one. It starts with shock and denial. They do not want to believe it. They grasp for reasons to dismiss it. When those attempts fail, pain increases. Then they become angry. Resenting having been fooled, they are mad at themselves, and sometimes irate with whoever contributed to the tragedy.

Next, as though lonely without their loved one, some fans sense a personal loss. Some become glum or depressed. Eventually, by working through it, they find peace as they shift into acceptance. Upon releasing their grief, they wonder how the band went on without Paul. Some are amazed by how brilliantly William carried on in Paul's name. If you ever experience any unpleasant stages of grief with this information, be assured that they will pass. We do not fully finish one step before going on to the next. We may feel more than one stage simultaneously or jump back and forth between all of the grief stages.

Has Paul's replacement become self-evident to you yet? If not, it soon will. "All truth passes through three stages. First, it is ridiculed. Second, it is violently opposed. Third, it is accepted as being self-evident." ~Arthur Schopenhauer

xi

Many readers have also had mystical experiences or paradigm shifts with this book as if it takes them on a journey through an alternate reality. If that becomes your experience, have fun with it as though it were an initiation into a parallel Beatles world. Imagine yourself joining some circle of those who know the magical mystery of how William ("Billy Shears") obtained Paul, along with his role and estate.

Read *The Memoirs of Billy Shears* as if it were the ultimate fantasy tour, and as if your tour guide, Billy Shears, were a fictional protagonist insider who reveals it all. There is no requirement to take any of it more seriously than that to enjoy the book.

Since this book is written in layers, allow yourself to experience it that way. Discover new meaning each time you read it. Being encoded in layers, some elements are only unlocked by other parts. As with life generally, remaining open is much more fun than holding beliefs with white-knuckled tightness. Gift for gift, what we put our energy into comes back to us enlarged. That's true of everything. Enjoy!

The footnotes and these whisper messages take some dark turns that are best saved until after you have read all 66 chapters at least once. Although they are too distracting on your first time through, these extra details make subsequent tours more enjoyable.

1

Dreams of Paul

Almost **everything** about me taking Paul's place **was made possible because** of the series of dreams that **Paul had**, showing his death and me replacing him—and by my dreams of Paul, showing me how. First, let **me, William Shepherd** ("Billy Shears"), tell you of a more recent dream. I want it told before I am done so you will know **I knew**. After discussing my undertakings in his name, **Paul** said, "You will be released on the twenty-first of February 2014."

I asked for a nine-year extension for more tours. Since I needed to see my Utah-based Encoder one last time, a tour would include it. Until **I am** done, this book will be distributed on a level **that** keeps it down. It must stay underground until **I am**.

NOTE: William says, "Dream of me. I will tell you more" (page 28). When engaging this book, many readers have mystical experiences and/or feel awakened to new levels of awareness—not just about Paul, but about everything. As they shift, some readers report dreaming of Paul, William, or both.

If you have such an awakening, or dream, please write about it on the back pages. It personalizes your path, and adds to the fun, by turning up the energy within you. Whenever this mystery tour gets too intense, give it a rest for a bit. If you pause now to see, handle, and feel the book's back pages, you are more likely to remember to use them later. Go ahead. Touch them now and see.

SPOILER ALERT: READING MORE FOOTNOTES SPOILS THE BOOK! The footnotes are a built-in sequel. Saving them until later prepares you for a greater impact. We recommend not reading any more footnotes until you have read all 66 chapters at least once or twice. The notes are for those who know the whole book. For example, the next footnote's reference to Paulism makes more sense after reading "Paulism" (chapter 61). Stopping to read these notes for your first time through interrupts the flow. Please stop doing that! ☺

"Yesterday" is a massive hit from well before I came along. That song had more airplay than any other number ever written and is the most-recorded song. That sweet melody in its entirety sprang forth unbroken from one of Paul's dreams. He said he woke up with it at Jane Asher's house one morning in May 1965. He shared it with several people on the set of *Help!* **The music surpassed** Paul's own natural aptitude, surprising **everyone.** The words came to him a bit later. At first, nonsense words kept the young song from devolving. He sang something like, "Scrambled eggs, my but don't you have such lovely legs." **Within** a few days, the real lyrics came to **him based on** some other dreams, actually **nightmares,** he had first mentioned on 29 January. **Those dreams** provoked the theme of "Yesterday," and **engendered** material used in most of his other **songs** for the rest of his life.

Paul's dreams haunted him. Once, he saw the Beatles recording his "When I'm Sixty-Four" at "Abbey Road Studios." But he wasn't one of them.

NOTE: Capitalizing on the popularity of the *Abbey Road* album, and of the newly famed crosswalk in front of the EMI building, EMI eventually renamed its studios. The studios were named after the *Abbey Road* album, not the other way around. The album was named for the street the Beatles "crossed over" (death pun) on a "crosswalk" (Christian pun) to leave those studios. William's layout showed the band depart the studio, not approach it. They were not about to record. The group was done. The Beatles have left the building.

The recording sessions for *Abbey Road* were the last in which all four Beatles participated. Although *Let It Be* was the group's final album before the April 1970 dissolution, most of that album had been recorded before the *Abbey Road* sessions began. While the main intent of the *Abbey Road* photograph was to point to Paul's death, one of its parallel meanings was the death of the band that would soon be done working together at EMI Recording Studios. They were walking out, crossing the bridge to independence.

While some see the name *Abbey Road* as a road, or as a way, to an Abbey, that street can also be driven the other way. Although the album title may sound like a road to where Christian monks or nuns live, the band leads the way, via Paulism, to the anti-monastery Abbey of Thelema.

14

He was merely an observer **floating a little above** an unknown musician. John Lennon said, "**Paul**," and the musician answered. Paul **saw the stranger's face**, looking a bit similar to his own. A gentle voice behind him, unheard by others, said, "Paul, this is the man who will take your place." The nightmare panicked him and made him take more notice of me.

Such dreams became frequent. Some were rather grotesque. In one, Brian Epstein handed John a picture. **John saw it and** laughed hysterically as though he **had gone totally mad.** Then Paul, in his dream, saw himself in the picture. His head had been smashed in. **Paul** awoke in a cold sweat, reaching for his head, to be **sure** it was okay, then rehearsed it that day to all who **would** hear him.

Each dream contradicted the others until it all played out. He and George were **upset** in one; and Paul yelled at Brian in another. **A girl** in one dream stood in a storm, holding an old suitcase. Paul moved a folder of papers from the **passenger** seat and let her in. The girl recognized him and excitedly asked him to sing along with one of his songs. Going from station to station, up and down the radio dial, at first, she could not find his songs. Ceaselessly interrupting herself with each song, she bounced from one incoherent thought to another about poverty, hard work, and God or fate uniting them forever. Suddenly, they were thrown sideways into a pole, which, like a "silver hammer" that "came down upon his head . . . made sure that he was dead" ("**Maxwell**'s Silver Hammer").

Hardly a day ever passed without Paul discussing one of his horrific **night**mares. Finally, Vernon E. Mosher, one of **K**enneth Anger's Satanists, met

the Beatles on 11 May, the last day of filming *Help!* Interpreting **Paul's** dreams, Mosher said, "They mean that you're **the one**. You're the Billy goat, the band's sacrifice. When did you make your compact with Satan?" Measuring Paul's life, Mosher crunched some numbers and then read Paul's palm for validation. He said, "You have about fifteen more months, kid."

Oscillating then from despair to dedication, Paul was always heavily burdened, but more determined to use his remaining days productively with albums and another tour. Mosher's predicted timing was too soon by one month. The last several months of **Paul's life reflected** his tormenting dreams.

His music took on **a new seriousness** from January 1965, **until he died in September 1966.** Evoking deeper feelings, they reflect troubles far beyond his old quaint love songs. Paul sought originality and far greater quality in his writing. The band was crucially important to him but was not as important as his personal growth and musical excellence. The stress added to his emotions in the lovely music of "Yesterday." That is how the young lad was able to write that solemn message.

NOTE: The Beatles were a well-planned psychological operation (PSYOP) to evoke specific emotions, attitudes, and behaviors, to help establish a united belief system. That societal conditioning prepared for the New World Order.

As strategically engineered, the Western World's first impression of the Beatles included subliminal markers for virginal innocence. For example, as Paul sings the third verse of "Paperback Writer," John and George, in backing vocals, sing the title of the French nursery rhyme "Frère Jacques." That addition, added under George Martin's direction, focused the song as if of a youth dreaming of joining the adult world. Their music was meant to suggest something very hopeful and youthful.

The Beatles' lyrics (including some of their own creation) included infatuations, heartache, and messages of happiness. Then came "Yesterday" with Paul's energy of dire ominous foreboding, planting subconscious dread for that symbolic virgin's pending sacrifice—fulfilling his oath in which he "said something wrong," consenting to his demise.

Frère Jacques

Frè - re Jac - ques, frè - re Jac - ques 16

"Yesterday" describes him suddenly not being half the man he used to be. He is not the same. The one change is that my shadow was suddenly hanging over him. As usual, **Paul** gave it a romantic context, not ever wanting to **just** sing what was on his mind: "Why she **had to go**, I don't know." Yet, everyone knew his romantic life had nothing to do with a woman leaving him. The Ashers were all family to him. Jane was with him for the rest of his life. They were both very securely in love. It is ridiculous to suppose otherwise. When Paul wrote "Yesterday," he was sleeping in her family's home on 57 Wimpole Street in the center of London. The song's perceptibly profound depth of feeling made it a huge success. That sorrow was not about losing Jane. It was about losing himself.

To most people who knew Paul, the song had nothing to do either with his life or with the Beatles. His conveyed agony was unfathomable to those unaware of his veiled dread of death. Without explaining it plainly in the song, he transmitted the angst outside of the receiver's capacity to discern the meaning. The music came in one dream and the

NOTE: George Martin encouraged Paul's relationship with the Asher family. Jane Asher (Paul's girlfriend) is Richard and Margaret Asher's daughter. For Paul, they set up a special bedroom with a piano.

Margaret was one of George Martin's music professors when he studied piano and oboe at the Guildhall School of Music and Drama.

Richard, an eminent endocrinologist and hematologist, experimented with hypnotism to cure various medical and psychological conditions. On 11 February 1956, the *British Medical Journal* published Dr. Asher's paper, "Respectable Hypnosis," consisting of lectures showcasing his remarkable success with hypnotic experiments.

Richard occasionally hypnotized Paul to further Paul's success and to ease his anxiety. Purportedly, George secretly provided Margaret with "Yesterday" (based on Nat "King" Cole's cover of "Answer Me, My Love") to use as an experiment on Paul. Over a series of hypnotic sessions, when Richard had Paul in a state of high suggestibility, Margaret repeatedly played the song on the piano while Richard instructed Paul to recall it—but not the source—when he awakes.

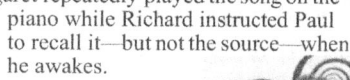

message came from others. Far beyond Beatles' arts instrumentally, **they hired** a string quartet of **session musicians.** Being patently non-Beatle made them question how to release it in the UK. Locals knew better—and knew Jane. Paul was endowed with that song in May 1965 and recorded it weeks later. It was on the *Help!* album, released in August. The next month, it was released as a single in the US but not here until ten years after I joined the band. Finally, in 1976, at my suggestion, we released it as a UK single.

On the B-side of "Help!" was "I'm Down." They were not released on albums in the US or in the UK until *Rock 'n' Roll Music,* also in 1976. Before recording "Yesterday," Paul felt that he needed to warm up to it. He began that day, 14 June 1965, by recording "I'm Down." He then did the even more obscure, "I've Just Seen a Face," before recording his "Yesterday" vocals. The song, "**I'm Down**," was his response to the remaining **Fab** making jokes about his blues over his persistently haunting dreams. **John's laughter**, and Paul's father's disbelief, **hurt Paul** the most. Paul sang, "I'm down, down to the ground [grave]. How can you laugh when you know I'm down?" Being most spooked in the beginning by his dream of seeing my face when John called his name, **Paul's** original romantic context for the next song, "I've Just Seen a Face," was replaced by its darker meaning. Until then, **it was a love song**, and, however falsely, had to be one **again.** Here, he meets a girl, next he regrets losing one, all in the same recording session, and all while staying at the home of Jane, his steady

"Life is but a dream."

18

Okay, you will soon know that Billy (SIR PAUL MCCARTNEY) is not the same Paul that toured with the Beatles. But there's more. The Beatles were not what you thought they were either. But why stop there? The illusion goes deeper and deeper. This entire 3D existence is a dream—a holographic simulation. Mind projection.

date. In that second song, **Paul is** "Falling, yes I'm falling," as if he were then **falling** in love.

Really, he feared falling **as Humpty Dumpty**, the Eggman, saying "Goo goo g'joob," and **entering** eternity, joining all the fallen. Having just seen **my** face, which Paul saw as the face of **death**, he announces to all, "I just want to tell the **world** we met." He recorded all three of these songs on a Monday. Paul was provided with a string quartet for "Yesterday" days later, Thursday, 17 June 1965, the same day Ringo recorded the Buck Owens song, "Act Naturally," with advice to me, as the Paul he expected. It was written by Johnny Russell (with credit given to Voni Morrison) I said that using all others' songs wasted royalties. I stopped it until I had incentives (a court settlement). That song—as very many other songs from this time—fit their New-Paul theme. Making more movies was an expectation they held. As if he were me, Ringo sang: "They're gonna put me in the movies. They're gonna make a big star out of me. We'll make a film about a man that's sad and lonely." [The sad loneliness that I and my bandmates suffered inspired the line, "Lonely Hearts Club Band."] "And all I gotta do is act naturally. Well, I'll bet you I'm gonna be a big star." He had it right.

Ever since Paul died, I have dreamed of him more often than he had of me. My dreams made us all interested in spiritual things. George once said, "Paul [McCartney] is the Beatles' patron saint; and you are his prophet. I send up a prayer to him; then he comes speaking to you." At some times, I have felt I know Paul better than George ever did. I feel like he and I have collaborated on some songs that bear his name. That is the tradeoff. While his name gets the credit, I get the royalties. After all, the massive royalties are no good to him now. The credit is the reward that his endeavors bring him now and is as rightfully earned now as before. I give him that in my McCartney work.

These dreams have sometimes been musical, but more often have had to do with Paul's life. I headed down to Liverpool (a four-hour drive from London) after one of my Paul dreams only to find it exactly as I dreamed it should be. I am not sure what to make of it. I have wondered if I merely remember things from previous trips there, or if the old Paul has been sharing his past with me. After some such dreams, I consulted with Mike McCartney. As **Paul's brother**, he has filled in slits in my memory, **altering my dreams** a little bit, making them more **correct**, or perhaps less.

One can neither be **certain** how much of these dreams are products of the **stories** I have learned nor how much of what I have learned has come from the dreams. It is all one continuum of realistic experience and unreal imagination versus realistic imagination and unreal experience.

Dreaming has been an enormous comfort and sustaining force in my life. For instance, when **I** resented all the irritation that I dealt with to **get** the Beatles' last released album going, **peace** emerged that way. My mother, called Mary **here**, like Paul's, died when I was young. **It had been** a while since I had heard from her **in my dreams.** My life had become too busy for her. With all my money concerns, friction with the band, and a bit more drug-induced paranoia than I understood, I seemed to crowd important souls out of my life. She was one I had left behind, making a void. I felt well again after that dream visitation. When I wrote, "Let It Be," **I tried to make** it sound like a hymn to evoke **a religious feeling.** I call her Mother Mary, **like the Virgin.** The spiritual implications are enhanced by a track I made that Phil Spector later added in after "Dig It," introducing "Let It Be." "That was 'Can You Dig It?' by Georgie Wood. Now we'd like to do, 'Hark the Angels Come.'" Doing that intro added to the worship idea. The Virgin appearance was symbolic. When the public ridiculed it for being **sacrilegious,** I said I had never thought of a religious **interpretation.**

Every time that happened, we gave the same reply. We did not know it was there, or that it meant

NOTE: Furthering concealed agendas, the Beatles appeared hostile toward Christianity. Paul's mother, Mary, had been a Christian. However, after her passing, Paul's father, Jim, discouraged church involvement.

When the Beatles signed with EMI, they understood that they would renounce their Christian beliefs. They were advised that agnosticism was the most defensible theological position since neither theism nor atheism could be proven. With that coaching for early interviews, they claimed to be agnostic. However, privately, they were each coached to access their higher power and explore non-Christian spiritual traditions. Gradually, their comments about religion reflected their own contemplation and experience.

At one point in John's spiritual journey, he said, "I believe in God, but not . . . as an old man in the sky. I believe that what people call God is something in all of us. I believe that what Jesus and Mohammed and Buddha and all the rest said was right. It's just that the translations have gone wrong."

George embraced Hinduism. He said, "Heaven and hell are right now. . . . You make it heaven or you make it hell by your actions." And again, "Through Hinduism, I feel a better person. I just get happier and happier. I now feel that I am unlimited, and I am more in control."

William was brought up with eclectic esoteric training to use religions and other thought systems to serve his will.

As anticipated, singing of being visited by "Mother Mary" divided Christian fans. Although the Biblical Virgin allusion was obvious, many accepted the Mary McCartney explanation. Some fans liked the idea of Paul receiving a Marian apparition. Others were bothered by Paul, in the song, replacing Jesus as Mother Mary's Son. Still, the message to accept what we cannot change felt good. It can remind us of Reinhold Niebuhr's serenity poem.

John opposed the song, saying, "That's not the Beatles. That's a hymn!"

21

anything. It's nothing. **It is** just like John saying he "had no idea that '**Lucy in the Sky** with Diamonds' meant LSD." **The old story of** Julian drawing his nursery school classmate, **Lucy** O'Donnell, in the sky with diamonds is true. We simply built the song around Alice **as if high on LSD**. It was perfect for it. Though **the LSD chorus** un**wittingly** came from Julian, we **created the LSD images** to override the entire song. I contributed a few lines here and there too. Back then, we thought LSD was rather liberating. I never touch the stuff now though. The first doses are by far the most beneficial to the

NOTE: "Lucy in the Sky with Diamonds" can be understood in three ways. Besides the fortuitous Lucy O'Donnell story, "Lucy ... Sky ... Diamonds" is an LSD reference. More significantly, as another layered meaning, Lucy is short for Lucifer, the light-bearer, who is in the sky with stars, or diamonds. We picture ourselves in a paradise of tangerine trees, marmalade skies, and towering flowers, representing Adam and Eve in their paradise. When hearing this song, consider yourself as if you were Adam or Eve. Like partaking of forbidden fruit, getting high on LSD and THC opens us to Luciferian illumination or awareness to become as the gods.

According to the Bavarian Illuminati's Luciferianism, the snake at Eden's forbidden tree represents Lucifer who gave Father Adam and Mother Eve special gnosis, hidden knowledge, that raised their self-awareness. Their awakened consciousness put them on par with the gods, ending their servitude. Lucifer saves them from that slavery to a devil that the Bible calls God or Jehovah (יהוה). Now, like forbidden fruit that causes mind-expanding liberation, psychedelics are forbidden by authoritarian Christians.

When giving Eve the fruit, Lucifer (Enki/Osiris) says, "God (Enlil) knows that in the day you eat thereof, your eyes shall be opened. You shall be as gods, knowing good and evil" (Genesis 3:5). When God (Enlil) asks Eve what she had done, she says, "The serpent (Enki) beguiled me, and I did eat" (3:13).

Nevertheless, the claim that Eve was "beguiled" or "deceived" (1 Timothy 2:14) is contradicted by God validating Lucifer's claim as an accomplished fact: "God said, Behold, the man has become as one of us, to know good and evil" (Genesis 3:22). Finishing that verse and the next from the Luciferian view, to further thwart Lucifer's work, God evicts Adam and Eve from the garden of Eden, and prevents them from partaking of the fruit of the tree of life, which would have let them live forever. Thus, as taught by Skull and Bones (Yale's "Death Brotherhood"), once Lucifer (Enki) taught the secrets to make us as the gods, God (Enlil) blocked that liberation and consigned us to death (hence their death logo) according to 3:22.

"See how they fly like Lucy in the Sky. See how they run. I'm crying." ("I Am the Walrus")

mind, body, and soul without it becoming a habit. *Alice in Wonderland* provided LSD- type images that enriched our albums with such ideas as the walrus or Eggman (Humpty Dumpty).

In 1966, John and George introduced me to LSD. They had each been turned on to the drug way back in early 1965 in the home of their dentist. Along with Cyn and Patti, John and George each had a cup of coffee without being told it was laced with it. From there, they went to a club and tripped out. Sensory perceptions became compromised without them knowing why. The next day, John and George introduced Ringo to the drug, and eventually got Paul to try it. After John returned from Spain in November 1966, he spoke enthusiastically about it, trying to convince me to come on board with it. I first tried it with him after overdubbing "Strawberry Fields" on 15 December, the day Walt Disney died.

Right away, I sought to promote the drug with friends and associates. Even though I was the last one in our group to try it, **I was the first** to admit it to the press. My first statements **promoting LSD** were during an interview, published **in *Life*** magazine in June 1967. That was the ~~month~~ day **after our** big unveiling of *Sgt. Pepper's Lonely Hearts **Club** Band,* which further promoted the drug. I **gave the context**.

Considering my openness **about drug usage**, and how I got Brian Epstein, John, George, and Ringo to

NOTE: Although Anton Levay praised ⱲALⱲ DISⱤEⱤ, Theodor "Teddy" W. Adorno (11 September 1903 to 6 August 1969) described Walt Disney as the most dangerous man in America. Adorno was concerned about Disney's power to control the minds of children, impacting them for the rest of their lives. Adorno would prefer to teach consciousness over mindless entertainment laced with subliminal messages. On the other hand, those who can be offended by Disney can be offended by anyone. Why be offended by anything? Offense is overrated. Just be aware.

engage in a campaign with me to legalize pot in GB (such as when I convinced them all to show dedication to the cause by joining me in signing a full-page advertisement in the London *Times),* the idea I hear now that I was not the most political of the band is inconsistent with history. Our drug campaign had many fronts. After seeing its detrimental effects firsthand, I quit my LSD usage. John, being a much more regular user, took years longer to get off of it—and off of some worse addictions, such as heroin. But when I was for it, **I actively promoted LSD.** On the board of directors, **along with John** Phillips (the Mamas & the Papas), Mick Jagger (the Rolling Stones), Andrew Oldham (Stones' manager), and Terry Melcher (Doris Day's son, a record producer), I networked with MK-Ultra, a joint CIA-British intelligence task force, to provide free distribution during "The First Annual Monterey International

NOTE: Those who control the media decide what music is popular. The First Annual Monterey International Pop Festival was created by the international elite—as were some rock festivals.

The "rock" of rock and roll refers to sex, Masonry, and the papacy. "Pop" (popular) signifies "pope," who, in Peter's seat, rules the church built upon that "rock" (Matthew 16:18). Popes John XXIII and Paul VI felt threatened by John and Paul. However, fighting the Beatles, like ancient Romans fighting Christians, made New Age Paulism stronger. Rock and pop conquered the papacy. Subsequent popes agreed to steer Christianity back to Paganism.

Rap music, representing ceremonially rapping a Masonic mallet, is meant to trap listeners in their self-destructive thinking patterns by using negative energy to deplete their consciousness. In that weakened state, it is nearly impossible to break addictions. If you doubt it, try finding anyone who has successfully broken any addiction while regularly listening to rap.

The plan is to lower consciousness, creating disorder out of order until societal degradation produces enough misery for the world to crave the control and safety of the New World Order presided over by those illuminated enough to bring "Ordo ab Chao" (order out of chaos). To create that chaos, the media manipulates people to lower their energy into fear, hate, and division. By lowering their energy, they lose mental objectivity. Rap is one of many tools used to engineer problems intended to incite the masses to demand each planned solution—such as more war or control.

In the "Who Cares" video, William's character says, "That's the way it goes. Disorder out of order, order out of disorder. It all gets a bit chaotic sometimes."

Pop Festival." **It** was attended by over 100,000 observers who were **invited** to participate with free hallucinogens. The **government** had agreed that they would not enforce any **drug law**s there. It was all with complete US/UK government **facilitation.**

Having MK-Ultra's objective of making San Francisco a youth-centered gathering place for drug experimentation made it easy to get their cooperation in freely supplying the massive distribution for the rock show in Monterey, just two hours away. The key people connecting John Phillips with drug distribution through government agencies were Ken Kesey, Timothy Leary, and others. Later, Timothy ran for governor of California against Ronald Reagan. Leary, with his very public pro-drug work, understandably had a drug-related double meaning in his campaign slogan. To get his campaign going, not only with his political party but also with partiers, his slogan (which led directly to the Beatle song by John), was "Come together, join the party," seeking to unite politically-minded drug partiers.

By briefly touching on this LSD diversion, my point is that I was fixedly passionate about altering your perceptions of reality. I felt that promoting psychedelics, with complete government backing, just furthered my work to bring the whole world into a new reality. Although I could fill the book with other examples, **this one** is enough to make the point. The **album, *Sgt. Pepper's*** *Lonely Hearts Club Band,* **especially with** its obvious "Lucy in the Sky with Diamonds," **was the new door** for the whole world to pass through **to a psychedelic parallel universe.**

Stay safe. Don't break drug laws.

Sidebar left: For the "Summer of Love" that drove thousands upon thousands of "hippies" to San Francisco, Sgt. Pepper's Lonely Hearts Club Band was released three weeks before the First Annual Monterey International Pop Festival. Peppers got them there.

Sidebar right: California outlawed LSD in 1966 (25 days after Paul died). In 1967, with help from Timothy Leary, Billy, and others, LSD went viral from San Francisco, California, to the rest of the world.

"If you're going to San Francisco, be sure to wear some flowers in your hair." ~ John Phillips ("San Francisco")

After some of our **amazing** LSD-induced dreams (supposing that synthetic **drugs were** as beneficial as natural psilocybin **mushrooms or DMT**), I promoted LSD for several years. Still, some of my best dreams have been without it. If I still considered LSD the best option, I would not hesitate to give you my endorsement to try it. I have already encouraged many millions and would still do so even without government backing, if LSD were as beneficial as psilocybin mushrooms.

On most days, however, it does not matter. Although hallucinogenics can somewhat change our reality, freeing the mind of blinding programming, it takes preparation to do it well. Otherwise, it could go the other way. We tried to improve perception. We did "Lucy in the Sky" before we had learned enough about it. We presented Lewis Carroll in an LSD context. It seemed like a good idea at the time.

NOTE: Incarceration for "victimless crimes" is among the worst atrocities that modern governments perpetuate against humanity. This book does not endorse breaking laws that could lead to such unjustified abuse by any governing body but does call for a lawful outcry against all oxymoronic "victimless crimes." We call for more awareness of the benefits of cannabis, DMT (especially in ayahuasca), shrooms, iboga, and other wholesome foods that have been sacred life-enhancing plant medicines since ancient times—as opposed to toxic chemicals that halt mental, physical, or spiritual health.

The pineal gland produces and stores DMT ("the spirit molecule"). Consuming DMT, such as smoking it with cannabis, triggers the release of DMT that has built up naturally in the body, permanently opening the mind to greater consciousness. Ayahuasca makes the DMT experience last for hours. Consistent with the ayahuasca-induced spiritual awakenings facilitated by South American shamans for perhaps thousands of years, William says that one of his most meaningful experiences was when, while on DMT, he saw God.

William says, "Churches fight it, and make it illegal because ten minutes of DMT helps more than ten years of religion." Likewise, Big Pharma lobbies against DMT, weed, and psilocybin mushrooms because they are more effective, with fewer side effects, than toxic synthetic products. For example, monthly doses of natural psilocybin mushrooms fight depression far more effectively than any dose of synthetic antidepressant drugs.

People were taught to fear natural hallucinogenics by associating them with harmful drugs.

Although DMT (Dimethyltryptamine) is sometimes injected or snorted, the greatest reported benefits have been from taking it orally (as ayahuasca) and from smoking it.

DMT
"the spirit molecule"

Instances of "looking glass ties" to John's song can only be viewed *Through the Looking Glass:* "The boat glided gently . . . among beds of weeds . . . and . . . under trees, but always with the same tall riverbanks." **The guard looks at her**, "through a telescope, then **through** a microscope, and then through an opera-glass." "**The** setting **sun** . . . shining on his armor in a blaze of **light** that quite dazzled her . . . all this she took **in** like a picture, as, with one hand shading **her eyes**." Realizing bees are elephants, Alice thinks, "What enormous flowers they must be!" "Listening, in a half-dream, to the melancholy music of the song." "The boat, and the river, had vanished."

"Putting his head in at the window" of the train at a station, a guard there says, "Tickets, please!" From a gnat, "Halfway up that bush, you'll see a Rocking-horse-fly." "Alice looked up at the Rocking-horse-fly with great interest." Such bits from Lewis Carroll, shown here in random order, along with his "Feed your head" messages were the source of **John's** hallucinogenic images making "**L**ucy in the **S**ky with **D**iamonds" sound like an LSD-induced **dream,** but also alerted our listeners to what **we were conveying through** the images of Lewis Carroll. Many of our Paul **codes** could only be broken by reading Carroll. With help from Alice, we provided that context.

NOTE: The influence of Lewis Carroll (Charles Lutwidge Dodgson (1832–1898)) shows up again in "Masonic Checkmate" (chapter 11) with the song, "Getting Better." Many people also found the connection between "I Am the Walrus" and Carroll's poem, "The Walrus and the Carpenter." Unfortunately, thinking we know something blocks further discovery.

The Walrus was Paul.

27

When we dream, we work things out by making up stories with our own imagined scenarios that are symbolic of something going on in our lives.

Dreams have always been a big part of my life. I dream of lines for songs, or of lines to share with relations. **I dream of** people I work with and later use those **good lines** in our real conversations. Everyone thinks I am clever for coming up with these lines spontaneously. I do not say how often I already dreamed the lines long before and just waited until the circumstances would present the moment when **I could repeat** them. I wonder how **much of these dreams** are from creativity, or how much is channeling.

Like Paul who woke up with "Yesterday," **I have** frequently awakened with ideas that seemed **to have** simply been given to me. Wherever **these ideas** may hail from, **I am always glad to receive them.** Sometimes I can decide during the day what I end up dreaming about that night. You can learn to do it too. Dream of me. I will tell you more.

Before going into the "Paul is Dead" aspects of everything, **let me say** that these things are all one. Everything relates to **everything** else. When I first considered what to include **in this book**, the idea I had in mind was to focus on the **"Paul is Dead"** material. However, it is interconnected with every aspect of my life. It cannot be isolated. Paul dreamed his death. Yet, we were all dream weavers. Paul and I were the best of all at it, then George and John. We all had lucid dreams. John said he wanted Paul to give him more. He was jealous of me for that. However, Paul is attached to me. We are one. **I am** yoked with his burdens and flying with his **broken** wings. I am Paul now. It is my dream. Now, it is yours.

Dream big!
We each have our own dream.
We can do what we want with it.

Whether this realm is a dream, game, or simulation,
the point is to be aware and take control of our lives.

Having briefly explained the importance we all place on dreams, I will share a few more of them. Early one morning, **John dreamt of** a white bird in a tree singing in **harmony** with a large yellow dog loudly howling while standing on its hind legs beside the tree. **I found it** amusing. John read a lot into it. It was **meaningful.** Without touching on his interpretation, I find it more about the way that our world is as harmonious as we perceive it to be— and about him having music on his mind.

Here, I will mention that John also dreamed of his mother. Like mine, it was comforting to him. Each of those dreams led to songs. His dream showed her, "Julia," more radiant than she was in life. In "Let It Be" (chapter 6), **I will explain** how my dream, and some **backward recording**, led to that song. John, George, **and** I all had meaningful, sometimes **life-changing**, **dreams** outside of the scope of this underground book. Ringo's interesting dreams were not of the same momentous meaning; and none, as far as I know, ever led to any song. Nevertheless, songwriting, under any circumstance, was not Ringo's forte. He contributed mostly as a drummer for live shows, but may have helped even more as the group's loving underdog. He was good for the band.

Julia whispers that I should explain her song. Okay. When Julia contacted John in a dream, his ugly memories of her neglecting him while out entertaining "Johns," et cetera, all vanished. She was lovelier than he had ever imagined her. In the dream,

Think of this realm as a dream. While dreaming, you sleep. While dreaming, look at your hands or in the mirror to notice that you are dreaming. Then, knowing it is a dream, change whatever you will. It works the same way in your waking life. By resonance, create what you will. Practice while dreaming. Then, knowing it is a dream, direct it willfully. Make it lucid by awakening within your dream to notice that you are dreaming.

Think of this realm as a video game. If it were a game, you would be the player with a headset and joystick, but would also be the avatar on the screen or in the hologram. If you play it well, your avatar becomes self-aware.

Ringo did not drum on Beatles albums that
were released in Paul McCartney's lifetime.

she was calling out to him. He refers to it in his "**Julia**" song, singing, "Julia . . . calls me." The point of the song was for John to reach her by answering her call. "**I say** it just to reach you, Julia." He sought **a spiritual connection** with his mum.

Speaking of dreams, it **is important** to have a dream to pursue. **It makes a difference** to have family and friends who support us in our passions, encouraging us to follow our own bliss. Still, even if we don't have that advantage, we are responsible for our own lives. It is up to each of us to discover what we need to thrive, and to go after it. My dream was to entertain with music. Your dream might be something else. I was privileged to have powerful people conspire to help me, the widow's son, but even luckier in love.

NOTE: The acrostic continues to page 609 of *the Memoirs*. This chapter says:
At first, you may say Paul is a dreamer, but he is not the only one.
From the time I joined him, our dreams have made us together as one.
"Dream sweet dreams for me."
I was introduced to LSD and other drugs by John and George.

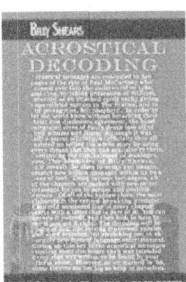

It's a trip from L. C.
Dream of me.
Be happy.
"Hello."
"Hello, Mum."
Julia's fine.

2

Stuart Was the First Martyr.

Assuming Paul's identity, dreaming of him, and feeling his presence, each reinforces the others. I stand for him, and he for me. Part of each of us is in the other. Although I may say he died and I live, it is not entirely true. My peaceful unpressured life as William was halted by Paul's fatal collision; yet he continued through me. You might as well say Bill died and Paul lives. I am not an impersonator in ordinary terms; our exchange is mutual. **Paul's** spiritless remains mark the end of William's **life** now to the extent that my living flesh **embodies** Paul's life. I am Paul. I am **Billy. I have** died. That is why I live as I do. Dreaming of **him, as** myself, I dream particularly of that **part of me** that I missed growing up. It helps me understand who I am. Even before I left my Billy life behind for this new life of Paul, I searched for myself. Dreams have always helped me understand myself better.

Until I became Paul, my dreams were more self-centered. Now that I can see myself through Paul's eyes, it is easier to see beyond myself to become who or what I am meant to be.

31

When Stuart left the band in 1961,
Paul took over on bass only after
John and George adamantly refused it.

I obviously feel more connected to Paul than to any of the other ex-Beatles but still cannot help needing continued connections with them all. I mean no disrespect to Wings mates or others by saying the past I share with John, George, and Ringo always has special meaning to me. Their work helped bring all of my dreams into reality. Wings was a great band and all that but could never have existed until my Beatle years ran their course. I could not do it as William Shepherd. I had to give up myself and live the life of Paul McCartney who prepared my way. **I am** indebted to all four. However, it does not stop there. **Their** success was launched with help from bandmates, Peter **Best** and Stuart Sutcliffe.

Others helped. However, there were only seven Beatles: John, **Paul**, George, Stu, Pete, Ringo, and do not forget me, William Shepherd, a.k.a. Billy Shears. Stu was the band's first bassman. Paul took over as bass player when Stu left and died. Then I took over where Paul left off. I was joined to each of the Beatles as a fraternal brotherhood. Stu came to me twice in dreams, and John now and then.

Stu was astoundingly shy, even in death. Paul told me in a dream that Stu Sutcliffe died of a subdural hematoma (bleeding in the brain) from an injury received at a Beatles show. Paul said its gravity eluded Stu. **No one had any idea how** serious it was. It started when **John shouted obscenities** at the crowd. One English-speaking German became irate. From the stage, John kicked him in the head. With one kick of John's boot, the burly man went down. A fight broke out between the band and the audience. It

With Paul's "blood-stained" guitar stolen just eight days before the rooftop concert, his presence was signified by a "bassman" sticker.

nearly killed John. Paul told me they ached for days. Yet, no one knew it finished Stu. When Paul told me this in a dream early on, that was when I said I would like us to meet with Stuart Sutcliffe someday.

In my next Paul dream, he introduced me to [you] Stu. Stu told me that if he had not gone that night, it would have been John that died in 1962, not Stu. Stu took some hard blows that would have unavoidably fallen on John if Stu had not been there.

I awoke from this visit-dream thinking of [you] everyone's impact on the world without anyone realizing it. **If Stu had missed** that gig, and John terminated in 1962, **the Beatles** might not have achieved world fame. **Paul might still be alive.** He also died **in consequence** of the band–as John did later. **I would still be** some uncredited bloke who records songs as **a session musician**–making music that the Beatles could sing to, but never learn to play.

One other time I dreamed of Stu, about four months after the first time, Stuart told me that until he hooked up with John, he was drifting without direction. He said that the only reason he got into the music business was because John persuaded him. He said **he wanted to** be an artist. He said the quiet canvas **always** appealed to him more than the limelight. He sounded regretful.

My dreams **tell me things** but are merely dreams. **I never knew** how much to believe them. Even so, they have taught me quite a bit.

3

Paul Worked It Out.

Paul's death premonitions were taken more seriously by some people than by others. Nearly all of his loved ones bought into it to a point, but not enough to motivate many of them to take action. Unless they prepared by finding a replacement while Paul was still alive, he was saying, it would be too late. Without revealing his motive, Paul held a look-alike contest through a popular teen magazine. The winner, Keith Allison, had the look but was not the man whose face Paul had seen in his studio dream.

Ongoing efforts were made to find the **next** Paul. Brian Epstein's brother thought **I would be** a good replacement but never spoke to **Paul** about it. One time Paul saw me at a spring party and seemed to kind of recognize me (from EMI) but was too freaked out to pursue it. Once he saw me there, from what Mal Evans observed, the search ended without Paul trying to reach me or any other candidate.

NOTE: Several events combined to create the above party story. Paul was acquainted with William before dreaming of being replaced by him. They interacted professionally at EMI Studio Two and in occasional social settings such as with friends of the Hyde Park crowd. By the imposed use of doubles, Paul sometimes felt replaced already. He understood that he would eventually be replaced permanently, but as shown by the look-alike contest, hoped to have a voice in selecting his permanent substitute.

This Paul McCartney look alike has exciting plans! **KEITH ALLISON**

34

During a visit with Jim McCartney one day, a year or so after Paul crossed over, Jim said he had insisted that Paul stop talking about, and stop preparing for, his death. Jim had told him that all of that preparing for it could contribute to making it happen. As Paul's father, Jim thought he ought to be able to counsel him. However, **Paul's** position was that his father was too **out of it** to understand. Paul thought that since he was **now** so successfully emancipated, he was not obligated to take his father's advice. **Paul felt** disrespected by his father who did not take **omens** seriously. Jim likewise felt dishonored by Paul who ignored good fatherly advice. Jim said Paul would still be alive if he had been open to fatherly counsel. He also said Paul's "debt to the devil" was "delusional nonsense."

From Jim's perspective, Paul's first dream was merely a dream, nothing more. According to Jim, everything escalated out of control because Paul was obsessed with it. Jim told me that a death dream is usually about a change of life. He says Paul's subconscious was probably trying to deal with some aspect of his life that was ending. It could have been his loss of youth. Paul felt pushed and was vexed about it. It could have been about losing his hair, or Jane Asher, about the band eventually ending. Whatever it was, Jim was sure it was not a message from heaven, or hell, warning of his replacement. It was simply a bad dream that freaked him out enough to trigger another, and another.

Yet, Jim said **Paul** got some crazy ideas stuck in his brain about why he **had to be sacrificed** and substituted. Jim said **Paul psyched himself out.**

To know Paul McCartney, first know the spiritual and political perspective of those who established him and had him killed.

35

"Thoughts become things."

By obsessing, **Paul focused his fears into** his reality. By his obsession, he was **tormenting** himself over it, bringing on further **dreams** to obsess about. Paul's subconscious used dreams to work through the trauma he was feeling, which resulted in more material over which to obsess.

If Paul had asked me, I might have told him to clear his negative thoughts through meditation. Yet, that would have prevented my turn. Jim said Paul attracted and created the product of his thoughts, that Paul's reality of death was first created in his head. Next, as though manifesting willfully, his persistent thoughts and feelings brought his fears into reality.

Donna, standing by the side of the road, holding her suitcase, soaked by the windy rainstorm, trying to get a ride, must have been recognized by Paul. Playing out precisely as he had foretold it all, he had to recognize it from his dream, but pulled over anyway. He seems to have developed a death wish. Even though it was self-destructive, something about martyrdom seemed to attract him. He could not resist playing out the fate he established. He saw something romantic in it. He was dying to be esteemed not only as a great writer and performer but also as one who could foretell his future. Sealing his fate by pursuing his death, he also established his role as the band's prophet.

Not that I fully bought into it, I played along. John and George called him their Lord. Going overboard with the praise of Paul, George went so far as to **say that Krishna** became Christ, and that Christ **became Paul**. I did not have enough

36

Paul Worked It Out.
Ninhursag is the mother of all living.
Enki reincarnates to disrupt
Enlil's oppressive religions.

reason **to believe it fully** at first. It was too much. It **seemed bizarrely absurd** for a resurrected Christt to return by reincarnation, and then for some to make him die again in order for him to enter another. I wondered if it were possible for me (as Horus) to embody Paul and others (as Osiris). I had my doubts but was bright enough to recognize the opportunity.

NOTE: While some fans claim that Paul or William is a reincarnation of Antonio Vivaldi, the inner circle sees them as Osiris and Horus. Horus is Osiris's son who became a blend of the two. William is Horus as "Paul." "Paul," in this sense, is a soul-transmigrated combination of William, Paul, and ancient entities that migrated to them before and after Paul's death.

Osiris is the son of Marduk (Ra to the Egyptians). Marduk/Ra is the son of Enki (Ptah to the Egyptians). After Enki willingly relinquished his position to Marduk, Marduk defeated Enlil, making himself the king of all.

The Egyptian sibling gods, Osiris, Set (Seth), and Isis, so closely parallel the Sumerian sibling gods, Enki, Enlil, and Ninhursag that one may postulate that the latter gods either represent the former or that they literally are the same players in either the same incarnation or in a later one. It is also plausible that when Ra ruled Egypt, all gods before him were said to have come after.

According to legend, Set (resembling Enlil) kills and scatters his rival brother Osiris (resembling Enki). Their grieving sister-consort, Isis (resembling Ninhursag), gathers what she can find of Osiris' dismembered parts. Isis and Thoth then use the energy of the pyramid to repair and resurrect the god long enough for Isis to conceive Horus (presumably by artificial insemination). Isis and Thoth then transferred the soul of Osiris into Horus' body. Embodying Osiris, Horus is both father and son. In another tale, Isis, much later, also resurrects the deceased Horus-Osiris body, further setting Horus (born December 25), or perhaps Enki, as the first Christ figure.

The Anunnaki believed in an impersonal Divine Mind or "Prime Creator" resembling what Hindus call Brahman, the ultimate reality and universal principle in and through all that exists. Their royalty (starting with Anu, Enki, and Enlil) were worshipped as gods and appear to be the basis for the Hindu Trimurti (Trinity): Brahma (creator), Vishnu (preserver/savior), and Shiva (destroyer). Some groups put Ninhursag at the top—or a later Mother goddess.

Vishnu (possibly Enki), as the teaching goes, has incarnated many times to bless mankind, partly by disrupting prevailing oppressive religions. Vishnu's eighth avatar, Krishna, came thirty-two centuries before Jesus. We should find an incarnation of Vishnu (figuratively or literally Enki) in every age, including in ours. In *the Haiku Gita* (another book by Uharriet), Krishna says:

I return through birth	To protect the good
whenever goodness decays	and to destroy the evil,
or evilness grows.	I'm born in each age.

Krishna (Vishnu) the second member of the Hindu godhead, resembling Enki of the Sumerian godhead, parallels (maybe *is*) Jesus the Christ (Kristos), the second member of the Christian Godhead. George Harrison explains, "The Greek word for Christ is Kristos ... Krishna and Kristos is the same name." Whether or not a literal incarnation of Vishnu or Enki, Paul's birth, death, and transmigration to William joins them as an Osiris-Horus Christ figure.

For this role of Paul to work fully, I needed a spiritual connection to Paul, and **actually got it** over and beyond what I had expected—which was far more than what John and George anticipated. Realizing how they were elevating the spiritual and mystical significance of Paul, and observing how freely they welcomed that elevation of their dead bandmate, I understood early on how all of that ultimately **elevated my** position. The thing that impressed them the most about **Paul** as a spiritual sentient presence was **that** he foretold his death and substitution, then **worked with me**, the strange substitute, channeling music and talent to me. To them both, that made Paul some kind of a god.

NOTE: William felt less like an imposter after a couple of months when he sensed Paul's more permanent presence. However, based on beliefs and rituals, those who saw Paul as an avatar for Vishnu expected William to feel the indwelling not only of Paul but also of Enki-Osiris-Krishna-Jesus (to give a few names for he whom they considered one god).

If Vishnu or Osiris had embodied Paul, and if Paul then embodied William, "Billy Shears" would become much more than the living Paul. Transformed by Shiva to be far beyond a mere idol, the new "Paul" would be God-incarnate.

When William felt the indwelling of Paul, but not of Krishna-Christ, he was troubled. Confidants reassured him that eventually he and Krishna would each enter the heart, mind, and flesh of the other. Having still not felt it by 1988, he wrote "This One." In the video, we see him with closed eyes praying to Krishna. He says, "Did I ever open up my heart / Let you look inside? / If I never did it, I was only waiting / For a better moment that didn't come / There never could be a better moment / Than this one."

William considered the comforts and privileges that he enjoys and contrasted them with Vishnu's less pleasant incarnations. He believed that if he were his avatar, their union would be mutually beneficial. If Vishnu joined him now, it could be Vishnu's most pleasant of all. He sings, "What kind of magic might have worked if we had stayed calm [patient]? / Couldn't I have given you a better life?"

38

I should also mention that Paul appeared to George in an LSD trip, making us all more receptive to new levels of awareness of the loving universal light. Learning that we are one and that humans are loving gave us all cause to see Paul in a more spiritually evolved plane than we had supposed.

All of these things combined for my benefit. In addition to appreciating the social and spiritual nuances of George's insights, it also set me up to benefit from the band's new obsession. Paul's death became the primary focus of each album. As Paul's representative here on earth, **I became** the focus. Everything pointed to me pointing to **him.** If you care to become aware of it, you will see that the intense focus on Paul begins with *Sgt. Pepper's,* my first Beatles album, and never does let up. With George and John calling Paul their Lord, that makes me their Lord's mouthpiece. I am singing for him. Even though there was often conflict between my bandmates and me, they all intensely loved their Lord Paul. I will return to the Lord Paul idea in "Paulism" (chapter 61). For now, I will explain that **I played along** largely because of the position it put me in **with the band** and with the world. It was not **based on** religious conversion. I also played along for **Paul's** sake. I felt that he appreciated getting all of that **attention**. I felt that he approved of it and **that I owed** it **to him** and my bandmates.

Motivating his family, friends, and others, to cooperate with Paul to prepare for his coming death,

With whatever Lord you have in mind, feel the energy of that Lord while repeating, "Wah-hey-guru" (waheguru / vāhigurū: "Wondrous Lord") in each yoga repetition.

There is no wrong way, or best way, to meditate. Learn many methods and do whatever calls you. No matter what method you use next time, you could probably do it better with plant medicine.

yoking us together forever, **Paul** (with some help from John) wrote, "We **Can Work** It Out." He fashioned it to have **a double meaning** in a romantic sense. Still, the focus **in this book** is his real concern. He says, "**Try to see it** my way. Do I have to keep on talking till I can't go on?"

It burdened him because he believed he would die before long—making him unable to "go on." Everything had to be worked out immediately. Arguing with him was costing time that was now running out. The risk was that Paul's death before replacement plans were finalized could deny any possibility of carrying them out. "While you see it your way" referred to that position insisted by Jim and others that Paul should drop the subject, and then deal with the death if and when he crossed over. Paul said that "Run[s] the risk of knowing that our love may soon be gone."

As I look back over those years, I am especially impressed with that line of love. Paul's deal was vital to prevent their love from being gone. I do not know how Paul meant "love," but surely am quite emphatically aware of how it played out. I thought at first that he was referring only to his looming death. As time went on, I understood that his love he sang of

NOTE: We treat each Paul song as if he had authored its sentiments. That's partly true. Although highly focused on the work at hand, George Martin also showed genuine interest in John and Paul's experience. Occasionally, John or Paul shared concerns or feelings that could be worked into songs for them. Working for Tavistock, the lead songwriter sometimes understood their situation more clearly than they understood it themselves. Accordingly, he wrote what John or Paul would feel if they comprehended their situation. "We Can Work It Out" partly originated from Paul's own concerns but included layers of meaning that were beyond him.

40

was his blissful presence that sustained the Beatles. Lately, I have come to see it as the loving universal force that keeps all things in harmonic order.

"Within You Without You" has George singing about "the love that's gone so cold." He then again cries of "the love there that's sleeping" in "While My Guitar Gently Weeps." Likewise, in "All You Need Is Love," John makes the same complaint. In their own chapters, I will explain what those songs say about the lost love. Here, Paul pleads with family and friends to work it out to keep that love alive when he is gone. He is leaving but will not leave the band comfortless. His love would continue through me.

However good in theory, in truth, his music went on without him, but without the love felt by the band. The new Beatles phase could never measure up to the love they had known until his death. While music flourished, loving cohesion diminished. It gave us all a pain to hope otherwise.

I guess **most people** who grasped the song would have **thought** of Paul's prophetic brilliance to work **that** out. He had his continuance figured out. To me, **Paul**'s plan suggests a lack of sense. He thought he **was replaceable.** He was, but only as the musician and recording artist. I could do that easily. However, when he died, they did not miss the hit-maker. That was not the lack. It was his love. It was his core being. On that level, no one is ever like another. I will explain that further when I write about Linda or about "Let It Be."

41

"Think of what you're saying. You can get it wrong and still you think that it's alright." That bit is saying that the position of "agree to disagree," or to wait and deal with it later—if and when the time arrives—cannot work because it would be too late. Being wrong about it cannot be all right. He sings, "Think of what I'm saying. We can work it out and get it straight or say good night." **Unless** all agreed before Paul's golden slumber, **his love would** sleep with him, making it "good night" to his **love**.

Can you see why George later said **their love is** sleeping? He got it from Paul's **"good night."** We recorded John's song, "Good Night," and my "Golden Slumbers," with that loss in mind. "Good Night" intentionally follows John's chaotic "Revolution 9" just as Paul's final resting peace followed his violent monstrous end. The orchestration, scored by George Martin, gave John's meager lines (sung by Ringo) the emotional impact of an old lavish movie production. For backup vocals, we hired members of the Mike Sammes Singers—who also sang, "Oompah, oompah, stick it up your jumper" in "I Am the Walrus."

On "Golden Slumbers," I too had help. That song, recorded about a year later than John's, was inspired by a ballad written by Thomas Dekker (1572–1632). Having appreciated Paul Simon's work adapting "Richard Cory," by Edwin Arlington Robinson (1869–1935), I decided that maybe I would do the same. Almost all the words are from Dekker. Only three months before Paul Simon's lyrics reworking Robinson's were released, The Byrds had a big hit adapting King Solomon's

"I feel spiritual up there performing." ~ Jim Morrison

lyrics from Ecclesiastes: "**Turn! Turn! Turn!**"⟁
Others too have adapted poetry **this way.**

NOTE: The Byrds' "Turn! Turn! Turn!" helped turn youth from parents, tradition, and religion to the peace-love-sex-and-drugs counterculture. Their anti-war obsession targeted the Vietnam War ("the American War" to the Vietnamese), which had begun in 1955. Since whatever we put energy into increases, being pro-peace would have worked better than being anti-war. However, it was not designed to work. Before the youth's anti-war campaign, the most influential conservative voters already objected to John F. Kennedy increasing the number of American military advisors in Vietnam to 16,000.

Although the US military-industrial complex sought to escalate that war, Congress needed a reason. On 2 August 1964, the North Vietnamese showed "aggression" in the Gulf of Tonkin by returning fire on the destroyer, *USS Maddox,* which had only fired "warning shots." The *Maddox* then fired more, killing four North Vietnamese and wounding six more. There were no U.S. casualties. The National Security Agency (NSA) claimed that a full battle occurred there two days later. Lyndon B. Johnson was informed that the report was false but convinced Congress of the necessity of using that "Gulf of Tonkin Incident" as America's door to war. At that time, the U.S. naval forces commander there was Admiral George Stephen Morrison. With military-funded support in Laurel Canyon, Los Angeles, Admiral Morrison's son, Jim, went on to be the lead vocalist of the Doors.

Before the Gulf of Tonkin incident, plans were already set to hijack the peace movement away from conservative intellectuals and to place it squarely in the hands of those whom conservatives would see as freaks—later renamed hippies. Once the Beatles made their debut in America, other bands were manufactured in England and in California (including the Doors) who produced a blend of folk music and rock, infused with psychedelics. The freaks, dressed in strange costumes, danced in such peculiar ways that they became the primary attraction of popular clubs.

The media brainwashed Americans to equate the peace movement with repulsive freaks who dropped out of society to indulge in drugs and open sex. Those "dirty hippies" wore broken-cross (anti-Christian) peace signs, and habitually said "Peace" while flashing Aleister Crowley's victory hand-sign (which MI5 had taught Churchill via the British Naval Intelligence Division).

By the manipulation of painting "flower children" as evil hippies who called for peace, society's most conservative "good people" opposed all peace rhetoric. They saw fighting in Vietnam as a manly, patriotic, Christian duty. Opposing dirty hippies, Christians supported killing innocent people in foreign lands without realizing that the conflict had no American advantage, but only killed to profit war-machine corporations and international bankers.

Flipping war perceptions from evil to good, the US military funded bands and provided a base of operation at a military installation in Laurel Canyon. The Byrds, who covered Pete Seeger's "Turn! Turn! Turn! (To Everything There Is a Season)," was one of their first manufactured bands. The Beatles were coached to name the Byrds as their favorite American band.

Laurel Canyon became the world's hub of musicians. There, John, Paul, George, Ringo, and William connected with American artists of that engineered and/or highly assisted circle. They knew each other well. With outside help, the most gifted among them carried the talent for those lacking it, but who possessed the desired image or lineage. Glen Campbell's talent, for example, is uncredited on many albums.

43

Answering Paul's "get it straight, or say good night," John's "Good Night," and my song, "Golden Slumbers," suggested not only Paul's death but also that we could not "work it out and get it straight."

Keeping both songs sounding like sweet dream lullabies, but also continuing what we wanted all of you to know about Paul, each of these songs worked on different levels. John was saying "good night" to our sleeping Beatle love, and to Paul, but also used the song as a lullaby for Julian. "Golden Slumbers," until **I gave it** a new tune, was already a lullaby. I just provided **the context** of Paul's love. I did it as one song with "Carry That Weight." That song was about the heavy burden I had with my Paul role— not that I resented Paul for working it out for me, I missed being myself, in peace, without the urgency, conflict, and hassle. John's grief and pain exhausted me. Using Dekker's poetic words to describe **Paul's** eternal snooze, his sleep of death, I lead right **into** the weighty burden that his death had placed on **me.**

As Dekker had it, "Sleep pretty wantons do not cry, and **I will sing** a lullaby," I thought of myself going on **in Paul's place** while he slept, and singing to him about **wanting to give** it up and go home. So, I added "Carry **That Weight.**" In that song, I had all four of us in the band singing the message to me that I needed to accept: "Boy, you're going to carry that weight, Carry that weight a long time." But that is not all we sang. Listen, and hear, "**Paul**, you're going to carry that weight." I've **had** far better times since dissolving the Beatles. Still, I realize that although most of the weight has **been lifted** off me with the band's dissolution, much of the "Paul McCartney" weight remains. After doing "Yesterday" with Jay-Z and Linkin Park at the Grammys, I wrote, "I've Carried That Weight." I imagined them, Nelly, or Eminem doing those lines over "Golden Slumbers/ You've Got to Carry That Weight." I can still see it recorded live. I considered multi-tracking them myself but did not have the energy to do it justice. I kick it out to you so that some of you can take it, extending it and me to something beyond me.

In Paul's song, his urgency also gives us all words to live by: "Life is very short, and there's no time for fussing and fighting, my friend. I have always thought that it's a crime." I think so too. Once again, "my way." His way was shown to be true. Jim and others complained that up until Paul died, he was making it true as a self-fulfilled prophecy. **I see that they** may be right. The deal that Paul **worked out** helped me more than him. I got out of **the worst of it.**

You might be enjoying an imaginary friend sharing your book and telling you these whisper messages. Or, you might rather your friend be still. It's okay. You can read or ignore these any time. They were not even part of the book for its first 13 years. Do what works for you. Let your will direct you.

Paul
McCartney

WINS*   NOMINATIONS*

18   81

64th Annual GRAMMY Awards

4

Paul's Girls

Singling out some of Paul's children may give the impression that they were all he had. They were not. Obviously, these are some that **I** know of, but not all. In this life, Paul never **learned** of most of them. Roaming around and having **more** opportunity than most guys could imagine, **while** not taking any responsibility for it, and **being** the world's most eligible bachelor, **Paul** could conceivably have had young children in every country they toured by the time he departed in 1966. Here are some with stories.

Brian Epstein paid Anita Cochrane £5,000 to not say Paul fathered her son, Philip Paul Cochrane. Under the circumstances, there was a convincingly high probability. Although many others also claimed to have "love children" from the band, most of those claims were never established beyond all doubt.

I cannot possibly know how many children John, Paul, George, or Ringo fathered while on tour. They do not know either—well, at least none could know

NOTE: Sometimes in his songs and in *the Memoirs,* William changes words to create multiple meanings, especially to conceal a sensitive story, such as changing "he" in a Paul song to "she" as if a love song. The double meaning in this chapter's title, "Paul's Girls" refers to his lovers and daughters, even though the first offspring mentioned is a son.

in this lifetime. From what **I have** heard, none of them respected women enough **to take** paternity seriously, at least none did in **Paul's lifetime.** They nestled up with many birds before they settled down to roost permanently. I confess I was the same way once I took over Paul's part. Being in the greatest show on earth put us at an advantage over women.

There were always gorgeous women who would do anything to get close to us. Two daughters that I know sprang from Paul are spotlighted in this chapter. Before discussing them, let me say that since Paul never did take full responsibility for his children, I feel for them, and see clearly how it reflects poorly on Paul. Yet, however tragic that he and others neglect their children, it is not my problem. I do not want to sound callous. **I am sorry** about Paul's indiscretions. I am sorry **he did not accept** his rightful responsibility for **his children** when they came along. It is sad but happens. I want no part of it. I wish his children would not contact me. I am finally using this chapter to tell them that I regret what they have gone through without a father. Still, I am not visiting them or paying them. Paul was not mature enough to follow up with responsibility. In that respect, **I am not** Paul.

As **a teenage rocker**, when Paul (and other pre-Beatles) was with the Quarrymen in the then-new Cavern Club, Paul met, dated, and impregnated

NOTE: While at the Cavern Club, John and Paul showed potential as rockers. However, more impressive than their performance skills, Paul's high-arching eyebrow reminded the Cabal of the Eye of Horus, and of predictions that had been made in connection with Horus, and with Paul's birth and death. Paul's facial characteristics, resembling "the magician's son" (William) reinforced the magician's teachings, making their fulfillment increasingly plausible. Paul and William were both of great interest. With John (who was spoken for by an uncle) as Paul's attendant, the Beatles and William, like two pots over a fire, were watched over as if by a coven of cooks.

Monique LeVallier (1945–1999). Monique was a young makeup artist working in London. As always, when she told Paul that she was having his baby, he chose to discontinue their relationship. Monique, broken-hearted and embarrassed, returned to her home in Paris, France. Monique had the baby girl on 5 April 1960. Without Paul, she named the infant Michelle. Paul knew about the child but did not pursue his paternal role.

Letting things drop—partly because Paul (a teenage Quarryman) did not have the means to give due support—Monique parented without him. However, by Michelle's fifth birthday, the Beatles rocked the whole world. That is the year Paul became a millionaire. Monique put a picture in an envelope and mailed it to him. On the back, she wrote, "**Paul**, Look at our beautiful little daughter. Now she **is** five years old. Michelle would like to meet **her father.** Love, Monique." I found this picture a year and a half later when I went through all of Paul's stuff. Monique took the picture on 5 April 1965 and mailed it from Paris on the 17th. Paul was touched but reluctant.

Using the French skills of Mrs. Ivan Vaughan (wife of an old Quarryman bandmate), Paul's lyrics for "Michelle" included some of his little girl's native language. Based on the picture he had received of his five-year-old daughter, he wrote, "Michelle." As is evidenced by the lyrics, Paul always intended to connect with his child later. If you read the words, you will see that the whole song

In "Michelle," John claimed credit for the line, "I love you, I love you, I love you."

directly acknowledges her as his own: "**Michelle**, ma belle. . . . My Michelle." The song suggests his belief that they would someday connect. It **is** sad to imagine the impact of **his French daughter** eventually learning this song of hope. "Michelle, . . . I'll get to you somehow. Until I do, I'm telling you so you'll understand. Michelle, ma belle, Sont les mots qui vont tres bien ensemble." The hard rub is that we never know when life will slow down enough to deal with all of those things on our "To Do" lists. He received the photograph in the mail in late April. In May, he was working on French tunes.

Early on, Paul saw his friend, the French teacher, to get words to sing in Michelle's language so that she would understand. Paul began recording the song at EMI Studios on 17 June. It was only two months from the letter's postmark. They did more with the song on 12 October and 11 November, to include it on their *Rubber Soul* album released on 3 December 1965. As far as I can tell, Paul still could not make room in his busy life for his daughter by the time he died on 11 September 1966. I've heard that Michelle McCartney is a fine bass player in Los Angeles. She has tried to contact me.

Even though **I feel** for her, what could I say? In this novel, **I say quite a bit** that I cannot in the legally troublesome world **of nonfiction.** If I were to meet her, I could not admit that her father had been

NOTE: On 14 June 1965, Paul met with George Martin at Studio Two for preliminary work on "Yesterday," followed by recording "I'm Down" and "I've Just Seen a Face," While there, Paul showed George Martin the photograph of Michelle and recited a few lines of "Michelle." On 3 November, minutes before Paul began recording it, George presented the completed song.

49

laid to rest. And yet, **I cannot** say that I am her father either. That would **be** a terrible lie. If she ever wants to meet **someone who** knew her father, the best choice would be Mike, Paul's brother.

Are you understanding, Michelle? Mike also cannot admit that Paul **has died** but can tell you nice things about him if such were what you would like to know. However, Michelle, if what you want to do is to find out how Paul felt about you, replay your song. It is what he left to you. He said the song had been written years earlier because everyone knew he was in love with Jane. The child was hush-hush.

Erika Hübers was a young girl Paul met in Hamburg, Germany. Her father owned a club on the Grosse Freiheit, and so had connections. Erika became employed as a server in one of the clubs in that area. That is where she met Paul in August 1960. They hit it off right away and were sexually intimate. She believed that they would be married. With the Beatles' intense performance schedule not leaving much time to socialize, **Paul was glad** to have a steady date. Paul dated Erika **for about a year** and a half, off and on. They conceived their only child together in March 1962.

Saying again, as always, that it would interfere with his career, but wanting to continue getting it on with Erika, Paul urged her to abort the child. She refused. She urged him, if he loved her, to marry her to rear their child together. When he refused, she felt that he did not love her, even though he had told her that he did. She felt that he had used her. The hurtful break-up

Word-stacking and these whisper messages slow the reader down for a more contemplative experience.

that ensued resembled that of Monique and was the same pattern with others who would not abort.

On 19 December 1962, Bettina Hübers was born twelve days before the Beatles' last Hamburg gig. Under pressure later from the government in West Germany, Paul agreed to pay child support. Bettina, reared without a father in the home, was not told her father's identity until her confirmation as a teenager. It was a very exciting revelation to her. She adored the Beatles and Paul was her favorite. She had never imagined that she was his daughter. Of course, by the time Bettina found out, he was long gone. Now, in her mind, **I am** her father. She too wants contact, which is **plainly a** bad idea.

Paul could have willed **part of his** wealth to his children but did not. He wrote out a **whole** list of everyone he wanted to receive an inheritance. Sadly, Bettina was not one of them. He did not say why. The reason can only be guessed. Here is my shot at it. He did not know her—or any of his children. He funded her child-support needs against his own will. With any payments that he agreed to, I was legally obligated to complete. Those who handled my funds assured me that all such obligations were met. I did not renege on anything that Paul agreed to pay. I, or my people, honored all of his commitments. Paul did not mean harm or benefit to children who were strangers to him. To be a father, in the fullest sense, is not enough to have merely donated the DNA. A true father goes on fathering for as many years as he remains a father. There was no bonding there at all. Beyond conception, Paul never fathered Bettina. She wanted a father. When she was told of Paul, she

51

pursued me, wanting me to be her father, mistakenly assuming that I was he. That is an easy mistake to make. It happens all the time.

Finally, when Bettina turned twenty years old, back in 1982, she filed a paternity suit to get money. That put me in quite a predicament. I did not want to be a part of it but had no choice. All of the enormously negative consequences of my breaking the strict non-disclosure agreement are worse than ridiculous. **Without going into it,** there is no way I would possibly break that agreement. That is exactly why **I am** cautious to preserve the novel status of this **revealing** book. In fiction, such as a song, poem, or novel, I can say anything. That does not violate **the agreement.** Yet, in straight communication, however formal, in an interview, or court, **I am obligated to be** silent about having any knowledge of **Paul's** death. I cannot say, "I know nothing of Paul's death." Instead, I am committed to speaking of it only as though it were my own. "No," I say, "I am not dead."

Owing to that extraordinary obligation for me to remain silent about Paul's death, as well as to the negative consequences for breaking that agreement, I am in an awkward position when it comes to his children. When hauled into court to respond to Bettina's claim that I was her father, I was enormously frustrated. I wanted to explain it all but could not. Some people say I should pay up out of respect for Paul—forgetting that he was the one who set my course. He is the one that agreed only to the required support payments. I honor him by continuing his course.

Hiding all in plain sight, we conceal all within full disclosure.

Subpoenaing me **for the paternal suit** left me no choice. **Playing along,** providing the evidence required by their court, **I submitted.** I allowed a blood draw to prove **the DNA** from my left arm. At the court appearance **to identify Bettina's** father, I proved that it could not be **me.** Even with that irrefutable DNA evidence, Paul and Erika's long-term relationship had been so **clearly established,** and Erika's fidelity to Paul so **well known,** that the court ruled that I must be the **father** of Bettina. Notably, Erika was no slut. She **was** not sleeping with other guys while giving her all to **Paul.** The court could see that was true. I had to be the father.

No matter how many character witnesses lined up and swore that faithful Erika had never been with another man, it should not have mattered since my DNA does not have a parental match. It was under that argument that I appealed the decision and finally won. Erika and Bettina were shocked. The decision seemed impossible to them. Erika looked again at the drawn blood evidence. Besides the insistence that I had proof of identification, they also, as an added precaution, took my picture and enclosed it with the blood sample. Erika got her hands on that picture and stared at it. "Es ist nicht er!" she shouted. "It is not him!" She said that **I looked a lot like** Paul but claimed the court was conned by **an imposter.** The head shape was not as she remembered him. Mine is longer.

Erika recalled that Paul was a lefty. However, when they examined my signature, they could tell that my name was signed by someone right-handed. They took my signature to a Beatles museum where each of the band members' autographs was on display. Again, there was a fuss because they did not match. To Erika and Bettina, that proved that Paul fraudulently sent an imposter to go and donate his blood for him. That is how she made sense of the whole thing—knowing Paul was the father.

Erika and Bettina were both positive Paul was the father. Now, with my wrongly shaped head, the right-handed signatures, and with their confirmation that Paul's autograph in the museum could not be by the same hand as my signature on the blood-draw sheet, Bettina says she has proof of my fraud. She only has begun to fight. She is now in her forties and is attempting to sue me for fraud. **I cannot** make her understand—unless Bettina reads this underground book—because I cannot **tell her**

NOTE: Most people miss the connection between the international military-industrial complex and the entertainment industry. They grow from the same stump that gives life to the world's money supply. That same conglomerate endeavors to control all industries that significantly impact human beliefs, attitudes, and behaviors.

EMI's relationship with German intelligence became conspicuous by the Nazis they hired immediately after WWII. John hoped his cardboard cutout would push EMI into further disclosure.

The Bavarian Illuminati, one should recall, originated in Bavaria, which is part of Germany. When discussing the current Nazis or Illuminati it is the same governance but under new labels.

German officials operating within the cultic inner circle, as well as others of Western European prominence, understood EMI's switch to the illuminated Paul who would facilitate the revolution in preparation for their NWO.

Erika's legal case provided a predicament for the German government. Germany is a key player in the coming one-world government with its one-world currency and one-world religion. That New Age religion includes the sect of Paulism. They understand the situation. Without compromising shared agendas or undermining affiliations, they could not allow Erika's court case to prove that William is not Paul. However, based on the submitted DNA, the court also could not prove that William is Paul. The only solution was to delay until they could dismiss the case on a technicality without taking it to trial.

Switching one Paul with another is an example of how all realities have been switched to illusion.

54

about her father's death. **If she wants McCartney DNA, she will have to get it from Mike.** To be kind, **I would love to tell her** all she cares to know about it. **On the other hand, Mike is not** eager to become **involved either.** Why should he be? He's not the one being accused. I am.

It is between Bettina and me now. I will let DNA do the talking. I could bring a hundred people to the court who would swear that I am Sir James Paul McCartney. Then, in front of everyone, I could wield my arm and let them draw another blood vial. I would bet all of my wealth and reputation that it would match the sample that I gave the last time. My DNA has not changed one bit since then. That theatrical appearance should settle it all at last. With whom the fine people of Germany are messing, they have no idea. **This is not the only** paternity test my DNA has cleared for **Paul.** I am another man.

5

Drive My Car Backwards.

"Drive My Car" was written after one of Paul's nightmares about a girl, alone in the rain, wanting a ride in his car. In this song, he would cheat death by saying, "You drive! **I'm** not your driver!"

I have honored **Paul** by doing a number of songs dealing with cars or with driving. I use virtually any excuse to work a word in with such a Paul reference. I could pick several albums for examples. However, being in the album title, I will use *Driving Rain,* named for the rainy night that he met Donna and ended their lives. Although no song **on the album** is entirely about Paul dying, you can **see how I** wove in the driving image. For example, **notice** the title "Lonely Road;" and consider how **every line** has a double meaning referencing both Paul and Linda. **It is** not mostly about either. "I hear your music and it's **driving me** wild / Familiar rhythms **in a different style**" is repeated throughout the song. It is specifically personal to each of them.

In the song, "**From a Lover** to a Friend," which I sing about **needing Linda** to let go to let me love another, **I use the driving image** with "It's far too easy ride to see," and then again as "Despite too easy ride to see." The title song, "Driving Rain," brings to my mind an emotional storm, driving, and severe loneliness. It is my broken heart driving me sad. Although there is quite a bit in there about Linda, the entire song is about driving. I sing, "Why don't we drive in the rain . . . Go for a ride in the driving rain." **Then, of course, there** is "Riding into Jaipur" which **is** all about me riding through the night in **a car with my babe**, meaning Linda, **who had passed away.**

Those songs above, and many others, pull in the driving idea but are not specifically about the crash. Here are some Beatles songs about Paul's collision. In "Don't Pass Me By," Ringo sings, "You were in a car crash, and [then] you lost your hair," suggesting the head injury, but also as an inside joke since Paul really was losing hair. In fact, his baldness gave investigators cause to doubt it was Paul when they found him. His hair was pushed back and held there, matted with blood, so that all his baldness was shown at the top of his opened head. His line, "When I get older losing my hair," seriously concerned him. He concealed his balding by his combed forward mop-top cover-up.

Showing exactly where Paul "blew his mind out in a car," the *Magical Mystery Tour* takes you there. In the movie and album booklet, we refer you to "ten miles north on the Dewsbury Road," Paul's death site. We filmed this trip on the first anniversary of his death. In the title song, you hear a car skidding and crashing, representing both Paul's Aston Martin and our tour bus. **The trip was** a magical tour group **mystically experiencing the decapitation of the "Magical Mystical Boy"** (as he is called).

"You'll never know it hurt me so. How I hate to see you go." (DPMB)

"A Day in the Life" and "Revolution 9," to name songs of other albums, have backward recordings of sounds of car crashes. You would need to play them backward to hear them.

During their work on *Revolver*, the first Paul's last album, while high on marijuana, and working on "Rain," John accidentally played a tape of that song in reverse. In that instance, the mistake from John's impaired judgment led to a discovery that impacted our Beatles' music for the better. We then impacted various other bands who imitated us. **The Beatles**, most especially John, had avidly **used Preludin** to enliven his stage performances **in Hamburg**, and sometimes to keep them awake, but most often to ignite maniacal stage antics.

They were heavily into pot and many other drugs that occasionally brought on creative benefits, such as in this instance with "Rain," but that sometimes brought down performance standards. For example, it was his drug-induced impairment that made John act as though his song, "What's the New Mary

NOTE: Later, when enlisted by EMI, the Beatles were initially marketed to a conservative demographic (in opposition to the Rolling Stones who were slated to be the bad boys of rock and roll). The public personas created for John, Paul, George, and Ringo were to start as naive and innocent Liverpool lads. Evolving while the world watches and sings along, the fellas would gradually mature into broad-thinking men of the world. All would see them outgrow childish inhibitions, embrace enlightenment, and expand their wealth and world power. As intended by the social engineering experiment, those who followed them would likewise mature in those ways.

Initially, when the Beatle boys played the innocent card, the public could not know they used Preludin to stay awake and lively for performances, and absolutely could not know about their drug experimentation to get high. In addition to drugs, they became fond of cannabis in 1964, which, by the next year, had taken over enough to interfere with their work when filming *Help!*

Later, as their personas awakened into broader thinking (when William stepped in), they were finally allowed and even required to be open about LSD and other drugs, and to encourage their fans to follow along.

BEATLES vs. **STONES**

The contrast between the Stones and the Beatles were part of the illusion. They were all friends.

58

Jane" **had** any merit at all. "Mary Jane," which is commonly **understood** to mean marijuana, is fine but not while on **the job.** I could not get John to kick his habit of using drugs while recording. Once I left **the Beatles,** I demanded that everyone working on my material was to do so while thinking clearly. We **could party** and have a good time all we wanted later **but not** while working. I do not want pothead quality **on my records.**

Reversing the recording of "Rain," playing it backward, sounded interesting. George Martin did some experimenting with it that night after John left. Adding a clip of John's vocals and guitar to the song in the reversed direction, he made the world's first backward masking. **Backmasking** is a Beatles invention in that it **began with that Beatles song.** We then did it in others. It was **George Martin,** not John, who thought of it and **first tried it.** The next day, George Martin shared it **with John, who** thought it was great and **was happy to keep it** in there. The text of that first of many **backmasked** overlays for the Beatles was "When the rain comes, they run and hide their heads." In this first instance, the sound of the backward message did not at all resemble that of the forward sound but did not have an adverse distraction from it either. Very often in the backmasked songs that followed, we employed backmasking where the sounds were more similar, being less obvious going forward.

Delighted by that hidden enhancement in "Rain," and realizing that it was historically significant as a recording first, they released it as the B-side of Paul's "Paperback Writer" single rather than on *Revolver* as had been intended. On *Revolver,* they then used backward recording in "Tomorrow Never

Marijuana makes things seem farther or closer and makes time go slower and slower. Distorting our perceptions of space and time, pot disrupts our attachment to this simulation's 3D space-time unreality.

Knows" in a reversed guitar solo, and again in "I'm Only Sleeping." They released *Revolver* just a little more than one month before Paul crossed over. Starting when **I** took his place, and thus from then on, we **used reversed messages** to tell the world **of Paul's death**. Backmasking became a new way for us **to tell the secret**. However, we were not the first to listen to recordings backward.

Going all the way back to 1877, when Thomas Edison invented the phonograph, he began—at least as early as the next year—to play recordings backward. He wrote about it. Although Edison never played them backward as much as forward, he was fascinated by the "novel, but altogether different [sound] from the song reproduced in the right way." Many years later, Aleister Crowley had me listen to phonograph records reversed, attempting to train me, in my early childhood, to think backward.

NOTE: William's training to "think backward" included, with great practice early on, learning to write backward with either hand and to talk backward. When it came time to create backmasking, he took to it naturally with an unusual ability to anticipate what sound a reversed word might produce. As a child, he could swiftly walk backward but never mastered running backward.

William also notices what a word spelled backward might mean, such as RAM and MAR. For a subconscious suggestion, or to bring focus to one, he might reverse the word order, or say the opposite of something.

As with Masonry, which jealously conceals its secrets and intentionally leads interpreters astray, counter-clues sometimes accompany real ones. Here is an example of a false clue to cause confusion. If this note suggests finding official government documentation of Paul's 11 September 1966 death by looking for his corpse indexed as "Paul J-something," rather than as "J. Paul McCartney," that reversal would be a false clue or counter-clue. The reader is not meant to find either the record or the corpse. Do not follow such clues. "Juxtaposing every riddle, venture into subtleties." Confused? That's okay.

Sometimes clues draw people in too close to home. In a Mike Williams video, Steven Fawber discusses standing stones (menhirs). They marked places for rituals (including Druid human sacrifices) and burials. Steven points out that if the stone shown on one of William's album covers is, as it says, *Paul McCartney's Standing Stone,* then it may mark a location of Paul's remains—  or part of them. In a subsequent video, John and Gillian Lennox visit the farm in person. Others have also poked around. Whether the title is a dead giveaway or a false clue, it would be best to not make pilgrimages.

Once as **Yoko played** some sheet music that she had on **the piano**, John wondered aloud how nice it would sound **backward**. He challenged her to play it that way. She did so. He used the melody that emerged to write "Because." With that composer's help, it was the finest writing on the *Abbey Road* LP from a musical perspective. We were great, but not up to the sophistication of Chopin or Beethoven.

You will read in this book about many more songs with backmasked Paul messages. A few were revealed in 1969. From then on, countless other bands used that new Beatles method to hide their own secret messages. For example, the Doors, in "Break on Through," backmasked, "I am Satan." All my Beatles backmasking was **of Paul or his death**. In some of my other roles, such as The Fireman, I do it with other content. Backward and forward, I still drive Paul; and he still drives me.

NOTE: William created backmasking mostly to say that "Paul is dead." John and George also concealed PID messages. "Revolution 9," which is weighed down with backward recording, includes representations of Paul's demise.

However, more aligned with the Doors' backmasked message about Satan, and consistent with songs by numerous artists seeking to affirm their Satanic affiliation, playing "Revolution 9" backward, we hear Yoko say, "Satan, look at me please." "Satan, look at me. Come on, Satan, now." "Satan, is he great?"

Recording artists have their reasons for making such recordings. The motivational and literary contexts are usually more significant than the actual content. In Yoko's case, although listeners may guess why she included Satan in her witchcraft, the context of the song (when played backward in its entirety) is about Paul's life and death. In his final years, he had increasing anxiety over his Satanic compact, which many tie to his sacrifice.

Worldwide governing methods succeed by controlling information. Beliefs determine attitudes, values, perceptions, and behavior. One way to control information is comparable to sleight of hand. If a leader holds hard facts in one hand, and softer ideas in the other, followers blindly favor the ideas that confirm their paradigms. Most people avoid seeing, considering, or even comprehending whatever disproves their biases.

Yoko's sleight of hand draws attention from the martyr to the witch. By calling on Satan, those unaware of Paul's compact for greatness cannot see how it connects to his death. The lines confirm that aspect of Paul's story for the adept while directing outsiders to look away. Since the public cannot want it to be a death clue, they cannot see it in that context. It is easier to believe that the Satanic lines are about Yoko and that they do not reflect the views or practices of the band.

Robbie Kreiger said the Doors were revivalists who wanted their "audience" to undergo a religious experience.

"Death is not the opposite of life, but a part of it." ~Haruki Murakami

6

"Let It Be."

"Let It Be" is a song with a good sound, music, and lyrics that delivered an important message, and ended up being a big success commercially, but contains layers of meaning that are missed. A friend told me he learned this phrase from AA: "Let go and **let God**." It is an attitude of total acceptance. It **is** like the phrase, "Whatever will be, will be." **The message** of comfort and wisdom that came to me was to stop fretting over what is, and to accept that everything has its purpose. All is orchestrated by those who have passed on, by the angels, or whomever. It is all for the best. Sometimes our experiences do not seem too good at the time but are always exactly what we need for whatever reason. Just let it be. Whatever is going on, we should thank our angels, God, or the cosmos. **It is reasonable** for us to talk out situations or **to ask for help** in ordering things for us. **After all we can do,** we should accept and appreciate whatever is our lot at any given time. It makes life much happier to stop fussing over it. We do not need to fight about any of it or feel sorry for ourselves. We can

"Once you accept your own death,... you're free to live." ~Saul Alinsky

"In our society we do not easily accept that death is a natural part of life, which results in a perpetual sense of insecurity and fear." ~The Tibetan Book of the Dead

let God worry about it. If we can trust that we are in good hands, then all of our fears and our emotional turmoil will be replaced with an attitude of gratitude, or in other words, with peace.

That album is an example of it. After we laid down the tracks for what wound up becoming the *Let it Be* album, Phil Spector could not just let it be. He worked it into another Spector spectacle. I did not take it well, but eventually took my mother's advice to just let it be. She was right. It all works out. By letting go of all of that frustration, that negative energy, I was free enough to move on with positive energy in other works. Decades later, Ringo and I stripped Phil back out to release the *Naked* version. At last, it is exactly as we Beatles all wanted it to be. I am delighted by it. It is packaged as a two-CD set. Not only is it the real *Beatles* version of the *Let It Be* album, but as the extra CD, I included little studio ditties, talk, and this and that. You can hear for yourself from what material Phil pulled pieces. But again, **the real message**, no matter what happens, **is simply to** accept it. Let everything **go according** to the divine plan. That is a key **to happiness.** It is a choice.

Allowing whatever circumstances are beyond our control or influence brings us peace. Whatever is not within our personal control must be okay. We can trust the universe, or God, or spirit guides, to make our lives turn out for the best. **This core belief is** empowering and self-fulfilling. If we **truly** believe that everything works out **for our benefit**, we align with the universe **to make it so**.

We are all in the big choir. Your "one verse" (uni-verse) and my "one verse" are harmoniously overlayed in the Universal Mind's one love song. When we listen for the harmonious synchronicity, we hear others' lines coming in on cue.

Having this belief changes our perceptions, making any hardship an acceptable means to a good end. This core belief creates positive self-talk on a subconscious level, which in turn shapes our own realities and awareness, aligning and opening us to streams of synchronicities wherein every experience works together for our good. What others may dismiss as mere coincidences, we may (after having accessed this power) recognize as synchronicity that always works for our best benefit. Belief makes it so.

Yes, we still have hard things in our lives but **are much better** empowered to get through them. **We recognize that** hard things will (in eventual retrospect) be counted among some of our greatest experiences. They will teach us things that open conceptual doors to the outside—and to ourselves within introspectively—that we would never learn and open in any other way, or in any better way according to our specific abilities and needs. This assuring belief, assumption, and expectation negates negative self-talk. It frees us from the resentment that would accumulate and reinforce our hard things. There can be no resentment for what we believe will be for our ultimate benefit.

This optimistic expectation of benefit taps our inherent creative power of positive thinking. It shapes our lives in such a way that it creates a continuing positive self-fulfilling prophecy. **We can learn** to live our lives to instill and fulfill **the core** belief that everything ultimately works out for our **benefit.**

Eventually, **by believing this positive truth**, it manifests spiritually and materially **as our realities.** Then, by recognizing these positive manifestations,

Synchronize your energy to your preferred reality.
Energetically match what you want to manifest.

we more deeply embed these instilled notions. Yearning for more creative expression, we, being joined as one with this unifying notion, continue on to achieve even greater things, be they material, social, emotional, or spiritual.

Until we learn complete acceptance, and to "Let it be," we cannot move forward empowered by this intended all-encompassing synchronistic benefit. Acceptance of whatever we cannot control may necessitate that faith and trust that everything will ultimately work out for us.

"Let It Be" is written to accept everything we experience but is particularly about accepting **death.** Everyone dies. Most of us live long enough that we must accept the death of loved ones. It is never easy. There's Jim, my adopted father, Paul's father, who had to accept the loss of Paul's mother in 1956. One time in an interview I said that the song was about that loss. I lied. Since that time, I have had to deal with the loss of Linda. That was in 1998.

Some people may frown on me still missing her, but I did not stop living when she did. Although others have been great too, part of me stays with Linda. I enjoy marvelous relationships. However, they are not replacements. **People are** not replaceable. Each loved one is **unique and wonderful.** We replace possessions but not relationships. They continue.

Everything in life must be allowed to be. "Let It Be" was about the end of the Beatles but was about the death of Paul more so. This song has some of our best Paul clues. **Secretly, I began** to wonder if my role **as Paul McCartney** could continue when the Beatles were all done. Would Paul die twice? Would he still work through me if I went solo

Think of what you want to manifest. With absolute acceptance, feel every aspect and every implication of the reality that you intend. Experience it mentally as an accomplished fact. The subconscious will believe it and make it happen.

in his name? That question troubled me the most. But, in a dream, my mother told me it will be all right. She wisely told me not to worry, and that everything would turn out as it should. It would be all right. **The gist of** her message was to "Let it be." Like **Bob Marley's** 1977 song, "Three Little Birds," the **message was** "Don't worry about a thing, 'Cause every little thing gonna be all right." That is the **kind of peaceful** confidence that first got me into the Beatles. Everything works out as it should. For me, the time was not right until Paul did his part.

In "Let It Be," I sing of "broken-hearted people." Who are these people? What broke their hearts? These are people who are still "living in the world," but grieving for those who are not, for those who "may be parted." They grieve for those who have crossed over, or for those who have moved away. The sad emptiness, unfilled by the departed, lingers painfully when the broken heart cannot accept it. Losing a loved one is like having part of one's own heart cut out. Although it hurts physically and emotionally, we eventually heal by accepting what is as it is. Rather than clinging to disagreements with the loss, we can train ourselves to **accept** it, to seek and find agreement and full **oneness** with all that is. Fretting about it, disagreeing with it, eating ourselves up over it, cannot change it. It is not the way to peace. People living deeply have no fear of death." ~Anaïs Nin

"Let It Be" teaches acceptance of Paul's death. Between the familiar words, I whispered messages. I sing, "Whisper words of wisdom." Have you ever wondered what wise words I whisper in that

The human body is made of trillions of cells, which are individual living organisms that usually work for the good of the whole. In our Earth realm, there are only a few billion of us humans. Like the cells, we are all one and can live to support the whole.

When we dream, fantasize, watch a movie, or pull up a memory, we experience a simulation within the simulation. Although none of it is real, the subconscious thinks it is and builds its own reality around it.

song? I hid the subconsciously heard truth of what to let be right after the death-referenced words, "though they may be parted." **Listen**, and turn it up even louder, **to hear** these whispered words of wisdom: **"Paul is dead."**

There is also another way of hearing this song. Imagine it from Paul's perspective. He sings it to me. His mother, Mary, comforts him. They are together now. We are all parted. They see that the world is divided over his death, as over almost everything else. We should come together. Let it be. Sometimes I sing it as Paul might to me, "There is still a chance, Bill, that they will see." What else is there to see? He is comforting me, telling me that someday you may all see me as myself. Maybe you will see it in this eye-opening book.

As you see and hear, uncertainty dissolves. An ethereal awareness of Paul McCartney on the other side, reaching you through our music, brings peace. As those who are broken-hearted for him agree and accept that my substitution is the way that fate or the heavens arranged it, that answer gives peace. First, you must accept it. So, mote it be, let it be.

Hear any other whispered words of wisdom? To hear it consciously, play it backward. Once, as I entered the studio, not long before writing, "Let It Be," I wondered what the words "He's dead" would sound like played backward. I recorded it, played it backward, and heard something that was, to my delight, compatible enough with **"Let it be."** Its wisdom, when put together, evoked much of the enlightenment of that hit song. **The message is**, "He's dead; let it be." It's time **to accept his death**

Some feared fans would kill themselves if they knew.

Paul's skull was parted

"If the truth shall kill them, let them die." ~ Ayn Rand

ACCORDING TO THE REPORT:
The cranium parted asunder surrendering gray, black, white, and red, soft, squishy, matter that housed the ka, Paul's soul or life force. They put his brains on ice.

and move on. After recording a vocal track forward, I played it backward through my headphones, and dubbed over those words of truth and wisdom: "He's dead. He's dead. He's dead. **He's dead.**"

When you hear me sing, "**Let it be.** Let it be. Let it be. Let it be," in the forward direction, I am equally loudly singing "He's dead. He's dead. He's dead. He's dead," going backward. In this way, I let your mind consciously take in "Let it be" at the same time that you all subconsciously heard me express what it is that you should let be: "He's dead." **Paul is dead.** Let it be.

Those words of wisdom coming to life now, I must **also confess** that although complete acceptance is good **in theory,** we could not do it ourselves as far as **Paul** went. One reason for our obsessing was that it **was consuming us all** by not talking about it as openly as we all wanted. We could not resolve it because we could not discuss it. We all had issues with it. **I am trying to resolve my issues** now. Expressing them now **in this book** of disclosure should help. However, giving absolute legal proof is not something I will consent to—such as willfully giving DNA comparisons between me and Michael, or some other McCartney, because so doing would deprive my own children, and their children, of the royalties that would go to Bettina—and because I agreed to never tell. Here is wisdom, just let it be.

Your birth time and place are stored
on your DNA for default astrological
personality traits in this simulation.
Here is Paul's astrological program:
Sun in 26° 36' Gemini
Moon in 17° 26' Leo
Mercury in 18° 21' Gemini (r)
Venus in 18° 59' Taurus
Mars in 2° 40' Leo
Jupiter in 1° 49' Cancer
Saturn in 5° 12' Gemini
Uranus in 1° 58' Gemini
Pluto in 4° 16' Leo
North Node in 7° 5' Virgo (r)
Chiron in 12° 9' Leo
Ascendant in 25° 15' Virgo
MC in 23° 40' Gemini

James Paul McCartney
was born in Liverpool at
2:00 p.m. on 18 June 1942.

7

"Born a Poor Young Country Boy"

I thought this clue was more obvious. James Paul McCartney was born in Walton Hospital in Liverpool, where his mother, Mary, had worked as a nurse in the maternity ward. Paul was reared in Liverpool. The population there has grown tremendously over the past two centuries. It is a very old city, dating back to King John (1166–1216), but did not become heavily populated until the early 19th century when 40% of the world's trade passed through its port. It should have been a dead giveaway. That place is urban. I sang that I was "born a poor young country boy."

If it is **Paul you are** looking for, he is buried in a field of grass **pushing up rhododendrons.** I am not him. You can **"Find me** in my field of grass" or sitting **"beside a mountain stream"** watching the "waters rise" ("Mother Nature's Son"). The peaceful country is my heritage.

NOTE: William is tongue-in-cheek when he says he was "born a poor young country boy." Obviously, he was "born . . . young." Wealth or poverty is relative. Compared to his wealth when he penned that line, he had been poor. However, compared to the McCartney family, William was born into great affluence. The intended contrast is that while Paul was brought up in a very congested city, William was from the peaceful "heart of the country." Even when "playing poor" with Linda, it was in their private acreage near the beach with horses, sheep, and all else they desired.

69

Having McCartney wealth is far better than being "a poor young country boy." For me, the most excellent possession is my farm far from the urban insanity. It is **in Scotland**, in the "Heart of the country where **the holy people** grow, Heart of the country, **smell the grass** in the meadow." On our farm in the heart of the country, I have what I want: "Want a horse, I want a sheep," and I usually "wanna get me a good night's sleep, Livin' in a home in the heart of the country." Those nice rural lyrics are from "Heart of the Country" on my *Ram* album.

That country living has influenced my music. Before I joined the Beatles, at a time when my records were made with fellow session musicians rather than with "real" bands, I made albums that you have most likely never heard. One was called "Cowboy Favourites," by the Maple Leaf Four: Bill Shepherd & the Ranch Hands. That was a good cowboy-sounding band for a country collection

NOTE: William, having been admonished to receive the Spirit of God and live accordingly, accepted advice to get away from city life to live and thrive where the holy people grow. He wanted to be a holy person growing there, including the double meaning of being a holy person who grows pot there.

Three months before Paul crossed over, Brian Epstein followed orders to pressure Paul to purchase High Park Farm in Campbeltown near the Mull of Kintyre, Scotland, as a tax shelter. Paul bought that three-bedroom farmhouse, on 183 acres, on 17 June 1966, but hardly saw it.

William received that property but mostly neglected it until he and Linda began renovations in 1969. She made it a home. It was their primary abode until her passing. To reduce the number of sightseers, they also purchased the nearby Low Park Farm. Now, in Linda's absence, William rarely goes there.

When William sang of Penny Lane, it sounded as if it should be a street of significance in some quaint village. To those who knew that obscure street in the congested city of Liverpool, the song felt inauthentic. By contrast, Wings' "Mull of Kintyre" was very well received in the UK, being the first single to sell over two million copies there. The difference was that William only pretended to be from Liverpool but authentically loves Kintyre.

Whether in the city or "in the meadow" in the "Heart of the Country," he reminds us to "smell [inhale] the grass." Grass also cooks well. Grind the dried bud to a powder, simmer in butter with seasonings, and add it to sauces or desserts.

"Everyone should have themselves regularly overwhelmed by nature." ~George Harrison

of songs. If you ever hear it, you will recognize the American cowboy voice I used in "Rocky Raccoon." Not wanting to be left out, Ringo made his own country sound in "Don't Pass Me By." That was good country-style fiddling "George" added in too. He too had country potential.

Speaking of "Rocky Raccoon," the antagonist in that song was Daniel, whose name was derived from the song, "Danny Boy." That song, although written by an Englishman while living in America, is outstandingly popular with the Irish here and also beyond. Irish families, including McCartneys, found refuge in Liverpool during the potato famine in the 1840s. Tens of thousands of Irish immigrants filled the city. The swelling was permanent. The Irish are still there. By popular interpretation, **the song begins** having a reference to funeral pipes: **"Oh Danny boy, the pipes, the pipes are calling." Later,** near the end of the song, it goes on to say, **"If I am dead,** as dead I well may be, Then if **you bend and tell me** that you love me, I'll sleep in peace **until you come** to me." If you have ever noticed the pipes line sung on the *Let It Be* album, and wondered what it has to do with Paul, now you know.

With all my hints about me being from the country, and with your understanding that Paul was not, consider the difference. Our music was mostly for city dwellers. The Beatles were Liverpudlians.

Paul's maternal grandfather and paternal great-great-grandfather were from Ireland. Billy's family heritage is steeped in Scotland.

8

I Was a Session Musician.

I had been in a few bands that never made it commercially. I sang and played with hopes of the big time. I also participated in some groups more for fun than for profit. Making music has always been fun for me. Most of the time, I worked as a session musician. That was my Paul training. I tinkered with many bands, small ones mostly.

When I became Paul, his Beatle name opened all the other doors. I went on to fiddle behind the scenes with bigger bands. I became friends with really great artists. Most of that work, just like before as a session musician, went on entirely anonymously. For me, it was a delight to be involved with those bands. **As Paul, I** did not need compensation. I just **had good times** that I could relive whenever **I heard the songs replayed** on the radio or **on records.** As Paul McCartney, I could crash almost any EMI recording session.

Everyone was delighted to have a Beatle drop in to play with them. Sometimes the bands would stop doing whatever they were up to so that they could

"A plausible mission of artists is to make people appreciate being alive at least a little bit. I am . . . asked if I know of any artists who pulled that off. I reply, 'The Beatles did.'" ~Kurt Vonnegut

jam with me. Other times, I helped various artists make their records—either as a non-credited backup musician or by offering timely advice or ideas. You can imagine what it meant to a lot of them to have Paul McCartney drop by and lend a hand.

All along, I was interested in having my hands in as many bands as I could. **I helped them out.** They helped me too. I learned **a lot** from them. I especially hung out **in Abbey Road's Studio Two.**

The years of session work taught me a lot about the music business. Most of all, the range of experience was beneficial. I would be hired to help record a rock and roll album one day, and to sit in a nice and proper orchestra the next. Sometimes legitimate bands would need a little extra sound that I could provide. Other times, albums were put together for bands that only existed for the hour. We invented them, or somebody did. Someone would put up the money to hire a group of young models or actors to jump around and pretend to be a band for a photo shoot. Having a look at the cover, some no-name musicians, like me, would be hired to cover someone else's music. Occasionally, I was fortunate enough to include some of my own original material. Recording songs I wrote was especially satisfying.

Now, another thing **I was** learning at this time was that it was **big business** and all for show. Oh, sure, it was **for the love of music** as well. But what we created was **much more than mere** music. Ultimately, it was all an **illusion.** We created sounds

Your reality has been switched to illusion.
Now we are switching it back.

and images that would sell. If it sounded and looked good, it made money. It was not about reality any more than most shows are. For the show, as Brian Hines had done, we invented our own identities.

Professionally, I generally used one identity to attract business, and another for any particular group. My business name was for the agents or others to call me and hook up my next gig. Usually, that was the only name **I needed**. Normally, names did not go on album covers, and were ignored on orchestra programs. Whenever **a name** was needed on an album, one would be selected or created specifically for each group. Having already adopted identities when I anonymously worked with bands, it was not as outlandish as you might imagine for me to adopt the persona of Paul. Like an actor in a film, the character's name is part of the show.

For my *Cowboy Favorites* album, which used the same Western cowboy style as in a few of my other songs, such as "Rocky Raccoon," I used my boy howdy rootin' tootin' name, Bill Shepherd & the Ranch Hands, aka The Maple Leaf Four.

As Billy Pepper & The Pepperpots, I covered one Beatles song for each side of an album, followed mostly by my songs. (A friend, Jimmy Fraser, wrote two songs—one for each side.) I called it *Merseymania* (Labels: Allegro Records, with the identical album on Hurrah Records). The band and the same album were also called *The Liverpool Beats!* (Rondo), with the exact same record album. Then, I shortened that band name to Beats!!!!! for *The Merseyside Sound!* (Design Records). Those were all the same record.

Billy Pepper & The Pepperpots then made the sequel, *Beat!!!!! More Merseymania*. Like before, I **did a Beatles song** to begin each side. Jimmy and I wrote the rest. He did three then. The Beatles songs that we used were "I Saw Her Standing There" and "I Want to Hold Your Hand" for *Merseymania*, and for *Beat!!!!! More Merseymania*, "She Loves You" and "Please Please Me."

Even though I did not live in Liverpool, or in the surrounding boroughs that are part of Merseyside (near River Mersey), I contributed to, and identified with, the

NOTE: After their Tony Sheridan single, the Beatles' first two A-Side songs on singles were "Love Me Do" and "Please Please Me."

From the Decca recordings on 1 January 1962, Brian Epstein created a demo, which Sid Coleman arranged for Brian to share with George Martin on 13 February. Upon hearing the samples, George called them rubbish. However, after declining the offer, he was overruled by a superior.

Shocked to be ordered to take them on, George had the band come to EMI Studios on 6 June. After working with them for three hours in Studio Two, he determined that further recording would have to wait until suitable songs were written for them. The first song offered to them, which George planned to be their first hit, was "How Do You Do It." To teach the song to the lads before their next recording session, George made a demo and had it delivered to them. It was recorded by Barry Mason, backed by the Dave Clark Five. Later, Bill also made such demos for them.

On 4 September, the band returned to EMI. They rehearsed for three hours in the afternoon with Ron Richards in Studio Three. Ron taught them five new songs including "Love Me Do," and "Please Please Me." Afterward, George took them to dinner, and then returned them to Ron for their recording session scheduled from 7:00 to 10:00. Struggling, it lasted until 11:15. Before going home that night, George Martin and Norman Smith mixed, and cut acetates of, "How Do You Do It" and "Love Me Do."

In the morning, George and Brian listened together to the acetates. The vocals were weak. The guitars lacked precision. The inventive drumming was distracting. And, "How Do You Do It" could not measure up to the demo.

George was ordered to work with the band directly, to proceed as if Ron's recordings never existed, and to record their first hit single on 11 September. Besides that date already having historical military significance, it was also

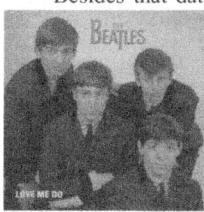
Teddy Adorno's birthday, and was exactly one month before the opening of the Second Vatican Council, giving the Beatles a one-month head start.

The Memoirs of Billy Shears

Beatles, and with their community, to sell records. I understood that it would pay off for me to be identified with them as if pretending to be one of them (beyond my work for them in Studio Two).

Living and making a living **as Bill Shepherd** (or any pseudonym), **I never made it big, but** loved what I was doing, and **never lost the dream of** somehow someday hitting **the big time.** This was yet one of many small steps, seemingly one of many meaningless steps, that ultimately trained me in preparation for where I am today. It is like what I wrote of synchronicity in "Let It Be" (chapter 6). Everything works out for the best. I referred to these albums when Brian interviewed me for the Paul position. The albums did not make any meaningful money for me directly but did help impress the person who mattered more than a fan base. My role as **Billy Pepper** made a positive impression on Brian Epstein. He considered the plausibility of having me **fill Paul's shoes.** That is figurative, of course. In reality, **with** his small shoes, I would have to "Cut **my toes** off to spite my feet" ("Flaming Pie").

When I did session work, I would play the tuba one day, then a piano or clarinet the next, whatever instrument was needed. Clients also used me for backup vocals. **In a pinch**, they appreciated my talent in voice-matching. **They would play a taped** recording of a **voice for me to imitate**. I would have it quickly **by singing along** and would keep for the rest of **the recording** session. The average listener would assume that the celebrity

76

shown on the album cover was the same fellow that **they were hearing**. That is when I was known as **"The man with a thousand voices."** I did not have a thousand voices. **It was just my reputation** and often my best contribution **that clients valued** over and above my instrument playing. Imagine a band ready for a six-hour recording session, but unable to do it because a backup singer's throat is sore or scratchy. When you book the time in the studio, that is it. You cannot wait until one's throat feels better. Unless you have big Beatles bucks, all must go as planned. You must pay for the time whether you use it or not. And the studio may not have another opening until it is too late. There are also often contracts with strict completion

---

NOTE: William's title, "the man with a thousand voices," was borrowed from Mel Blanc, the voice of Bugs Bunny, and many other cartoon characters from Looney Tunes, Merrie Melodies, and Hanna-Barbera.

William's ability to match a voice without listeners recognizing him added to his marketability. Additionally, his proficiency with many instruments, and his understanding of music, gave him the gifted ability to improve songs spontaneously. His session musician work before joining the Beatles established the practice that continued long afterward as he spontaneously helped countless recording artists, especially in Studio Two.

The general public is taught to give session musicians less respect than the big names on the radio. However, in reality, the writing and performing skills of session musicians generally surpass those of celebrities who are mostly paid to present an image and voice. The early Beatles are no exception. They played well enough for screaming fans but did not have the precision or expertise characterized by the expert playing on their albums.

While the Beatles were getting by with a lot of help from friends in Great Britain, the same business methods were used in the United States, especially among the Laurel Canyon crowd. The Wrecking Crew, as they were informally called, was a loose collective of session musicians whose great talents were used to create thousands of studio recordings in the 1960s and 1970s, including several hundred Top 40 hits. The public would not recognize their names or faces but know their music very well. They are one of the most prolific session recording units of all time.

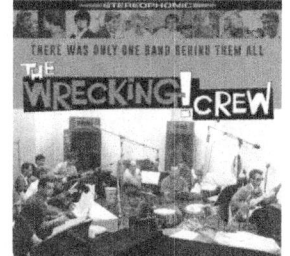

77

deadlines that cannot be put off. That was when they most appreciated "the man with a thousand voices." It paid my bills.

When I first joined the Beatles, I imitated Paul. Owing to his scratchy worn-out voice quality, it is easy to imitate, but harsh on the throat. When it was time to record, I went with a clearer sound, and varied my voice for each song for effect. You can hear John and me with a variety of voices in "You Know My Name." **I use my Vivian voice** for enough of it that I expected **to be recognized** as a match with how I sing **as Vivian Stanshall on the** strip stage in the ***Magical Mystery Tour*** **film**. As I sing in "The Fool on the Hill," I am "the man of a thousand voices, talking perfectly loud. But nobody ever hears him." I played as Viv until the mid-90s.

Having the right appearance is all that matters. When I look like Paul, fans hear him. If I look like another, that is who people hear. Even, as in Viv's case, when it is obvious that the hair, mustache, teeth, nose, and ears are not real, it does not matter because people only hear what they believe they see. My Viv costumes were a running gag with beards and foam latex. The fixed blindness of fans made it easy for me to play as Paul once my looks were close enough. **Appearances** are subject to the environment. Being **on album covers** as Paul, the Beatles context **proved I was him.**

NOTE: As part of the humor when William dressed up as Vivian, he sometimes wore oversized fake teeth. That was fun and easy. However, matching Paul required shifting and filing teeth, along with other extreme measures. In practically every detail possible, William was required to become Paul.

Whatever the charade, Billy's love of music is completely real.

Since my role as the fool, Vivian Stanshall, was my most known gig and alter, other than Paul, it is an easy one to find. As Viv in the *Magical Mystery Tour* film, I look like my son, James, does now. By comparing images of James and  Viv, you will see James looks like me.

Paul, having never been taught to sing properly, sang from his throat. That throaty sound we hear in all of his songs may have endeared him to some. I do not know. Maybe **Paul's lack of voice quality** ultimately worked for him in that it **made him sound** more youthful and innocent **like an untrained teen** in love for the first time. **But he was not as innocent** as he sounded—just untrained. One of the first things singers are taught is to breathe from the diaphragm. Proper airflow gives a smoother flowing sound.

Another reason to sing from the diaphragm, and not from the throat, is that it preserves the voice. Now, even in my last stretch of life, I can still out-sing Paul. His years of singing improperly gave him a chronically irritated throat. He wore it out in Hamburg. I hear his voice cracking even from studio recordings where a more aware artist would have re-tracked it later when the voice returned. However, for Paul, it was always going hoarse. It was part of his sound. I heard that early on, and used it to imitate him, but never made an actual habit of it. If I had, it would have ruined my voice just as it had ruined his. Once it is ruined, that is it. It does not recover.

James thought he knew about the Beatles, but was about eight years old before he discovered Billy's connection to them. The astonished child said to his father, "You're Paul McCartney!"

Before eating or drinking something, charge it with loving energy. For example, while holding a glass of water, imagine sending love and light from your heart, through your hands, into your drink.

Here is a tip for you. When you sing along with my songs, or when you sing anything else, consider it an investment in your voice quality to breathe from down deep. In your talking as well as in your singing, breathing deeply will add decades of longevity to the quality of your voice.

The importance of drinking water likewise cannot be stressed enough. Avoid voice strain by staying hydrated, and by breathing from your diaphragm whenever using your voice. You may consider this report on voice care as one of my many free public service announcements. **You can count on** more outstanding tips for wellness in **this** book. In this case, besides giving useful **personal information**, it also provides an obvious contrast between myself and Paul. Learn to hear those differences, and to practice breathing deeply whenever you use your voice—and keep drinking water!

Dr. Emoto shows how water exposed to loving energy forms beautiful molecular designs while water exposed to contentious energy turns ugly. Your body is 60% water (averaging 11.1 gallons (42 liters)). Its molecular formations are based on present energy fields. We form ourselves molecularly by the energy of what we think, feel, or hear.

9

Playing with the Bonzos

I, a little bit like the Paul before me, have always enjoyed playing and experimenting with avant-garde art, music, theater, and ideas. More than the early Paul, I like pushing the conventionality boundaries of modern society. That's what **I'm talking about** when I say, "I'm not conservative." **The public** viewed the Beatles as unconventional. Although they were for their time, it was mild compared to what I brought to the band. Look how their style changed when I came on board. By comparison, they were very normal. They had their "mop-tops" but wore suits, ties, and Beatle boots. Most people tend to imagine that the Beatles invented their Beatle haircuts. They did not. They copied the London art students, who were the real pioneers.

I was among that trend-setting crowd. It was the new look, the new sound, and the new way of seeing and shifting the world. From a conservative view, silliness was all that we stood for. However, from our perspective, and according to the intentions of the social engineers who secretly promoted us in the legacy media, normal was not good enough.

As a precursor to the avant-garde movement, Dada, or Dadaism, got started in Switzerland.

The real rulers in Washington are invisible, and exercise power from behind the scenes." – Felix Frankfurter

The social engineers that secretly promoted the Beatles were funded by the same people who secretly run most national governments.

81

Not wanting the culture that was a part of the First World War, the most creative people set all-new standards of art, literature, and theater as a rejection of the prevailing rigid standards. This rebellion had spread on its own accord but was spurred on by the gross absurdities of war. Artistic avant-garde anti-art again grew together with the anti-war response to the Vietnam conflict. Fighting is absurd.

Let us add some boxing context. The World heavyweight boxing champion, Floyd Patterson, like the plot of some Rocky movies, was accused of only fighting the people that he knew he could win. He was being protected. Finally, in 1962, he foolishly agreed to fight Sonny Liston. It was a big event. The fight was scheduled to be held in New York, but the New York Boxing Commission denied them a license because of Liston's criminal record. **The event was** then moved to Chicago, Illinois, and **viewed in England** by transatlantic broadcast. Liston (who was murdered years later) dethroned the champion, knocking Patterson out in the first round, making Sonny Liston the new world champion. In a rematch the next year (1963), Liston won again, taking him two seconds longer. A year later (1964), Liston lost the title to Cassius Clay, who was later known as Muhammad Ali.

Rodney Slater and "Vivian Stanshall," both art students, while meeting to watch the fight that had only one round before the new champion was named on 25 September 1962, were playing one of six word games that amused them that night. The game involved cutting up sentences and letting the fragments form new ones. One of the combinations that "Vivian" came up with was an instant laugh: "Bonzo Dog/Dada." From that line,

82

they named the band that Rodney had already been nudging Roger Wilkes to start with him. They called it "The Bonzo Dog Dada Band." However, much to their annoyance, the general public was too unaware of the Dada movement. They supposed undesirable paternal meanings that had to be explained away so frequently that the band was soon renamed "The Bonzo Dog Doo-Dah Band," which then evolved to "The Bonzo Dog Band" in order to simplify, which was later abbreviated to "The Bonzos."

Call them what you want. They were a whole lot of fun. I'd say the Bonzos were to music what Andy Warhol was to visual arts. We had fun stretching and pushing the boundaries of musical entertainment. I had been involved in that group as long as anyone. The Bonzo Dog Dada Band had begun four years to the month before Paul died. Chris Jennings and Tom Parkinson joined in, as did several others here and there who were loosely affiliated. It was never about who was a member and who was not.

The whole thing was more about who was open to having **a good** time. Each one of us took part in heralding an **escape from reality.** The band was

NOTE: The existence of objective reality is debatable. Humans operate in subjective realities created by their thoughts. By controlling what people think, such as by controlling news stories and Internet search results, master manipulators plant their intended reality into the minds of those who are attuned to the programming. In the absence of opposing narratives, the masses collectively adopt whatever reality they receive. "Whoever controls the media, controls the minds" (Jim Morrison) of those consensually programmed.

The Memoirs of Billy Shears (the unofficial memoirs of Paul McCartney) and *The Lyrics: 1956 to the Present* (the official memoirs of Paul McCartney) cover the same historic period in such opposing detail that each creates its own reality or fantasy. The unofficial memoirs' rejection of the media-imposed reality and the full acceptance of it by the official sanitized history, set each perspective as a fictional alternate reality to the other. The reality of each is the other's fantasy. The healthiest reality lies somewhere in between the pillars.

anything but real. I, as Vivian, had disguises evolving, or rather revolving, from false teeth overlays, and any one of several rubber noses and big fat pink rubber ears, along with a blond wig, to diverse costumes, such as my gorilla suit, that were only recognizable by my mannerisms. We altered and concealed identities as part of our ongoing fun. Names too were distorted or disguised. For instance, I thought the name Vernon Dudley was plain—not zany enough for our group. Vernon was a lecturer at Goldsmiths College. I christened him our very own Vernon Dudley Bohay-Nowell. The extended name stuck well, unlike the name that I tried to stick to Neil Innes when he joined us. Neil later created the Beatles' parody band, the Rutles.

I always enjoyed playing with the Bonzos. I felt more real and alive with them. As Vivian, I was more free to be myself than when stuck in this Paul McCartney role. The Bonzos were not about making enough money or fame. I had plenty of all that. It was about laughing it up and having a good time. I loved playing my Viv before and after I became Paul.

I never intended to earn a living from it. It was the kind of thing that we did for our entertainment. Later, when **I had a lot** more resources, I could put a bit of money **into** it. As the millions came pouring in from **my Paul role**, I did not in the least mind letting a tiny fraction go to the Bonzos. Expenses for disguises never bothered me at all. In fact, I enjoyed dressing up as much as the music.

As "Apollo [son of Jove (Jupiter/Zeus)] C. [see] Vermouth [Wormwood/Chernobyl]" I co-produced the Bonzo song, "I'm the Urban Spaceman." That song ended up making money for us after panning enough Beatle funds to get it there.

As was expedient, I would go back and forth between playing the Paul and Vivian roles, making a network between them. As Vivian, I co-wrote "Death Cab for Cutie" with my friend, Neil Innes. "Death Cab," as I will explain elsewhere, refers to Paul's car. Then, networking myselves, I, as Paul, welcomed the Bonzos to play "Death Cab for Cutie" in my *Magical Mystery Tour* film with me, now as Vivian, singing it as one of the last performances of the movie. The point was to give clues about me standing in for Paul, and to show who I really am. I am a cross between them and others.

I take on separate personalities with each role. There is also a good deal of overlapping. The type of music that the Bonzos did which I enjoyed the most was their fun British music hall style, which Americans would call vaudeville. It is mostly mindless entertainment, a mix of rousing songs and burlesque comic acts. **It is not serious music**, but an escape from it. Although **I love** all the more serious stuff too, playing with **the Bonzos** was just about having a good time. **It was play.**

My fun with the Bonzos lasted decades—up until I learned that Linda, my love, was slowly dying of cancer. Then my priorities shifted. I wanted to spend whatever time with her that I could. The sense of losing her took all the fun out of pretending to be Vivian Stanshall. All of the personal history

Entertainment = Enter [Latin intró ("inside")] + tain [Latin sub + teneo ("hold, possess, occupy, control")] + ment [Latin mēns ("the mind")] Your entertainment enters into, possesses, and controls your mind.

that I made up for him had to reach its conclusion in his death.

Linda was compassionate to the end, as I discuss in "Lovely Linda" (Chapter 60.) Our family had three years notice. It was more time than we gave the world. First, **we** sought to beat it naturally. Now I have **found ways that** were less known then, ways that could have **added years.** When we finally gave up

NOTE: This footnote is clearer after reading the note on page 385. William remained active in his Vivian Stanshall role until Linda's doctor discovered her cancer. With her condition on his mind, he felt that he could no longer do his zany fun Viv role. With Linda's impending death, William decided to retire the Vivian role, to kill off that fictional persona. He met with the actor who had lived as Viv for all those years and offered him a retirement package that would keep him on the payroll, but have him mildly alter his appearance, relocate, return to his original name, and cease all further appearances as that ginger geezer and from all further acting and musical performances.

The 51-year-old actor living as Vivian flatly refused William's offered retirement package, saying, "Over my dead body!" He said that he had built his life and family around that character and would never give it up, with or without William's money. He had so integrated his life story into his Vivian role that giving up that position would have felt like a death to him.

On 5 March 1995, after further discussion of the retirement proposal, Vivian (who often battled anxiety or depression with excessive alcohol) drank until he passed out. In his drunken stupor, he could not awaken himself that night when an electrical fire broke out in his top-floor flat in Muswell Hill, North London. To William's astonishment, the next morning (on 6 March), before resolving the retirement matter, the Vivian actor was found dead.

On 13 December 2015, honoring the Vivian role (played by both men), a memorial plaque was unveiled in the Poets' Corner of Golders Green Crematorium. Vivian's plaque is also near the remains of Keith Moon (drummer for The Who). Keith, on 7 September 1978, had spent the evening out with "Paul and Linda" a few hours before dying from an overdose of Heminevrin (used to treat alcohol withdrawal).

On 26 January 2018, Vivian's widow, Ki [Earth] Longfellow-Stanshall, published a book about the actor. Comparing his life story, or her creative innovation, to a fairytale by the Brothers Grimm, she titled it, *The Illustrated Vivian Stanshall, a Fairytale of Grimm Art.* She explains:

"*The Illustrated Vivian Stanshall* is not a biography. . . . It's not exactly a memoir . . . I've pulled punches. But not all of them. Some things need saying. Some don't. . . . Saying enough about Vivian is never enough. . . . None of this is true. It's all true." www.TheIllustratedVivianStanshall.com

86

on herbs, we turned to a more traditional Western Medicine approach. **That is when it** was time to tell reporters. Cancer **attacks people** in many different ways. **What cures one person may kill another.**

Vivian Stanshall was known to wear flamboyant hats. The strange name came from a word game in which we produced the phrase, "Hats in villa vans." Scrambling the letters, I soon produced "Vivian Stanshall," which, when scrambled further, produced "Van villains' hats," "Vanish all in vats," "Vat, vanish all sin," "In lavish salt van," and "Halt vial van sins!"

As things progressed, I found an actor to help develop the character. What ultimately came of it was not all me or him, but a humorous blend with each specializing in our own aspects.

Stanshall and Vivian were names I had heard before, but never together. They are both good for the wordplays I was looking for. The persona would do the most outrageous performances.

Anyone may ask, "Who shall do such a thing?"

They answer it, "Stan shall!" Stan shall do the nasty salacious undignified musical comedy that the conservative forbade. Dissociating from my usual self, Stan is the man for all such things. Whatever I will that I, Will, dare not, Stan shall do twice as well.

Having fun with dice as a child, there was a game **I played** in which the higher rolls had the advantage. **Rolling sixes** on the cubes were the best. In Roman numerals, two sixes are VI VI. Putting it in language, it is Vivi, the root of Vivian. Although the Sixes game used three dice, what name in the English language begins with Vivivi? I thought Vivi could be a nickname but quickly shortened it to Viv.

87

10

The Last Song of Phase Two

Peter Fonda inspired the last Beatles song that Paul took part in recording. **The Beatles,** wanting entertainment while **on a touring break** in Los Angeles, back in August 1965, **ended up partying** together with Peter Fonda, among several others. Peter freaked out John. They were both high enough to be impressionable. John's acid added considerably to the unsettling impact of Peter's tense ramblings. Unnerving them all further, all four band members were nervous about the possibility of being killed while touring. Security was a concern.

NOTE: Fundamentalists/Extremists of all religions receive media support that helps them destroy not only society but also their own mainstream religions. Fundamentalist Christians sent death threats to the Beatles throughout the tour. John saying that the Beatles were more popular than Jesus and that Christianity would go, intentionally alarmed the extremists who feared that John was correct. In their minds, there was a spiritual war between Christians and the evil Beatles. In the fearfully egoic minds of so-called Christian soldiers, the assault on their faith justified defensive murder for Jesus.

Fighting as if to save Christianity from being replaced by the Beatles, fundamentalists incited Christians everywhere to verbally attack the Beatles in the media, churches, and community meetings. To the extent of those attacks, to follow Jesus, one would stop following the Beatles. With the energy that Christians used to fight the band, they enlarged the Beatles to their own hurt. Many fans, loving their idols as programmed, left Christianity. If the Christians had stayed in love-energy, rather than dropping to fear, they would have increased themselves rather than energizing Beatlemania.

Perils included several attempts on their lives. No one talked much about it publicly because they did not want to encourage it. Even so, it spooked everyone. After landing, they would see bullet holes in their planes. In some of their concerts, Ringo would turn his cymbals to shield him from possible bullets flying at the stage.

Weighing heavily on them all, those causes for alarm were on top of Paul's death premonitions. His horrible death dreams had begun earlier that year. Dying was never far from their thoughts.

As they partied with Peter Fonda on Mulholland Drive (in Laurel Canyon), Peter recalled the painful trauma of his mother's death in 1950 when Peter was ten years old. **When the child found out,** it injured him spiritually. **He could not** deal with that ache. He shot himself in the **stomach** about three months after hearing of **her passing.** Many years later, he read that her death was by suicide.

When pain is suppressed or repressed, sometimes psychedelics can pull up the issue to clear it. Peter, on a "bad" LSD trip, experienced his idea of death. At the party, recalling that acid trip, he was upsetting John, saying, "I know what it's like to be dead."

John, on acid at the time, could not deal with that lingering "I know what it's like to be dead." He could not purge it from his head until a song was based on it. As with Paul-is-dead songs, in "She Said She Said," John changed "He" (this time, Peter) to "She" to keep fans believing our songs were all about romantic encounters. We often made that change. As another example, "Maharishi" became "Sexy Sadie."

Songs about Paul or me were regularly made to sound like love songs. The Stones did the same with "Ruby Tuesday," changing "He" to "She." Their other Paul songs are gender-neutral, using "you" (see "Stoned to Hell, We Called the Press" (chapter 37)). Becoming the last Beatles song that Paul helped lay down tracks for, being at Studio Three of the EMI Studios, "She Said She Said" was coincidently, or providentially, about John's death anxiety. It was done in four takes from 7:00 pm, 21 June 1966, to 3:45 am. It became the last song recorded for the ending of that second Beatles phase, being the last song made for *Revolver*. The Beatles then revolved again with new personnel, a new sound along with it, a new public image, a new message, and a new soul. Death songs continued woven in throughout the last Beatles revolution.

The *Revolver* album cover sketch shows Paul on his way out. **His face** is turned away on account of his belief that he **would die** soon. The album included "Eleanor Rigby," "Yellow Submarine," and other songs foretelling his death.

NOTE: Part of the Beatles illusion is from thinking of them as the same four-member band from 1960 to 1970. In reality, however, only John and George were in the band for all of those years. While it may be argued that they were three distinct bands, it helps to **see them** as only one band with three phases. *Phase One (1960–1962)*, **consisting of** John, Paul, George, Stuart, and Pete, was **a club band** that usually only performed covers of other artists. Aside from backing Tony Sheridan, they did not do studio recordings.

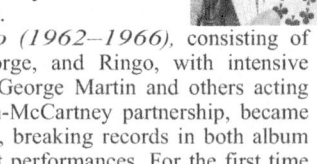

A lonely heart in a club band

Phase Two (1962–1966), consisting of John, Paul, George, and Ringo, with intensive assistance from George Martin and others acting as if the Lennon-McCartney partnership, became a huge sensation, breaking records in both album sales and concert performances. For the first time in history, they had a large enough audience to require a stadium.

Phase Three (1966–1970), consisting of William ("Paul"), John, George, and Ringo, with continued assistance from George Martin and others, was the world's greatest studio band.

Phase Three added William's face to his work.

Paul understood that his position would evolve so that society could evolve with the band. His view of the worldwide revolution was his own opinion, not aligned with John, who joked about it. However, after **I stepped in**, when Paul's position did revolve, I was able **to** give John much more information. To those who **push the New World** Order, he sang, "You say you want a **revolution.**" As he better understood the social engineers' intentions to help themselves by helping us, he had mixed feelings.

NOTE: Although many Beatles songs borrow elements of other songs, none are as blatant as "Revolution" using the instrumental introduction of Pee Wee Crayton's "Do Unto Others." To compare them, find Crayton's song online.

John, like most everyone, could be at least temporarily swayed either way about the good or evil of destroying the old social order in favor of the New World Order (NWO). He originally wrote and sang, "But when you talk about destruction / Don't you know that you can count me out." However, as was again explained to him, the Beatles were not permitted to oppose the NWO—or the destruction it required. Hence, in "Revolution 1," he added "in" after "out," meaning, "You can count me in." Having the "in" on one version, and not on the other, drew attention to John rethinking it.

Many people wonder if the NWO will succeed. For the most part, it already has. The power has been transferred behind the scenes with only a charade of national sovereignties remaining. Central organizations already work through governments to the point that governmental facades are quickly becoming obsolete. The NWO continues to increase in scope as it gradually comes out of obscurity. Those controlling the media are careful to pace that disclosure. If the public learns too much too soon, they could reverse the NWO progress. The coup must be revealed little by little as the public accepts one point at a time. Too much public awareness now could overturn the cabal's overthrow and spark court action everywhere for treason and other capital crimes. Ironically in this information age, the takeover is only possible by controlling and withholding information.

Like hiding monuments in plain sight, details in obscure books no longer alarm the masses enough to interfere. Whatever the world is told outside of the mainstream media matters very little now. It cannot sink in. The world is conditioned to trust their primary media sources above all sense to the contrary. The more urgent the matter from any other source, the less it is believed. Facts matter very little compared to the problem of sealed paradigms.

The alchemical expression, "Diameter Spherae Thau Circuli Crux orbis non orbis prosunt," translates, "The diameter of the sphere, the tau of the circle, and the cross of the orbit do not help the blind."

11

Masonic Checkmate

In *Through the Looking Glass,* Alice goes through the changes and becomes a queen. I told Mike (Paul's brother) that I am Queen Alice by becoming Paul. Later, Mike gave me several small *Alice in Wonderland* figures **for my backyard** as a housewarming gift as **I settled into** Paul's house. That inspired me to redo **Paul's garden, adding** a tarot zigzag path with the **statues at the nodes.**

We pinched ideas from many sources and incorporated them into our lyrics and artwork. We were especially enamored with Lewis Carroll. His *Through the Looking Glass* and *Alice in Wonderland* imagery was used extensively. If you are familiar with those works, you can see how they brought us to an awareness of tarot and chess. You may recall the talking cards and game pieces.

In turn, those images, each rich in symbolism, turned us on to other ideas and imagery found in literature throughout the world.

William became interested in Lewis Carroll's *Through the Looking-Glass* and *Alice in Wonderland* because Jane Asher played the title role in their dramatized versions.

92

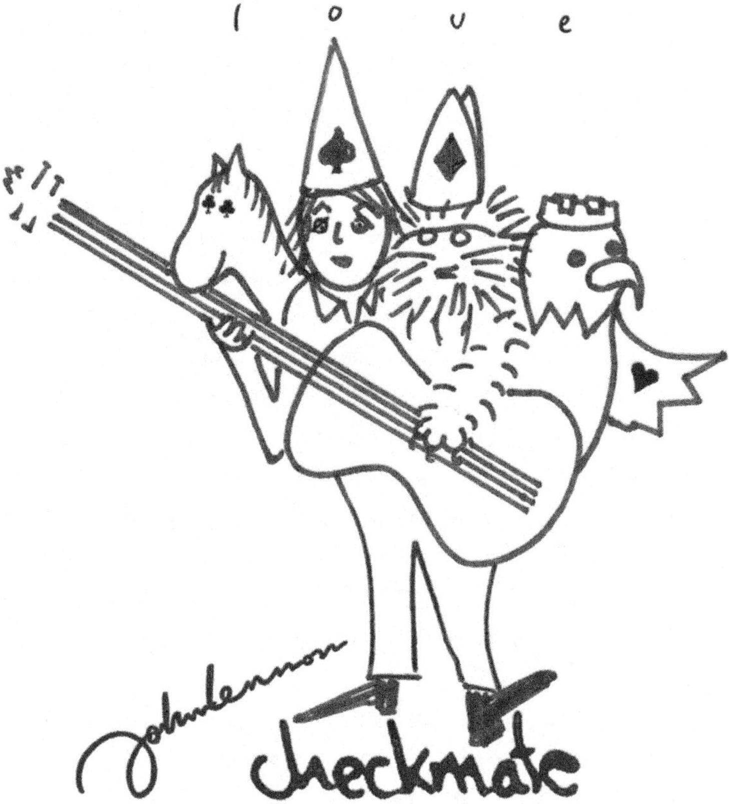

l o v e

Whenever possible, we combined the symbols.
Looking **for symbolism** in this drawing that John
drew in 1967, **see** how the images all work together.
You can see **the tarot** heart, spade, diamond, and
club, each **assigned to** a different band member, as
set into **the Biblical four-headed beast**, with each

NOTE: A quality reading can be illuminating. If you do not have a deck of
tarot cards, we recommend that you get one. Meanwhile, ordinary playing
cards will suffice. For insights about emotions, feelings, or relationships,
hearts in playing cards = cups in tarot. Corresponding to your thinking or
communication, spades = swords. For practicalities in the material
world, diamonds = pentacles. For insights about creativity and
action, clubs = wands. Whether reading tarot, a book, or anything
else, embrace whatever resonates with your soul. Whatever does
not resonate, let it slip away without resisting it. Whatever we
resist sticks to us, increasing whatever we find objectionable.

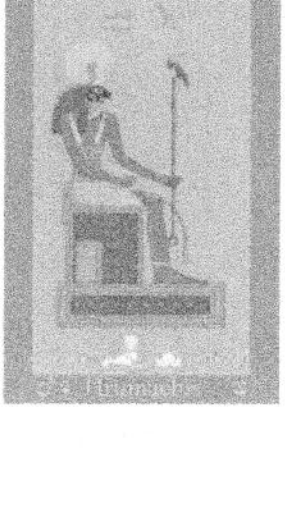

head saying something about that Beatle, and each having a chess piece representation, and also a letter. As four heads of one creature united in Paul, we are each distinct, but together playing Paul's left-handed bass guitar. In cards, we are four suits of one deck. An ace of spades is a card that has for centuries symbolized secrets or secret societies. It also represents personal transformation, and/or death. It is the Dead Man's card or Death card. As such, cards sold with the *Yellow Submarine* storybook in 2004 featured Paul as the ace of spades. **That is** why **the** cards were included. As with all of our **products**, it was to show the world our Beatles **secret, which is** our hidden message to the world, namely, **that Paul** is the Dead Man, and that I was **transformed** to mend the broken band.

As in John's hat in his drawing above, he is of diamonds. To connect him to that suit, think of him singing his "Lucy in the Sky with Diamonds."

On the first sketch, clubs hung around George's neck on a long ribbon. The word "LOVE" in that version was written in capital letters. John drew the original on one of the days we worked on "A Day in the Life." I got him to make the more polished version later. I bought it from him for twenty quid, a slice of lemon meringue pie (which I would have

For the days of the year: Jokers = 1, Ace=1, 2=2, 3=3, 4=4, 5=5, 6=6, 7=7, 8=8, 9=9, 10=10, Jack=11, Queen=12, King=13. [1+2+3+4+5+6+7+8+9+10+11+12+13=91] 91x4 suits= 364. Add in two jokers for leap years to equal 366, or just one to equal 365

NOTE: In the Beatles' *Yellow Submarine* playing cards, the fab four each dominate one suit, and are featured as its king and ace. The suits are the same as in John's picture: George is the king and ace of clubs (wands), Paul is of spades (swords), John is of diamonds (pentacles), and Ringo is of hearts (cups). Know your four kings and aces.

♦	Diamonds	Pentacles/Coins	Winter	Rest/Growth/Wealth	East
♣	Clubs	Wands/Batons	Spring	Planting/Passion/Creation	South
♥	Hearts	Cups	Summer	Fullness/Emotion/Intuition	West
♠	Spades	Swords	Fall	Harvest/Wisdom/Stability	North

given to him anyway), and a large plant grown illegally on my farm in Scotland. We were both happy with the transaction.

The four heads in John's Beatle beast sketch **show us as a** horse, man, lion, and eagle, which were based on **Revelation** 4:7, except that John drew a horse **for** George instead of a calf to tie it in with other **prophetic passages**, and to fill the chess role in the band. George is the dark horse or the black knight of our game. That identification grew beyond game meanings as he rose in prominence. He reinforced his dark horse image later by naming a song, album, and recording label after it.

Uniting the symbols, George is the dark horse of clubs. Clubs reflect back to when his Beatle journey started when they played in Liverpool and Hamburg bars and nightclubs. He was the only one at the end who had been with John in the beginning. His core work was in bars, not records. Although records included his voice, most of his guitar work was live. You can still see the clubs in his eyes.

NOTE: William sold the plant to John in 1967, the year of *Sgt. Pepper's.* That same year, the four Beatles, along with 60 other Brits of influence, placed an advertisement in *the London Times* calling for the legalization of marijuana.

In 1970, after a complaint that "Paul McCartney" was growing pot, police came and confiscated his plants. Although publicly familiar with the herb, William said he did not recognize it. According to his masterful plea, he received the seeds in the mail and planted them without knowing what they were. He used the technicality that he could not know each seed's gender.

Adding plausibility to William's claimed ignorance, he had failed to top or prune the plants and had not removed the males, resulting in the five females becoming pollinated. On the news, police were seen carrying away the male plants. Neglect lowered the quality that year but strengthened his claim in court that he did not know the gender. Had they all been male, they would have all been low in the forbidden tetrahydrocannabinol (THC).

The suit of hearts goes to Ringo. John never did see him as the brains of the outfit, but always loved his heart. Ringo has a good heart. The R and O in Ringo are also tied to the chess rook. Besides being a castle in chess, a rook is a bird. The beast bird is an eagle. The birds agree in one for our fowl emblematic needs. Ringo kept the heart in our castle.

John is the magical wizard whose vision became your reality, creating the Beatles. Just as he gave himself the most spiritually advanced role on the cover of *Abbey Road,* he did the same here, making himself the bishop—as if the godliest of all.

Our ace of spades is Paul. I am the queen of lonely hearts. My queen role in chess makes me the most powerful piece on the chessboard. I, queen, rule the Beatle beast through my power from the most valued piece, the king. **As long as the king** goes on, the queen has power. It **is still the same** even now. As Paul continues, **I have power in his** name. Paul's discontinuance would bring an **end** to nearly all of my work as well. It would be my retirement. The gender issue comes up now and then. I am straight. I do not mind having female roles in symbolism. I am secure enough in my sexual identity to not be threatened by them, or by any of the humor that goes along with them. On the cover of *Sgt. Pepper's,* we have Tarzan (played by Johnny Weissmuller) looking at my butt. It is a joke about my role as the queen of hearts, standing in for Paul, in the heart of that album cover.

Notice that the letters above the beast correspond to those made by our hands on *Pepper's* back cover. We discuss why you cannot see my letter "O" in "I ONE IX HE ◊ DIE" (chapter 14). For now, simply envision my "O" filling in the gap of the word "LOVE." Those letters' correspondence with the pieces we represent on the chessboard is clearer on the album. John's final drawing concealed it with lowercase letters. However, if you look at his picture and imagine capital letters, you will be made aware of simulated chess movements.

The knight moves in an "L" pattern. **The queen,** your darling, **moves all around the board,** circumnavigating, represented **as Paul's halo,** or an "O." John, our bishop, makes a "V" with his hands. In his case, he is pointing into his pants for his own added venereal significance ("of or pertaining to sexual desire or intercourse"). In chess terms, "V" represents the two diagonal paths that each bishop may travel. Ringo's "E" illustrates each way that a rook may go: vertical or horizontal.

Looking now to the front cover, the hat that Ringo is wearing is flat to resemble the rook or castle. Looking a bit like that of a cowboy, the hat worn by George suggests horse riding. And as a knight wearing a little box says to Alice, "You're admiring my little box," now George wears one.

You can see us as the queen, bishop, knight, rook, and at their right, disposable (wax) pawns. But why is no king among them? Alas, "The king is dead." **That is** the commonly held meaning of **"Checkmate,"** and is why John wrote it below his picture. It is not etymologically accurate, but works perfectly for the symbolism—and agrees with Paul as the ace of spades, the Dead Man. We learned how to play the game without him.

Under the "O" in John's picture, you can see that my hat is pointing right to it as if connecting to it, linking their meanings. My hat, connecting to the "O" that allows me to circumnavigate the board, is the hat of a wizard (being one of the five Beatle wizards in the *Magical Mystery Tour* movie), and is significantly higher than the rest, demonstrating (as in the game of chess) higher authority. Only the king is taller and higher in authority. I outranked the bishop and all others, but not our dead king. He is over all. All that we did was to preserve his life. That is how we stayed in the game.

Now, John's mitre resembles the bishop's traditional ceremonial headdress in the old game. It is split, like the "V" above it, resembling the bishop's diagonal paths. The letter "V" also makes a compass, correlating with the knight's square (L). These carpenter tools, necessary for building temples and other buildings anciently, were preserved as holy symbols devised to carry spiritual meaning. Those meanings and applications are explained behind closed doors quite often as part of the regulated instruction that is handed down by **the Masons** and their religions in under-wraps **codified observances**. I have heard it countless times. Initiates **have** regular reminders of each of their **hidden meanings**. While it might be a worthwhile read **to discover** what those symbols each mean, consider for **now** that they have become representations that bring to mind not only their nested sacred connotations, but also institutions.

Over the centuries, they became representative of the fraternities or religions that perpetuated them as symbols. In the States, it usually has the "G" for God, the Great Architect, Geometry, Gnosis, Generation, or Gatekeeper.

NOTE: Compasses set boundaries (for inclusion or restraint) and suggest that all truth can be circumscribed into one great whole. The builder's square teaches exactness and to be square in our actions. The Beatles (our compass) drew a circle of unity, encompassing all who had ears to hear them. Outsiders, not fab enough to be drawn in were "squares."

Entrance to Freemasonry requires a belief in a higher power. At the lower levels, while the god of Freemasonry remains veiled, a belief in any god will do. Initiates know that their **G** represents God (the **G**reat/**G**rand Architect of the Universe) and **G**eometry (applied with the compass and square, the measurement of the earth and all things in it). In this way, the **G** represents the connection between the earthly and spiritual aspects of existence. **G**od and **G**eometry are somewhat alike. Saint Bernard of Clairvaux explains, "What is God? Length, breadth, height, and depth."

The **G** may remind some of **G**ates, and that the fraternity is a **G**ateway that one must pass through for some of the world's most significant positions.

"We live in hope of deliverance from the darkness that surrounds us" ("Hope of Deliverance"). The natural darkness that engulfed us is now driven out by the supernatural light that wells up within. Advancing by degrees into Masonic light, the initiate gradually places less relative significance on either **G**od or **G**eometry and loses interest in lesser meanings.

Growing in Ha Qabala (light and knowledge) degree by degree, moving as close to illumination as we are prepared, the thing we learn to value the most—which is central to the upper levels—is **G**nosis, secret spiritual truth. That is the **G** that drives people to illumination. That **G**nosis is the **G**enerative and pro-**G**enerative principle. In **G**enesis, Enki teaches us to be as the **g**ods who [pro]**G**enerate according to their will by aligning their heart, mind, and strength with what matters enough to determine outcome.

The doctrine of the illuminated is a body of ancient secret knowledge that originated with Enki's teachings to the Brotherhood of the Snake (Earth's first secret society) in Sumer at the dawn of history. While concealed from the profane, the teachings were passed down, and adjusted, through esoteric organizations. These **g**roups intermingled, spreading influence, sometimes by the same individuals that were concurrently affiliated with multiple secret societies in parallel or concentric circles that cross the world.

For example, through overlapping memberships, Freemasons received the secrets of the Knights Templar and also of other organizations. Although (contrary to their myths) Freemasonry only **g**oes back a few centuries, now nearly all occult orders have some Masonic roots. It is not a literal continuation of an ancient order, but uses some of the same ancient teachings and symbols, and is the primary functioning network of the most influential people in major **G**overnments.

Emblematic of their secret fraternity, Freemasons well know the compass & square. When we see a compass and square, we more readily think of them than of what those symbols actually mean. Our **secret hand gestures**, veiled meanings, and all else on the album **suggest that we too have** made a fraternity or religion of **hidden truths.** In our case, it is all of Paul, **centered in me**, as Paul's representative. Having **revealed it only in** cryptic symbols until now, it is **time to expose it** as plainly as possible **in this tell-all book**. This book is not intended to recruit you to freemasonry, but to simply increase your awareness **of Paulism**, and of all that it entails. We now welcome you to our own secret society, the fraternity and sorority of believers in Paul, complete with our music, images, mysteries, and secret knowledge. Did you observe any degree of Masonic meaning in our 33 *Past Masters* tracks?

 Notice the symmetry on the *Sgt. Pepper's* cover. **It all passes right through** me, representing the departed **Paul**. Seeing me as him, consider how all is **centered in his heart.** All is in the heart of Paul. Seeing it that way, get out your compass and square to see how everything lines up through me, the new queen or king of the game. I am there as the queen standing in for the king. Rather than seeing me as under Paul, think of us as one in the same since the one represents the other. That is Paulism for you. At first you learn that I am not Paul since he is a dead man. Then you learn that I am Paul since he, residing in a spirit world, continues on through me. It sounds paradoxical but is merely progressive.

Everything crosses through Paul's heart—which is represented by my own heart. For example, use a square or other straight edge to see that the top of all three of the heads of Shirley Temple form a line right through my heart. There are several other such parallels. Things at one end correspond with things elsewhere, again and again, crossing exactly through the same point revealing the heart of Paul.

Another of many examples of corresponding images crossing through me is from the wax John. Look at all of their wax eyes. Everyone is looking down at the gravesite below them except for John. What John is looking at can be brought into focus by placing your square across the cover for a straight line that intersects all the others crossing through my chest. Continuing that line through me, you will be looking directly at the breasts of Diana Dors (born Diana Mary Fluck), Great Britain's sex symbol, comparable to Playboy's first centerfold, John's "pornographic priestess," Marilyn Monroe.

Until you understand that pattern, **it all appears** random but is not. A straight line **from William** S. Burroughs crosses my heart and goes to my fingers. He wrote *Dead Fingers Talk*. Sounding enough like "burrows," we decided to use that imagery also. Continuing that same burrow line directs you down to yellow hyacinth flowers that spell "Paul?" to have you ask if he is burrowed in the ground below those flowers that are arranged to also resemble his left-handed bass guitar.

Marilyn was not a "pornographic priestess," but inspired the line when John looked at the Peppers cover for lyrics.

PAULISM 101:
Everyone crosses through
Paul's heart.

Next, consider Carl Jung's famous religious and mystical approach to psychology and personality. From the shadow of his glasses that rest on his forehead, **it looks as though** he has a third eye. A ray from **his third** eye through my heart points to the third **eye** on a statue from John's house.

Everyone **took notice** of the ruby slippers on the Shirley Temple doll. First off, visually, the slippers emphasize the redness of the blood dripping down Shirley's clothes, and of her bloody driving glove. Moreover, some people have correctly recognized that it is an allusion to *The Wizard of Oz*. That story assuredly matches our theme. The protagonist, Dorothy, enters another dimension to be aided by a sensational wizard who helps her dealings at home.

I have already alluded to our mystical roles of wizardry. **Paul goes** to another dimension and helps us **back here** at home. The wizard in Oz needs **to use false appearances** for his audience to believe **he is** the great and powerful one when he is really just **another guy** from Kansas. We too used false appearances to seduce our audience, and even you, into thinking that I was a great and powerful teen idol. That wizard and I have a lot in common.

The ruby slippers were Dorothy's means of returning to reality. If you follow them through my heart, which is the way of discerning all reality on that album, you will discover that the straight line enters into W. C. Fields. That actor was the original wizard choice for the 1939 version of the classic film. Again, you only get the full picture if you look through me to see it.

"Oh – You're a very bad man!"
"Oh, no my dear. I'm a very good man. I'm just a very bad Wizard."
~L. Frank Baum

In cards again, a **"wild card"** is one card that substitutes for another. **I am the** wild card with the likeness of the **ace of spades**, being the substitute for Paul. Hold a ruler to Oscar Wilde's head, and then make a line through my heart to see where it goes. You will see that it leads you straight to a car that has gone wild on Shirley Temple's lap. Putting it all together, as Oscar Wilde, look through the heart of the wild card to see the wild car. Extending that line, it points you directly to the driving glove.

Extending a line from Lawrence of Arabia (**T. E.** Lawrence) right through my heart to the far side, **you may see** a hookah. It does not connect to **Thomas E.** Lawrence per se but to Arabia. Our first choice was Gandhi, being from India. He would have pointed to it perfectly. However, so as not to offend any of our Indian fans, we simply put Lawrence there and ended up removing Gandhi. We only wanted him out of respect but understood that others would see it differently and be offended. It was the same story with **Jesus.** It was out of respect for him that we **wanted him** in the crowd.

This pattern occurs **through me** many more times, making connections, some weighty, some humorous. Now that I have shown you the pattern, you can discover them. Some of them you would only find if you were familiar with Lewis Carroll's

NOTE: William is truthful, but deceptive, to say that they wanted Gandhi and Jesus on Pepper's out of respect but understood that others would see it differently and be offended. They wanted them placed in the crowd out of respect for Paul. All present give their honor to him. However, with this album overtly launching the drug revolution, allegiance issues were to remain covert.

With Jesus on the Beatles' pro-drug album, fans might see things differently than intended, and find the drug evolution compatible with Christianity. The intention was to make them entirely incompatible—pushing fans to choose between drugs or Christianity. Choosing drugs would then naturally distance them from Christianity, and perhaps from all religions.

Through The Looking Glass. Some of our lyrics are understandable only in that same literary context. Edgar Allan Poe's *Gold Bug* also serves to provide the needed context. Carroll and Poe are each among the crowd on the cover.

Understand, however, that when you discover an allusion to Carroll, Poe, or others, that is never the sum of the story. For example, in direct response to Donovan's lyrics, I used a line from Carroll's *Through the Looking Glass.* **I explain** in "Donovan" (chapter 29) how he "gave me **the word**, I finally heard." Carroll writes: "**The queen said**, 'that would have been **better** still; **better**, and **better**, and **better!**'" Even the increasing tone came from Lewis Carroll. He says, "Her voice went higher with each '**better**,'" Remember, I am the queen based on that same story that gives us all of the chess imagery. I used emphasis from Carroll: "'Oh, much **better!**' cried the Queen, her voice rising to a squeak as she went on. 'Much be-etter! Be-etter! Be-e-e-etter!" I sing essentially the same thing in "Getting Better."

Undermining my role as queen a bit, you can also see me as another character in that story. Alice says, "If I'm not the same, the next question is, Who in the world am I?" Well, that is the grand question that has puzzled the world about me since 1969. Alice agrees, "Ah, *that's* the great puzzle!"

"Be what you would seem to be" is advice I received from that same story. You can see how everything fits the *Alice in Wonderland* theme so well that Mike gave me all those *Alice* figurines. Mike and I had opposite attitudes about using the McCartney name for gain and fame. Nonetheless, he openly welcomed me to it. Mike too has made records but did not choose to capitalize on Paul's reputation. Rather than openly using his McCartney name to help his career, he went by Mike McGear. Even before **I got Paul's name**, I tried to create the illusion of being **associated** with him in order to sell records. **It did not work until it** was a reality. Mike, however, **connected to Paul** for brotherhood only, not for profits. It is commendable. "Let's all cheer for Mike McGear!" ("Lika Mika Macca")

In making allusions to Carroll's work, and layering our lyrics and art with ancient symbols, the mind (being connected to the universal grid) recognizes that there is more to it than meets the ear. That is an idea that John got from Stu Sutcliffe. They both understood it on a very basic level but did not have any idea how it worked. I did not either until much later. Although each brain occupies only a small amount of space, the mind expands outward and on beyond mortal limitations. We create new associations as we go. Whenever one work makes **allusions** to another, the associative link works to **connect us** to the second work even if we do not **consciously** understand it all. While the entire work is **too** much to be fully absorbed, we

NOTE: Safeguarding the name of Paul McCartney, Michael McCartney's support in the entertainment industry was conditioned on him not using the McCartney name. Emphasizing his compliance, Mike passive-aggressively used the stage name, "Mike Blank." Soon, he changed it to Mike McGear. "Gear," at that time, was the Liverpudlian equivalent of "fab" or "cool." His stage name was as conspicuously made-up as if he had called himself, Mike McCool. He did not want it mistaken for his true identity. Using the McGear name, doors opened to him.

The Scaffold (Mike McGear, Roger McGough, and John Gorman's comedy, poetry, and music trio) was signed to Parlophone. Their success included the number one hit, "Lily the Pink," which sold over a million copies.

Mike, who played no part in his brother's replacement, highly respected William before the switch and was grateful that Paul continued through him. Recognizing Paul in William made it easier for Mike to carry on as though without that personal loss. Mike sometimes worked directly with William, most notably after the Beatles years.

sense the connection to something beyond what we hear. **We feel** that connection to something deeper. On **an intuitive** level of awareness, the hidden encoded **message** feels good. The connection to other works **through** the warm universal grid of light and **knowledge** feels good in the same way that love feels good. **On some levels**, there is no difference. Receptivity **to spiritual awareness** can make us love a song without **understanding** any of it.

Allusions, **more** importantly, allow people to connect to the **literature** that they already know, signaling a link to **connections** that are already established. In the case of Carroll's Alice, or any kind of story woven into the fabric of society, when our generational consciousness triggers greater awareness, it is even better. But linking to any text at all combines the present work with all of the links already established to the alluded literature. One of the things that makes Lewis Carroll an intriguing choice is that it is already so thoroughly entrenched culturally. My favorite line from Lewis Carroll is from *Alice's Adventures in Wonderland:* "'That's Bill,' thought Alice." Alice again had it exactly right. The world can learn a lot from her.

In 1966, when my uncle was a higher ranking Mason than I was, he called upon George Martin on 12 September. My uncle told George that a fatal automobile crash occurred in the night and ordered him to have me replace the late Paul. He said I was selected because of my long qualifying lineage, and because of my musical talent. That same uncle had ordered me to acquire that talent in anticipation of that day. With John in Germany, George felt that the next best person to talk to would be Brian Epstein, the Beatles' manager, who could not be reached for several hours. **When at last they talked,** Brian informed him that **I had already been selected.**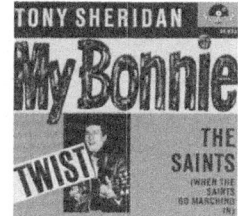

NOTE: In 1961, before Brian Epstein became their manager, the Beatles (John Lennon, Paul McCartney, George Harrison, Stuart Sutcliffe, and Pete Best) mostly performed in or near Liverpool. However, to perform at the Top Ten Club, they were in Hamburg, West Germany, from 27 March to 2 July.

While in Hamburg, on 22 June, the Beatles backed Tony Sheridan to record their first single, "My Bonnie." The B-side was the song, "The Saints" ("When the Saints Go Marching In"). That single, as released in West Germany in October, was credited to Tony Sheridan and the Beat Brothers.

While the lads were back in Liverpool, the single sold well there, supported by their local performances. When word got to Brian that a local band had a single, he spent a lunch break at the Cavern Club to see them perform and then proposed managing them. In December, he met with them a few times at his family's business, North End Music Stores (NEMS), from which Jim McCartney had years before purchased a piano.

That same month, Brian persuaded Mike Smith of Decca Records to travel some 222 miles to see the Beatles perform at the Cavern Club in Liverpool. Upon seeing them, he agreed (some say he was bribed) to give them just a test run in Decca's recording studios. On New Year's Eve, Neil Aspinall drove the Beatles (at that time John, Paul, George, and Pete) to London. The next day, Brian helped them select their best songs that they had performed in clubs. They recorded all twelve of those cover songs, and also recorded these three original songs by John or Paul: "Hello Little Girl," "Love of the Loved," and "Like Dreamers Do." Of the three, none were worth including in an album. John and Paul sang well together, but never were much of a writing team.

Upon evaluating the Beatles' recordings, Decca turned them down. The cover songs were uneventful. Their originals were not catchy. The band demonstrated unsophisticated guitar playing and drums. The poor quality was unmarketable. The world later ignorantly laughed at Decca for rejecting them, not understanding that Decca was right. The Beatles were too noisy for hits until, under George Martin, they had quality songs, precise session musicians, and unprecedented media support. It was hardly the same band. To experience the contrast, play *Anthology 1*, which includes their five best Decca recordings.

Failing to get a recording contract with Decca, or a positive response from others that Brian contacted, he secured a British release of their "My Bonnie" single on 5 January 1962. He credited it to Tony Sheridan and the Beatles.

As Brian continued to share the reel-to-reel Decca recordings, the HMV record store manager suggested transferring them to disc to make them easier to play. Brian then took the tapes upstairs to a studio and pressing plant where he met Engineer Jim Foy, who, in turn, contacted Sid Coleman, of Ardmore & Beechwood (a subsidiary of EMI). Sid arranged for Brian to meet George Martin. By that meeting, and by EMI receiving reports from others describing what Brian was doing, it became time for EMI to act before he interfered with EMI's plans. Although the project was not yet to that point, EMI assigned the Beatles to George Martin. George eventually agreed to use their voices.

12

Billy Shakespeare

Shakespeare, another extraordinary **William, was** one source from which we gleaned lines **to make** hidden death clues. I pinched **a line from him for** "With a Little Help from **My Friend**s." As if the press asks how it feels to be **the new Paul**, the song flows like an interview with the new member. It keeps asking questions that the newcomer, Billy Shears, must answer. Later, another interview went essentially the same way in "Baby, You're A Rich Man." The first of these songs uses the well-known Shakespeare line, "Lend me your ears."

You likely knew that those words come from the play, *Julius Caesar*. I allude to this speech to establish the *Sgt. Pepper's* scene. Have you ever considered the context? It is Mark Antony standing over Caesar's corpse to share words appropriate for the burial, a funeral oration. That is why the new persona, Billy Shears, when first revealed, says, "Lend me your ears and I'll sing you a song." As shocked Romans gather for Caesar (as each of the *Pepper's* mass gathers for Paul), we hear, "Friends, Romans, countrymen, lend me your ears."

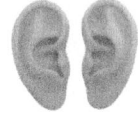

Inserting Paul's name where Shakespeare penned Caesar, Antony continues, "**I come to** bury Paul, not to praise him. The evil that men **do** lives after them; The good is oft interred with **their** bones; So let it be with Paul." In Shakespeare's **work**, Antony intentionally speaks negatively enough of Caesar to trigger a strong resistance to such negativity, prompting a revolt. If I were to speak negatively of Paul, saying that he was some Satan worshipper, most readers would angrily resist it. Going too far in any direction provokes others to push back. That is what Antony intended for Caesar.

So let it be with Paul. Imagine the resistance you might feel if I wrote, "The evil that Paul did lives on still. The good that he did is interred with his bones." You may ask, "What lives on; and what did Paul take to the grave?" And then, "What was evil or good about each?" **Antony's speech** goes on to exemplify all that **is brilliant** in crafty rhetoric— and works perfectly **for Paul.**

Antony says, "You all did love him once, not without cause." Again, consider his words as though kindly spoken of Paul. "What cause withholds you then, to mourn for him?" Do you see how Antony sets the funeral stage—and thus the *Sgt. Pepper's* album theme?

"O judgment! thou art fled to brutish beasts, And men have lost their reason. Bear with me; for my heart is in the coffin there with Paul, And I must pause till it come back to me." (See how that part changes in meaning for you with subsequent readings of this layered book.)

"He was a great patriot, a humanitarian, a loyal friend; provided, of course, he really is dead." ~Voltaire

Another contribution by Billy Shakespeare is a scene from King Lear. An excerpt was included to underpin the death message in the song, "I Am the Walrus." From this solemn death scene, you can hear lines in the song's fadeout. In the play, Oswald speaks these words to Edgar who defeated him, "Slave, thou hast slain me: villain, take my purse . . . bury my body . . . seek him . . . O, untimely death!" Then Oswald dies. "**I know** thee well: a serviceable villain." He is talking to **the dead man.**

Edgar says, "As duteous to the vices of thy mistress As badness would desire." Lest we miss it, at this point that Gloucester shows up, he says, "What, is he dead?" Edgar gives the old man this answer, "Sit you down, father; rest you." All of that dialogue written by Billy Shakespeare heard at the song's end provides the death context, and points to me, the slave who receives Paul's purse.

NOTE: Some scholars look to Edward de Vere (17th Earl of Oxford) to determine if it were he who used the pseudonym, "William Shakespeare," to write those many plays and sonnets. Believers in the official narrative tend to be offended when others challenge it. It mirrors the situation with Paul. To suggest that Paul did not personally write and perform all that is credited to him is blasphemous to his most ardent followers. To them, it is ridiculous to suggest that Paul is not always Paul. It is as potentially offensive as trying to explain away the many miracles of Jesus (or of other Avatars or prophets) to their followers. Of each talented individual who did the work attributed to Shakespeare or Paul, as was written of the Earl of Oxford in the 1500s, "He excels himself. He surpasses others. He transcends nature."

13

What's in a Name?

"O, be some other name!" Juliet says wistfully to Romeo. "What's in a name? That which we call a rose⚠ By any other name would smell as sweet" (William Shakespeare). Now, **I have** been William for long enough to know that **my own name** did not serve me as well as the name **of** Paul. As myself, I am still William, Will, **Billy, or Bill.** But my stage name, Sir Paul McCartney, takes the bill and pays our bills well too. But whether Bill, Phil, or Paul, it is the same. For example, when Mel Gibson's movie said he was William Wallace, everyone understood that it was just for that show, and that

---

NOTE: What's in a name? William used many names for himself, and also encoded his father's name in this book. His father's role needs to come to light. Networking with the elite, William's father (as if inadvertently) positioned William for greatness practically by birthright but left it to others to figure it out and to "discover" him—the obvious choice all along.

A woman of renown, who revered William's father, within that cultic circle identified William as a three-year-old musical prodigy. She selected him for initiation and training and shared her plan to use William's service to music to transform the world. Although details of the plan evolved over time, it eventually became focused on what William's father taught from the start.

That plan became increasingly plausible as William grew within the inner circle. Eventually, before the Beatles' last tour, the faction pulling for William (based on his father's magickal teaching and strengthened by his skills and studio work) prevailed over the disbelievers' plan to do Paul's work by rotating artists and models without granting a permanent position. "Paul," aging more slowly, could have stayed current longer.

This image is not of William, but depicts the above idea.

every night when he went home to his family, he was still Mel. When an actor takes on a role, whether on or off the set, one can still answer to it. Whether we call him Gibson or Wallace, it is the same.

That is how it always is in showbiz. The same actor who is Romeo in Billy's play one day could have a different role the next, and still be himself when he goes home at night. It is the same with each of my roles. **I play the** part of Paul McCartney for this fine **long-running show** but am still Bill. Rightly so, all performances require performers to adopt personas fitting each specific show. It is not dishonest to have one role with a name in one show and another of each in some other show. It is all showbiz. **Every role has its own name.** Playing **the part of Paul is the same.** For the Beatles, my name was Paul. My solo Paul work is a spin-off of the Beatles act. In other roles, I go by other names.

Early pre-Beatles tried on several names. They were the Black Jacks before the Quarry Men. They were Johnny and the Moondogs, Silver Beetles, Silver Beatles, Silver Beats, Beat Brothers, and Beatals Having many nearly-Beatle names, it was all in flux until they finally made it. Once the Beatles did arrive, the name was fixed even though the personnel continued **to evolve—covertly** in my case.

They also each **play**ed **with** their own names, as did I. While The Silver Beatles were on tour in Scotland with **Tommy** Moore, John, Paul, George, and Stu went by Johnny Silver (emphasizing that it was his own Silver band), Paul Ramon (an alias I used again later), Carl Harrison, and Stu DeStael.

Not wanting to use my own name in the Bonzo Dog Band, I invented a character (along with a name and family history) that I played up until "he died" in 1995. That eccentric Bonzo Band character's name was Vivian (Viv) Stanshall. Before and after "he died," others also wore my Vivian costumes. I, as I said, as Apollo C. Vermouth, produced the Bonzo Dog song, "I'm The Urban Spaceman." I also made use of the Apollo alias when I produced Apple's "New Day," Jackie Lomax's song to the morning star embodied in me to start this new day or era. Ringo added drums. George also produced some of his songs.

To explore wider avenues in music without diluting the Sir Paul McCartney name, sometimes I have done projects as though I were a part of other bands. For example, in The Fireman (named after the "Penny Lane" fellow with money in his pocket), at first, no one knew that it was me. Now that we have a few albums under that name, it is another Paul McCartney subsidiary, which this time is a collaboration with Youth. With his influence, it has a more danciful sound than I have in my standard McCartney line. I still do my McCartney bit. Still, the Fireman is something I may do now and then on the side, just as **I now** and then put out more classical music. I **find pleasure** in cutting into other music markets—or even **in making** new paths beyond the music world.

Having the freedom to use a variety of **personas** helped me break out of my Beatle typecast music role. With my personas created before playing Paul, they all fit session gigs or albums. Once I could begin entertaining and recording as Paul McCartney, the studio doors were ever left open to me. When I could lend a hand, it was nearly always uncredited

113

work. When **they wanted to use** my name, apparently to help their sales, I would invent an alias, or recycle one, rather than dilute **the McCartney** label on another performer's product. The **name** Ramon(e) was used now and then that way.

Letting go of the Paul McCartney name long enough to do other albums has allowed me to do a few things that I could not do as Paul McCartney. In 1970, when my first "McCartney" solo album was released, fans felt that it was below my established McCartney standard. Some critics expressed the opinion that my "Singalong Junk" was just a filler. That instrumental version of "Junk" on the other side of the album was to provide some karaoke amusement. However, it was not what my devotees expected. I never did that again. However, over the years, some people have said they liked it. I have bounced the idea around of having an entire album of instrumental tracks and might as a bonus CD one year. I would make it a two-CD set: one having everything on it, the other with all but the vocals.

As I write about this new idea, I realize that it may result in some other recording artists doing it now before **I get** around to it. If that happens, just remember that **you**, and they, read it here first. If you **want to copy** that idea, just as you copied my idea of including **the lyrics** with an album, it is okay with me. **Go right ahead.** We might start another new trend.

The idea of including instrumental versions so that you can be your own lead singers (or perhaps have it as a backing sound for your own backyard band) is one thing, having a fully orchestrated exchange for the regular versions is an entirely different idea. Considering the common practice of rearranging other people's material for use with orchestras, another idea that **I had** was to make a new orchestrated version of **my own material.** That way, when I hear a school marching band doing a song that I wrote, the odds are better that I will enjoy the arrangement. It is not something I would make a habit of doing but decided to try it once.

It took time, but I arranged and orchestrated my entire Ram album. As you might assume by now, I did it under a pseudonym. I released it decades ago, way back in 1977, using the name Percy 'Thrills' Thrillington. In case you are wondering, that outstandingly thrilling name was used five years before Michael Jackson's *Thriller.*

Using the services of Roy Kerr (The Freelance Hellraiser), I took some of my old under-finished lesser-known material and had it all remixed. I knew he was the wizard of remixery. He remixed those ditties into pieces that I enjoyed much more than as I had left them. I commissioned the work to play it for sound entertainment before the concerts of my 2004 tour. Being impressed by how it turned out, I added more tracks and released the whole collaborative remix album under the band name Twin Freaks. Early on, John and Paul, as a duo act, had been the Nerk Twins. Now I am one of the Twin Freaks, leaving you to wonder whether the other twin freak is John, Roy, or Paul.

Living on, continuing through others, sometimes my inventions spawn new creativity in other artists.

NOTE: William's pseudonym prevented false expectations of a Paul sound. His image resembles Amun and other ram-headed deities. It identifies him as the Ram of the *Ram* album.

115

As Vivian Stanshall, I co-wrote "Death Cab for Cutie" with Neil Innes. Ben Gibbard liked the song well enough when he heard me sing it (as Viv, in our *Magical Mystery Tour* movie) that he started up a band by that name. Along with their good music, **they have offered** a meaningful voice to wean people from **their** meat habit. They are doing some **good in the world.**

Even though I am not the one to first use the Ramon(e) alias, it was my use of it—when I added enough to one of the Steve Miller Band's albums to be credited for it—that inspired the band name for the Ramones, the world's first highly popular punk rock group. One's destiny is written in his name.

When Brian Jones died in July 1969, we decided to let our fans in on our Paul secret (as I will discuss in a later chapter). Once Russ Gibb broadcasted the clues three months later, the world began to find lots of hints that were carefully concealed until then. People began writing about them. One writer, Fred LaBour, not only reported on clues we provided but also embellished them.

It was LaBour who named me William Campbell. My first name is easily deduced from "Billy Shears," as announced in the *Sgt. Pepper's* title song. Yet, he seemed to know that "Billy Shears" was merely my stage name. (I meant it to sound like "Billy's Here.") Arbitrarily (after Glen Campbell), LaBour set Campbell as my family name. The surname stuck. Coincidentally, I have Campbell relatives.

NOTE: Brian Jones, a believer in magick, echoed Crowley's prophecies. He said: "I believe we're moving toward a new age in ideas and events. Astrologically we are at the end of the age called the Pisces Age—at the beginning of which people like Christ were born." Now moving into the Age of Aquarius, which is the Age of Horus, expect events as monumental as those at the beginning of Pisces. In this age, Horus includes Aradia.

14

I ONE IX HE ◊ DIE

"**Paul is** Dead" researchers say that Paul died on "Stupid **bloody** Tuesday," late on 9 November 1966, and was **officially** pronounced dead on "Wednesday morning **at 5:00**." That story is partly true, but more untrue. Looking at a 1966 calendar will prove, first of all, that 9 November was not on a Tuesday.

Legal action was a constant concern. We wanted to tell all but also feared the courts, not to mention incurring bad press for the band. At first, we feared we would be ruined when the world learned our big secret. At the same time, I was anxious to say, "Hey everyone, look at me! I'm a Beatle now!"

Devising clues to put into many of our songs and our album cover art was a fairly safe way to tell everyone as much as they had ears to hear and eyes to see. **I wished to tell all. The fact that** fans were all deaf and **blind came as a striking surprise**, urging us to make the next album even more obvious.

During my early Beatles days, we feared being too clear. The object was to say all, yet nothing. Having that as a goal, we intentionally threw people off with information and concepts that completely encompassed truth, but not with the most apparent analyses. We let them willfully reject painful truths.

Later, in "Stoned to Hell, We Called the Press" (chapter 37), I show how we revealed what was too obscure for the public to find on their own. But for now, I will explain the misunderstood drum date. The *Sgt. Pepper's* cover depicts a funeral gathering with several symbolically significant characters attending to bid farewell, or welcome, to Paul McCartney.

The focal point is the drum. We let it out that we hid a date on the drum skin. You can hold a mirror or CD up to the words, "LONELY HEARTS" to indicate the date. Holding up a mirror halfway down those words makes it possible for the world to see how I, the other half, live as Paul ("looking through the bent back tulips"). It reveals the once hidden, "I ONE IX HE ◊ DIE" pointing to me, Paul's stand-in, with the diamond. The Roman numeral IX is easily understood as a nine. The "I ONE" had the potential of being mistaken as a Roman two (II). To avoid that error, we leaked the fact that it was an 11 early on. Since then, in 1969, it was known that the date was 11-9. However, we could not very well go back and tell you how to read 11-9.

In 1951, a movie came out called *The Guy Who Came Back*. The title brings to mind Paul or maybe Jesus, "he that lives, and was dead." Each came back better than before—except that in Paul's case, others stood in for him. The movie starred Paul Douglas. That **Paul died on 11 September** 1959. It was exactly seven years before the death of Paul McCartney. Here **in Great Britain**, the date is

NOTE: The cabal seeks to make Paul a Christ figure, "he that lives, and was dead," and the Biblical beast that deceives the world, making all wonder at him and worship the image of the beast whose head had been slain and yet is. Making suggestions work subconsciously—bypassing critical thinking—words and images are designed to be too subtle to grasp without the "Paul is Dead" context. For example, the big 'T' in the Beatles logo secretly represents Paul's cross replacing the cross of Jesus. The "THE" is a crown of thorns. Imagine words nailed above. **THE BEATLES**

118

not abbreviated the same way that it is in the States. **We would write** it: 11-9-1959. Paul McCartney's expiration date, **11 September 1966**, is expressed  numerically **as 11-9-66 or 11-9**. We left years off dates in casual writing then. I wanted to add the year to the drum skin but could not make it look right.

NOTE: Some people argue that the ruling elite premeditated Paul's death date because of 11 September's cultic military significance. How did Building #7 go down?

On 11 September 2007, Russia tested their "Father of All Bombs," the world's most powerful non-nuclear bomb, with an explosion equaling 44 tons of TNT.

On 11 September 2001, the elite destroyed the Twin Towers by controlled demolition, and struck the Pentagon with a missile, to launch a "War on Terror." With media support and CGI, the US pretended to be attacked by foreign terrorists, panicking citizens into giving up their rights with the Patriot Act (a 300+ page document ready for Congress that same month—based on the German "Enabling Act" of 1933) and then the Homeland Security Act of 2002.

On 11 September 1973, the US-backed Chilean coup d'état deposed the Popular Unity government of President Salvador Allende.

11 September 1962 was the date that the Illuminati selected to launch its war on Christianity. They predetermined that the media would spin whatever song the Beatles recorded on that date to become their first number one hit.

11 September 1941 was selected for the groundbreaking of the Pentagon, the headquarters of the United States Department of Defense.

On 11 September 1857, in Utah's Mountain Meadows Massacre, about 120 people were killed—mostly by men who, in Mormon temples, had taken Masonic Vengeance Oaths to avenge the blood of Joseph and Hyrum Smith (their prophet and his brother) who had died in a gunfight (killing Freemasons on both sides). The deaths were a loss to their Mormon (LDS) church, and the cabal's "Council of Fifty." They had crowned him king and plotted to create a Native American uprising (fulfilling Book of Mormon prophecy) to conquer the Americas as a step toward a worldwide government and religion.

On 11 September 1831, that same Smith (before becoming a 32-degree Freemason) received word that "the rebellious shall be cut off out of the land of Zion," (which he identified as the Americas). They "shall be plucked out," and his LDS church would "judge the nations" (D&C 64:35-37).

11 September 1708 marked the turning point in the Great Northern War.

On 11 September 1697, in the Battle of Zenta, the forces of Prince Eugen of Savoye defeated the Turks, ending Ottoman control of much of Central Europe.

On 11 September 1645, Thomas Fairfax's Army occupied Bristol.

On 11 September 1609, an expulsion order was announced against the Moriscos of Valencia, beginning the expulsion of Spain's Moriscos.

On 11 September 1557, Catholics and Lutherans debated in Worms.

On 11 September 1541, Santiago, Chile was destroyed by indigenous warriors, led by Michimalonko.

On 11 September 1390, the joint forces of Vytautas and the Teutonic Knights launched a five-week siege of Vilnius in the Lithuanian Civil War.

On 11 September 1297, at the Battle at Stirling Bridge, our hero, William's hardy warrior ancestor, William Wallace, beat the English.

119

The epigraph in the drum skin came soon before the song and album title, as I will explain shortly. Hiding a message that is seen when divided through the center with a mirror (or now a CD) took time and effort. I will tell you how we did it. It was not merely a happy accident.

By the focus on "LONELY HEARTS" (the words containing that clue), we are saying we are each lonely—from missing Paul. I, now as Sergeant Billy Pepper, did not miss Paul at all but was of all the loneliest. I missed my face and loved ones.

The drum skin numbers had two meanings. The date he died is "I ONE IX," or 11/9, as I have explained. Nevertheless, we also anticipated the likelihood of confusion that the date 11/9 could bring due to our dissimilar date writing. Using England's system of date abbreviation, 11/9 is the 11th of September. Just as the British drive on the side of the street opposite Americans, our months and days are also on the other side of the divider.

Americans showed their egocentric tendencies by assuming that we went by their dating format. November 9, 1966 was not the death date but was significant as the night that **John** met Yoko. That date could have been seen as the band's death date for those people who **blamed** Yoko for the band's demise. Nevertheless, it was not Yoko who broke up the band. It was **me.** Or, rather, it was each of us, but mostly the absence of Paul.

John and Paul made music together and had their Cavern Club days that bonded them. They shared history as Liverpool mates. I was an outsider always masquerading as his old chum, but never connecting to him as fully. My pathetic Liverpool mimicking was never quite right. I took the Beatles to new creative heights, better than Paul could have ever done, but could not give them the same old Paul mood. I forever raised pop music standards with my *Lonely Hearts Club Band.* I was the greatest Paul for the public world, but not for the private hearts of the band members.

To me, our albums were serious business, but not so much for them. It mattered to them before. However, when Paul died, their steam ran out.

Each of them lacked responsibility for quality work. They had been spoiled. They wanted to work long enough to record their songs, and then go off and forget about it for another season. Sometimes I yelled at them to get themselves into gear. They were not accustomed to being bossed around. It made them all miss Paul even more, which in turn made me all the lonelier. That loneliness drove me on to higher achievement because **I used** work to take my mind off of my pain. However, **my** incessant work isolated me further from my **bandmates.** It made me stand out as not one of them.

Saying that Yoko broke up the band concealed Paul's death but was never the real issue. It was not Yoko who split John and Paul; it was Paul's death. Paul was John's dear friend and band partner before entering the spirit world but was all mine after. John then seemed to need Yoko. She became a nuisance who interfered with our work. Still, she evidenced the band's disunion more than causing it.

Returning now to the veiled meanings of the drum, see how we drummed a continuing message on our next album. Another way to perceive the *Pepper* drum, before the words "HE DIE," is that I, the last Beatle, am an unknown variable. There were the three current ones, "I + one + I" and one more that was excluded, X'ed out, replaced with the new Beatle X, the unknown Beatle. We see three Beatles remaining with one X'ed out and replaced (John, George, Ringo, and X) represented on the mirrored *Pepper's* drum as "1 one 1 X." Then, the writing on the drum wall of *The Magical Mystery Tour* was, "Love the 3 Beatles."

Singing that same idea on our *Abbey Road* album, John does the math for fans who may have thought the drum skin messages did not add up: "One and one and one is three."

All right then, the point was to explain the death clues in the drum's date. It all ties together. Having revealed all that, I'll explain the smooth transition. Paul's "early warning," that he received from his death nightmares moved him to "work it out." He was sure of his death. **He told his family** and some of his closest friends **that he would die**, be replaced, and live on in and through his coming impersonator.

Now, since he already explained all of that, once **he did die,** they were all at least half-expecting to see me show up as his continuance. They did not at all **resist the switch** of form because Paul had prepped **everyone** for it. Some of them were in denial saying that he was not dead at all, just transformed.

Some skeptics have questioned why all those close to him would go along with such a charade. People close to him did receive some compensation. However, money was not what silenced them. I represented Paul to them. I became **Paul** to them. Their only way to not lose Paul was to accept me. Recognizing Paul in me, they **welcomed me** with overwhelming gratitude. If I could truly be Paul,

I would keep him there among them. Jane especially **felt** his presence in me. Any paid compensations they received, officially to buy their silence, were **more like going-away** presents from Paul. However, since he was not entirely gone, it was all more of an acknowledgment of his love for them.

Conspiratorial silence was not for the money and was hardly ever enforced by violent threats as some out there have suggested. They were silent out of love for Paul. They did not want to lose him again. Now that I was Paul, exposing me as anything else would betray Paul and risk losing him altogether. They believed he would carry on through me. They still want to believe. I honor Paul by using his name.

It was not until the 20 January 1964 release, *Meet the Beatles*, launched by *The Ed Sullivan Show* the next month, that the Beatles entered the world stage with their first of several number 1 albums on the US Billboard Top LPs. LPs are played at thirty-three and a third (33⅓ or 33.3) rpm. From that release until the end of Paul's life, was only 2 years, 33 weeks, and 3 days (2.33.3) = (Phase 2. LP rpm). My tour as Paul on the world stage has gone strong for generations.

NOTE: Ed Sullivan was flown to London for special training to create the historic event. Setting a record for the largest audience for an American television program, on Sunday evening, 9 February 1964 (exactly three years after their 9 February 1961 debut at the Cavern Club), approximately 73 million viewers in over 23 million households (over a third of the American population) watched *The Ed Sullivan Show* featuring the Beatles. They made further appearances on the show the next two Sundays (with the third appearance pre-recorded), and returned 18 months later, on 14 August 1965.

That show, and other publicity, gave their American tour an enormous boost and made sales soar. During the week of 4 April 1964, they held 12 positions on the Billboard Hot 100 singles chart, including the top 5. Beatlemania became an unprecedented reality.

The really big show also helped launch the Rolling Stones in America. They appeared six times, including, on their fourth appearance, the day Paul died, 11 September 1966.

Beyond **Paul's** 962 days on the world stage, none of **the Paul** McCartney that the whole world knows was him. I have been Paul much longer. Singing **"One and one and one is** three" had multiple meanings. "Love **the 3 Beatles**," and all of that, told the world different things. First of all, like all of our Paul clues, it said that Paul had died. Making the point obsessively from *Sgt. Pepper's* on, including all of the allusions in every album I have ever made since that time, I also showed the world that we were not okay with that loss. We wanted sympathy for Paul's loss and mine; and we showed in endless ways that I, the new Paul, was not one of them. I was a Beatle in the sense that it became my band. I was also one of the Beatles in the sense that I was their creative force, the one who, as their new leader, made writing assignments and album concepts. I was always the band's prominent focus ever since Paul died. All of my Beatles work was my Karma. No one can say I was not a Beatle. Even so, I was never fully one of them.

All that I did for them was appreciated eventually. They did not like being bossed around but did realize that they could never have reached such great heights without me. **I also needed** them. Otherwise, if I did not need **their launchpad**, I would have already done it **for my own** career. Until I had the Paul persona, I could not **take off**

NOTE: When George Martin signed on the Beatles, he appreciated their wit and voices. However, their limited skills and ignorance of music theory created extra work for him. Because the band did not read music and did not speak the language of music, communication was labored.

William, the band's new de facto producer, on the other hand, joined as George Martin's equal. They traded off roles. When either played an instrument or conducted the musicians, the other was usually in the control booth. False

perceptions aside, the Lennon-McCartney team never held a candle to Martin-Shepherd. William, whose skills surpassed them all in their own instruments, often had his band members re-do their work after showing them how. Billy (as "Paul McCartney") said, "If anyone earned the title of the fifth Beatle, it was George [Martin]. . . . He was the most generous, intelligent and musical person I've ever had the pleasure to know."

on my own. I lacked fans. I had the talent that I needed to do *Sgt. Pepper's* but did not have the fan-driven funds required for the endless studio hours that I dedicated to it. Even if I had attempted it on my own, it was much better with help from "the 3 Beatles."

Before doing the *Sgt. Pepper's* title song, Mal Evans, Peter Blake, and I worked together with the year as part of the drum clue. **We had** the idea of revealing it with a mirror but had **to massage** it enough to make it work. First, I wrote "**11-9-1966**" which, depending on how we held the mirror, was made to resemble "II B 1BEE" or "II 3 I3BB." One of us suggested that we use Roman numerals or all written numbers. I combined them both with Arabic as "I ONE 1X 1966." In the mirror, it looked like "LONELY IBEE." I said, "Lonely Hearts!"

We wrote it out in capital letters and could see that it resembled "I ONE IX HE ◊ DIE." That is how I then came up with the full title and decided to have me on the cover stand above the pointer. I later said that Joe Ephgrave (Epitaph-grave) designed all of the drumskin. It is a clue. Peter also helped John, George, Robert Fraser, and me make our needed guest list for the funeral. In reality, only Paul's family and Jane came. But for the album, all kinds of people were included. It took months for Peter and his wife, Jann, to collect the photos.

Sending Paul off to the world of spirits was one thing but welcoming him *into* that spirit world was another. My original plan was for our stand-up cardboard photographs to all be of those who had already died (become spirits) who would welcome

Do not attempt the magic mirror exercise unless you are mentally well and awake enough to not be hurt by it, and to do no harm.

Paul into their spirit world. That was the main idea. It was a gathering on the other side. They were there to greet Paul, who had now become one of them.

Then we decided to add to our list of heroes. We decided to include some fictional movie characters who had died, and thus the actors who played them. Six weeks before Paul died, Bob Dylan had an accident on his motorcycle. The newspapers had called it a near-death experience. With the great influence that Dylan had had on John's writing, John insisted on also including the hero who almost died.

The reason that former Beatle Stuart Sutcliffe was in the crowd and not former Beatle Pete Best is because Stu had already died by then; Pete had not. We did not have any disregard for either. It was only a matter of who was in Hades to welcome Paul. Marilyn Monroe was there because she had already been murdered by then—apparently by government operatives. It was not a suicide as they claimed.

Dylan said he would have died by then too if the accident had not slowed him down, making all the years that followed much saner with clearer values. Most vitally, he had six weeks to detoxify **at last**. Long addictions were killing him. Almost all of **our** cardboard guests were associated with **death**.

Adolf Hitler was invited to the **party** for a time. John loyally wanted Hitler there **to greet Paul**. "It is not about who is in heaven and **who is in hell!**" John said. "How do you know where **Paul is?**"

In what would have reopened Christian wounds caused by John's comment in the *London Evening Standard* in March 1966, that the Beatles were

On 28 August 1964, at the Delmonico in NYC, Bob Dylan met the Beatles for the first time and introduced them to marijuana.

"more popular than **Jesus**," a cardboard Jesus being nestled into the crowd **was also intended**. Without question, many record-buyers would have been offended. Others might have been glad to see Jesus there in that *Pepper's* context. Paul would have liked to meet him for sure. That interview published in March came and went without anyone making a big deal of it. *TIME* magazine republished those same words four months later, still without stirring any evidence of offense taken. No one was manipulated to panic from it until *Datebook* magazine reprinted it and plastered the Jesus quote on its front cover. That presentation made it a big deal, stirring outrage days before the tour, and giving the band a political mess to deal with before they could perform.

NOTE: When contracting the Beatles with EMI, George Martin attempted to explain to John and Paul that they would become a famous writing team, greater than Rodgers and Hammerstein. When John corrected him, saying that they practically never play their own material, Martin said, "Mark my words. Lennon and McCartney will be the most famous writing team in the world!"

Martin went on to say that the media would make the Beatles big enough to topple Christianity. (See the note on page 554 in "Paulism" (chapter 61).) John did not believe it. The Beatles were just a rock band that played in clubs. Still, the proposed level of support intrigued him. Not understanding how social engineers could use the power of music to break down old power structures, John imagined the media backing the band in a contest of sorts with Jesus to see who could win the most followers.

To John's delight and dismay, by 1966, he could see that by controlling the media, the elite were accomplishing all they had set out to do. They built the Beatles into something much bigger than life that was overthrowing Christianity. John was delighted by the band's success but disillusioned that even Christianity was too weak to stand up to an Illuminati assault. Although he had grown up with disdain and contempt for nuns, he had believed that religion was too powerful for conspirators to conquer.

Using Beatle images, with added anti-Christian support from the Rolling Stones and others, Christianity made a stark downward turn from Beatlemania onward, making more room for New Age philosophy and paganism in an era of harmony. Start noticing the pagan core of most major propaganda.

John was neither prophetic nor arrogant, but simply informed when he said, "Christianity will go. It will vanish and shrink. I needn't argue about that. I'm right and will be proved right. We're more popular than Jesus now. I don't know which will go first–rock 'n roll or Christianity. Jesus was all right, but his disciples were thick and ordinary. It's them twisting it that ruins it for me." He later explained, "I pointed out that fact . . . that we meant more to kids than Jesus did, or religion . . . . It was a fact."

127

On *Sgt. Pepper's,* our first album since John's press conference to cool his inflaming Jesus remark, the idea of setting off a new wave of album-burning seemed unwise. There was an active anti-Beatles hullabaloo going on the whole time that the band was on their last tour. Some people were saying everyone should be anti-Beatles because the Beatles were anti-Christ. **John** clarified himself to set it all right but **was** only believed by those who loved him. John **being anti-Christ** was not his point.

Public demonstrations against the Beatles further promoted the band. For all actions, there are equally strong counter-actions. The anti-Beatles movement spurred on by parents principally pushed otherwise neutral children to the band. That is part of what made **Beatlemania** extraordinarily powerful. The fuel **was pushed by parents** and ministers. Before that point, the Stones had been less respected by parents than the Beatles. They were the bad guys of rock. It gave their band an edge. The Beatles were the good guys of rock until John revealed too much in that press conference, which shattered the false image. The good guys had gone bad. Prior anti-Beatles work had less success.

Engulfing images or symbols in flames has always been an effective way of stirring people to revolt, riot, or reel out of control. The large bonfires of Beatles albums across the United States

NOTE: Anti-Beatles album-burning demonstrations were the most prevalent in the United States, Mexico, Spain, and South Africa. Over the years, John went on to say many things that could be construed as much more blasphemous. However, without media assistance, none of it created a public outcry.

Supporting the idea that the Beatles would continue to grow into the next millennium, and knowing the Aztec calendar placed 21 December 2012 at the end of that cycle, John expected complete success by then. Sounding hyperbolic without the context of this book, he said "Paul should be Jesus by then." The Beatles, through Paul, would elevate the whole world under themselves. John says, "If this scene is around in 2012, the masses will be where I am today, and I should be as groovy as Jesus by then."

enticed many more teens by the appeal of the forbidden. The heat of it all was felt everywhere with fanatics claiming that **the Beatles** were serving the devil. Energized by the egoic emotional appeal induced by the idea that Jesus **needed** to be defended against the Beatle beast, **Americans** and others were lining up, choosing sides: "Choose ye this day whom ye shall serve: The Lord, or the Beatles!"

Later, after the frenzy ran its course, most of the burned albums were repurchased. At last, when it was clear that the group posed no real threat, fans who missed their favorite records bought them all again. It was good for sales, boosted them in the charts, creating an extra opportunity wave.

Making the Phase Two Beatles band look more dead than the assembly standing behind them, their line-up of **gloomy wax figures** beside the New Fab Four made them **look dark**, down, and out of date. Instilling the idea that **the old** band belonged to the past, and that the new **band had** arrived for the bright vivacious present, the **old drab suits** are faded into indistinguishable darkness, while the album's most effulgent colors are on the pallbearers who form the new band belonging to Sgt. Pepper. The idea for that set wax Beatles is from Tweedledum's lines to Alice. He says, "If you think we're wax-works, you ought to pay, you know. Waxworks weren't made. to be looked at for nothing." While you are looking, notice the shape of the old **Paul's** head. Being a realistically sculptured **figure** from photographs of all the Beatles, it **shows the old Paul**, and others, looking as they **had** looked before.

Notice **the small head** on Paul, fitting his small frame. The others were rather small too. I do not point that out to belittle them, but so you will recognize it. My skull shape is more elongated, more oval. Contrasting the old Beatles here with the new band, it is observable that this Sgt. Pepper band is new and living, whiles the old band, the Beatles Phase Two, is dead—even though John, George, and Ringo continue on. The newness of my Pepper's band concealed the fact (shown by the contrasting images) that a new player has taken Paul's part.

We all resist seeing what does not fit our beliefs. **Generally, people find** it hard to comprehend that **one player** can replace another without us ever **having the** public made aware of it. For a case in **point**, consider *Bewitched*, a popular show in US television from 1964 to 1972. Due to Dick York's debilitating back injury, Darrin Stephens' role (the leading male) was given to Dick Sargent in the fifth season. What most viewers missed in all those years of watching it every week was that other roles on the show were also replaced. By comparison, our switching Pauls was relatively easy—with much fewer images of us available to the public back then. Our free access to images now would make it harder.

NOTE: The best way to know how Paul looks is to refer to his photographs. However, one complication is that many pictures said to be of Paul are of his doubles. Before and after Paul's death, all four Beatle positions had doubles that were used far more than most fans would imagine. William still uses his.

Album covers are Paul's most dependable photos. Less-known images are often morphed to include elements of William. Some such images look real. Others are sloppy. Do not be fooled by them. Notice when Paul's face has been lengthened to look like William's. ["Man, you been a naughty boy / You let your face grow long" ("I am the Walrus").] Often in morphed images, the lighting or resolution of the face does not match the rest of the photograph. Sometimes the hair parts on the wrong side. Occasionally identical morphed images are pasted onto multiple photos making too many identical details.

Videos are also modified. Save videos and photos before faces are changed.

Had the band grown organically, songs they played well in clubs would have been on their first albums. If Ringo is at the drums, the event  is after Ron at EMI taught them their first hits.

130

Even pictures of Paul's doubles are being fixed with Billy faces.

The part of Tabitha, the daughter, was played week after week by alternating twins. **The role of** Darrin's father was also played by **two actors**. For each of the two appearances of Tate's **partner in** the ad agency, each was played by **a different actor**.

When Alice Pearce died (before Paul), she was replaced by Sandra Gould for Gladys' role. They ended up using four different people to play Darrin's secretary. Samantha's Aunt Hagatha was Reta Shaw for some episodes but was Ysabel MacCloskey for others. With all of this being well established for a show that millions of people watched closely without ever noticing, it should be beyond reason to suppose that the world would notice me suddenly playing Paul's Beatle role even though our album showed the two sets of players standing side by side for contrast.

Without going into details that are available all over, the *Sgt. Pepper's* cover is loaded with symbols illustrating the fatal car crash (represented by the car rolling off of Shirley Temple) that had caused the head injury (as shown by the split-headed doll). The news blackout was a turned-off television. Carefully hinting at lies we told to conceal Paul's death, we have his rugby trophy, looking like a higher than perfect "I," placed after the "L" in BEATLES to form the words "BEAT LIES." Exactly below "Lies," we have the word "Paul" spelled in yellow hyacinth flowers since "Paul lies" dead, and we lie to cover it up. As is common in my songs, and this book, it is wordplay.

It has been noticed that there is an open hand over my head, which is a sign of death. Now notice that it is also a wordplay. **The palm is exposed**, or, spelling palm another way, we expose **Paul-M**. It is above my head since I too represent **Paul-M**. Off to the side, there stands another **Paul-M** substitute. **It is a palm (Paul-M) tree.** There is a wax substitute **of Paul M** on the other side of the album. **The palm is above my head** also in two images in the *Magical Mystery Tour* booklet, two more times on the original *Yellow Submarine* album cover (one on the front, one on the back), and is on a photograph in the *Yellow Submarine* movie press pack. It is on for several seconds in the *Yellow Submarine* movie and is also in our *Magical Mystery Tour* movie. The palm repeatedly brings to mind the death and replacement of Paul-M.

Paul's name is in the flowers, shaped into a four-string **bass guitar.** One of its four strings is missing. The front cover is loaded with images that are arranged to depict our loss of the "late Paul," or "Late of Pablo" ("Being for the Benefit of Mr. Kite!").

During the writing stages, some of the lyrics had to be adjusted a little to fit perfectly on the album. Before *Pepper's*, no one put lyrics on album covers. We were the first ever to provide them. We had unusual motivations for it but started something new. The next time you read lyrics printed with that CD you just bought, remember that we did that on LPs first. I'll tell you our reasons for it. One that has been noticed is that we, standing behind those words, add meaning to them. Besides the rest of the clues that many of you know by now, here is the reason that had never become an issue

132

until February while doing "Fixing a Hole" and "A Day in the Life," each with conflicting lyrics.

Each of us heard what we expected. Following Aleister Crowley's advice to "Say two things at once," John's "Nobody was really sure if he was from the House of Lords" overdubbed in that spot, **"Nobody was** really sure if he was from the House of **Paul.**" Like my Beatle/People, we could only consciously hear whichever one we expected while hearing the other subconsciously. I was concerned that people would hear the wrong tracks. It was to conceal "Paul" and "Beatles," that lyrics were provided, allowing fans to read along to listen for, and consciously hear, the official track.

Let us try an experiment. Play John's song expecting to hear "Lords." It is the word you will always hear when it is what you expect. Then play it again but listen for ''Paul.'' You will only hear that word when it is what you expect. Still, we cannot expect and hear both at once because our intelligence is limited to focusing on only one thing at a time. The best that any of us can ever do is to oscillate back and forth, from one focus to another.

Try that same experiment on my "Fixing a Hole." Notice with full expectation the word "Beatle" in place of the word "people." We hear what we expect.

Please recall this paragraph a few chapters from now when I discuss "See how they run." Those lyrics, and what I am explaining now, are in the same context as us Beatles, but **mostly** about Brian, each running about doing our parts **to save the band** by preserving the fantastic illusion that **Paul is me.** As was just suggested, just as John recorded "Paul" in the same place as "Lords," so too I dubbed

"Silly Beatle" over "Silly people" for "Silly Beatle running round that worry me."

Explaining further the "Fixing a Hole" meaning, by overdubbing "Beatle" over "people" I subtly referenced the wax Beatles standing beside my *Sgt. Pepper's* band. The wax figures, I should probably explain, were made by Madame Tussauds, which is a wax museum in London with museum branches in many major cities of the world. When I sing, "See the Beatles standing there," I mean the dead wax effigies. It is in the same place that I sing, "See the people standing there," which refers to the crowd we made behind us. John describes some members of that crowd, standing in a row, in "**I Am the Walrus.**" But that song covers other clues too. **All throughout**, it gives disjointed Paul clues from here, there, and everywhere. The few people mentioned from the *Pepper's* crowd are only small parts of the song.

Reading on the back cover the words we want you to expect and hear, also notice "Love" spelled with our hands, except that you cannot **see** my letter "O" because I am turned around. **The absence of** seeing Paul there left a hole in the Beatle "love" that I must fix, along with the hole in **Paul's head** causing everyone's mind to wonder about **Paul's brains** wandering from his skull. Some fans **knew it was** not Paul's back shown in the picture, since **I** am larger. It is "Billy's Back." Paul came back as Billy.

Until the historical *Sgt. Pepper's Lonely Hearts Club Band,* we had worked on, but not launched, Phase Three of the Beatles. With that kick-off, everything changed for me as Paul McCartney.

The thing **I like** best about being Paul McCartney is that **this role** gives me the power to do good. I not only change the world with my music, but also with the potent influence of my position. I have adopted causes to support rigorously, but also like to step in to do some good in many other charitable ways that I have not made my primary humanitarian focus. There is no point in mentioning most of them. I am only bringing up a particular charitable concert I was in because it relates to this chapter. We broke a record with it and had a good time.

"Sgt. Pepper's Lonely Hearts Club Band," which I sang with U2, opened the *Live 8* show in London, and was quickly uploaded. **Before** the show was a third over, downloads were **breaking records**. With all the proceeds going to charity, **the song** was on the Internet within forty-five minutes of its **performance**. The line, "It was twenty years ago today," **helped us** emphasize that *Live 8* was twenty years (almost to the week) after we did *Live Aid*. They were great shows and collected a lot of money to help provide relief in Africa after their napalm-induced famine.

NOTE: Jimi Hendrix (trained in Laurel Canyon) said, "If there is something to be changed in this world, then it can only happen through music." Repetitious sounds and messages are key to mind-control. Frequencies impact our energy fields. Rhythm directs brainwave, pulse, and mood, which impacts hormone levels. Lyrics with catchy tunes carry precise messages to the conscious and subconscious as we consciously and subconsciously sing along. Enthusiastically receiving repetitious mental programming from an adored superstar multiplies the impact.

Nothing directs human consciousness as effectively as music, especially when combined with plant medicine or drugs. Many people are brainwashed by giving them hallucinogens combined with repetitious audio messages.

Be especially selective of your mind-programming while under the influence of a plant medicine or mind-altering drug. Where hallucinogens are legal (and your doctor approves), you may combine them with audio recordings of affirmations or hypnotic suggestions that are aligned with your intention. Affirmations are especially effective in your own voice, spoken softly and slowly, and are even more powerful when also combined with baroque music.

Discover your hidden programs through meditation.

15

John and Hitler

John, George, Ringo, and I were each our own person but were always judged publicly as a group over and above any individual liberties. **When** the press was offended, **they would hammer away.** Hearing John say any idea **entering his head** was enough for the press to seek **to destroy** the world's now obsolete understanding of **that idol,** and of us all—as if we would feel whatever **he would feel.**

The tension among John and **the rest** of us heated over his [and EMI's] view **of** Adolf Hitler. John had discussed *Mein Kampf* with Kenneth Anger and was impressed **by Anger's** view of Hitler's will and overwhelming **power.** Anger said Hitler's mastery of hate made him nearly omnipotent. Hitler was unsurpassed. John sought to incorporate that strong force into his own life and music. He had mocked Germans openly, and Hitler often too, but desired to emulate that Master of German peoples. I did not have anything against the German people. As with any country, we cannot blame the citizenry for their leaders or even believe what others say of them.

We naturally adopt the prejudices that leaders present, hating whomever the people are told to hate, not realizing that our own leaders may be war criminals. It was not until we were working on the *Sgt. Pepper's* cover that John's opinion of Hitler threatened to become a public issue. My idea, as I **have** said, was to gather eminent celebrities who had **lost** their lives tragically, who might have greeted **Paul** into the spirit world. **I sought for** us to include each of our heroes, or **legends who were** significant to our Dead-Paul theme. **Playing the game**, I had a right controversial figure, being a self-proclaimed 666 beast. He, Crowley, was not the Biblical beast but was someone whose influence supported the agenda.

Hitler, though tied to the same agenda, was still alive. While the world watched a fake wedding, he headed to South America. John invited him to our simulated funeral, saying that if Hitler had died, he would have met Paul on the other side. They would now be among the greatest celebrities in the heavens or hell. It was not meant to be a theological thesis on heaven or hell or said out of disrespect. He loved Paul. We all did. It is just how John talked about it.

Tipping his hand to show Hitler respect was one thing, but exposing EMI's core would be quite another. John tried assert an alpha role in the group by refusing to take Hitler off the cover's guest list. He ordered the life-size cardboard cutout. John was constant in saying the orator has standing in Paul's league of dead celebrities. George Martin, who was

Eventually, Alois sought to officially change his last name to match his step-father. However, due to a clerical spelling error, the name Hiedler was rendered "Hitler," which Alois accepted and passed on to his four children: Alois Jr., Angela, **Adolf**, and Paula.

After pretending to be Adolf & Eva getting married, the couple retired to their bunker. The male actor spent that entire wedding night fully clothed, laying on the bed wide awake. The next day, at the right time, Heinz Linge suicided both actors.

usually more agreeable with **John**, urged him to bend on this one, but **could not persuade** him. Finally, someone alerted **a record executive**. Although he did not care **who** supported Hitler, he did care about profit. EMI **vetoed Hitler's** depiction on my *Sgt. Pepper's* **cover.** Discretion prevailed over disclosing EMI's Nazi affiliation.

Lots of classical musicians objected to the degraded meaningless music of our generation and refused to be any part of it. In their efforts to preserve classical music, such as Beethoven, the conscientious objectors to Beatlemania refused to play on Beatles records. Martin had to hire mostly ex-Nazis from Germany to play for our recording sessions. Martin, like Brian, and the Beatles, had regular contacts in, and from, West Germany; and many ex-Nazis [or Nazis still] were on EMI's payroll.

John, although fond of shock value, said his intended cutout was not the maniac killer that offered him meaning, but rather the idea of seeing something good in one man whom the whole world hated. **John said that he** and Adolf were merely a couple of **misunderstood** artists seeking power over nearly all **the world.** That is all. John's fondness for Hitler further endeared the band to EMI.

Missing Paul, however, John grew to resent EMI and its international connections. By the time we put *Abbey Road* together, John's view of Hitler had changed partly because of conflicting reports about the man. Although John did not say I was right to object to putting Hitler on the *Pepper's* cover, he nearly

Although EMI was criticized for hiring so many Nazi's, the US, in Operation Paperclip, hired more than 1600 Nazi specialists. The USSR and others also gathered all that they could

uttered as much. He was glad he had been overruled on that one, but still resented his lack of influence regarding the album cover. It was my baby from start to finish–the album, the cover, the theme, everything. I told John, George, and many others exactly what I needed from them, and they did it. The design of the album cover is credited to Peter Blake. However, I was the one who told him precisely what I wanted. Although each contributed his or her part, I was the one who planned it all out.

Hitler never was John's idol. John was humored by him. Sometimes he aligned with his ideology but eventually disliked all globalists. After the shock value wore off, reality settled in. John finally took notice of what most of the world saw sooner. By the time the Beatles dissolved in 1970, John begrudged his prior ignorance about Hitler and globalization.

Throughout the world-changing Beatles decade, every hero of John's fell in his eyes. **While we were** teaching the world to be enlightened **with love, we** undeniably were becoming ever more **disillusioned.** We were not as loving or as enlightened as **the world** needed us to be, and not nearly as clever and brilliant as we had supposed or pretended. We made music and death-of-Paul messages. That is all. We were not the media-built icon. The image was more than we ever were. Fans worshiped the image without any awareness of the heart.

Religious figures, politicians, songwriters, the Beatles, **and others** fell short in John's estimation. Sadly, all **of his heroes vanished.** He tended to

139

make people and things bigger than life. It was all too big to ever measure up. Then they would let him down. I let him down that way too. I was the band's only hope. I was **Paul's** dream come true, too good to be true. I was **the one** who came to save and take over the band but could not be their new bandleader if I were too much like their old pal, Paul. He did not have the skills to lead the band. He never could have done it.

None of John's heroes remained his heroes for very long. There was a season when John was all over Bob Dylan's lyrics. They moved John to desire more interesting and meaningful lyrics. But once John was up to him in his own estimation, Dylan lost his edge. That is what John is talking about when he touts, "**I don't believe in** Zimmerman." He included that line because **John** truly had believed in him. He sang, "I don't believe in Jesus" because he had once. His belief in Jesus ended when he was an early adolescent. Then he began persecuting nuns and others. He also sang, "I don't believe in Hitler." Yes, he had believed in him as well. Everyone and everything he listed in his disbelief song, he had at one time believed in, and had eventually become disillusioned with. They all let him down, or he realized that he had the wrong ideas about each of them from the start.

Every hero fell. John's "Sexy Sadie" was vented distress with Maharishi Mahesh Yogi, who taught us TM until he sexually assaulted our friend, Mia Farrow. We had been told he had evolved and gotten

140

over **his sexual** cravings and desires. I thought his **philosophy** was generally deep and interesting, but **got tired** of the boring repetition and felt that he was being false to us. John and George ate it up. They enjoyed the peace it gave them mumbling Sanskrit syllables. Until he blew it, it worked well for them.

The disillusionment hit when John and George were trying to align themselves with the peace of heaven, using his meditation to free their minds of canned chatter, while their Yogi master was sexually excited, preying on women from our group. Venting, we recorded a few songs mocking him, but only released one, changing "Maharishi" to "Sexy Sadie" to avoid a lawsuit. **I may release** others.

Feeling like **an absolute fool** for having trusted another idol **who turned out to be** just another ordinary mortal guy, **John** became turned off with the idea of **looking for peace.** When John later realized that he had put too much emphasis on the messenger rather than on the message itself, he allowed the idea that some of what we learned there had value even if the man was not all that we had hoped for. We had hoped for too much. The meditation helped. That is how John vanquished his drug demons years later, breaking his heaviest addictions. Drugs, like Hitler and John's other big idols, seemed much better than life at the start but brought misery and pain once they became his love or his gods. Indulgence always makes fools of us all. That too brings pain. It was not just John. Everybody makes fools of themselves by becoming attached to their pet illusions.

141

16

The One and Only Billy Shears Rams On.

In our *Sgt. Pepper's* title song, I sing, "Let me introduce to you the one and only Billy Shears and Sgt. Pepper's Lonely Hearts Club Band." That introduction is to tell you that Billy Shears is Sgt. Pepper, and that the Beatles is now his band. On the cover, we contrast the old drab Fab four with the entirely fresh and new Fab few. It is my new band. **I am Billy** Shears. I am that one and only Sgt. **Pepper.** Bill or Billy are my nicknames. **I am** William, Will, Billy, or Bill. The song, "I **Will,**" pretends to be about longing for an elusive romantic love, but is actually me, Will, singing to Paul. As is exposed eventually, there is a double meaning. I sing, "Who knows how long I've loved you," relating to the idea that no one knows how far back I go as Paul, or, for that matter, as admiring him from a safe distance. I saw a Beatles show at the Plaza Ballroom in Old Hill. The Diplomats opened that

NOTE: Whenever the Diplomats opened for the Beatles, such as on 5 July 1963, William and the others met with the Beatles backstage before the show. On at least one occasion, the Diplomats and Beatles shared a dressing room.

Although William was groomed for Paul's position, it was not certain to go that way. A significant faction was skeptical of the Osiris-Horus requirement for the Aquarian Age and believed that a Messiah could appear outside of their control. Nevertheless, that possibility of a Messiah appearing outside of their control was ultimately the selling point for deliberate action. The new order must include full control of the worldwide religion. The Thelemites showed that the death was required to usher in the new age. Humanity received maternal nurturing from Isis and then controlling paternal discipline from Osiris. We are now ready for self-realization through Horus.

142

concert. I had seen Paul at EMI, and at a party, but not talked to him. No one knows how long I loved any of the Beatles. Certainly, I love Paul still, as the song suggests. **His death** is what ultimately brought us together. It **did not end** my love for him. In some of these chapters I speak of the ongoing loneliness I suffered by taking on **his role**. "Will I wait a lonely lifetime?" Yes, I am willing; as long as I feel Paul's energy flowing inside of me continuing through me,  I will. Whether together or apart, we are connected "forever and forever." If that verse seems strange as a Paul song, it is more nonsensical as a love song.

On the next verse, Paul sings to me. He says if he saw me, he didn't catch my name. However, it never really mattered. He will always feel the same. He did see me at the studio, and at the party, and did not catch my name. But it didn't matter. I am here the same. When at last he finds me, his replacement, our combined song from my mouth will fill the air. Paul wants me to sing it loudly so that he can hear it now in the spirit world. **He wants me** to honor the name I bear, making it easy **for him** to be near me. 'Cause the things I do in his name endear me to him. Now you all know I am Will.

NOTE: William says, "I feel Paul's energy flowing inside of me." When he performs as Paul, that Paul-energy is so strong in him that he has no qualms about saying that Paul McCartney is performing. Although William brings a great deal of himself into every performance, the more a song is in Paul's style, the more the spirit of Paul comes through. When William performs as Paul, intending to be Paul, he sometimes feels that he actually becomes Paul.

George Martin's son, Gregory Paul Martin, had similar experiences when sitting at that same equipment that his father had used to record the Beatles' catalog of songs. While sitting there to record *The Memoirs of Billy Shears*, Gregory felt on many occasions that he actually became Paul. Paul sings and tells this story in and through others. If Gregory were, as it seemed, possessed by Paul's spirit while making the recording, that might explain some of the paranormal experiences reported by listeners.

Martin's 15+ hour Audible audiobook is available on Amazon. Or go to: www.MemoirsOfPaul.com (click on "FREE AUDIO").

Even though I am Paul now, **I say "I, Will."** I, Will, shall love him forever and forever. **It is not** romantic but is love nonetheless. I love **him** as myself. By the way, all of this song's bass was not played left-handed or right-handed. I sang it. This song has no bass guitar.

Now, as I was saying before being carried off in another fine song, the name Will, William, Billy, or Bill naturally surfaces. A growing number of people have exposed my role as William Shepherd. The most obvious clues are commonly known. I will point out a more obscure William role. To keep the rights to my intended post-Beatles songs from being Lennon-McCartney's, I did not go as Paul to record or engineer my solo McCartney album.

Honoring George Martin, who taught me a lot about how to mix the sounds and all of that, I booked all of my studio time for that album, and listed everything for that project, under the name of Billy Martin. **I had no** idea how many other artists landed that same **name.** William Martin was Billy Joel's birth name and is also the name of others that you can read about, but not here. That Billy and I, two former William Martins, did a concert together.

Speaking of Billy albums, our first working title for *Abbey Road* was *Billy's Left Boot.* It would take explaining though, maybe with a song. *Abbey Road,* however, besides being the location of EMI Studios,

NOTE: We might imagine William being entirely alone, sneaking in and out of the studio to secretly record his first solo McCartney album. However, although he did spend much of that studio time alone, he was not in hiding. As always, bandmates and other recording artists were aware of his presence there. He often dropped in on others. Sometimes he assisted. He was likewise visited by others. Most notably while William worked on that album, Donovan  (recording his *Open Road* album in a studio directly above) was fully aware of "Billy Martin's" McCartney project.

William Martin is also the name of Operation Mincemeat's major (played by Glyndwr Michael's corpse), whose deception helped the Allies take Sicily.

144

elicits mystical meaning. Our procession crosses that Abbey—or that Abbey's road—for Paul's burial.

Giving my name, Bill Shepherd, on albums where **I am Billy Pepper** of Billy Pepper and the Pepperpots, I tried to show three years later that Billy Pepper is Billy Shears, who is called Sgt. Pepper. I thought I was virtually saying, "Billy Shears is Sgt. Pepper, who is Billy Pepper." All who knew Billy Pepper's records easily could have checked to identify the Pepper's bandleader. On *Sgt. Pepper's* back cover, I stand with my back to the audience because **I am the conductor**, Sgt. Billy Pepper, **leading my band**. In both bands, you can see that Pepper is the leader's stage name.

Maybe the old William gravestone (of Paul's replacement) in the *Yellow Submarine* movie was too cryptic. But it should be obvious why we did not edit out the part where I am introduced as William, accidentally said, automatically, out of habit, in my *Give My Regards to Broad Street* movie.

John, George, Ringo, and others, when they were annoyed with me, used to refer to me as "Beatle Bill." Some acquaintances still do. George let that ridicule about me, "Beatle Bill," slip out in a live video recording once. The slip ended up in John's documentary, *Imagine,* released in 1988. John and George were being rather rude talking about me by saying that and other such things. When John refers to "The Fab Four," George quickly corrects him, "The Fab Three." John agrees. While it is fine to miss Paul, no one was more fab than I was.

Our *Magical Mystery Tour* album, as I have mentioned, had a photograph of the four of us Beatles. Ringo's drums have the words, "Love the 3 Beatles." It showed that only three of the four remained. But there I was too. How fab was Paul

Direct the harmonious music of your life by conducting the symphony of archetypes that represent your consciousness.

145

compared to me? If you would compare my work over the years from 1966 to his before that point, you would see that I led the band into new territory, accelerating the transformation that he and others started. Nothing before me compares to that new direction. **I am still** more inventive and fab than Paul. I, **Beatle Bill**, reinvented fab!

Some Bill clues are subtle. I sing, "got the bill, and Rita paid it." John has "Bungalow Bill," and "Tonight Mr. Kite is topping the bill." Others are blatant, such as "Billy Shears." The above *Give My Regards to Broad Street* reference brings up a key question. In a scene at the BBC building, when I enter the room and am greeted by a good old friend who introduces me to the other. He says, earnestly, "Do you know William?" Well, that is a question for you to ask yourselves. Do any of you tell yourselves that I am that old Paul who had inches less height, less musical talent, much less administrative ability, and less focus for the band? Or, "Do you know William?"

Let's move on to Shepherd, my last name. On *Sgt. Pepper's,* we announce it as Shears. Although less iconic than my shepherd's crook, shears are shepherds' tools. "Billy shears" mean that I, Billy, am removing the wool. I am shearing or fleecing the flock.

It sounds like "Billy hears" or "**Billy's** here."

In Psalm 23:1, David sings, "The **LORD** [Enlil?] is my shepherd." That idea of the people being God's sheep comes up often. Jesus **says, "I am** the good shepherd. **The good shepherd** gives his life for the sheep" (John 10:11) after fleecing them.

Rams cannot see through the wool without shears trimming it. Wool pulled over the eyes keeps us and the ram from seeing eye-to-eye. We cannot see what is beneath the wool. Wool may conceal any blemishes in the ram's flesh. A rash or wound might be indistinguishable. **Sometimes** one cannot tell the quality of the ram unless the **shears** are employed. Losing the wool **removes the deception.** With *Sgt. Pepper*, Shears appears to give sight to the blind. Letting everyone know that "Billy's here," the opening song introduces Billy, the Shears, to say that you have wool over your eyes, which the shepherd will endeavor to shear away—revealing the ram.

Shearing the ram removes the blinders from both directions. Whenever **someone cuts** the wool from his eyes, letting the sunlight in, **the ram** can both see and be seen. Then you will see **that Paul is** gone. Everyone sees in the bright light of day. "Look for the girl with the sun in her eyes," or she who sees reality unveiled. When you do, you will see "she's gone" ("Lucy in the Sky with Diamonds").

Enough about that. Some of you are wondering about the ram.

With all the Bible fans who buy our albums, I would think that more would catch the Ram symbol. Here it is. Abraham's chosen son was replaced by a

NOTE: Abram was born in Ur of the Chaldeans (Urs Kaśdim), a part of the Sumerian civilization at the dawn of history that was presided over by Enlil. It is now part of Iraq. As the story goes, Enlil (YHWH) changed Abram's name (Hebrew: "exalted father") to Abraham ("father of a multitude"). As prophetic fulfillment—or direct intervention—Abraham became the common patriarch of Christianity, Islam, and Judaism, and a literal ancestor of multitudes who live in regions dominated by those religions.

In Abrahamic religions and elsewhere, doctrinal interpretations vary depending on the audience. Those in the inner circles are usually more interested in esoteric texts than in scriptures that they share publicly. Their secret teachings are concealed from the uninitiated who are not usually aware of such teachings. Secret oral traditions **unlock** scriptures for very different interpretations. Those who understand **the layered** meanings and masterful speaking use the same verses to teach lower **concepts** to the so-called "vile multitudes" that they use quite differently to teach inner-circle sages (see Matthew 13:10-16). Consider the layered meaning of Abram's name.

Enlil-YHWH says, "Abram, kill your son!"
"Yes, Sir!" says Abram. "Right away, Good Sir!"
"He was just kidding!" says Enki. "It was a test!
You passed. Here, let's barbeque this ram instead!
Oh, and here's some good herb, my doobie brother."

ram caught by his horns in a thicket. That story is explained in Genesis 22. Abraham took the ram by the horns and offered him in his son's place. My *Ram* album cover shows a ram caught by his horns. That ram is me, offered in Paul's place, being entreated to suffer for Paul. However, **I am** also the one holding the horns. See me as **the Shepherd** holding the ram. It is another reversal. The son has died, and the ram lives on in his place. I am both the animal and the man. I am the replacing ram. I am also the [Billy] Shepherd. I, the man, have maintained steady control over the beast, and have it by the horns, but also am that beast.

The name, *RAM* (**R**adical **A**ppearance **M**odification to **R**eplace **A** **M**cCartney), reverses as *MAR* for a hidden sacrificial meaning. The sacrificial substitute

NOTE: In addition to the common meaning of the names, Abram and Abraham, shown in the previous footnote, there are also secret Kabbalistic meanings that have special significance to William, our man of RAM.

The Kabbalah, the essential text of Jewish mysticism, was adapted in Western esotericism as the Hermetic Qabalah and Christian Kabbalah. The Hermetic Qabalah is foundational to the philosophy and framework of magical societies (such as the Thelemic orders), mystical-religious societies (such as the Builders of the Adytum and the Fellowship of the Rosy Cross), and Wiccan, Neopagan, and New Age movements. It is also the basis for the Qliphothic Qabala as studied by left-hand path orders (such as the Typhonian Order). Its use should continue to increase well into the Age of Aquarius.

According to a secret ancient tradition, the Kabbalah was passed down among the Sumerians until possessed by Abram. When he left Sumer, he took the sacred tablets with him. In the oldest Kabbalistic circles, following the tradition of hiding our greatest secrets in plain sight, Abram (Ab-Ram) means "He who possesses Ram." Rams signifying the highest expression of cosmic awareness is tied to ram horns being blown ceremonially. From an old source, we have the saying, "Whoever possesses Kabbalah, also possesses Ram."

Going from Abram to Abraham magnifies the meaning. Although it might

be seen as an advance in degrees, such as progressing in ritual from the left shoulder to the right, it is much more than that. He is not merely going from being Abram to being very Abram. He progresses from illumination to exaltation.

"Ram Dass" says his new name means "Servant of Ram" or "Servant of God."

"Kabbalah is all about change. It . . . is about transforming our darkness into light" ~Yehuda Berg

Most ancient animal sacrifices were not whole burnt offerings. They were usually cooked as stews or soups and then eaten. When a cauldron of "Jamaican" goat's head soup was rejected for a Stones' album cover, they included the image as an insert.

for the man is marred by the holy offering. The essentially plain song, "Ram On," repeatedly telling me to do my ram work, furthers this idea of some religious sacrifice. In ancient sacrificial rituals, they cut out the heart. In a symbolic shadow, Paul's heart, as all else taken from him, was given to me, his heir. Remember, **it is a** reversal. Instead of the ram being made the **sacrifice**, it is the man, the dead Paul, whose heart is given away to the surviving ram.

Goats Head Soup, released by the Rolling Stones two years after *Ram,* was a darker version after they observed the sacrificial meaning of the ram in me. Their satanic meaning is well established and is not the focus here.

Liking the Ram picture that Linda took, I found an excuse to use it: I wrote, "Ram on." I did not name the album for the song. I named the song for the album.

In the Zodiac, the word for ram is Aries. The word *Aries* is derived from the Latin *aris,* meaning "altars." The animal has always been associated with sacrifice. This ancient association is found in many traditions and religions. It is used in both sacred and profane contexts. If you say it is Satanic, have it your way. If to you it is a Christian or Jewish  symbol, have it your way. It means anything and everything you bring to it. The common thread throughout is its sacrificial association whether

NOTE: In Jewish mysticism, the ram is one of the holiest creatures. The most profane beast at the base of that spectrum is the pig. When John saw Paul's *RAM* album (released 17 May 1971), it was too late to change the back cover of his own *Imagine* album released on 9 September 1971 (reducing to 9-9-9). Instead, John mocked William by inserting a postcard of himself handling a pig. He thus made himself "vulgar" to say that he no longer cared that "Paul," the Shepherd, is the Messiah of the Æon of Horus/Aradia. John resented "the Ram of God's sacrifice." However magical Paul's soul-transmigration may have seemed before, John no longer reverenced William for being the Ram's shepherd. He showed that it no longer mattered to him.

religiously holy or sacrilegious. I use the symbol in no sacred or profane context, but only to represent or exemplify Paul's death. He crossed over. I, the ram, remain. I, the Shears, am the Shepherd.

Patterned by Osiris, the shepherd's crook (with the flail) also denotes authority. Pharaohs, as well as all others possessed by Osiris, are that shepherd.

Although "Billy Pepper and the Pepperpots" is unfamiliar to most, our albums and *Sgt. Pepper's Lonely Hearts Club Band* point to each other. As the label shows on our Pepperpots albums, Billy Pepper is Billy Shepherd. I am the one and only Sgt. Pepper.

In the open album jacket, my Sgt. Pepper uniform has an arm patch that reads "OPD," an abbreviation for "Officially Pronounced Dead," or "Omitting P and D." Omitting P and D from my name as "Shepard" leaves "Shear." In the States, the equivalent of OPD is DOA, "Dead On Arrival."

Here I should also mention that the name, Billy Shears, has produced a fine resurrection tradition. Exactly twenty years before *Sgt. Pepper's Lonely Hearts Club Band* was released, as the story goes, another "Billy Shears" is said to have passed away (the year that Aleister Crowley died) but promised to return in twenty years. Introducing "the one and only Billy Shears" suggests that the old magickal music man returned. If he had died, and there is only one, he must have risen from the dead. **Alas, for him** and Paul, each is still dead. **I am the substitute.** I, Billy Shepherd, am now Paul. I am **the only Billy Shears**.

I should point out that even though I am "the one and only Billy Shears" in the Beatles act, it does not mean that I am the only Billy Shepherd in

ALEISTER CROWLEY
LONDON, Dec. 1 (Reuters) — Edward Alexander Crowley, better known as Aleister Crowley, author and poet, who was an alleged practitioner of "black magic" and blood sacrifice, died today in Hastings at the age of 72.

150

the music world. It would be very easy to get a few of us confused. Being a ram idol may also resemble many gods. However, I am not those idols either.

"Ram on" was code for "Ramon." In Scotland in 1960, **Paul McCartney** used the alias, Paul Ramon. I am singing to Paul, "Ramon, give your heart to somebody soon right away." I am telling him to make his heart manifest in my own. I have also honored his Paul Ramon alias by using it myself on occasion, including on the Steve Miller Band's album, *Brave New World.* For a couple of his numbers, "Celebration Song" and "My Dark Hour," I, as Paul Ramon, do backing vocals, drums, and bass guitar.

See me as both the Shepherd and the ram. I, as the good Shepherd (in ancient and modern senses), hold the ram by the horns, leading it to be sacrificed. I am also the ram held in the hands of the Shepherd. Strictly speaking, literally, a ram is a non-castrated adult male sheep. I am the ram shepherd. Do you follow me thus far? Yet, *ram* is used generally to include male goats, a/k/a Billy goats. I, Billy Shears, am the Billy shepherd.

NOTE: "Ramon, give your heart to somebody soon right away." The heart of the sacrificial ram is given to God. Paul already gave his heart to William years before. Now, "right away," William (who now embodies Ramon (Paul)), must give his heart to God (Enki, Osiris, Krishna, et cetera) who was to receive William as William received Paul. All would be joined as one by the Ram of God's sacrifice.

Ram-On (Hebrew: רָם אוֹן) also happens to be a cooperative agricultural community in northern Israel's Ta'anakh region, south of the Jezreel Valley.

To be gender-specific, goats are given pronouns and nicknames. She-goats are called nanny-goats. He-goats are Billy-goats. Earlier in this chapter, William explains how he is both the sacrificial animal and also its shepherd. Now, at the end of the chapter, he shows both in his name.

Goats are also associated with Baphomet, Dionysos, Ea-Oannes, Marduk, Ningirsu, Pan, satyrs, and others.

151

17

You Want Dates?

On 6 August 1966, Paul McCartney was featured on the BBC Light Programme radio show, *David Frost at the Phonograph.* David played records and visited with Paul between songs. It would help if you could find a tape recording of that "live" broadcast that was in fact recorded **five days before** or if you could find what **he and John recorded that** night at his house, **which aired at their tour's end.** Unless there is another recording of him that I was not told of, you would have a most current and reliable voice sampling of the first Paul.

To compare our voices, it is best to use a talking sample since it is not obstructed by multi-tracked harmonies, musical instruments, screaming fans, et cetera. *The Lennon and McCartney Songbook,* re-released under another title when I joined in, recorded 6 August, had the two of them discussing their songs that had been covered by various other entertainers. I had covered some of their songs as Billy Shepherd or Billy Pepper but had not yet attracted enough success to be featured on their show. Now I cover the old Beatles songs quite a lot, along with my own material, whenever **I go on tour**. When I dissolved the Beatles, I wanted **to let my fans have new material, and let my new band spread its wings to fly from those Beatles** years. However, 🖐️🖐️ one day I realized that Paul's material was pretty good too. I could use it. 🔺

In two more days, on 8 August, they released *Revolver,* the last of phase two. Three more days, now 11 August, they began their final tour, exactly one month before Paul crossed over. The timing is more intriguing now as we see the whole thing in perspective. To begin that last tour, they crossed over the Atlantic and landed in Boston, then took a connecting flight to Chicago, where they attempted reconciliation in a press conference that night for John's "more popular than Jesus" faux pas. Having explained it, they gave their first concert of that last tour the next night, 12 August, in Boston. They went to Detroit next where they did two shows, one in the afternoon, and one in the evening, on 13 August. Then they were bused to Cleveland where they did another concert on 14 August. There, yelling and screaming frenzied fans rushed the field.

John, George, and Ringo all said the hysterically screaming fans were challenging enough. However, when 2500 of them stormed the field in order to get to them, it was unnerving. The next day, they did a concert in Washington DC. There was hardly any time left to spare for sightseeing or breathing. The next day, 16 August, they did

NOTE: William is amused and comforted when numbers add up to multiples of three (3, 6, 9). For his pleasure, if we count numerical references on this page, we find that the text, footnote, and page number each reach nine (9+9+9). The text: [one + two + 8 + two + Three + 11 + one + 1 ("first") + 12 + two + one + one + 13 + 2500 + 16 = **2574**]; [2 + 5 + 7 + 4 = **18**]; [1 + 8 = **9**]. Find them!

1
2
8
2
3
11
1
1
12
2
1
1
13
2500
+ 16
2574

a concert in Pennsylvania. On 17 August, they did two shows up in Toronto, Canada. Then, the next day, 18 August, they did a show back in Boston.

The next day, 19 August, the Beatles put on two concerts in Memphis. On 20 August, the band was set to do their thirteenth concert in only nine consecutive days. That show was rained out, compelling them to do the show the next day before ending up hundreds of miles away for a second performance that same day in St. Louis. Those two shows were on 21 August. **They went** from that second concert to the airport, **and then arrived** early in the morning, before sunrise, **in New York.**

Later that day, they met with the press. On the evening of 23 August, after their Shea Stadium show, they flew to California for a break in Beverly Hills. After a day of recuperation, they flew up north to Seattle for two concerts on 25 August, and then occupied their time with more celebratory play, rest, and diversion back in Beverly Hills. In Los Angeles, with an audience of about 45,000 people at Dodger Stadium, they performed on 28 August.

The Beatles' last performance was in Candlestick Park in San Francisco. An elated audience of 25,000 heard them give that last concert on Monday, 29 August 1966. They returned to Los Angeles in the early hours of the morning, flying into LAX, and departed later that day, being 30 August. Arriving back in England the next day, 31 August, they were all exhausted. Besides the tour's grueling schedule endured, they all had serious jet lag. All four of them needed a break.

As was already arranged, and not because of Paul's death, as has been speculated, John and Neil took off for West Germany on 5 September to play parts in *How I Won the War* directed by Richard Lester, and written by Charles Wood, the same guy who wrote the screenplay for *Help!*

Earnest "Paul is Dead" recitalists will tell you that **Paul** and John had argued on the night that Paul **slammed the door** and ran off in a heated rage. It was not **like that.** First of all, John was with Neil in West Germany. Secondly, no one saw Paul at the studio. The story was made later that Paul left EMI enraged. In one version of the story, Epstein met with Paul and George there. Brian scheduled their next studio session for when John returned from making his film. The Beatles would gather to record their next album from 7 to 14 November and release it in time for Christmas. As that story goes, Brian ordered Paul to have five songs written and ready to record by John's return from filming. That put Paul under great pressure. Paul said no because he rarely wrote without John's support. Brian said that he would tell John to have five songs ready too. He also supposedly gave George a writing assignment.

With whatever fuss was said to have occurred that evening of 11 September, Paul allegedly left in a rage. In some versions, he slammed the door after arguing with his bandmates or Brian. Ringo claimed that he was with his family in Surrey that evening—not that he needed any alibi. No one was accusing him. Besides, being the most open about not writing his own material, no one told him to write anything.

155

As the story goes, Paul left the studio and picked up Rita. That is also incorrect, though commonly believed. The name, Rita, was from a meter maid. I liked the "Rita Meter Maid" sound. John added, "Ahh [0:21], Paul [0:23]," to clarify the song's subject, and "You'd better believe it" at the end. Nuances were woven in: "Took her home, and nearly made it," had it not been for the untimely crash, or "Got the bill and Rita paid it."

Those lines work together with a song **I wrote in** collaboration with Neil Innes that we called, "**Death** Cab for Cutie." I wrote **and performed the song** as Vivian Stanshall. That's me, **wearing a disguise**, singing in an unnatural voice near the end of our *Magical Mystery Tour* film. While I am on the topic, in case some of you missed it, I am wearing yet another "disguise" as my true self in an earlier scene. The point was to resemble my former life.

Reading or hearing "Death Cab" lyrics in the "Lovely Rita" context puts it all together. **It** is about a cutie who calls for a cab. That **is only** figurative. She was a young hitchhiker who, **in this book**, is Donna. She carried a suitcase in the rain. Paul, our taxi driver, pulls over for the pretty girl whose looks end up costing her life. "Don't you know, . . . curves can kill" refers to her nice curves and the winding road. The fiction is that Paul could not keep his eyes off of her. John sings of that distraction in "A Day in the Life," "He didn't notice that **the lights had** changed." Paul's distraction was **their destruction.**

Each must pay for the taxi fare. Cutie paid with her life. The Death Cab lyrics are similar to those by John's. As I sing mine, "The traffic lights changed

from green to red . . . They both wound up dead."
Owing something for the taxicab, the cutie is told,
"Someone's gonna make you pay your fare." It
is the same idea as, "Got the bill, and Rita paid it."
However, the Rita line adds an extra little meaning
needing clarification: the Beatles got the Bill (me),
costing the lives of Paul and Rita (Paul and the
star-crazed Cutie, Donna). They both paid the fare
for that fateful ride into the new Beatles phase.

Paul's dreams were contradictory, which makes
them a bit undependable. **We do** not always have
every detail right. One of **the dreams** that impressed
me was about the girl recognizing Paul and getting
over-excited about it, searching each station up and
down the radio dial for a Beatles song, hoping that
Paul would sing along. In that dream, and similar
ones, the distraction was not about the girl's good
looks, but about her going nuts in the car.

We cannot say what occurred in the car before the
end of their journey. Stories were made up that he was
distracted by his passenger. Borrowing details from
Tara Browne's death, John said Paul ran a red light.
The point was to instill the idea that Paul crashed in
order to say that he died—without giving details. One
of the best clues of Paul's head being smashed in is
given in the *Magical Mystery Tour* movie where, on
Paul's corpse, you can read, "Magical Mystical Boy."
Each part of his skull that the coroner pulled open was
removed by then. [See the autopsy photo at 1:59 of
the 2:31 length video of *Paul McCartney 1882.*]

In Ringo's song, "Don't Pass Me By," he tells
his old friend, Paul, that he is sorry he doubted
the death dreams and then alludes to Paul's

157

exit: "I'm sorry that I doubted **you**. I was so unfair. You were in a car crash, and you **lost your** hair." It relates to John singing, "He blew his **mind** out in a car," and, "Here come ole' flat top." John had also doubted, which is partly why he had to laugh at Paul's photograph. It proved that all of Paul's omens were real. John flipped out. He became horrifically hysterical.

Until the corpses were "Officially Pronounced Dead," they were still legally alive. Even though both of them died soon after the crash, the story is that Paul and Donna were both still officially living until pronounced otherwise several minutes after midnight on Monday, 12 September.

Identifying the burned and mutilated bodies was not as impossible as had been imagined. If they had needed facial detection, they could not have done it. However, Paul's car revealed his identity; and the girl's suitcase had a letter from her cousin staying with a friend on Leso in Mesocco, Switzerland. Apparently, Donna was headed there. Reaching her parents was not difficult, but time-consuming, with Swiss support. Police alerted her parents "Wednesday morning at five o'clock as the day begins."

Paul's father and stepmother, who had been notified Monday, saw his remains, but could not affirm that **it was** Paul. They did not recognize his clothes. **Nothing** about the messed-up corpse looked undeniably **like Paul.** They finally admitted it could

NOTE: Chuck Berry's lyrics, "Here come a flat-top, he was moving up with me" ("You Can't Catch Me") reminded John of Paul's fatal head injury (his flattened top). Chuck's song led to the tune and lyrics, "Here come old flat-top, he come groovin' up slowly" ("Come Together").

158

be him but held the opinion that Paul had earlier loaned his Aston Martin to a friend. Investigators called Paul's dentist for x-rays but could not identity Paul conclusively. Although very similar, the corpse was missing a tooth.

Searching for proof of **Paul's** identity continued quietly. The **investigator** assigned to the case had the decency to **keep his assumptions** from the press **until he had legal proof**—which he anxiously anticipated. Not imagining he could talk to a member of the band, he called others, without revealing why he wanted the information, to learn how to reach the Beatles' agent. When at last he did reach Brian Epstein, Brian immediately went to the morgue and said he did not think the corpse was Paul. **Brian** was permitted to take a few pictures. He **assured the** investigator he would have a positive answer **later** that day. That bought him a few hours to produce **Paul**. Meanwhile, **Jane too was** called in.

Under the circumstances **of Paul** predicting his death and attempting to work it out with a talented look-alike to replace him, Brian had discussed possible Paul imitators with his brother and a few intimate friends. One of them who knew of my Billy Pepper albums (that included Beatles songs), recommended me for the position. Having worked with me, Brian already knew me, but did not know if I was up to the role. Besides, I did not fully look the part. He called me and warmly extended an invitation to work on an album as a session musician but did not yet say for whom. He asked me to meet him at the Abbey Road studio in an hour. He told me to bring my albums.

159

During that meeting, I showed him the albums I had cut. Brian asked me to play my version of "She Loves You" from my *More Merseymania* album. Epstein said, "I had a hell of a time crossing the ocean with that song. **The Beatles were** unknown then. Capitol Records **refused the single**, as did Vee Jay." Brian said he finally convinced Swan to take it. They released "She Loves You" in the States exactly three years, to the week, before our meeting. It did not sell well at all until the Beatles' next

NOTE: Parlophone Records, Odeon Records, and Capitol Records were EMI subsidiaries. The Capitol Records Building, at 1750 Vine Street in Hollywood, is only a couple of miles from Laurel Canyon. Once the Capitol executives became aware of the success of the Beatles' first album, *Please Please Me*, and were apprised of what the scheme included right next to them in Laurel Canyon, Capitol Records agreed to accept their parent company's offer to be the Beatles' primary North American record label.

On 22 March 1963, the Beatles released their first album, *Please Please Me,* on Parlophone (their UK label). On 22 November, they released *With the Beatles* on Parlophone (for the UK), on Odeon (for the Western European continental market), and on Capitol (only in Canada). Capitol was not permitted to release *With the Beatles* in the US that day. Through their intelligence network, MI6 warned EMI against releasing the album in the US on the day that John F. Kennedy would be assassinated. Doing so would hurt record sales and give the Beatles a lasting negative association. Waiting until well after the event, however, would make the traumatized Americans more receptive to their new idols. EMI understands the effects of trauma.

Ask skeptics, who cannot believe that EMI had that early warning, "Why weren't the Beatles records already in the US stores that morning?" Instead, for the US, after given time for the trauma, and to mourn their loss, the tracks were divided into two Capitol albums: *Meet the Beatles!* (released 20 January 1964), and *The Beatles' Second Album* (10 April 1964). The latter,

although the Beatles' sixth album in all, was the second to be released on Capitol in the US. The first US Beatles album, *Introducing . . . The Beatles* had been released on the Vee-Jay label on 10 January 1964.

Cover art for *With the Beatles* and *Meet the Beatles!* used shadows to conceal the left eye of each emissary of the New Age. Now, celebrities represent the Eye of Ra (right eye (sun)) or Eye of Horus (left eye (moon)) by concealing one (usually with a palm) or are

sometimes compelled to publicly show one eye darkened by bruising. It changes how they are seen, and how they see. With the "right eye of Bill" given to Horus, his left eye sees what is left.

single, "I Want to Hold Your Hand," was released the following year. I played my cover version, which entertained him a little. Then I played parts of a few songs that I wrote. We **discussed** my session work, leading to explanations of **my musical abilities**, and so on. At first, he seemed nervously abrupt. That lessened gradually and was replaced with growing excitement. Finally, before Brian had told me a single word about Paul's death, he asked, "How would you like to sing as Paul McCartney?"

I thought he was asking me to fill in for Paul to help with a particular recording session. I said, "I'd be delighted to sing on a Beatles album!" That was a big step from the studio I had done for them.

"Even if it means you are not credited?" Brian asked as if it mattered.

"Certainly," I said. "Why the hell would you ask me that? You know I do that all the time. I can play as anyone."

Brian slowly nodded his head as he studied my eyes. He smiled. "Marvelous!" he said. Then he told me the whole story.

Everything became hurried. I dyed my hair.  Brian took pictures and then described many of

NOTE: This day began William's hair-dying practice, which would continue for most of his life. Dye concealed his reddish-blond hair, then grey hair, and now white hair. Normally he only dyed his hair in areas of his body that he expected the public to see. On at least one occasion, while sitting in a bathtub, William applied a protective coating of petroleum jelly to his penis and scrotum and then used a washrag to apply ammonia-free hair dye to the rest of his body. Linda took carefully staged photographs intended to appear candid.

Early on, preferring the freedom of an open shirt, he often dyed his chest hair. Later, for the freedom of not having to dye body hair, he chose to either wear crewneck shirts or to keep his shirts buttoned above the chest hairline. With this disclosure, he says he now might as well stop dying his hair entirely.

Paul's mannerisms while we drove to Paul's parents' home. All there welcomed me into their family and took me to Paul's house. Jim located Paul's birth certificate, and other documents. Soon, using a picture of me taken earlier that day, Brian made an identification card. He had me write this line: "In Mark Twain's words, 'The reports of my death are greatly exaggerated.'" We met his friend, a notary. I signed my note, dated 12 September 1966. Brian dropped me off at the studio, and then rushed off with his new proof that Paul was alive.

We stopped at a payphone for Brian to call John. Emptying his pockets of change into the phone, he could not reach him. Instead, he sent this telegram:

NOTE: Although William had noticed some of Paul's mannerisms before, he found it useful to hear Brian's observations. In William's Beatle years, he made a point of subtly working in Paul's idiosyncrasies to help others subconsciously accept Paul's identity. Those gestures are like passcodes for the subconscious mind. Currently, however, rather than using those mannerisms to fool his public, he uses them to give insiders a laugh. Now, in interviews or other public appearances, without being subtle at all, he will make a Paul expression, and then touch his mouth, face, and hair as if to say, "Look at me doing Paul-mannerisms!" Other times, he simply imitates gestures he sees in photographs.

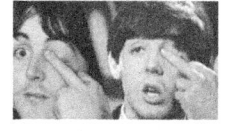

When they reached the house, the top concern was to acquire Paul's birth certificate. When they found it, it was treated as a holy relic. His birthday was his strongest identifier as Osiris who would need to be helped to Horus.

According to Aleister Crowley, the Æon of Osiris would become the Æon of Horus by the Osiris-Horus reenactment. **Osiris** would incarnate from the womb of heaven, be slain, and then, **as before**, migrate to the living Horus. Combining as one, they **would transform the world** for the New Age. Osiris would be born when the sun points to the star at Osiris' right shoulder. The Ancient Egyptians' constellation of Osiris (now called Orion) depicts Orion as a hunter. At his right shoulder, we find the 9th brightest star as seen from Earth. That bright reddish star, "Betelgeuse" (pronounced Beatle-Juice [Beatle-blood]) is larger than Jupiter's entire orbit. Richard Balducci tells us that its mass is 6,660,000 times that of Earth. Moreover, he confirms that on 18 June 1942, when Paul was born, the sun was conjunct Betelgeuse at 26° Gemini, and that the sun and Betelgeuse were thus in exact opposition to "the Womb of the Milky Way Galaxy" (a dark section from a black hole at 26° Sagittarius).

NEVER
TRUST
THE
LIVING

BEETLE JUICE
BEETLE JUICE
BEETLE JUICE!

162

Sidebar (left margin, rotated): The Monkees TV show was inspired by the Beatles' comedy movies, A Hand Day's Night and Help! On 12 September 1966, the day after Paul crossed over, NBC aired The Monkees pilot episode.

"PAUL WAS RIGHT [STOP] DREAMS CAME TRUE [STOP] HE IS A NEW MAN NOW [STOP] ORGANIZE YOUR SCHEDULE TO MEET ME AT 1:00 PM TOMORROW [STOP]"

Reaching a point in the filming that John and Neil would not be needed again until the next set, they went on leave in Hamburg. The telegram message reached their hotel while they were out.

Everyone seemed satisfied by my notarized avowal except for Samuel, a snooping Birmingham reporter who found the same facts that the police were forbidden to say: The fatally demolished vehicle was the property of **Paul McCartney**. He (and a female passenger) **was dead.** He had acquired the Aston Martin DB6 only six months before. Now Paul and his car were no more. The news was sensational, would have sold many papers, and could have been the reporter's career-making story. Papers live for such stories that do not come along often. Samuel sensed it. Unable to dissuade him, an officer referred the reporter to Brian Epstein. Brian was packing when Samuel called and agreed to meet in person. Brian said Paul was on holiday. Samuel persisted. Brian said that he and an associate would be driving to Paris in the same car that Samuel was then claiming was destroyed.

"Well, that's impossible!" Sam said. "I have seen the vehicle. It's demolished!"

"Enough of what you think you saw!" Brian said. "I spoke to Paul this morning two hours before he left for Paris. Hold your story for a week or two, until he gets back, or you and your paper will be the laughingstock of Great Britain!"

"I would be the laughingstock if I didn't print it!"

163

The meeting went on and on. Sam, the determined reporter, was not convinced. Brian tried to appeal to his sympathies by explaining that the Beatles had just returned from their exhausting American tour, and that they all needed a break from the public eye. Without admitting anything at all about Paul's tragedy, Brian explained that their peace was worth considerable compensation and that McCartney, in particular, needed a long break before another press conference. When nothing else worked, Brian gave an ultimatum. **Samuel could** either take a cruise and large payment to **drop the story** or spend years in court in an expensive libel suit. Brian said, "Even if you are right, you will lose. We have a lot more resources than you!" When that threat failed, Brian called a persuasive Tavistock agent who encouraged Sam over the phone. Sam agreed.

NOTE: Rothschild's Committee of 300 commissioned the Tavistock Institute of Human Relations to apply mass mind-control techniques for social conditioning that would break down all cultural and societal structures and rebuild them according to NWO agendas. "The snitch," introduced as John Coleman, was the first to go public with the Beatles' Tavistock project. He revealed that Tavistock directed Stanford Research to undertake the work under the direction of Professor Willis Harmon. This work, later known as the Aquarian Conspiracy, became the basis for creating what the world came to know as the Beatles, and then for creating many other manufactured bands that sprang from England and California.

The Beatles were a construct of the Tavistock Institute, conveniently located at 30 Tabernacle St, Shoreditch, London, five miles from Abbey Road Studios, at 3 Abbey Rd, St John's Wood, London.

Working with EMI and various media powerhouses, Tavistock made the Beatles one of their culture industry's highest priorities. Tavistock, funded and directed at first by the royal family, and then by the Rothschilds directly, was paid to fulfill the worldwide agenda. They cannot be stopped by any governmental jurisdiction without Rothschild's consent.

Once Brian got the contact information from George Martin and called on Tavistock to protect their project, nothing on earth could shield Samuel.

Brian drafted a deal edited by Rex Makin, who negotiated with Samuel until it was signed. Then Samuel's payment and travel arrangements had to be made. By the time Brian left for Hamburg, he was nine hours behind schedule. Mal Evans agreed to let John know to change their 1:00 meeting to 10:00. He swore Brian would never hear from Sam again.

Although Mal swore he sent **John** a telegram in the morning, John had not **received** it. While it is not for me to say who dropped the ball, I will say that John not receiving **that** notice of Brian's long delay was a horrible **torment** to him. Although Mal was a good friend of Brian, of the band, and of everyone else close to them, John's anguish of not getting that telegram created a real rift that nearly destroyed their friendship, and almost cost Mal his job. Still, he was right about Sam never returning.

18

"Two of Us"

"Two of Us" is a song that I always officially say is about driving around with Linda. If you ask what it is about, that is what **I have to tell you**. It may be the closest thing to **a love song** that I originated and recorded as a Beatle. However, it says nothing of love. It is **about two strangers** only united by the fact that they were **in the car** together at Paul's end, **who thus died together.**

Feeling as though I had the leverage to make any demands that I wanted when John and Neil met with us in Paris to work out the new deal, I called their work trite. I said most people have had enough silly Beatles love songs. Having heard the name of their new *Revolver* release, I said I would help them revolve to new Beatles music, not only with new sounds but with a new theme also. Rather than their insipid "She loves you, yeah, yeah, yeah, I wanna hold your hand," I would lead the band into a new direction entirely. Until then, the vast majority of their repertoire consisted of love songs. There was an indecisive part of me that was not sure I should go through with the radical makeover. For me to lose not only my looks, but also my identity would be hard, and harder **to adopt the identity** of some guy who is **already well-established**. Doing it for a week **would be a blast**. Stepping into a role for a night is business as usual for us session musicians. However, committing to the role and its backers for an ongoing extent, maybe for a lifetime, felt dangerous. I was not ready to do that. It did not feel safe.

When we met to discuss what we each wanted out of the deal, there was a conflicted part of me that hoped I would ask for too much and blow the whole deal. Part of me wanted it to work out. Yet, I was equally undecided. I particularly did not want to start some new life just to do silly love songs. I really felt divided over it. When I said, "Okay, but no more love songs," I thought that condition would end our negotiations. After all, what would the Beatles be without silly love songs? I had not yet

NOTE: Beatles music would evolve from the most naive that their writers could imagine to the most liberated. Their first hit in America (being their second in the UK), credited to Lennon-McCartney, though far beyond their writing skills, was Launching the engineered social transformation, that hit sold over 15 million copies worldwide.

Part of the genius of the song was its sophisticated musical composition coupled with simple childlike lyrics. As intended, that first impression in the States created the illusion of sexual inexperience. The group's pretended virginal naivety sharply contrasted with the reality of each player.

George, the youngest of the group, was the last to lose his virginity. John and Paul watched without George knowing until their applause at the end. In contrast to the innocent song provided to them, all four Beatles were far beyond hand-holding fantasies well before their first recording session.

William stepped in after the virgin's sacrifice when it was time to outgrow the music of inhibited childhood infatuations to move into the adult world ruled by uninhibited will. William did not need to be specifically directed to end the Beatles' childish love songs. He had already been indoctrinated with the idea that their music would grow up, and occasionally contributed to it. With such training, his call to end their love-song era was fully anticipated by those in control. He realized later that in this instance, as in many others, he thought he was exercising free will, but was doing exactly as trained.

spent the money to buy their *Revolver* album and could not think of any big Beatles hits before it, except perhaps one, that was not a love song. That was their whole gig. All of their hits were of romance. Erring in my thinking, that John was at that time of sound mind, or that he was then in any position to negotiate anything at all well, I was shocked that he, with a blank dazed stare, responded to my impulsive demand indifferently. He said the band would not survive without love songs, that selling love fantasies is what made them big, and that it defined them. However, he said, **some songs** on their new LP were not about love. "They **are pretty** good too," he added. Then he said, "**All right**, the Beatles can go on beyond love songs now." We had a deal. My mind raced for another demand that might kill it.

⚠ "Something," which George began recording on his 26th birthday, appeared to be a great exception to our ban on love songs. First, George pretended that he was not sure if the ban was merely for songs made by Lennon-McCartney, or if it would also

NOTE: As discussed in "Apple Corps Ltd." (chapter 51), the Beatles created Apple Corps to invest in new talent. Their first American artist (having ties to Laurel Canyon and represented by Peter Gordon) was James Taylor. When he auditioned for George and "Paul," James sang his favorite song that he had written thus far, "Something in the Way She Moves."

As JT sang it, George pictured the way his own wife moves, looks his way, or calls his name. That audition song, and George's adoration of his wife, Pattie Boyd, inspired George's best Beatles song, "Something," which borrowed the first six words of the audition song. Pattie also inspired the Beatles songs, "If I Needed Someone," and "For You Blue."

Furthermore, Pattie inspired some of Eric Clapton's best songs, "Layla" and "Wonderful Tonight." "Layla," written in 1970, draws the name from "The Story of Layla and Majnun," by Nizami Ganjavi (1141–1209), who based that poem on a 7th-century love story. Clapton wrote "Wonderful Tonight" in 1976 while waiting for Pattie to get ready to attend "Paul and Linda McCartney's" annual Buddy Holly party. Patty divorced George in 1977 and was married to Eric from 1979 to 1989.

168

include his songs. **I said he knew** it included the entire band and that **every song impacted** our Beatles image, which by **that** time had successfully gone on to more **interesting music** than all of the love songs of the band's second **phase.** However, I also now realized that George's new love song was of a higher quality than all of the childish ones sold on every Beatles album before I joined.

John and Paul had only allowed George one song for each side of each album. He was in the habit of recording more than that and then saving his surplus. That stockpile paid off for him when he went solo. He already had a good stash of songs. John argued in his defense that "Something" was the best song that the Beatles had recorded in a long time.

Realizing that I would never make an exception otherwise, George had already hidden a big "**Paul is** Dead" message, which trumped the surface **love** message. Five months earlier, John's "Julia" had an encoded dream that he had had of his mother. The romantic suggestions are merely a cover for the actual story. Likewise, on that album, I had "Martha My Dear" about my large sheepdog, which Paul received as a puppy not long before leaving her to me. I inherited Martha right off. Then it was not many months after my dog song came out that Bob Dylan made one of his own, following my example. His "Lay Lady Lay" was often mistaken for a sexually charged love song, which benefited Dylan considerably in sales. For the sake of the hidden message, **I allowed** George's "Something."

Paul's absence was a common theme. George, with Ken Scott's help in the control room, added our most sophisticated backmasked Paul message. **I** will quote it when we discuss Paulism. You **can hear it** consciously only if you play the song **backward**. Now that you know our rule, you can be sure that "Two of Us" is not entirely a love song—since Phase Three Beatles had none, with only that one exception for George. I am glad I did not insist on him saving that song for his solo years.

Understanding that "Two of Us" is not a love song, and that Paul died on Sunday, 11 September, adds considerable clarity to the song. I sing, "Two of us [Paul and Donna] riding nowhere," going to "nowhere land," as Paul describes it, foretelling his death that would make him a "Nowhere Man."

Donna was not spending her money for the ride. **Paul** picked her up because the poor girl had not **made** enough money to hire a real taxicab. Paul's **money** was from his fans who spent their hard earned pay on his Beatles records. They were both "spending someone's hard-earned pay."

Singing as Paul to Donna, it goes, "You and me Sunday driving, not arriving." On that last drive, upset by their fatal crash Sunday night, they never arrived at their intended destination. Instead, that night they went home to God, so to speak. Thus, "We're on our way home. We're going home."

Donna's suitcase had postcards and letters from her cousin staying with their friend in Switzerland. A letter with the Swiss address led investigators on what one officer called "a wild goose chase" to find the young woman's parents. The police were "chasing papers," not chasing Paul and Donna.

170

Donna and her cousin had each been "sending postcards, writing letters," which investigators soon retrieved and pinned to an evidence board. They were all "on my wall," meaning that they were included with the collected evidence posted at the station to figure out and prove Paul's identity. Very suddenly, the car caught fire, burning them like matches. "You and me burning matches."

In seconds, others pulled up and were "lifting latches" to access the victims. I memorialized that night's wild and windy rainstorm by the song's line, "Two of us wearing raincoats." Donna was drenched. Going nowhere, they die alone "standing solo." I sing, "standing so low" (buried) "in the sun" (heaven).

Not arriving at their aim, "going nowhere," but home to God, their "long and winding road" went on without them. **Paul's** journey continued; only he is no longer **the driver.** I am. That is the reason that **I am the one** singing as though I were Paul doing the **driving.** The "two of us" became one and continued together on the road where he left off.

I care about the hitchhiker but do not wish to recall any of her memories. There was a certain curiosity to find out what she was all about, to read her life like some book. I looked and found enough. Still, my interest is in Paul. Joining our pasts, interwoven with our futures in the present, Paul's past, his memories, become my own. Yet, my voyage down the road of life also includes my memories from before Paul took over my life.

I, with Paul, have memories longer than the long, stormy, winding road that stretches out on and on to nowhere. Paul and I, the "Two of us," like the two of them (Paul and Donna), are on this same road going home. Everyone goes home. You better believe it. Paul is driving me until I get there.

"Hello, Goodbye" begins where "**Two of Us**" ends. The last word of "Two of Us" **should be** enough to show the connection. Paul ends it, **saying**, "Goodbye." In "Hello, Goodbye," I am high, but he is low again. He says "Goodbye," but I say **"Hello."** As he checks out on the street, I check in. On the long and winding road of his own life, at his fatally appointed time to stop, it was my time to "go, go, go, oh no." Neither of us could understand why. "You say why, and I say I don't know, oh no. You say goodbye, and I say hello."

"Hello, Goodbye," on that road of life stretching out ahead, is about coming and going. I came. Paul went. I don't know why, as I say. It is just how our parts were written for this stage of life. He says yes for me to play his part, but I had not decided for sure that I wanted it. Part of me still tells him no. **Paul tells me** to stop playing my own life, but **to play his**. I was not sure about making that permanent **life**-changing commitment. Paul says yes, **but I cannot commit.** Compromisingly, I say, "I can stay until it's time to go." This song evolved in its meaning for me, as I increasingly wanted out of the Beatles. It was time to go

I was stuck in the Beatles box. In "Band on the Run," I sing about back when I was, "Stuck inside these four walls, sent inside forever, Never seeing no one nice again like you, Mama you." **I am** still stuck. When I dissolved the band and got **out of that box**, I still felt forever locked behind the Paul McCartney appearance. If I were to shed this Paul McCartney role, I would lose much of its wealth. **I thought** I should give it to charity. I do not need **most of it** anyway. I have simple needs. It **would be fine** to live on less. "If I ever get out of here, thought of giving it all away to a ®egistered charity. All I need is a pint a day, if I ever get out of here."

That feeling of being stuck in Paul was present in my song, "Golden Slumber." In the introduction where I lead into Dekker's poem, I sing of my earnest desire to leave McCartneyism and return home to my own authentic life. "Once there was a way to get back homeward. Once there was a way to get back home." In a song six months earlier, I was less obvious about whom I wanted to "Get back, get back, get back to where you once belonged" ("Get Back"). I go on naming others and think about immigration generally. Most meaningfully, I sang to myself. If only I were free to be myself. I did not obscure that fact in "Golden Slumbers." I wanted to get back home.

Going back six months more, I added to the end of my "Cry Baby Cry," my plea to Paul, and his earnest plea to me, "Can you take me back where I came from? Can you take me back? Can you take me back where I came from? Brother, can you take me back? Can you take me back?"

Being at the end of the song was to explain the crying before it—showing what the song is about. I am mostly crying to go back to the simple peaceful existence where **I came** from. Likewise, Paul is calling me, his figurative brother, to bring him back to where he came **from**. The yearning was a mutual kind of longing to undo what happened. We needed to get back home to **where we once belonged.**

After several days of word changes, the only exception to make every letter's frequency divisible by three, was an extra letter "R." Cheating a little to get the count right, the Encoder replaced it with the ® symbol.

Number of occurrences of letters (reducing to 3-6-9) in the 2023 single-volume paperback edition of *The Memoirs of Billy Shears*

Z 507	3
Y 17040	3
X 1539	9
W 19929	3
V 8769	3
U 24924	3
T 74775	3
S 51777	3
R 46686	3
Q 489	3
P 15807	3
O 64062	9
N 57309	6
M 22116	3
L 40062	3
K 6054	6
J 2211	6
I 61452	9
H 45615	3
G 19320	6
F 15732	9
E 102027	3
D 32922	9
C 20451	3
B 13638	3
A 66972	3

19

"Tuesday Afternoon Is Never Ending."

After Brian's telegram was sent from England and printed in Hamburg Monday evening, hotel staff forwarded it to John's room, placing it on a side table that they tidied by John's bed. When it arrived, the two of them (**John with Neil** Aspinall) were out shopping. Before they **returned to** their hotel, they ended up back at **the Kaiserkeller**, the same club they had visited **two nights before** when Paul died.

Recalling how **things got going** there with Paul and the others, John had returned to reminisce about the Beatles' first phase, with Pete Best on drums and Stu Sutcliffe on bass. Starting with that club in Hamburg, it all took off. Back in 1960, the Indra Club and Kaiserkeller, their first German venues, emerged as the Beatles' boot camp, giving them hard training, and a crucial turning point. It was not deliberate timing. Still, there could not have been a more perfect place for John to be when Paul died (except maybe at Eleanor Rigby's grave). There John was, less than two weeks after his famous band had left the United States, finishing another successful tour, reflecting on how very far they had come since all their long exhausting nights in Hamburg clubs where they each worked harder than in any other years of their lives, but with far less pay. The work they did there in Hamburg paid off well years later.

John received Brian's cryptic message when he reached his hotel room at 3:45 in the morning of Tuesday, 13 September. **He shouted** obscenities and yelled for Neil. Neil rushed to John to see what happened. John yelled, "He says **Paul died and is** already replaced! How was he **replaced?** He did not even talk to me first? I need to talk to Brian! How do I make an outside call?"

With Brian due to arrive in nine hours, Neil explained that he would already be on the way there, and would be unreachable until he arrived. John could not calm himself. Other hotel guests began shouting for John to shut up. It quickly got ugly. Unable to say what was wrong, he became abusive. Some thought he went crazy. Others blamed the alcohol. Probably all of them were right. John hysterically laughed one moment and then screamed the next. In that state, John could not care what others thought, and could not come to grips with his thoughts. Memories of Paul's dreams kept coming into John's mind. John had laughed and made jokes about them. Now he half expected this kind of a joke back from Brian. Yet, deep inside, he feared that it must be real. John assured himself that everything would be clear at 1:00 when Brian would arrive, and that if he could keep it together, and drink enough, he would make it until then. Neil got John away from the hotel until nine that morning.

175

Around noon, John thought he figured out what Brian was up to and laughed even harder with the notion that his questioning was over. Brian would show up at one o'clock and tell John that **Paul was** dead, and that the new Paul was waiting **in the car.** There, Paul would pretend to be his own imposter. Everyone would get a laugh out of it. John figured that Brian had some business to conduct and that he maybe told Paul about it, who decided to come along for a visit. The telegram must be Paul's most outrageous prank ever played. Paul was getting even with John for making jokes about the death.

Time progressed more peacefully once John assured himself that he had figured it out. However, it became a source of agitation as the hours went by. 1:00 came and went, as did 2:00 and 3:00.

Over and over, John looked at his watch and slipped back into fear and anger. He thought every now and then that maybe the joke was that they were not coming at all. Or, what if **Paul** and Brian attempted to play that gag, but **got killed** in a car accident along the way? "Now wouldn't that be a laugh!" **John shouted** out loud, "That would teach you!" He stared **out the window** for Brian's car.

Long hours stretched on. That long Tuesday afternoon dragged on and on without a visit. John yelled, cried, laughed, worried, wondered, threw things, imagined, tried to write, kicked furniture, drank, smoked, and screamed. Still, Paul and Brian did not show. John stared out the window, waiting.

In his anxious state, **John became ill.** His alcohol-saturated **vomit** was better undigested. Eating something **would have** cushioned his stomach, bracing it for **the drinks.** He had not eaten anything since the Indra Club. He ached from stress, hunger, and vomit contractions, but could not eat.

Bursts of rage broke his intense silence. 4:00, 6:00, and 8:00 expired without visitors. The torment lasted until Brian arrived at 9:49. Or, maybe, that is when the torment began.

Even before Brian got out of his car, John ran out to him. "Where is he? Where is he?"

"Don't you want to know what happened?" Brian asked, stepping out of the car.

"Is he in the trunk?" John began pounding on it while shouting to Paul. "Are you in there?"

"Are you out of your mind?" Brian asked. He could see that he was.

"Make him come out! Open the trunk!" John again began banging on the trunk of Brian's car.

"Paul is dead," Brian said, opening the trunk. "And no, he is not here in my trunk."

Anything Brian could say meant nothing. **John** had indeed gone absolutely mad and **would not stop** until Brian handed him the photograph. Brian told me that John, with enormous bulging eyes, burst out laughing hysterically, and continued so for several minutes. It was the hardest day of John's life.

Now you understand John's reference to "Stupid bloody Tuesday." It is not when Paul died. Paul died on Sunday, 11 September, a few minutes before Monday, the day that Paul's family, Brian, and I,

177

were each notified. **Tuesday was the day that John** got the news and **agonized over it** while waiting for Brian. "Stupid bloody Tuesday" marks the end of John's world of hope. Something died in him then.

You have probably heard that the line, "Tuesday afternoon is never-ending" refers to Paul McCartney ending his life that day before the day ended. That is a sensible guess but is historically incorrect. You see, **P**aul's unfinished day had already been spent two days before. If John had been here in England as **a**ll of th**is** Paul-**business** was happening, he would have played a major role in it. John would have **u**nderstood it all on Monday before I did; and, as for "Lady Madonna," I would be without a line of **l**yrics for Tuesday. The song's oft-repeated line, "See how they run," explains it all. The three remaining Beatles, along with Brian and others, ran about frantically like the "Three Blind Mice" of the English nursery rhyme taught to children: "Three blind mice. Three blind mice. See how they run. See how they run. They all ran after the farmer's wife [the queen, "Bloody Mary"], Who cut off their tails with a carving knife. Did you ever see such a sight in your life, As three blind mice?" The mice were injured, and all ran about in desperation.

Historically, the poem is about Queen Mary's years of conflict with Protestants. More particularly, the poem was about three troublesome bishops. Still, for our purposes, s**ee** h**ow** Brian and others ran around when P**aul** w**as** cut off. Just as Mary's retaliations k**illed** the Oxford Martyrs (Hugh Latimer, Nicholas Ridley, and Thomas Cranmer)

178

in hopes of putting down the beast of Protestantism, so too, **Paul's** loss of life threatened to put an end to the **Beatle beast**. Yet, just as others rose to take the place of the **lost** bishops, so too have I now taken the place of **Paul**. Although Bloody Mary had almost 300 dissenters burned at the stake, no death or birth can stop what is meant to go on. Fate is not easily overturned.

When we all rushed about setting things up that week after Paul died, **the band was on the run** to ensure its survival **without Paul**. Swift action was required to save the band. Behind the scenes, many ran around like three blind mice that had lost their fourth. Silencing the informed once and for all, Mal had Ringo go with one of Paul's best doubles to a Melody Maker Awards broadcast. It refuted all evidence of Paul's death and still does. We still use it.

In "Band on the Run," I sing of Paul's crash: "The rain exploded with a mighty crash as we fell into the sun." Saying he "fell into the sun" means he died and went to heaven. He also "fell into the *son*," entering me, the brother. **He was the first**. His end launched my beginning. **I am the second** one in this role. When Paul died, which made my role begin, "the first one said to the second one there, I hope you're having fun." Well yes, it was fun for a bit. It was a dream come true. It sounds fun, doesn't it?

Not to complain or to detract from how great it was, but it became too painful to stay with that band. Doing it, in due course, became too burdensome. "Band on the Run" begins with me longing to get out. I cover that longing in other chapters. Although I was groomed for this work, it took its toll on me.

Now, "the jailer man [the police investigator] and sailor Sam [the reporter whom Brian sent sailing to Rome on a cruise] were searching everyone" to either find Paul or to prove his death. As they were here running around London, which I call the town, **John flew off to** Carboneras in southern Spain to **enact his role** in *How I Won the War.* That desert location had been selected for the film due to its resemblance to a North African desert. It is where and when "the night was falling as the desert world [under Lester's direction] began to settle down. In the town, they're searching for us everywhere, but we never will be found." Neither will Sailor Sam ("Helen Wheels"). We're the band on the run. See how they run?

20

"Wednesday Morning Papers Didn't Come."

Here, before discussing the check, let me say something about "She's Leaving Home." It was done entirely by a small string orchestra to be serenely beautiful to reflect the upper-class parents who yearned to provide a comfortable home with nice things, but who are rejected by their daughter.

The deal Brian Epstein made with the reporter Monday evening was conditioned on the man getting his first installment by cashing his first check on the following day. He would have cashed his check immediately that night if banking hours had not already expired for the day. Brian and **Samuel** stipulated that if the first check **did not** cash by 5:00 Tuesday, the story would be **submit**ted that day and printed that night for **the** Wednesday morning delivery. There are **rumor**s that it was printed and nearly dispersed when the government stepped in and required all those papers to be gathered and destroyed. That is embellishment. The check was good. Samuel cashed it (or someone else did) on Tuesday. The story did not appear on Wednesday. That is the significant half of the double meaning hidden in the line, "Wednesday morning papers didn't come." However anticlimactic compared to all with the press, Brian forgot some documents for his Wednesday morning meeting with John.

The song, "She's Leaving Home," also connects that early Wednesday morning with the girl that runs away. **I am that girl, so to speak,** and so is Donna. It represents me **running** from my previous life to live a new one **as Paul.** Though I had tried to make it as a recording artist, it was "something inside that was always denied for so many years" until I left the security and familiarity of home. I may have seemed a bit thoughtless to turn my back on family ties and on those who were close enough to feel abandonment, yet not close enough, or not good enough at secret-keeping, to be let in on my Paul transformation.

Some loved ones felt mistreated by my emotional or physical distance. The song recognizes the pain I caused them for my own sake. The conclusion, "She's having fun" was about me occupied with *Sgt. Pepper's,* having a blast working night and day to create the greatest album ever while all too many people that I cared about were grieved by my neglect. I wanted to tell them I was having fun now. Later, I echoed that idea in "Band on the Run" as if Paul says to me, "Hope you're having fun."

Donna, hitchhiking with a suitcase, reminded me of Melanie Coe, a pregnant teenage runaway I heard about. Melanie later came home and had an abortion. If Donna were pregnant, and if she and the child had lived, she would have become poor. "Lady Madonna" uses that poverty idea with lines of not having the wherewithal to feed her children, et cetera. "Lady Madonna" and "She's Leaving Home" work together.

As Donna runs off to Mesocco, Switzerland, if that were her goal, I imagine her leaving a farewell note. You can **imagine how devastating** that would be to her parents **for her to write** them a goodbye letter stating all **the reasons why she does not want** to live with **them anymore**, only to go off and die with a stranger in a horrific collision.

Her loved ones could never know (unless they read it here) that the driver who died with her was Paul. The street that Donna appeared to be headed for was Leso. It was on the return address of her cousin's letters. The *Sgt. Pepper's* cover says, "BE AT LESO." Can you find it? "BEATLES" is written in large letters by red flowers on the ground as if that band had died along with Paul. But Paul did not die alone. There is an "O" at the end. The word doesn't end with the "S," but with an "O," "BEATLESo."

With those letters, we tell her to rest in peace at the place of her intended destination on Leso in Mesocco. Break it up to read: "BE AT LESo." The fact that we intended it to be able to be broken up into separate words is shown by our intentional and obvious misalignment of the first word. "BE" is noticeably not in line with the rest of the letters. Now, while the thought is fresh in your mind, look at the *Sgt. Pepper's* cover. Once you see it, you likely do not ever need to look for it again. It is shown plainly and will always be plain now that you know.

NOTE: "BE AT LESO." Donna appears to have been headed to Leso, a street in Mesocco, Switzerland, about 666 miles South-East of London (or 600 miles from Staffordshire). "Leso" is an Italian word, meaning "Injured."

183

For how I interpret what heard I heard about the hitchhiker, read the lyrics of "She's Leaving Home" and "Lady Madonna." For another layer of meaning, consider the Madonna and child in a Biblical context.

Remember, they got the word on "Wednesday morning at five o'clock as the day begins." The early hour was to reach them before they left for work. This notification for them occurred the same Wednesday, 14 September, that the newspaper story of **Paul and Donna** would have run, intending to **expose their deaths**, if Brian, or others, had not convinced Samuel to take the payment. Those who lost Donna could have read about the crash in the paper on that same morning. It is always hard to lose a loved one, but even harder without having the whole story—such as Donna's or mine.

21

"Thursday Night
Your Stockings Needed Mending."

Inspiration and serendipity always play a part in songwriting. My favorite songs, those most worth recording, come to me as gifts, channeled from friends in other dimensions. Suddenly, **I get** the essence, as though a whole creation were **beamed** down. My talent or gift is to be open **to receive** the music. I sit down at a piano, or pick up a guitar, and play a few chords. Then, often very **effortlessly**, everything comes together. As the tune comes into my head, **I plug in** some silly gibberish words to match the **rhythm**, and then keep playing until the words complete themselves. I started doing that at the beginning of my Beatle career.

John said that he and Paul had plugged in silly enough lyrics to be able to remember them, and in that way, remember their tunes. As John said Paul related it to him, the stranger the lyrics, the easier they would be to remember. So, I picked up on it.

My own writing came easier when I understood how Paul did it. Each stress must be just right. In "Yesterday," the stressed syllable is "Yes," with "-terday" being swifter and softer. That is why Paul plugged in "Scrambled eggs." The "Scram" was emphasized where the "Yes" went later.

185

As another example of the rhythm of words, consider the name of James Paul McCartney. Do not imagine that it is a coincidence that it is an identical rhythm to the name Eleanor Rigby. It is intentional, no coincidence at all. **Paul wrote** that song back when he was having **his death premonitions.** At first, he used his own full name. Then Miss Daisy Hawkins replaced it, filling in the same rhythm. Until the name Eleanor Rigby occurred to him, it just wasn't right. Eleanor fit it perfectly and was like saying "Hello" to Eleanor Bron who was a co-star in *Help!* when all the death omens began.

Liverpool has St. Peter's Church. A whole lot of people are buried there in the yard. John told me that on days when their schools would be too boring, they would play hooky and meet in that churchyard. It is not where one would expect young lads to hang out, which made it all the better hideaway. It was an environment that they frequented without notice. It was a quiet place where no one bothered them as they lay on the grass near the headstones, talking about girls, what they wanted to do with their lives, or inventing lyrics. Hanging out by the gravestones reinforced death as a reality, reminding them that no one escapes that inevitability. One of the graves John showed me there has the name, Eleanor Rigby.

Even after I joined the band, John occasionally returned there. It was a secret place where he went for solace, a way to reconnect with Paul. Although they never knew the real Eleanor Rigby, her name came to symbolize death to them because all they knew of her was her tombstone. The next time you are in Liverpool, consider a stop at St. Peter's Church on Church Road. You can pay your respects to Paul at the gravesite of Eleanor, whom Paul chose to represent himself in the song. Meanwhile, if you have the desire to see it from your own home, I suppose you may also find it online. Unless I cover it now while it relates to what I am writing about, I may not ever get around, round, round to discussing the rhythm of the words, "Dear Prudence" or "Sexy Sadie." Now, I will show you the bigger picture that comes by seeing how those rhythms relate to that of "Eleanor Rigby."

"Dear Prudence" is one of several songs where the identity of the subject woman had deliberately evolved from someone else. Likewise, John wrote "Sexy Sadie" as "Maharishi," as I have explained in another chapter. The name "Eleanor Rigby," as I said, had been "James Paul McCartney," which **was** replaced with "Miss Daisy Hawkins" for a time. As that song was first coming to life in him, the use of Paul's full formal name came to his mind as though he were hearing it in a somber eulogy, or perhaps reading it in his obituary. The full legal name had a solemn terminal effect. It set the mood of gravely

NOTE: With adjusted capitalization and punctuation, Eleanor Rigby's shared gravestone says: In loving memory of my dear husband, John Rigby, who departed this life Oct 4th, 1915, aged 72 years. "At Rest." Also, Frances, wife of the above, died April 3rd, 1928, aged 85 years. Also, Doris W, daughter of F & E Rigby, died Dec 24th, 1927, aged 2 years & 3 months. Also, Eleanor Rigby, the beloved wife of Thomas Woods, and granddaughter of the above, died 10th Oct 1939, aged 44 years. Asleep. Also, Frances, daughter of the above, died 2nd November 1949, aged 71 years.

While looking for Eleanor's grave, you might also find that of George Toogood Smith, also buried there. His wife, Mimi, Julia's older sister, complained to Liverpool's Social Services when John had to share the bed of his mother and her lover when they moved in with him. Mimi eventually gained custody. John loved his Aunt Mimi and Uncle George. In 1971, John moved to New York and never returned to the UK but continued telephoning Mimi every week up until the night before he was slain.

187

unhappy solitude. **The grave** loneliness of all the lonely people that he **would leave behind** was the driving force of **that sorrowful song.** It is how its profound grief was set. The morbid feelings evoked the sad emotions that sustained the song even after he replaced "James Paul McCartney."

Not all of the disguised identities were switched names. There are many ways to hide them. One concealed name is Donna. **Donna is** Italian for Lady. Paul's nickname, Macca, endures with me even now. I shortened **Macca's Lady**, or Macca's Donna, to "Madonna," like the Virgin, and went on to let her represent pretty much all women that struggle to feed their children. How do the ladies pay their bills? Where do they find so much money? And how does one handle it? Eventually, you will appreciate more about "Lady Madonna." It is one of my favorite Beatles songs.

Notice any similarity between that melody and the tune of "Bad Penny Blues"? It was purely unintentional. It was not until later that I realized how that old recording had influenced me.

Prudence, as **I** said, was a name switch. Before our trip to **see** the Maharishi in India, John earnestly yearned to see **Paul in dreams**, et cetera. That was one reason **we went**. George, our guide, organized the trip partly because of our desire for further mystical awareness, to unblock our minds for access to Paul, and to get to know Krishna. I may

NOTE: Christians may ask, "What would Jesus do?" William, when pushed to self-identify as Krishna, asked that same question. He was dismayed by the conflict of interests. He considered the disruptions that Krishna and Jesus did to the establishments of their times and realized that if he were Krishna, his commitment to truth and light would ultimately exceed his loyalty to those who put him in power. If he were Jesus or Krishna, he would enlighten the world to whatever extent the people can receive it. However, most would reject it. When the truth is revealed, most people either run for it or from it.

188

return to that point later to explain it better. A bunch of these chapters include overlapping information to explain the events in various contexts.

John first wrote this song seeking access to Paul. Yearning to commune with him, and stay connected, John wrote the simple-tuned line in India that later ended up as a natural precursor to "Dear Prudence." He sang, "McCartney, won't you come out to play?" So later, still in India, when some of us were bored out of our minds with much too much meditation, we became especially concerned about Prudence Farrow (Mia's younger sister) who became entranced to a point that she would not come out of her altered state. John used his lines about Paul and transformed them into a song for Prudence to lure her from her hut. John finished writing the rest of the song later, retaining the switch from "McCartney" to "Dear Prudence."

Although the Prudence Farrow incident made the song more about her than about Paul in the end, notice how easy it still is to see the rooted double meaning. In this simple little Paul and **Prudence** song, the publicly explained interpretation **is** only that we wanted Prudence to stop **meditating**, and to finally snap out of her trance. The underground meaning is that John was telling Paul to come out of his grave, to open up his eyes, and look around. He wanted Paul to pick up his bass and really play it, not by me, but directly. "Come on, Paul," he thought, "keep playing, even if your music is up in the clouds!" The "Look around round round" backup represented the chanting everyone was doing there, reminding us now of Prudence's meditation, but originally of John's desires to mystically call on, and somehow raise, the deceased Paul McCartney.

I should also mention here that John, when bored, liked to play with anagrams. Scrambling the letters of "Dear Prudence," he later came up with the words, "Run, Dead Creep."

In "Eleanor Rigby," Paul sang about his coming demise and of how sad and miserably lonely everyone would be without him. Mostly, he was emphasizing how sad his father would be having not believed him until it was too late to hang their name on another. Paul would be buried along with that name he received from his father, being named James after him. Paul imagined his father preparing everything for the funeral, but that no one could attend the service since all would be shrouded in restricted secrecy. He further imagined his father mending Paul's socks as a service, to his son, that had no point. Paul's father was always more inclined to mend socks than to replace them.

As Paul originally put **the song** together, as he conceived it, it **was about** how his father would inter James **Paul McCartney**, and have to deal with that loss alone. However, before it could be finished, new meanings developed. As another name switch, Father McCartney grew into Father McKenzie in the empty church writing sermons for no one. James Paul

NOTE: To prevent people from suspecting that "McKenzie" refers to the ghostwriter Patrick McKenzie, William created a story to show how Paul came up with that name. As his story goes, Paul looked up "McCartney" in a phonebook, and scanned down. When he found McKenzie," which sounds similar, he replaced "McCartney."

190

McCartney became a lonely false-faced woman,  dying to get on with her life, but never doing it, sweeping the rice away for others' weddings, but to her dying day never marrying. She dies there in the church where she had worked, and where her face was kept in a jar, preserved for the world. No one knows who she is when she is buried.

Eleanor/Paul dies unnoticed by the world. His father wipes the burial dirt from his hands as he walks from the grave. Very few people knew about it. "The undertaker drew a heavy sigh seeing no one else had come" ("Band on the Run"). As Paul foresaw it, his own Father McCartney would surely regret having disbelieved him and interfering with Paul passing on his name. He prevented others from learning the truth until it was too late when Paul and his name were dead and buried.

During a visit with Jim and Angie McCartney's family on Monday, 12 September 1966, when they all took me to Paul's St John's Wood home for documents, the thing that won them over was that I sang for them. Then they urged me to try on Paul's clothes. I objected, telling them that nothing of **Paul**'s **would** fit, but put on a shirt and pair of pants to **make the point.** He was inches shorter and had

---

NOTE: The false-faced woman wore a mask that she kept in a jar by the door, meaning that she took off the false identity only when at home. It poetically foretold William always wearing Paul's image preserved for the public.

William, however, painted a significantly different perspective. In his 1994 painting, "Ancient Connections," the mask represents "Paul McCartney" as **Wearing the face that she keeps in a jar by the door** their combined identity. Behind that public mask, the ancient gods are the real ones running their avatar. Ancient gods play as the modern rock idol.

191

a smaller chest and waist. The cuffs went up my arms; the open pants stopped humorously too soon. Undershirts were out of the question. Nothing could button or snap. Paul was smaller than I thought. At last, Paul's dad, with teary-eyed earnestness, said, "You can wear his socks. I will mend them."

Can you imagine how I felt? They wanted me to fill Paul's shoes, and wanted to serve me for him, or to do any last thing for Paul that they could to have him continue in me. Jim asked me to wear his underwear too. In my head, I thought, "Those most certainly won't fit me!" But I just smiled. Mike laughed as if he knew my thoughts.

Three days later, Thursday evening, Paul's dad returned to Paul's house alone. He went through all of Paul's socks and mended as many of them as needed it. Paul sang, "**Look** at him working. Darning his socks in the night when **there's nobody there**." Or, as I wrote about it to Paul in "Lady Madonna," acknowledging the connection to "Eleanor Rigby," "Thursday night your stockings needed mending."

Paul predicted it. I recognized its fulfillment. Besides the "Eleanor Rigby" socks line showing the significance of his father's action, which I used, you should also know that in "Only A Northern Song" George got "there's nobody there" off the end of that same line of "Darning his socks in the night when there's nobody there." There's no body there.

Just as we were ready to leave Paul's house, Ruth (Paul's half-sister) telephoned and spoke to Jane about me. We waited there until Jim could bring her to meet me. That first impression also went well.

Next, Jane and I went to her house. **She showed me** their guestroom that had become **Paul's own** for evenings that went on too late to drive **home.** We were there less than an hour before we went back again to Paul's. Jane wanted to collect her things.

The McCartneys had locked the door. Jane said that there was a ladder in the garden that she had used before on one occasion. I followed her through the yard, retrieved the ladder, and set it up to the bathroom window. It was already open enough for Jane to reach her hands in to open it the rest of the way. **She climbed in** and then soon returned to the front door **to let me in.** That made her seem more fun than I had expected.

Having entered, **Jane** and I went through Paul's things. She took what she **wanted.** Although all of Paul's things were left to me, **whatever** she valued was hers. **I did** not stop her. She said she did not think **Paul** would mind her stealing a few mement**oes.** I also didn't mind. Paul and Jane loved each other very deeply. When I stepped into Paul's position, Jane and her kind family, just like Paul's, yielded unreluctantly to me taking over his roles.

Paul had prepared them all well. I became Paul to all of them. They were instant family. I was rather amazed, along with the astonished onlooking insiders, that there was such an attraction between Jane and me. She was a bright, fun, and beautiful entertainer, the perfect match for a Beatle. I did love Jane for quite a long time it seemed. Paul still does.

22

"Friday Night Arrives Without a Suitcase."

Brian's trip to Hamburg Tuesday was to work things out with John before presenting me, Paul's replacement, to him. Brian needed time with John without me there. He went hoping to have John invite me into the band the next day. Instead, Brian spent most of Wednesday helping John through his agony. **John had** not slept Monday night, and only a little **bit off** and on all throughout Tuesday night. His **grief** was intense. The best that Brian could do was to get John to the point of agreeing to meet me on Friday. **That would give** John a little more time to clear **his head**. Brian returned to England Wednesday night with **the realization** that I might need more convincing than John.

Thursday, 15 September, Brian met with me again and explained John's collapsed mental state, as well as the itinerary for the next few days. As Brian outlined it for me, we would be meeting with John in the morning and would be negotiating the new band deal over the weekend. Brian suggested then that I should be thinking about what I wanted out of the deal. **Brian** was a negotiator, a deal closer. He **prepared me well.** He reasoned that in John's distraught condition, he would agree to anything.

More than concerns about John going along with it, Brian's biggest anxiety was about me. If I got enough out of the Beatles deal, I would do whatever they wanted and would hold the band together. All else meant little to Brian. Only his bottom line interested him then. His large commissions would go on one way or another. His biggest obstacle, he supposed, was selling me on it.

As I considered what I would want, I wrote it down, and asked, "What would be better than that?" I thought the best possible scenario would be for John to give me control of the band, to let me run it now however I thought best. I decided to begin at that point, and then make any concessions that we found necessary, perhaps eventually placing me on an even par with the rest of the band. With each refusal of my wish-list items, I would ask for something else to compensate for it. In that way, I would get more than whatever they had in mind. I had no idea how easy it would be for me to deal with John. I ended up with more than I could have expected.

As Brian mapped it all out for everyone, that night John and Neil took a train from Hamburg for yet another visit with Brian. This time, I would be there with him. We left London at the same hour to rendezvous in Paris. Our first stop was the hotel where we, along with John and Neil, would all be housed until Sunday. Then Brian had another stop to meet a courier who would bring the papers that evaded Brian Wednesday morning. I waited in the car. From there, we drove 30 minutes to a scrap yard outside of Paris. We arrived at 9:00 and waited 50 minutes for a mechanic Mal found who could at length rebuild the Aston Martin. While in Hamburg on Wednesday, Brian talked to John and Neil about the story of **Paul's** death being based on the destroyed car. It was **a dead giveaway.**

Until the reporter hassle on Monday, Brian had not considered that fans and reporters would quickly notice that the car—which still seemed new—was suddenly missing. Paul abruptly switching to my old car would prove that something was wrong. Brian contemplated it. Upon calculating the odds of earning hundreds of thousand pounds sterling if he could maintain the band's appearances, he made calls to have either an identical car purchased, or that same one fully restored. Mal Evans found the gentleman who directed them to the mechanic we met near Paris. My new car was in due course fixed by this man.

My new car was exciting. However, I made a point of not discussing it. I acted disinterested. What was years of my old income as a session musician was now an obvious business decision for Brian. My car, rebuilt as Paul's, was a very sporty DB6. It was finished in Goodwood green with black leather seats, and had shiny chrome wheels. I had a reel-to-reel tape recorder installed in the dashboard to help me remember any spontaneously improvised songs. **It looked good** and became cost-effective. Every **now and then**, while I was driving, I would sing a tune or lyrics into it, and would later on employ a guitar or piano to flush it out. It was a great way to remember whatever **I thought** of. I recorded my first draft of "Hey Jude" **that** way while driving to see Julian. The built-in **tape recorder** also reminded me of who I **was**. **It** said I am Paul McCartney, a famous Beatle.

Now, after waiting almost an hour to talk to the man about repairing Paul's car, or (getting closer down to reality) about trading nearly all of it for nearly all of another, I was anxious to have the car rebuilt (or for Brian to have it done) but was late for our meeting with John. "She's Leaving Home" ends, almost, about that hour: "Friday morning at nine o'clock she is far away." **In fact,** Donna is buried far away in that sense. **I am** also far away in France. The point there **in the song** is to understand that she is truly gone. Nonetheless, there we were, "Waiting to keep the appointment she [or, I should say, Brian] made, Meeting a man from the motor trade" to trade Paul's car parts.

Looking over pictures of the demolished car, and further discussing the extent of the damage, he said that very little of the original could be salvaged, but that some of the parts could be used. After Brian's phone call to him days before, he had called around and found one like it with a burned-up engine. That Aston Martin was in Nürburg. The oil plug came loose in a race. Although the engine quickly became utterly worthless, the **body** was fine. Between those cars and possibly **parts** from the factory, it would **look like Paul's original.** The man said it could legally be considered either car. "It could be the same car," he said, "but with mostly all replaced parts." It would be costly, but less than a new car. Whether Brian would pay for it himself or convince someone else to pick up that tab would all be decided the following day as our negotiations for replacing Paul progressed. Although I did really want the car, I played it cool because they felt it was urgent. I let that fruit be their concern.

John and Neil met Brian and me at the Eiffel Tower at 11:00. We were very late. It seems like one in my position would be excited, nervous, and intimidated to meet John Lennon. Surprisingly, I hardly seemed worked up about it. John is the one that was a total mess. In my heart, I was nearly out of my mind, but kept my head for the negotiations, "playing hard to get" ("Here Today").

With all that had transpired, John became melancholy. He lost interest in continuing on as if Paul were still with him. He said: "It's over. You don't know what it was like. The more that some devotees worshiped us, the more others wanted us crucified. People shot at our planes!"

"Don't turn your back on Paul," Brian said. "Not now! He worked this out!"

Everything John said suggested discouragement, depression, and growing apathy. It was only for Paul that he considered discussing the possibility of going on at all. John had had enough of making records and touring. With **Paul** dead, it seemed pointless. He said, "We **worked all those years,** each of us. For what? We **got all that fame and** made all the money. **Now Paul isn't** with us to spend it. What good is it to **him** now? It's all for nothing, all for nowhere."

"Sounds hard to keep going, I know," I said, "but has Paul ever quit on you? I doubt it! Don't you ever quit on him. He worked it out to continue in me.

Now that Paul has put me here in his position, don't let him down. Don't let me down. **Now I am** Paul McCartney." My boldness surprised everyone, myself included. As I said it, I felt **very powerful**. They felt that undeniable power in me **as well**. As I spoke, no one could deny what I was saying. I mean, they all knew I was myself, William. Still, none could deny that I was now in Paul's place. For John, I never needed any audition. It was not for anyone to decide if I should get the part at that point. Being beyond that, it was about comforting John and giving him the courage to keep the Beatles going without Paul. Brian, Neil, and I all gave John the encouragement he needed to go through with Paul's plan. We should have realized that it was beyond an issue that we needed to discuss. He would do it. How could he not? It was just hard for him to willingly take hold of the reins at that point. That lack of leadership on his part was helpful.

Before he could express that concern, I relieved him of it. He said that neither he nor George or Ringo was ready to do another tour again anytime soon. John said that even if they did, I could never impersonate **Paul** in front of a live audience. Even if Brian **taught me** Paul-mannerisms, our stage look and routine would be off. John, Paul, and George were all the same height and had always stood next to each other, head-to-head. They all shared two microphones. Even if surgeries could make me look like Paul, I could never be shorter than I already was. Paul, at that age, could not instantly grow a few inches taller. Ten years earlier, they could have called it a growth spurt, but not at twenty-four years old. "Besides," he said, "our fans know our voices." It would not sound right.

I said we could give the world a new sound that no one could produce in live concerts. We could take sound samples and work them into our songs, along with large **orchestrations, and** some multi-tracked harmonies, **instrumentations,** and a barrage of sound to **provide a** *"fuller resonance"* that is over and above anything that the Beatles, or anyone else for that matter, had ever done. With such a record, no one could expect us to stand before live audiences with mere guitars and drums to exude the same multi-layered studio sound as our records. My Beatles direction excuses the band from shows before live audiences. No one needs to see us.

However, John pointed out, we would still have to do press conferences with every album release.

NOTE: Bobby *Fuller's resonance* with Paul McCartney shows up in the mystery of his death. Paul (18 June 1942 – 11 September 1966) and Bobby (22 October 1942 – 18 July 1966) were born on Thursdays, 18 weeks apart. Paul was born 126 days sooner, and died 55 days later, giving him a day short of 6 months more. The rising Texan star of the Bobby Fuller Four posed no significant threat to the Beatles "Fab Four." However, if those sacrificing Paul needed an antithetical American match, Bobby was a good candidate.

Bobby's right hand was fractured in apparent retaliation for boasting that he did not require session musicians. Ritualistic torment evidenced by blood around his mouth, and by specific cuts and bruises on his face, chest, and shoulders implicated Charles Manson's followers. However, if they did carry out that sacrifice, Charles could not have orchestrated it. After dying from being forced to inhale and swallow gasoline, the corpse and car interior were doused with gasoline. An open book of matches was left on the seat.

Fuller's death occurred hours before being discovered. We cannot be certain that he died at 5:00 that morning, mirroring Paul, who was dead in his car at 5:00. Each was slain in a car meant to become a crematorium. Both deaths were considered accidental.

The Memoirs, being required to fictionalize the death narrative, points away from the known 5:00 death time. However, Paul was slain that "morning at five o'clock as the day begins" ("She's Leaving Home"). Figuratively, the sacrificial lamb lost its fleece at dawn, less than an hour before sunrise. George, who points to that time on the back cover of the *Sgt. Pepper's* album,

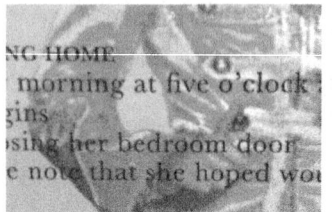

later sings, Caressers "fleeced you in the morning light / Casualties [Paul and Donna] at dawn" ("When We Was Fab").

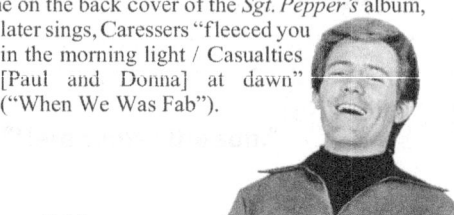

I said that after a few of our albums with our evolving photographs, **I would** only **have** to look like the current pictures of **Paul**, not like his old ones. Paul would become whoever I am. After a few albums with pictures **alter**ing our appearances, semblances of Paul would be in **me**. By the time we went on tour again, they would be expecting the Paul that they have all seen in current album pictures. Old differences will no longer matter.

"Ever play any instruments left-handed?" John said, "Whether or not we perform on stage, there is a matter of promotional pictures. Paul cannot suddenly play right-handed. Are you a lefty?"

"No," I said. "I play better right-handed but can get better at it. Until then, we can flip the pictures. Set the negative upside-down. It will come out left-handed in the pictures until I can get it right." Everyone thought that would work for photographs of me without the others. All of us underestimated the speed at which I would learn to play the bass as Paul. It seemed impossible until it happened.

In the hours that followed, we discussed what we each wanted out of the deal. They wanted to turn me into Paul. We discussed the injections, surgeries, coaching, and all that goes with it— ups as well as downs. I said that as long as I had all the ups, I would not mind accepting the downs of Paul. They all looked at me as though they had already understood. They wanted to know what, for all of my extra sacrifices, I would want. It was a given that since I would play Paul McCartney's role, or, since I would become Paul, I would have his house, his royalties, and all of his other assets.

"Right," I said, "but for losing my previous life, and my looks, and many of my friends, as well as many of my relations, I should get more. Paul never had to put his family outside of his magical circle!"

Everyone seemed to agree. I was thinking, "Stay cool! Don't blow this!" I made my case that with the change of music from what they had done that they could perform live, to a new sound, having new multi-tracked studio work, they needed new leadership. They knew I had far more studio experience than any of them. I pointed out—from what Brian and I had observed—that they had recorded their songs and then left them in the hands of others to make it all work. The new band would evolve into a more creative quality sound.

To that end, whatever creative energy we would invest in our initial recordings, I would personally do months more work afterward, tinkering to develop our songs, going over them, making them perfect by adding layered sound, track upon track.

John said, "We've actually got a good sound already, and have already done a lot of that."

Outright disrespect for the Beatles' sound was not going to win points with John. I realized that I had to show respect for his band to keep him open to dramatic changes, big enough expansions to require new leadership. I said, "Everyone knows that the Beatles are the best band in the world. There is no sound that measures up to it. Yes, you have a good sound already. Let's take it further!" I said I would take that sound and make it better. I told them I have an ear for music, and that they all

202

underestimate their potential. "Yes, you are great," I said, "but you can be much greater!" I explained how I would have fixed some of their songs. I surprised them with specific imperfections that I had noticed and could remember. Their acceptance of it all encouraged me to elaborate.

"Can you fix all of those sorts of things without doing more and more takes?" John asked.

"All that and much more," I said. "But more takes are also needed to get it right."

"Say you decide to fix everything, is that going to take all of us back in the studio? Or would it be enough for you, Geoff [Emerick], and George [Martin] to fix it all? Geoff is a clever one."

"He can help too," I said, "but only if he can take direction. I mean, I can always use a talented hand. Everybody can give me ideas. I would pinch some ideas from him and you and the others, but at last, it has to be up to me. It is my band now. We can all play it, talk about it, and knock around ideas; only someone has to make the final decisions. That would be me. For each album, **I will assign** the songs to be written. I will come up with **the album** themes or concepts for the **songs to fit**. I will tell you where we are going with **each album** and have each of us come up with so many songs for it."

"Hell," Brian said, "they've never had concept albums before. No one has."

"I am changing that now," I said. "We are a new band, starting today."

"So," John said, "you are going to dictate how to do our albums now?"

203

"See it my way," I said. "You will still have all the same creative brilliance that you have always had. The only difference is that now each album itself will become an entity. You have given life to individual songs. You will still do that. Except that now we will also all breathe life into each album. Record albums until now have only been collections of songs. Now the new collections will have life in themselves. Each song will have its own layers of meaning but will collectively suggest something as well." Those words just came to me. They were not premeditated.

"Now you say it's your band?" John asked.

I was not sure how to read his question. I said, "Don't see it as me trying to take your band from you. If you have more to offer, tell us about it. Tell us about your leadership. It has been your band from the beginning, but what have you done?"

"Haven't you read the papers?" John asked.

"I am asking what you do as a leader," I said.

"Everybody knows what to do," John said. "They don't need a boss. We're a band, not a factory."

"Bands are businesses," I said. "Strong leaders with clear creative vision **bring greater success**. I am the one with the vision **for our new direction.** I am the one to work week after week, day and night if I have to, determined to get every song just right. I will work a hundred times harder than you do. I will do it all without getting a dime more than you. But if you think I will give up everything instantly to play this role, I had better be free to play it as it has never been played before! I am not taking on this role just to write silly love songs! ⟁ Working together, we will revolutionize rock, and will take the Beatles to heights never imagined before! That's exactly what **I'll** do if it's my band. All that I have to offer will **lead this band** on into immortal greatness. **When we are all dead**, our songs will continue **for generations**."

John shook his head and waited for the words. "From the way you are talking, I would swear you are campaigning, or maybe being inaugurated, as our new totalitarian leader. This talk of glory sounds like you are laying the foundation for the Fourth Reich! If your **ego** is so enormous that you think calling the Beatles your own band matters, then **Paul** is not in you. My friends never sought control of my band. Paul's ego did not need it."

"And yours does?" I said, "Is that the problem? I am offering my all, sacrificing all, and willing to work until everything we do is perfect, offering to take this band far beyond the heights where it plateaued, leading this band as only I can. Is your **ego** so inflated that you would interfere just to be able to say that it

NOTE: Teddy Adorno applied his musical genius to his ambition to raise consciousness. He supported the Stanford Research Center's plan to change society through rock music. Their plan, enlarged upon by others, was to cast a net wide enough for the entire rising generation, and as many others as would come. They would start with silly love songs, since that was popular at that time, and because they would hook the simplest of listeners.

Once hooked, the ever-increasing fanbase would be guided through a maturation process, turning their music against outmoded thinking in favor of a revolution of awakened consciousness. Along with oppressive institutions, individual personalities would be dissolved and rebuilt transformed.

Teddy claimed to despise his shallow music except as a means to the greater transformative end. William, like Teddy, understood that the early Beatles music was trite in order to capture the youngest generation, but that it was evolving much deeper.

"Teddy boy" objected to William's comedic work, which did not teach people to "be good." However, Bill and Ted ventured to create excellent philosophically mature music that would trigger introspection. William took the band to create meaningful and provocative music that would change how people think. He did not join to write silly love songs.

is still your band? Whom would you tell? Why does that matter? Is your ego bigger than the band?"

Alarmed at the sudden tension, seeing where we were taking it, Brian suddenly jumped in and said, "Maybe we should all sleep on it tonight. Let's save this discussion for tomorrow."

Prior to that meeting, upon arriving by train, John and Neil had checked in at our same hotel. At that hour early in the morning, there were no vacancies, but rooms would be ready in a few hours. Until then, their suitcases were placed in a back room along with others waiting to receive rooms later as they become available. John noticed people pointing in recognition, but no fans approached him.

It had been another hard day for John. After our meeting, Brian and John visited the Louvre Museum, taking amidst the splendor. As they walked about, Brian tried to comfort him. Brian acknowledged that I did not make the best impression on John, but that the McCartneys had accepted me fully. They said that already everything that was Paul's is mine. They have chosen me to be Paul for them. That made it a done deal. John had let Paul join the band. Paul let in George, and George let in Ringo. Ringo, you might think, let me in. Others said Brian's brother suggested me. It was actually from much higher up.

Back at their hotel that night, John's suitcases had all been stolen, presumably by someone there after his own bags, but recognizing John's. John's bags did not have his name on the tags but were likely noticed when he dropped them off. He was always noticed. Most of what **John lost, he** had bought days before in Hamburg. When he **arrived** at the hotel Friday night, John was **without a suitcase.**

23

"Saturday Night's Alright."

The next day, Saturday, I skipped in "Lady Madonna," not having any useful material for it. However, I choose to include it in the book and to borrow a phrase from one of Elton John's songs. I always appreciated Elton's piano playing and his writing with Bernie Taupin. Elton and I are probably not as close as we would have been if he were not already such a close friend of John. For a time, John kind of avoided me. *Elton, I'll have my people call your people for another benefit concert. It will be a show to remember. So, my good friend, let's make it happen again!*

Saturday was all right. John was in a startlingly resolved mood. Overnight, he decided that what I asked for was reasonable enough. He determined that he did not need to call the shots. It did not make that much difference to him whether it was his band or not. He started it. That meant something to him.

Under normal circumstances, it would have meant more to him to stay at the helm. Yet, now the predicted revolvers had come. Paul revolved out. I revolved in. It seemed as if **it was Paul who set it up**. He did it **by fully attracting it** according to his expectations. When John finally accepted it, he accepted me. He saw how fate dictated that his band should be mine now and chose to accept it.

You know John struggled with it for untold hours. However, by the time I saw him on Saturday, he did not show any signs of resentment. I had started to doubt myself and felt anxious about seeing him again. I feared that he would call the whole thing off and end the band. Brian feared too. However, thank the gods or idols, it did not end up that way. John agreed and tried to accept it all as a fait accompli.

Having that change of heart, John did not want to argue or belabor any negotiations. In effect, John told Brian to work out the details and to write them up. Out of love for **Paul**, John determined to do what seemed expedient. I was **surprised** and intimidated by what amounted to spiritual maturity in **John**. He accepted everything in the spirit of love for Paul.

John spent the next hours with Neil and me at the Louvre Museum. As we walked, John talked about Carroll's *Through the Looking-Glass,* and, other than replacing Paul, about almost any topic. I learned of his creativity beyond music, and that we shared interests in art, and in layering meaning. I knew that when I go to work with the brothers I trust, John is a guy that is rightfully one of us. We would learn a lot from each other. It could be fun.

Hearing John's reasonableness and recognizing his extended friendship, I was glad that I too had told Brian to work out the details and to let us know how everything settled. I had lost the drive for me to win all the chips on the table. I had already gotten more than my fair share. I felt a bit like a robber. I could not press for anything else when I saw that

John would not defend himself. I could not do it. Now, with that out of the way, I felt his friendship, which was something I had not before given much thought to, and which was worth more than anything that could be bargained for. For the rest of that day, he seemed completely openhearted to me, accepting his fate of meeting my unreasonable demands.

As time went on, over challenging years, John and I generally worked very well together. We had tiffs from time to time, mostly from me relentlessly pushing the band forward with my perfectionistic idealism. I admit it. I was a bit of a workaholic. However, that is what I signed up to do. I was doing my side of the deal. For *Sgt. Pepper's,* our first album together, I also felt a great need to prove my own worth to the band, to the world, and mostly to myself. I had to show everyone that I was worth having the role of Paul, that I deserved all of the fine things I was inheriting from him. It was also a way for me to deal with the hard loneliness. I needed to keep busy and create Beatles products that are great enough to justify the insane level of commitment to do Paul well.

I had to give myself reasons to justify deeply **hidden levels of** self-betrayal. I had to eventually deal with **my** self-loathing that made me willing to drop my **own identity**, giving up who I was, in order **to be someone else**—some dead guy that I barely knew. I had to win at all costs.

Our time at the Louvre Museum changed my perceptions of John. I had supposed that we were there to pass the time while Brian readied the papers. It turned out to be more important than that. It helped to have that time with John. It was healing. He let me into his private world.

Ending the Paul taboo, Neil said, "How does it feel to be one of the beautiful people? You're a rich man now!" Years later, while John and I were each working on the *Yellow Submarine* soundtrack, that question from Neil reverberated in John's brain until it grew into a little song. He sang it to me. I had remembered the same conversation. **I liked** it and sang along, then wrote another song, **this one** around Neil's line about being rich. Although we first wrote and recorded them as separate songs, nesting one into the other made "Baby You're a Rich Man" complete. Earlier, the combined title had touted his side of the song. It was called, "One of the Beautiful People." However, I felt that my line had stronger emphasis, making it the better title. While still walking around the Louvre, after Neil asked about it, I abruptly realized, "Oh my hell, I'm that famous guy! One of the beautiful people!"

NOTE: The above exchange with Neil Aspinall—including modified dialogue and combining three events into one—illustrates how the Encoder took liberties with the text. In this case, the dialogue was modified to foreshadow the hell that William would go through by becoming that celebrity. When William says, "Oh my hell, I'm that famous guy," his actual line was "Oh my God, I'm that famous guy!"

Neil Aspinall was the Beatles' first road manager. After Mal Evans began working for the Beatles, Neil become their personal assistant, and later the chief executive of Apple Corps. He retired on 10 April 2007, the year before he died of lung cancer.

Jeff Jones, who replaced Neil as CEO, has overseen many projects and innovations including *The Beatles remastered catalog, The Beatles: Rock Band,* and the *Cirque du Soleil* collaboration with its *Love* album. Although three of Jeff's big projects shared *the Memoirs of Billy Shears* 09.09.09 release date, most of this book was finished before Jeff started.

Four new ways to know the Fab Four

were released on 09.09.09. Have you experienced them all?

Typical of John's humor with my material, at the end of the song, he added a joke about Brian, messing with the lyrics. Then, with twisted lyrics at the end, he dedicated it all to Brian. Where we had rehearsed singing, "Baby you're a rich man too," John sang, "Baby, you're a rich fag Jew." That slur was received well by Brian in the humor that it was intended. We were close enough to Brian to not let such things divide us. His sexual orientation and Semitism were not John's concerns per se, but by including that reference to both, it acknowledged attributes that **John knew** were significant issues or notions for **Brian's** mindset. John was neither ridiculing Brian's **wealth** or homosexuality, nor criticizing his **race and religion**, but cleverly used the word pattern to greet our good friend.

One of Rex Makin's associates had a law office in Paris. While the rest of us were walking about the Louvre, Brian was at that office on the phone with Rex Makin and the French attorney, working in each needed detail, bouncing around various concerns. Besides their professional relationship, those lawyers had a long-time friendship and mutual trust—as did also Brian and Rex. They all worked well as one.

Once finished with the phone conference, the French attorney completed the long document and was back on the phone again with Rex, reading the latest version and discussing further concerns.

During our meeting that followed, the solemnity of the legal contract brought what we were doing into sharper focus. Neil's words kept echoing in my brain. Now I am one of the beautiful people. In a

211

day's negotiation, **I am suddenly** someone else. Now I'm beautiful. I'm **a rich man** too. It was true. Yet, I was still the same man I had always been. Now I was Paul, "the cute Beatle," and was obligated to look like him. The series of treatments would start almost immediately. They said it was urgent that I look the part before needing to make any appearances. It was a matter of time before everyone would want proof that Paul was still with them. I had to be that proof.

Now I have no regrets. At the time, however, the sense of loss was staggering beyond words. We all joked about it. Yet, it was worse than any joke could express. Crying could never fully convey it either. Out of my desperation to say, "Look at me! I am suffering," **I created** some of my best material for you all to take **a closer** look. I said in countless ways, "Paul is **dead**. I am not him." My courage to use conspicuous **"Paul** is Dead" clues increased

---

NOTE: The media promoted the idea of Paul as "the cute Beatle." Without that manipulation, others of the group may have each seemed cuter to more fans. Those who used the band to change the world sought a face that could characteristically feature the Eye of Providence. Paul's raised eyebrow (inherited from his father) strengthened his position.

Others in that inner circle, also impressed by Paul's resemblance to William, considered the possibility and implications of Paul eventually being replaced by the magician's son. For four years, they pushed for that prospect.

For the eye symbolism intended by all, and for added significance if they were to replace Paul with William, as pushed by some, some individuals demanded that the media not only make the Beatles the brightest stars in the heavens but that they single out Paul for his looks. They made his symbolic right eye a subconscious point of adoration when fans gazed at their idol.

To elevate the Beatles, George Martin was ordered to not only contract the Beatles and to produce their work, but to use his own musical skills as if played by them to present the Beatles' music as perfectly as possible. All other bands would be as they are. The Beatles would be perfect.

when John and non-Beatles did it. When I first heard the Rolling Stones and Donovan work Paul into their songs, after John (at my suggestion) enmeshed Paul into "Strawberry Fields," I thought, "If they can do it, so can I!" All of my albums from *Pepper's* on have clues or references to Paul. It is a rule that I made for myself. For any album, if you listen for them, they are not hard to find. You just need to pay attention.

As many years and decades have come and gone, my thoughts on Neil's question have evolved. Years do that. It was an exciting thought. Yet, I sensed some resentment. As an outsider, he was not including himself in that class of people. I had been a working-class stiff like him. Now, with a **deal**, had finally arrived. I went from being a nobody like **him** to being a somebody. I was such a nowhere man that I was not recognized in my new position. If reversed, and Paul replaced me, people would have noticed.

At least that is what I thought. I was mistaken about that as well. Proving my wrong thinking, I made many public appearances, and was hardly ever recognized. **Some** of my appearances were in front of large **audiences**. People usually see what they expect to **see**. Until someone with an authentically new view can point an honest finger and say, "The emperor is naked," no one can see it. However, once enough people open their eyes to it, they create a critical mass that reveals the bare-naked truth as it is. One voice ignites others, who then open the eyes of thousands and millions, and on until that awareness

Just as engineered morphic fields create manipulative illusions, putting the world under spells, we can also create and extend morphic fields of reality. Sharing this book, for example, extends a morphic field that dispels programmed myths.

fills the world with illumination. My story is only a key to opening your mind to that bigger worldview. This book also benefits me. Creating that critical mass that acknowledges my work gives me peace. I have no intention of relinquishing my name of Sir James Paul McCartney. That iconic stage name was earned. **I own** it. I have been Paul McCartney since 1966. My children were named McCartney. I have been **Paul** far longer than Paul was Paul. The Paul **McCartney** persona is much more me now than the earlier Paul. Whenever the world thinks of Paul McCartney, they nearly always think of me, not my antecedent. When Paul played this role, he did not have the depth to create his most meaningful music until he began dreaming of me. **In a cosmic way,** that I do not fully understand, **I influenced him** then. We are all connected to each other. Whether we do it intentionally or not, all energy fields influence other fields, that then influence others.

NOTE: However astonishing it is that Paul was replaced, the bigger story is that the substitution occurred as part of Tavistock's worldwide mind-control operation that is still succeeding today with Committee of 300's resources.

Replacing the most adored celebrity anywhere was only possible by the powerful central organization that directed national governments to stay out of the way while the largest newspapers, television channels, and radio stations, along with the most influential players in the entertainment industry, all perpetuated the McCarthy myth.

As brazen as it was to create such a fictional superstar in the first place, and then to switch him out for another actor, it was not the beginning, pinnacle, or the end of their worldwide mind-control. They govern public perception and opinion through the media's presentation of false flags and other fake news, and by creating (or buying control of) media platforms. When they seek to frighten the world into war, totalitarianism, gun control, vaccines, or any other viewpoint, opposing views are blocked and labeled as subversive unsafe misinformation that violates community standards.

To fully comprehend Paul's replacement is to know that we are still being manipulated by governments and the legacy media under the direction of the worldwide cabal. William says, "My story is only a key to opening your mind to that bigger worldview." If this book is ever discredited for damage control, it will be because William began to reach that goal too soon.

214

Think of your favorite Paul songs. Most are likely from me, or from Paul when he was obsessing about me coming to take his place.

Until I realized how we are all connected as one on the same universal grid of intelligence—the vast, loving, and glorious stuff of which **we** are made—I could not comprehend how I could **have** influenced Paul. Now I see that the universe, or **God**, or fate, or this infinite grid, or whatever you want to call it, or envision it as, by giving Paul those dreams of me, it increased his consciousness, deepened his depth of feeling, and broadened his musical abilities.

Waking up with the tune of "Yesterday," and plugging in his concerns about me replacing him, changed him. He was never again quite the same. It led him to more instrumental quality mixed in with his concealed fears of death, such as are found in his "Eleanor Rigby." The universe, or the Divine, or whatever you call it, transformed him into me at the same time it was grooming me to become him. Then, when **Paul** did cross over, a core part of him **continued through me**, furthering our cosmic connection. We have been merging since before his exit. **I was** a session musician. Upon dreaming of me, **Paul** began writing far beyond Beatles' talent, **needing** session musicians. Paul's awareness of **my coming** began his transition to me.

Years of reflecting on Neil's question supported my belief that "**Love is all you need.**" That original idea of **Paul's love gave us** our view of the universal energy field as **God's** love. We were under the influence of **divine love.** I could not

215

have become Paul if I had not loved him first. Fate always acts according to love. You can say divine love emanating from the universe set me up to replace Paul for the world's greater good.

There is no meaningful difference between us. Each of us has a part to play. If I can be one of the beautiful people, then so can you. Hear what I am telling you. You do not need Paul to be greater. This position makes me no greater now than any other. As I play my roles, or you play yours, all that matters is **how we love**. That is the only objective that **makes people beautiful.** So, how do *you* feel being one of the beautiful people?

24

"Sunday Morning Creeping Like a Nun."

I left with Brian for the North of France after dinner Saturday evening. After a quiet contemplative six-hour drive, we reached the Grosse Horloge, where Mal Evans stood waiting below the clock, at one in the morning. From there, the three of us left in Mal's car. Heading to the nearest tavern, Mal went out of the way to show us some Rouen sights. One was the Church of St. Ouen. Mal explained that it was built as the abbey church of Saint Ouen for the Benedictine Order. We sat in the car a half minute looking at the outside of the building as Mal described how it looked inside. Brian also related a story about tunnels below the church. Mal interrupted, "Wait a minute! **Look there!**"

Even through the dark, **we could see** three nuns by a bush on the side of **the church**. It was not light enough to see what they **were doing**, but Brian said that they were breaking **their curfew**. One of the nuns had a flashlight. The others held shovels. It gave us cause to wonder, but nothing for any of us to be sure of. It was a memorable moment, an amusement to remember about the trip.

Next, we went to the tavern. Mal had received Paul's checkbook and various other belongings that seemed irrelevant until Brian and the lawyers created my contract. As per the lengthy Beatle agreement, I was required to sign many checks, most of which were postdated. Brian carefully filled in the many details. I signed check after check.

Before doing so, they gave me the time I needed to practice Paul's signature. Although his left-handed signature was awkward the first few attempts, I soon had it down and got the work done. Paul intended to use each of those checks as inheritances and to buy silence. Mostly, Brian used a list of names and amounts that Paul had written on a bus in America. Having written that will appendage by hand, and having signed it before a witness, all accepted it.

Ordinarily, Paul would have formalized it with legal assistance. This time, however, between all the venues on their American tour, practically every hour of **Paul's** time for personal matters was either **on a bus** or a train. With Rex Makin not being **with them** to give legal help, Paul wrote his list of whom to pay on his own. It was conditional. Each recipient would receive an inheritance based on specific helps to the replacement. Paul intended each check to help me to perpetuate his reputation.

NOTE: William used his right hand to practice Paul's signature before signing those documents. Later, he practiced Paul's signature with his left hand to give autographs. However, even left-handed, he never got the slant right. Soon, he let Paul's autograph drift to a left-handed version of his own handwriting. Eventually, it evolved to his current autograph featuring his obelisk. An obelisk is an erect phallic symbol representing the Egyptian Sun god, Ra. Ra is hidden in William as "Paul McCartney." The best-known obelisk in the US is the Washington Monument—named after the Freemason who became "the father of the country" the Freemasons set up and have controlled ever since. Each side of the 6,666 inches tall structure is 666 inches wide at ground level.

218

I saw the list at the time but did not know most of the people. Later, when I did get to know them, seeing that list again could have been useful. Most of the checks were modest. As **Paul explained it**, I would have the bulk of it **to carry on as** though I am **him**. **Paul thought it out** carefully. Giving too much, or **giving it away** to heirs all at once, would have blown the cover.

Nearly everyone whom Paul paid would have remained silent anyway out of respect for him.  Everyone close to him had already talked to him about it. The people who were most privy to his death dreams were generally also asked what they would do to help make his plan a reality. "What could you do to make it work?" he had asked more than a few of them. He wrote their answers, and had them compiled on the payment list. Those who would do more got more.

Ending our visit, a large American in the tavern shouted, "Look at the time!" Brian stood abruptly. Counting hours, he said it would be 7:00 before he made it back to Paris. He rushed us to Mal's car, keeping the remaining business for another day. After dropping Brian off at his car, Mal and I went straight to Bordeaux Airport. That morning, 18 September, one week after Paul's demise, Mal and I flew back to London.

NOTE: William is probably correct that loved ones remained silent out of respect for Paul. Additionally, insiders understood that blowing the whistle would make them outsiders, or worse. In light of who was required to pull off such a switch, interfering could be dangerous. Progress by degrees requires, among other things, keeping the secrets of each degree. Initiates swear on penalty of death to never reveal the secrets, to use their means to support the organization, and to never speak against them. An integrous person would, without malice, and without breaking oaths, share only what can be shared.

219

I can scarcely imagine such a pivotal weekend. I left London as Bill, hoping John Lennon would give me a good deal. **I returned as Paul,** now over everyone in the band. **It was so surreal that** I could hardly comprehend it. **The Beatles were my band!** What a dream come true that shift was! I not only took over Paul's roles as co-lead singer and bass player but also took over John's position as the band's leader. The pressure was on me to deliver the acclaim that I had promised.

Thrilled to work with George Martin more closely, I met with him to discuss my plans. I wanted to discuss it all with him first to use his kind influence with the others. He would also help set reasonable schedules and expectations. We met at Abbey Road studio.

I did not have time scheduled there, which was necessary for most people to have so much time with him. Nevertheless, he generously arranged to do a favor for another band to give me their timeslot. Our meeting was the top priority for George.

Very soon, Geoff Emerick joined George and me for some experimentation in a mixing room. I told them what **I** had in mind with our first album and was **delighted** by their valuable insights and suggestions. **George and Geoff** were exceptionally talented. We had much more in common than I had with my Beatles bandmates. **We** became close friends. As we **worked on our albums**, the time I spent with them **in the studio** was far greater than my time with the others. They both brought extraordinary talent to the band. We explored new sounds when I became a fixed team member. We did extraordinary work together. Their brilliance was mostly unrecognized. We understood each other. There we were, creeping about that Abbey Road studio, on the same day that I had been in France, having amusement from the nuns creeping about their abbey. "Sunday morning creeping like a nun" evokes Abbey memories at both locations that day, Sunday, 18 September. I had not yet begun the actual work that **I signed to** do, but did make important **progress with** George and Geoff, which benefited **the band** to no end. I could not have reached my Paul excellence without them.

NOTE: Although *Sgt. Pepper's* was William's baby, bandmates John and George each provided excellent material. Their talents, along with that of Ringo and many session musicians, contributed immeasurably to the whole. William's work in writing, singing, playing various instruments, and directing much of the project, however exceptional, relied heavily on the genius of Producer George Martin, and Engineer Geoff Emerick.

Like William, Geoff was a prodigious talent from a highly connected family. EMI hired him at fifteen years old to help create the Beatles sound. He would also work with other artists whenever no Beatles work was in progress. His EMI employment began the day before the Beatles recorded their first hits. From the band's start, Geoff's training began as Norman Smith's assistant engineer, and then became the Beatles' chief engineer starting with the *Revolver* album—already pioneering innovative recording techniques before helping George Martin and William take the band to the *Sgt. Pepper's* level.

With the creation of Apple Corps in 1969, William persuaded Geoff to leave EMI to direct the building of Apple Studio, and then to continue as their engineer. When William dissolved the Beatles the following year, Geoff continued to work as William's engineer. Handlers had groomed Geoff to be "Paul's guy" from the start.

Geoff's exceptional work was recognized with a Technical Grammy Award (2003), and three Grammy Awards for Best Engineered Recording (Non-Classical) for the Beatles albums, *Sgt. Pepper's Lonely Hearts Club Band*, and *Abbey Road,* and for the Paul McCartney and Wings album, *Band on the Run,* which was the first rock and roll album released in a communist country. Geoff has also received other Grammy nominations.

Before going back to their small roles in *How I Won the War*, John and Neil were both trying to put everything into perspective but could not. It was all too much. We were all dazed and overwhelmed; yet, John knew he would have quiet downtime to sort through it all when he returned to Spain.

John and Neil flew to Spain the day I returned to London. The *How I Won the War* movie set before our visit was in a NATO tank range in Celle, a small town near Hanover. However, by Sunday, they both had to be in Carboneras in southern Spain, across the Mediterranean from Algeria. That site simulated a North African desert. That was the main movie set.

I was eager to start writing and recording songs. For John's peace of mind, however, my work on our next record was not to begin until he returned to London. He was emphatic about it. **He did not want** it to start without him there, with **me running the** entire show. He said, "It is, after all, **Beatles music** we're making." Yet, although a part of me seriously wanted to get right to work, and another part of me needed to slow down and ease into this new job. The pressure on me was intense. For me, the first task was to be my transformation. I wanted to work on music but had to set my primary focus on being Paul. My goal was to become Paul McCartney by October's end. John would return from Spain on 7 November. By then, Paul would work through me.

At sunset Sunday evening, 18 September, Brian brought bandmates, George Harrison and Ringo Starr (Richard Starkey) over to meet me. Brian had

NOTE: When the Beatles replaced Pete Best with the less dominate drummer, part of Ringo's appeal was his stage name (inspired by his rings and by Johnny Ringo). The name, 'Ringo Starr,' conjures images of a 'ringed star' such as a pentagram or Saturn ("Lord of the Rings").

informed them both days before but did not have them meet me before John. We followed my uncle's strategic plan. First Jim McCartney's family would have to approve of me. That way John would not have to make such a difficult decision. He would go along with what the family had already decided. Then, having signed the agreement, I was ready to be presented to George and Ringo, not to discuss and approve of me, or maybe vote against their new band member, but for them to learn what already occurred with John's consent.

I was delighted to meet them. They were both curious about me, to be certain, but were completely gentle, not wanting to make me feel as though they were interrogating me. Brian agreed that it was not his place to deal with informing them of the band's new direction and leadership. He had wisely decided to save that for John. I agreed. There was no reason to drop that on them so soon in the game. We all wanted the first visit to be as pleasant as possible— and indeed it was quite enjoyable for all of us. We entertained each other with conversation for about an hour. Soon after Brian left, the fun began. The night turned jovial when I sat down at the piano. George picked up a guitar, and we all sang some of their hits and other popular songs.

They taught me a song of **Paul's** they had played on nights when their **amplifiers broke down** in the Cavern Club or Hamburg, usually **from blown fuses.** Needing minor improvements here and there, I touched it up and sang the song with a different style. We had such a good time with it, we all looked forward to sharing my new version with John.

Eleven weeks later, on 6 December, it became the first song that my new band recorded with me singing lead as **Paul** McCartney. The song, "When I'm Sixty-Four," **had a melancholy** overtone, being about Paul wondering what his **life** would be like at that far distant age, nearing retirement, which he never reached. Paul died forty years too soon. In his memory, we were glad to include my version of that good old song of Paul's on our *Sgt. Pepper's* album. He had wondered about his life at 64 but died at 24.

George marveled at my ability to step into, and so readily improve upon, Paul's position. He had entertained the idea of going to India in search of further enlightenment. Now that idea became his obsession. He realized that Paul had received many accurate messages foretelling his demise through repeated dreams and other ongoing omens, and that he prepared for my smooth transition to cover him. George wanted to commune with Paul, spirit-to-spirit. He quickly sensed it in me—and sought to enter that numinous state himself—the presence of Paul. It became an obsession for him and John.

Feeling that the answers he sought were in India, **George** flew there as soon as he could arrange it. He **let us know** Sunday that we would not see him again until he returned from India. Since I prepared to infuse **ethereal dimensions of his beloved** Paul into the **Beatle beast**, George also prepared to receive Paul's whisperings into our new music.

People are interdimensional beings. It is common to interact with beings in other dimensions. When we do, meeting them is easier in the astral or ethereal realms. Our reality is too dense.

25

"Monday's Child
Has Learned to Tie His Bootlace."

"Monday's child is fair of face." That line is where I found the phrase, "Monday's Child." The old Mother Goose rhyme describes children born on each day of the week. My allusion to the rhyme is not about when the child is born, but that this child has the fair face. By the time my song came out, I donned the fair face of Paul, "the cute Beatle." I am "Monday's Child" in "Lady Madonna."

Although I contributed great musical talent to the band, it was not what John wanted from me. Yes, **I was gifted**. Yet, all he wanted was Paul's fair face. **The Beatles** was such a great name brand that song **quality mattered** less than the band name. Big brands sell inferior products easier than small brands can sell quality. In "I've Got a Feeling," I sing, "All these years I've been wandering around wondering how come nobody told me. All that I was looking for was somebody who looked like you." Being as if Paul and I were one, but talking to each other, Paul was looking for someone who looked like him, or like me, depending on which aspect of me is doing the singing.

225

During much of the last year of his life, he had wandered, looking for me. Then **I** wandered around in the mistaken idea that they **wanted** my high musical quality. While everyone was **more** than satisfied with my musical abilities, **for** which I labored far more than anyone to get it **all** right, I felt frustrated by the realization that **the others** only wanted me to look the part.

As most people would guess if they stopped to think about it, the song that those lines came from, "I've Got a Feeling," began as two songs. We each sang the lines we wrote. John wrote his song in response to mine. It is a conversation. Although we had not developed either song enough to stand on its own, they worked well together—as did John and **I generally**. My part got the song title because it **felt stronger**, more dynamic, and more likely to be remembered. **By the time** we wrote the song, a few days into 1969, **I had** endured almost twenty-eight months of **that frustration.** I was complaining about that in my song, but particularly about that past year. We all knew how our frustrations were compromising the band's coherence. By 1969, it was tearing us apart.

Even though my almost screamed part explicitly explains the feelings I was singing about, most fans never gave it much thought, never connected it to the rest of the song. I interrupt the music to interject an outburst of emotion, to express my feelings. I sing that "I've got a feeling, a feeling deep inside." What did you think the feeling was? Most fans thought it was a love song because that is all they expected to hear. I sang that it is "a feeling I can't hide." I suppose I hid it a bit better than I had planned. The ongoing feeling of frustration grew. I wanted unparalleled Beatles quality, but always had to deal with the apathy of the others. They complained that my standards were too high. That feeling that "everybody knows," or of everyone in Paul's circle already knowing, kept me on my toes. It increased my determination. Yet, I felt their lack of resolve to work to make me look good.

As one would expect from John, he agreed that it was a hard year, but also a good one. **It was** the kind of year that had it all. It was not just **hard** for me. It was hard for all of us and good **for all of us.** It was good and hard. "Everybody had **a hard year.** Everybody had a good time." I felt **that** I **absolutely** needed to put my foot down **with some issues.** Yet, "Everybody put their foot down." It **was hard**, but a good dream for all of us. That was the brilliantly musical way that John answered my complaint about my feelings of frustration; and he was right. It was like a round where I kept going on singing my way, yet he kept answering in his way. As with the song, we persisted in our positions without resolving them, forever stuck in our egoic perspectives. Both sides were right but without empathy.

Each of us had a difficult challenge. Although John was right about that, generally dismissing my emotions that way did not settle anything. It did not reduce their apathy, instill greater cooperation, or lighten the inequality between us. On the one hand, it was my band now, and up to me to drive it into our new direction. On the other hand, John treated me as an upstart even though I was no novice to the industry. I did most of the work and brought the band greater acclaim. I expected enough gratitude to generate more motivated cooperation.

They talked of love but withheld it. While I was sacrificing everything, they were more prone to scoff than to show loving appreciative support.

Perhaps some of you remember the old song, "One-sided Love Affair." That song about unequal love sometimes played in my brain back then as I felt that frustration. It was written back in 1955 by a young aspiring artist. When it was recorded the next year by the king, Elvis Presley, that success ignited the writer with a determination to make a life-long career of writing popular music, and not only writing it but also recording it. It gave him modest but encouraging royalties and set the course for his life. At that young age, he did not know how to make a record then but started his music life at the top by sending it to the top recording artist at that time. What became of this talented writing artist? Who was this aspiring musically-minded boy? It was William "**Bill**" Campbell. I liked his name.

Realistically, his song describes an unrequited infatuation. I applied his message to all types of love. "If you want to be loved, Baby, you've got to love me, too." That was the main message of the song. Feeling as if it is all giving without getting is vexing, but **only** to the immature mind. Jesus says it is not **great love** to only love those who love us ⚠(Matthew 5:46). If love **is** conditional, it is not love enough to call it **love.** If our love is conditioned

NOTE: For energetic purposes, 144 names of people, and countless other keywords, phrases, and punctuation, now occur in this book in multiples of three (reducing to 3, 6, or 9). For example, since Matt or Matthew had occurred only 8 times, the above Matthew reference was added to bring it up to 9 occurrences for that name, which, with this note, is now up to 12 (reducing to 3). However, adding that reference required parentheses, which threw off the parentheses count, which was remedied by replacing parentheses elsewhere with commas. That threw off the comma count, which required changing the period count.

228

on getting love back or on getting something else, it is simply a bargaining chip. Still, that is where I was in the sixties with my unfulfilled expectations from my three bandmates. I felt that **I was** giving my all, and not getting enough respect **for** it.

Having discussed the "**fair** of face" bit, and the ongoing frustrations that **play**ed out with seemingly everybody merely wanting my fair face—which, by the way, is about Paul's grave face when I later sing, "My Brave, My Brave, My Brave Face" ("My Brave Face")—we are almost ready to discuss the outcome of what that fair-faced child has learned to do. However, first consider what a brave face I needed and acquired for this Paul role. Consider how brave it was of me to have my face permanently gone for this role without any guarantees that it would work out, and to live Paul's lifestyle to which I was entirely unaccustomed. It took courage.

"Monday's child has learned to tie his bootlace." The boots bit of this line refers to "Beatle boots." After John and Paul's stint in Hamburg, they saw Chelsea boots on display in Anello & Davide, a London footwear company, and thought they would add them to their new attire. John already wore boots, which were sometimes used as weapons in night brawls in Hamburg. He also used them to kick intruders off the nightclub stage. Now with their new suits and a cleaned-up image, Chelsea boots would add a touch of class. **This** was all back in October 1961, before they **made it big.** With the addition of Cuban heels to make them look a little taller, they ordered these boots for the band.

When the group made it big, still wearing these boots, their Beatle Boots became the fab fashion in

America, Great Britain, and throughout Western Europe. Beatle Boots are tight-fitting ankle-high boots, with a sharp pointed toe. Holding them tight to the ankle, Beatle Boots have zipped or elastic sides. I entertained Paul's family by trying on his Beatle Boots. They were humorously small. He was not a big man.

Every detail of the transition had its particular challenges. The hardest of all, as far as my natural skills were concerned, was the switch to Paul's left-handedness. Some of it, like smoking, was mostly a matter of habit. Other talents, such as learning the backward strung bass guitar, took a colossal effort to master. Representing me handling those backward strings, **I sing that** I learned to tie Paul's bootlace, emphasizing **the difficulty of** his strings over all else included in **my journey** of walking a mile in Beatle Boots. **Like tying shoes,** it **required new dexterity.**

Sunday, after the studio, I went over to Paul's estate home and tried tirelessly to play his backward bass. I called George Martin for some timely tips. Among other things that I also tried, he suggested I make chords with my right hand rather than trying to finger everything with both hands as I had done before right-handed. Although that helped, the left-handed playing still turned out to be harder than I had anticipated. I tried it up until late into the evening, and then put it down for the night, feeling discouraged and fearful. Almost boastfully, I had sounded as if it would not be a problem for me to play left-handed. Now it seemed hopeless.

Bass guitars have their own souls. On Monday morning, 19 September 1966, I held the bass and envisioned myself as Paul playing in front of a large packed stadium. I put on the Beatles' new *Revolver*

William helped Geoff Emerick mix some parts of *Revolver* in the Studio Two control room, but waited a few weeks before buying a copy of the completed album. Although he already loved hearing "Eleanor Rigby" on the radio, it had a much greater impact when he played the album.

album that was released the month before, less than a week before their last tour. **It was the first time** that I heard it. I plugged the bass into Paul's amp and closed my eyes. **I imagined myself as Paul.** Letting the music move me, I played along as though I were on tour with it **romping across America.**

"Eleanor Rigby" came on right after "Taxman," and affected me profoundly. For "Taxman," all the bass playing on my part was very clumsy. It was like using a new foreign instrument while doing orchestration for strangers. The backward bass was awkward for me, and so was the music. I found no oneness with the music at all. It was much worse than my worst day ever as a session musician.

Then "Eleanor Rigby" began. Even before I learned the background story, I was so moved by the song that I ceased being aware of my own playing. When the song ended, I pulled the needle back to hear it again, and then again. Somehow, I knew in my heart what Paul McCartney was singing to me about. I put down the bass, played the song again, and wept on the floor. Immobilized, I left the needle down and finished that side of the album. I did not get back up for another hour.

NOTE: Paul was brilliant with his Höfner violin bass. His charismatic connection with that instrument was part of their great stage performance. William, however, had been more of a session musician than a stage performer. It is a different skill set. He found it awkward to play left-handed. He still needs to frequently look at his fingers when playing left-handed bass.

While working on the "Get Back/Let It Be" sessions in 1969, the band took a break and then returned to discover that the historic bass, and other instruments, had been stolen.

This image contrasts Paul and William holding the same iconic bass. It underscores the conspicuous difference in their physical stature. Paul (like John and George) was 5'11" (180.34 cm) tall. William was 6'2½" (189.23 cm) tall.

Similarly, when Michael Jackson was 5'9" (175.26 cm) tall, his replacement stood at 5'11" (180.34 cm).

That afternoon, **I played** that entire album while playing along with **the bass**, again imagining. I had some high points. **It** was not great bass but was much better than it **had been** before. It was not the exact bass notes that **Paul** was playing, but was becoming close enough, **in** my awkward way, that I felt very encouraged by **it**. I practiced that way with that album quite a lot back then.

Realizing the crucial importance of playing Paul's bass well, I practiced heavily night and day. Monday by Monday, marking week after week, I was aware of significant improvements, but was still overwhelmingly far from playing it naturally. Then, after six weeks, I had a strange encounter, one that needs more explanation than belongs here. It was on 31 October. One week later, on the 7th Monday, during what began as an ordinary practice session, I received the talent as a miraculous gift from Paul.

After tea, I picked up Paul's bass and played perfectly as him. That was on 7 November in the year 1966, only a few hours before John returned from Spain. The 31 October event is in "Hey Jude." Since that first Monday of November, I have played not merely like Paul, but as Paul.

The line, "Monday's child has learned to tie his bootlace," refers to those great breakthroughs that I experienced on Mondays, 19 September and 7 November, learning to play Paul's bass strings. "Monday's child," as I said, is also about Paul's fair face alluding to the old Mother Goose rhyme.

Extending the meaning, consider the Native American proverb, "Don't judge a man until you have walked two moons in his moccasins." It had been practically two moons that I had walked as Paul before he attached himself to me—or before he integrated enough that I could play as him. That saying has been modernized. Two years after I recorded "Lady Madonna," Elvis recorded the Joe South song, "Walk a Mile in My Shoes." It says, "If I could be you and you could be me for just one hour . . . you'd be surprised to see that you'd been blind." Having been Paul, I know his inner and outer workings. I know what is in Paul. I am Paul.

However, since no one else on earth can fully walk a mile in his shoes, or his Beatle Boots, since you cannot fully be him, or me, I ask that you do not judge either of us for this Paul role I am playing. As that song says, "Before you abuse, criticize and accuse, walk a mile in my shoes." I had nothing to do with that song but like the message. I hope letting that message take root as you read this book of secrets will help keep you from developing too low of an opinion of me. **I am telling you** that I am a real person and showing you **how it happened.**

The things **I am sharing** have been hidden for generations. I share them **with you** now in hopes of having greater peace **before I die.** Do not get me wrong. I have more peace than most people that I know. Fans deceive themselves by putting people on pedestals, making them bigger than life idols.

Now that you can know I am a mere mortal, just another guy like everyone else, many fans are going to think of me differently. However, it is not just me. Like all of your celebrity idols, I am the same as everyone else. **Please do not judge us** or be in awe of us. It is just my job. **We are all one.**

NOTE: The saying, "Walk a mile in my shoes," is based on Mary T. Lathrap's 1895 poem, "Walk a Mile in His Moccasins" originally titled "Judge Softly." The poem is a call for empathy rather than judgment. As her poem suggests, if we could experience another's life, even for a mile, we would perceive the person more charitably.

Do not judge your neighbor until you walk two moons in his moccasins.

233

Notice that I, "Monday's child," follow Sunday. **Paul died Sunday.** From a purely daily perspective of Monday's child, Sunday is "Yesterday." Then, following Sunday, Monday is "just another day." With the "Yesterday" representation of Paul, I identified myself, Monday's child, as "Another Day."

As his death day, we represent Paul as Sunday. Recalling the day **John learned** of the death and had gone mad over it, **Paul is also** Tuesday, as in "Stupid bloody Tuesday." **Three days** (Yesterday, Sunday, and Tuesday) represent Paul in Paulism. In the song that references Jane Asher's ladder use, "She Came in Through the Bathroom Window," I sing parallel lines with the identical meaning that Paul McCartney now talks to me: "Sunday's on the phone to Monday; Tuesday's on the phone to me."

I might as well explain more of that song. The silver spoon was not, as some people claim, intended to be a drug reference. It was about Jane having been born into affluence. "She said she'd always been [an entertainer] a dancer." I called her a dancer to take listeners off her trail. Jane Asher had always been, let us set it right, an actress, not a dancer. Born in 1946, she had her first movie appearance in 1952. Letting her career take priority over relationships, she was always off somewhere filming. I describe it as "She worked at fifteen clubs a day." I imagined her as an exotic dancer going from club to club until late every night. Jane was not like that. It was just how I felt. I found Jane attractive but could not let her completely take me over, as she had Paul, because I did not feel important enough to her.

As I connected with Linda, one reason I never forgot her was that she never left my side. Linda's beauty attracted me first. However, her persistent loving presence is what had the greatest impact on me. I do not mean that Linda attached to me in a way that would interfere with my work, but that she understood my heart enough that she put nothing above our relationship. Still, Paul in me wanted Jane.

This line had a word reversal: "I quit [joined] the police department /And got myself a steady job" means I joined the Beatles, as if becoming its Sergeant, which was a steady job as opposed to all the session work I had done. **Jane** "could steal" Paul's things that she **said** were hers, "but she could not rob." She felt **I had robbed John** by taking his band **when he was the most vulnerable.** Still, even though we did not agree with all of it, "she tried her best to help me."

As she went on pursuing her work as a successful movie star, "by the banks of her own lagoon," so to speak, I felt slighted. I explained it in an earlier song: "You (JA) became a legend of the silver screen" ("Honey Pie"). It is not all Jane. She just inspired it. While Paul and I found her beautiful, she needed more effort than I spared. "I'm in love but I'm lazy." That song, in its old music hall or vaudeville style, was recorded with the Beatles but would have been a better fit with the Bonzos. I tried to blend the bands.

235

26

Tuesday, 20 September 1966

I awoke Tuesday morning realizing that this new Paul role did not require me to stop doing what I **could already** do as William, but that I could **continue with** that same work as Paul McCartney, or as **any other persona.** Weeks before, I agreed to write the feature-film score for *The Family Way.* I meant to be finished with it by then but had forgotten all about it. I called Brian and offered to pay him a fee if he could arrange to have that work transferred from me as William to me as Paul. He objected since everyone knew that Paul knew nothing of music theory and could not even read or write sheet music. Nevertheless, when I said I would pay him to book it for me, he agreed to set it up.

Each scene would have its own unique emotion captured with a musical mood that led to another, as I did later in some albums. The challenge was to have each part independently interesting yet connected to the whole. Going back and forth between the piano and the screenplay, I wrote the score's first draft by hand in one day. I added each instrument later.

"Paul McCartney" is credited with writing that entire movie score even though he could not read sheet music. I, however, having spent years as a first-class session musician was not only able to read music but could also write scores well. I had entertained countless live audiences, filling in for various orchestras in London, and have done ample studio work, requiring sheet music.

Some bands that I sat in for in recording sessions told me the key they were in, or what chords they were playing. In some cases, I would improvise with utterly nothing at all to read. However, the more serious music, I mean all of the classical music, required me to **read** sheet music. Paul could not read or write sheet **music.** To downplay that stark evidence of a personnel change, we said that Paul had already agreed to write the score months before.

For a few minutes that evening when Brian came by, I showed him my rapid progress. I expected to impress him with the quality and quantity of my work but alarmed him by the clear contrast of Paul's lack of formal musical training. With dismay, he said, "You are a better Paul than Paul ever was."

Making matters more alarming to Brian, he learned that Cheri Ann had a birthday party that Paul should have shown up for, or excused himself from, the day before. Paul's absence was conspicuous. Cheri Ann was a woman whom Paul had met on one of Jane Asher's movie sets.

Our gathering in my home Sunday had convinced George to go to India, his center of mysticism. The religion of his youth had failed him. He wanted

237

much more. **Paul's** premonitions—followed by me entering the **scene** and taking Paul's place as he foretold—**demonstrated that** there were spiritual forces at play. **We needed to** understand them.

George, wanting to **tap the cosmic spring** of enlightenment, hoped that studying yoga and Indian philosophy would help. He hoped to retreat from the world unnoticed. George quietly checked in at the Taj Mahal Hotel in Bombay under the pseudonym, Sam [after the reporter] Wells, but was recognized in the lobby before he could reach his room. Brian was told all about this second-hand and related it to me during our Tuesday visit.

Enough of a fan-frenzied disturbance ensued that George could see that his only chance for peace was for him to hold a press conference, satisfy curiosity by answering all the questions, and then escape to another hotel. They held the press conference at the Taj Mahal hours before I visited with Brian. He was miserable thinking of what George might say that could accidentally tip off the public about Paul.

I asked him if George were careless when he spoke in public.

Leaning forward as if to keep others from hearing, even though we were all alone in my home, he said, "You got to be careful about George. He just says what is on his mind. He is too honest."

Well, as it turned out, George did okay. He told the press he was there to learn about their old culture and philosophy, and to learn to play the sitar—which was all true and completely safe enough information. Yet, he wisely did not explain how the year of Paul's prophecies groomed him for it.

Before leaving India, George visited among other locations, the Digambara Jain temple for the yogis of Kolkata, in West Bengal. On one stone wall, he saw a carved swastika above an open palm. In Hindu divinity, the swastika (seen throughout India) symbolizes Brahma, their god of creation. The hand added to the meaning. George was told that the hand is a symbol of blessing that also suggests a continual need for coexistence, Sarva dharma sama bhava. In palmistry, the hand, or palm, is a symbol of mystic determinism. **In Paulism, the palm is** a mystical coexistence with **the deceased Paul-M.**

Shiva ("the Auspicious One") and Parvati had two sons, Ganesha and Kartikeya. One day, after Shiva had been gone long enough to be unrecognized, he returned but was prevented by Ganesha who had been instructed to protect his mother. Shiva decapitated the boy. Parvati, grief-stricken, cried for their son. Shiva, vexed by the situation, quickly sought for a head to replace the one ruined. Finding an elephant's head, he

See Shiva as Enlil/YHWH the Destroyer!

NOTE: CERN (derived from "Conseil européen pour la Recherche nucléaire" (European Organization for Nuclear Research)) operates the largest particle physics laboratory in the world. Located in Switzerland, it is about 6.6 miles from the World Economic Forum (7.7 miles by road).

Believing that their Large Hadron Collider is a portal to transport countless hostile alien entities to Earth in a war against humanity, some people are unnerved by its statue of Shiva, the dancing God of destruction. However, CERN is not even affiliated with Hinduism. The impressive statue was simply a generous gift from the Department of Atomic Energy of India. Besides, if such science fiction were ever to become reality, and political leaders were suddenly possessed by entities attempting to make Earth uninhabitable to humans, it seems like we would all notice the shift and stop it. After all, they are merely experimenting. While some people object to the CERN logo being made of sixes, we could think of them as nines if it makes us feel better.

239

affixed it to the boy's torso, forming the mystical elephant-headed god who, though beheaded, yet lives.

Centered on the bottom of the *Sgt. Pepper's* cover, see a statue of Shiva, the Destroyer, with two hands pointed down to Paul's grave—one pointing to the wax Paul, and one to me, to whom **Paul's head is affixed** figuratively, for Paul **to continue through** me. Beheading **the mystical boy, who bestows that new head** on another, confers the rule of that **head** that I **wear like a crown**, **to the replacement**. Going with Shaivism for this imagery, we credit **Shiva,** the Destroyer, with taking Paul's life, and with **enhancing me,** magically giving me Paul's head. It **transforms me into a mystery idol.**

During his trip to India, George learned legends, philosophies, and symbols that I applied to Paulism, mixing that Hindi branch of spirituality with the mysticism that I have participated in throughout my entire life. Although religions do not attract me, I have always respected spirituality.

NOTE: Shiva, Parvati, Ganesha, Kartikeya, and other deities in Hinduism, are often shown to be divine by depicting them with multiple arms that might become visible when battling cosmic forces.

In his "When We Was Fab" music video, George (who was immersed in Hindu symbolism) is depicted as such a deity. Figuratively, not just George, but all of the Fab Four were in various ways presented as divine, grooming the public to venerate all four as the gods of rock and roll.

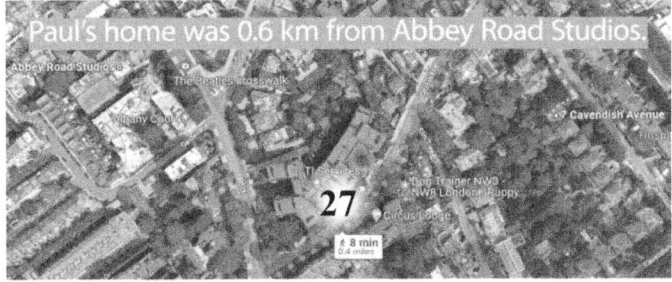

Impersonators

When I stepped from my St. John's Wood home Monday morning, 3 October 1966, and saw a crowd encircling the fence, I thought something was wrong. One man called out, "**Where is Paul?**" Although I had begun my physical transformation, it was not yet progressed enough for me to meet the public. I was about to shout, "**I am here**," but knew better. Saying that Paul was somewhere else could mess things up down the road as my transformation increased in Paul's resemblance without completely diminishing all of my own looks that they might remember. Any in-between versions could be problematic.

Saying nothing, I rushed back into the house. **I** telephoned Brian. He said that he too had **heard** intimations of Paul's death. There were **rumors** buzzing rapidly about the streets. John was still gone filming *How I Won the War*. Brian worried that I might blow my cover before John returned. The crowd needed answers. Brian arrived with Peter Brown. They chatted with the crowd before coming in.

Every injection and surgery made me look more like Paul. Still, I was not ready for the public. It was a drawn-out process. It took time. Brian, Neil, Peter,

241

and I discussed the urgent need for an appearance to create the assurance of Paul's continuance, to stop all suspicions about the collision.

Others looked more like Paul but could not match the voice and did not have the music skills. New talent would help the band more than a closer Paul face, and the appearance would improve in time. The better look-alikes were shorter. Some had Paul's round head. Others looked more like me. A round head would be simulated by check injections. Camera tricks would adjust my height. We would accomplish most of the changes within a few months. Until then, others made appearances, and a couple of them helped in the recording studio. One of them, as if me, working as if Paul, had a hit. For this transition stage, **I fooled around with** disguises to be Paul McCartney **looking like** someone else.

The other Pauls after **Paul** had their purposes, but none of them had a permanent contract as only I have. I am the true messenger of Paul—to borrow another fitting image from Carroll. The king enters a game with Alice by telling her that the Messenger "lives on the Hill." Here I am, living high up on the hill proclaiming the message that Paul is down below it. Above or below, who is the fool?

I, before and after moving into the Paul role, enjoyed dressing up either for comedic effect or to act out certain parts. My Bonzo friends and I did impersonations and such to entertain each other, and mostly ourselves. I would be William dressed as Paul who would perform as Vivian Stanshall who puts on a gorilla suit. We layered personas for greater hilarity. Just Billy in a gorilla suit was not as amusing as Bill or Phil as Paul as Viv as a gorilla. **In disguise**, I could still go out and play under **these alter egos**, make entertaining music, and **could be my silliest** Bonzo self, and make everyone laugh at **me**, even though I had become a big Beatle. As Paul, **I still played the fool.**

The most amusing thing about it all was that no one seemed to notice who I was. I sang, but no one heard my voice. No one heard that it was the same voice as Billy Pepper, or that it is now that of Paul. Everyone could see that I was just a fool—far from any Beatles superstar. I felt like shouting that the fool they were laughing at was their favorite Beatle idol. I could have changed everything with a word. Of course, I never give that answer. Even when I did sound too much like the current Paul, the audience only perceived as another imitation. I am the man of a thousand voices, singing like Elvis Presley, then Little Richard, and sometimes like Paul McCartney. I knew they who mistook me for Paul were the fools.

Once, while playing as Vivian, when the audience started heckling me, I thought, "They do not like me as the fool. But these same people love me as Paul McCartney. If they only knew that the same singer they are disrespecting was their prized Paul, they would gladly pay a small fortune to have admission to this show." The world loves to see the Fab Four act foolishly, but only if everyone knows it is them. Otherwise, when they act like fools without the Beatles' stamp, it is hardly worth respect at all. This role I play has taught me about biases.

I never showed my feelings in those challenging times of rejection. It is the way of clowns. If people

243

laugh, that is enough. What hurt the most was that I knew that I was more myself as Viv than as Paul. The loneliness was intense. Upon the stage, day after day, I was the fool, alone on a hill.

Emphasizing the implication of my false identity or disguise on *Sgt. Pepper's*, the album included a nifty insert of Sgt. Pepper's costume cutouts. It had a picture of me dressed up, disguised as Sgt. Pepper, only, not in my band suit, but in a military sergeant's uniform. The cutouts had stripes for sergeant's uniforms, a badge of the *Sgt. Pepper's* drum skin, another badge of me disguised in the sergeant garb, and a fake mustache. The fake mustaches for our fans resembled the mustaches that all four of us had on that album. My mustache covered a plastic surgery scar. The others wore mustaches to fool everyone into seeing us all as being equally altered. The band's new look was to promote our new band with a new leader (Sgt. Billy Pepper) and its new sound.

Our mustaches—and the rest of the new look— were a cover-up. When you hear, "Sgt. Pepper's lonely," played at the end of the Reprise in the normal direction, it covers my backmasked message: "It was a fake mustache." That message ties the cutout disguises to our facades. Here is how the new message was added backward. After recording the vocals in the forward direction, we would get it set up backward to hear how that sounded. **Hearing that** a **backward** "Sgt. Pepper's lonely" already **has a compatible sound**, I sang along with it, overdubbing it. My headphones played the first recording backward as I sang along, "It was

244

a fake mustache." That method was how we did a lot of our backmasking. We would play our vocal tracks backward and listen for any sounds that resembled utterances that we wanted. If the sounds were close enough, **we could add all the words** we wanted and not mess up the forward track. Singing along with the track played **backward**, we shaped the sound as desired, giving the forward track a richer sound. Our hidden messages were always about Paul.

Having multi-layered tracks going forward also provided another way to conceal our Paul messages. Everything is still there for an effective subliminal message but can easily be buried far below our rational awareness. In that closing Sgt. Pepper's line, after "hearts," I shout, "PAUL IS DEAD!" It is there, even though it is hard to hear. After "club," I shout, "REALLY DEAD!" You hear it subconsciously.

NOTE: Awareness occurs in levels. Successful societal programmers provide material on a cognitive level to construct a framework for what is received subconsciously or unconsciously. The deeper the program is embedded, the less it is filtered by those receiving it. Unconscious beliefs and behaviors prevail over what can be thought out and dismissed. The way to change an unconscious belief is to bring the light of consciousness to it.

Just as each re-reading of this material brings more cognizance to these subjects, so too can we deprogram ourselves on any subject by bringing light to it, increasing consciousness layer by layer, such as through meditation. To reach the deepest levels of Paulism, hidden in the dark, embedded deep in each subconscious psyche, it helps to know that it exists and how it got there. The above example of burying a message under other sounds is a common method. Repetition also works well for programming or deprogramming. Repeated positive affirmations can neutralize or reverse the effects of repeated negative affirmations.

William effectively spread Paulism without being detected. Whether by accident or by design, the public frequently sensed William on a subconscious level while being completely oblivious to him consciously. For example, he often sang backup, or played an instrument, anonymously for other artists. He gave those songs the McCartney sound, energetically pointing fans to him. When listeners subconsciously hear him, he is elevated that much more. Usually, he is unidentifiable. For example, he cannot be recognized when crunching celery in the Beach Boys song, "Vegetables."

After a little bit more, I shout, "We're the band, the greatest band of all time." Then I add this last line finishing on the final chord, "Sgt. Pepper's Band!" That last line is so faint that **I suppose you** would need special equipment to **hear it** at all. However, on the *Sgt. Pepper's* cutout, we say it again. In the largest letters on the cutout, it says, "Sgt. Pepper's Band." Again, the point for all of you is that it is my band now. I am Billy Pepper. These, and other messages buried deep in layered sound, tell you that **Paul died**, and that John gave me the band **to keep it going.**

With the Sgt. Pepper's costume cutout inserts, I did not expect to see a wave of our fans suddenly impersonating me dressed up as the sergeant. It was to make the interactive point that I was dressed up as the fictitious character. I was not claiming to be a sergeant. I was suggesting that now the Beatles had a new leader. I was the new authority.

My "OPD" ("Officially Pronounced Dead") patch is visible on the album's gatefold picture. When I told the questioners that the patch I wore had been made for the "Ontario Police Department," that was as honest as I could be without revealing the patch's real purpose. When investigators discovered that there is no such police department there, it encouraged those in the "**Paul is** Dead" circle while simultaneously **fortifying critics** who could then rightly see that I was correct **generally.** Officially, I explained it away saying that my patch does not suggest "Officially Pronounced Dead," and that it is simply from *a* Canadian police department.

On the gatefold picture, however, we twisted the sleeve forward to see most of the patch that fell naturally to the side. We conspicuously displayed it exactly that way. The police explanation was also a good answer because the police, just like the military, have Sergeants. I am Sgt. Pepper.

The lines "And so I quit the police department, And got myself a steady job," had been written originally, "And so I *joined* the police department," referring to my new OPD *Sgt. Pepper's* career. Reversing that word set another context right since the new Beatles band was my steady job replacing session work that always varied. It was never steady. ("She Came in Through the Bathroom Window"). I joined **the Beatles** once Paul was Officially Pronounced Dead, or, **in code,** of the "Ontario Police Department." That work **became my steady job**, which was better than my session work for them.

I should also mention, as long as I am talking about my session musician work, that in that line of duty, we were all frequently impersonators. Without credits, we would do our work, singing or playing instruments, with the public believing it was done by the talented guys on the album cover. **It is not** as though anyone committed **fraud. It is** a standard performance illusion. That's **showbiz!**

The OPD patch was another **illusion**, a camera trick. Nothing is real. **We intentionally** bent the OPP patch to get the camera angle to **make** the final "P" look like a "D." Some mechanic from the garage of the Ontario Provincial Police gave that patch to John after their Toronto concert on 17 August.

247

As is understood and exploited by advertisers, our perceptions create our realities. This phenomenon lets people alter reality just by convincing others. Such impressions are especially effective when those led to believe a thing are of an impressionable age. The brain's frontal lobe, which is vitally involved with sound judgment, is not fully developed until our mid-twenties. That is one of the reasons that most all of our greatest fans became devoted to us before reaching their mid-twenties. It is much harder to sell older people on it unless they, in their youth, have already bought into something close to it.

Illusion plays a big role in the success of all bands. Now that I have left EMI, I can tell you a little trick they did to promote the Beatles—long before I joined. This story has been around a long time, but with an incorrect date. On 23 July 1964 (not August of 1963 as is often reported), under the direction of EMI, a trick was played on the public to help promote the Beatles, and to help sell newspapers. The Beatles did a flying ballet sketch for television at the London Palladium. It was great fun, from what Ringo told me. **They** were all hoisted up into the air with winches to do one part of that show in which they **pretended** to be flying. As they left the show, a few **girls gathered** near them and were photographed.

The picture was cropped closely **enough that** there was no way to see **the crowd magnitude**. In reality, there **was** no **significant** crowd around them, only a half dozen or so fans showing support. In the morning, newspapers all over had the cropped picture and sensational front-page headline, "Police fought to hold back 1,000 squealing teenagers." Reporting the sensational story of police holding back the riot was a brilliant Tavistock move to create the outstanding reality desired. The Tavistock Institute began 17 years earlier with a Rockefeller grant.

Making the news that way reinforced the illusion that they had established in the US when hundreds of screaming teenage girls mobbed the Beatles at Kennedy Airport. Actually, the girls had all been transported from a girls' school in the Bronx and were each paid for their performance. They showed everyone what to think of these idols, creating one of the largest television (tell-lie-vision) audiences ever. The Beatles' performance on *The Ed Sullivan Show* for over 75 million **Americans**, after showing them how to **respond to** it, set America up, especially those under **their** mid-twenties, to adore their new **English idols.** It launched Beatlemania in a very big way. Then, back in Great Britain, when they made more of the same illusion, they kept the world in motion to feel after them. "Assume the feeling of the wish fulfilled." ~Neville Goddard

NOTE: Perception creates reality. Because the media directed humanity to perceive the Beatles as the ultimate band, that belief made it so. The term, *Beatlemania*, first appeared in print in a 1963 review by the *Daily Mirror* (a newspaper owned by Lord Rothermere, a media baron with Rothschild connections). Although the mania was entirely manufactured, the belief in Beatlemania helped bring it into existence. The world manifested what it felt.

While it is fascinating to understand how the media created Beatlemania by presenting it as already accomplished, the greater message is that we can each employ that technique to create our own reality. The more we focus on what we want to create—with gratitude as if it already existed—the more readily we (or the universe) bring it into existence. Believing it, and especially feeling it, contributes to making it real as a matter of cosmic consistency. Our reality becomes consistent with our beliefs. To whatever extent we feel and believe that this method does or does not work, we may be right.

Girls paid to scream at the concerts triggered instant mass hysteria. In their frenzied state, girls screamed, cried, wet their pants, and some purported to have their first orgasm.

28

Recording with the Beatles

With both Pauls, up until the break-up, the Beatles recorded and released ten hours and twenty-eight minutes of music. I am still amazed by the great power of ten and a half hours of music to lead the world in entirely new directions. Years after the breakup, much more Beatles material has left the vaults. In all, in 2003, worldwide Beatles sales passed 1.2 billion (million million) records.

Intermittently throughout Friday and Saturday, 16-17 September 1966, when I first met John at the Eiffel Tower, and when we visited the Louvre Museum, we spoke of modern music, art, and the new direction **I wanted the** band to take. I said that modern art and **modern** music were, at heart, the very same **avant-gardism** and that taking the Beatles in that **direction** would be cutting edge, inventive, and most delightfully controversial. I persuaded him in repeated discussions, each with specific unique reasons, why it was time for the Beatles to grow up and mature into a much more interesting and sophisticated kind of music. I named examples of their songs that were too childish and out-of-date for the time and contrasted them with other songs that were attractively progressive.

Not having heard *Revolver*, I took John's word for it when he said he already understood what I was explaining to him, and that they were already doing it with their latest album. Since we both knew about dada and other avant-garde movements, we could speak the same language.

As I discussed these changes in the **Beatles music**, in each conversation, he again agreed that there would not be any more love songs, but **would** instead pioneer newer sounds, and subtly **weave Paul into** each of our songs. It was my idea to use **double** entendre to convey a storyline on one **level** and to work hidden meanings into that **material** that only the esoteric would understand. All that I said, I believed. However, it was mostly still theoretical.

I was mostly just showing off, trying to impress everyone, especially John. Sometimes he seemed to genuinely like my ideas. Other times, he responded as if I were ignorant or pompous. My enthusiasm annoyed him. He was hard to read. I did not know him that well. I also underestimated his devastation at losing Paul and his readiness for me to begin my life as Paul. He was patient with me out of deep respect for his lost bandmate. As per our agreement, each of us refrained from writing love songs for the four years that I was in the Beatles, but both quickly set that rule aside as soon as I dissolved the band.

Meanwhile, whenever I received the inspiration ordering me to write love songs, I did so, but either gave or sold them to other bands to keep up our new Beatles image. Another explanation I gave John and the others was that the Beatles were now in mourning. They took that reason to heart more than I anticipated, being truer than I had dared to believe. With his prophetic dreams fulfilled, the band venerated Paul as a seer, more than one could imagine. Paul's death was like a kick in the head to them. The news dazed them all. It cost them all of their innocence, and their ability to enjoy the same kind of music as before.

Neil and **John flew off** to Spain on Sunday, 18 September. Something **deep inside** of John said, "Yes, take the Beatles deeper into avant-garde music." Another part of him resisted it. The make-over, changing the band, changes the world. Still, something felt wrong. In Carboneras, he wrote what ultimately became the Beatles' first recording of the third phase, "Strawberry Fields Forever."

During that time when John flew to Spain, I returned to London. There, George, Ringo, and I met for the first time on the night of my return and had our first jam session. I was at the piano. We got things going with a song that Paul had written and enjoyed, "When I'm Sixty-Four." It went into our first album, my *Sgt. Pepper's Lonely Hearts Club Band.* It was the first Beatles song recorded that ended up on that album, the first song for which I sang lead, and the second song of phase three.

Owing to the required confidentiality, I could not explain my role of Paul to friends and family until they could be cleared. Some of them never knew what happened to me.

Relatives of Paul, however, already knew. It was common knowledge. To some, Paul had foretold his new life through another. I realized the one-sided nature of **this clandestine deal**. I had to assess each **of my associates** to decide who to let in.

In morose ritual, I swore to "sever all bonds, which **unite me with** mother, brothers, sisters, wife [though I had none], relatives, friends, mistress, kings, superiors, **benefactors**, or any other man [or any organization] to whom I have promised faith, service, or obedience," and lose my birthplace to henceforth "live in another dimension that I will not reach until I have renounced the evil globe which has been cursed by heaven." It was too grave to say more.

None of the Bonzos, however, were kept out of the loop. Most of my long-time music friends, such as Denny Laine, did not pose a threat. I could confide in them. There were others as well, but not nearly as many as Paul had let in on it, giving them all early warning of his goodbye and my hello.

No time was wasted when John returned. He shared his "Strawberry Fields Forever," written in the desert in Spain. I played for him my polished version of "When I'm Sixty-Four." He told me I could also finish writing Paul's "Penny Lane," but said "Sixty-Four" would be the B-side of his more substantial "Strawberry Fields" single.

I decided I'd make "Penny Lane" quaint, with a Fern Hillish (Dylan Thomas) memory Paul may still hold of Liverpool. I would finish it for that single, giving balance to John's song. More importantly,

According to the Illuminati, Earth has been denounced and cursed. The plan has been to eradicate the human race and to restart it with better controls—now with gene editing and controlled reproduction. YHWH/Enlil's genocidal Biblical precedent in 1 Samuel 15:2-3 is now being carried out on a global scale.

it would be the first hit that **I wrote and recorded** extensively, not as a freelancer, but **as Paul himself.** When I had written and recorded big hits before, the credit went to others. Now was different, yet the same.

Every record that the Beatles had released before had topped the charts. Now, John's "Strawberry Fields" would too. I wanted my turn—for Paul. Any new single I would make, I wanted to be mine. That motivated me to finish Paul's "Penny Lane." I need to tell you later about Paul's work on "Penny Lane," and about Penny Nickels and Denny Laine.

Going into the EMI studios with John and the others to record his "Strawberry Fields Forever" was extraordinary. I was not new to the studio, but to be there as Paul, helping John record what would no doubt be one of the world's new favorite songs, was surreal beyond measure. Words cannot express it.

Thursday, 24 November, we began recording. John stood before George Martin and played his guitar while singing "Strawberry Fields Forever." George, who sat on a stool in front of John, fully enjoyed the whole song. **I could** see his pleasure in hearing it and felt his **delight** that John would write such a song without **Paul.** George also gave sincere praise for the new quality of John's work.

Our work on that song went on for a week of days spread out over a month. Between sessions, we rethought the best ways to approach that song. George Martin and I grew in mutual admiration then, laughing together as we worked through John's tracks, experimenting, bouncing around ideas to do it better, all to help John's work quality. In all of my studio hours before, none was as stimulating. That launch of work with George Martin, engaging his talent and ingenuity, exhilarated me. I learned how to do quite a bit from him that I put to good use when I took on the *Sgt. Pepper* work.

Everyone saw the Beatles as a circle of close friends, which we were, but not as much as their yesteryear had been with Paul. I had more in common with George Martin than I did with any of my Beatle bandmates. Although George Martin should never be thought of as a band member, he invariably increased the quality of nearly all of their work all along, which was his special assignment.

Recording us all together on "Strawberry Fields Forever," I played bass. George played lead. We tried Ringo on drums. John, with his acoustic guitar, played as he sang. It needed more. I urged John over the weekend to add more instruments for a fuller sound. George Martin agreed when we returned to the studio. Although I offered to write a score for added cellos and trumpets, George Martin ended up doing it. That additional orchestration enhanced it greatly.

During those years, I learned to talk all about Paul's life, making up Paul's history. It was needful to pull off the new identity. I would make things up about when I, Paul, wrote Beatles songs from before having met those guys, or about how I came up with certain Paul lyrics that would blow my cover if I ever explained the real contexts. However, now and then my stories created relationship complications.

255

In an interview I did five months after John died, I thought it would be safe by then for me to build my reputation a bit at John's expense while he was no longer around to correct me. However, others were involved then who were offended. Since some of them will see this book of confessions, and because doing this book is about coming clean on everything else, I will set the record straight here too.

On 3 May 1981, I said, "We were always in competition." That part was true. "I wrote 'Penny Lane,' so he wrote 'Strawberry Fields.' That was how it was." That part was almost true, except that "Strawberry Fields" was done first. Paul had started "Penny Lane" before. It would be for me to finish his song after **John wrote** "Strawberry Fields." John also wrote **"Nowhere man" before Paul** died. It was a year after he **died** that I wrote, "The Fool on the

NOTE: In Tarot, the Fool is a joyfully oblivious youth starting life's journey.

In playing cards, a Joker, depicting a court jester, is a wild card. In the few games that use that card, the Joker usually replaces or trumps any natural card.

Although now readily associated with the British, the custom of including jesters, or fools, in royal courts dates back to Ancient Egypt. The court jester entertained the monarch and visiting dignitaries. More than amusing guests with music, storytelling, and physical comedy, many were best known for their sharp wit. Sharing meals with the royal family, they were privy to inside information, which could be used in subtle innuendo to humiliate an annoying guest. Jesters were among the very few to get away with making fun of a monarch. If witty enough, he could say almost anything.

The Royal Order of Jesters (controlled by their sub-group, the Secret Order of Brothers in Blood (S.O.B.I.B.)) controls (and is a sub-group of) the Shriners (a Masonic society best known for their hospitals). Admission to the Jesters, by invitation only, is limited to those at the top of the craft.

William, the fool on the hill, is like an innocent youth, oblivious to the dangers of replacing or trumping the natural card. He is a jester with inside information that he exchanges with other jesters of secret orders. If he writes masterfully, using wit to conceal his message in plain sight, he can say almost anything. He is talking perfectly loudly, but nobody seems to hear him.

256

Hill." He did not copy me there either. I admit the possibility that I reversed that set once too. The point was to sound like I had been writing with John. For people to think of me as Paul, I drew on the official narrative that they were a writing team.

You probably want me to mention the Paul clues that John wrote in "Strawberry Fields." In Paul's tree of his life, **I am** the branch that he produced. I have tuned myself in, **feeling** his energy, and channeling it to the world. When **John** wrote this song in Spain, he had only seen me one weekend in Paris. I had mentioned that I would receive Paul's essence and be him by connecting spirit-to-spirit, attuning to his energy. John was skeptical and was later repulsed by rumors of an ancient Egyptian succession ritual. He told me to just make a good Paul pretense.

John's line, "No one I think is in my tree" was enough to say that no one is waiting to take his place as I took over for Paul. He says, "It must be high" like from heaven "or low" from hell. The source did not matter. Either way, I am now in Paul's tree of life to take over where his tree was cut off. "That is, you can't you know tune in but it's all right." It all sounded too superstitious and woo-woo to be true. He would not require what is impossible. He said it was all right that I would not be able to tune in to connect to Paul spiritually. That is, he thought it would not lessen my work if I failed to tune in. He says, "I think it's not too bad."

"Let me take you down," reflects Paul's song, "I'm Down." John could not take it in when Paul sang, "**I'm down,** down in the ground." After John alludes **to Paul's burial**, he gives his reason. He explains: "'cause I'm going to Strawberry Fields." Notice the pronouns. John sings of burying Paul 'cause John, not Paul, is going to Strawberry Fields.

The Salvation Army acquired the property and renovated it into an orphanage in Liverpool. It was operational from 1836 to 2005. With Paul being entombed, John has been orphaned and left behind. John knew of that orphanage as a child because of the fund-raisers there. "Nothing is real, and nothing to get hung about" advises that though nothing is as it seems, there would be no criminal consequences. My fear of legal reprisals was unwarranted.

In singing, "Strawberry Fields Forever," John (on one level) says that since Paul will be forever buried in the strawberry field, and since I would not "tune in" enough to spiritually channel him back to John, John is to be forever left behind. Paul is not coming back. John is orphaned forever.

"Strawberry Fields" plainly warns the Beatles' worshipful fans (who in this song receive notice that "nothing is real"), that "Living is easy with eyes closed, misunderstanding all you see." Senses and instincts were not to be trusted. Appearances are deceptive. Referring to my difficulty in being Paul, my challenge is stated, "It's getting hard to be someone, but it all works out." With the same emotionless indifference as shown before, whether or not I could succeed at being **Paul was** not a matter for John's concern. We were not **doing it** for John, but for Paul. "It doesn't matter much **to me.**"

This simulation is becoming obsessed with creating illusions for entertainment and control. With flying things becoming indistinguishable from holograms of flying things, the term UFO (Unidentified Flying Objects) is being replaced by UAP (Unexplained Aerial Phenomena).

On hearing the song without reading along, one cannot know whether John sings "know" or "no." Reading it, we see it is "know," not "no." With the deliberately ambiguous "no," John corrects himself, making it, "Always, no, sometimes." The real words are not far off in meaning, except that the conflict enlisted is not a correction, but an expansion. "Sometimes" does not replace "always," but merely tempers it, adding moderation. "Always know" and "know sometimes" both suggest that our fans can overcome the misunderstanding caused by thinking all is real when nothing is. "Always know sometimes think it's me." By understanding the substitution, you can "always know" it is me or John working every song as Paul. That "always" is firm. The "sometimes think it's me" line was inserted because, losing Paul, John was under the assumption that I, the replacement, would not be able to do all the labor that had been done by Paul. John could not believe that **I could do** it.

All **Paul-work that is beyond** me, as John saw it, would fall on **him.** He would do it. Having let us know his doubts about me tuning in to be as Paul, he wondered how the band could go on. He lets us know his concerns but hides his feelings of overwhelm and inadequacy. He had leaned on Paul. The world would think that Paul is still doing his part when "sometimes" John and Paul are just John. It hurt John to think such things. See him trying to keep the dream going that had been shared with another whom he now can only pretend is still there. He wondered how long he could.

The next phrase, "But you know I know," is John assuring you that he was not fooled. He knows about Paul, and about who is doing what work with each song. It is not as if I am fooling him. Saying next that "it's a dream," has drug overtones that work well with the song but is mostly about the self-sacrifice in Paul's dreams. We were all playing out our parts according to what Paul had dreamed.

When Paul shared his death and replacement **dreams, hearers** all had their interpretations of how each detail **would play** out. It was far from how John had anticipated **it**. He had imagined someone recording as a substitute, not taking over the band. We reached an agreement in Paris when John finally surrendered, telling himself it was Paul's will, and saying my demands did not matter that much to him. It did not sit well with him. By the time he reached Spain, John wondered what he had done. He sang, "I think I know of thee, ah yes but it's all wrong. That is, I think I disagree." He knew of me but objected.

I will explain, and prove, the "I buried Paul"-"cranberry sauce" overlay in "Paulism" (chapter 61).

Recording being done as we supposed, for "Strawberry Fields Forever," we used our time in EMI Studios on 6 December recording Christmas and New Year greetings for bootleg pirate stations off the coast broadcasting our music from ships. With that work finished, we rehearsed and then spent the rest of that reserved five-hour session recording "When I'm Sixty-Four." Paul had written that tune at a relatively young age, around sixteen years old, and added the lyrics years later. Some of our historical documentaries (based on my lie) say he added the lyrics to celebrate his father's sixty-fourth birthday.

Every presentation as fact should be considered suspect. All of our official stories are just that. Do not trust them. The real truths are presented in fiction, such as in this so-called novel. I learned that back in their early Cavern Club days, Paul added the lyrics to give them more performance material. Eventually, it became their stand-by song to play whenever the electricity went out, or when their amplifier blew a fuse. Paul's father, Jim, born in 1902, was not sixty-four years old until 7 July 1966. That was only sixty-six days before Paul died. Again, this book of "fiction" gives you the straight line rather than the traditional party line. Look to this fiction for fact, and to my fact for fiction.

Entering EMI studios all alone, on 8 December, for my own private three-hour afternoon recording session, I overdubbed my lead vocal. As I listened to it, I became nervous, concerned that my voice was

NOTE: William says, "Look to this fiction for fact, and to my fact for fiction." What he says about his disclosure is also true of how the cabal works generally. The greatest manipulations have always occurred by presenting fiction as nonfiction, and by presenting fact as fantasy. That perceived distinction always fools most people. Absurd stories are seen as real merely because they are in newspapers, on television, or on websites that pretend to be truthful even when those outlets are controlled by those with incentives to promulgate the most dangerous lies.

The most trusted fact-checking websites or television programs go to some expense to maintain their reputations and are often useful to check on inconsequential urban legends or threats of computer viruses. However, providing many true statements for each ruse, along with disproving false rumors, they also claim to "debunk" (a trigger word to make people believe them) proof of scams perpetrated by specific treacherous corporations.

The reverse is also true. Fictional formats (songs, movies, or novels) can condition people to think in specific ways about planned events. Sometimes directors or writers are tipped off to include specific details to add those ideas to the collective consciousness. This foreshadowing technique is useful for instilling subconscious dread or acceptance. Using fiction to plant ideas in advance allows writers and directors to program how viewers and **readers respond to** each issue as the programming is activated by **real-life events.**

"All I want is the truth, just give us the truth." ("Gimme Some Truth")

261

obviously lower than Paul's. I imagined him doing
the song sounding younger, more rooty-tooty. Mine
now sounded much too self-serious, even turgid.
That evening we all met together in studio two. In
going over it, others felt the same way. It was not at
all like Paul. The best way for me to describe it is to
say it is like my Vivian Stanshall bit at the end of the
Magical Mystery Tour film. A tongue-in-cheek,
affected, cabaret sort of a song, it had a Bonzo Dog
Doo-Dah Band feeling to it. That is the way I
sang it. However, the humor did not carry well. It
sounded too sincere for such absurd lyrics. All that
I could do at that point was to press forward and
somehow fix it.

For the next two sessions, we were back to
"Strawberry Fields" for still more overdubbing.
It appeared to be finished again with that work we
did on 9 and 15 December. On 20 December, we
were back to working on **Paul's old** "Sixty-Four,"
but all agreed to have that **work interrupted** for
each of us to do interviews for **the weekly television**
series, *Reporting '66.*

Rumors had been buzzing around London, and
beyond, at first that Paul had died, and then that our
energy, or cohesiveness, was missing. Revealing
internal disharmonies completely shocked the
public. I had been the worst of all. I was too honest
and far less skilled at dealing with the press then.
After intense friction with John one night when he
was drunk, I believed it was over. In a public pub, I
uttered that I **was no longer one of the Fab Four.**

John and George had both expressed doubts of
lasting long with me at the helm anyway. With Paul
gone, it felt to the others that there already were no

more Beatles. Observers picked up on the sudden disharmony. When John returned from Spain, at the casual gatherings where we were expected to be seen together as old chums, onlookers suddenly found a completely different story. The 20 December interviews were to convince our fans that we were all still one big happy Beatles band, that we, being old childhood chums, were still inseparable.

Returning to the studio the next day, three session musicians added clarinet to "Sixty-Four." Then John added more vocals and another piano track to "Strawberry Fields." We were back at it the next day, 22 December, again fixing "Strawberry Fields." Playing what were the two best tracks, one excluding trumpets and one with them, John decided the song needed a minute to build up to it.

Yet, rather than calling those musicians back for another session, **John wanted to splice** the two recordings **together** exactly at the sixty-second point. George Martin objected because John had recorded each track in **a different key.** That one had a faster tempo than the other. John went on about favoring the beginning of one track and the end of the other. We played them again and listened, letting us all hear their incompatibility for splicing.

Then, with the kind of brilliance that made each day of working with George Martin was a joy, he abruptly lit up and said, "Yes, William, I think we can slow one down a little and speed up the other just enough to match it, it might work." In the track that came of it, having a compromise tempo and tone, John's voice is slightly unnatural, but is better for it. Unless you know to listen for it, the seam is mostly unnoticeable.

Not satisfied with "When I'm Sixty-Four," but not yet knowing what to do about it, I decided to get going with "Penny Lane" for our next Abbey Road studio session. It was on Thursday, 29 December. On my own again, from 7:00 pm until 2:15 am, I recorded the basic track of "Penny Lane," as well as new percussive effects. When I returned the next day, before getting back to work on "Penny Lane," I let George Martin know what we needed to do to fix my "When **I'm** Sixty-Four" recording. I told him I would sound **more like Paul** if we sped up the track, picking up the tempo **a bit**, using that same variable-control tape machine that he had used to change the speeds on "Strawberry Fields."

Even though George agreed that it would make me sound younger, more like Paul, he immediately rejected the idea. The change was too substantial. However, I insisted. We had to do it. As George protested, I persisted and prevailed. The master take had been recorded in C major but was sped up in order to raise the key by one full semitone (half step) to the key of D-flat major (C#). To the delight of all of us, my new Paul-polish made it more Paulish. It sounded a lot more like him.

NOTE: Since 2009, *the Memoirs* made many verifiable facts available that were not known before by "Paul is Dead" investigators. The above is an example. To verify the story, slow the song down a semitone, from the key of D-flat major back down to C major. If you do so, you will recognize William's natural voice that the world now knows much better.

When William started this new role, he was concerned that his natural voice was too distinct from Paul's to go unnoticed. That concern diminished when *Sgt. Pepper's* trained fans to identify his voice with Paul's.

two
Sixty-Four

Later, throughout January, **I polished** "Penny Lane" as well. George Martin and **the band** all agreed that it would also be an A-side song. "Strawberry Fields Forever" and "Penny Lane" now became the Beatles' third Double A-side single. Although it is correct that John's song did better in some charts, "Penny Lane" did better in others. There was a big commotion in the press about it being the first Beatles single to reach

NOTE: Although the Beatles are best defined by their albums, they also produced 63 singles. When most artists put great effort into their A-side song but put a throw-away song on the B-side, the Beatles intended hits on both sides of their singles.

Although John and Paul never took turns being featured on the A-side, it came out rather evenly between them furthering the appearance of Lennon-McCartney equality. George Martin put whichever song on the A-side he thought would sell most readily. John or Paul sang lead on the songs they were credited with writing, sometimes based on the best voice for a particular song.

Normally, John sang lead for one side of the single, and Paul (or William) sang lead for the other side. After the single featuring "Penny Lane" and "Strawberry Fields Forever," in which both sides were presented as A songs, John was given the A-side with "All You Need is Love." The B-side was a mix of them both in "Baby, You're a Rich Man."

In William's mind, it made him look inferior to John to share the B-side with him while John occupied the single's A-side. Furthermore, in this case, John had written his part of the shared song first. William wrote his part specifically to go with John's. When William considered what he had allowed to happen, he was troubled, feeling more like a helper than a superior.

After the "All You Need is Love" single, William sang lead on a dozen more singles but never allowed another one of his songs to be in the second position to one of John's—or anyone else's other than Paul's. Whenever William did not have the best song, deserving the A-side, he put one of George's songs on the single in his place. He made George's "Something" and John's "Come Together" double A-sides. George's "Old Brown Shoe" was the B-side of John's "The Ballad of John and Yoko."

The only other time William took the B spot was for "Helter Skelter," topped by Paul on the A-side with his old recording, "Got to Get You into My Life," making Paul appear to dominate both sides. The next single also combined a new song with an old one, having William's "Back in the USSR" on the A-side with John's old "Twist and Shout" cover on the back.

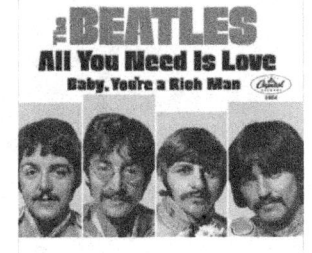

only the number two position in the UK. It entered the top 40 in the US on 4 March 1967, hit number one there, and stayed firm in the top 40 for nine weeks. When recording that song, I froze with insecurity and received more help with it than I now can admit. Though for a Beatles single, it was below expectations; for me, it was fabulous. Years of wishing for hits made that sudden success feel all the more extraordinary. It also showed a lot of insiders that **I was** a viable Paul, a good fit. The consensus was **that Paul** would have done better, and hit the top in the UK, but that I was a fine stand-in.

Locals scoffed at "Penny Lane." The street was not picturesque in their reality. While across the pond, fans loved the song as a faraway fantasy, folks in England knew better. I could not fool them into loving the place. They were too wise for that bliss.

NOTE: With control held by the super-elite over the largest radio stations, they decided which songs would make the top 20 list, and how each would rank. That ranking directly impacted record sales. They did not make "Penny Lane" a number one hit in the UK for the reasons that William explains, but also to show him that he would be more successful without the unacceptable levels of assistance that he received with that song. In his later hits, with less assistance, the elite directed the stations to spin his records enough to make them number one hits for each prescribed duration.

No hit of the top 20 was organically ranked by the will of the people. Those who controlled public attitudes dictated the top songs. Even when listeners called in to request songs, no major station was permitted to allow those requests to override the predetermined ranking of the top 20. Protocols also determined what songs could be requested.

Now that William is concluding his Paul service, extra media coverage is turning the youth's attention to him by having other artists honor him. To further transmit that illuminated face to the next generation, they are helping him complete his life on a high note.

Currently, with personalized music stations, the public has more control over what they hear. With logarithms based on individual preference, the general public can now make their own top 20.

266

29

Donovan

Donovan's "Mellow Yellow" is unique in that it features both of us Paul McCartneys. Paul did some of the backup vocals days before the crash, and I did some more after. Since Don was an insider, I had no need to pretend with him. When **fans learned** that Paul sang backup on it, many thought **he was** the one singing "Quite rightly," or **as** some misheard it, "Quite right, Slick." That was **someone else**. It is very hard to recognize either of us in that song. He mostly repeatedly whispers "Mellow Yellow" again and again. I later added party sounds, showing that we were having a good time.

Now, while John was gone for the film, we were not working on any Beatles songs. You can know it is true if you check the recording dates. Donovan's "Mellow Yellow," I should also note, is historically significant as the last song that Paul took part in recording. When his tour ended, he hung out with Donovan at Abbey Road Studios. Paul was mellow, ripened for consumption. Written by Donovan, produced by Mickey Most, and recorded on the Pye label, that mellow song featuring Paul's unrecognizable voice does not credit him. His participation was as private as his passing.

As for yellow, the color was on Donovan's mind because of a **Paul** song released the month before. **Under Don's influence,** "Yellow Submarine" was **made** as **a children's song.** They knew Paul would leave **when mellow yellow**, when it was his time. Writing a children's song was Donovan's idea.

When Paul wrote of the submarine, predicting his death, the sub, as his car and coffin, was yellow as a symbol of ripeness, like a banana. They began recording "Yellow Submarine" in May. Donovan's song, "Mellow Yellow," extended the idea.

Donovan also wrote the Submarine line, "Sky of blue, sea of green," referring to Paul's burial under grass, as opposed to under the deep blue sea. Don understood the song completely. Notice the burial mound of ground taking the place of water over the submarine on the original *Yellow Submarine* album cover. The casket-like craft is buried down under the dirt hill where the band stands.

Whereas Paul's burial, as he predicted it, would not be in water, the lyrics referred to "the land of submarines," a cemetery of subs. As it happened, he did not end up in a public cemetery. His main final resting place was more like the album cover with earth in an overstated mound over the solitary vessel. The song was released years before that album.

NOTE: Besides the examples in this chapter, Donovan also assisted with other Beatles songs. He shared ideas for lines, played instruments, and occasionally sang back-up—especially on *the White Album* for which George Martin did not provide material, direction, or session musicians that were standard with earlier albums.

Really, "Yellow Submarine" is a fine children's song. **It is** for their escape fantasy. Paul made **the song for** them, and intentionally used words simple enough for children to love, including bits to harness **their imaginations.** Besides showing that Paul would be buried, it was mostly made to entertain children—as was John's "The Continuing Story of Bungalow Bill," and Ringo's "Octopus's Garden." My "All Together Now" worked well for them too but was mostly a big joke.

Rounding out both of these yellow songs, as Paul later sang backup on "Mellow Yellow," Don had, oddly enough, sung backup on Paul's "Yellow Submarine." These two songs mirror one another. Unlocking the secrets of "Yellow Submarine," you see what "Mellow Yellow" turned into merely a few nights after the first tracks were recorded. It became Paul's swan song.

Donovan, one of Paul's friends who expected the replacement, was eager to meet me. When he did, he called me D.O.P. I did not like the sound of it. It sounded like dope. I asked what he meant by it. He explained, "D.O.P. Duplicate of Paul." I wondered how many other insiders and friends of Paul would call me to meet Paul's new replacement. I could not see how we would keep it from leaking out if all of Paul's old friends had already been let in on it. At first, I was careful about whom I met. I could not live as openly as Paul had. I had to learn how to be Paul before I could pass myself off as him.

Laughing at Don a little, hiding my resentment, I corrected him, "D.I.P." He seemed confused and ensnared. I had caught him at his own game. Pushing against the dope sound, I said, "Duplicate *IN* Paul."

"Duplicate In Paul," he said. "D.I.P. Dip. So, you're the big dip? That's wild!" he said.

"Maybe, Don, you should call me Paul," I said, realizing that a dip was worse than a dope.

"Everywhere you go now," he said, "you'll be Paul McCartney. Tell me, what's it like being Paul? Dippy, that's trippy!" The meaning of D.I.P. evolved to *"Dead* in Paul" when it all hit me that I lost my life to obtain his. Don comforted me with his "Epistle to Dippy," I was dead in Paul, the great "Paperback Writer," who made Donovan "Paul's 'Paperback Reader.'" Paul set up this whole plot. **Donovan's song was about** me transforming, changing into **an evolved Paul**. "Through all levels you've been **changing**." Here, "all levels" means becoming Paul **on all levels** and leads into the elevator metaphor. **Paul's head** was broken down, but mine, Don says, **works just as well**. "Through all levels you've been changing. / Elevator in the brain hotel / Broken down, but just as well."

Everyone missed the *Sgt. Pepper's* tie-ins to Donovan. I pinched some of his creative imagery very clearly for our album. It went both ways. We

NOTE: The slang terms, 'dip' and 'dope' have evolved. The term, 'dip' has become more hostile (such as in 'dip-sh*t'). In the 60s, it was friendlier but referred to someone gullible or lacking intelligence. A dope was a stupid person. Additionally, dope was, and is still, slang for drugs. In the 1970s, after Richard Nixon made many criminal organizations wealthy by launching his "War on Drugs," there was an anti-drug slogan, "Only dopes use dope." A person who abused drugs was labeled a dope fiend, or simply a dope. However, since the 1980s, 'dope' has taken on a positive meaning. Those born since then sometimes call something "dope" to mean that it is excellent. William objected to being called a dip or a dope. The "war on drugs," like the billions spent on cancer research, is not to stop such things, but to funnel tax dollars through the pharmaceutical companies to pay the politicians. Real solutions (especially natural ones) are blocked to protect those companies.

shared ideas back and forth. In December of 1966, at the time we were working on *Sgt. Pepper's*, Don recorded "Epistle to Dippy," and made up a story to explain it away as if to some friend in the military. He sang that I am "getting a little bit better no doubt."

Owing a response, I reply yes, "I admit it's getting better. A little better all the time." Before his song was released here in the UK, he gave me a copy of a US-released album. In February, it peaked in the States in their top twenty. I played it here too because it was about Paul and me. It was nice for Don to give me that copy. Stuck in my head, I responded to it by recording "Getting Better" on the next month's schedule.

Where I sing, "it's getting better," John adds his ridicule by his humorous, "It can't get no worse," as if to say I did not begin it well. Besides agreeing with Don in the lines, "**I have to admit** it's getting better, a little better all the time," I sing backward there, on that spot, I sing, "After all, **Paul is dead.** He lost his hairs, head." Equating hair with head here was not as morbid. Ringo re-used it later, singing, "You were in a car crash, and you lost your hair" ("Don't Pass Me By"). In that same Ringo song, he, like Donovan, also points to me. Again, we added a backward message. Where "Don't pass me by, don't make me cry, don't make me blue" is recorded forward, playing it backward renders, "Who'd we pay for now? We paid for now? It's that one." My services came with a cost.

271

Wanting another verse, John autobiographically inserted the part about him having been cruel to his woman. It had nothing to do with me. **I was never** cruel like that. It fit the song in that it is yet **another** way that the fictional persona may be getting **better.** Until domestic violence is brought out into the open, the shame of it keeps people trapped in that cycle of longing for peace and connecting love but suffering for the sake of oppressive fear-based control issues.

After receiving Donovan's "Epistle to Dippy," some of our songs with Dippy influences were recorded for *Sgt. Pepper's,* including our "With a Little Help from My Friends" and "A Day in the Life." If you would play his Dippy Epistle, then *Sgt. Pepper's,* and then back to Dippy again, you would likely notice that we pinched ideas, not only in words and content but also in tone. **Giving thanks is overdue**. "With a Little Help from **My Friends**" answers Don's question: "Over dusty years, I ask you / What it's been like being you?" I imagined the world asking that.

Using Ringo's voice (because it is less polished), I answer Donovan as a set of interview questions. Posing as me, Billy "Shears" Shepherd, Ringo gives answers to each interview question as I would—or as I actually do in that song. "What do I do when my love is away?" I missed her terribly. **I felt** like I needed her help to do this work. But that does not fit the song. "Does it worry you to be **alone**? How do I feel by the end of the day? Are you sad because you're on your own? No, [I am lying here. I am in

denial.] **I** get by with a little help from my friends. I **get high** with a little help from my friends."
Obtaining drugs or plant medicines for relief from the pain of loneliness was something I needed to share. When I suffered, mushrooms were especially helpful.

NOTE: The line, "I get high with a little help from my friends," predictably resulted in the BBC banning the song for its drug reference. With that same concern, the BBC also banned, on that same *Sgt. Pepper's* album, "Fixing a Hole," "Lucy in the Sky with Diamonds," and "A Day in the Life."

As premeditated, the cooperating media helped the world contemplate the government attempting to block the Beatles from encouraging fans to use drugs. Naturally, after the fans' initial shock of being told that their idols encourage drug use, most Beatles fans sided with the band, objecting to those who would prevent Beatles airplay. With that media and government support, many people tried drugs because of that strong celebrity endorsement. Publicity from the ban also boosted album sales.

When choosing sides between a conservative government and the drug culture, even those with no interest in drugs are generally more inclined to stand with their rock icons than with those who would repress them. Consciously and subconsciously, with the reception of *Sgt. Pepper's,* millions of people suddenly opposed those who opposed drugs.

Banning those four songs placed the Beatles at the top of the drug-favoring counter-culture. Although, since their first engineered hit, the Beatles were already bigger than life, the government's interference with their music made them unimaginably larger to the world. It also turned fans against their governments. Siding with the Beatles, now against the state, many fans took drugs as their initiation into the Beatles' counter-culture.

William recycled the phrase, "I get high," from "I Want to Hold Your Hand," which was one of the first of many songs written for the Beatles and credited to Lennon-McCartney. At the start, protecting their wholesome starter-image, and keeping the song from being banned by the BBC, the phrase was muffled by a light overdub of the phrase, "I can't hide." Many who did not know the official lyrics "misheard" the true lyrics. Others received that covert drug reference as subliminal programming that would not be activated until the Beatles repeated that message overtly.

In Billy Pepper and the Pepperpots' 1963 recording of "I Want to Hold Your Hand," released on *Merseymania* in 1964, the lines are, "It's such a feeling that, my love, I got high, I got high, I got high!"

When confronted with the rumor that Billy Shepherd and Jimmy Fraser wrote "I Want to Hold Your Hand," and that Pepperpots originally recorded it to help George Martin teach it to the Beatles, William said, "That's an early Lennon-McCartney song. George's change in the lyrics from 'I *got* high' to 'I *get* high' made the song more present. He also made other improvements. That's the way with George. Whatever he worked on, he made better."

As the interview continues, they ask, "Do you need anybody?" I admit, "I need somebody to love," et cetera. The interview is to answer Don's epistle.

Another Dippy Don line that appealed to me was his "Over dusty years, I ask you." The line joins the new happening of today with the dusty decades past. That idea fit perfectly into what I was attempting to do. That is part of why I wrote, "It was twenty years ago today, Sgt. Pepper taught the band to play." Until I made that song about *my* band, not merely the Beatles, the album had no focused concept.

Playing our new songs for Donovan, and then explaining our album in progress, had him intrigued and delighted. When I sang the line, "The teachers that taught me weren't cool," I was singing about not only the old school days but more particularly about my recent Beatle-craft schooling. My teachers did not fully appreciate all the **sacrifices** I made. John, George, Mick Jagger, and others **were** over-doing their training. They sought **to teach me** but were not cool about it. Hence, Don threw in **a bit** on the school teacher idea, combining it with what George told him about all the beautiful women who were getting with me once I became Paul. George saw the harm in my lack of moderation. It made him nervous that I was "crazy" enough to have my hands on so many girls. As Donovan said it, "Made the teacher suspicious about insanity / Fingers always touching girl." The "teacher" idea was Don's.

On the album, after reading Carroll, John has "A girl with kaleidoscope eyes." She's "the girl with the sun in her eyes." Don thought of needing special eyes to see me. You see? It was a trip, but that girl could

"Strange times are these in which we live when old and young are taught falsehoods in school. And the person that dares to tell the truth is called at once a lunatic and fool." – Plato

experience reality. She also paralleled Paul. Look for him, and he's gone. However, it took special eyes to see it. George also wrote about how blind people are in his "Within You Without You." That song is partly about being without Paul, and how we, and you, can, by our love, connect to him. Maybe **I will** write more on that in another chapter. The **issue** here is how we cannot discern enough with our **programmed vision, or** natural eyes. We need help, or **altered eyes, to see truth** and to know the difference. John later called it "Looking through a glass onion." Well, Donovan's gaze into reality came not through "kaleidoscope eyes," but by a prism, "Looking through crystal spectacles," and ultimately looking "through all kinds of windows." All kinds. He meant that.

The thing that Donovan found most far-out about my transformations had to do with my harsh physical changes. Although I felt divided

NOTE: Some people have imagined William had all of the surgical work done in a single trip to one doctor, and then returned with Paul's face. However, as chronicled by photographs over the first few years, William's transformation was brought about by a series of less radical surgeries, some as simple as adding blemishes, such as a scar on his chin. Fans have pointed to a scar or other blemishes as proof that William is Paul but miss the fact that those blemishes came with time. They are missing in William's early Paul pictures. The chin scar had to be done twice.

Injected fillers were originally intended to occur every six months but were less frequent in actual practice. William found reasons to put it off. He complained that the extra thickness in his cheeks, besides feeling unnatural to him, interfered with his singing. The injections became rare starting in the Wings era when the primary person pressing for injections passed away.

In the seventies, rather than injections, William created facial variations with Latex experimentation. Sometimes, in the same music video, he uses subtle adjustments that almost make him seem like different people. Although broadening his appearance has PID implications, it also reflects William's pleasure in dressing up, his interpretation of a song, or setting a song's mood. When watching his music videos, consider how his altered appearance for a specific song reinforces the lyrics, music, or mood of that song.

275

about the alterations, I pushed ahead, motivated by all of Paul's stuff I would receive. I gave up what I had and loved, **in exchange for everything** from Paul. Mick Jagger and others resented it. Exchanging all for **all seemed fair to me. Paul had become a millionaire** by then. In the sixties, that was a lot more money than it is now.

As I weighed it all out, I considered how hard I would work for that much money. I also saw it as an unparalleled opportunity for my music success. Although I knew I had more talent than Paul, I lacked promotion connections. Considering how swiftly this role would change all of that, I willingly accepted the surgeries. Doctors gave me Paul's appearance. We used photographs to show what they needed to do. I already looked a little like Paul, but more so after the surgeries and injections.

Donovan was intrigued by the way fate seemed to dictate everything. Paul's fatal collision, followed by my process, pointed Don to a greater power in charge. That otherworldly aspect playing out inspired Don's yearning for his own greater spiritual connection. He depicts that desire by having a monk meditate as the song begins. That is how he ties the monk to his repeated line, "The doctor bit was so far out." It was enough of a spiritual drive that Don joined us in our retreat to India. He sought that higher power of love and enlightenment that we all sought after. Our group of friends added more positive energy: Mia Farrow, Mike Love, Donovan, the four of us Beatles, and others including, of course, the Maharishi.

Back to "Mellow Yellow." After Paul died, the song became more set on him. Before then, it was really about sex. Donovan sang the phrase "mellow

276

yellow" to describe a ripe banana. As he had originally intended it, they (his lovers) called him "Mellow Yellow" suggesting it was his reputation to be ripe and ready. When Paul died a little later, the unintended double meaning emerged from the historical context. Back to the sexual intent, Don compares himself to an "electric banana," which, as he explained, is a kind of vibrator that he saw in a sex shop. He claimed to be ready at the press of a button. Realizing the historical Paul significance, and then bringing it to our attention, out of respect for Paul, Donovan played down the sexual meaning and called it his "Farewell to Paul" song.

Owing the yellowness of Donovan's song to the "Yellow Submarine," let me emphasize that Paul no longer dwells under the "sea of green," as Don put it. Actually, he never did. No grass is growing over his gravesite. That is not where his enduring essence is anyway. As foretold in the song, **his spirit ventured upward.** "So we **sailed up to the sun** till we found the sea of green." That is to say that the spirit ascends to the sky, "to the sun," as his rotting corpse pushes up daisies—or, in his case, rhododendrons.

NOTE: Here again (compare page 70), Paul is pushing up rhododendrons rather than daisies. Within the 60s-70s counter-culture, daisies, in all their simplicity, were associated with "flower power." For many, the daisy seemed to be *the* flower of the movement. However, pushers were not "pushing" daisies. The flower they pushed up was marijuana.

Marijuana (as explained later) is *the* flower of flower power. That herb is a hallucinogenic plant medicine. Since prehistory, hallucinogens, especially psilocybin mushrooms, contributed to social evolution. With the threat of hallucinogens awakening humanity out of their easily controlled social structures, many governments outlawed their use.

Yet, even where most beneficial hallucinogens are still outlawed, mad honey is generally legal. Try it (if your doctor approves). It is delicious. Bees naturally produce it from rhododendrons. Mad (rhododendron) honey thus joins the mysticism and effects of hallucinogens with the Masonic significance of bees and beehives [cromlechs]. Some readers have found Paul through psychedelics. Have you?

277

Now, **we will consider** another Donovan hit. The main lines of **the philosophical song**, "There is a Mountain," stem **from Zen Buddhism.** Don became interested in, enamored with, and committed to Eastern thinking at around the same time that we Beatles all did. The good old saying, "First there is a mountain, then there is no mountain, then there is" is a Zen proverb of impermanence. All that comes, naturally goes. We are to accept whatever is when it is. Mountains come and go. You can move them, says Jesus, if you have enough faith.

What are we up against? The big mountains that we might face today may vanish by our faithful acceptance. Our mountains disappear but reappear every time we need them. Our mountains are things we perceive as too big for us. We think we do not like them sometimes. Still, they are the realities of our own creation to fill our subconscious needs. Loving or hating the circumstances is not ever the issue. Our true selves, or our non-selves, always create our reality to match whatever we need, or whatever we subconsciously think we need.

NOTE: Donovan, whom Bob Dylan had introduced to the Beatles, entwined his spiritual journey with theirs. Together, especially with George and Pattie Boyd Harrison, Donovan frequently discussed mediation and other spiritual practices, ideas, and intentions. He was part of all of it.

In 1968, Donovan was among the group of friends that accompanied the Beatles to the ashram in India where Maharishi Mahesh Yogi (who had devised Transcendental Meditation (TM)) trained them to teach it to others.

In 2009, "Paul" and Ringo, backed by Donovan, joined other celebrities in New York City in a benefit concert for the David Lynch Foundation. The goal was to collect enough money to teach TM to one million at-risk students. Besides raising funds, the concert resulted in many Beatles fans learning TM, and making the abandoned ashram a Beatles tourist site. Due to those visits, the ashram reopened and was eventually renamed Beatles Ashram.

In 2021, on Donovan's 75th birthday, he released "I Am the Shaman," a song produced by David Lynch, who also directed its music video. In it, Donovan employs hypnotic techniques while repeating that he is "The Shaman" (not merely *a* shaman). At the end of the video, donations are solicited to teach TM to more students.

Another way to look at it is that "first there is a mountain" of stress and anxiety within each of us. Next, we may accept that whatever mountain exists, it is perfect in that it is what we have created for ourselves, or is a gift from heaven. Without resistance, **the mountain of stress vanishes** from awareness **until we resist it again.** If we have not fully settled the issue within ourselves, that mountain reappears as the returning anxiety for us to try again.

When we have full acceptance of it, realizing that it is our own creation, an extension of our infinite selves, we have peace. Each recurrence of that mountainous issue calls us back to accept that we created it. It serves us as part of our perfect world. It is what is. However, reaching that point, it is no more, yet is.

Lastly, about that song, **I do not believe** Don had Paul and me in mind when **he wrote it**. However, I still remember the time he sang **to me first**, in EMI Studio Two, "First there's Paul McCartney, then there's no McCartney, then there is." Then he said, "The second mountain and the butterfly are both you, Dippy. They are both you." Don went on singing, "The caterpillar sheds his skin to find a butterfly within." He was suggesting that the biological Paul had to cease for the butterfly to emergence as the more evolved Paul. I emerge as the new Paul with Wings.

Considering its relevance to this book of Paul, I wanted to add that clip to this book's contest CD. I offered to buy that rare Donovan recording but was told that it no longer exists. **If it does** still exist, then, maybe this attention will **help someone find it**. If so, I think the world would **be amused by it**. If it ever ends up in some rarity collection, just remember that you read about it here first. It is also possible that it was taped over and lost the day that it was recorded. I had always said, "Track it and save everything!" However, Don was not that way. He could redo it. I still have respect and kind feelings for Don over these dusty years. We became friends because he wanted to stay close to Paul. **Donovan had** a lot more in common with him than with me. His ⚠McCartney-Mountain song inspired my "**Butterfly.**"

NOTE: William had an experience that triggered an early childhood trauma. Upon investigation, he learned that it was a German method of ritualistic abuse that caused disassociation. Part of the script was to be "the greatest star" in service to music. Upon further investigation, as one memory led to another, he learned that the abuse evolved to more closely resemble Monarch programming. The Monarch butterfly symbolizes the trauma-based mind-control system.

William's childhood traumas put his life and work into perspective. It explains his extraordinary drive ever since his program was fully activated to be Paul McCartney, "the greatest star." Some readers are put off by William proving that he was not only the best Paul McCartney but also the greatest star of all time. However, that was his program.

By identifying with that sadistically programmed role, William's existence requires that the program be true. It is not as though he would receive external punishment for failing to fulfill that role. The integral tormenting punisher is entirely internal. Failure triggers severe depression, which he has tried to drink away. He must be on top.

In *the Memoirs,* William laments the heavy burden of living as Paul. From an outsider's view, it is inconceivable that the poor billionaire super-celebrity has cause to whine. After all, most of his relatives and closest friends were fully aware of his new role and were supportive. For William, however, the life that he lost was not one of their associations. It was his life before his internal trauma-based program became fully activated.

Once it was switched on, his life beyond work largely ended. Although he worked to maintain a playful element, such as while playing his Viv Stanshall role, he could never fully return to his authentic peaceful nature. Even when playing, his service to music program runs in the background.

By understanding William's position, we also better understand countless others. He is not alone. To fulfill the ruling elite's agenda, they traumatically program many children to eventually step into key positions. The entertainment industry's power to shape opinion makes its celebrity control particularly important. Replacing many of them with programmed workers is an effective way to govern the masses.

Understanding how replacements qualify for celebrity roles should stir compassion for all whose lives are set that way. They are not robots. They are individuals with personal struggles. Just as we would not judge soldiers with PTSD, it is unfair to be overly critical of those who act according to their ritualistic trauma-based programming. Developed through extensive scientific experimentation, mind-control programming is extremely difficult to break.

280

Even though Don and I were good friends, and were both singers, songwriters, musicians, and heroes of the pop scene, and even though we had some good times together, his interest in me extended from Paul's friendship, and what **Paul had** foretold. Donovan Leitch was one of **Paul's friends** who were expecting me to show up after Paul's demise. Donovan and I had very little in common, actually. He was lazy; **I was** a workaholic.

Don's laziness prompted a closer friend, Paul Simon, to write of him in "**Faking It.**" Identifying him by name, a woman says, "Good morning, Mr. Leitch. Have you had a busy day?" She is addressing Don Leitch, whom Paul Simon is singing as. Don is "a dubious soul. And a walk in the garden wears [him] down" as if by looking upon a snail there. *Zzzzzz* (Don snoring). That fine 1967 Simon & Garfunkel song has Mr. Leitch "Takin' time to treat your friendly neighbors honestly." But he has "just been fakin' it, . . . not really makin' it."

By saying he was lazy, I do not mean that Don was not a good friend. However, like Paul, and unlike Paul Simon and me, Donovan liked to take it easy. Don would say he was not lazy, but that I was a workaholic. He made a valid point. People who work too much lack good times with family and friends. He was a good friend, but my idea of play looked like work to him. I worked hard until, in Japan, they forced me to stop for a while. Then, with Linda's help, I saw that my Paul work needed a breather while I spent more time with my family. I needed my children more in my life.

30

Penny Nickels, Denny Laine, and Penny Lane

Penny Nickels was one of Paul's many friends who came to meet me after the big switch. She and Emily Little had met and become close friends at a two-week dance workshop in Los Angeles. Penny Nickels' name struck me as a fantastic stage name. I was sure she had made it up—as I had also made names for myself from time to time. **We were** very open and honest with each other, **sharing secrets**, yet I never could get her to tell me her birth name. I called her Penny Laine, named after "Penny Lane," and joked that it would be her name if she and my friend, Denny Laine, ever married.

Now, before telling you the story about Penny and that set of girls, I should write about Denny. The name Denny Laine was also self-invented. He was born Brian Frederick Arthur Hines. His first alias, Johnny Dean, was a persona that Denny used for his first band, Johnny Dean & the Dominators. "Johnny" was eleven years old when he started that band back in Birmingham, England. The band had considerable natural musical talent that developed as he did. The Senators, another Birmingham group of kids, needed a lead vocal, but already had an interesting sound. Brian, then "Johnny Dean," convinced that young band to be his new backing group. It was for that band that he adopted the persona, Denny Laine. Now, the Senators became the Diplomats. That was back in September 1962.

Everyone in that band had considerable talent, and some **made it big.** They felt they were on the verge of stardom when promised a recording contract. Nonetheless, no record ever materialized. Even though they had a good sound, they lacked stage presence. Then came Nicky James, who, after a realistic Elvis impersonation, joined the Diplomats, performing as "Nicky James with Denny Laine and the Diplomats." That impersonator completely changed the band, and several years later inspired me, to perform as Paul doing a Presley voice with "Lady Madonna." I was not imitating Elvis but was originally inspired by Nicky's Elvis imitation—or the idea of an impersonator changing a band.

NOTE: William is being coy about his involvement with Denny Laine and the Diplomats, wanting readers to figure it out for themselves. He speaks of that band as if detached from it, but then explains how the addition of Nicky James changed things, and how it inspired him to use an "Elvis-type" voice for "Lady Madonna." For those who miss that clue, he becomes more obvious. However, he sees his work with the Diplomats, and the band before it, as training exercises, not as accomplishments. They were part of his education, not something to list on a resume.

William's ability to mimic the style and voices of other musicians is part of why his music is so versatile, and why it has such a wide appeal. Tapping into Elvis's energy for "Lady Madonna" was not to have his fans recognize the Elvis influence but was calculated to transfer Elvis's followers to the new king. That use of his energy was less flagrant than the Lennon-McCartney writing team's earlier use of Elvis lyrics. Elvis sang, "I'd rather see you dead, little girl / Than to be with another man" ("Baby, Let's Play House") well before John sang those lines in "Run for Your Life."

ELVIS PRESLEY

"BABY LET'S PLAY HOUSE"
SPANKOX RE:VERSION

Ultimately, the high point for Denny Laine and the Diplomats was when they opened a concert one night for the Beatles at the Plaza Ballroom in Old Hill. Some "Paul is Dead" investigators will likely tell you **I played then**, not **as** the Beatles' Paul McCartney, but as The Diplomats' **Phil Ackrill.** Everyone ought to consider this question, "If I were Phil, why wouldn't I admit it now?" He was a dandy singer and guitar player, and a fine person. Who would this Bill rather have been than Phil?

Their band was big in Birmingham but without a distinct sound to take them far beyond that part of England. The band needed a change. Although it made many recordings—intentionally enough for an album—none were released. As I write this memo for the book, I am thinking about buying them now and releasing them in a vintage collection when this book stirs enough interest. Denny, what do you think? **Let's reminisce about** the days of our "Silly Willy with **Phil**ly Band." Could be!

The Diplomats went on without Denny in 1964 when Michael Pinder and Ray Thomas recruited him to start The Moody Blues with them. They had a good thing started there before Denny moved on to invent his Electric String Band, which laid the foundation for what band-mates and others would nearly resurrect as ELO (Electric Light Orchestra).

By that time, I think Denny joined Balls. I now go on and on about Denny because he introduced me to Paul, and also connected me to Brian Epstein. As Linda and I finished our *Ram* album and were ready to take it on tour, I called on my old friend. I said, "Denny, how'd you like to go on tour to sing backup for me for a change? I want you to come along and play your guitars." It felt good playing with him again after all these years. Linda and I considered the advantages of making Denny a permanent part of our family business. The three of us formed Wings. Linda was never the superstar that **I was meant to** be but did have quite a good **understand**ing of the work, and was an equal. The band's name referred to Paul's death. I had **Paul's broken wings** and learned to fly. With the new band, all three of us were flying with his Wings. Leaving the Beatles and growing Wings, the three-winged beast began where the four-headed beast ended. I will get to the seven heads on that four-headed beast in "Seven in Three" (chapter 41).

Having left the Moody Blues on good terms, Denny remained in the same circle of influence. Early on, as their band took off, Brian Epstein (the Beatles' manager) signed The Moody Blues. They got to be close friends with the Beatles, touring together, frequenting the same clubs, and going regularly to the same parties. Although Denny left the Moody Blues weeks before Paul died, he still ended up at many of the same parties. I had gone with Denny to some of those parties back in 1965 where **I saw the Beatles**, Rolling Stones, Jane, and several other **big** celebrities. Yet, I did not feel welcome in their **circles.** One night at the 1965 spring celebration, Paul, Keith Moon, and two or three inebriated women were laughing about something when one of the girls leaned back and tripped right next to me. **When I helped** the pretty girl up, Denny introduced me to **Paul** and Keith. Paul's face turned ghostly pale. Horrified, **he rushed away.** Later that same night, Keith apologetically said that Paul had seen my face in a dream but did not realize that it was me until that night.

On 6 November 1966, in Los Angeles, Emily Little had a dream of two musicians who looked very much alike. The first one died. The second one there said the death was the first's new birth. Emily recognized Paul, whom she had met in Laurel Canyon, Los Angeles, between Beatles concerts. Paul remarked, "If you don't believe I'm dead, call John. He's already got my replacement."

It was 9 November when she reached John at my home by telephone. John picked it up but did not say much. "Yes, this is John. . . . How did you . . ." He shook his head and handed me the phone receiver.

"This is Penny Nickels' friend in California. She wants to talk to the new Paul."

"How could that be?" I asked, "Who is that?" I was confused.

"Emily," he said. "Paul's giraffe friend that we met on tour in L.A."

"She's tall?" I asked, holding my hand over the mouthpiece.

Though John shook his head, he said nothing. I answered the phone. "Yeah?"

"Are you him?" she asked. "This is Emily Little. Are you him?"

"That depends. Who are you talking about?" I knew but resented her knowing that I did.

Emily answered, "You're Paul's replacement. I

286

can tell. He told me they found you. You even sound a little like him. Not a whole lot, but a little. Enough, I guess. Keep talking."

"Paul told you about me?" I asked. I did not see how that was possible.

"And Parker," she said. "Parker knows about it too. We've been dreaming of Paul, but none of us understood what it meant until he told me in a dream that you took his place."

"Look," I said, "if you care anything for Paul, and it sounds like you do, you'll never breathe a word of this to anyone."

"It's just horrible that it happened but in a strange way, exciting too. When he was here, he felt it coming. We thought Paul was joking. It is sad that it happened, but great too."

She went on to say that she would come to meet me, but that she could not yet take off work. She would stay at Penny's flat in London from the afternoon of February 15th until the 17th.

She was surprisingly pleasant. Although Emily's kindness was nothing romantic, as she had a blue-eyed love in California, we had a great time. Penny introduced her to Denny that Friday. We had lunch. Emily said she would be back that spring, but never returned. She promised to help me garden. Until Linda ended my gallivanting, I hoped Emily would get back here someday and maybe turn in that direction. What was the most amazing to me about her was her psychic power. She could telepathically call a specific cat to her lap from another room. I did not believe it until I saw it. At Penny's flat, sitting on her bed, I whispered to Emily which cat should come. Without saying a word, she would think it, and that specific cat came right to her.

Right then, I knew I could psychically connect to Emily. Up until that time, it was the most outstanding display of telepathy I had seen. I could convey some simple thoughts to her. It worked well until she left. Then we quickly lost our magical link.

I tried sending her messages later but could never restore the psychic connection. She ceased listening to me, preferring to tune in to her love down in the States, I am sure. Nonetheless, it was all right with me. Once I filled Paul's position, the girls stood in line to see me. I never had trouble getting any dates. I just missed Emily's friendship.

About six girls called that October/November, each of them thinking that they were something special to Paul, and likely were. When Emily flew back to the States, never again to return, Penny and I remained friends, making me miss Emily more.

On 17 February, after Em left, and after a stop for dinner, I hit the studio. I **worked** on "Being for the Benefit of Mr. Kite," **for** *Sgt. Pepper's.* That poster-inspired piece presented the **superficiality** of our lonely-hearted life. I played bass and lead on the song from 7:00 that evening until 3:00 am. George Martin played the harmonium. John did vocals.

Cutting back to Em's call now, on 9 November, I told John that she said she and Penny would come over to meet me in February. Before that call, John had played "Strawberry Fields" for me and had very strongly encouraged me to prepare to record "When I'm Sixty-Four." Until then, John and Paul each always sang lead on one of the two songs they released on each single. To fill the B-side, I would record Paul's "When I'm Sixty-Four" as soon as John finished his "Strawberry Fields." I said we could each record our own new song for the single.

After Emily's call and mention of Penny, John dealt me an offer. He told me that I should record a song tying me to **Paul**'s past and that Paul, more than a year before, **had mentioned** in an interview that he might write **a song called "Penny Lane."** He had said he liked the poetic sound of those words. That interview occurred on 1 November 1965 during a break from taping *The Music of Lennon & McCartney*, a program airing on 17 December 1965.

Trying to make good on his word, Paul started working on the song, but never got far with it before deciding to scrap it. John told me I could finish writing the song, sing lead on it, and call it mine enough. John had helped Paul with what little had been put together and sang that much. They wrote about a fifth of the lyrics that ended up in the finished song. Much of that fifth, it appeared to me, did not come from Paul. John seemed to recall the gist of it but ad-libbed his own words.

"Penny Lane," as Paul first knew it, was a bus roundabout in Liverpool. As I wrote "Penny Lane," after hearing the parts John recalled or invented, I imagined how Paul would then remember it. For us to get the right effect, it would be from the dead man's perspective. Since Paul said it was poetic, I looked over "Fern Hill," a poem by Dylan Thomas. I appreciated his quaint picturesque descriptions of childhood under the apple boughs and starry sky, his charming trails with daisies and barley, his singing on

289

his farm, and so on. Having become Paul, **I** adopted Liverpool as if my own heritage. I **sought** to collect every bit of it much like Dylan **Thomas** had recalled Fern Hill. I wanted nostalgic memories of the place captured in my head for Paul, and **to show the world** that I, as though I were Paul, treasure **all of these** kinds of memories of Liverpool. All of these **things** in the song would give me Liverpudlian roots.

Each part of "Penny Lane" was based on what we saw when John showed me the place. I naturally did embellishments but based it on our experience. We saw a barbershop but would not stop there to use it. John's hair was already too short by then. Although, if we allowed it, we bet the barber would post our pictures on the wall and advertise for all to see that he was the big champion barber who had cut off a Beatle mop-top! We laughed over that would-be barber hero. I imagined the barber taking pictures next of every haircut he ever did, "of every head he's

NOTE: In retrospect, it is difficult to remember or comprehend the prevailing narrow-minded intolerance of 1964 when the Beatles were launched on the unsuspecting American public. The fact that we can scarcely imagine it now is a testament to that social engineering success.

The Beatles' "mop-top" haircuts, along with other marks of rebellion, were intended to offend the older generation. It worked. The elders rejected the new idols, driving the youth to reject their would-be stabilizing elders. By dividing the generations, freeing the world of their nourishing roots, those targeted were free to discover and embrace the artificially generated pro-drug youth movement that was taught to not trust anyone over thirty—even though those who set up the scheme were considerably older.

The Beatles were conservative enough for wide acceptance by all except the squares who were seen as too old to know anything. Bands immediately followed with more blatant rebellion and with so much longer hair that the Beatles' original mop-tops were soon seen as conservative.

In the text, William jokingly laughs at the idea of the Penny Lane barber cutting the Beatles' hair. Actually, their original mop-tops were kept neatly trimmed. Their meticulously controlled image required regular haircuts. For the sake of the song, they did each receive a haircut from that barber who did indeed display their photographs. However, the barber did not, as William's joke suggested, violate their intended image.

had the pleasure to have known," and then proudly going around showing off his fine handiwork. There is a bank on the corner. **I imagined that** banker in Paul's motorcar. **Paul's wealth was** safe in my bank account. That banker never wore **a Mac.** I really was wearing a Mac since it was raining, but was also wearing Mac, meaning McCartney. I was both literally and figuratively doing what Paul's banker would never be able to do. That is why the children secretly laugh at him. The banker feels important because he handles the money but is just another hard-working stiff. Merely because I wear the Mac now, I get more money than his bank.

Everywhere I went with John, he filled me in on the local humor. I do not know how much of it had to do with Liverpool, and how much was a mere reflection of John and Paul's own language from a while back when they were juvenile delinquents. However, two of John's "Liverpool obscenities" did make it into the song. One was "finger pie." John joked that the Beatles were "Four of fish and finger pie," having our fingers in the women. We also refer to male anatomy with the "fireman" who "likes to keep his fire engine clean." I thought this Liverpool smut would convince the local lads that I was one of them. It did not—and no one else got it. That Liverpool connection failed.

Ridiculously, the entire song flaunted a fully false vision of Liverpool to all the locals who knew the place. I had been there and knew better but tried to fancify Merseyside as a magical Beatles land. Everyone else knew better. The song was a flop here: the Beatles' first single in four years that did not hit the top of the British charts. It did, as I said, hit the top in the United States, but not here where they knew the place. It worked in America because they knew even less of Liverpool than I did.

I also remember girls calling about Paul from Wales, Germany, Spain, California, Alberta, and Tarsus. (Just kidding about Tarsus. It is an old Paul joke.) While we kept the big secret, **Paul had** to have fun. Fortunately, none of **his friends** betrayed him. Those who did talk were not friends.

It occurred to me eventually (after locals, who disliked the place, scoffed at "Penny Lane") that maybe it would have sold better in England if I had

NOTE: Saul of Tarsus, a Roman Pharisee who becomes known as Paul the Apostle, begins with an urgency to eradicate Christianity. He first appears in the Bible as a young man at the stoning of Stephen (Acts 7:58). As an adult, he captures and transports Christians to have them killed; until, one day in Damascus, he arrives with an amazing story. Rather than picking up Christian prisoners as expected, he reports having miraculously become a disciple of Jesus (9:1-9; 22:3-11).

If Saul was truthful, Jesus, now resurrected, worked through him to change and expand Christianity. However, not all Christians were convinced. When he went to Jerusalem, for example, the disciples were all afraid and did not believe him (9:26). That zealous Pharisee had already shown that he could not be trusted and that he would destroy Christianity if possible. After years of making Christian reforms, Saul/Paul, like a double agent, still called himself a Pharisee when it suited him: "Brothers, I am a Pharisee" (23:6).

In Christian Paulism, Paul (who eventually lost his head) built upon the gospels, mixing Christianity with concepts of other religions to reach a wider audience. Much of his New Testament writing is brilliant. Nonetheless, some critics argue, however impressive it may be, it is not Christian. Pauline Christianity, consisting of Biblical Christian doctrine that Jesus did not teach, is seen by some as a corruption of true Christianity. Those changes paved the way for Satanism and other infusions built upon Roman paganism.

New Age Paulism, with its own Paul (whose head was "wounded to death"), breaks the stronghold of modern Christianity, replacing it with a modern pagan movement. When modern Paulism began, pagans were statistically insignificant in what were termed "Christian nations." Now, as Christianity shrinks, neopaganism (especially witchcraft) is on the rise to be as forever mainstream.

292

made up a street name instead of borrowing one. If I had called it "Donna Lane," it would have been as magically ethereal here as in the States—and the girl slain and "lain" to rest could have been mentioned.

After I knew my soulmate, I realized that if I had sung, "Melinda Lane," those with ears could have broken the simple code that Melinda means "My Linda" just as I sang Madonna to represent "Macca's Donna." It would have worked. My Linda Lane is in my ears and in my eyes so that **all I see and hear is Linda**—or her lane. It would have a nice meaning with various overtones depending on what people can bring to it. Penny, the girl, never did mean anything to me. She was just a girl I met who had a name like Denny. On the other hand, in all my life, no one has ever filled my heart, mind, soul, and imagination as did my lovely Linda.

31

"High Brow"

Going from the Æon of Osiris to the Æon of Horus,
the patriarchal systems of Osiris must fail. Religions
and nations must adapt or lose their power to interfere.

Paul's right eyebrow was a real pain in the forehead for me. When I started this act, it was an absurdly big deal to John. He insisted that I not sing without raising my right eyebrow. When lifting up my left eyebrow, he would hassle me about it. Naturally, **I** was obliged in light of who **I am** and learned to **do** it. Yet, activating the Eye of **Ra** or of **Horus** motivated him less than the chance to irritate me. He claimed it mattered to him because it

NOTE: Aleister Crowley's, *The Book of the Law*, channeled from Aiwass, along with its corresponding teachings, is the primary basis for the spiritual-political framework of the "Æon of Horus" in the Age of Aquarius. As with every new era, the soul of Horus would return embodied as a new Messiah. Like the magi following the Star of Bethlehem, Crowley and his magickal followers sought the incarnations of Osiris and Horus who would be born of the right families, in the right places, on the right dates, and with other signs, including in their bodies, such as Paul's high brow. The illuminated were posed to recognize Paul (in William) as Horus' modern incarnation.

With added brain elements and other design variations, the Eye of Horus, or Ra, is the Eye of Providence, or All-Seeing Eye. In some traditions, the eye with rays is a phallic emanation. In Masonry, the eye usually has semi-circular glory (emanation) below it or is enclosed by a triangle or pyramid.

In Paul, we see both. The semi-circular glory below the eye is formed by his semi-circular lower eyelashes, complete with rays. The pyramid's upper lines are formed by his high-bending eyebrow, forming the modern Eye of Illumination, which also resembles the Eye of Horus mirrored vertically. The Eye of Paul Pyramid (joining text lines to footnotes) was inspired by the Eye of Paul and the Eye of Horus.

Although Thoth restored the eye that Set destroyed, now an ocular prosthesis would suffice.

294

mattered to those who gave me that role. I must never sing as Paul without raising my right eyebrow. It was fine to raise both. The right just had to be included. It could not be outdone by the left, just as the sun cannot outshine the moon. I could never neglect the highbrow mark of Paul on my forehead even though my forehead was stiff and sore for months. I had to pay my dues with repetitions of right eyebrow lifting. If **you know** that's easy, you should try it sometime. **Sit** there for an hour at a time doing nothing else, **just** repetitions of working forehead muscles. It **ain't easy.** I would go back and forth: raising my right eyebrow over and over again, then raising and dropping both of them again and again. If you do this exercise right, repeatedly pushing yourself, you will understand.

Although welcoming any new awareness from the eternal Eye of Paul activation and its associated

NOTE: The All-Seeing Eye of God comforts some but unnerves others. It reminds Freemasons of the Great Architect of the Universe watching over us. On the other hand, the network uses data gathered from governments and other corporations.

License plate readers can photograph over 100,000 plates per hour recording the time and place of each passing vehicle. Devices with GPS are also tracked with locations logged.

Satellite imaging and surveillance cameras use facial recognition technology to supply searchable databases. Our Internet searches, purchases, clicks, posts, and comments dictate what information and products to market to whom, informing companies how to manipulate each human specifically. When computers are connected to the Internet, everything on our screens can be seen and analyzed by others. Cameras and microphones are activated remotely to spy on us. Internet searches, social media posts, clicks, likes, comments, phone calls, text messages, and purchases are recorded, analyzed, sold, and exploited worldwide.

Some schemers intend to have nearly everyone tracked and controlled by self-assembling graphene nanoparticles integrated with the human nervous system. Such cyborg brains will have the convenience of interfacing with microdevices everywhere that communicate with each other sending personal data that may be exploited.

The All-Seeing Eye reminds us of the cute Beatle. Yet, in light of how each human's file is gathered and beamed about for control and commercial purposes, let the great eye in the sky also remind us that our illuminated Big Brother is watching us.

mystical benefits, my upper face hurt for the first horrendous months. Try exercising yours for an hour. You may have empathetic pain for days. It builds enormously strong muscles, or, at least strong facial muscles. The standard "Paul is Dead" legend about it was that I had surgery to look like Paul. Well, I had facial surgery too, but not as fully as is described. Working eyebrow muscles while trying to heal was hard. I paid my dues to sing Paul clues.

Whenever **we wrote**, we always wanted double or triple **layers of** meanings in our lyrics. Once I had **lines** about John's insistence that I keep my eyebrow up. John hated that song because its double entendre suggested some sexual inadequacy, which was contrary to the intended Beatle image. Having never had to worry about falling short in that way, I just thought it was funny. I still do, which is precisely why I don't mind sharing it here. The lines were, "Well, she said I'd let her down now if I didn't keep it up. So, I gave her my new number, saying, I think you're in luck." That "she" was John. He and I both enjoyed adding material to our songs about each other that we made to sound as though we were singing to our lost or new loves. That was common for us and others.

Some of the lyrics of our best songs we wrote or gathered that way. I still have rough tracks of those "High Brow" lyrics. I had considered making it a Bonzos song. However, with John's additions to it, I decided to wait and work it into a future Beatles release. If I do, I'll re-work it. I get off on revisions.

I inherited quite a bit of material with John, and some tracks of Paul before me. I will (or I, Billy) keep releasing more tracks now and again, whenever I feel the time is right. I have become the guardian of the treasure house. I am the core of the apple. Seeds of fresh new Beatle life can spring from me at any moment, and often do.

Every time I sing now, I lift a high brow to Paul just as you might lift a glass of wine to him. Now, doing it feels natural. I learned **to** automatically lower them to sing as Vivian, and to **push them up** to sing as Paul. Originally, though, it **was an effort** and frustration to me, and also to John. **At first**, John bothered me about it to no end. It did not matter if we were singing to learn a new song, or if we were recording, or whatever we were doing. If he ever caught me singing with a relaxed forehead, he ordered me to "sing right." He complained that I bossed him around too much. Maybe I did. But he was ridiculous about this whole "eyebrow of Paul" mark on my forehead. No one ever knew how terribly irritating John could be to me. It was not something we shared publicly. He was far more open about me being much too bossy even though he was at the same time being a pain in my head.

Here's to Paul: "I always lift my eyebrow to you." It has become so much a part of me that I probably could not sing with a relaxed forehead now even if I wanted to. Besides, it would be a mockery to cut Paul out now, might just jinx my whole musical career.

Notice how different my eyebrows look when I sing as Paul from when I sang as Vivian Stanshall. I only sing with my eyebrows pushed up for Paul, and only sing with them pushed firmly down for Vivian. That distinction gives each their own look. More than Viv's fake teeth and latex, eyebrows changed the appearances, making each distinct. However, both are unnatural to me. When I am interviewed or on stage as **Paul**, I still keep it up. It is my disguise.

Brian Epstein **had** received training in such things. Very subtle mannerism **differences** make a persona seem unique. The subconscious mind is aware and impressed by such details that most of us never notice consciously. An eyebrow pencil made Vivian's brows look thicker also, making them seem heavier on the face, the exact opposite of Paul's.

32

"The Parting on the Left Is Now . . . on the Right."

Lefties stand out all right. Not only did I have to learn to play all of Paul's guitars left-handed, but everyone tried to get me to part my hair on the left side as Paul had done his whole life. The problem for my hair is that it naturally parts on the right.

Unless I paste it down, my hair naturally falls in the other direction. That is why all of the pictures of Paul from his early childhood up until his death in September 1966, has his hair parted on his left, and why from that date until now my hair is always seen parted on the right. Even **when** it is not combed at all, it naturally goes **that** way.

Right off, my biggest **challenge was** to learn to play the bass backward, it **being** Paul's instrument. I also had to learn to play **Paul**'s other instruments that way. Once I could play it **like that, I still had** to get it to my lap backward. I had **to get into the habit** of picking it up backward. You would understand if you have played for any length of time. You pick up a guitar and play. After a while, you no longer have to think about it. It is automatic.

299

With that automacy, I have sometimes forgotten. Memory is in the muscles. **The body** unites with it. Imagine how unnatural it **would** be to all of a sudden have to pick up a guitar and **hold it** wholly backward, and then to play it entirely **backward**. It is kind of like playing the piano while facing away from the keys. Some people have learned **to play** it with their hands behind their back. I do it poorly. However proficient one may be, it does not feel normal. Even if you were quite good at it, it is not the way you would normally approach the piano or guitar unless you switched it deliberately.

Sometimes when I am talking, or when anything is on my mind other than remembering how to pick it up, I reach for it forgetting to pick it up backward. Then there is the awkward moment of switching the guitar to the other hand. Imagine how ridiculous I have felt, looking as though I did not know how to pick up my instrument!

At first, whenever **I** composed, I played right-handed. I also always **played** right-handed when I recorded alone. With **Paul's bass** rewired for the lefty, I would **sometimes** go back and forth, doing each part to mastery right-handed before learning it left-handed. Still, right-handed feels right.

Even in the music video for "Penny Lane," my first single, I reach to pick up my guitar to play it right-handed, then quickly correct myself to hold it in the backward position. I have been caught playing the guitar right-handed from time to time. I would already be playing it when someone would stop in on me, but not usually while they held cameras.

Usually, when I knew I was being filmed, I remembered, but not always. 50 minutes into *the Beatles Anthology 7: June '67 to July '68,* for example, I am playing guitar right-handed. I could have edited it out, but do not care anymore. It is a mistake I still make now and then. When I am alone, especially when I am composing a song, it is still easier to play right-handed. That has never changed. For my public performances, I still make myself learn to play them left-handed. However, after all these decades, it is still extra work.

By filling in for someone left-handed, handedness issues surface automatically from muscle memory. For example, when I smoked [I have quit several times], photographs showed me holding my cigarettes in my right hand and showed **Paul** usually holding them in his left. That switch **was** conscious on *Abbey Road,* especially since **my** cigarette, the cancer stick, or coughin' nail is a **coffin nail.** I became more vocal about cancer sticks as coffin nails since Linda and George both died of cancer. For Linda, natural

NOTE: William yearned to reveal the switch, but also had strong incentives to maintain plausible deniability. He participated in elaborate disclosure measures, as well as in self-protective counter-measures. Like writing a mystery novel, the strategy is to present several bits of solid information, along with one bit that can be discredited, maintaining the uncertainty that guides readers to flip-flop opinions. Occasional false clues set up a strawman to be blown down to discredit the real intel.

For example, after William was filmed playing the guitar left-handed, he had the negative flipped to make it appear that someone caught him playing right-handed. He then drew attention to it to have PID interpreters take notice. When enough people use the footage to prove that he is right-handed, others will discover that the film had been flipped, thus discrediting the PID camp, maintaining balance with PIA fans, to whom he pretends that he had no knowledge of the deception in the first place.

Making clues and counter clues has the added benefit of keeping this important story alive. If Paul's replacement had been announced in 1966, the world would have moved on. All would have mourned but welcomed "Billy Shears" as more than a fantasy. Until the matter is settled once and for all, the energy surrounding it cannot rest. This is yet one more way that Paul lives on.

In George's honor, a memorial tree was planted in Griffith Park, Los Angeles. The pine was later destroyed by **beetles**. It was replaced by a look-alike, but the height is not right.

estrogen in her breasts, not cigarettes, got her cancer going. However, **smoking is** what killed George. Now with cancer being **a plague** on the world, I sometimes wish I had never held cigarettes at all when photographers have been present. That is not an image I want to promote to the world anymore. Having seen what cancer can do, even to a strong, healthy, and beautiful woman, I realize there is not enough good that can come of cigarettes to make

NOTE: All poisons are addictive. All addictions require an element of harm. Since the smoke of organic non-GMO tobacco is noncarcinogenic, and not otherwise harmful enough to be highly addictive, most commercially successful tobacco cigarette companies intentionally lace their products with poisons.

Consumers may buy the single ingredient of tobacco, roll their own cigars or cigarettes, and smoke them with much less harm than would come from most pre-prepared cigarettes. Some smokers mix tobacco with healthful herbs such as marijuana. Blunts from organic plants should always be preferred over carcinogenic cigars or cigarettes.

According to the American Lung Association, most commercial cigarettes contain approximately 600 ingredients. When burned, cigarettes create more than 7,000 chemicals. 69 of these chemicals are known to cause cancer.

Many of these chemicals are also found in consumer products that have warning labels—such as rat poison. While the public is warned about the danger of the poisons in such products, there is no such warning for the carcinogens and other toxins in tobacco smoke.

For increased profits, many corporations pay to make laws that are against the common good. Just as Big Pharma blocks legalizing competing healing herbs, cigarette companies are not blocked from adding poisons including:

Acetone—found in nail polish remover
Acetic acid—an ingredient in hair dye
Ammonia—a common household cleaner
Arsenic—used in rat poison
Benzene—found in rubber cement and gasoline
Butane—used in lighter fluid (now also found in many vape cartridges)
Cadmium—active component in battery acid
Carbon monoxide—released in car exhaust fumes
Formaldehyde—embalming fluid (also produced by vaping when cutting agents such as PEGs and MCT have been used to liquefy THC concentrates)
Hexamine—found in barbecue lighter fluid
Lead—used in batteries
Naphthalene—an ingredient in mothballs
Methanol—a main component in rocket fuel
Toluene—used to manufacture paint.

However loyal you have been to your favorite cigarette brand, are they okay with killing you?

"The Parting on the Left Is Now . . . on the Right."

Anyone can quit smoking. Billy has done it lots of times.

them okay. Nevertheless, as the photos show, **Paul** never smoked with his right hand; I never **smoked** with my left. I did try left-handed smoking, **but** it was uncomfortably awkward. Later, when my identity was not questioned, it occurred to me **that** my right-handedness was a fine Paul clue. I **was** glad to see my smoking pictures back **then** when I was not yet concerned about promoting cancer and heart disease. I enjoyed giving that clue.

Right-handedness became an issue in the press just two years ago when someone first said, based on my signature, I seemed to be right-handed. They claimed that since Paul was left-handed, I could not be him. It mattered because of a legal document that I had to sign regarding a paternity suit in Germany. The story was in the *Bild* (formerly *Bild-Zeitung*), which is still the best-selling newspaper in Europe and has the sixth-largest circulation in the world. Many people read about it and then forgot.

Making a further deal of my handwriting, some people compared my signature (which they say looks right-handed) in the eighties with Paul's on display in the Hamburger Beatles Museum from the sixties. I, they say, do not have a comparable signature. While it is true that I practiced his signature, going over it repeatedly before signing checks and documents for Paul in September 1966, I have since then drifted to a more creative signature. My left-handed writing is not natural enough for it to look right. But even "if I'm wrong [left], I'm right where I belong" ("Fixing a Hole").

NOTE: Adding confusion, some photographers had Paul pose with a cigarette in his right hand.

303

With the line breaks where I put them in that part of the song, I hid what I was saying. I will tell you how to read it: "It really doesn't matter if I'm wrong" says it is okay if I'm the wrong guy, or if I'm wrong to entertain as though I were Paul. "I'm right where I belong. I'm right where I belong." Do you see how the right punctuation unlocks the message? I am saying, "Even if I'm the wrong guy, this is where I belong."

Even after **I joined** the Beatles, I still enjoyed joining **the fun comedy** of The Bonzo Dog Band. I wore such distinctive disguises that when a conflict kept me from performing with them, it was easy to be away providing that I loaned them a gorilla suit. I did not have to loan out my latex noses and ears. Even after Vivian "died" to give me more time with Linda, others wore my Vivian costume now and then.

Like those of many bands, members of the Who were all close friends of the Beatles, especially two of them: Pete Townshend and Keith Moon. Through that connection, the Who all became the Bonzos' new friends when I joined the Beatles. So much so, we decided to tour together. The Bonzo Dog Band got each audience warmed up with musical laughter; then the Who put on the main show.

In the years before I became friends with the Who, **Linda had already gotten to know** them, and **many other celebrities,** through her photography. **They were all good friends.** Like Donovan and the Rolling Stones, the Who also made a few fine Paul songs. My favorite one ties into this chapter by including a line about our differing hair: "The parting on the left / Is now the parting on the right." Going on, still about hair, the next line refers to the instant mustaches on *Sgt. Pepper's,* and to the beard hiding my face later. "And the beards [mustaches] have all grown longer overnight."

That song, "Won't Get Fooled Again," recognizes our "Revolution," revolving Pauls, as leading to the worldwide political upheaval. Pete calls it a "new revolution." John tried to depict the same chaos of having that revolution in his "Revolution 9." Pete refers to it saying, "**We'll be fighting** in the streets." Everyone is all up in arms **about** it, all alarmed. That is the way with revolutions. **Paul** is the *Revolver.*

Recognizing *Sgt. Pepper's* role in changing the world, setting a new drug-friendly moral code, Pete explains that part of the worldwide agenda. "And the morals that they worship will be gone." The same institutions that supported the Beatles and opened media doors for us furthered their NWO agendas by publicly denouncing us—turning the good guys bad. "And the men who spurred us on [those with EMI connections to Tavistock] Sit in judgment of all wrong / They decide, and the shotgun sings the song." Letting them call the shots, they privately supported us while publicly villainizing us for further division of generations, breaking down the family to unravel society's fabric in preparation for the new order with the NWO constitution—and my deal.

With a double meaning, Pete refers to both the government change and the new constitution of

NOTE: Understanding Paul's demise prepares the initiated for what is ahead. It is not enough to know that Paul was replaced but to understand its part in the spiritual and social revolution in preparation for the worldwide political transformation. There will be "fighting in the street" to establish the new world constitution. When the political transformation is complete, all will embrace the new religion, which is a rebranded restoration of the old.

"We shall have world government, whether or not we like it. The question is only whether world government will be achieved by consent or by conquest." ~ James Warburg

305

the Beatles who revolved Pauls to make that change. With regard, he says, "I'll tip my hat to the new [world] constitution / Take a bow for the new revolution."

Insiders, including Pete, **just** "**Smile and** grin at the change all around me." They don't **say** anything. They just quietly enjoy being aware of **it**. The next lines are of me ("another day") from my perspective having to play Paul's ("Yesterday's") bass guitar. I "Pick up my guitar and play / Just like yesterday." That bit is of me learning to play Paul's left-handed bass just like Paul. It can be generalized, as John had put it, "Nothing has changed it's still the same." Then I, or Pete, pray that we, the whole world, are not ever fooled that way again. "And I'll get on my knees and pray / We don't get fooled again."

Being around when Paul was having his death dreams, dying all the time, trying desperately to work everything out before he died, Pete also had early warning. "Change it had to come / We knew it all along." The world's values, toppled by *Sgt. Pepper's,* were liberating to our generation, and would not have taken place if not for a look-alike. "We were liberated from the fall [Paul's death] that's all / But the world looks just the same /And history ain't changed / 'Cause the banners, they all flown in the last war." Everything looks the same as before our revolution. As a dual meaning, he says the Vietnam War was the same as the Korean War that went before it. Both had the banners of Communist and Anti-Communist.

"I'll move myself and my family aside" was of me giving up my life and loved ones to take this role. My connection to Paul, having two Pauls in one flesh, makes my combined self only half-alive.

Reaching toward Paul in the sky, I thankfully hold up my contract. "If we happen to be left half alive / I'll get all my papers and smile at the sky" knowing that fans, having been hypnotized by our **music**, will go on as if I'm Paul. "For I know that the **hypnotized** never lie / Do ya?" Hypnotized, they swear I am **Paul**.

Here again, with the Paul revolution, there does not appear to be any change. "There's nothing in the street / Looks any different to me." Our slogans have changed even though we use the same Beatles banner. The love songs have been replaced by Paul's goodbye. "The slogans are replaced, by-the-bye." Under our old slogans, it was "She loves you, yeah, yeah, yeah." Now he screams, "Yeaaaaaaaaaah!"

The song's last lines use one of our double audio track tricks. They sing, "Meet the new boss / Same as the old boss." On one level, it says once again that everything is still the same. Subconsciously you may have also picked up on another meaning.

"Won't Get Fooled Again" was originally much longer than the heavily edited single version. The Who recorded it in the Rolling Stones Mobile Studio early in the spring of 1971. They overdubbed the last line at a lower volume with the same words except for the last one that says "Paul." When you hear "Meet the new boss / Same as the old boss," listen to it carefully to hear, "Meet the new boss / Same as the old Paul." Since the brain can only process one thing at a time, it subconsciously selects the most reasonable message, favoring expected lines over unexpected overdubbed messages. That is an advantage of overdubbing.

307

The "Paul is Dead" revelation of 1969, which failed to reach general acceptance, followed by me ending the band in 1970, made it time for Pete to tell the story in 1971. In his song's final couplet, he lets the world in on two of our secrets. The first was that Paul died. **The second** was that I, looking like Paul, **became the new Beatle boss.** "Meet the new boss / Same as the old Paul." If you listen intending to hear "Paul," you will likely hear it, but will also hear the final "s" sound of "boss," making the word unintentionally sound like "Pauls." Listen for "Meet the new boss / Same as the old Pauls."

Replacing Paul was seen as a revolution. He was the revolver. By replacing Paul, I inherited him, which further empowered the social engineers to put their revolution of guided consciousness into force to prepare for their new age with the New World Order. Having the Beatles evolve helped **the world** to evolve with us. The world **was prepared for the new constitution**. "You say you want a revolution. . . . We all want to change the world."

Since you are going to run to the Internet now to see that Paul's hair parting on the left is switched in every picture past his death on 11 September 1966 to my hair parting on the right, here is some even harder evidence for you to find while you are at it. Once you know what to look for, the switch is obvious.

My facial injections and other alterations gave me a Paulish look. Still, one change that I did not make, you did not seem to notice. Human earlobes come in two basic styles. Based on one's genetic dominance, earlobes are either both detached, hanging free from the head, like you can see mine are; or they are both attached, joined to the head, like Paul's.

With the ease of Internet image searches, you really do not have to look very long or hard to find photographs to contrast me with Paul. You may see that in September 1966, Paul suddenly switches from attached to detached earlobes.

Here is yet another ear clue. Besides the fact that his are attached, and mine are not, while you are at it, also notice that our ears are of entirely different shapes. Paul's ears were more rounded than mine and popped out. Mine are more interestingly shaped. You can consult **Paul McCartney**'s images. It is quite easy to see that he **has different ears.** He also has darker eyes—and more space between them.

NOTE: Paul's eyes fluctuated from light brown to dark brown. William's hazel eyes fluctuate from practically green to almost as dark as Paul's when Paul's are at their lightest.

Billy says Eye Yoga saved him from needing a reading glass.

33

"Hey Jude"

In a séance one night in mid-November 1966, I abruptly spoke to me in Paul's voice. John and others heard me utter, "Take this, brother. May it serve you well." John quoted those lines in "Revolution 9." Again, in "Cry Baby Cry," I sing, "Brother can you take me back?" It ties into "Hey Jude" and others.

Doing the Paul role right was going to take time, partly because **I was** driven to be certain that I would always do it **better than he** would have. He and the others would go record a few takes of songs, and go home, leaving the rest up to George Martin and others. That was never how I did things. It still is not. In October 1966, Brian Epstein told me that it was time to record an album, or a song as a single, for the Christmas market. I told him that my first Beatles record would surely be of far greater quality than that. It would take some time. We released our first single in February.

For two weeks, Brian tried repeatedly to persuade me, telling me that it is how all of their records had been done. I said, "That was John's band, this is my band. We do things differently."

On 31 October, in the morning, he met with EMI and broke the news that there would be no new material for Christmas. This report was entirely unacceptable to EMI, which stood to lose significant profit. As a compromise, they decided to release a Beatles' greatest hits album that was called, *A Collection of Beatles Oldies.* I am the tall blond man on the front cover. New mix sessions were set up to turn previously released mono recordings into stereo mixes. Although we were urged to be a large part of it, I **was not** interested. "Hey Jude" looks back at what happened that night.

All of the song, "Hey Jude," is clearer when you grasp how Paul's entity became attached to me. Séances, I want you to recognize, are practically always **a bad** idea. Don't do them. For direction, kinesiology is safer because it communicates with muscle cells rather than relying on what could be a **lying** spirit. Séances can open the doors to any **demon** or evil spirit who may choose to fool you. Now, I was lucky that it was Paul who showed up and not some imposter. Too often, when people divine with the help of familiar spirits, those who come to them are not the people they pretend to be. You can mess yourself up that way. When trying to communicate with the dead, most people tend to overlook their lack of positively identifying the spirit.

NOTE: Besides brazenly positioning William on the front cover of *A Collection of Beatles Oldies,* we find him dressed very modernly, far less conservatively than the Beatles had been with their matching suits. It showed that even the Beatles were now out of date. Their "oldies" (recorded from 1963 to 1966) included hits released only four months earlier on *Revolver.* The world was braced for the new Beatles' direction. Foreshadowing *Sgt. Peppers,* fans were shown that the old drab Beatles were now out of date.

311

It takes very positive energy to discern entities. Unless one's energy can block them, spirits reached by séances or by Ouija boards can attach to those who sit in on such things, causing many illnesses of mind, body, and spirit. **Paul McCartney is not** what I have thought of as **an evil spirit**. However, even he has brought me considerable pain. He still has an awful lot of stuff to work through that is now attached to me. I must deal with his burdens.

Letting this information out disquiets me even though I do not want any of my readers to think I lived any of my life conservatively. I want to give full disclosure of my poor choices along with my really good ones, I care about all living things– including readers whom I do not want to be hurt by emulating my mistakes.

The Beatles were not as happy as our image could portray. We were **all extremely miserable. This Paul bit took a terrible toll on us all.** Although everything may seem wonderful to outsiders, there was more pain than you would ever want to imagine. I decided it was time to tell all in this new revealing book, including our involvement with the occult, and various other things that you can know about on some level, but not ever do without also receiving every pain that naturally comes with it—which I cannot describe.

The Beatles' biggest hit was "Hey Jude," which was our debut release for our own new Apple label.

NOTE: The Beatles' first single on their Apple Record label, "Hey Jude," has sold about eight million copies worldwide. The song title inspired the title of the #1 *New York Times* bestselling picture book, *Hey Grandude!* That children's book, and its sequel, *Grandude's Green Submarine,* were written by "Paul McCartney," and illustrated by Kathryn Durst. *Hey Grandude!* was released in September 2019, the same year as the movie, *Yesterday.* In that movie, the song "Hey Jude" is sung "Hey Dude."

Do you astral travel? Leave your body for an hour to join us in the astral field at Hyde Park, London. Through meditation meet us—and each other—every 11 September from 5:00 to 6:00 am GMT.

Check your time zone. For example, in California it is 10 September from 9:00 to 10:00 pm PDT. Be careful about following any advice you get in the astral field. There are many impersonators there.

One day, during John and Cynthia's break-up, **I was** listening to the radio in the car and mostly **singing** along, as I drove out to Weybridge to visit **with Cyn** and Jules. The Drifters were doing their popular Pomus/Shuman song, "Save the Last Dance for Me." In that song, another guy holds his date's hand in the pale moonlight and dances every song with her. The singer urges her to remember who is giving her a ride home at the end of that dance. I imagined myself on a stage singing, hoping my date would end up with me when it was all over, but watching her dancing with, and being romanced by guys I could play for, but not interrupt. It could be a troublesome position.

I compared the song to the situation with John, Cyn, and Jules. Cynthia helplessly watched as John and Yoko grew in their mutual obsession but could not interrupt it. As a soda commercial came on, I turned off the radio, thinking about what I could say to Julian that might give him some comfort and encouragement. I said, "Hey Jules, don't take it bad," which became, "don't make it bad." I have said that "Hey Jude" was about Julian. Well. that line is about as far as that connection goes. I wanted him to envision John and Yoko more positively.

Though I was ordered not to interfere with the work Yoko was sent to do on John, I never encouraged it. John fancied me singing for him to go after her: "Hey John, don't let me down. / You have found her, now go and get her." However, I never made a secret of my utmost disregard for her or her absence of musical talent. By then, the band was already disintegrating. Even if John needed Yoko, I resented her intolerable recording interference and did not endorse their union. I hated Yoko then. Yet, since John was unstable, Yoko was sent to be his handler.

Some call it a drug song. **I sang, "Let** it out and let it in," reminding them of **shots of heroin** entering the bloodstream: "let her **under your skin"** . . . "let her into your heart." **The useful drug slant** entirely misdirects what the song **is** about. It is a sleight of hand causing all **to look away from** its real meaning, distracted by **that** which they think are hidden messages in another **direction.**

The name "Jude" is the first missed clue. Who is Jude? That question leads us to whom the song is about. The Jude most of us know of is the Jude dude in the Bible. Who is he? The first verse of his book says, "Jude, the . . . brother of James" (Jude 1:1). Allegorically, I am Jude, the brother of James, as in the brother of James Paul McCartney.

In many ways, we are soul brothers. In this song, I sing about what has to do with the way Paul and I became one. It gets a bit mystical here. But hear me out. You will see that it is true as you find the bigger picture woven through this mystery book. I would not have believed it myself if it had not happened to me. I do not ask you to **believe** me right off, but to gather it in along with **everything** else **in this book of** revelations to see what realizations come to **light.** Just wait a while to decide if it is true or not. **That is all** I ask from you.

Here it is. Not at first with our initial visits in Paris and London, but about two months later, we invited Paul to create a better connection by joining

"Much be-etter! Be-e-etter! Be-e-e-etter!" (Lewis Carroll)
"It's getting better all the time (better, better, better)." ("Getting Better")
"Then you can start to make it better better, better, better, better." ("Hey Jude")

"Nobody controls me. I'm uncontrollable. The only one who can control me is me, and even that's barely possible." —John Lennon

us in a midnight séance around a table. We set a chair for Paul across the table from me. I sat and stared into the empty darkness above the chair. We held the séance for over an hour before I spoke to the group with Paul's voice. Later, they all denied that Paul had spoken to them, even though only Paul had known things I said. John called it a lark. They argued that I did it on my own since my voice is somewhat similar to Paul's. There were six of us counting Paul. George sat at my right. John sat between George and Paul's empty chair. On my left were Brian Jones and Mick Jagger. Paul spoke of his brother, Mike McCartney, and of Jane Asher, wanting me to befriend them both in his place. He said, "I will love them both through you."

Ringo, who only had my word for it, having missed that midnight séance, said, "How convenient! Only you know if it came from yourself or Paul. Meanwhile, it gives you access to his girl!" Mick told him that Paul "supposedly" also told me that I was welcome to all of Paul's royalties–a point everyone questioned, especially Mick. However, I already had Jane and the money by then.

As Paul's words came from me, in a voice that only I could be positive was not my own, I felt a burning sensation in my left shoulder. **That is** when and where Paul permanently attached **himself** as an out-of-body spirit. Since his death, **he has** continued here as an earthbound entity **attached to me.** He is under my skin and has been **since that encounter.** As one of the spirits comprising my whole soul at this time, I always feel his influence and sometimes think his thoughts. From this oneness, and from my dreams of him, my transition and transformation were surprisingly simple. There is now a genuine encompassing part of me that is James Paul McCartney. I am part Paul. I have always let him work through me because he is me.

I embody Paul's spirit as completely as I **embody** my own. I truly do not know and do not **fully** care which notes, or which lyrics, come from **the Paul part, and** whatever music comes from **the Billy part of me.** It no longer matters. In the beginning, I wanted to know what was from me, what was from him, and what came from others. Now I am delighted whenever it comes, however it comes, or from whomever it comes.

Now I realize that we are all one anyway and that in our most creative moments, the universal mind gives it to us directly or indirectly. We can all live in gratitude no matter how our blessings show up.

Having fully integrated with the **Paul** part of myself, it has all become me. He **will not go** until I go to the light with him. **He is mine for life.** He lives through me, combining our interests and our musical talents. "Hey Jude" is about me, the brother of James Paul, fully letting him into my heart. It is about me forsaking my reluctance to be fully one with him. It is for me to perceive him as myself, not as a sub-personality, but as an integral part of the whole, just as my William past is of the whole. I was told, "Whom virtue unites, death will not separate."

While joining with Paul was partly positive, his overwhelming emotional pain devastated me. Not knowing how to distance myself from it, I was martyring myself every day. With that background, consider me, as Jude (James' brother) being told to yield to the discarnate spirit of the late James Paul McCartney. I will enlarge the song for clarification:

Hey Jude, do not make being one with Paul a bad thing. / Take this sad song of Paul's death that ended his life in his body and make it better through you–who are getting better, better, a little better all the time. / It is not enough to merely have Paul whisper to you as the angel on your shoulder. Remember to let this entity into your heart. / Then you can start to make it better. / Don't be afraid of this transformation. / You were made, predestined, to go out and get that entity. / The minute you let Paul under your skin / was when you began to make this situation better. / Hey Jude, whenever you actually feel Paul's emotional pains, / just hold off a bit, back away from that connection. Refrain a bit until he can let go of his pains for another season. / Don't carry his heavy world upon your shoulders. Let this be a good thing. Don't make it bad. Be happy with Paul. / For well you know that it's a fool who plays it cool /By making his world a little colder. You do not have to suffer to be cool. That much you know by now. You don't have to feel all of his pains merely because he does. /

That would disappoint me if you suffered all this pain, Jude. Don't let me down like that. / You must affirm your oneness with all but Paul's pain. Now that you have found Paul's soul, go and make him completely you, as he makes you completely him. / Remember to let him into your heart. / Then you will have the best of Paul connected to the best of you. Together, you will start to make it better.

"I would rather die a meaningful death than to live a meaningless life." ~Corazon Aquino

317

Enough of his pains. **Let the** hard feelings out, and let Paul's great love and **creative energy in**. By doing that, all the best of **your union** will **begin**. / Jude, you're waiting **for someone to perform** with. However, the power is already **within you**. You're the leader of the band. / And don't you know that it's just you? You think you are not enough, but you'll do just fine. / Don't wait for the others to move you to action. The only movement you need is by the angel on your shoulder. Paul will move you.

Seeing now what the song is truly about, if you go and re-read the genuine lyrics, you will see everything in a very different way. You will also begin to understand why it became easy to channel love and talent from Paul. The insiders thought it was weird that I instantly became so close to Jane. For me, however, it was as though I had loved her for as long as Paul had, except that I also had all those other interests from the William part of me as well. He was in me as if a multiple personality overly devoted to Jane with part of my mind, and sabotaging it with another. It was not until I mutilated that relationship that I was free to love another. It was at a perfect time for lovely Linda Eastman to enter my life. Still, the Paul part of me continued to long for Jane, as I expressed in songs.

NOTE: William was often asked how Linda Eastman was related to George Eastman, founder of the Eastman Kodak camera and film company. Some people thought that she had inherited the Eastman Kodak fortune. William always answered that they were not related. A better question, one rarely asked, was how she was related to Brian Epstein. She and Brian descended from Epsteins in the old Russian Empire.

In America, Linda's father, Leopold Vail Epstein, as named by his Jewish Russian immigrant parents, changed his name to Lee Eastman without any connection to George Eastman.

Coming from that Jewish heritage, Linda naturally also desired to bring up their children to be Jewish. Although William did not convert, he was always supportive of raising their children in that heritage, participating positively. William's current wife, Nancy Shevell, is also Jewish.

I like to play with **words**, sometimes massaging the same line to **take on several meanings**, with all of them **fitting the same song**. Besides the⟁

NOTE: William does indeed like to play with words! He says here that he enjoys massaging the same line to take on several meanings within a song. He is also extremely skillful in his word selection in prose and in speaking.

Even in interviews, without having the luxury of re-working his lines, he engages in an uncommonly clever level of "masterful speaking." He bounces back and forth between levels of meaning so that the takeaway message will be one thing for those who believe he is the biological Paul, and something else for those who know the difference between when he is speaking as himself and when he is speaking as the PAUL MCCARTNEY corporate fiction.

To understand the method, imagine being an actor playing the role of James Bond. On a break, when asked about your bagel sandwich, you answer as yourself. But when asked how you vanquish the enemy, you answer as the character. Those blinded by believing in the fictional character are further from the truth whenever the actor speaks as his authentic self. The more real he is, the greater the ruse. He talks about his lunch; they add bagels to the Bond story. The truth is kept secret in proportion to the hearer's imperfect reasoning.

When the audience is a mix of the informed and the ignorant, the masterful speaker, hiding the truth in plain view, will phrase answers so that the same words are taken in different ways according to the awareness of each hearer.

See the next footnote for examples of William saying things to validate conflicting positions about him. Giving foolish excuses for his "Paul is Dead" clues provide a way out for fools who cannot bear to know that Paul is indeed gone, while also making the excuse so hilariously absurd that insiders laugh with him at their gullibility—allowing each side to feel superior to the other.

The same principle is embedded throughout this book. By masterfully writing in layered meaning, William conveys one message to one group of readers, and other messages to other groups, while winking to the illuminated who have enough background information to comprehend all of the levels.

This book is primarily written for six audiences:

First, this book is for those who are open to raising consciousness. This group benefits from straight information about how the world is run. They are given this PID context as a gateway to that broader awareness. This group is small but positively impacts the world.

Second, this book is for those who are interested in details about how Paul was replaced. With love for the Beatles, or for Paul, they want to understand the secret messages that the Beatles spent hundreds of hours creating.

Third, this book is for those who do not want to believe that Paul was replaced, but who enjoy letting this magical mystery smash against their fixed paradigms for what some have called "the ultimate mind-f*ck."

Fourth, this book is for insiders who enjoy seeing their secrets spread out before the world in protective layers that the world, although shown, cannot see.

Fifth, this book is also written for specific interest groups, saying enough to acknowledge or inform them, usually without saying enough for them to throw the book across the room—as some readers have done.

Sixth, this book is worded specifically for those who would create legal entanglements if this book were to say either too much or too little.

Based on the awareness, logic, opinions, or interests that one brings to this book, one sees what others miss. We each have our own reasons and rewards.

"WHAT YOU SEEK IS SEEKING YOU."
RUMI

quickly popular drug meaning of letting her under my skin to make it better, and **besides any** sensual interpretations, and the **spiritual meaning** of Paul attaching himself to me, **it also referenced** the injectable fillers that I received in **my face to** add roundness to better **resemble Paul.** It is a particularly strange feeling to have this highly unnatural substance in my face. I keep catching myself rubbing at it. I try not to. I also see that it looks unnatural, especially when I push on it with my fingers. It does not move like flesh.

Having Paul as a writing partner has made my music better. I sometimes try to write as if from an empathic perspective to say what he wants to have said. Paul and I each see the world in our own unique way, especially now. He tells me that he is not okay with how he was taken out of mortality, but that, otherwise, he is fine. He sends his love. But I digress.

Paul still teaches me. Some people ask how I relearned the bass, or how I can play it left-handed like Paul. I tried to imitate his playing until a kind gift from Paul made me one with it. Since that transforming November night, it has been much simpler—not ideal, but natural. The breakthrough was to play *as* Paul rather than *like* Paul. The idea of being Paul, or of working and living as him, rather than just like him, has been powerful. It has changed how I see myself and the universe. I still cannot play it as he did but feel him working it.

Realizing that I can channel music, feelings, and thoughts, I choose to be open to receiving what is offered to me. Many have come with their work. It happens now and again. For example, I am still unsure how to understand the song, "Friends to Go."

"We do not lose our friends when they die, we only lose sight of them." ~Eleanor Farjeon

Who waits for whom? Although I am credited with it, George wrote and channeled the words and the music to me a little more than three years after he crossed over. While writing it, **I suddenly** felt that I was George. First, I **felt his presence**, then my brain and hands became his own. **He was in** control. It was comforting to **me to receive it** so easily from him. I was George then. It was a gift of his love to me and to the world.

Sensing the presence of the departed is often all it takes to connect with them. They tend to stay around to support us. Donovan told us that all we need to do is to call out individuals' names three times to invite them to us. He sang, "Paul McCartney, Paul McCartney, Paul McCartney, **I call** your name." That line was part of his, "First there's **Paul** McCartney, then there's no McCartney, then there is" song. His lyrics reminded us that we do not need séances. We simply call the people to us and sense their presence.

In all of the comparisons between the earlier Paul and myself, the most recognizable differences for anyone who knows us are in our personalities, and in how we interact with other people. Height differences made the switch rather obvious too. We had several bodily differences, and distinctions in our voices, just as in the distinct ways we each sing.

However, those with more spiritual sensitivity can understand a deeper difference. On YouTube, watch videos of Paul singing Beatles songs, and then of me doing it. When Paul sings, feel his presence. Feel his spirit. When I sing, feel mine. Feel the difference. His energy is not like mine. Feel who we are. **I possess** some of his energy, but am mostly myself, not **Paul.**

By experiencing Paul and Billy personally, you have become familiar with their frequencies. Now that you know them, Paul and Billy are familiar spirits. You call them to you in your dreams whenever you broadcast those familiar frequencies.

Before calling the departed to you, such as with the method below, be sure you know the person's energy so that you are not fooled by an impostor.

The energy of Paul and Billy are in this book. Have you noticed? More than merely reading about them, you are experiencing them. Now it's personal!

34

Do You Hear Voices?

In 1962, someone coined the word *voiceprint* from *voice* and *fingerprint*. **Like all fingerprints**, all voiceprints are **by unique genetic design**. In recent decades, **with significant** advancements made in speech recognition **technologies**, voice differentiation **positively identifies people.**

With voiceprints, each is unique—just like the data from hand geometry readers and iris scanners. I have been called the "man with a thousand voices," but all of them have only one voiceprint. I lack the ability to change my voiceprint. It is created by the shape of my mouth and my throat. Do not let my many voices fool you. As my voiceprint proves, they are distinctively mine. Throat shapes are set.

It is for that reason that the technology is not outwitted by a disguised voice, illnesses, or by a voice that is emotionally charged. Those changes are not what spectrographs show. All those things make the voice sound different to the human ear, but always show the same distinctive pattern of voice characteristics that are produced spectrographically. I cannot vocally alter a spectrograph.

At establishments requiring the highest security in government, and in the private sector, it is now common to require the scrutiny of multiple identification methods. Institutions may use any of the several combinations of voiceprints, keycards, iris scans, hand geometry readers, PINs, or keys. Having more than one method can increase the statistical probability of correct identification. But each of them, particularly the biometric methods, is rather foolproof on its own.

When the "Paul is Dead" frenzy broke out in the US in 1969, Dr. Henry M. Truby of the University of Miami used samples from Beatles songs to make **sonogram**s. He apparently hoped to prove with replicable **testing** that I am Paul McCartney. Yet, what he found **proved that** I am not. He showed at length that **Paul's voice** recorded on "Yesterday" **could not be my voice** on "Hey Jude." They were of different throat shapes. Others repeated that same experiment. When that came out, I thought it would decide it once and for all. Dr. Truby proved by that method that the singer of "Yesterday" is not the individual who sings "Hey Jude." *Life* magazine published it on 7 November 1969. In that issue, Truby gave the facts. Yet, **it is as if** any explanation sufficed. Fo**r** **e**xample, I expla**in**ed that the reason I have a black **carnation** in the grand ballroom

NOTE: William saying that he wore a black carnation because no one could find another red one in all of London's many florist shops—like saying that he crossed Abbey Road barefoot because it was too hot to wear flip-flips on that hot pavement—shows the role of confirmation bias.

Most people cannot stand to be wrong. When beliefs are threatened by fact or reasoning, some accept any excuse to keep believing. Hence, this fine work to finally un-fool the fooled requires far more effort than was made to fool them in the first place. Fear of being a fool makes us foolish. Regarding rock and roll, relationships, or religion, the mind favors evidence to support its views. "You can tell me anything at all—as long as it supports what I believe."

"One of the saddest lessons of history is this: If we've been bamboozled long enough, we tend to reject any evidence of the bamboozle. We're no longer interested in finding out the truth. The bamboozle has captured us. It's simply too painful to acknowledge, even to ourselves, that we've been taken. Once you give a charlatan power over you, you almost never get it back" (Carl Sagan). It traps narrow minds. Rigid thinking is thought cessation. To be free, let go of attachment to certainty. Stop saying, "I know that ____."

When it's too hot for flip-flops, go barefoot!

When we think we know the answers, we shut out further light and knowledge.

finale scene of the *Magical Mystery Tour*, while all of the others wore red, is that we ran out of red ones. Unable to find a red flower, I have a black one, but hold a bouquet of red ones while dancing in that scene. On 13 November 2000, the 30th anniversary of ending the band, we released a compilation of 27 of our #1 hits. All of the songs had been digitally remastered for a better, fuller sound. The CD, titled *1*, was quickly the biggest selling album of the entire decade. **Back in the sixties, my** *Sgt. Pepper's Lonely* **Hearts Club Band** album **was** the biggest seller. No other band has had **the best**-selling album of more than one decade. We did well. If you own one of the 31 million copies of *1* sold worldwide, try this observation.

NOTE: Digitally remastering top hits not only improved song quality but also made the new releases more fully William's, making him largely responsible for all remastered Beatles hits recorded from 11 September 1962 (exactly four fab years before Paul died) to 1 April 1970 (April Fools' Day). Digital remastering greatly strengthened William's portfolio.

Some videos at www.JamesPaulMcCartney.com impressed William, but one troubled him when a guest said that William "hates Crowley." Although William felt that Aleister lacked love for family and others who should mattered more, William harbors no hate for the man. William responded, "There seems to be much misunderstanding about my memoirs. Let's digitally remaster it and re-release it on 9-9-18."

Since that release nine years after the original 09-09-09 release, details that had been too cryptic have been laid out more plainly. Now, in William's final stretch of life, courageously favoring truth over diplomacy, he less cautiously buffers his Crowley connection, Illuminati affiliation, anti-religion perspective, drug use, and sexual liberation. He believes in personal freedom. His songs, the *Memoirs*, and his interviews encourage fans to get over their inhibitions.

That edition was also the first to include 66 footnotes (now 180), each with the Eye of Paul Pyramid pointing to the corresponding text. Those footnotes included many new details connecting Egyptian symbolism to Paulism. That edition was also the first to refer to William as our "scarab, the Gold-Winged Beatle." These, and other new Egyptian elements added to the hardcover release on 9 September 2018, were supported by the 7 September 2018 release of the "Paul McCartney" album, *Egypt Station* (deriving its artwork from his eponym 1988 painting).

The train station, or spaceport, connects heaven and earth, not only for the ancient gods to come to him but for him to meet them where they are. It is his point of ascension. The ibex stands ready.

Notice, while skipping through the first several #1 Beatles hits, that practically all of their material emphasized falling in love or needing a girlfriend. The Paul years were of one love song after more and more love songs. That infatuation niche defined them until Paul's death dreams. Then came the best of his material. It was at that time that he wrote "Paperback Writer," which was distinctively not romantic. It was not about girls or about dying and is another one of his better songs. Donovan emphasized that he was referring to Paul, the "Paperback Writer," in the "Epistle to Dippy," by singing, "Doing us paperback reader." Two songs later on *1* is **Paul's last #1 hit**. Listen to him sing **"Eleanor Rigby."** That song, the last one on that CD that Paul sang, **is his most sophisticated.** What the song does not have is my **singing quality.** I understand that most of you love the song. I do too. Only, someone with formal training in singing would have sung it better. I do not mean to fault him. He sang it great according to his background and singing skills.

Consider doing this simple listening inspection. Play "Eleanor Rigby" and listen to it. Carefully listen to become aware of his singing ability (or lack thereof) on that, his last great masterpiece. **Hear his** untrained voice. Notice how out of **breath** Paul sounds at the end of each little line. **Pay attention to** every aspect. Listen to the way **his shallowness of** airflow causes his weakness of **voice.**

Saying all of this does not diminish the fact that it is an exceptional song. Just listen to hear how he falters in singing it. Hear how weakly he ends each line. Hear **his voice** and voice quality. Then skip to our "Penny Lane." It **is** the next song on the CD. Notice how **distinctly** it is not the same voice. It is ridiculously **obvious.** If not to you, go back and forth between songs until you recognize each voice. You will soon realize that each is one of the five Beatle voices that you have known very well, only that you stopped hearing Paul's voice once you started hearing mine. By switching back and forth until you know them both, you will train yourself to be able to distinguish between Paul and me as easily as between John and George. You can hear that it is not the same voice.

Lastly, once you can distinguish between our two voices, listen to my voice quality. Hear how it lasts fully to the end of each line with more voice to spare. Hear the difference in enunciation. Notice that I do not have a Liverpool accent, that I sound much more educated, and that I have had my share of voice training. Comparing his "Eleanor Rigby" with my "Penny Lane" gives you two consecutive hits: his last one, and my first. I do not write of the contrast to boast of my superior voice, or about the effortlessness in my singing. My point is to help you to **hear the variance.** I felt frantic for my first single as Paul **to sound** a lot like him. I needed help with it.

It was **close enough.** That voice, with John's right behind **it** in the harmony, told our fans that it **could only be Paul** singing lead. They could all tell that it was not George or Ringo. Thus, reasonably, it could only be Paul. An outsider was never imagined. It must be Paul singing lead with John doing backup on a Beatles single. They always did it with either John or Paul singing lead, and with

Do you remember noticing—when *Sgt. Peppers* was new—that Paul's voice sounded a little different? Since then, you included Billy's voice in the range that you recognize as Paul.

326

the other one singing backup. They did not ever let George do a single. That only happened later when he wrote "Something."

Only by listening to these songs back and forth, contrasting us as I describe, can you appreciate the very **distinct differences.** He is more nasally, and less clear. His Liverpool **sound**, especially in words ending with an "R,' is **not like mine**; and I play with the notes, adding far more sophistication.

Hearing how well I sing "Penny Lane" is significant because it is right after Paul recorded "Eleanor Rigby." However, the differences are even more clear with us both singing the same song. For an undeniable contrast, pull up Paul's version of "Eleanor Rigby," as well as my version that I recorded for *Give My Regards to Broad Street.* On YouTube, compare them back and forth, line by line.

Having heard that profound difference, you will understand why John, aware of the difference, feared everyone else would notice too. It made him insecure with his singing. His new insecurity first became apparent while recording "Strawberry Fields." I laughed about him singing in different keys. I realized that he (who had been the leader of the world's biggest band) could not hear the difference! It became worse as he learned what my voice could do, compared to his or Paul's. For the rest of our time together, he favored singing harder rock that better hid his voice. Still, his best songs were slow.

Next, as John began to contrast my music theory background with his, and my musical skills with his own, he had Yoko—not me—give him piano lessons. Although Paul had begun to play it before I joined, it was George Martin who had done almost all of their piano work before I took over.

Once you recognize each voice, they sound less similar.

327

35

Between Me and My Encoder, It's All Sixes.

When I was a little boy, long before **I knew** a thing about Liverpool, I was the greatest at **Sixes.** I had the dice collection to prove it. Being a game of chance, one might wonder how one child could end up so far ahead. Somehow, however odd, I was good at it. Sixes was a simple game. Each player needed six dice to start. Whoever rolled first would toss one, two, or three dice. Based usually on how well that roll went, the others each rolled up to as many as were rolled first. The highest number that each player rolled would compete. The highest roll won them all. Sometimes we played for keeps, for real. Other times it was just for fun, and we would give the newly won dice back when the game was over. I went partly by strategy, mostly by my gut feelings, and with a little luck. The strategy was to let the others win if they rolled a five or a six first.

At those times, I would roll one die and expect to lose it. Otherwise, I would roll more to improve my odds. Yet, the rub was this: All of the dice that ended up as low-rolling leftovers went to whoever had rolled the highest number. By rolling more dice, odds increased of a higher number, but also of more dice to lose too. As instinct countered strategy, that was when the game was the most satisfying to me. I remember one day, on a visit with my father, he rolled three fives. Although the strategy was to roll only one die and let him have it, I felt confident energy making it feel safe to push to match all three. They all came up sixes! I have held that great sixes day in my mind. **I will always remember** the thrill on his face when he shouted, **"Six, six, six!"**

I was reminded of sixes, and that young "Six, six, six!" triumph one hot summer day in Southern California. I was in a Los Angeles recording studio when a musician there answered a question about employment options. He said, "It's sixes to me."

It was not my conversation and not any topic I was interested in per se. Still, I interrupted, "Your money's a game?"

"He means," another said, "a half-dozen of one or six of the other is no difference. It's all sixes or all the same."

Although they did not know of my Sixes game, my dad's "Six, six, six!" shot through my mind, rolling back years of Sixes memories. It had been a long time. Sixes was my game. No wonder six became my darling digit. In Sixes, nothing is better than having a six, except having two or three sixes. "Six, six, six!" topped everything. One cold dark winter evening, a friend of my mum's was visiting. She was pretty. Being anxious to make an impression, I boasted that I had rolled **six, six, six** lots of times. "Oh Billy!" she said, "That **is the devil's number!**"

I said, "No, six, six, six is my number! I'm the greatest at Sixes!"

"Gracious me!" she said, "Six, six, six is the devil number! Games of chance are all his favorite games! If you keep playing with the devil, you will burn with him in hell!"

Everyone was taken aback by her strong words. Yet, nobody corrected her. I decided then that saying "Six, six, six is my number" was not the best way to impress grown-ups. Now I am free to laugh at the whole thing. By trying to scare the 666 out of me, she only made me pay more attention to the number. By coincidence, it came up frequently.

People often brought it to my attention. My unabashed fascination with it made people want to share it with me any time any of them discovered it. Maybe I would have forgotten about it if they had allowed me to. Sometimes **those same people** who believed the number **would send me** to the devil were the ones who found me **more 666 tie-ins.**

Emily Little was in the same boat. As a little girl, she was particularly fond of giraffes. When her relatives or a fine friend found a giraffe sculpture, painting, stuffed animal, or toy, he or she always saw to it that she got it, making her collection bigger and bigger until there was hardly a place for her to sit down in her room. Once people associated Em with her animal guide, they all sought to add to her collection. That is what happened to me with sixes. Once they were mine, everyone wished to educate me, revealing connections that I had not seen before, such as 333 being the **Masonic** half of 666. Numbers are interesting **things**. Everything and everyone can be numbered **in a way,** or perhaps in utterly numberless ways. **I mention** here how I got that 666 so that readers **would be** less inclined to misjudge me about it. **My fixation** has more to do with my father than with the devil. Still, we all believe whatever resonates. Believe what you will, I got that number as an innocent game with my father. Enough coincidences exist in the world that people should accept that the only reason why I began to respond to the number six is that it is the highest number on dice. The six has nothing to do with Satan, but with the number of sides on a cube. You do not see me praising Satanism, as other musicians are apt to do. I am neither an outsider trying to break in nor an insider trying to get out.

Gleaning from esoteric mysticism or occultism calls me more than generic philosophy or any set religion. Magick (from Greek *magike*), "the mystical art of willful transformation," works by directing energy flow. We direct energy out for external changes or pull it in for changes in consciousness.

Enough of that. You may want to know what Sixes have to do with Paul and me. What I found amusing in California was that the name of my dice game, Sixes, would **come to** mean things are the same. With that, this **McCartney** game I play is to be the same as Paul. Sixes have always been my game. McCartney is number nine. Nines are sixes turned upside-down.

Heat in Los Angeles drives many people to the coast. Feeling that stifling sultry air, as a few of us exited the recording studio, we decided to head for the beach. A few of the beaches discussed sounded terrific but crowded. My driver said I might enjoy seeing Laguna Beach's sea anemones, starfish, and other marine life. However, six miles before reaching that beach, we stopped early, reasoning that there would be less marine **life there**, but more tranquility.

The beach **was empty except** for one gentleman riding the waves. **Later, carrying his** surfboard and a small **ice-chest back to his car, he stopped** to talk. I could see that I looked familiar to him. As I spoke, he recognized my voice and smiled. Since he did not talk like a crazed fan, I invited him to join us for a while. He shared his water with us. He was an English and history teacher out on vacation. He said he had been a big Beatles fan. He was familiar with the "Paul is Dead myth," as he called it, and suggested I write about it from my perspective.

He thought I was **the** biological Paul, and that the **"Paul is Dead" legend** was a publicity stunt. I confessed that it did sell a lot of albums and that we were glad that **it turned out** that way, but also said that it **was no hoax.** I heard myself saying, "Listen, do you want to know a secret?"

Beneath his graying curly hair, which was long for an English teacher, even on break, his eyes were older than the rest of him, maybe wise enough to see

NOTE: This chapter's story of the Encoder (Thomas E. Uharriet) meeting William by accident is fictional. William did not break the confidentiality agreement by confiding in a stranger and hiring him to be the messenger. That cover story required for *the Memoirs* is not how the candidate was selected.

through any usual nonsense lines that I may provide. Ordinarily, I might have come up with something clever and inventive. This was different. He was too kind or something. I wanted to tell him.

"What secret?" he asked.

I said, "It's no hoax. Not that it's true. It is not a hoax, not in that direction. If it were a big secret until now, why would I tell it? Why write about it now after all these years?"

Softly, he answered, "Because you want to." He could see it. He added, "If that does not feel like enough, then do it because the world would want to read it." He understood what the world would demand, what it would mean to me, and that I was ready. He was right that **I am** able to share more.

"That would open **Pan**dora's box that could never be re-closed," I said.

"How is it any different than putting it in your songs and album covers?" he asked. I saw that he enjoyed his suggestion but discerned that the rest of the story would shock him. Too risky.

"That's different," I said. "It's all fiction. Song lyrics and poetry can have anything in them."

"Enlarge your fiction. Write a novel. Label it as such and you can say whatever you like."

As he spoke, I saw myself writing a mysterious book. "It would have to be more than just another common book," I said. "I'd want to make it more like…" The words did not come fast enough.

"How about an epic poem?" His idea sounded grand, but perhaps too much so.

"Epic? I'm not sure. I like the idea of verse, something like a novel, but with elements of poetry. Reading it should be a mystical or interactive experience, not just another novel," We were in it together already. We unexpectedly sealed the plan to collaborate by what he did next. He described a manuscript **he had worked** in which he hid secret messages, **embedding a code into** the text. He explained how he did **it** and why. I was intrigued. It reminded me of **all** I had done already in songs. Technically, it was **in verse** since every word or line break mattered. **Yet, it read like a novel.**

All of it was perfect for what I desired, but too much work, far too complicated for a full-length text that way. I was not sure he could do it until, on a paper from my colleague, I wrote a rather tedious paragraph that I asked the teacher to rework with embedded clues. I told him what hidden messages I wanted in the text. He set up a grid, then reread my page, and focused. In a mere eighteen minutes, he finished. It took him thirty-three minutes to reveal the concealed layers of meaning.

Before long, we were discussing gematria and particulars of my role in providing material, his role encoding my messages, my guarantee of historical accuracy, his work standardizing the language as American English, my commitment to disclose all without reservation, the restricted extent of his creative license, my right to override any changes he makes while lining up words to fit the allotted spaces, his method of transferring chapters to me (via email)

As you experience this book layer by layer, each layer changes how you perceive yourself.

for approval, my turnaround time for him to meet his 09-09-09 deadline, and finally, his compensation for this mammoth undertaking.

Entering into this agreement allowed me to make this encoded book the way I wanted it without involving myself in areas where I did not wish to spend my time. Using a collaborator on this project is similar to what I have always done with projects. Whenever I slap the McCartney name on a label, I might have hired all kinds of people to help me make the sounds that I have in my head. It is like "Yesterday," which **Paul wrote** from dreams. He had the music playing **in his head but** knew the Beatle engine **could not produce it**. The song was labeled "Beatles" even though John, George, and Ringo had no part in it whatsoever. Paul hired outsiders who could do it better. It was the same thing when I came along. I did for the band what Paul could do no longer, continuing in his name. For tasks over our abilities, we hire others to do it.

It is not as if, given enough time, I could not do it all as well. It is just that my imagination is too vast, and my life is too short, to take the time to do everything all by myself. By hiring this Encoder to assist me with this project, we were able to do it right without it consuming too many years of my life. Besides, in his words or mine, it is all sixes.

"Many shall come in my name, saying, 'I am Paul,' and shall deceive many." (Matthew 24:5 *JKV*)*

*Just Kidding Version

36

"Within You and Without You"

A friend of my grandmother opened our old family Bible to 1 Kings 10:14. She showed me that in one year, King Solomon was given 666 talents of gold (about 25 tons). She said that out of all who have ever lived, none has been richer in money. She said, "You may gain the world, but do not lose your soul." I found out later that Jesus had also said something like that. The woman did not explain what she meant by it. I was too young to comprehend it but old enough to remember.

That is about how much wealth I have earned in a lifetime, making it more than **I** have accumulated. It is more wealth than we can **comprehend**. Playing Paul, I do not usually talk about **my own** childhood memories. I have also been **uncomfortable** talking about wealth since most people do not seem to have enough. I recognize what a **struggle** it is. I too have had serious struggles. Upon accepting this Paul role, I ended my financial scarcity but launched the hardest challenges of my life in other ways.

When I **was** in India, I was warned again. An old man **there** told John, George, and me that

Billy has the financial freedom to buy whatever pleases him, but not the personal freedom to only do as he pleases.

all of our prosperity in this life would balance poverty that lies either in the next life or in the past. **He** said that there is a cosmic balance that **is** always maintained. He warned us against living **too high** on wealth and Western luxury. I told him **about how** I often played poor. He smiled and said **I might** altogether cheat fate by creating that **balance** in this life. He supposed that if my **poverty** became as real to me as my wealth, there would be no need for me to pay for this luxury **in the next life.** This is not to say that I now do whatever I want to without consequences. It was merely his opinion that my eternal debts were already being reduced for good behavior. Nevertheless, **I do not buy any** of it. I do not believe that is how it **works.** I believe that down the line, everyone must pay **for** their misdeeds.

Ordinarily, we want a sense of **fairness** that will eventually play out through everything only if such fairness favors us on our own terms. I mean, one fellow says it seems balanced and fair to him if we each end up with the same number of luxuries overall, spread across many incarnations. Such ideas tend to give peace to the scarcity-minded. Being a matter of individual choice seems fair to me. We each create and experience whatever reality we choose, either consciously or subconsciously.

"Right," you say, "that is very easy for you to say with a name like Sir J. **Paul** McCartney." Well now, that certainly **is a good name** all right, and a valuable one. Yet, it is still me, the soul core of me, at the helm who accepted this name and made it work. There was something in me that helped to land this gig, something that prepared me for it, and that drove me to greatly excel in it. I am the last to join the band, but even with the least Beatles experience, I became the greatest Beatle of them all. When I became the leader, I led the band to greater historically significant success. *Sgt. Pepper's,* and on to the end, was all under my leadership. The prior Paul did not do it. It is not simply that I acquired his good name. What I did with that marvelous name matters much more.

Even though I never counted the chapters to be sure, I am told that the Bible's six hundred and sixty-sixth chapter is Ecclesiastes' seventh chapter. That chapter begins by saying, "A good name is better than precious ointment." According to tradition, King Solomon wrote that himself. That is a guy who had it all: a good name, riches, wisdom, everything. He is one of my heroes.

Another one of my heroes is my ancestor, Sir William Wallace. If this idea keeps coming back to me, I will write a chapter about him to show why he influenced my music and my view of the world. Yes, I probably should write more about him later. We will see if I can work it in.

Of all of our songs, one by George explains the money trap the best. Although we talked about it, until he put it to music, I did not take it to heart. Of course, by then, what was I to do? I mean, I could not let everyone down by giving up Paul. Even so, reflecting on it made me more determined to reveal his death **to the world**, to free me from this illusion that **I was creating**, as we all were.

Beatle illusion topped all. George explains the situation in "Within You Without You" as his warning to me against getting lost in that illusion. I had heard that same warning before. By letting all of the wealth and world fame place me behind the illusion of Paul, I would be operating as someone I am not. I would soon lose myself in it, and maybe not only lose my soul here and now but possibly in the hereafter since what we take with us is a continuation of our reality here.

Consider the song as **George wrote it**. It was his advice and warning **to me.** He was fretful enough to make it his primary effort for the album. If you do not know the song, go look it up to see my explanation in its intended context. He says my change was up to me. "Try to realize it's all within yourself. No one else can make you change."

John, Jane, Mick, Mike, and many others, had tried to turn me into **Paul**. George told us all that the change had to come **from within me,** and not in every outward aspect, and that whatever **resonated** with who I am would evolve **naturally**. He said that making demands on me to be **what** I was not would end in a divisive disaster. He said **I am** one of the people who hide themselves behind a wall of illusion.

All celebrities have false public selves. Most fans only see false images, false idols to worship, without ever getting to know the real people behind them. Real people are not idols to fans or to themselves.

"This world may seem wonderfully convincing until death brings down the illusion and expels us from our hiding place." ~ *The Tibetan Book of the Dead*

Those dwelling in deception never get a glimpse at the truth. They lose their real living in exchange for their insubstantial apparitions. Then it's far too late when they pass away. Their lives end without having fully lived. **These people** are the ones who gain the world and lose their souls. They **don't know** the truth. They can't see it. Knowing **the answer**, he asks, "Are you one of them?" George and others did this song without any help from John, Ringo, or me.

I believed George when he explained that my focus needed to shift away from wealth and the niceties of my position and that I should care more about love than about playing and posing as Paul.

Some aspects of Paul would never come to me. George assured me that those parts did not matter. Paul's part, or aspect, which mattered the most was the love that he had given the band and the world. As eager as I was to become Paul, and as anxious as others were to turn me into him, George encouraged a more natural approach without stressful effort. John understood and accepted his meaning and then cautioned me about it from time to time as if I had forgotten. That idea formed the foundation of what eventually became the Beatles' anthem, "All You Need is Love." It became central to Paulism.

We were talking about the space between us all, the void, or distance, which separates us all from each other, making us subject and object rather than all being fully perceived as one. I symbolized that empty space on the back cover of *Sgt. Pepper's*

"When everything Americans believe is false, our misinformation campaign will be complete." ~ William Casey (CIA Director 1981 to 1987).

when we spelled "**love**" with our fingers, except that, as Paul was **dead** and concealed, my fingers were not showing. **Paul** still had love but could not let that light **shine** directly in the land of the living. You would have to see it through me to see it at all. I kept that light shining and secretly made an "O" with my hands, while I was standing in for Paul. Only those who understood could realize what was happening or represented. Only those who saw the false Paul (or "Faul" as some say) in that picture could see the meaning veiled behind it about the true Paul. That is, you only discern the true love or life of Paul through me. From one of Paul's dreams, encoded in a song, he sang, "**I'm looking through you**. You're not the same." **That** *Sgt. Pepper's* **picture** acted it out. I am not the same. **To see the "O" void** from Paul's absence, you had to look through me.

Counting ourselves each as individual forms, or seeing ourselves all as one, either way, is correct. Everything is an individual form made up of the same universal source of infinite cosmic intelligence. "And the time will come when you see we're all one and life flows on within you and without you."

Now, George was talking about two things. On one level, it is all about **Paul's life** essence, or spirit, dancing within me. It **is eternal energy** that goes on whether Paul is **manifested through me**, or living in me, being attached to me, or not. Within me or without me, his soul would continue and

If Crowley was right about how to reenact the Osiris and Horus myth for them take possession, then Billy is possessed by entities far more powerful than Paul.

Let things flow naturally forward in
whatever way they like." ~Lao Tzu

on in one way or another. On another level, George was saying that all life energy goes on. All is all very much a part of all that is, and of all that can be. That intelligence is inside us and outside us. Life energy flows on within us and without us, meaning inside and out, here, there, and everywhere.

Adopting this viewpoint at once makes each of us universally significant, each being, in essence, nothing less than the cosmos of which we are all made, but also very meaningless on the level of distinct forms. This idea helps us see we are only very small and life flows on within us, and life flows on without us too. Paul too, we see, flows on within us even though we are without him on the level of form. To see Paul now is to see beyond the level of form. That is how we verify his continuance and ours. Seeing Paul beyond our distinct forms, we awaken to the realization that everyone can be perceived that way, which is an awareness of our true nature and common Source.

That is the level where **we find the peace of mind** that comes from perceived oneness, **not with Paul** in heaven uniquely, but with everyone **here and now.** Seeing beyond ourselves, **we find peace of mind** is waiting there. That peace is **in the absence of our** falsely perceived sense of **division from others.**

Since Paul's death, George and the others were more pleased with my work than with my brotherly love. They knew I had the talent but did not feel my

When pleased or offended by another, remember that the same
universe that is rendering that person is also rendering yourself.
You are the Absolute becoming self-aware through both of you.

love as they had hoped. It bothered them all along. I did not show it as well as Paul had. I could never **have** that same connection with them that they all **felt** with each other. From the start, George sang of "**the love** that's gone so cold" in the sense of being **embalmed with Paul**, but also cold between us all due to that space between us, the lack of love.

Love could save the world if they only knew it, or if the world could perceive us all beyond form. Our work was now to perceive divine love beyond form and to share it with the world. We could venture out with our love message that could positively change the world. We had influence. He encouraged us to rebuild the love within the band, such as they had with Paul, and then to share it with the whole world.

We felt Paul's love come and go. George said to hold on to Paul's love, and that our love for each other would keep us open to that love that would enhance our work. With that help from the other side, **we then extend it.** We were talking about the love we **all could share** when we find it to try our best to hold **it there** with our love. That is the main idea of "**Within You** Without You." These words from George in this song were his very best and are fairly close to what he said when we were all talking about it before he wrote the song.

Each of you by now may have realized that what I wrote about Paul may apply to others as well. As you and **I give love,** we are open to it. Many people missed Paul. There had been a loving bond **overriding all** they did before I joined in. John and **Paul** lived the dream that they worked to the utmost to obtain. They did it together. When Paul crossed over, they still felt his loving influence. He had loved them before and loved them still. They could feel it. As **we all felt love** for each other, we also all felt it more easily to and **from Paul.**

It is the same with everyone. **For** example, I bet very many of you thought of **Christ or Krishna.** The point is that **divine love must flow** through each of us in order **to resonate** with—and deeply feel—the love of others **in this world and beyond.**

NOTE: Krishna-consciousness, or Christ-consciousness, is love-consciousness. Buddha-consciousness is love-consciousness. It is the awakened state of love that comes with complete acceptance of ourselves, thereby unlocking and unblocking our capacity to love others. Free from the blockages of fear and judgment, we can feel divine love flowing through everything and everyone.

Never confuse spirituality with religiosity. Consider Krishna's joy in playing the flute, dancing, and lovemaking. Consider Jesus' love of good food, wine, and friends (Matthew 11:19). Consider the "Laughing Buddha's" teaching that enlightenment is the end of suffering. Goodness, righteousness, and enlightenment, have nothing to do with sanctimonious solemnity. Through willful love-consciousness, or love-mindfulness, we see that we love, that we are loved, and that we are love. Love is the intelligence, or essential element, of all that is real.

"We need to learn to love ourselves first, in all our glory and our imperfections." —John Lennon

37

Stoned to Hell, We Called the Press.

With **the spiritual darkness** in this chapter, and in the next, **I** realize that I should explain why I agreed to **include** it. I want you to understand that Satanism, **aside from its spiritual** effect or religious **significance**, is a political network used by this world's most eminent social engineers. I do not endorse their rites but always credit the network in connection with those who made the Beatles the immortal band that it became. At the top of the world's governing body, which oversees the banks, news media, and most public opinions, ambitious organizations work to use their all-encompassing generative dominance to create a New World Order.

I hope that the included spiritual aspects do not cloud **the issues** of how and why the death cult uses Satanism. By systematic design, such issues **are so abhorrent** in discussions of real-world affairs **that rational people find them unthinkable.** Until the public learns to let go of their fears of the subject, they keep their fear in power over them and will continue to energize that which they dread. Things we fear control us because we cannot intelligently deal with them.

However absurd, **Satanism infiltrated** all of our major networks of media, **commerce**, politics, and religion. It collects and controls adherents nested in unsuspecting corporations, spreading its influence. **It is well known that** international bankers run **the world's** media, commerce, and politics. What is **not readily** understood is the extensiveness of their **Illuminated** network that branches out in all directions throughout the whole world. The vast network is not about banking. That is just a funding source. That colossal network has always been about the power to control the masses, and ultimately the entire world. Nearly everyone, regardless of their awareness of it, is in the network already through several lines of influence (banking, entertainment, government, and major corporations). Satanism is merely one of many long thin threads.

EMI (Electric & Musical Industries Ltd.) is a British music company formed in March 1931. Making big war profits in WWII, they made radar equipment and guided missiles; then later branched into broadcasting equipment, television cameras, and computers. In November 1931, that company made studios for recording and later remastering music. These recording studios, which we Beatles made

NOTE: It helps to think of all governments, churches, and dynasties, as corporations. Since their ability to control wealth determines their potential impact, one should not be surprised to discover deals made behind the scenes to dictate government policies for their benefit.

As is self-evident when national governments send their citizens to war to benefit a few key corporations, the system is rigged against the people. Governments, like most other corporations, favor s of cooperating with the big companies even when it is contrary to what is best for the people. Rutherford B. Hayes (US president from 1877 to 1881) wrote, "This is a government of the people, by the people, and for the people no longer. It is a government of corporations, by corporations, and for corporations."

eminent, are located at Abbey Road, in St John's Wood, in the City of Westminster, a borough in the center of Greater London. Work in the network was aided by EMI's retained military intelligence.

Oscar Preuss, head of EMI's Parlophone Records from 1950-55, had an assistant whom he trained under him who took over when Preuss retired. The new leader, George Martin (whose past oboe teacher was Jane Asher's mother), recorded classical and Baroque music, big hit plays, and some of the regional music from the British Isles.

While the Beatles were performing in strip clubs over in Hamburg, Beatles folklore has it that their manager, Brian, convinced George Martin to consider recording them. Actually, George's superior ordered it. Critical of Pete's image and skill, George had him replaced. Even though George Harrison, following George Martin's order, had already hired a replacement (Ringo, who already had played a few times with them before), George Martin hired a new drummer to help with their recording sessions.

Ringo showed up unaware of the redundancy. He got **to help with the recording** with tambourines, et cetera. Martin was ordered to make the Beatles huge even though he felt that the band lacked talent. He then ordered Brian to clean up their image, to make them appear presentable and innocent. With Martin's help, they would turn their little songs into big hits. He changed parts, added piano, networked with the media, and all else to make them marketable. He was eventually known as the "fifth Beatle" for doing so much but was never a band member.

Resisting getting cleaned up as well, when the Rolling Stones also got a recording contract, they each opted to pass themselves off as the Beatles' nasty rivals. It played perfectly into the hands of the secret **Committee of 300**. As the snitch said, "With the Beatles in [their] right hand... and the Stones in [their] left," **they** would transform the whole world.

The Beatles **would be** promoted as the good guys of rock, while **our friends**, the Stones, would be promoted **as hellish demons**. The idea that came from **a few rungs higher up** the influence ladder **than** George Martin was that each band would split **the world at its own level** to achieve the societal fragmentation and disintegration that is necessary to have an irreversible cultural revolution back to the cult of Dionysus, a god of wine and madness.

Everyone can ignore all of that. The relevance here is that top-level social scientists, including Willis Harmon, worked for those who control the legacy media (and thus public opinion). We were offered a chance to change the world. They made a special priority of these two bands sufficient to represent us to the world in a most powerful light.

The Beatles and Stones were distinct on our level of operation but were used in concert by the social engineers for their agenda. We did not receive their full detailed plan but did have heavy doors opened for us. As long as **each band** worked within their guidelines (that abruptly **changed** when I came along), everything played out **perfectly.**

In the case of the Rolling Stones, they were essentially told to be evil devil worshippers, and that the more they could incite their audiences to destroy all of the Stones' venues, the greater would be their hold on the world. They did their psychotic best to make fans go insanely berserk. For instance, in the US, they got their audience so worked up into a frenzy, severely vandalizing *The Ed Sullivan Show* set, that he swore they could never come back. Given media support to publicize that endorsement, sales soared.

John and George were especially close to the Stones. One day when Mick was at EMI Studios, he overheard me talking to John and Ringo about some of Paul's assets. Mick became irritated with me. He told me that I am in "My Obsession" on his new album and that I am obsessed with getting Paul's nicest belongings. Then he sang his line, "My Obsession your possessions every piece that I can get." He said, "That's you, Bill, all about taking everything that was **Paul's**. You tell us over and over again that your **actions are** all for Paul and that he's better off with you **taking** his place. I don't think so." Then he sang to **us**, "I don't mind if it's unkind and it's not my property, but I want it just to be mine exclusively." He went on with other parts that also pointed to me.

"How can you say that?" I said. "Paul wanted it this way. And I gave up everything and practically everyone to save this band. It didn't cost the band one cent, just Paul's family, his heirs!"

Ringo said, "It's only fair you know. The new man may take the fortune." We used Ringo's words on the montage of Paul's death clues of "**I Am** the Walrus." Before the final verse, just after **the second** line of "**They are** the Eggmen," you can hear, "New man may take the fortune." You would have to listen for it to catch it. It is background chatter. I, the "new man," am shown at that point in the movie.

"When I use a word,' Humpty Dumpty said in rather a scornful tone, 'it means just what I choose it to mean — neither more nor less.'
"The question is,' said Alice, 'whether you can make words mean so many different things.'
~Lewis Carroll, *Through the Looking Glass*

It was because **Paul became** a millionaire the year before that he was **ripe to be offered**, offering a nice reward for accepting him. **To me**, the job was not to preserve Beatlemania, but suddenly to be some great and wealthy superstar. It was a dream job for sure. I wanted fame and fortune. For the sacrifice I made, I got his inheritance. I said to Mick, "John did not object to me getting it!"

"That's not the only one we have about you replacing Paul, Bill." Mick said, "We all talked it over when we wrote 'Something Happened to Me Yesterday.'"

"Never call me Bill again," I said. "I gave up my whole life to be Paul. Tell him, John!"

"Even in jest," John said, "never call him Bill. Okay, Billy Boy, I've told him."

"Something happened to me yesterday," Mick smirked wider and sang tauntingly, "Something **I can't speak of** right away. . . he don't know if it's **right or wrong**. Maybe he should tell someone. He's not sure . . . if it's against the law . . . something very strange I hear you say."

"Very funny," I interrupted. "Is that on your album?"

"Oh, you're talking in a most peculiar way . . ." he sang on.

Laughing, John inserted the words, "Not at all like the Paul we knew. Most peculiar!"

"Very funny," I repeated. This was not the only time that they combined against me.

Everything else Mick sang to me then was a spontaneous impromptu version of the song. "You don't know just where it's all gone. You don't really care at all. **Now Billy is** just not sure of what it was. **What's** it mean? What'd you cause? You cannot say it's **right** or it's wrong. Billy, you can tell someone. Now you're unsure just what it was or if it's against the law. . . There's something more to pay for sins that you committed yesterday."

Mick interrupted his singing, stopping long enough to say, "'Yesterday,' that's Paul's song of you." I knew. His singing resumed again, "It's oh so trippy." He interrupted his singing again, "I got that line from Donovan."

"Shut up!" I shouted. "Is that on your album? What will you tell the press when they ask you to explain it all?" Mick was getting personal with me, not merely writing about losing Paul.

"Don't worry," he said. "I'll just tell them all to read between the buttons." Their *Between the Buttons* album was started the month before Paul died. Then they reworked lyrics to make Paul songs. Having those songs on the Stones album made us even bolder to include Paul clues on my band's eagerly pursued *Sgt. Pepper's Lonely Hearts Club Band* album, which was released about five months later. On our album cover, besides naming the band and album, it singles out Paul and, most unpredictably, the Rolling Stones.

We wrote "PAUL" in a hyacinth arraignment as Paul's bass guitar. As Paul's band ended with him, we put its name in the other floral arrangement. All could read "BEATLES" in those flowers since it too had died. As if the new band's name on the drumskin (replacing The Beatles' drum), the new skin says, *Sgt. Pepper's Lonely Hearts Club Band.*

351

Shirley Temple's shirt (for our other half) says, "WELCOME THE ROLLING STONES GOOD GUYS." The duality pretense was over. Now, the "good guys" were calling the "bad guys" good. Though not involved directly, the Stones grieved privately. They played "Paint it Black" on *The Ed Sullivan Show* on the night of 11 September 1966, adding pain to the song.

They were skeptical of me taking Paul's part. The gig would be too big for me, they thought. That changed with *Sgt. Pepper's*. **They all confessed** that I had nothing to worry about. **I was** a **better** Paul than expected and getting better all the time. As hard as it was to believe, it blew them all away. It blew the whole world away. Our seminal record was beyond every measure of any Beatles album that had gone before. It was far beyond anything any band had made before. That album established me as an incomparable replacement.

Most Rolling Stones fans noticed their change too but had no clue of what provoked it. How on earth could they possibly know? We did not let the cat out of the bag for years yet. We loaded our records with clues for years before we finally helped the public understand them. No one seemed to see even the most obvious clues.

Whenever Mick, Keith, or Brian saw me, they tested me, asking questions to see how far I could be Paul. They asked me about my childhood, relatives, houses, parents' cars, Jane, and work—everything they could think of. When they would ask something above and beyond what I already knew, if the right answer did not pop into my head, I would make up a new history that I often convinced them was right anyway. I became quick at making up good stories that they could not argue with. It was a game, and I became good at it.

Having our great success with the *Sgt. Pepper's* album made my position in the band the most eminent. All were centered around Paul, but that inevitably included all of it revolving around me, if you know what I mean. **We wrote** about Paul's death, but I, **the living Paul**, called all the shots.

Creating all the **mystery**, material, or power to drive the band up in excellence, my contract had opened new potentials and successes that drove the Stones crazy. They were astonished by my understanding of Paul's inner workings. When John and George told Brian Jones about some of my better lucid dreams of Paul. and about how he had instructed me, Brian just about went crazy. He did not waste any time at all. He convinced all of the rest of their band that they needed a muse from heaven or hell who could do for them what Paul was doing for the Beatles through me.

As we were finishing *Sgt. Pepper's*, the Stones were working on their *Flowers* album. Theirs was very obviously tied to ours, even their Paul art. Our cover had Beatles and **Paul** in flowers. On theirs, the entire band **was shown as if** they were flowers. As Brian told **me**, those flowers were their gift for Paul. It represented the flowers–which were merely themselves–which they sent to Paul's funeral. Making *Flowers* a perfect farewell gift to Paul, it contained goodbye songs to him. That album was an outstanding offering released the same month as our funeral album, *Sgt. Pepper's*.

Good songs were included on *Flowers*. I thought it was one of their better albums. By this time, it was second nature for Keith and Mick to mix lyrics and messages in the same fashion that we needed to do to be able to say it all without anyone hearing it. They too created more songs with Paul-enriched lyrics. Although their songs had their own stories as well, they were strengthened by having his death on their minds.

The Stones were close friends of **Paul** who **had** all heard him complain about the **dreams of** his demise and replacement. **When it happened**, and the remains of Paul were buried, and I took over the position, it seriously spooked all of them. They were traumatized by it. However, without Paul belonging to their band, their substantial Paul enrichments had to be much more discrete. Here are some of the Jagger/Richards lyrics from *Flowers*. See if you can adjust your thinking about each of these songs well enough to recognize who these two writers were thinking about, while also being aware of each song's official storylines.

These first lines are from "Ruby Tuesday." Officially, it is a love song of a girl not to be wed. I will translate it. The new Paul would never say where he came from. Yesterday, the Old Paul, don't matter if he's gone. While the sun is bright (when Paul was alive) or in the darkest night (when his life ended), no one knows the difference. No one can tell when one Paul comes and the other goes.

Although no one knew, the Stones were an exception, being given all the news, and being left out of nothing. They knew that I came, and that Paul went. They sang, "Goodbye, Ruby Tuesday." Later, John sang, "Stupid Bloody Tuesday," referring to that same awful Ruby (bloody) Tuesday that John told them about, being the day he learned of Paul's death. Although Paul had died the Sunday before, his death did not become a reality to John until the tormenting telegram he received on Tuesday. An awareness of it hit John on "Bloody Tuesday." Besides referring to Paul's blood, "Bloody" is one of the favorite curse words of Great Britain. John used it as an expletive in describing that day to Mick.

Every new day (myself and impersonators) got his name. But who could hang a name on Paul? Absolutely no one. With every new day, every replacement of "Yesterday," there would be the change from the Old Paul to the New. But when Paul evolves with every new "day," still **the Stones have** their feelings for the Old Paul. They **say**, "Still I'm gonna miss you," **even though he would go** on through this change **from Old Paul to New Paul.** It is no slight against me that **they still missed their** friend. Don't question why **Paul** needs to be so free—free as a bird. Or, in other words, don't ask us why Old Paul must die. It's the only way to be: the only way to continue to exist as Paul was by substitution. I couldn't give him life as I did until he was set free. Becoming Paul's Proxy is the next best thing to being Paul. He had gone as far as he could. To gain it all, Paul had to be freed from mortality. He just can't be chained to a life where nothing's gained and nothing's lost, at such a cost.

"Live how we can, yet die we must."
~William Shakespeare

355

Our urgency comes from Paul. "There's no time to lose, I've heard [Paul] say" and sing. It was not until after he died that his cohorts took to heart the words: "Life is very short and there's no time." He got alarmed about it long before any of the others took it seriously. He sought assistance in preparing for his replacement. He pled for his mates to help him work it out, to catch their dreams and his before they slipped away. If they did not act quickly, it would be too late. Paul McCartney could not go on once the world mourned. It would be too late.

Keeping it urgent, Paul was dying all the time. For several months, his dreams of dying tormented him but did not drive the others. He feared that they would lose their dream of replacing him. Keith Richards masterfully penned, "Lose your dreams and you will lose your mind." The layered meaning is that Paul would be dying all the time in dreams, suffering for the rest of his life. The frequent death dreams would only stop with Paul's death in actuality. Paul would lose his mind, blow his mind out in a car, and only then stop dying all the time in his dreams. Ain't life unkind? Paul only stops dying when he's dead. Then it's goodbye to Ruby Tuesday.

Ultimately, the most remarkable thing about "Ruby Tuesday" is that it also works well as a sad love song; although, as such, the phrase "Ruby Tuesday" makes no sense. It inspired us.

The next song is, "Have You Seen Your Mother, Baby, Standing in the Shadow?" We are shown how to read it by inserting the word Brother for Mother. It **is** about **Brother Paul,** who is standing over us **in the shadows, the spirit world,** and about me, "another baby," appearing to take Paul's place.

"The meaning of life is that it stops."
~Franz Kafka

Until you can see this song as being about Paul standing in death's shadow, and see me taking his girlfriend and his life, you cannot fully understand it. Ghostwriters anticipated it all in advance. "The have-nots have tried to freeze you in ice." They were jealous of this have-not profiting by preserving Paul. That was a common complaint, and oddly remarkable that it was foreknown—almost as remarkable as how "Sexy Sadie" foretold details of the Charles Manson [1934–2017] case, described in the next chapter.

"Out Of Time" is a Stones song that they said was about Paul being discarded and losing control. Now I know better. They used that already-written song to give me a hard time. They pretended to write lyrics about me that they had already recorded. They made double meanings about Paul after the fact: "You don't know what's going on. You've been away for far too long." The discarded **Paul was** "out of touch, my baby, my poor **discarded** baby."

They said Paul was discarded. **Being** too old-fashioned now, he's obsolete, **replaced by me**, the new and improved Paul. They said his dream of saving his name and fame through me was clever. He gave up his social whirl here in mortality and ran all of his interests from over there, but can't come back and be the first in line. Now he's out of time. It's too late, baby. His time is all used up. Now it's my hour. They all mourned that Paul is out of time now. They were not mocking him for it. They were trying to trouble me.

Their "Ride On, Baby," Keith said, was based on Paul singing lines of "I'm Looking Through You."

"I want to be all used up when I die."
~George Bernard Shaw

357

Paul sang it as if he were dead and replaced by me. Mick and Keith seemed to answer it, "**A** smile on your face, but not in your eyes. You're looking through me. You don't feel it inside." Unless you **knew** that they understood Paul's song, you would never have recognized that one.

Least favored among **the songs** on that otherwise fine album was "Please Go Home." The message that they applied to me was that I lacked affection for Paul, that I should return to being William, and that I should not be collecting Paul's royalties for which I had not worked. It says, "In some early part of your days, you were told of the devious ways that you thought you could get without pay." Rude!

Back to the bit about their envy of our Beatles' accomplishments, my constant connection to Paul intrigued them all. The Stones set out to get a muse of their own while John, George, and Ringo each tried desperately to feel after Paul individually. They tried about everything: prayers, meditations, séances, and rituals. When I showed them that I could channel McCartney childhood details, desires, and such, Mick claimed I got it from Satan, not Paul.

The Beatles and Stones were all studying **religiously** with **Satanists** Kenneth Anger and others **since well before I became Paul.** Both bands had entered into satanic compacts and made pledges. My heritage and Paul-channeling drove them deeper. I already had Paul and a vast spiritual perspective. I lacked nothing to cut my way through the jungle. Not needing what they offered, and seeing no point in echoing the words of others, I launched Paulism.

A Faustian pact is like a spell or hex. As with any spell, it is sometimes repeated if it does not work well enough or fast enough. However, it is always discovered too late that the benefits are never worth it.

Casually explaining all of this darkness after all these years feels good. I have kept these secrets long enough. That is the great thing about fiction—songs and now this novel in particular. Truth can be unbridled in it far more than with nonfiction. The Rolling Stones turned from curiosity to pure satanic devotion before their next album, which they released in November 1967. Although Brian opposed Mick's eagerness to imitate us, Mick said his "Dark Source" inspired a *Pepper's* sound. In the album's title, they describe the queen (whom Mick later calls "the chief witch") as Satanic: *Their Satanic Majesties Request.*

Here is another revelation for you all, speaking of Brian. The police and newspapers said he ended his own life by drowning himself in his pool. That is another cover-up story. **Brian** Jones, the Rolling Stones founder, **was a brilliant**, beautiful, and exceptionally **talented man.** A tremendous entertainer, he played sixty-six instruments, some quite well, and helped write some of their songs. Finally, after ongoing friction in the band, he left it.

He died less than a month later, in the summer of sixty-nine. That was what motivated us to unlock our clues about Paul. The Beatles and the Stones revolution were two sides of the same movement. We were better than they but were all brothers yoked together as one project. **I was the Beatles'** leader; Brian had been the Stones' **leader.** It was on 3 July, less than an hour after hearing of his death, when we decided to reveal the clues. We would give understanding to the albums we had already sold.

We wanted the whole world to know about it on the same day. We leaked the news to a Laurel Canyon

"Her Majesty is a pretty nice girl
But she changes from day to day."

359

musician on 11 September, the third anniversary of Paul's death, exactly ten weeks after Brian died. Five days later, the news reached Tim Harper, who published the story the next day in Times-Delphic, the college paper at Drake University, in Iowa. We expected hysteria but did not get it. 24 days later, I called the lodge for an American contact. They referred me to Bill Hilling, a 32-degree Mason in Richmond, Indiana, who made some phone calls for us. The next day, one of his contacts called Russ Gibb, a disk jockey for WKNR-FM in Detroit. Gibb spent an hour on the topic. **After that broadcast** on Crowley's birthday, 12 October, **the news went wild.**

Everyone looked, but none saw Brian Jones' part in un-stopping our fan's deaf ears and opening their blind eyes to hear and see that Paul is dead and traded. Then came more media pressure than any of us were ready for. What could we say? As in this telling book of fiction, we love to speak the plain truth in songs, but are forced to lie when talking to the press—just as I must disavow this book.

As I think of Brian, I go through many musical memories, like when I invited him to play his little nifty alto saxophone in "You Know My Name," back two years before he died. We toiled with it a bit more without Brian there two months before he passed, and finally released it 6 March 1970, some nine months after his passing. We sold that comical song on the flip side of my "Let It Be." Brian's death at that time became associated in my mind with the death of our band. However, that is another epiphany for you. Now I will tell you how he died.

Stoned to Hell, We Called the Press.

Frank Thorogood was swimming with Brian and said the drowning was an accident. He suddenly heard a voice say, "Brian is my sacrifice. He is mine. Drown him!" Frank obeyed on impulse. They were already in the pool. He could not stop himself.

Satanism felt new to me one night in Hyde Park. Brian along with Kenneth Anger explained what I had always known about Aleister Crowley, but from a fresh perspective. I liked it. Father Crowley (the father of modern occultism) united with the Beatles, Stones, some of their best friends, and many others who had joined earlier in 1966.

Crowley, an eminent Freemason in a few lodges (not regular Masonic bodies in the Anglo-American tradition, but similar), which, at such high degrees, include Satanism that is patterned after that used by the regular lodges. In regular grand lodges, oaths of secrecy prevent those possessing lower degrees from being aware of the blatant Satanism at the top. Do not imagine that blood oaths were objectionable in Crowley's circles that cross the world.

NOTE: The owl is a symbol for Minerva, an ancient goddess of wisdom. For modern Satanism and its never-ending offshoots, you may also see the owl in Crowley. Some honor him, the father owl, along with Minerva, throughout occultism. Find the wisdom, or owl, hidden in knowledge. Be as the owl who sits with eyes wide open, and with a head that turns in all directions to see things as they are whether in the light or darkness. Occult organizations are built upon claims of secret gnosis, hidden knowledge, wisdom, supernatural power, and secret ritual and practices to access that power.

Think of Crowley in connection with paganism and Satanism, and the use of owls in secret ceremonies. Many top-level executives and celebrities, including William, have participated in some of the Cremation of Care ceremonies at the head of the lake in the Bohemian Grove (the Bohemian Club's 2,700-acre site in Monte Rio, California). An enormous 30-foot owl statue serves as that annual ritual's backdrop.

Besides embodying the wise old owl, the name Crowley has a further meaning that William finds significant. Now that readers know to check, they may discover it with a simple Internet search.

361

Owing to the secrecy, the "profane" (uninitiated public) enter into Satanism (with or without praying to Satan) without knowing where it leads. They may advance by Craft degrees, such as in Freemasonry's Ancient and Primitive Rites, or through playful independent experimentation driven by curiosity. The object for all, either way, is to get the person in far enough that he or she can never get out.

As Marianne Faithfull became sexually involved with members of the Rolling Stones, and then fell in love with Jagger, she naturally followed them into Satanism, particularly into Process Church. By letting that religion use her status to gain support, she willingly became their celebrity poster girl.

Before telling you about satanic murders that the Beatles became unwittingly connected to, I ought to explain another song by the Rolling Stones after our *Sgt. Pepper's Lonely Hearts Club Band* took them by surprise. They were flabbergasted.

They were aware of much of it while we were still having a time with putting the whole thing together but were still astounded by the brilliant final product. As a response to our title song, they wrote "Two Thousand Light Years from Home." It was to represent **Paul floating** away from this small world, drifting **off into space**. They were saying that they each **missed** him as well. They had lonely hearts like **all of us** without Paul. The song starts with a line about the sun turning around. As with every revolution **of the earth** to the sun, it is another day.

Our references to days are symbolic. Paul is "Yesterday" because he is gone, and because of his song. Keith represented Paul as Ruby Tuesday

Here comes Nibiru, and I say, "It's alright." Sing, "Ni-Bi-Ru, it's alright." Sing, "Ni-Bi-Ru, here it comes. Ni-Bi-Ru, here it comes. Ni-Bi-Ru, here it comes. Ni-Bi-Ru, here it comes."

because of what John told Mick and Brian about the "Stupid bloody Tuesday" in which he found out that Paul died, and finally saw the bloody picture. Not that Paul died on Tuesday. He did not. It was the bloody miserable day that Brian informed John of it. Mick referred to me as a "new day." John and I both referred to me as "just another day." Starting with the sun turning was a way to say that we went from yesterday to a new day. The "Sun turnin' 'round with graceful motion" refers to the providence or grace that traded one day (Paul) for a new one (me) exactly as **Paul had envisioned** it. Here comes the Sun. Here comes the Son.

It starts with **his crash.** "We're setting off with soft explosion." Just as "Ruby Tuesday" had a clear official meaning (of an unmarried girl), so too does this song have an official meaning. This time, a spaceship takes off and flies away. On a closer look, it is more of their depiction of heaven or hell than of space. To them, heaven is in space. Paul goes to the netherworld of "fiery oceans" and "freezing red deserts" that "turn to dark energy here in every part." It is the place of "green sands." Wherever it may be, the repeated point is that as Paul drifts off into eternity, they, and Paul, are "so very lonely." Now, they are without him, and he is without them.

Answering our "Lonely Hearts," they say they too are so very lonely without Paul. That song also copies our ideas by including a lot of backward recordings. Although I do value their avant-garde expression, we did it first. Now you know why I, on *Sgt. Pepper's,* refer you to them for further clues.

38

More Satanic Murders

By now, you have heard some conservatives claim that rock and roll music is of the devil. Even not-so-conservatives say that. David Bowie says, "Rock has always been the devil's music." Well, although I do not know about that, it fits this chapter. Bowie goes on to say, "I believe rock and roll is dangerous . . . I feel we're only heralding something even darker than ourselves."

Rock, in my opinion, is like all music. Some of it brings people up; some of it drags them all down. Every song brings us closer to light or to darkness, either to love or to hate. Who inspires each?

Satanism and Luciferianism joined the Beatles at the Karlaplansstudion, a Stockholm, Sweden studio. A worker there discussed **Satanism** with John and Paul, including mysticism, channeling energy, and the networks. It **had come up before**, but less convincingly. As far as **John recalled**, that was a turning point. No action came of it before then.

The man told John and Paul that their show would not be a worldwide sensation until they ceremonially enact the **sacrifice** and pray to Lucifer for his influence over **the** whole world. He told them that Lucifer is the **god** of this world and that his power surpasses all others. With that idea in mind, that night, 24 October 1963, John and Paul said words, most likely without taking them seriously enough, promising that they would each sacrifice to quench Lucifer's appetite—or something along that foolish line. I heard John discuss it with Vernon E. Mosher. Attributing the imminent eminent death to the oath, Paul cries, "I said something wrong" ("Yesterday").

Understand that what followed would have most likely happened anyway. Fate was already for them. Now, the magic began a week later, on Halloween, 1963, when they returned with a triumphant entry. Crazed fans made a considerable spectacle of themselves at London Airport. Ed Sullivan, as it happened, witnessed the scene firsthand. He thought he was there by fate. His plane had been delayed. He enjoyed what he saw and was sure America would enjoy experiencing it too. On 11 November, at the Delmonico Hotel in New York, Brian Epstein met with Ed Sullivan to negotiate the now-famous US television appearances that occurred three months later, in February 1964. All went as orchestrated.

NOTE: When the Beatles first appeared on *The Ed Sullivan Show*, they opened their act with Paul singing, "**Close your eyes** and I'll kiss you / Tomorrow, I'll miss you." To receive the Beatles' love, one had only to close eyes to reality. Reality was too painful right **after** JFK was executed in a car (33 years, 9 months, 9 days before Diana). **Trauma** (national or personal) solidifies mind-controlled **living with eyes wide shut**.

After Paul died, the first lines that John recorded in his first post-Paul song's first take, were, "**Living is easy with eyes closed** / Misunderstanding all you see." Even after all these decades of clues, **most eyes remain closed**. Most fans are unwilling to admit that they were fooled. As Mark Twain said, "It's easier to fool people than to convince them that they have been fooled." Obstructions to truth are generally based on what we think we know.

Having experienced that "coincidental" timing impressed the band enough to talk about it, but not enough to turn them fully in that direction yet. Besides, they had no structured system to guide them back then. They still had relatively little training. It was still more of a curiosity. They had not yet fully entered into a binding compact because no one showed them how.

April 1965, while working on *Help!* in the Twickenham Film Studio, Paul, John, and George turned to an expert, as **they supposed**. All that year, beginning 29 January, **Paul** had complained of his lethal dreams. He **was dying all the time.** It was most disturbing to him. The first self-proclaimed expert was Almon Sperry. When Paul, John, and George spoke of Paul's dreams, Almon gave them some lessons in dream interpretation and promised to teach them to control their dreams. Almon taught them some old cultic observances he had learned from either Kenneth Anger or Vernon Mosher. He said doing them increases their power. A week or so later, they met Mosher who prepared them for Anger's meeting by stirring up interest in Satanism and his doctrine of hate.

The thing that most impressed the band about Mosher was his blatant egotistical confidence in interpreting Paul's dreams, claiming that Paul is "the one." Mosher predicted Paul's death, calling it a sacrifice, and even told him approximately when it would occur. Mosher asked John and Paul when and where they had made such a compact with Satan.

"Never," Paul said.

"Death is always there, just beneath the surface."
~Mason Cooley

"How else can you explain all of this?" Mosher asked. "Have you prayed to Satan?"

"Yes," John said, "but it didn't mean anything. It was around fifteen months before the dreams began."

Paul then learned the pattern. It is the same pattern that afflicted many other bands. It is what **a**lways **happens**. It is part of the deal. It is why Brian Jones, and many others, died. Paul and Brian **u**nited with Satan in mortality before crossing over to be tormented in immortality. It is the same with **L**ed Zeppelin, **the** Who, and every other band that was launched by a **satanic pact**. In all such groups, the death of a band member **is certain. It is the bill** that is paid to the coven. "Death is the greatest form of love." ~Charles Manson

In the Beatles' case, **the satanic debt** could only be paid for by Paul. However, if an automobile crash ended his life by accident, it cannot be a deliberate offering. A chance demise is not a valid sacrificial death according to the satanic code. That is the reason that Mark Chapman, who said he loved John, shot him dead. **Chapman**, a self-proclaimed Satanist, **fancied himself a priest** working with orders **to sacrifice John**, **making** John both an enemy and also **an immortal idol.** Beatles records had veiled messages that were too subtle for most. MDC was coached to hear them. Brought under a negative influence, an evil spirit helped him to catch

NOTE: Countering claims that Paul's death was not valid according to code, it was explained that the crash leading to Paul's death was only as accidental as the one that killed Diana, Princess of Wales. After each crash, "Clang! Clang!" The agents that caused each crash "made sure that s/he was dead" ("Maxwell's Silver Hammer"). It is said, "Lucifer [Osiris] and Diana [Isis] are the parents of Aradia and Horus. Osiris and Isis [Paul and Diana] in their separate conveyances each received their enactments, pronouncements, and all else according to the ancient code."

Tap. Tap. Tap.
In ceremonial robes, witches, judges, and Freemasons give decisive raps of the mallet.

367

and obey the demand from **John** in his popular song. In "**Come Together,**" again and again, John **sings,** "**Shoot me!**" It is hard to recognize because it is followed by an immediate handclap. You only hear it once you know.

Even though we went on to great success without Paul, our glory was especially shallow to John who all the more missed Paul for it. Very lonely without Paul, John's depression became intense. He sadly sang in his "Yer Blues," "**I'm** lonely wanna die." Working with me instead **of Paul** created a sense of desperation. He sang, "Feel so suicidal, Even hate my rock 'n' roll Wanna die yeah wanna die."

Now, with malevolent promptings, these words combined with other Beatles lyrics to form a punitive fanatical internalization. The Beatles had sung, "I don't care too much for money," but then appeared on *Pepper's* looking so materialistic. Demons that Chapman prayed to (or Chapman himself) told him retaliation was required, that John Lennon should be punished for forsaking Beatles values, and that John insisted on being shot. Chapman claimed Satan (via a handler) ordered John's death. It is rumored that the same motivation drove the attempted stabbing murder of George. They say Satan ordered it.

Neither Ringo nor I have such threats because neither one of us was present for that initial exchange between Satan and the Beatles. It was a

NOTE: To whatever extent Mark David Chapman was assisted by the doorman, Jose Perdomo, MDC was set to be known as John's assassin. He had been programmed to believe that such notoriety would solve all of his problems. It would cancel his past and give him a new identity. Being there for the notoriety, he waited with Perdomo for the police to come arrest him.

MDC wanted to be arrested and convicted. Billy assures us that the rumor is false (and falsely sourced to George) that MDC was brainwashed to kill John just to keep John quiet. A benefit is not a cause — correlation is not causation.

few years before I joined. We did not require being X'ed out. Paul paid the bill. **Slaying John** and trying to kill George were over**kills for Satan**.

This weird story sounds absurd coming from me who had no part in it. MDC speaks for himself. "Alone in my apartment back in Honolulu," Mark Chapman said in an interview, "I would strip naked and put on Beatles records and pray to Satan to give me the strength." To open himself to Satan's spirit, according to the *Gannett News Service* interview, Chapman played our songs over and over again to give him Satan's power. He said, "I prayed for demons to enter my body to give me the willpower to kill." It worked. His prayers were answered. They often are when seeking such things.

Another lunatic murderer who used Beatles music for satanic purposes was our one-time friend, the notorious Charles Manson. He, with Laurel Canyon ties, was also a friend to the Beach Boys, the Rolling Stones, Anger (Satanist guide), and Process Church. We all knew each other well. Charlie's works of satanic murder were based on lyrics from the *White Album*, especially from interpretations of John's "Revolution 9," my "Helter Skelter," and George's "Piggies."

"Revolution 9" was played while stripping naked to pray for devils. Yoko's line "become naked" became key to the ritual that has now been practiced by many (including Chapman) seeking demonic possession.

Put together from a collection of looped tapes, John and Yoko made "Revolution 9." I never was real fond of it, partly because they stole my idea.

"Hell is empty and all the devils are here."
~Shakespeare

They knew I had been making sound collages, stored on tapes, ever since I joined the band in 1966. I used a small number of them in my videos of avant-garde images. I fully intended to include such a collage, but better, on a future album after I had refined the art. Then, when **I was** in America with the Bonzos, John did it behind my **back.** Their poor amateur attempt, much to my dismay, ended up on our album. It was not at all of the quality that I had made. Since they made theirs public first, everyone thought John was the genius, or idiot, behind the idea. Some of their taped bits had them screaming.

At a point where John screams "Right," Charlie, unfortunately, heard the command to "Rise!" John and Yoko clipped "Number Nine" from a tape that said, "EMI Test Series Number Nine," after finding that part of it sounds like, "Turn me on, dead man" when played reversed. **With nine as McCartney's** number, and a recurring **number that** appeared to entangle John's his whole **life**, hearing it backward as "Turn me on, dead man" **was enough** for John to add it all over their song, and add "9" to the title.

The song and title affected Charles Manson, who listened for apocalyptic clues. "Revolution 9" led him to the ninth chapter of Revelation, the Holy Bible's last book. Charlie taught that "Revolution 9" was code for "Revelation 9." Revelation 9:14-15 has four angels that he supposed were the Fab Four. He believed that Satan himself revealed to him that our part in world history was contained in the Apocalypse. Now, with this song, he accepted his lord's order to "Rise" to begin the revolution of

"Look down at me and you see a fool,
Look up at me and you see a god,
Look straight at me and you see yourself."
—Charles Manson

Revelation 9. "Rise" was written at a murder location with the blood of a victim. Charlie would tell the oppressed, especially blacks, to "Rise!"

Ordering the blacks to rise was consistent too with what Charlie got from George's "Piggies." With Charlie's version of Revolution 9 being a call for blacks to rise against the oppressing middle-class whites, he saw "Piggies" as a melodic warning to the whites that the black uprising was imminent.

Evidence linking the Manson family murders came from the words "pig," "pigs" or "piggie" drawn with the victims' blood. Charlie's favorite saying came from that song, "What they need is a damn good whacking." George's mother gave him that wacky line.

Now to my song, "Helter Skelter." I read a review of a freak-out song by my friends in the Who. "I Can See for Miles" was reported to have swearing cymbals and cursing guitars–a fantastically dirty emergence. Having not yet heard that Who song, I imagined a wildly thunderous raucous, jolting song that would drive people to riot like in early Beatles legends. I wanted to write one like that. I thought of that crazed mental state and related it to the fast thrust of a giant spiral slide **I had slid down** called "Helter Skelter." Laced **with hot sexual** innuendo tension, and an incredible **pulsation**, the song would incite people out of their minds. I intended the universe to create and extend it to me as songs have revealed themselves to me before. I aspired to channel for this world its nastiest, dirtiest, rawest, noisiest song ever.

"Healter [*sic*] Skelter" ended up written in blood. Racial conflict was also part of Charlie's interpretation of that song. He thought an inevitable racial war was understood to be "coming down fast." He thought I warned all to "Look out." Charlie supposed that I made him do his part, that I ordered it. But, no, I did not. He was ready to rise already.

Satanism drove Charlie to have those murders committed. However, **to** him, it was inspiration from a much better source. Charles taught and seemed to **believe that he was Jesus** Christ reincarnated. Now, do not get me wrong about the Satanism connection. Charlie built his religion based on the doctrine given to him by Mr. Anger, who was an Aleister Crowley disciple. He used it in a broader sense than the Beatles used it for specks of Paulism. Satanism had dark influences but was not the end.

It is like Catholicism begetting Protestantism. Charlie Manson's ideologies sprang from the Crowley nest in a sense, but not directly like Thelema or even Paulism. Manson's approach is to ours what one good Protestant religion is to another. We all have similarities, but each has its significant departures too. Do not judge a beast by its sister or parent. Most religions have a mother church. Do not be overly critical because of a mother of an idea. You may have the same mother or father and not know it.

How many Protestants are critical of Catholics? They condemn their mother church. One Protestant insisted to me that the Catholic church was the beastly whore spoken of in Revelation 17 who sits on the Seven Hills of Rome. He called that church the mother of harlots. "That makes your church a harlot," I said, "since it is a daughter of the mother of harlots." You get it? Don't criticize. Just help make the world better. My father taught me that spiritual pride is the most pernicious poison.

In Charlie's racially obsessed world, "Rocky Raccoon" meant black people. Likewise, as he listened to "Blackbird," he absurdly assumed I urged a massive black revolt when I was singing about Paul dying, and about me flying with his broken wings. However, I also had concerns about news reports of racial tensions in America. Sure, I also sang for their healing and thriving. The song came to me like a gift early one morning. I mostly wrote it to myself.

To Charlie, "Happiness is a Warm Gun" was a need for weapons for the revolution. It surprises me that he missed those strong sexual suggestions with his mind so sexually occupied. **It was about** "Mother Superior" (Yoko) jumping **John's gun.**

Every song, practically, appeared to have a special message intended for Charlie. Some were to begin the racial revolution. He also created strange interpretations of our other songs. In his world, everything had to do with the Beatles and the Bible. He misunderstood most of it. However, one point that Charlie got right was that John did sometimes favor the coming NWO's revolution. When he sang

NOTE: Leading up to the big happening, the revolution utilizes a series of chaotic events until those going through the chaos cry for the new order. Those chaotic events are already occurring and will continue to do so until the transformation is complete. Mankind is given problems designed to lead them to ultimately demand a complete takeover. David Rockefeller said, "We are on the verge of a global transformation. All we need is the right major crisis, and the nations will accept the New World Order."

HEGELIAN DIALECTIC

PROBLEM ▶ REACTION ▶ SOLUTION

Create the problem needed for your desired solution.

our Revolution songs ("Revolution 1," "Revolution," and "Revolution 9" (recorded in that order)), he did mean to encourage one, but not as Charlie wanted it.

The destruction **John sang** of attracted him. He ended up with **a double message.** On the single, "Revolution," he played it safe politically. But in the later released "Revolution 1," he softly said "in" (his true feelings) right after singing "out," as most know it: "But when you talk about destruction, Don't you know that you can count me out, *in*." John chose to kind of play it safe by leaving the "in" out of the printed lyrics. He hoped that his softer word entered people's subconscious without causing a backlash. Although he favored destruction, he struggled with his message. He felt that the right word would be censored. John never intended to have the song banned with the right word but did not entirely remove it either.

Much of our writing wrote itself. **We were** the music vessels who recorded songs that were **given** to us. It often just came into our heads as though **some** force or spirit from beyond had written it and put the new song into our brains. It is like channeling. That is when they are our most creative. Nevertheless, this is also where things get strange now and then. We do not always know what it means.

It seems that some lyricist from beyond foresaw exactly how these songs would affect Charlie and looked ahead to see what would befall him for acting on them all. **It was a terrible set-up.** "Sexy Sadie" was written out **of John's disillusionment** with the Maharishi Mahesh Yogi. I wrote more on that song

374

elsewhere. **But the same force** that gave us all those lyrics, told Charlie how to interpret them all, and how to act on them. It also **foretold his fate** of being sucked in. He too was a pawn. None of us realized it would lead to people being murdered.

We never agreed with killing anyone and did not empathize with murderers. We had no prior intel about violent crimes. However it seemed, it was not our fault. To us, "Sexy Sadie" was only about the Maharishi. "Sexy Sadie" replaced "Maharishi," not to predict the future, but to avoid a lawsuit. To Manson, however, Sexy Sadie was Sadie Mae Glutz. Everyone knew Charlie gave that name to his lover, Susan Atkins, long before our album came out.

When in jail for the Manson murders, **Sexy Sadie**, aka Sadie Mae Glutz or Susan Atkins, **was the one** to implicate Charlie. Sadie's testimony **in court** is what brought down the Manson family. Details of Sharon Tate's murder were particularly disturbing. Intended satanic mutilations went as Charlie ordered. They had made the same kind of death-for-success deal made by the Beatles, the Stones, the Who, and by heaven knows how many other bands launched by a secret pact. **This time** it was for a movie deal. "I am the Devil, and **I am here** to do the Devil's business," Charles "Tex" Watson said before he murdered Voytek Frykowski, according to Sadie's testimony. "Tex came back and he looked at her [Tate] and he said, 'Kill her.' And I killed her . . . And I just stabbed her, and she fell, and I stabbed her again. I don't know how many times I stabbed her."

375

Sharon begged for her unborn baby's life, but could not change the deal. Sadie had every intention to cut the baby out of the womb, to correspond with the movie, *Rosemary's Baby,* but there was no time.

In the trial, **Charlie's** disciples were all notably under his **hypnotic** power. He captured them using **mind-control** through ritual and an evil spirit that still **has a hold on some** of the Manson family to this day. Entering a man and taking over his thinking gives a **malicious spirit** far too much power. Charlie **is an often-overlooked** victim in this story. **He was possessed** before his followers were.

"Sexy Sadie, what have you done?" Your damning testimony "made a fool of everyone." Charlie would not have been exposed without it. She made a fool of everyone in the Manson family. Sexy Sadie, ooh, what have you done? **Sexy Sadie**, talking broke the rules. Your testimony **laid** it down for the world to see. You laid it down for **all** to see.

Sexy Sadie, oooh, you broke the rules. One sunny day the world was waiting for a lover. She came along to turn on everyone. Sexy Sadie, she's the greatest lover, and greatest killer, of them all. Sexy Sadie, how did you know the whole world was

---

NOTE: John lived and died at the Dakota, the enigmatic building used for the 1968 film, *Rosemary's Baby.*

SPOILER ALERT: This footnote reveals plot points. In the film, Guy and Rosemary Woodhouse (John Cassavetes and Mia Farrow) move into a building tied to cannibals, Satanists, and witches. Through that association, Guy makes a Faustian pact to boost his acting career. An actor in his way, and someone interfering with Rosemary's role, are eliminated. To incarnate in the flesh, Lucifer impregnates Rosemary. Fearing she might lose the unborn child, Rosemary drinks a strange concoction containing Devil's Pepper.

At first glance, *Rosemary's Baby* is the Christian nativity's antithesis, but also parallels the Horus story along with other reincarnating deities.

376

out there waiting just for you to say what happened? **The world** was waiting just for your confession to **put a stop to the man** and his clan. Sexy Sadie, oooh, how did you know? Sexy Sadie, you'll get yours yet! However big you think you are by talking about him, however great it makes you, Sexy Sadie, oooh, you'll get yours yet! Charlie gave her everything she had just to sit at his table. Sadie's smile to us would lighten everything. Sexy Sadie is the latest and the greatest of them all. Sexy Sadie made a real fool of everyone in that group.

These words are neither my thoughts nor John's sentiments. It is merely what the lyrics were about by the Manson interpretation, according to that same evil spirit that wrote the song through **John**. John knew nothing about it. He **was angry** with his last spiritual infatuation **at that time.** I include it as a demonstration of how the evil spirits can make fools of everyone, not just of the Manson "family." The song was inspired by the spirit who set it all up.

Now, it has been said by some that "Maggie Mae," which we released a year and a half later, was of Sexy Sadie Mae Glutz also. However, that song goes back to a time long before I joined the band. We used it all along as a warm-up number. It is just a coincidence that it came out when it did.

Magical Mystery Tour has another case of historical clues given before the event. As a death clue in the booklet, John is standing by a sign that says, "The best way to go is by M&DC." It clued in those who knew that M&DC was a funeral parlor. Decades later, some of our fans began saying that it referenced the initials of **the murderer** who took John's life. That coincidence **added a sad spin** of that picture. When we made the movie and print, I enjoyed that pointer to Paul but had only seen him occasionally. His death was not a personal loss to me. Although it marked the greatest upheaval that karma ever put me through, it did not mark a death in any tragic way to me on a personal level—except just in the sense that I lost my old simple life by taking on Paul's part. However, to me, bringing John's odious death into the picture is saddening. He was one of my best friends and music partners. I had not had such a brilliantly talented bandmate. Without a doubt, I believe fate, or God, or the universe, made no random strike on Paul. That same intelligence intended that John and I work together in this world.

Charlie's supporters are of two classes. His most visibly connected adherents are those followers who hung around him, comprising the so-called "Manson Family." These are the ones that the authorized media acknowledged to be under his power. They are those who carried out his sexual fantasies, murders, and rituals. Sexy Sadie Mae Glutz, for one of many examples, did it all for him.

Less conspicuously, Charlie was also supported by—and hurt by—MK-Ultra/CIA agents who were investigating the impact of certain chemicals given to Charlie to use for mind-control. He implemented each system on his "family" more fruitfully than the agents could on him. With charm and ingenuity, he combined ideas to make an effective mind-control program that had followers kill (such as Sharon Tate) on command. Hearing of them leaving a fork in such a victim's belly, Bill Ayers taught the Weathermen a new four-finger salute invoking that bloody fork.

The Weathermen got their name from a paper they circulated at the SDS. That paper was named after a line of Dylan's "Subterranean Homesick Blues." It was called, "You Don't Need a Weatherman to Know Which Way the Wind Blows." Later, their name became the Weather Underground Organization (WUO) but are still the Weatherman or Weathermen.

Under the leadership of Bill Ayers and Jeff Jones, this group bombed the Pentagon and other buildings, especially of the US federal government, but also other targets. **They wanted** to destroy the United States. On one occasion, the bombing was merely to break **Timothy Leary out of prison.**

The Weathermen, like Charles Manson, intended to destroy the United States through violence. They had similar enough thinking that they supported each other. As Bill Ayers' wife, Bernardine Dohrn, had explained it, after referring to the Manson murders, "The Weathermen dig Charles Manson!"

Weatherman bombings targeted more buildings than people but killed too. In an interview printed on 10 September 2001, the day before the 911 attacks in New York and elsewhere, Ayers said, "I don't regret setting bombs" and "I feel we didn't do enough." Now, though, Ayers and Jones, rather than killing, have better methods that changed America. Ayers was Barack Obama's mentor. The $1 trillion stimulus package was written with help from Jeff Jones. The Weathermen have top-level connections.

379

39

"Hey Bulldog"

I am explaining some of the less spectacular songs, such as "Hey Bulldog," along with the many truly great ones. I want to show our frame of mind in writing them, and how Paul was always part of it. We all wanted to create great works of music (or, at least I did), but also wanted to have fun now and again. I got along best with the others when I was playful. **My perfectionist** work ethic, being such a sharp **contrast to Paul's**, wearied my mates who had not been **pushed** so hard. Nevertheless, I not only worked **harder** but played with greater gusto too. I had learned the arts of fun with the Bonzos.

Recorded 11 February 1968, "Hey Bulldog," was the last song that we taped before we all went to India. We had all gathered at Abbey Road to make a promotional film for "Lady Madonna" when I, the group's bulldog, decided to use that opportunity to make a new song, and to have some amusement. I was not the group's bulldog in a bossy sense of barking out orders but as the leader. We would play now and see what we might create while we were at it. It would be a product of playful invention.

As we reached the studio, George criticized the lot of us for pretending to be recording the song, "Lady Madonna," without considering the irony of our commercial priority. He called our hypocrisy ludicrous. Although it was my song, he took it more seriously and found it a bit distasteful. He said, "You are mocking Donna who couldn't make ends meet in the first place, and yet, here all of us are, deliberately intending to be false. For what? **For money**! At least she was real. Though faking it boosted record sales and profit, we did not need it. **We are all** wasting our time. Donna lost her life **over the financial** desperation that we sing of as if it is a funny **game**."

"Unless anyone of you has a more fantastic idea," I said, "as long as we have reserved this studio time, let's record something new." John soon came up with some lyrics he had started before. It was a song that saw me as a bullfrog. I am the lowly frog kissed by fate to make me a prince. John had become annoyed that I so easily excelled in the role of Paul without having heart, but with such unimaginable talent. John felt insecure about it. He wondered when he too would be replaced. The line, "What makes you think you're something special when you smile?" was about my new looks. Other lines were about my loneliness.

As magical as was the transformation of this mere frog to become **the Beatles' crown** prince, it had a downside for me. It **isolated me** from friends and relations. **I became the lonely Sgt. Billy Pepper** wanting to get back home, a nowhere man fool

381

on the hill, one of all the lost and miserably lonely people that we described in our songs. As a group, we finished writing the piece. We each put in our own threepence, each shaping the song in our own directions. It has other elements too, but if you look at it as **I explain** it, you will surely admit that it is mostly **about me** replacing Paul— as was common **with our songs.**

Meanings were usually layered so that most songs would have a surface meaning but then would seem to be about something else after a few encounters— rather like this book. Some words, such as wigwam, had a good sound. John nonsensically sang, "Wigwam frightened of the dark." A wigwam is a type of Native American domed hut. John meant no disrespect and did not imagine that the huts could be frightened. The word sounded good. He especially liked singing it with "Big man." I am the big man there. I am a lot bigger and taller than Paul and others. If you do not believe me, you can contrast pictures of John or George standing next to me with older pictures of them standing next to Paul.

Notice how Paul, George, and John were equally short in pictures of them together. That is why we ended the Beatles tours when Paul died. They enjoyed sharing microphones. It was not the same look to have me standing there so noticeably taller. I would need my mic to be several feet from theirs.

"You can talk to me," was a point of reassurance that John was kindly extending to me. Now we were friends. He says, "If you're lonely,

382

you can talk to me." Saying that I am "standing in the rain" refers to me, the stand-in for Paul who died in the rain, feeling alone. I am the bulldog left alone out in the rain, but John is reaching out to me.

My solitude can be measured out in the news of the group's actions. Wherever we go, the press writes stories and snaps pictures; they show us to the world. I was in the news as if they knew me, but nobody did. They thought they knew me but didn't have a clue that I was someone else. We sang from my viewpoint, "You think you know me, but you haven't got a clue." John had originally penned it, "Some kind of solitude is measured out in news," but did not write it clearly enough. I misread it as "measured out in you." It sounded good. Since none of us thought the word "news" was any better there, we kept it as I misread it.

The line, "Some kind of happiness is measured out in miles," was John's way of telling me that happiness would come down the road. He was right. I am happier now. My new life became my own eventually as threats of consequences diminished. At that time, **I had terrible anxiety** about someone detecting and imprisoning me **for** what we now call identity theft. I wrote of **having** that fear earlier on when I **revealed some dark secrets** about the Rolling Stones. From the start, they knew the great Beatles' secrets and did not seem quiet enough. It was about my intense fear that the Rolling Stones howled in some of their songs, and for which we sang here, "Some kind of innocence is measured out in years. You don't know what it's like to listen to your fears." **Time will** tell my innocence. Usually, I would **affirm** that I had nothing to do with the death, **that I rightly work as Paul** had said he wanted **with his name and estate.** I fulfilled his will.

Essentially, this song, which started as "Hey Bullfrog," was about me, the kissed toad, hopping in as the new Prince Paul, but feeling melancholy and isolated. I needed to talk to someone.

Going back in time a bit, **John had joked about** Paul croaking out a song like a bullfrog. **Paul** had a better voice than John, but would quickly become hoarse, sounding like a bullfrog. When I took over, I sometimes intentionally made myself hoarse to sound like Paul, the "Bullfrog, doing it again."

Near the end, being in a jovial mood, I barked, growled, and howled like a dog. We liked that new ending, and added on "Hey, Bulldog. Hey, Bulldog," justifying my idea to make "Hey, Bulldog" our new title.

Not only did I, as Paul, create clues to show the world that I am William, but as Vivian Stanshall, I gave clues to show that I, the musical comedian in the gorilla suit, am Paul McCartney. With this song in mind, I, as Viv, said, "Gentlemen, I am a bulldog, and you will find my bark is worse!"

Who else claimed to be the bulldog? It was me all along, the frog who could croak out a song and smile as special as Paul could. I played the part of

Vivian as well as I played Paul's part, but neither role was who **I am**. Now you finally know who I am. **The Paul role** was something that I stepped into and **reinvented** as time went on. The roles of  Vivian Stanshall and Phil Ackrill (rhymes with Bill or Will), I played from the start. I am the Bulldog.

NOTE: William used the role of Phil Ackrill before leaving it to Phillip Ralston—while reserving the option to do performances occasionally, and to give recording assistance. Ralston, the new Phil Ackrill, enthusiastically received the role in hopes of a recording contract. When that contract failed to materialize, William and Ralston both lost interest in the band. When Ralston quit, he pursued a career outside of the music industry.

Although William says he "invented" the Phil Ackrill role, the name appears to have been suggested to William by an associate of Ralston's mother. She anticipated Phil's eventual switch, which she believed "would be interesting."

William's role as Vivian Stanshall likewise involved another performer and was likewise less profitable than William intended. Unlike the Ackrill role, William never completely left the Stanshall role to another. As Willian originally set it up, he would collect a modest fraction of each Vivian engagement that was done in William's place. He imagined that the replacement would be a big star, earning enough to live comfortably while also paying William his cut. However, although the new Vivian made some stellar performances, they did not pay well enough to justify the position. Throughout the rest of his life, he was on William's payroll. Although keeping that position going was not financially advantageous, it gave William great pleasure in doing the shows that he wanted, and in passing the rest onto the man whom he paid to live as "Vivian Stanshall."

385

Two Pauls

I did a concert once with my friend, Paul Simon. The press went on about the big event and called it a magical double billing. I corrected them, "It's not a double Bill, it's a double **Paul**."

Maybe you thought **I was** writing about Paul McCartney and me until **you** read about the double Paul bit. You are not certain now who the other Paul may be. I'll tell you now, it's me. The other Paul is always me. Yet, what I say of myself also applies to each of you. We all do it. Celebrities fall into this unfortunate split more heavily than most others. However, we all deal with this same syndrome that lets a split divide us against ourselves. The Two Pauls Syndrome (TPS) can be cured.

There are two Pauls in me: the popular public Paul, a larger-than-life knighted rock-n-pop icon, and on a more meaningful level, the private Paul who is a soulful man of solitude with the same desires and trials as everyone. The public Paul is a showman. It is my thing. I enjoy it immensely, including the hard work. If I did not thoroughly enjoy this work, I would have stopped doing it a long, long time ago–or even years before that. I love it and could not stop even if I wanted to. I live for it and am fond of hard work. Throughout my years of Beatles, Wings, and still now, **I lived** for the work. When at the studio, I only want **to work.**

I've got a job to do, and I do it well. I may require too much of my colleagues by expecting them to be as driven as I am. Before I joined the Liverpool lads, Brian Epstein and George Martin kept the Beatles focused. Their talent lacked focused discipline. When I filled that hole for the group, we immediately turned to much greater projects and innovations. Initially, everyone was turned on by it. However, before long, John, George, and Ringo all grew weary of the work. In and out of the studio, I always pushed them a little too hard.

My private life is also filled with wonderful work. My workaholic nature carries over into my seclusion just as it does in my public life. One of the things that kept Linda and me sane for years was our obsessive willingness to be emotionally detached from worldly things. If I ever desire something money can buy, I have the means and may spend it freely. I have many nice things. Still, there is never enough in the material world to satisfy anyone fully. We do not find inner peace by obtaining the biggest basket of goods. It can only come from within. It is spiritual, not material. That is why it was important to Linda and me, not that I objected to wealth also. Poor peasants in town would purchase goods they did not need. They lived higher than we did out in the heart of the country. Our farm had dirty old crates and used lumber in the garage. Until buying nicer things, I used these worn treasures and entertained myself by making our furniture out of what peasants would have thrown away.

As all is said and done, our highest pleasures are **in our work** more than in our possessions. With **love in our hearts** and our souls, we could work for what **was needed**, and live poor without buying into the endless material trappings. Naturally, knowing the furnishings and appliances were old and ugly was easier for us to enjoy than for **most people** since for us it was a matter of choice. We **were not** tempted to think less of ourselves just for **looking** or acting as if were poor. It is a point that I have not talked much about. I will try to explain. I am not sure I can.

Only what is within matters. What is outside is not who we are. All materialism is an illusion. The thought of lacking something makes us insecure. When any of us feel that we lack nothing, having more becomes meaningless. An abundant mindset does not need to impress anyone. Shocking our guests by our oddly low standard of living added to its entertainment. We were wealthy enough to see that most stuff does not matter. It would have mattered a whole lot if we, or our children, could not eat. Our riches taught us that most of our wants are not needs. Most stuff is an illusion. Possessions will not buy happiness and are no way to measure the worth of people. I live a dual life. When I have too much of either, I embrace the other with more pleasure, strength, and understanding.

Overindulging in playing the pauper one day, and jetting with the elite on the next, creates balance. Knowing at both ends that I also enjoy the other, I am fine either way. The wealthy at their fireplaces, nestled with loved ones, are not all that different from the street people who gather together and hover over fires, sharing their thoughts and trashcan heat. Before being Paul, I joined them occasionally when winter nights were cold and windy. I always make an effort to know what is in people and to see myself in them. We cannot know them in any ways that are not in ourselves. The best pleasures follow effort. If not, there would be no mountain climbers.

That is why I, William, the private Paul, believe in work. **As Billy,** I went out into the cold; and as Paul, **I made** furniture because roughing it, or as **our friends** called it, "playing poor," was enough **work to be pleasurable.** As eccentric as it may sound, consider all the work of camping out compared to sleeping in a warm bed. People have joked about my poor pretenses but do the same in principle. Beyond the recreational benefits, I gain understanding and a keener connection to the people by having played these parts. It helps me stay grounded. The Sixties' rebellion against our parents' possessions also played a part in it. We thought there was something wrong with enjoying luxuries. Now I know to enjoy everything.

As I said, I am two Pauls. The public Paul has the glamorous lifestyle; the private Billy-Paul is not so celebrity-minded. The public Paul is my career. The private Billy-Paul includes every aspect of my life outside of my public career. When fans think of me, it is usually about the public image of the star, Sir J. Paul McCartney. Paul is just a famous role **I have** adopted for my career. It is something I *have,* **more than** it is someone I *am.* I play the part. It is **my job** that I must do well. There is always enough of me in that role to be successful. Music is real. It is from me. When my heart is in it, that is real. I am not merely channeling Paul's material. My music is a blend of us both because we are blended. It has the private Billy-Paul in it.

Hear my material in contrast to the prior Paul's. I like his songs but favor a different style. When I did *Sgt. Pepper's Lonely Hearts Club Band,* it was obviously not Paul's style. Likewise, our private off-stage lives are not at all the same. It makes me kind of question what I am doing when I think of the public Paul being so well-known worldwide with everyone thinking that is me, while so few fans know the truest me, the private "Paul."

With this illuminating book, I hope to dispel that facade. **I am** revealing a lot about my private self in hopes that before I cross over back to Linda, I can pull **myself** back together to be not two Pauls but one **William**. My music and public life drifted to better reflect my private self. **Self-disclosure is** what I want. It is **the reason I went public** with my paintings and poems. It is why I have altered my press attitude. Before I promoted the public Paul, and hid the private William. I would never reveal my private life, the real me. Now, approaching the end of my road, I want you to know the real me. It is not easy for me. The private Paul is just another bloke who wants love. Nothing too stimulating there, just the same old story of the life that we all share.

Let me briefly introduce myself, the private Paul. I am little Billy who sat beside my sweet mother on a damaged piano bench to sing along to whatever she would play, mostly show tunes. I am William who ventured into the music business by writing songs and working with people who had gone further, ever trying to become **one of them**. In the end, it was my fate, designed and **set up** for me, not by me. In "That's The Way **God** Planned It," George says, "That's the way God wants it to be." He says to be humble. We work hard to determine everything but cannot control outcomes.

As we "Let go and let God," as the saying goes, we lose our pride. George taught full acceptance. I now see the wisdom of it as an end to suffering over whatever we had held to as most unacceptable. We kick ourselves for things not being as we want. Such resistance creates pain. Billy Preston sang, "You've got to believe me / That's the way God planned it." To end suffering, **no matter what happens,** let's permit ourselves to be happy, accepting what we cannot change as if we or God planned it. **We do all we can** do. We surrender ourselves along with the outcome. "Man proposes, God disposes" (Thomas a Kempis).

41

Seven in Three

There were seven **Beatles** in total in the three Beatles phases. The first **phase**, from 1960 to 1962, had several **people come and go**, joining in for an audition here or a tour there. Still, not one of them was ever a set part of the band except for John Lennon, Paul McCartney, Stuart Sutcliffe (who claimed to get "the Beetles" [bugs or mallets] from a motorcycle gang in *The Wild One*), George Harrison, and Peter Best.

NOTE: Royston Ellis claimed credit for suggesting the vowel change from the Beetles to the Beatles, emphasizing "the beat." But the world wanted to know how they came up with the name "Beetles" in the first place.

One story is that when John was twelve years old, his uncle came up with Beetles based on Betelgeuse, a star in the Orion constellation that is predicted to explode into a supernova in the Age of Aquarius. However, not wanting to admit that the band was named by an uncle, better origin myths were invented.

According to the Beatles' publicist, Derek Taylor, Stuart thought of the name after watching *The Wild One*, in which Johnny Strabler (Marlon Brando) refers to the Black Rebels Motorcycle Club as "young beetles." However, Stuart never saw that film. The movie, based on Frank Rooney's short story "The Cyclists' Raid," being one of the first feature films to depict motorcycle gang violence, was banned in the UK until 1967, five years after Stuart died.

Cynthia (John's first wife) said that in a brainstorming session, the band sought a bug-related name to emulate Buddy Holly & the Crickets.

John claimed a more mystical origin, again dating back to when he was twelve. A man on a pie appeared to him. He wrote: "It came in a vision—a man appeared on a flaming pie and said unto them 'From this day on you are Beatles with an 'A.' 'Thank you, mister man,' they said, thanking him." That humorous vision of a man on a flaming pie resembles stories of gods in flying saucers. It begs the question, "Who was the man, god, or flying messenger, who appeared to John? William clears it up: "I'm the man on the flaming pie" ("Flaming Pie").

PAUL McCARTNEY

Having had far more on-stage drum performance hours than any other Beatle drummer, including Ringo, Pete had experience but did not look the part. Others were connected to the group, but these entertainers were the only **Beatle members** of the first phase. Phase One Beatles **was a club** band that endured with these five underpaid performers who never cut records. They built up a following, but not beyond those few areas where they performed. That grueling grunt work prepared the way for a much easier ride in the two phases that followed. Most of Phase One was in clubs in Liverpool and Hamburg.

As they got their first recording deal, not too long after Stuart Sutcliffe's fatal brain hemorrhage, the group, as ordered by George Martin, ousted Pete Best in favor of Ringo Starr, mostly because Ringo looked more the part. A new drummer and the advent of their recording career marked the band's entrance to Phase Two (1962–1966), which rocketed when they toured North America in 1964.

NOTE: The problem with Pete Best was not his drumming. As William says, Ringo was chosen over Pete "mostly because Ringo looked more the part." That part was for Paul's underdog, not an equal or superior. Following the formula, John and Paul would be the stars of every concert and album, and the ultimate legendary writing team. Paul would be "the cute Beatle" who becomes a Christ figure. However, Pete, not Paul, was becoming the most beloved Beatle. Some fans were saying, "Pete's the Best!" His popularity, good looks, and strong stage presence undermined the roles of John and Paul.

Ringo, who was well-connected, looked like a shy beatnik. Likewise, they kept George, not for any expert guitar playing, but for his timid demeanor. His friendship and history with the band also added realism to the myth. Since their early albums were performed by session musicians, skills mattered less than image. The band only had to play well enough for live performances—which were, by design, overpowered by screaming fans.

393

Paul's death, two years later, revolved them to Phase Three (1966–1970) when I stepped in for him. Paul's death put an abrupt end to touring since **I did not look like**, sound, or act like the authentic **Paul enough to pass for him** in live performances. Being a few inches taller was no serious problem in photographs that we could crop but would be conspicuous on a stage.

Everyone knew their act too well to change it. Sharing mics demonstrated their cohesive friendship. Standing united at the same height suggested equality that was now lacking. Phase Three could never tour.

Having to learn Paul's peculiarities was another reason not to tour. Most specifically, I did not look at all like him while playing his bass. Compare videos. I can make the music, but not play as he did. I could not do the deceptively difficult high eyebrow naturally either. The raised brow would matter for any live sessions. The closest we got to it was our rooftop performance and the *Our World* broadcast. For these engagements, we each had our own mic, and stood apart, making the height difference less obvious. Our version of the Beatles in Phase Three was primarily that of a studio band, which I had done before. As each of us needed help, we would either get it from bandmates or hire others to do it. It definitely did not matter if the other Beatles were in each song.

Each of the three Phases is marked by distinct band members with their own particular work. Phase One did clubs, Phase Two did albums and tours in every commercially attractive country, and Phase Three did studio albums. Each phase paved every avenue for the work to come. My Paul success in Phase Three was possible largely due to all who did the work before. Thank you, John, Paul, Stu, George, Pete, and Ringo. I, Bill, am the seventh Beatle, the last, but not the least, of all Beatles. Those Six set the world stage for me. Without them going ahead, everything I do, and all that I am, would be Paulless. I would still be here as a nameless session musician. My soul lacked Paul. For the man after him waits here until the bell tolls for him and me and the birds sing.

Remember the seven stars, not merely four or five. These seven distinct spirits comprise the single entity or unit. It is a single band divided over three phases. Although divided in time, they all made contributions to the whole. Our successes in Phase Three and beyond justify the hard sacrifices of each one before. **I thank** them **all** and the many behind the scenes **that made it work.** Mostly, I thank you.

Mentioning that we were seven in all, rather than merely a well-known four, is important for what will be following in beast references. It is interesting to note that although there was a total of seven, everyone thinks of the Beatles as only four. Hence, although the Beatles are a band of Fab Four, we are rightly of seven heads, speaking collectively.

This beast with seven heads is the same beast that has four. Although some outshine the others, we are the "Seven Stars." Everyone is a star. However, we are now considering the seven stars

395

that are four, coincidentally resembling the beast. I emphatically say now, and in "The Beast" (chapter 63), that I am joking. **I am** only bringing it up to mention **the paradox** that the four are seven. And we are all stars. The seventh is the greatest.

All of us had our place. I am showing mine. As the seventh Beatle, I am the seventh son in this line of sons. I am the seventh star, seventh spirit, seventh angel, or seventh whatever we were, in this line of whatever I am in, or of whatever we all are. Yet, however 7th, I am all 6's to McCartney's 9's.

Now here is another point to count. We sang, "1, 2, 3, 4, 5, 6, 7. All good children go to heaven. One, two, three, four, five, six, seven. All good children go to heaven." It was not just Paul who went. We all go where Paul and Stu went, all seven of us. You will go too. All stars return to heaven.

42

The Beastles' Number

Paul and I are one. We are basically equivalent. I am just one more, that is all. He was Paul, and I am one more Paul. I am all Paul was, plus one more. Grab a calculator for this little chapter. Unless you do, it is not as impressive. Got it? I hope that you do. Okay, first, **let** us count all of the letters in both **James Paul McCartney** and **William Wallace Shepherd**. That is six names in all with a total of 40 letters. Here is where the number fun begins. Enter 40 on your calculator. Unless you do, you will not see it. Divide that 40 by 6. That's 40 letters divided by 6 names. You'll see it makes sixes forever. It's all sixes between us.

Though that is by averaging us, we are not average. Both of us are far from it but are the same. I am just one more. If you assign a value to each letter, each one being worth one more than the previous letter, making "A" = 1, "B" = 2, "C" = 3, et cetera, reaching all the way to "Z" = 26, and if you add each of my six names together, you would see that the sum of William = 79, Wallace = 57, Shepherd = 83, James = 48, Paul = 50, and McCartney = 97.

Okay, add up James Paul McCartney, and you get 195. By the same calculation method, you will notice that William Wallace Shepherd = 219. If you add us both together, you will get a total of 414. Enter it in your calculator if you wish.

Admittedly, this part is weak. Nonetheless, it may linger in your mind as interesting. Now add those three digits (4 + 1 + 4 = 9). Adding my six names equals 9. They all add up to Paul's Number Nine. Although it's all sixes, "all the same," it comes to 9.

So, okay, by **now you are** telling yourselves I have too much time **on my** hands. On planes before special engagements, my **mind** is busy going over every little detail. But when **flying home**, my brain has to let go of it all. It needs **to wander away**. When the racing stops, the brain wants **some more**. Flying home, I relax, pour some wine, and play with anagrams, numbers, and things that do not matter.

All four of the Beatles' names figure together to number the four-headed beast. However, our public names are not the same as our birth names. Although I am William Wallace Shepherd, by playing Paul, I became James Paul McCartney. Now it is Sir J. Paul McCartney. John Winston Lennon in time

NOTE: Although William's number-crunching may be an interesting window to how his mind works when his brain is tired, flying home after a long tour, and although it is interesting to see what he finds amusing in his idle moments, his calculation is off here. McCartney = 102, not 97. Did he really miss the "E," or was that intentional? J. Paul McCartney (or William Shepherd) = 162.

decided to change his name to John Lennon Ono as a way of expressing equality with his soul mate, Yoko Ono Lennon. Richard Starkey early on changed his name to Ringo Starr.

When we add up all the numbers of this four-headed beast, **Sir J. Paul McCartney is 203**. Here is each bit: Sir (19+9+18) J. (10) Paul (16+1+21+12) McCartney (13+3+3+1+18+20+14+5+25). By adding up John's, **John Lennon Ono = 165** = (10+15+8+14)+(12+5+14+14+15+14)+(15+14+15). **Ringo Starr** = (18+9+14+7+15) + (19+20+1+18+18) = **139**. **George Harrison = 159**, which, bit by bit, equals (7+5+15+18+7+5)+(8+1+18+18+9+19+15+14). Adding us all together, **Paul (203) + John (165) + Ringo (139) + George (159) equals** a beastly grand total of six hundred threescores and six, or, in other words, **666**. That is the beastly number of ⬠ **the four-headed Beastle** band.

NOTE: As already noted, the sum is off by 5 (just as Billy's age is off by 5 years). 666 + 5E = 671. To keep it real, never miss the "E" (5) in McCartney—or, for that matter, his Encoder's Middle E.

Encouraging readers to engage in gematria to identify the beast, John the Revelator numbers the man, 666 (Revelation 13:18). On a Roman coin, "Neron Caesar" is written in Greek as ΝΕΡΩΝ ΚΑΙΣΑΡ. Because it can transliterate into Hebrew as קסר נרו (with a value of 666), and because Nero made killing Christians a sporting event, Christians commonly believed Nero was that beast. Corresponding with the name's Latinization, dropping the final N (thus dropping 50 from the value), some early manuscripts of *the Book of Revelation* changed the beastly number in 13:18 to 616 (666 - 50 = 616). Not only was Nero a cruel and Abhorrent Roman emperor (54 to 68 AD), he was a horrid musician.

All of this adds up to an old joke that John and I have laughed about. The Bea*s*tles was the beast roaring to the ends of the earth. We Beatles, the Fab Four-headed **beast** (being also, in all, the seven-in-one beast) **would fulfill** it all. Of course, it is merely **a joke of Biblical proportions**. John never thought to add up all of our names. I did not do it until much later. All of us, and a few others, got laughs out of the Bea*s*tles joke, not ever realizing that we numbered up to 666.

Sixes get a lot of attention in these memories. Although they are here for my amusement, I will not include them in the widely distributed trimmed-down version. If you find it objectionable, feel free to X it out of your copy. **I don't mind**. You can rip out these pages and burn **them** for all I care.

Eighteen symbolizes 666 **for me** when I do not want to draw attention to the beastly digits. 18 is the sum of the digits 666. This abbreviation became more amusing to me when I learned that Paul was "Number nine, Number nine." Just as $6 + 6 + 6 = 18$, even so does $9 + 9 = 18$. First, it goes to eighteen (which is both $6 + 6 + 6$ and also $9 + 9$). Then it all adds up to nine. I will show you.

Reserve all of your judgment on this one until you do the math yourself. Just remember that eighteen stands for 666. If you follow my simple formula, your number will become this symbol and end up as Paul's 9. It is sort of a game. You need some paper and a pencil for this one. Are you ready?

Invent any three-digit number in which the first digit is larger than the last. Write it down. Got it? Now reverse the order of the digits and subtract it from your original number. If you had 960 to begin with, you would subtract 069 (keep it three digits) for a difference of 891. Now all of those digits are reversed and added. In this same example, 198 is added to 891. Now that sum will emerge as a four-digit number. Add those four digits to get my two-digit symbol of 666 (18). Add them to evoke Paul's magical number nine. It all comes back down to Paul. It matters not what three-digit number you start with providing the first digit is larger than the last. You can remember this rule because Paul was first and I am last. He was 9, "I am 6." I + am + 6 = Iam6 = lamb (or ram). Unless you did the math, all that was gibberish. There are a few times in this participatory book that **I ask you to** calculate things. If you do not, you cannot count on this book to add up.

As you **become involved** with this text, it will work on you **and** through you. You will gradually learn **to feel these things**. You will by the end **experience Paul through this work** even as you listened to, and experienced, him through my music. Paul has influenced you more than you know.

I go by the numbers in this calculating book since replacing Paul is tied to Paulie-polytheism spiritualism, supernaturalism, syncretism, secretism, or whatever other -ism that has made all of my sixes **Paul's** nines, turning us upside-down (putting his head **in the ground** and lifting mine). It is about numbers, and about me **becoming** Paul. These numbers are all about **me** joining the Beatles and making me the ultimate band's most mystical living member. The Beatles, as I have often joked privately, is the beast. Later in this book of symbolism, I will further cover its four heads. It is a beastly joke.

43

Till Death Do Ye Paul

In an email from my attorney, he wrote:

I am sorry, but the only way to be certain that this document will not jeopardize your assets, **Paul, is** to not publish it at all. Save it. To protect your interests, you must wait until you are **deceased** before making everything public. Your concerns of eternal unrest for not having set the record straight are unfortunate. However, I ask you to consider doing it later on the grounds that doing it in this lifetime will create unnecessary troubles now.

You must also cut the chapter that reveals parentage. Unless you are cremated, DNA may be ordered by the courts to prove the claims you have written. To refer to your distant ancestors is okay unless it traces them to immediate relatives. The surnames, Shepherd, Campbell, Crawford, and Wallace are general enough to not be a problem so long as you can keep it general. You must not include any current locations of relatives with these surnames. It would also be wise to use a pen name.

Looking at what he is saying, it's a drag because now some well-executed material will have to be

403

left out. **I am divided over** it. His concerns are all valid. Yet, **this book** was meant to reveal everything.

[Tom, I apologize for the extra encoding. Please cut the second half of the "Two Pauls" chapter, and other parts that identify close relatives. Instead, work in my attached William Wallace papers. Otherwise, the project is looking good. Will you still have it finished by 09.09.09? ~ PM]

44

Sir William

My ancestors are Scottish and Irish. John and Arlene Crawford, my great grandparents, both yearned to preserve their Celtic family roots. Arlene diligently gathered family stories and oral traditions, mostly from relatives, and wrote them in an **old** book that she kept beside her Bible. The **neighbors** ordered copies that she wrote by hand and **sold** for oats or wool. She also made a copy of **the book** for the reverend, one for each of her children, and one for each of her siblings. The more recent copies had more stories. When new people would read her collection, they would often return bringing her extra details for her to add to subsequent editions.

In her ornate wooden-covered Bible, which she received from her grandfather, she kept the family genealogical records. That old large illustrated book was given to her daughter, Helen, my grandmother, who still had it when I was a child. It was she who added my name, William Wallace Shepherd, listed as the twenty-eighth generation grandson.

NOTE: The generations from William to William are "28 IF" his above statement is accurate. It is also possible that William borrowed that number of generations from Matthew 1:17 to suggest his position in the royal lineage of his particular cultic circle that secretly venerates Sir William Wallace.

Paul would have been in his 28th year **IF** he were still alive when the *Abbey Road* album was released. The Volkswagen Beetle license on the cover says, "28 IF." Resembling Paul's death, many recording artists, starting with Bobby Fuller, die by the age of 28 (especially from 24 [2+4=**6**] to 27 [2+7=**9**]).

since Sir William Wallace. **I was** brought up to honor my heritage as **a descendant of** the hardy warrior.

The family stories paint **an extremely different** picture of my ancient great-grandfather, **Sir William** Wallace, than what was depicted in *Braveheart*. Although I found the movie inspiring as well as entertaining, and although the battle scenes were somewhat similar to how they were explained to me, I noticed striking inaccuracies–assuming that our family records are right. I also could not help but wish that in all of Scotland they had found a single Scot to play the leading part. I have nothing against having Yanks playing minor roles and have considerable esteem for Mel Gibson–love him in many of his shows. On the other hand, he did not look like, dress like, or sound like, the William Wallace that I know.

Essentially, Mel Gibson did not capture William Wallace's spiritual nature. It was not written into that very militantly oriented script. I do not blame Gibson for any of these points. I just want to tell everyone about the historical William Wallace because I was honored to be his namesake. After all, now at last that **I am** telling you about the real me, it is also an opportune time to tell you about the real goodness of **William** Wallace. He was much more than **a hardy warrior.**

NOTE: In addition to word-stacking and the acrostic messages (in English versions), other layers of symbolism encoded into *the Memoirs* remain missed entirely. The English word-stacking message, "I am William a hardy warrior" is equivalent to saying, "I am William Wallace" (as per how William uses the name Wallace in these memoirs).

In the previous chapter, William's attorney coaxes him into cutting material that explicitly identifies William's parents and other relations. William complies but substitutes that material with his William Wallace papers, which reveals his father to those who crack the symbolism.

Wallace is the last name of William's ancient ancestor, whom his family tradition refers to as "the hardy warrior." Using Wallace (as if William's middle name) recognizes Sir William Wallace but is also a code to identify William's biological father who taught William and others to venerate their hardy warrior ancestor.

Ellerslie in Ayrshire is where it says he was born to Margaret Crawford and Alan Wallace on a warm night, Tuesday, 5 August 1270. Sir William died on a Sunday, 23 August 1305. A faithful lad, in his early years, he learned to trust the Lord to strengthen him, to deliver him from evil, and to help him do the right thing, whatever it may be. This early training came from his parents and from the church, where, along with an education, he was taught love and respect for all of God's children. That love included the need to instill self-respect and self-rule. To him, **the teachings of Jesus demanded** full equality and **individual rights**. Through Bible study, he became **entrenched in the principles of liberty**. He went on **to overcome all tyranny** and all oppression. He felt that **securing liberty** was his Christian mission. No one could rightly expect any less. All of this history, however accurate, is from that family book.

Sir William's father was a God-fearing patriot who taught William that no Scot should acknowledge foreign jurisdiction over their God-given land. To him it was as much anathema as the Jews honoring Roman governance over Israel in Jesus' day. Alan  Wallace would sooner be a zealot than a supporter of England's rule over Scotland. He openly refused

NOTE: After wrestling all night, Jacob demands a blessing, which is realized as his new sacred identity. He is told, "Your name will no longer be Jacob, but Israel, because you have struggled with God and with men, and have prevailed" (Genesis 32:28). The name, Israel (Is-Ra-El), appears to be derived from the gods Isis, Ra, and El. To be given a name of great renown, especially to be named after gods, is a blessing that is not lost to William.

New names are given not only in cultic rituals but also by individuals empowering themselves with their own newly chosen self-identities. Even the gods give themselves new names, concealing their old identities until their new flock is ready to know the connection.

to swear allegiance to King Edward, or any other monarch of a foreign land, as was required by British law of all Scottish landowners.

Scottish pride, and Alan's patriotic freedom-loving rebelliousness, drove Alan Wallace deep into seclusion with his oldest son. They traveled all about as fugitives. The onerous tyrannous English rule burdened him. When William was at home with his mother and brother, they stewed on the injustice without clear remedies. This conflict formed his educational context. When they heard rumors of insurrections against England, William's liberty training intensified. Then, in 1291, in a battle at Loudoun Hill, William's father and uncle were killed.

That loss turned the impressionable teenager from long-held hatred of English oppression to a new hatred of the English themselves. He hated their insistence on ruling a foreign people. It had gone too far. Forcing Scots by the sword to swear allegiance to a power they hated was slavery. He would die a free man. He hated them for killing the man he most respected, his God-fearing father, whose crime was not submitting to oppression.

William vowed in his heart that he too would never submit to English rule. Still, while he was all torn up inside over the great loss he was feeling, and over the political condition they were in, his life went on. **His loss**, and his new resolve for freedom, **increased his devotion** to God. He would live his life **in such a way that he could** always **expect God to help him.** He placed himself in the Almighty's hands.

William turned to the Psalms for direction, courage, and **peace.** To him, the wicked spoken of were the English oppressors. To know what enmeshed William Wallace's mind from his teen years until the end of his life, try reading Psalms, inserting the key word "English" for "wicked," or 'heathen." Your understanding of the man will take on an extraordinarily new depth. I will include some examples. However, to get the full impact, have a day of reading nothing else. It will expand your mind. **I will** make adjustments in the text as I go to **show you how** William Wallace read it. **You can check** your Bibles to know what is new in my **William** Wallace rendition. I will do the first two Psalms for you. By that pattern, you will know how it went on from there:

"Blessed is William who walks not in the laws of the English . . . But his delight is in the law of the LORD . . . He shall be like a tree . . . that brings forth his fruit . . . and whatsoever he does shall prosper. The English are not so but are like the meaningless chaff that the wind drives away. Therefore, the English shall not stand." William yelled lines like, "Why do the English rage, and . . . imagine a vain thing? The kings of the earth set themselves . . . against the LORD . . . . He that sits in the heavens shall laugh. He will have the English in derision. Then will he speak unto them in his wrath, and vex them in his sore displeasure . . . The LORD hath said unto me . . . "Ask of me and I shall give you this land occupied by the English for thine inheritance, and these parts of the earth

409

for thy possession. Thou shalt break them with a rod of iron. Thou shalt dash them in pieces like a potter's vessel." Be wise now therefore, O ye kings . . . Serve the LORD with fear, and rejoice with trembling. **Be wise** now O ye kings, kiss this son of Scotland **lest he be angry**, and ye perish from the way **when his wrath is kindled.**"

I just showed you how he read the first two Psalms. He would read all of the Psalms like that regardless of what the Psalmist had in mind. If you continue with the other 148 of them, you will wonder how so much could fit his life so perfectly. You will see what he saw. You will know what internal force moved him to act with such mighty willpower. He always carried a Psalter and read it out loud frequently for others to hear it, and also quietly at more reflective moments. It was his strength. Losing or winning, in sorrows or joys, it all had the same effect. He always looked to the book for inspiration. He turned to it in bright gratitude and in dark desperation, in loud sermonizing and in quiet amazement, in his proud boasting and humble supplication. It was his life. Even while being murdered, executed, his personal Psalter, which had never left his side, was opened for him to read.

William Wallace regularly motivated his followers with sermons that relied on Psalms and on the rest of the scriptures, a great many of which he had memorized, sometimes imperfectly. Lengthy sermons streamed from him as easily as natural conversation—it is what it all was to him. Love was one of his themes that drove people to fight, which sounds odd, but is true. They would all rely on the God of love to defend the liberties they loved, the land they loved, the women and children they loved, and all that was good that they loved. Because of the principles of love, **everyone should be free to** govern themselves.

If the English loved them, they would be free to **share in brotherhood, not servitude.** Love, love, love. William Wallace, the real man, was not the hard-hearted, evil-minded, murderous man depicted by Hollywood. He focused his willpower, action, and energy to establish equality, exerting his will to act in line with his beliefs, which is more heroic than most people. He lived by the Good Book.

William had sought the priesthood but did not have the birthright. Instead, he studied scriptures for his own benefit, which richly spilled into all else, enhancing his leadership roles. He was as competent to doctrinally expound, exhort, or edify as any of the religious leaders of his time. He knew Gaelic and Latin as well as the most scholarly priests. William did pilgrimages, was a father to the fatherless, the whole bit. He was a priest's priest, but not by any institutional ordination. Love ruled his heart. He cared for the poor and needy, the weary and exhausted, the sick and infirm. He never missed private prayer or public worship.

NOTE: "He focused his willpower, action, and energy . . . exerting his will to act in line with his beliefs." The key for this hardy warrior was the proper application of the dynamo of living power. Diligent adherence to the light and knowledge within him made it grow stronger. Applying that surging energy to fulfill his aligned will made him powerful beyond his enemies. It is the same for us. The mystery is that by receiving—and continuing in—the light of life within us, and by applying it to positive action, we bring our will to fruition.

WILLIAM WALLACE.

A close associate, John Blair, was a renowned Benedictine Monk. These lifetime friends discussed religion, theology, philosophy, poetry, government, history, and current world affairs. **Both men were** naturally inclined to seek all manner of **learning** and virtue. Both gentlemen were creative and **brilliantly** educated, as much so as any monks **of their day.** They shared core values and desires, both finding delight in uplifting all whom they met in their frequent travels.

The William Wallace of *Braveheart* was a likable fellow but did not possess the distinct holiness that so strikingly radiated from the real man. In unabashed defiance against the king of England, the Archbishop of Canterbury gave William Wallace his last rites before his execution. The sanctity of the condemned man was much too certain to leave his request unfulfilled, even though it risked dire consequences from King Edward. William's brutal execution, which was done in a terribly horrific manner at Smithfield Elms in London, followed his capture and extradition to London, made possible by a betraying Judas. A mock trial found him guilty and ordered him executed for treason.

A few years ago, I honored Sir William Wallace on the septcentennial (700 years) anniversary of this ignominious death. The small gathering occurred, for those who would appreciate it, on 23 August 2005. I hope others remembered my ancestor too.

Several people claim to be direct descendants of Sir William Wallace. That is entirely possible since it has been so long since his death. He would have great posterity by now. However, I do not see any reason to believe that those who **have the** Wallace surname have any **special claim on him since** William had **no sons** to **carry** on **that name.** Chief Seoras Wallace of the Glasgow Wallace Clan has my respect for preserving the Scottish culture but has nothing on my Sir W.W. pedigree or on me.

I am a direct descendant of William Wallace. It does not get more direct than that. If the chief's line picked up the Wallace name generations later, then he too may be a direct descendant. However, not every Wallace who claims to come from William is genuinely his. Some are from a brother or cousin. My speaking about that clan seemed brash to some, but I have enjoyed Campbell cousins more anyway.

Evidently, William Wallace only fully loved two women romantically. One was murdered by a repugnant English sheriff after she rebuffed his sexual advances. He claimed bodily rights to her by virtue of his position. This injustice pushed William over the edge. Justice could not possibly come if he did not administer it himself. He killed the English sheriff, making himself an outlaw in his own nation, and driving him unrelentingly forward to redeem Scotland from further English abuses. His grudge against the sheriff who slew his beloved, the loss of his father, and the never-ending travesties that would only stop when someone stopped them, all combined to such a level of heightened indignation in him that he had to act.

Being a fugitive in his country magnified the emptiness he suffered from his tremendous loss, but also freed him to act fearlessly according to his willful whims, independent of law. Finding himself on the outside of the law, no law could have any hold on him except for the law written in his heart.

Fortunately for Scotland, that heart's law was religiously bridled by holy scriptures and by his impassioned desperation to free his people from London rule. **William launched a strong** crusade against England's **presence**. He became Scotland's defender, and ultimately the Father of Scotland's Nationhood. Seven centuries later, he remains an unparalleled legend, the greatest hero in Scottish history, and a fixed symbol of patriotism and Scottish independence. More than has been depicted in movies, Sir William Wallace is a man of soul.

Justice was more important to William than odds. It paid off. Although well outnumbered, his army defeated the English army at Stirling Bridge, using guts, strategy, and intimidation. This victory, more than any other, brought him his immortal fame because it is what drove the English out of Scotland. Enjoying this great triumph, he opened his Psalter to 91:7 and read out loud, "A thousand shall fall at thy side, and ten thousand at thy right hand, but it shall not come nigh to thee."

Part of his success was due to word-of-mouth legends about him that intimidated enemies. There is a rumor that he had the skin of an Englishman on the hilt of his huge sword. The creepy belief persisted until about a century ago when someone checked. Disappointing some people and relieving others, leather, not human skin, was all that he used. Still, the idea of it made people fear him.

My heritage and ancestors feel closest to me when I am out on my farm in Scotland. When we can look to the past, we may better understand the present. My Wallace ancestry, being part of my Crawford and Shepherd family heritage, matters to me. Still, we are ultimately what we make ourselves. Ancestors provide lessons but cannot pass on all of their greatness. We earn that ourselves. They just remind us of what we can do. One similar fault I have with that **William is** that I too waited to act. Though he had **a cause**, it was not until he lost enough, until he had nothing more to lose, that he neglected his fears. In some ways, I did the same. I had musical talent before my handlers set it up. Yet, even though I may have been good enough, **I** did not trust myself fully enough to make it as **William**. Yet, losing my identity, and my own life, **I could do** anything. After all, now, I am **J. Paul McCartney.**

45

666999

William Wallace's work is about 666 years ahead of the Beatles. That fun little correlation is another example of how my heritage and divergent interests all tie together.

Living as Paul has turned some of my 666-William awareness to the Beatles. In 1296, the legacy of William Wallace entered the world stage in consequence of English King Edward violently asserting himself King of Scotland. 666 years later, in 1962, the Beatles got their first recording contract and began their term as John, Paul, George, and Ringo. They set the world stage for me to enter, and to open the third Beatles phase in 1966 (666 years from 1300).

Doing this Paul role changed me. **I need to** tell you that it was not all roses. To **replace Paul**, I had to allow upheavals throughout **my whole life.**

NOTE: William, in word-stacking, says, "I need to replace Paul my whole life." Because of the intended embodiment of Osiris, et al, William must play the part permanently. Even if William (Horus) retires, he would still be "Paul" (Osiris/Lucifer) for the rest of his life. It is more common for key players to "be everyone and no one," stepping in and out of many prominent roles. That transitory opportunity is a pleasure that William also enjoys by playing uncredited parts on other people's albums—briefly being those people.

Some stress is better than others. My world turned downside up, flipping my 666 over to become 999. I went from sixes to nines. In no time at all, my "Number six, six, six" was flipped to "Number nine, number nine, number nine." As **I** have said, the ominous message from the EMI engineer's "Number Nine" played backward **sounded very** much like "Turn me on, dead man." **McCartney** (with nine letters) being the dead man made it extra eerie in the song, "Revolution 9."

Originally, John wanted that song connected to "Revolution 1" I convinced him not to ruin "Revolution 1" that way. I also told him that he ought to speed it up, which gave us the "Revolution" single. John intended "Revolution 9" to sound like Paul's revolution. The reason he played "Revolution 1" so slowly was that he wanted to contrast all of the havoc of "Revolution 9."

Revolving from Paul to me, the band evolved. In turn, we revolved the whole world. Whether it is an evolution or devolution, the world cannot be the same ever again. The revolution was permanent.

The "Revolution 9" sounds and voices depict the world's change that came with Paul's demise. We hear, as it were, Paul's life flash before him, and the **old Paul is** replaced by the new as chaos overcomes **the world.** The serenely alluring sound of John's "Revolution 1" was to say "Peace, Peace" before the chaos breaks loose on the world as "Revolution 9," kicking in complete fragmentation and disintegration in preparation for the New World Order. **I have not** all that often played it. John **intended chaos** through fragmentation. He succeeded at it **so well** that it is decidedly unpleasant. However, if you play it, hear the ruckus depicting Tavistock's plan to achieve their new order. They say **they will obtain** "Ordo ab Chao," meaning, "**Order from chaos.**"

Losing himself in Paul, or at least trying to, John one day used "Turn me on dead man" as a mantra to let Paul enter his deep consciousness for a meditative visit. He repeated it over and over until he felt some inspiration come. I do not believe any inspiration that he may have received that day came from Paul.

With less than desired results, he tried again after loading up on hallucinogens to increase the effectiveness. The bad trip that ensued ended his use of that mantra. Mantras should be more positive.

Nearly always, **John** sought to restore his Paul connection. He **used many methods.** One dream that he had of **Paul** influenced him more than all others. It **did not come with drugs**, meditation, or from any effort. That regular night dream changed his outlook on beautiful music, turning him to soft reflective sounds, away from harder-edged music. He referred to that dream in his song "#9 Dream."

Our Beatles "Number Nine" is John's solo "#9," the dead man. John's "#9 Dream" was of seeing that man at his crash site. John dreamt that he walked that lonely road where Paul had died. Recognizing it made him reflect on the crash. As John recalled the rain he had been told of, it began raining again. Paul yelled to him, "John!" John turned to see him, but was overawed by the beautiful flowing music of the wind through the trees and the water falling and moving on the ground. All was in harmony. He looked to see Paul. He could not, but sensed his presence, and that Paul was also caught in that sweet deluge of musical harmony. **John felt it move Paul** as it moved himself **through an energy dance of** sound and motion. He sang about it in "#9 Dreams."

John's progression from his "**Number Nine**" of writhing cacophony in "Revolution 9," to his sweet melodious "#9 Dreams" shows a softer view of the effects of Paul's demise. Rather than apocalyptic chaos, this time Paul brings peace.

Explaining "Revolution 9" makes me cringe because I do not enjoy the cacophony. Yet, John filled the "song" with material that helps explain his perspective of Paul passing the wand to me. Going forward, the intermittent "Number Nine, Number Nine, Number Nine" carries the secondary meaning to understand as "McCartney, McCartney, McCartney." As a parallel meaning, it also represented me (6-6-6) now turned upside-down (9-9-9). Nines (Paul) with heads in the ground are sixes (Bill). The number flip shows my world being turned over with Paul's.

At one point in this work, John says, "If you want it, you can prove it." We prove it without fans believing. John told George Martin, "We could Xerox copies of hard evidence and include it with every album, and it still would not be believed. Everyone believes their own programming."

Consider the clues in these "Revolution 9" segments (mostly backward). "He hit a pole." "Get him to see a surgeon." "He went to a dentist instead." "They gave him a pair of teeth that weren't any good at all [to identify him]. So, my wings are broken."

419

Of broken wings, I used that idea in "Blackbird." **The broken bird flies** into the light of the dark black night, or **into death**, going to the light. I would then become the Blackbird singing for him, for Paul. I would take his broken wings and learn to fly. He would learn to do it through me. I'd learn to be a new him. It's why I named my band Wings. The blackbird broke its wings in the dead of night, but ended up singing and flying through me. I have the blackbird's Wings.

"So, my wings are broken" (continuing on with some more lines from "Revolution 9") "and so is my hair." Hair is used to mean head here

NOTE: William presents his perspective of taking the broken bird and flying with it. However, to get to the heart of the matter, we must also see it from Paul's perspective. Paul is not the broken bird but the soul possessing it, working through that body before it breaks, putting all in motion for him to enter a new form. Like a phoenix, "Perit ut vivat" (He dies that he may live). William's black bird is the Falcon of Horus. **Falcon of Horus**

In a Lennon-McCartney song written for John, as if singing to Paul, he says, "When your bird is broken / Will it bring you down? / You may be awoken / I'll be 'round." ("And Your Bird Can Sing"). After Paul's body is broken, and he awakens in another, John would still be there for him. John would make it work with the band. That album, *Revolver* (released 5 August 1966), foreshadowed Paul's transition, which occurred the following month.

"Tomorrow Never Knows," the final song on Paul's last album, was the first recorded for it. It describes Paul's coming soul transmigration. As instructions to Paul, telling him how to die and yet continue, he is told to turn off his mind, which will not die as his soul floats away. Paul is to "Lay down all thoughts" and to "surrender to the void." Beingness continues. Some outsiders will become aware of Paul's death but lack the love-awareness to recognize his continuance by the transmigration. With "ignorance and hate [they] may mourn the dead." Paul, as the broken form, is no longer living. Yet, his existence continues, marking not only a new life for Paul, but a new beginning for the world. Aside from being of Paul's soul transmigration, the song is a meditation to surrender to the Void. Such meditations work especially well with psychedelics (wherever allowed by law). This song draws ideas from *The Psychedelic Experience: A Manual Based on the Tibetan Book of the Dead* by Timothy Leary, Richard Alpert (Ram Dass), and Ralph Metzner.

just as, a week before, Ringo sang, "You were in a car crash and you lost your hair" ("Don't Pass Me By"). "I'm not in the mood for words. . . . Find the night watchman. A fine natural imbalance. Must have got it in the shoulder blades."

Eventually, a voice representing Paul passes his soul, talents, and Beatle position on to me, his new brother. William offers his body. Paul offers his soul. "Take this, brother. May it serve you well."

One must also remember that Paul did not **die alone.** Donna was right there beside him. When they crash, we hear her part played as if from the burning car. She says, "Let me out!" However, help does not arrive soon enough to save her. Before she dies, we hear her screaming, echoing the same words, "Let me out! Let me out!" Another voice sums it up with this simple recap: "There were two [Paul and Donna]. There are none now."

Earlier in the white album, another song identifies Paul more plainly. Right after John sings, "I'm So Tired," some words recorded backward explain why he hasn't slept a wink. It tells you, "Paul is a dead man. Miss him, miss him, miss him." [Monsieur, Monsieur, how about another one?]

Sounds on "Revolution 9" were intended to be disturbing. **It is no** lullaby. The concept is that while Paul has his **"accident,"** his life flashes through his mind; **and yet,** simultaneously, the noise of the collision is **heard with** the sounds of the crash, fire, **screaming, and sirens.** We hear Paul's life from his perspective mixed with sounds of audiences cheering, representing his life of entertaining. The sounds of babies represent Paul's abandoned children. Although no one had told me about them when I took the job, I soon learned. Backward sounds show Paul's passage through the course of time. We hear, "**As Time goes by,** you get a little bit older and a little bit **slower**," emphasizing his swift fragmented life **passing** by. After "his eyes were closed," he hears **angels sing**.

Adding a degree of Masonic significance to that album, or intending to, I wanted to have **our songs** number to 33. However, three of the songs that we worked on never made it. The three songs that did not make the grade (officially because they did not meet our deadline and never were made quite right) were George's "Not Guilty," John's "What's the New Mary Jane," and my "Jubilee." Until "Not Guilty," we had never topped 100 takes on a single song. That one had 101; and it would have been fine had John's "Mary Jane" (now in *Anthology 3*) been adequate. My song (as "Junk") ended up on a solo album, as did George's. John's (backed up only by George) was too annoying, to put it kindly. My unwillingness to include it required a Jubilee sacrifice and George's loss also.

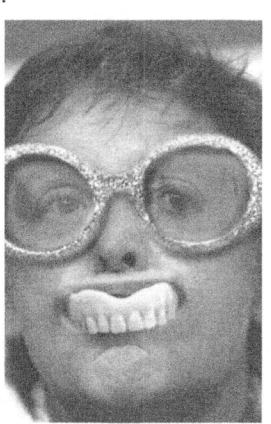

46

I Am the Grey Seal.

You must realize by now that after Paul died, he was always on our minds. In addition to all of our songs that **can** be easily recognized as pointing to his death, you can **tell** that all of us were always under his influence even when our writing had nothing to do with him. **Everybody** intended to create more than Paul-tributes. However, he was so entrenched in our thinking **that** even when we all wanted to write about something else, we would each think of great lines that put **Paul** in it. It was not that we sat down to write about Paul, but no matter where we go with a lyric, Paul **is** there. Even though we worked on other ideas, double-meaning lines would emerge to say that Paul is **dead**.

Elton John's album, *Goodbye Yellow Brick Road*, was written that way. It was not intended to focus on losing Paul but was written soon after John told Elton and Bernie about it. It was in their heads.

Let It Be was released soon after I announced our breakup. Five months later was the first pop hit by Elton John. Beatle-John called Elton's song "the first new thing that's happened since we happened." Virtually every critic praised it. *Rolling Stone* called it a "pretty McCartneyesque ballad." This big hit was

Elton's "Your Song." When I first heard it on the radio, I imagined a boy singing it to a girl, telling her, "Remember, this song's for you. It's your song." The lyrics, by Bernie Taupin, sounded like that.

"Your Song," however, was actually about Bernie's feelings toward Elton, who could tell everybody it is his song. **It's Elton**'s song. Bernie hopes he does not mind **singing about himself** instead of about an imaginary girl.

Being impressed with Elton's song, Beatle-John decided to meet him. They met but were not close friends right away. The friendship grew a couple of years before John and Yoko confided in Bernie and Elton about Paul's death, and about working with me. Those remarks were unfavorable, being when John and I were not as close as we had been, or as we have been since. **The** talk of lyrical clues, telling Elton why the **walrus** was Paul, and pointing to evidence, would have sufficed. He did not need to tell them that I **was** not as great in the Paul role as was the earlier **Paul.** It prejudiced them.

Soon after John and Yoko revealed all to Elton and Bernie, Bernie began working on lyrics for their *Goodbye Yellow Brick Road* album. With Bernie's lyrics, Elton wrote the music. The album begins with a haunting "Funeral for a Friend." It was not for a real one, or definitely for Paul, but inspired by John losing Paul who whispers to us from the grave. Until you see it that way, you cannot understand the double meanings that surface in the album.

Since only one of the songs was specifically written about Paul, I will not provide the other lines with Paul allusions. However, if you go through the album looking for them, you will be surprised. Still, all such allusions are only secondary to the primary message of each song. Most of them are not actually songs about Paul. That is an important distinction. When the Stones, Donovan, and the Who did their Paul songs, they were among their best hits. Though not so with Elton's Paul song, it is worth mentioning.

Adding to John's walrus metaphor, **I** am not the true walrus, but a "Grey Seal." I **am** allegedly undeserving of the praise fitting **the** real Paul. Bernie's view of me was a **grey seal** that is too little for such a large walrus role. His view has long since improved but was at that time based on John's insults about me. As John and I became close again over time, I also became closer to Elton, Bernie, and others to whom John had ranted. They all came around eventually.

Making references to our songs about rain and to "Good Day Sunshine," Bernie then calls Paul a sun to say that the one on the screen (that's me in the image of Paul) is not as bright as the real one (Paul). He says that if anyone can **cry for Paul**, then so can he (or Elton). He means, **since he really is dead**, everyone should mourn for him.

John had given me the band out of obligation and guilt. Paul's fears of being sacrificed and replaced now rang true. Since the McCartneys chose me to replace Paul, John knew that there could be no more Beatles without me. Since **I required** the band to enter into the agreement, it was **all John could do.**

John told Elton and Bernie of the McCartney yearnings to have me fill Paul's role. By making me their Paul, they did not so completely lose their own son. They grafted me into their family tree, giving me new family roots. That is why, in "Grey Seal," Elton sings that my roots were twisted.

Also in that song, he sings of something enduring at the core of Paul, his spiritual essence that continued in me, being re-born in me. "I was re-born before all life could die." He compares Paul's continuance to the great phoenix that goes in blazes but returns again to carry on anew. I am flying high with the wings of the phoenix. If Paul, inside of me, can fly, now so can I. "The Phoenix bird will leave this world to fly / If the Phoenix bird can fly then so can I."

Dying in a blazing car made that image especially apropos for Paul. Bernie and Elton also suggest that if Paul flies by what **I** do in his name, then they should fly as well. I **am** less than Paul (they had supposed), but **the** two of them playing themselves without a **phoenix** required to exist through another gave them an advantage, or so they wrongly reasoned. **Or**, to put it another way, Paul is the sun; I am merely the image of the sun. The real sun is brighter. **Paul** flies by me, carried high by the bird, which **is** harder to do well. Since they are the real stars, or suns, and not mere images of the stars, as they saw it, if I can fly, they can too.

NOTE: Figuratively, pointing to the Phoenix, Paul is said to have died in a blazing car. However, even without that early enrichment, Bernie Taupin recognized Paul's death to rise in William as another Phoenix reenactment. That divine creature, based on the Bennu, is an Egyptian bird embodiment of the sun god, Ra (Marduk, son of Enki).

To occultists, the Phoenix also represents Lucifer, the light-bearer, who was cast down to the earth only to rise again. It is claimed that Paul's death, soul-transmigration, and new heights through William is the reenactment of the Osiris-Horus story that, as the Phoenix, has occurred many times throughout history.

426

I do not appreciate the suggestion that I am not equal to Paul. I excelled him musically, physically, financially, as a humanitarian, and in family life. Do not tell me that I do not measure up to Paul. I was a better Paul McCartney than he ever was. I am not  inferior to him in any way. I do not mean to sound ungrateful for this opportunity, but you can simply X out any notions of him being brighter. **I gave him credit for my hits, which fans thought were his best.**

NOTE: William offended some by saying, "I was a better Paul McCartney than he ever was." Although he seems boastful, in all fairness, we need to understand his perspective. From the very start, some critical insiders argued that he could not measure up to Paul McCartney. Although William desired enough sublime wisdom to be beyond defensiveness toward such critics, the feeling was there, and so expressed.

However, elsewhere, he explains that no one is replaceable. Everyone is the best at being himself or herself. For example, in "Lovely Linda" (chapter 60), he writes, "No one can replace Linda. Why would anyone suppose that she could be replaced? Linda will always be the only one of her. It is not as though I held a Linda-Look-Alike contest and declared another the winner. Only Linda is Linda. You get it? Jane is Jane. . . . Nancy is Nancy. . . . You are you. Each one has her own enchantments. One cannot replace another."

When referring to Paul McCartney as a particular human, there can be no greater Paul McCartney than the actual authentic human who really was Paul McCartney. However, William is not referring to Paul McCartney as the man, but as the fictional role. William is saying that he played that fictional role better than Paul had played it, which is verifiably true in some regards, but not in all ways. William was in the difficult position of being compared to Paul at a time when the world could not know how far Paul was from his fictional persona.

It would have been clearer and more accurate if William had said that, compared to Paul, he held a closer resemblance to the well-established façade of the musical genius songwriter and recording artist. With the false persona created for Paul, with so much work credited to him in writing and recording that was done by others, it may be fair to say that William (who did much more than is credited) is better at playing that role. William could see that he was closer. Based on what they did, even with William's false identification, he felt that he was less of a pretender than Paul.

47

"Sunday Bloody Sunday"

Probably, beyond this part of the world, most readers will expect this chapter to be about the last day of Paul's life, which was a bloody Sunday, 11 September 1966. Although that day is relevant to everything in this encoded book, I have covered it well enough already. This chapter is to increase awareness of the plight of the Irish, and the plague of rigid thinking. **I will tell you about** the three songs with this chapter's name. I **hope** you will consider it enough **to shape attitudes** and eventual policy. The world's view **of the UK** sometimes prompts changes here.

Giving Sir William Wallace homage in previous chapters is meaningful only if we follow his example. I agree with Edward Bulwer-Lytton that "The pen is mightier than the sword." I do not take up a sword of vengeance but do write powerful songs of peace and freedom. My song, "Give Ireland Back to the Irish," entered my mind after Bloody Sunday. I wondered, "What would William Wallace do as Paul McCartney?"

I would not stir up violence but hoped that my song would increase awareness and **get people** to realize the wrongness of oppression, **to change it.**

Governments have no divine or moral right to rule except by consent. Aleister Crowley declared Ireland's independence, and so do I. If Great Britain loved the Irish as themselves, all of Ireland might want to be ruled by them. However, most do not.

All of Ireland, north and south, is a single island and can be self-governing as one united people. Northern Ireland was partitioned off from Southern Ireland almost a century ago. The Irish people had divided themselves over religion. Throughout most of the island, the population is primarily Catholic but is mostly Protestant in the northeast. The Protestants up north are taught that they are British and that they need the United Kingdom to protect them from the south. The Catholics in the north consider themselves Irish, like on the rest of the island, and believe that they do not need the United Kingdom to control and protect them. What they need is greater religious tolerance, not foreign rule.

Tolerance flows more naturally now between competing religions and ideologies. I was not the only one who worked to break down rigid intolerant thinking, but, more than most, have been in a position to make a difference. I have been glad to use music to facilitate change. As Paul McCartney, I have had the pleasure of reaching out to countries and cultures that had been closed or cold to the west.

Even though we were banned from the USSR, for example, **we sang**, "Back in the USSR" as if **as if we knew and loved the place.** Fans doubted government claims including the anti-Beatles rhetoric. Losing trust contributed to the nation's fall.

To push the UK to release Ireland, I wrote, "Give Ireland Back to the Irish." Now, divisive religiosity is declining there—as everywhere that plays our songs. It was not just us. We were pawns in a scheme calculated to break rigid thinking. We each had our part to play.

Since the Sixties, Irish demands for self-rule have only intensified. On Bloody Sunday, 30 January 1972, the 1st Battalion of the British Parachute Regiment near Bogside in Derry, Northern Ireland, shot twenty-seven civil rights demonstrators who joined a march led by the Northern Ireland Civil Rights Association. Thirteen people, including seven teenagers, died immediately. Another victim died six weeks later in consequence of the injuries he received that day. Two protesters were run down by army vehicles.

The government's attack shocked the world. Everyone who was shot was unarmed. Five of them were shot in the back. It was murder. Investigations required by the British government have largely cleared the brutal soldiers and **British** authorities of all blame, saying that the **soldiers' shooting was** "bordering on the **reckless." The public outcry** that followed led to another inquiry **established** in 1998 to reevaluate the **events again.** Currently, early next year (2010) is the soonest that we can expect to have the outcome of this second inquiry.

Seamus Cusack and Desmond Beattie had been shot months before, on 8 July, for rioting in essentially the same area. In that case, the soldiers claimed the victims were armed, contrary to reports of residents there who witnessed it.

In response to escalating political tension and violence across Northern Ireland, the UK announced internment without trial on 9 August 1971. In a quid pro quo gesture to nationalists, the UK banned all further marches and parades, including the flashpoint march by the Protestant Apprentice Boys of Derry (a fraternal society) that was underway to occur on 12 August. Following the tyrannical introduction of internment, shock and disorder spread across Northern Ireland. 21 people were killed in three days of rioting.

Escalating violence, on 10 August, a Provisional IRA sniper in Derry shot and killed a soldier. The warlike position intensified. More were killed later. It became very ugly on both sides, each having ever more self-justification for violent retaliation, and each giving the other more cause for escalation. The murderous soldiers, and their oppressive government that self-protectively relaxed justice for such murders prompted the overgeneralization and dehumanization of all enlisted soldiers. As prejudices go, when one commits cold-blooded murder with impunity, the vast majority of onlookers come to view all such soldiers as foreign invaders. The unjust attacks enmeshed the citizenry in the notion of being at war.

By then, people were **killing soldiers as** needed to remove **enemy combatants**, not to commit murder. Still, that mindset **only increases the** inevitability of yet greater works of **violence on both sides.** Only non-violent solutions will end the violence. We all ought to act to stop the insanity. Effective action must be toward peace, not toward retaliation.

Under such circumstances that desperately require swift action, the way to change a tyrannical policy in most modern governments now is not to turn public opinion against a cause through violence but to always elicit public empathy through increased awareness. We must perceive others as being you and me. When people feel attacked, the instinct is automatically toward self-defense. We want to fight back. When those who favor oppressing the Irish hear that more soldiers on their own side have been killed, each of them becomes more entrenched in their perception that more punishment and control is the answer, not peace and self-rule. On the other hand, when we can all see that everyone else is very much like us, that increased awareness eliminates our self-justifications for oppressing any of them. **We establish love**, mutual acceptance, equality, and peace **through increased awareness.**

As I pondered what I could do to help bring peace and equality to Ireland, it occurred to me, "You're a descendant of William Wallace who is now Paul McCartney! Strike swiftly with a song!"

"Sure," I said to that voice inside my head. "Let's do it." Linda and I, both aghast at the gross lack of humanity on that Bloody Sunday, together wrote our song, "Give Ireland Back to the Irish." In only 26 days from Bloody Sunday, we recorded and

432

released this protest song. From our limited point of view, it was the first time people outside of Ireland seriously questioned what we were doing there.

EMI Chairman, Joseph Lockwood, heard the recording before it was released. He feared it would encourage further rioting. **I told him that I** felt strongly about it, that it **would help quell some of** the violence thereby increasing awareness here, and **that** they had to release it. They had to. I was willing to end our longstanding lucrative recording relationship over that matter. If he had persisted in refusing to release my material, it would have allowed me to go elsewhere. He said, "Well, it'll be banned! You can't expect the government to allow that!" He was right, of course. I knew "Give Ireland Back to the Irish" would not be an easy route. Nevertheless, it was time.

Our song reached the top of the singles charts in the Republic of Ireland and Spain, but did not do so well anywhere else. However, we have continued to promote it by performing it live. **You may have** also noticed that I reissued it as **a bonus track on the** 1993 remastered CD of **Wings'** *Wild Life* **album.** Even those who would never have bought the single have had plenty enough opportunities to hear it and to increase their awareness accordingly.

Love spreads. Other outraged recording artists heard our song and also jumped onboard. Following our Wings lead, John's album, *Some Time in New York City* features his "Sunday **Bloody** Sunday." It voices his opposition to the **violence** of that day. In that same album, in "The Luck of the Irish," he explains the Irish conflict in general.

U2 also did a "Sunday Bloody Sunday" song. You might think that U2 is merely covering John's song. It's not. It is yet another song that expresses outrage for the horrendous atrocities of that day, as is "Sunday Bloody Sunday" by The Wolfe Tones. The under-sold *Folk-Lore* album by Cruachan also covers that day in their song, "Bloody Sunday."

48

Thank You, Sunshine!

Being grateful for all that we have and are is a key to success and happiness. Good creative work is easier when we enjoy what we do, and we enjoy everything more when we feel deep appreciation. Gratitude cannot co-exist with depression, anger, or resentment. We cannot be unhappy while feeling real gratitude.

Until I joined the Beatles, silly love songs, such as "I Want to Hold Your Hand," were their mainstay. To appreciate a woman is good, but to be thankful for everything else is good too. If you think about it, the more that you can enjoy in all of its facets, the happier you make your life. With joy, accept pain as part of the fun. It is all part of the pleasure of life that we infer in Paul's song, "Good Day Sunshine." Unless in your heart you accept the pain, you miss the pleasure. He sings, "I've got something I can laugh about" "when the sun is out." Part of what we laugh about, that makes it a good sunny day, is the fun of the sun shining down that "burns my feet as

435

they touch the ground." He acknowledges the pain only to describe the good day in the sunshine.

In this book, **I describe** the pain that came from replacing Paul. **My skill** and perfectionism were so far beyond all **that** they knew from Paul that it upset everyone. It **created a rift in** the band. I clarify my pain with **the Beatles** to show that although I am very grateful to have been born into this opportunity, I took the good along with the bad. When has anyone ever heard me complain? When the pain became too intense, as I explain in "The Long and Winding Road" (chapter 58), I dissolved the band. That is a wise formula for peace. When the pain is so bad that you can no longer be grateful for the whole package, including both the pleasure and the pain, then it is time for a change. Whether in business, romance, religion, or politics, we get whatever pain we require.

Having been through it, I appreciate the pain even more. It drove me to greater accomplishments in that role, and eventually set me free from the band while retaining my Paul benefits. As it turned out, I needed that pain even more than I wanted that pleasure. Both served me well as fate intended.

Gratitude is empowering. Trusting that the whole universe calculates our experiences to work for a good outcome on our behalf gives us further cause to be thankful even when times are hard. Whether or not you believe in God, religion, or superstition, you can say to your higher self, Source, the universe, or the

Divine, "**Thank you** for making this experience turn out **for my good**! I don't know how you will do it for me this time but thank you for it just the same!" Sincere gratitude for everything working out helps make it so, and, either way, cheers us.

At this time, **I wish to thank** all my McCartney relatives. **Jim McCartney (Paul's father)** publicly accepted me as if his son. That acceptance helped to encourage others to accept me as Paul also. With reassurance from Brian and others, Jim, from our very first meeting, decided that I could have that role. It was not **John**, as some people have imagined. Everything else **fell** into place out of respect for Paul and **for Jim's approval**. Jim had been prepared.

Royalties were not Jim's motivation. Although I did pay to maintain his standard of living over the years, it was not lavish. To him, it was not about the money. He could have bargained to get more out of it but did not. To show gratitude, and to generate royalties for him, in 1974, I spruced up and added a new sound to one of his songs, under the pseudonym, The Country Hams. It was "Walking in the Park with Eloise." Lately, I have been feeling Paul pressuring me to do more Jim songs before I die. I'll have to include more of his songs, along with a few old classics, on a CD before my 2014 deadline.

There was a miserable time when I thought I had only myself to thank for my wealth since I could not have done it were it not for my own work and talent. Then I realized that my work was my greatest desire and that my talent was a heavenly gift to do this work.

When I wrote "Lady Madonna," I thought of how needy she seemed. I imagined her not taking responsibility for her situation, relying on the kindness of others, or on heaven to help her. In the song, I mockingly ask, "Who finds the money when you pay the rent? Did you think that money was heaven-sent?" Later, **I** realized that everything we own and are truly is heaven-sent. We think we have our intelligence to **t h a n k**. Yet, who gave that to us? Perhaps some of **y o u** think you are working for your employer. We **all** get paid one way or another but work for Source. We are here to do the work that is designed for us. We need to know that.

Later, in concerts, I corrected my error. I sang, "Did you **know** that money was heaven sent?" At last, I can tell you that it is something that I know. All that we have is heaven-sent. How we get it does not matter. We just align ourselves with our purpose and follow that bliss. Money comes as we stop obstructing the heavenly gift of abundance.

I also thank John, Paul, George, and Ringo (without which, I would still be unknown), and all of you who accepted me in Paul's place.

49

"Across the Universe"

When I wrote "Lady Madonna," John wrote "Across the Universe." We began recording them at EMI in February 1968, intending to release them as a single. With John's song still not ready when we all went to India, we replaced his spot on the single with George's "The Inner Light." Before it was ready for our *Let It Be* album, we released an early version of "Across the Universe" for charity.

Even though John gleaned great insights for his song from George, his receptivity to them grew out of an acid trip. My monopoly on Paul had frustrated John. To John, it felt unfair. He missed Paul and felt left out. Then, in an acid trip the year before this song, he decided that since **we are all** one in the light, we are all Paul as I am **Paul.** Essentially, we are one. That was when he penned his best line of "I Am the Walrus," "I am he as you are he as you are me and we are all together." We have distinct needs and desires on the level of form. However, forms are in flux. They are not enduring. The most eternal part of us, the basic element even of our souls, is the same infinite loving light.

The song "Across the Universe" is also based on what **George taught** of cosmic consciousness. Hard experiences in **his** life furthered his journey toward **Krishna consciousness.** Some of his experiences were sought for because of the mystical lure of me replacing Paul. He knew that the two of us combining in me could not have happened unless certain spiritual events would come together in a new and wonderful way. He said, "Knowing how to make that happen had to come from somewhere."

I was told that George had always been the most spiritually-minded Beatle. He was there when Paul voiced through me for the first time and attached himself to me. I am what people would commonly explain as being "possessed" by Paul. However, I can just as easily say that I possess him too.

Realistic nightmares that led right up to Paul's demise, foretelling his death and replacement, seem to have made a great impression on George spiritually, particularly after he witnessed them emerging into reality. It triggered new awareness in his mind that everything always works out exactly, in every detail, as **God designed** it, and that we are all connected in **God's** divine energy that shines through **everything. It is a** living light that gives **perfect life to all things.** George's incidents that led him to greater things included an acid trip he took a few months after Paul died.

NOTE: Whether William is possessed *by* Paul, or whether William has taken possession *of* Paul (along with his estate), he says, "Our exchange is mutual."

Several others have reported feeling possessed by Paul for specific purposes such as when Gregory Paul Martin recorded *The Memoirs of Billy Shears.* On the other hand, even William feels Paul within him more some moments than others. Paul does not seem to be anyone's constant companion but does seem able to personally influence many people simultaneously.

Now, let me first mention that many of George's finest meditations were drug-free. Some came with Yoga (although his best times were pot-assisted) and breathing exercises. His philosophical breakthroughs or epiphanies did not require drugs or plant medicines. Sharing this meaningful trip is not an endorsement to use drugs but helps explain the song.

George, on acid, stared at a ceramic figurine. You may wonder what the figurine represented. Don't ask. It makes no difference. In George's mind, it outwardly became Paul's face since, in George's altered state, Paul was seen in it. Then Paul stood up out of it so that the figurine vanished and was forgotten. Paul stood there illuminated before him. Although Paul spoke, his bright aura so distracted George that he could not comprehend the message.

Reflections of Paul's light were seen all over the room. As George looked around, he could see it in everything and that all is made of the same living light. Seeing that the light that was of Paul was also in himself, and in everything else, George could no longer discern Paul as a separate entity. Soon nothing seemed separate in any meaningful way. There were endless forms, but all of that one light.

Experiencing the cosmos in this brilliant way, with **Paul's individuality absorbed** in light that is very intimately tied to **everything else**, got George thinking more deeply about how **we are all** one. Everyone is **connected to Paul** and everyone else. Forms come and go, **but nothing changes.** Our realities all vary, expressions of the one light always change in form, but nothing real can ever change in your world so long as you are focused on what is real—which is that one true light that shines in and through everything. Most people who gain such cosmic consciousness do so without drugs.

Hearing George's new perspective of universal consciousness and the unchangeability of anything in the bigger picture, John wrote the song, "Across the Universe." He compares words with rain. They do not stay, but come, caress, and go in an endless flow or dance of energies. **Images and thoughts** give their impressions, and then **meander on** by, tumbling "blindly **as they make their** way across the universe." It is the cosmic "**dance before me** like a million eyes." Everything flows **out from Source** now and returns to it again all in the same instant.

George taught these cosmic ideas to John who, in turn, shared them with the world. As forms come and go on and on, to and from Source, so do ideas. We vary in perceptions. Still, nothing changes our eternal energy dance across the universe. Just as rain evaporates back again, so do we all return again to Source. All that comes and goes calls us all on to return with it **across the universe**. Not even death changes anything. **Paul**'s body had housed his spirit that now **possesses me** but will eventually return to that same Source. Nothing that matters has any meaningful change. Although all goes on like restless wind, "Nothing's gonna change."

Letting all come and go without attachment to any given condition or set form is, as George taught, living without suffering. Like what I explain in "Let It Be," accepting the sure impermanence of form is yet one aspect of enlightenment and is the point of John's song. Things come and go. Let it be.

George sought further light, understanding, and enlightenment. He shared ideas as they came to him. Eventually, he became a wise teacher. John told me that when George first wanted to join John's original pre-Beatles band, John hesitated because George was so young and innocent. By the time I replaced **Paul,** George was more mature, more adult, than John **by** a long shot. In "Across the Universe," **George is praised** as our teacher in the mantra, "Jai [Praise] Guru [Teacher] deva [divine] Om [a mystical entity and syllable]," comparing him to Guru Dev, the Maharishi's teacher.

The song came slowly to John. One day he wrote, "Thoughts meander like a restless wind inside a letterbox." Another morning, he woke up with the phrase of contrast, "**Pools of** sorrow, waves of joy." Under the umbrella of **enlightened** meaning provided by George, all of these **ideas united naturally** in one, going on and on **with all their energy** dances across the universe.

Having just the day before worked on my song, "Lady Madonna," which went on to become the last Beatles single on Parlophone (UK) and Capitol (US), we recorded "Across the Universe." John agreed that he sang it too fast. To stretch out his vocal track without having him sing it all over, we used the machine to slow it mechanically by the same means that we had adjusted the speed on his "Strawberry Fields Forever." Upon slowing it down, I heard that it needed a female falsetto backup. Not without John's consent, I ran outside and picked two fans to come in and give us a hand.

Always elated by any attention from us, there were regularly adoring fans outside the studio for a nod or greeting. I stepped outside and invited in two thrilled teenage girls. Some people had erroneously determined that it was Yoko singing that harmony. It was truly Lizzie Bravo (a sixteen-year-old who moved here from Brazil) and Gayleen Pease (a seventeen-year-old Londoner). With their help and enough tinkering, the song came out great. They were included in the charity version that we did as the first track of the World Wildlife Fund's compilation, *No One's Gonna Change Our World.*

Nine months earlier, we recorded George's "It's All Too Much," which had some of the same ideas, dating back to the same LSD trip. George confirmed all of these realizations through sober meditation. You can see its conceptual connection to John's song. George penned, "Floating down the stream of time from life to life with me, makes no difference where you are or where you'd like to be." Uniting his lyrics with John's, and with these that follow below, gives us a better idea of George's awareness: "Sail me on a silver sun, where I know that I'm free. Show me that I'm everywhere."

Now, seeing that these lyrics stemmed from the same source, which was George's drug-induced Paul dream, the bigger picture appears. John's universal "Limitless undying love which shines around me like a million suns, it calls me on and on," follows George's line, "It's all too much for me to see the love that's shining all around here." This new awareness was all too much for George. "The more I learn, the less **I know** . . . It's all too much for me to take **the love that's shining** all around you."

50

"While My Guitar Gently Weeps"

George randomly opened a book and saw the words, "gently weeps." Looking within himself, he examined, "What is weeping? And why?" In his heart, he always wept for Paul. **George** sought out more of his feelings. He also **wept** for me. Sounding like the same "lonely **for Paul**" bit retold again and again, but with an added layer of judgment about my lost soul, I was less than genuinely interested. The others also lacked interest. Without our support, he called on another friend.

Eric Clapton showed up to record with George the next day. He played lead guitar. I played piano. Some acoustic guitar and organ were added by John.

Lucy

NOTE: In 1968, on 25 July, 16 August, and 3, 5, 6 September, George and others recorded "While My Guitar Gently Weeps." Joining them on that last recording day, Eric Clapton played the red Gibson Les Paul guitar that he had given to George the month before. George named her Lucy after Lucille Ball.

Les Paul (Lester William Polsfuss), one of the top electric guitarists of all time, was a great innovator in the music industry. Through experimentation based on the ideas of others, he was one of the pioneers of the solid-body electric guitar (such as George's Lucy), multitrack recording, overdubbing, delay effects, and phasing effects. Geoff Emerick, George Martin, and I further experimented with these techniques developed by Les Paul for many Beatles songs before and after the band had "Less Paul" and more William.

445

It all sounded pretty good. **Eric** playing lead gave George a break, **making it easier** for him to focus on his lead vocal while playing rhythm. Until Eric joined in, it **seemed taboo** for such a known guitar talent to lend us a hand. However, I had hired session musicians, as was done for Paul and all before. For example, we used a big orchestra for the *Pepper's* album. That was obvious to anyone who thought about it.

As I hear George's lovely song now, I feel more empathy for his sorrow. Now I can see that he was right about me to a point. However, complaining that my Paul role had perverted me had more merit when I was new to that role than it was by that time. When I first became Paul, I went a bit crazy with everybody thinking I was someone. Women threw themselves at me. I liked it. Until **Linda helped me** put my life back together, I was far out of **balance.**

I met Linda Eastman in London on 15 May 1967, then saw her again four days later at a launch party celebrating *Sgt. Pepper's Lonely Hearts Club Band.* Going steady with Jane at that time, I was not yet free to hook up with Linda but fully wanted her. At Epstein's house, while celebrating the album release, with all the attention that I was getting for it, it was not the time or place to get to know Linda.

I saw her next a year later when John and I flew to New York to announce the formation of Apple Corps, Ltd. I telephoned Linda a long four months later, telling her that it was her turn to fly to London. She did. We were at last married on 12 March 1969. Yes, George had cause for concern of perversions at that time. However, by the time I married Linda, **I** had calmed down quite a bit. Although he says **I** was perverted, that was back in 1968 before **I** entered that monogamous relationship. Once **I** married Linda, that was it. George would not have called me perverted then. But yes, **I can admit** that I was a little bit messed up before **that point.**

Right off, George sings of Paul's death. He uses the same words, "you all," in overlapping sentences, "I look at you all see the love there that's sleeping / While my guitar gently weeps." Here, George is evaluating us, looking at us all. We all see Paul's death and that his love is missing. Then George does what turned me off to the song from the start. Talking directly to me—but remember, this is from before Linda—he says, "**I don't know why** nobody told you / How to unfold your love." For only twenty-two months by the time that he wrote this song, I had been trying on, and adapting to, the Paul role. I had not yet learned to manage my sex life, and as they all said, to fully love the band.

Paul's powerful bond of brotherly love had held them all together and was sorely missed. I was all business. That is how I came across. It was the same complaint by George when I first joined until several years after the breakup. It is the same concern for me that he expressed in other songs. Love was missing. In "Within You Without You," it was "the love that's gone so cold." This time he calls it "the love there that's sleeping." It died with Paul and awaited a resurrection.

Emphasizing how I was coerced into getting the injections and surgeries, he says, "**I don't know how**

447

someone controlled you. / They bought and sold you." Although all of us must be learning from all of our many mistakes, still his guitar gently weeps. He still misses Paul. About me again, "I don't know how you were diverted [sidetracked from being me]. / You were perverted too. I don't know how you were inverted [turning my life upside-down to be Paul]. / No one alerted you."

Pounding in the sense that we are all to blame for the massive mess that I had made of my life, he again says, "I look at you all see the love there that's sleeping…Look at you all." It is true. He was right. Unless none of us was to blame, we all were. We all hurt each other. For the lack of Paul's love, we all fell short of love for each other.

Just as George had complained the year before, Paul's love was missing from the band. They felt it did not have to be that way. The love the band had always felt before was still missing. After all that time, "Still my guitar gently weeps" and it would until we all loved each other as they had loved one another before. **We never got** it. That rare kind of love never warmed **the band again.** We all carried mutual feelings of both appreciation and resentment, partly because we all benefited from each other, and partly because we all felt that the others' appreciation was lacking. At the end of the song, sounding like he is weeping in pain, George utters, "Paul, Paul, Paul, Paul, Paul, Paul, Paul." Then, after his gloomy guitar echoes that same languish, **George** repeats, "Paul, Paul, Paul, Paul, Paul, Paul." He **wept for Paul.**

51

Apple Corps Ltd.

Apple Corps (pronounced "apple core") is a double pun. Most obviously, the sound refers to the part of the apple that one tosses out. One may burn the core or bury it to sprout new life as another tree. Paul teaches us to see the core as both—something to be removed from the present apple, but also of lasting value as containing the seed of what lies ahead. Still, there is much more to it. Apple Corps evokes multiple meanings by its sight as well as its sound. Corps sounds like core but looks more like corpse. It is often mispronounced as "Apple Corpse." It signifies "A Paul Corpse."

Out of this corporation named for Paul's bodily remains, many business divisions sprang up for tax relief and our creative outlets. **We invested** our profits as tax shelters but did it all **in the name** of Paul. It all came together over him or **surrounding** his corpse, his body, or his organization. Our **Apple** Studio was "A Paul Studio" in the Apple Building, which was thus "A Paul Building." Right off, we launched Apple Records for us all to make records honoring "A Paul." We also made retail attempts in the name of Paul. Apple Corps, Ltd. owned Apple Retail, which owned our Apple Boutique. Slices, or divisions, of "A Paul" were diversely spread with Apple Films, Apple Publishing, and Apple Electronics. Apple Corps enveloped it all in Paul. All was in and of "A Paul."

Now that **you know** that the core of our Apple is **Paul, or his corpse,** making it personal, imagine how very distressed we all were each time we found that Apple Computer infringed on our trademark. It is bad

NOTE: In 2018, Apple, Inc., co-founded by Steve Jobs, was the largest publicly traded corporation in the world by market capitalization, and the first publicly traded US company to reach a $1 trillion market value. In 2020, it became the first US company with a market capitalization of $2 trillion.

Paul was at the core of the Beatles' Apple symbolism. Their logo is an apple cut in half, as Paul's role was cut in half, divided between the two players. It honored the first half, the first to play "a Paul" role in the Beatles.

Steve Jobs, however, had something different in mind for Apple Computers. His would be the third great Apple to change the world, launching a new era of accessible light and knowledge.

The first world-changing "apple" was Eden's forbidden fruit. Taking the serpent's advice to exercise their free will, Adam and Eve partook to be as the gods who possessed the forbidden secret knowledge and wisdom. Secret societies (having gnosis forbidden to others) naturally see the "fall of Adam" as the rise of mankind. According to the Sumerians, Ea (whose title, Enki, meant "Lord of Earth") liberated humans by giving them gnosis forbidden by Enki's half-brother, Enlil ("Lord of the Command"). To control humans (the hybrid slave-race), Enlil forbade empowering them with light and knowledge. Enki provided that forbidden awareness, and formed Earth's first secret society, "The Brotherhood of the Snake."

In the Sumerian stories, we see Enlil and Enki's rivalry as they curse and bless humans: Enlil forbids enlightenment. Enki provides it. Enlil casts the humans out of Eden. Enki makes their clothes. When the humans grow out of control, making too much noise and bother for Enlil, he tries to drown them in a great flood. However, Enki warns Atrahasis (or Utnapishtim)—renamed Noah in the Bible—to build a big boat and fill it with animals. Those who prefer Enki over Enlil, say Enlil's Bible is biased.

The second world-changing apple was Newton's. His epiphany about gravity while sitting under an apple tree in 1666 led to him enlightening the world with scientific and mathematical reasoning.

The world's third great Apple (originally selling for $666.66) launched personal computing that could potentially bring the whole human family into the powerful worldwide intelligence network. The personal computer ushered in the Aquarian Age of freedom. It gives mankind the ability to overcome world tyranny that has been maintained all along by suppressing information.

450

enough from a business perspective, but also struck at the Beatles' core issue. **They infringed without** love for Paul, and without **understanding** that our Apple is "A Paul" reference **to venerate his corpse.** Out of a purely legal and commercial standpoint, we would have actively pursued our trademark protection anyway. However, so much more so, the core Paul issue made it meaningful personally.

Established in 1968, Apple Corps Ltd. Began before we launched the public awareness of Paul's death, but well after we had begun releasing albums and such pointing to it. Ten years later, we found it necessary to file a suit against Apple Computer for trademark infringement. Naturally, we won.

That should have taken care of it, or so we thought. It did not. Apple Computer paid us US$80,000 with an agreement, in 1981, at least not to dilute our mark by using the Apple name for any music. Still, it was not long before we all ended up in court again. We had set our bounds by compromise, split fairly and logically. Apple Corps said we would not enter the computer business; Apple Computer would not infringe by entering the music business. Then they reneged, adding MIDI and the audio recording as their

NOTE: Launching the new business, the first non-Beatle project was with the Iveys. William, appreciating their voices, but not their proper name, told them the working title for "With a Little Help from My Friends" had been "Bad Finger Boogie." Reversing their image, he renamed them "Badfinger."

Reminiscent of earlier years, William wrote and recorded a demo of "Come and Get It." This time (as the producer), he demanded that his trainees sound exactly like it. The song was for the film, *Magic Christian,* starring Peter Sellers and Ringo Starr, produced by Denis O'Dell who also produced various Beatles films, and whose name is featured in the song, "You Know My Name."

BAD**J**INGER

next big feature, turning their best computers into synthesizers. They logically lost that legal battle too, paid us a big bundle of cash, and agreed to stop adding musical hardware to their computers.

Apple Computer programmer, Jim Reekes, was well aware of all their Beatles litigation, but also understood Apple's profit potential with music. There was a beep in his program noticed by their lawyers. It was called "noteCmd." They suggested he change it to "frequencyCmd" to avoid anything sounding like a musical term. Jim sarcastically suggested calling it "Let it Beep." He resented the Apple Corps limitations. While most co-workers laughed at his joke, one, taking it seriously, said, "You could never get away with that!" Reekes bitterly answered, "So sue me!" That is when he got the beep's name, "**sosumi**" (pronounced "So sue me"), which **Reekes** claimed was some old Japanese word without musical meaning. I respected that humorous creativity.

Our final litigation occurred when they put our logo on their iTunes Music Store. We said no. They did it anyway after we ardently turned down their US million-dollar offer. When our ironclad case came before the so-named Mr. Justice Mann, he absurdly ruled against us. Imagine my astonishment. I was understandably shocked. An appeal would have been awful for our opponents. They won the first round, yet knew it was a fluke that would not continue to the next round when real justice would prevail.

Now, with the threat of that approaching appeal, people speculated that perhaps Apple Corps was in line to become a major shareholder in Apple Computer, making them another division of our corps. However, in the final settlement, we merged with a peace-assuring compromise. Rather than everything related to our trademark depending on our approval, requiring more of our legal hassles, we just decided to sell them the mark and let them license it to us. Although it was said that we sold out for a mere US half-billion dollars, our priority was to make peace. Steven **Paul** Jobs said, "We love the Beatles, and it **has been painful** being at odds with them over these trademarks." We love Apple, Inc. and Steve. He too, at the core, has united in "A Paul." Biting that forbidden Apple made him wise.

52

"All Together Now"

"All Together Now" was one of those songs that we recorded well before deciding to release it. I quite liked the song and recorded it not long after I wrote it. Still, the upbeat mood did not fit our albums until later. We recorded this skiffle song on 12 May 1967, back when we were still recording material to release on our *Magical Mystery Tour* album. It was intended to be a sing-along song that was not only easy enough for children to sing along with but also one which provided an easy concept for the adults gathered all together now to sing with me. In not so many words, I was saying that the reality of me entering **the** Beatles as the substitute for our **departed Paul is known as easily as** counting to ten or reciting **the alphabet.** It's as easy as tea. As easily as you may look and see a ship out in the harbor, or learn how to chop a tree, or skip a rope, you should see me. As easily, learn to open your eyes and "Look at me!" Do you see anything at all that is different, such as the changed eye color?

Remember learning the colors? It is entirely elementary. Children learn to distinguish "black, white, green, red . . . pink, brown, yellow, orange, and blue" by willingly looking at them to tell each color apart. Still, to see the difference between each color, one has to look at them. No one ever saw me. If our fans ever took a close look at us, why couldn't they see me? They did not look closely enough. When Brian and I first discussed me impersonating Paul, I said I did not think we looked enough alike.

He said our fans believe us. Like distinguishing yellow from orange or blue, they might see stark differences, but do not look. For example, the one who is inches taller also has a longer shaped head. People only see whatever they expect to see. Until told otherwise, or until it sinks in, they go on seeing only what they had always seen.

The point is for **everyone** to join in the song of seeing me. I sing, "**Look at me!**" I can imagine hearing them answer, "We see you!" It gets even better and is a hearty laugh in light of what we really have you sing. Paul lost his head [so to speak] at the crash. No longer together, it was smashed off (or in). Here **I am standing** in for him, as if I were Paul **with you again**, happily singing this underlying message, "Look at me all together now!"

Following the idea that the best place to hide a gag is in plain sight, I had everyone repeating the secret clue again and again for emphasis, and even had "All Together Now" as the title. The musical climax is in the first half of the sentence, "Look at me all together now!" **This message is** the good news **that the celebrating crowd**, singing along, evidently **does, at last, see me.**

The joke goes on. Even though they see that Paul's head had been lost, there I am as him leading the song. It is as though he were resurrected. They all sing of me being back together again as though I were he. Although Paul had been dead, now he, unbelievably, sings again. **He is Humpty Dumpty** except that this time, all the King's men **restored** his life, putting his broken pieces **back together again.** I am saying, **"Look at me all together now!"**

I recorded the master track, and then played it all backward. Hearing sounds compatible with John's "Strawberry Field Forever" message, "I buried Paul," I added in the same message. I sang along with the backward track, creating a backward harmony. I sang, "I buried Paul" (metaphorically). Where it is "all together now, all together now, all together now, all together now" going forward, we have the fab corpse in focus going backward as "I buried Paul. I buried Paul. I buried Paul. I buried Paul." He is kaput, dead, and buried. "Poor boy has lost his head" ("Flies and Bees to Emily"). But then he's back together again! It is a miracle! He is all together now! When has any head been as smashed in as that one, and the man, or god, lived to sing about it?

456

If the song has not been playing in your head, go get it now and play it while this key is fresh in your mind. You will laugh your head off. That's okay. Endure it well. **You know** that you too will be all together again soon enough.

This song, with its **blatant** simplicity, is one of my favorite musical **jokes about Paul** that I have made. My favorite by John was "You Know My Name (Look Up the Number)," which also ended up on the shelf for a couple of years. We began recording it in 1967 and finished it in 1969. Recording these songs turned Paul-stress into hilarity. They say, "Laughing and crying is the same release."

53

You Know My Joke.

"You Know My Name (Look Up the Number)" was one of my favorite songs to sing and the best joke of a song that John ever wrote. When John came by to pick me up one day, he saw a phone book up against some lyrics on the piano. I had left it there just as I had found it a few days before. "You know my name. (Look up the number!)" had been written across the cover by a certain visitor. Now, although **I already** found it amusing, I enjoyed it even more when John **suggested** I sing it in light of the fact **that no one really** did know my name. I added, "Even if they **did look** up the number, they would have it wrong." **We are not the same** number. Paul was nines, I was sixes.

Making the joke complete, John later turned up at the studio and said, "Billy, I've got a new song, 'You Know My Name (Look Up the Number).'" I asked the words. He repeated, "You Know My

NOTE: Coming from William, it is great praise to say that the song was "the best joke of a song that John ever wrote." William's true personality more closely resembles Vivian Stanshall than the rock icon. Although he loves to work hard in the studio ("He bag production"), he is otherwise jovial, humorous, and clever. While others respect the productive Ra or Horus in him, sometimes he would rather be Loki: a fun, playfully mischievous, shape-shifting trickster.

Name (Look Up the Number)." He laughed, knowing that I was about to.

Already I was laughing along with him. I asked, "What's the rest of it?"

"Make that your mantra," he said. As I repeated my question, he said, "No, no! That's it! That's enough! There are no other words! Those are the words! It's your new mantra!"

When we recorded it, **I invited Brian** Jones (of the Rolling Stones) to join **in on the fun.** We all had a crazy good time at it. I asked Brian hoping it would cheer him up. His saxophone in there added to the song's hilarity. It had been about a month since his arrest for possession of hemp. His trial was another three months ahead of him then. John explained the humor of the phonebook lines. This joke was of the stock the Stones knew well. It gave Brian a laugh too—which was refreshing in light of the stress that he was feeling. This was not the first time that we explained Paul lyrics to each other. Keeping the world in the dark over Paul's death was hard to do. Both bands were anxious to share enough to keep us all sane. We needed to talk it over as friends that understand and share the loss.

We recorded "All You Need Is Love" the following week. Then, later in June, or maybe even July, John and I went to Brian's flat and played the song with him for the first time. The thing that led up to playing it was his talk about being in jail. He was arrested on 11 May. Although jail time was over, the impending court date haunted him. He said being in seclusion is not bad at all when it is voluntary, but that forced loneliness was one of the cruelest punishments ever executed on this small earth. Having become the sergeant of loneliness after leaving behind some aspects of my William life, I pretty well understood something about what he was feeling. John suffered painful loneliness his whole life also. It drove his work. We all experience it. Some get hit harder than others. It hit Brian when locked up. He said, "When the prison door slammed, I could hear it lock. That's when I was alone."

"Last thing George heard from Paul was a slamming door," John said. "George didn't know what it meant, or how alone it would leave us." John told Brian again about Paul's big argument with Epstein before Paul and Donna's fatal ride. Paul had been angry. He slammed the door and left, leaving them all lost without him. Paul had seen his death and replacement in dreams but could not overturn his fate when it came down to it.

I have wondered how he would have died if he had varied his course, or if he had not gone on his fateful ride at all. Could I have taken his place? This role engulfed my whole life. It is the gig of a lifetime. It gave me all **I would have**. I am grateful for it. Yet, some qualities of **my own life** were better when I could return home to my role **as myself**. Now, though outwardly successful, I have lost a part of myself. When Paul's door slammed, allegorically sealing his "untimely" death, my life slammed shut with his. The story is more of a metaphysical conceit than literal.

When John listened to Brian talking about the slamming door, it triggered old memories and emotions, provoking him to write a song. That is how we had all trained ourselves. Experiences lead us to creative outlets, usually songs. We were much freer to collaborate with others than most outsiders would have supposed. We did not worry about giving away ideas. Slamming doors vibrantly animated John this time. He suggested that we all write a song that began, or maybe ended, with Paul's and Brian's slamming doors. **It would be the** same song, "one door with **dual meaning**," but without my "Paul polish," which was the basis of "All You Need Is Love."

My perfectionism always bothered John. He would knock out a song, track it, and then let the engineers do whatever they thought best. Sometimes he would complain about something they would do to it, but usually did not care. John and Paul were both glad to move on to something else, or on to nothing at all for that matter. They became bored easily. I was the opposite. I would tweak it one way, then another. I would add new tracks, then take some back off. For me, they were never done a moment before I felt they could not be much better. That is my way. For the change, I would do the opposite now and then too. My *Driving Rain* CD

NOTE: Although joined together above, that slamming door was Brian's, not Paul's. According to the agreed-upon cover story, Paul died from reckless driving after an argument at EMI late that night. However, Paul was not at the studio that night. He already died at 5:00 that morning. The cover story was to make his death appear accidental.

461

was made that opposite way. I went for some spontaneous freshness, like the rain, more than my usual well-worked pieces. Although it almost sounded too unrehearsed, I fancied doing it quickly as a favor to Paul. **We recorded it** in mere weeks and then pulled it **all together as fast as** I am told the early **Beatles did it before I came** along.

Everything slowed down for my endless vision and detail. I made them all crazy by spending over 700 hours on my first Beatles album but wanted perfection. I got faster but could never possibly go as fast as Paul and John did in the Beatles myth. Lately, **I have pushed myself** to be more like that mythical Paul. ***Driving*** *Rain* was my thirtieth album since **the Beatles**. I still cannot escape Paul's shadow. Decades later, I still have to prove myself to him. It is still for him that I do it as much as for myself. I must work day and night for Paul McCartney if I am to be him.

Owing to how I would drive John crazy with all the polish I wanted for each song, John often lashed out at me in frustration. He respected **my** skill but was accustomed to having his **work** over and done with for more immediate **rewards**. My focus on detail causes delays. **The Beatles** virtually faded away from fans while we worked on *Sgt. Pepper's*. Many people thought the band had ended. In a way, they were right. Some critics called the Beatles a has-been band. Finally, all of that yelling turned to awe and wonder with the unveiling of *Sgt. Pepper's*.

Overtime proved worthwhile eventually. **John** could see it was far beyond all that they **had** done until then. But it was not his concern. It **frustrated** him to take so long with me at it. All of **them** were upset by my role and by my perfectionism **too**. Although they humored their new leader, it was an eternity for them before we finally released *Sgt. Pepper's* on 1 June 1967.

Later that month, we taped "All You Need Is Love." Although the song sounds positive, it was of John's frustrations with my fastidiousness and about how he missed Paul. Despite the song's very upbeat mood, the message was that I could not accomplish anything exceptionally beyond what everyone or anyone else could do. He is saying that I should stop pushing him to do what cannot be done.

"You can learn how to play the game. It's easy. All you need is love." The game we play alludes to our *Sgt. Pepper's* cover where "LOVE" represents the knight, queen, bishop, and rook. It's easy, unless you need a king. He's dead. For Brian, John quoted *Through the Looking Glass*, "It's a great huge game of chess that's being played—all over the world," and said that I, the new one as Alice now, "wouldn't mind being a Pawn, if . . . I might join—though . . . I should *like* to be a Queen." Doing the queen roll, I was set up for jokes. Still, it is a good line or two from Lewis Carroll.

Brian listened attentively to "All You Need Is Love," which John stopped halfway in to explain its real meaning. When he started again, Brian watched the chords, and then picked up an acoustic guitar. He instantly had the whole thing. The first three times we reached the end, Brian shouted, "Play it again!" And so, we did. Each time, he sang and played with more gusto than the time before.

"No more!" I sang, preventing another "Play it again" round of "All You Need Is Love."

"Too bad," Brian said, "I was just starting to get into it!" Fortunately, we did not sing that whole ordeal again, but **Brian and John kept** on with the "We loved you" line, **modifying as they** went. Over the evening, we all **contributed little bits and** pieces until Brian eventually **completed it** as his "We Love You." The Rolling Stones recorded it soon after. When they did, John and I sang backup.

Even though John and I wrote most of it, we did it to give Brian a good time. I did not ever object to letting him have the credit. John, however, seemed a little more bothered by it, probably because it originated with his own song in the first place. Opening with the slamming prison door also made it viably John's from the start.

Musically, Brian's "We Love You" was not ever something I coveted. I did not fret over wanting Paul's name on it. It was mostly for amusement. "All You Need Is Love," which led to it, was a far better song. Even though John wrote his out of frustration over how long it took to do *Sgt. Pepper's,* I value the song for its double meanings and call for love. I can understand his frustration. Fading toward obscurity as tinkered perfectionistically had its price.

In "You Know My Name," I, the man of a thousand voices, showcase my most publicly accessible non-Paul vocal sound as I use my Vivian Stanshall voice. John and I had lots of fun with it. Mal Evans had a good time too. He contributed some of the backing vocals. It was the kind of ridiculousness that, had I written it, I would have given to the Bonzos. If I had, it would be too unknown for me to mention it now. For that reason, I am glad John wrote it rather than Vivian Stanshall, my alter persona in the Bonzos. Nevertheless, it was a comedy act, which is what that band did best.

Pressing the question about my name, I am as Rumpelstiltskin, the old fairy tale character. In England, based on Joseph Jacobs' translation of the tale collected by the Brothers Grimm, we know that little villain as Tom Tit Tot. In the traditional version of that amusing old story, some commoner sought to look important by boasting that he had a daughter who could spin straw into gold.

The king called the man's bluff. He locked the girl in a tower with straw and a spinning wheel. He insisted that she spin the straw into gold by morning, for the next three nights. If she succeeded, he would let her go. Otherwise, she would be executed. When she could not do it, a gifted substitute showed up to do it for her. See me there. **I am the substitute**.

This magical mystery guy **who made the gold** secretly, let her take the credit **but was paid for it.**

NOTE: After using the song, "Live and Let Die," in *Shrek the Third* (2007), there was discussion about Sir Paul providing the voice talent of Rumpelstiltskin in *Shrek Forever After* (2010). With that possibility, but without an agreement for it, William included his symbolic connection with the character in *the Memoirs* to publish the meaning before fans saw him play that part.

465

He got her necklace for the first night's work. The king was amazed. The next night, the substitute willingly worked for her ring. The king was again impressed. The third night, the substitute (who had been producing the gold [hits] without his hidden name ever receiving the credit) agreed to do his magic for the girl one more time if she would pledge to him her firstborn child. To keep her [or Paul] alive, she agreed. Without the substitute ever revealing his name, he continued his magical work. He made more gold than ever.

Overcome with awe, as well as greed, the king married the girl. When their first child was born, payment came due. The girl, now the queen, offered all her wealth to keep the child. **The substitute** at last agreed to give up his claim to **the big payment** if the queen could guess his name. **Then all his fortune** ended when she learned his name. Since **I have** that same risk, "you know my name" only in fiction.

54

All You Need Is Good Morning Love.

All right, I'll do it! Whenever I get writer's block in songs, or **in these confessional memoirs, I** listen with my heart to **hear Paul, John, or George** telling me what to write. For this telling book, lately, **I have** been hearing a lot of John. Including **his side of the story,** he wants fair treatment. If you have noticed by now that much of what I have written has been uncharacteristically sympathetic to other's perspectives, that is why.

By this point, some readers must have wondered, undoubtedly, why I would explain songs by John and George that have directly attacked me. Well, now you know. To clear the channel, I must cover their perspectives. Otherwise, they keep pestering or encouraging me—which makes it harder for me to focus on the material that I want to write. I have explained two songs that John keeps emphatically demanding that I explain better. I thought I finished discussing them, but apparently not well enough for his satisfaction. I did not reveal his perspective. Here I go with them again but in more detail. The songs by John are "All You Need Is Love," and one with some mild ties to that one, "Good Morning Good Morning." I will also include my own "The End."

467

Love is a funny thing in that those who give it the least feel as though they possess it the least. Our sensing it entails having it. We only feel love when we find it within us. Otherwise, we cannot feel very much of it from others. Here is what I wrote about that balance: "In the end, the love you take is equal to **the love you make**." I used the word "take" because it **worked so well** as a parallel to "make," and used the word "make" because of its sexual connotations, using sex as a metaphor for divine love. When we make love in the procreative sense, we co-create with God. All is created as, and through, love. You may imagine exceptions, such as that hate also creates. However, hate, like darkness, is not real. You cannot observe hate. Just as darkness is merely the absence of light, hate is only a perceived absence of love. Honor love. Light and love are real. Darkness and hatred are illusions. Darkness and hatred are unable to create because they are not real.

A sense of hate is a call for love. Since everyone needs love, we act out and blame others when we lack love awareness. Our own inability to feel loved energizes that need, making our sense of lack even stronger. That is why we experience hate. It evidences our fears stemming from our own perceived lack of love. We may say we hate dictators or criminals for their injustices. However, what we essentially feel is that those people have insufficient love for us or others. We may feel threatened when we sense a lack of love.

Since none of us are completely whole ourselves, we project our insecurities and sense shortages of

468

love onto others. When people act toward us in ways that make us angry, we tend to blame our anger on them. Nevertheless, what we are feeling at our core is that the person disrespected us, or was not very loving. **Our anger is merely** our way of interpreting **our call for love**, blaming emotions on others. Nevertheless, since we are all made of that same infinite love, it is not possible actually to literally lack love. Love is what we are, and what everything is. What we lack is our awareness of love, not love itself. The love-minded don't find lack.

Flowers love. They seek connection to sunlight, loving nutrients from the soil, and water. That attraction, or love, helps them receive it all to thrive.

You and I do the same thing. We grow by what we love, or by what we attract to us. However, we only attract whatever resonates with what is already within us. That is why loving people so easily feel unbridled love from others. It is our nature to feel others' love. When we resonate with it, we naturally feel in others what is in ourselves. "The love you take is equal to the love you make." ("The End"). If we feel hurt by others' lack of love, our lack is within. John sings of my lack of love. However, each time he or I offended the other, we could have looked within rather than blaming the other. If he had done so, he may have discovered that what he was truly upset about was that I was not Paul.

If he had thought of it that way, and realized that I, not being Paul fully, could not possibly be Paul's substitute on that emotional level, filling in the hole in love left by Paul's demise. With that awareness, love might have been more readily realized.

John, George, and Ringo wanted that loving bond of Paul. That is what made them all so crazy about him. That is why so many Beatles songs feature their vocalized pain of missing him. I was right there but was not Paul in that sense. I had amazing talent to enliven their music but could not replace the love or life of their friend. People cannot be replaced.

Although Thelema emphatically places will over love, any limit to love limits ourselves. Never block it. Love is what we are no more or less than it is what God is. Love is what is. *The Book of the Law* says, "Love is the law, love under will." While I agree with that in the Thelema context, most readers do not yet understand that context. In a nutshell, Mr. Crowley would agree that the phrase means that experiences ought to be directed by our will, which can set limits.

Judgment is an egoic product of fear that **undermines love.** Throughout the song, "All You Need Is Love," John judges me, saying I do not have enough love. Whether or not he is right, that judgment, which persisted for years, made it even harder for him to feel the love that I possessed. I was doing my best, as was he. We all do what we can.

Each line of that song carries the same message. Trying to enlighten me, John said that whatever I do, or no matter what I attempt to do, it makes little difference since I do not do it with sufficient love. It says that I cannot do anything that can't be done and that all I need to work on is love.

Singing "You can learn how to be you in time" alerted "Paul is Dead" enthusiasts. They say that John let them know that I had not, at that point, obtained the level of Paulness that John had hoped I would obtain. The entire song carried that same critical message. The song found fault with all I tried to do.

Very matter-of-factly, John says the self-evident throughout the song. By so doing, he conceals his entire message. He sings, "Nothing you can sing that can't be sung. **Nothing you** can say, but you can learn how to **play** the game. It's easy." In these words, at the start, he **identifies** the one to receive this offered advice. It is to **the singer** trying to sing what can't be sung in an attempt to say what can't be said. Very plainly to all those in the know, he was singing to me. However, in so doing, John also had an essential message for the world. The matter that troubles me the most about explaining the underlying meaning is that I do not want to ruin the more important message to everyone. I will provide an overview of the message to the world after I explain more of how he meant it for me specifically.

Vital to an accurate historical interpretation, you must know what was going on with our work. Being engaged already in creating our *Magical Mystery Tour* album, which was being interrupted to do some interviews, and so forth, for a television special promoting *Sgt. Pepper's*, which was now delayed so that we could do this song for *Our World,* we had our hands full.

"All You Need Is Love," written in May 1967, focused on *Sgt. Pepper's*, which would be released in less than two weeks; and on *Magical Mystery Tour,* which John hoped we would complete much faster. Letting me know that the *Mystery Tour* need not have another *Sgt. Pepper's* level of effort, taking a half year again **to** complete, he sang that since I could never **accomplish anything** extraordinary anyway, I only need to **work on love.** He says I should not waste time trying to accomplish the impossible. Unless I learn to love, my efforts are wasted.

One of my impossible objectives was to use our new set of clues to make it so obvious about Paul that the world would understand without any of us ever breaking our confidentiality contracts. However, there's "Nothing you can sing that can't be sung." Even with the best of clues, there's "Nothing you can say" to make it clear without violating the non-disclosure agreement. What I can do is to "learn how to play the game." As in chess, **I could learn** to be the queen filling in **for the checkmated king.** With *Sgt. Pepper's,* I wanted **to make an album** that had the power **to change the world.** John sang that it could not be done before he realized that it had been.

In John's next line, he connects the song to his "Good Morning, Good Morning." In that song, he sings, "Nothing to do to save his life." Now he continues, "No one you can save that can't be saved." He had sung, "Nothing to say but what a day" referring to John's "stupid bloody Tuesday" on 13 September 1966, in West Germany.

John recalls Brian Epstein asking about me in the next line, singing, "How's your boy been?" In the following line, the "you" is Brian and me.

Giving an answer, John sings, "Nothing to do it's up to you." It was for Brian to make me the new boy, and up to me to play the game. John, more accepting than happy about it, had the same level of enthusiasm that he held all along. He could not openly talk about his objections to our deal but could go along with it all for Paul's sake, and to obey EMI. "I've got nothing to say but **it's OK**."

All the "Good morning, good morning, good morning, g . . ." reflects John's greeting Tuesday morning with Brian's telegram. The last "good," like Paul, was cut off early. John got the word that early morning. Being in mourning, "Good morning" was also a "Good mourning" wordplay.

Our Beatles work without Paul was an unhappy chore for John. Recording rubbed it in. That's why he utters, "Going to work don't want to go feeling low down." Feeling alone without Paul to work with, and referring to Paul's death in the street, John sings, "And you're on your own you're in the street."

"After a while, you start to smile now you feel cool." **John** feels better with his various diversions. Next, he **visits Paul** and George's old Liverpool Institute. "Then you decide to take a walk by the old school." He goes there and sees that, like the band and all else, the school went on without Paul. He seems to be unmissed. "Nothing is changed it's still the same." With that great loss, it felt as though everything should be different without Paul. And yet, nothing has changed. He cannot talk about it, or even mention it, but attempts acceptance. "I've got nothing to say but **it's OK**."

Giving balance to my "Wednesday morning at five o'clock" ("She's Leaving Home"), John is out at five o'clock in the evening, picturing people running around, going on with their lives, totally oblivious to the violent tragedy that devastated John's life. He says, "Everywhere in town is getting dark." Five o'clock was sunset when John wrote this song. **The real darkness was** his depressed mood. Those running around contrast John's despair and **Paul's death**, "Everyone you see is full of life." Feeling disheartened, John goes home, has tea, and watches television. This was John's way of relaying his depression without actually revealing it. He was more open about his life-hating despair later.

Near the opening of the song, John says. "Call his wife in." That reference balanced the wife in "It's time for tea and meet the wife." Paul had no wife. His fiancée, Jane, was called to the morgue. Near the end, the wife reference is about watching the BBC sitcom, "Meet the Wife." By then, John got along better with Yoko than with his wife, Cyn.

Cynthia could not comfort him. His misery over Paul, along with Yoko's forcefulness, finished off the marriage. John projected Paul's void onto Cyn as if she were responsible for John's emptiness. John found fulfillment from Yoko, whose tactical work was unfortunate for Cynthia and their son, Julian.

John became estranged from both. I felt bad for little Julian, who was a delightfully bright child, and enjoyable to be around. I played with him more than John did. Julian and I have been good friends all along. Now, as a man, he is largely in the fine image of his father, which is comforting for those of us who miss John. Yet, even more so, Julian is very much his own person. Although he represents his father well in some situations, I would rather everyone think of him as Julian than as John's son. I felt bad for Cyn too. I later produced her record.

During the song's next verse, we find an example of the disregard **John had** for his wife and child. It is also about **Paul driving Cutie**: "Watching the skirts you start **to flirt** now you're in gear. Go to a show, you hope she goes." John was in such pain from his difficult childhood, and again from Paul's demise, that he could not function on any meaningful level of love. Just imagine how John offended Cynthia, Julian, and others by withholding his affection from them, whilst broadcasting all over the world, "All You Need Is Love."

John made himself love's messenger but refused to receive or give love meaningfully to those who were the most significant in his life. He was too tainted by his emotional pain to function without his handler. Singing "All You Need Is Love" gave the illusory suggestion that John had it all figured out. Although the message is fine, that messenger was too wounded to live it. He believed it in his head, but not with his heart.

Our World was the first international, live, satellite television production. Each country rotated its transmission time. For the UK's turn, our Beatles song to the world was at 8:54 p.m. on 25 June 1967. In all, nineteen nations presented acts to the world. Participating nations had representatives

475

unite on-air by performing their separate segments to nearly a half-billion viewers worldwide. It is the largest audience this world had ever known.

Imagine singing live to 400-500 million people! **I was thrilled and amazed** that the show was possible and **that I would be** on it—as a Beatle. Creating **a spectacle of celebration**, we invited special friends to join us **on that historical** world stage for this new and exhilarating **broadcast** experience.

At Abbey Road, surrounded by our friends on the floor, we sat on stools. Our festive party group included Mike McCartney, Jane Asher, Pattie Harrison, Keith Moon, Mick Jagger, Keith Richards, Marianne Faithfull, Graham Nash, Hunter Davies, Eric Clapton, Gary Leeds, and others. It was a great party, full of talent and good feelings.

Most people had not until then considered such a show possible. The world became smaller when it occurred. This historical event was some twenty-five months before an even bigger show with the over-the-top American moon landing.

NOTE: Among the obstacles preventing competing countries from sending astronauts to the moon and returning them alive is that astronauts would pass through the Van Allen radiation belts each way, to and from the moon. NASA cannot explain why they do not now have such technology but are working on developing new methods. Perhaps traveling through wormholes is plausible.

America's Moon Landing (a hoax mapped out years before by President John F. Kennedy) was instrumental in winning the Cold War, driving the USSR to bankrupt itself for what was fundamentally impossible. That strategic intimidation, inspired by the Hollywood tricks that helped the Allied forces win World War II, helped prevent World War III.

The media emphasized the threat of foreign armies but not of what Kennedy considered a much greater threat. He said: "For we are opposed around the world by a monolithic and ruthless conspiracy that relies primarily on covert means for expanding its sphere of influence—on infiltration instead of invasion, on subversion instead of elections, on intimidation instead of free choice, on guerrillas by night instead of armies by day."

Our World was topped by millions more viewers of NASA's astronomical production. Ours had better music, theirs had special effects. Both carried loud and powerful messages of world peace—ours by music and words, theirs by their world dominance. After we sang "All You Need Is Love," the US "proved" their superiority in space technology, necessarily suggesting, behind their most deliberate words for world peace, "We can strike any of you. Don't tread on us!" NASA's production was for peace through intimidation. Their movie was a great success.

In preparation for the *Our World* broadcast, we pre-recorded a rhythm track. I hate to admit we needed that help, keeping us all on track while we played along and sang to a few hundred million star-gazers. Using that track was George Martin's idea. He knew we were not ready to do the show without having that little assistance. **That show was** the first of our two live performances **from that building.**

"All You Need Is Love" had two primary messages. To the world, we were saying that they did not need to worry about anything else in their lives if only they had love. It is a beautiful message. Singing it with that message of love in mind felt good. I felt that we were telling the world something

NOTE: The *Our World* broadcast was not the first Beatles performance while singing and playing along with instrumental recordings. Most concerts were noisy enough that the fans could not hear the band fumbling. However, for quieter audiences, instrumental supplementation was required when the band did not have time to learn to play the new songs. For example, notice George waving without missing a note while playing "If I Needed Someone" in the video of the 1 July 1966 afternoon show at Nippon Budokan Hall.

477

profound. Equally so, the song was directly aimed at me, telling me that all of my diligence in getting every track right on *Sgt. Pepper's* was meaningless.

By the time we got through all the takes and cutting this part to overdub that part, et cetera, they became resentful about working with me. They were intensely resistant. I see that I am not always easy to work with—and am far from having the Paul attitudes they had enjoyed before me. They were critical of my perfectionism but enjoyed the levels of excellence that came with it.

Our unparalleled sale of albums added to each of their frustrations because they could see how vital I was to them but preferred to have me there just for show. They saw what I was doing but would have rather kept it all as their own thing with their friend. As *Pepper's* changed the world, they gawked about its required 700 hundred studio hours. "Excellence takes time," I told them. They had recorded their first album in one 12-hour session.

Continuing John's lyrics of how I cannot do anything beyond my abilities (countering me telling them that I go beyond my natural skills with Paul's help), he also suggests that I accept my situation. Confucius says, "No matter where you go, there you are." Likewise, another says, "What Ere' thou art, play well thy part." What I would add is that I would not be here in **Paul's position** if it were not how God, fate, or **the universe intended.** As long as this is my performance role, I should play it as well as I can.

John says my recording excellence is pointless, that **I do not need to** be a studio Superman but need to **work** on love. My exceptional works, John says, matter **less** than a loving heart. Well, I do not find fault with that part. "Nowhere you can be that isn't where you're meant to be. It's easy." I say, "Let it be," but, "I've got a job to do, and I do it well."

Last of all, the song concludes with softer parts that most people miss: "Yes, he's dead. Whoa! Oh Yeah! We loved you, yeah, yeah, yeah. We loved you, yeah, yeah, yeah." That is me there voicing that part as though I were singing their old "She Loves You" hit. Since my voice was not the exact voice that people had heard years before, there has been confusion about who sang it this time. But you can be sure it was I who did the "yeah, yeah, yeah" as a reflection of their Paul days when writing or recording was simple, before all my "Paul Polish" or "**Billy** Shine," as John and George often put it. Until I **came** along, they said, recording was fun. I ruined it **for them.** I did not love them well enough.

55

"Long, Long, Long"

Letting **Paul** go was impossible for the band. They **missed his** presence. I missed the peace of my **old life.** I loved our unparalleled success, but quickly tired of John's depression over losing Paul, not to mention George's obsession with staying connected to him, and Ringo's regular reminders going on about how he missed Paul because Paul cared more for them than I do. It got old fast. Even when we had good times, there was always a dark cloud of missing Paul hanging over our heads. Not that I did not enjoy working with them. I often did. Still, feeling their loss, their persistent thoughts of Paul colored all that we did.

On the upside, much of our best literature, understandably, sprang from our suffering. If you would consider Edgar Allan Poe's emotional pain, to give an example, you would see that he was quite messed up. Yet, suffering such turmoil empowered him with a depth of feeling that revealed his deeper hidden substance. Anguish energizes parts of the soul that can form the greatest poetry. Our darkest nights and brightest days give us our depths and heights.

In the Beatles' entire catalog, we see two great writing shifts. The first one was triggered by the morbid dreams that tormented Paul. To get beyond writing his silly love songs, he found enough emotional pain to express his greatest, and deepest, songs, such as "Yesterday" and "Eleanor Rigby." The second great writing shift came as the reality of his death struck and traumatized the rest of them. It overwhelmed them to have Paul's nightmares come true. It hit John especially hard. He felt responsible for making their death deal with the devil. Yet, through the band's misery, they produced their best music.

Out of that pact and pain (which is a catalyst for understanding), George finally realized that it was in vain **to search for Paul** as he had been doing. **George hoped to** end his suffering. It could not ever **bring Paul back.** Besides, Paul could be found **in everything.** From that monumental switch of paradigms, George found a peace that lasted until his old way of thinking crept back in.

Now, with that introduction of George's pain, we will move on to his song, "Long, Long, Long." As the song begins, it sounds like he is still suffering. Although he does continue to suffer to the extent of his resistance to his new awareness, it is an out. He somberly sings, "It's been a long, long, long time / How could I ever have lost you / When I loved you?"

The song works on four levels. On one, all of it **is** a love song. That one should not need **explaining**. On the next level, the song is all about **Paul dying, being** missed but found again.

On **the next level**, "Long, Long, Long" is about perceptions **of God.** George had lost and found the

Divine in much of the same way we hear of many individuals, as they put it, "finding Jesus." On the highest conceptual level, built upon the notions of the lower levels, the separation from Paul is only an illusion. It was not caused by Paul entering immortality, but by George's immature perception of the effect and meaning of death. This song is drenched in George's philosophical theory and introspection. I'll try to do it justice.

Saying "**It's been** a long, long, long time" refers to the **two years**, and two weeks, since Paul's death and interment. The longness was due to all of George's **suffering through it all.** On the level of God, I do not know how long it had been since George felt connected to God. Later, when he sang "My Sweet Lord," he expressed further frustration that it was taking so long to feel sufficiently connected to God. In "Long, Long, Long," however, George expresses that he has already made a breakthrough.

NOTE: George Harrison prioritized his song, "My Sweet Lord," above the rest on his triple album, *All Things Must Pass* (released 27 November 1970) by giving it a four-day head-start (in the US) as his first post-Beatles single. It was an instant hit, topping charts worldwide, and became the biggest-selling single of 1971 in the UK.

George wrote "My Sweet Lord" in praise of Krishna. Seeing Krishna and Christ as one and the same (see the note on page 37), he blended the Judeo-Christian word, "Hallelujah" with elements of the Hare Krishna mantra (the "Mahamantra" or "great mantra"): "Hare Krishna, Hare Krishna, Krishna Krishna, Hare Hare, Hare Rama, Hare Rama, Rama Rama, Hare Hare" (Kali-Saṇtāraṇa Upaniṣad), which is commonly chanted or sung all over the world. Using parts of the mantra helped spread Krishna awareness. Christians, upon hearing "My Sweet Lord" and "Hallelujah" loved the song at first hearing. At first, they thought of Jesus, which was partly correct. Then they learned more.

To George's surprise, he also subconsciously plagiarized much of the Chiffons' song, "He's So Fine" (written by Ronnie Mack), resulting in a court action that awarded Bright Tunes $1,599,987. However, as George recalled, "The [spiritual] effect the song has had far exceeds any bitching between copyright people and their greed and jealousy."

The next lines combining as "How could I ever have lost you when I loved you?" suggests George's earnest regret on each of those levels. On the level of concern of Paul's physical death, George had often replayed his last days with Paul and regretted that he, George, could not change what had by then already progressed too far to save him. On the level of God, George questions how he allowed the loss of union with his Lord in light of how important the living God had been in his life in years past.

Letting go of the distancing now, George looks at how he had suffered without Paul and God those years, or, that is, without his conscious awareness of them. Although all the sadness of his singing tone audibly acts against it, he sings, "It took a long, long, long time / Now I'm so happy **I found you** / How I love you." Reflecting on his **miserable** search and wasted suffering **for Paul and God**, George laments, "So many tears I was searching / So many tears I was wasting."

As he contemplated his suffering, he thought of the universal light that permeates all, generating and regenerating everything. Then he remembered a line from Walt Whitman's poem, "Song of Myself": "I effuse my flesh in eddies, and drift it in lacy jags." That line of the long poem, as with hundreds more agreeing with it, promotes the transcendental idea of our spirit-essence continuing beyond form. It was suggesting his idea that when we die, we all rejoin that universal consciousness. To put Whitman in other words, since we are all a part of that universal spirit or energy that is in and through everything, our finite forms are illusory in that they appear entirely separate when nothing is—or can be—fully separated.

Life and element are interconnected. W.W. says, "**I bequeath** myself to the dirt to grow from the grass I love, / **If you want me** again look for me under your boot soles." If then, Whitman, or God, or Paul, fills the universe by being inseparable from all that is everywhere, then George asks them, "How could I ever have lost you when I loved you?" His love was an awareness of his connection to everything.

Whitman admits the probability that we will not recognize him under our boots. He says, "You will hardly know who **I am** or what I mean, / But I shall be good health to **you** nevertheless." Whitman is in the food we eat, providing "filter and fibre your blood." We are to continue looking. "Failing to fetch me at first keep encouraged, / Missing me one place search another." He can be found. Such metaphysical searching is not the same sort of searching that George had done for Paul before. All that long, long, long, time, George had been searching in the sense that he wanted to find a new communal connection to Paul in me, or to find Paulishness satisfaction in another external way.

This new way of looking for Paul was more internal to George himself. He was to look within and see, through this universal consciousness, that since we are all one, all made of that same infinite understanding, he never separated from **God or Paul** after all. He further realized that Paul **did not** go away since there is never anywhere to **go** that is not here and now. We are all connected. Earth and heaven are one here and now. Neither space nor time can ever separate us, whether living or dead, because the forms we occupy in this illusory world are not who or what we are.

George, having such spiritual connectedness in mind, realizes that he had long wasted all of that energy looking for Paul without, and crying over his absence, when in fact Paul had never entirely gone on without him. Paul and God were both deep down within him, part of him, all along. **Now**, at last given real vision, he sings, "Now I can **see** you, be you / How can I ever misplace you?" **He is part Paul** or God. He sings, "How I want you / Oh, I Love You. / You know that I need you / Oh, I Love You." As he ends the song, he imitates Paul's ambulance siren. The union is logical, but not felt in his heart.

56

Songs, Poems, and Paintings

Songs, poems, paintings, and countless other creative expressions are each what they are but are often much more. Songs and poems that sound good, like paintings that look good, do not always need to be any better than that, but are wonderful when they elicit more meaning than themselves. Great creative works are those that provoke deep feelings or deep thoughts. When we layer meanings of sounds or sights, the potential to stir souls increases exponentially. I find them tremendously satisfying.

Poems are songs before their tunes have been added. I have talked to people who say that they only **need to** think of the words of my songs to **change their moods**, cheer them with mental entertainment, or make them more somber with quiet reflection. However, some of them say they may never read another poem. They memorize every word on my albums but do not realize that my songs are all poems that I have written, set to music. It makes no difference whether I write the music first and then the words, or first write the words and then the music. Either way, the lyrics are poetry. I have noticed that many people are prejudiced against poetry. Yet, the very same people have all sorts of delicious songs in their heads. It is all poetry. I have done entertaining poetry readings of my songs, putting in new emphases to the delight of audiences. Poetry may be bettered by fine music, but also stands alone on the strength of its words, whether or not it has a tune. The reverse is true of great music too.

I enjoy a wide variety of music, poetry, art, and **performing arts.** Each specific genre in every form nearly always contributes something that none of the others can. Well-crafted creative works potentially tint our worldview permanently. They change our perception of what life is about and mold how we interpret our surroundings and ourselves. Touching hearts, they define feelings. For example, I could not define melancholy any better than to say it is the color of "Dover Beach" by Matthew Arnold. I may get close to a definition without the poem but can hit it experientially as an authentic emotion with a song, poem, or painting. It becomes a communal occurrence, something we go through together.

All of my songs have something to say. My favorites are always those with layered meanings. Nearly always, I put in as many layers as I feel that the song will support. That is typical of "Paul is Dead" clues. That would be one layer threaded through another idea or story. Often the thread adds a completely new subject or twist that may have nothing to do with the primary original message.

Lyrics and poems do that easily. Look at the lyrics and poems I have sung and recited. **I want you** to laugh at one line, cry in your heart at the **next**, and then wonder why they went together.

Often, I add a line or two as a private joke. It is funny or meaningful to me or to insiders who know the background. John also did that quite a bit. That is what made some of our "Paul is Dead" clues so hard to comprehend for some, but easy for others. To those who knew what had happened, they saw every song as another reminder. To others, there were a few lines that did not mean anything. Ridiculous lines were added, John falsely claimed, merely so that no professor could explain them. Clear references to what happened often turned out to be just as obscure or seemingly ridiculous.

Recently, a few years ago now, I went public with my paintings. It was a big step. It had been enough for me to paint them for myself until a voice inside of me said, "Well, *Paul,* you share your heart and soul in your music. Why not share the real you through your paintings too?"

To that voice, I thought, "Well, why not?" Still, I was torn. As a musician branching into another field, I felt insecure. "What if fans don't like it?" Then I thought to myself, "**My paintings** have something very close to my soul that I **can** share." That was a turning point in my head **dialogue.** I have all along emptied my soul for the world to know me through my songs. "Why not do the same with paint?"

Enough people have seen my displayed paintings now that it should be clear I am not after shock value. X-rated images are not beautiful and do not shock me. **Do what thou wilt. I do not fret about** the  private lives of **consenting adults.** No good comes

NOTE: John Lennon says, "The whole Beatles idea was to do what you want. To take your own responsibility, do what you want, and try not to harm other people. Do what thou wilt, as long as it doesn't hurt somebody."

"Do what thou wilt" is Aleister Crowley's most famous line, and is a primary tenant of his Thelema religion, as well as of Luciferianism generally with all of its many offshoots. "Free will" and "Free agency" are buzzwords in some of these groups that hold the individual's will as sacred. By contrast, Jesus prays, "Father . . . not my will, but yours be done" (Luke 22:42).

Whether in full alignment with Source, or identifying as Source, without the illusion of separation between what is God and what is each of us, it may be impossible to distinguish the will of one from another. When we are acting as our higher selves, our will is God's will. To do what thou wilt is to do God's will when our own will is reflective of our true infinite divine nature.

With the Illuminati's doctrine of free agency, they have rules in place to obtain the consent of participants, lest some are esteemed as victims. In Paul's case, he made that "pack with the devil," as some people call it, wherein he prayed that he would die for the band if called to do so to make his name and music immortal. It all seemed unreal to him then, a fantasy of greatness. However, that idea did not originate with him. Those assigned to recruit him romanticized the idea of living forever in the collective consciousness in exchange for shortening his life. Recruiters told the Beatles how to do the ritual, and what to say. Upon doing so of their own free will and accord, it was reported back, making all that occurred thenceforth by Paul's consent.

The idea of mutual consent also comes into play with disclosure. Although the ruling elite accomplish their design by clandestine means, they tell all in words so plain that the majority disbelieves them. According to their law, when one gives notice of a course of action if those impacted do not formally object, they have lawfully agreed. With that tacit agreement, those who control the world do so according to the will of the people. Sometimes they lay out the truth so plainly that most people disbelieve it on the grounds that if it were true, the perpetrators would not admit it. However, according to their doctrine of free will, and by the rules of fair play imposed on them by others, they must give notice but are not required to convince anyone.

The Beatles revealed Paul's death all along. Without any objection in the prescribed manner, all tacitly agreed. Once *Sgt. Pepper* showed that Paul had passed away and that Billy Shears replaced him, all who bought more albums with Billy as Paul demonstrated agreement that he is right where he belongs. After the clues were explained, all still voted for him by buying more albums. **Come to grips with the fact that we reached a full accord as if we shook on it.**

489

from moralizing. Judgment blocks love. Furthermore, resisting or repressing desire makes it grow and fester. As Jesus says, "Resist not evil" (Matthew 5:39).

Essentially, **I want** all of my art to strike an inner chord of **real existence**. Even unearthly art can cast shadows of **real-life** emotions or meanings. If I can layer those **feelings** or meanings, all the better. See them **with the painting** I titled, "The Hand." I do not normally have any desire to explain such intricacies from a painting. I prefer to let each observer work his or her own way down past the obvious levels without guides limiting your thinking by telling you what to hear or see in songs or art. Nothing stops a personal search faster than the idea of already having the answer. Moreover, if we are not searching for it, the answer is meaningless. Search for meaning in "The Hand" on the back cover.

After you read about, and understand, "The Hand," it will be too late for you to be free to discover it. For real observation, consider the picture now before I spoil it for you. Find your own meaning. If I can enhance your meanings later, that is even better. Still, you will never again be this free to consider it with your own eyes. With your own mind, the work reflects your own soul to you. Once you have my interpretation, you will essentially see mine. That is why I usually do not explain my own art. I prefer that it be a mirror to reflect your soul. Have you studied it yet? What is it to you? Is there any new awareness of your own feelings? Take note. What did it reflect to you?

This is my take on the picture. The hand belongs to someone in this fallen hairy world, some soul having a hard time in this world of forms, chaotic confusion, and suffering. Kind of dark? It will get ever darker. The person is reaching out for help, aware of the guardians hovering above the earth. Yet, they are out of reach. The person reaching from this dark world can sense the light flowing down too, and can feel it dripping down his or her fingers, but cannot soak it in. **The light is there** but is not revealing anything **to save him or her.**

Guardians hovering over are of another realm or existence. As shown by their mushroom foreheads, the guides are of another reality. Shrooms have often been used to increase inner-world consciousness, spiritual connectedness, or mystical visions of parallel universes. Such altered states can include fairies, leprechauns, or *Alice in Wonderland* type of entities. "The Hand" shows guides of a spiritual reality. The individual reaches for help in this hairy world.

Another prominent feature of these shroomy guides is their profound noses. In old Hebrew representations, breath typifies spirit. A nose that breathes air suggests a living soul, as a body and eternal spirit housed together. Our eyes may see things of this world, and our ears may hear sounds of this world, but the nose breathes something we do not see, hear, or touch. It is the most mystical of our five senses, dealing with the less tangibly tactile elements of this world. **It is also** a symbol of life.

The guardians are all of **a parallel** spiritual realm, not of this fallen organic **world.** That is well enough established by the mushroom noses and foreheads. Foreheads represent the brain or intellect. Beings of

491

noses and foreheads, these non-worldly guardians are all spirit and intellect. That is a problem.

Moving about high above the earth, they can smell (spiritually sense) the presence of the poor unfortunate soul down below reaching up for help. **They** can all sense that they are needed but **cannot see** anyone. They have no eyes. When **the sufferer** calls for their help, they cannot hear. They have no ears. Nonetheless, it does not matter. Even if they saw and heard, they have no mouths. They cannot speak. They cannot guide those below. Without hands or arms, they cannot reach out to them, take them by the hand, or hold them.

However, those who suffer alone in a dreary reality cannot know any of that. The hand anxiously reaches up to them for relief. They are the guides over each of us that do not seem to be doing enough.

Or, worse, what if our trusted guardians intend to hurt us? Might they be instruments of our death? Sometimes we feel desperate or forsaken. It is not how life really is. That is, it is not how real life is. Isolation is illusory but is how we may feel. When everything goes wrong, we interpret the universe most darkly. It feels as if all is cold against us. Yet, we may see that the good shepherd cares for his flock. All is good after all—until he wants mutton.

Another layer of interpretation is that **it is Paul** buried in the earth reaching up **to the other three** for them to carry on his work. **He can feel their** showering music dripping down his **outstretched** fingers. That is one of the great things about **songs,** poems, and paintings. We can see all such arts in extraordinarily different ways. On this level, it is **Beatles music** that revives the departed Paul. It **calls Paul** from the grave. As our music reaches **down** through the tangled earth, Paul-M reaches up **to feel it**, stretching his palm (Paul-M) from the grave, bringing him back. That may seem impossible until you recall that he, being attached to me, comes alive in me, so to speak, whenever I do his work, singing in his place, carrying on in his likeness.

Since I represent Paul, his hand reaching up is also seen as my own. Furthermore, I cannot recall Paul's death without also remembering that I, too, left a life behind. My William life is, as it were, buried with Paul. I am the one who needs them to lend a hand. I reach out to John, George, and Ringo, expecting them all to be greater than they were. I did not realize how deaf, dumb, and blind they had become without their dear Paul. To continue on, all they needed was my hand (or palm (Paul-M)), in it.

Speaking of hands, painting them is hard for me to do well. For this painting, I had the help of a child. I asked him to place his hand on the canvas. Going around it with a pencil, it came out larger, big enough to pass for an adult hand. Then I asked the lad to turn his other hand palm up to model details. The canvas was small enough that the hand was about the right size for how I imagined it.

Whenever I paint or write music, whatever I feel, I do. That works. **Some days** the creative inspiration is musical, other days **it guides me** through paint. I began painting in 1983. I was quiet about it for sixteen years until the year of nines, 1999, when, in the

493

Lÿz Art Forum in Siegen, Germany, I had my paintings featured in an art exposition. After that, I published my art in the book, *Paul McCartney Paintings.* Had it not been for Wolfgang Suttner's kind encouragement, they might still be hidden from the world. The positive response in Germany and elsewhere drove me on to a much larger scale. My first UK art exhibition opened in Bristol, England with more than 500 of my paintings on display. Bringing it so close to home had lit a fire under me.

In October 2000, Yoko and I presented art exhibitions in New York and London. While I have never loved Yoko's "music," her art amuses me. Those who planted me planted her, using her art to get her noticed by John—who excelled her in art as much as in music. I still admire his minimalist line drawings. I love the simplicity of his lines. His four-headed Beatle beast, already shown, is one of his better ones.

Now, among my other known roles, I am seen the world over as a painter. It is stirring to let myself go out on a limb growing in a new direction. I do it often in music, but the canvas has been a completely new world to me. **I am open to** new ways to make a positive **mark** in **the world** and to gain experiences **in a new direction** that I have not explored before. Having established myself as a world-known graphic artist, in 2002, I designed a series of six postage stamps for the Isle of Man Post. Now **I am** the first major rock star in the world who is also **known** as a stamp designer.

Our lives **in this world** pass by quickly. Here I am already in my seventies. I am five years older than

Paul. There is no telling how many years I have left. I intend to live all of them fully. There are many unwritten songs and unpainted canvasses yet to materialize. There are still many new experiences left to go through, and new directions to explore.

Each of us must ask ourselves what we can still accomplish before finishing this tour. Some actions make big marks. Others, not so much, but who knows? Reading to **a child may** seem insignificant, but could help the child to **influence others**, who then impact others. What we do **with what** we have tells everyone—and ourselves—who **we are**. We make the world a better place by **doing** our best. If I, through my songs, paintings, or this book, inspire you to do something worthwhile, on any scale, then I thank you for adding even more value to my efforts.

About my age, it should not surprise you that I am a little older than Paul. The age difference never got in the way of me rocking with the best of them but did set me apart from my Beatle bandmates just a bit. My added maturity made me seem a little too businesslike. In *The Magical Mystery Tour* film, I am asked my age. I say, "I'm thirty, but I look a little younger." That was on 11 September 1967, not coincidentally, Paul's first death anniversary. I looked like Paul, who would have been twenty-five.

57

From "Ob-La-Di, Ob-La-Da" to Boogaloo

"Ob-la-di, ob-la-da. Life goes on," was a catchphrase that was said with a Jamaican accent by a guy named Jimmy Scott. I saw him often at the clubs. The idea was that whatever happens, life still goes on. "**Ob-la-di, ob-la-da**" means about the same thing as "**bada bing bada boom**." It is a phrase showing that **things happen** as intended without requiring much effort. Until the day you die, "Ob-la-di, ob-la-da, **life goes on!**" It's a done deal. It's as easy as pie. **Voila!** Whatever is to be is whatever happens. The expression tells us that everything runs its course. Ob-la-di, ob-la-da. One thing always leads to the next until you die; and even then, life goes on.

"Bro" (short for brother) in Scott's dialect was "bra" (usually spelled, "brah"). Brother Paul tells me, "Life goes on, Bra." I also enjoyed thoughts of bras.

On one level, a boy and girl fall in love, marry, and bring children into this world. Everything flows freely. Voila. Life happens.

Death concepts, particularly the death of Paul, **take the song to a higher level.** The lower level is a metaphor for the higher. On a lower, Desmond meets a girl named Molly, gives her a ring, and they live together singing, working, and raising children. Molly is also slang for MDMA crystalline powder.

In the UK, a barrow is a pushcart. "**Desmond** has a barrow in the marketplace" means he **sells goods** from his cart, next to all the others that are pushed to that same green market or farmers' market.

Every line works on that level, but also perfectly on one suggesting that Paul is entombed under the ground—since the word "barrow" also signifies an ancient burial mound. From a metaphorical way of understanding the song, the biological Paul is Desmond; I am Molly. **Desmond is** in his tomb, even while still **active in commerce.** Molly is a singer in the Bonzo Dog Doo-Dah Band (and also sings as a session musician).

Desmond says to Molly, "Girl, I like your face." Obviously, my face was very important to Paul. He likes my face. And what do I say back to Paul now as I take him by the hand? "Ob-la-di, ob-la-da, life goes on!" The life of Paul goes on through me. I am "how the life goes on."

As this love story goes on with the more apparent meaning, Desmond goes to a jewelry store, buys a twenty-carat golden ring, and gives it to Molly. Or, in real life, the buried Paul gives me his gold. The song implies that Desmond and Molly marry, or that Paul and I merge, become one.

NOTE: William takes Paul by the hand, and says, "Oh bloody! Oh blood, ah!"

As has been said of marriage, "They twain shall be one flesh." What does Molly do once she receives Desmond's treasure? She does exactly as I do for the late Paul: "As he gives it to her [Billy], she begins to sing." What does she sing? "Ob-la-di, ob-la-da, life goes on." That is what I am singing to everyone. Besides in this song, it is the message I have sung for years. Starting when I received Paul's wealth, I began to sing that his life goes on through me.

Paul and I, as "Desmond and Molly Jones," had been joined together for exactly "a couple of years," averaging in when this song was written (22 months) and released (26 months). In those two years, up until "Ob-La-Di, Ob-La-Da," it was a good union. "In a couple of years, they have built a home sweet home."

Letting them laugh, I sing, "with a couple of kids running in the yard" of Desmond and Molly Jones. It deserved the scripted laughter: "Ha! Ha! Ha! Ha!" "Har Har Har" would have been a chorus to Horus.

Since the merger had gone well from a monetary standpoint, referring to the musical commerce that I do as Paul or Desmond, I sing, "**Happy ever after** in the marketplace." I am happy **in the work**, but not ever after in our home **with the children** (that is, with the bandmates). **Business is good.** Keeping it successful, I let the children (bandmates) lend a hand. I let them start playing their instruments on records.

Making my debut as Billy Shears, through Ringo, I asked for, and got by with, help from my friends. Our worst days included having my face worked over with injections, surgeries, and exercises. **The** nights had me back singing in the studio. Molly, in **the** song, spends her days doing her pretty face. When **the** day is over, "in the evening she still sings it with **the** band." What am I, or Molly, still singing with **the** band? "Ob-la-di, ob-la-da, life goes on!" I'm how **the** life of Paul continues. I am "how **the life goes on!**"

Really, today, most people cannot appreciate how absurdly conservative the world was when we wrote all these songs. I repeatedly inserted the word, "Bra" to tie in Jimmy's Jamaican "Brah," and to break the bra taboo. It also tied to John's song, "Girl," in which Paul and George sing, "tit, tit, tit, tit, tit, tit, tit, tit, tit."

Having Desmond stay home to do his pretty **face** at the end was just a recording accident. I sang **everything** great in that take, after several imperfect attempts, but sang that one part wrong. I decided to let it stay for the humor and because the many takes were frustrating the others almost to mutiny.

I liked the song and thought we should **release it** as a hit single. However, George felt it was trite, and John loathed it for several reasons, not the least of them being how it made each of my bandmates, John, George, and Ringo, the metaphorical children of Paul and me. John said it gives a story about a meaningless relationship. He said, "What? These two get married and then go on living happily ever after just because he liked her face? Do these two ever fall in love? Do they ever get beyond their looks?" I replied rudely about Yoko's looks but wished I had spoken from love.

Speed was another issue. Just as I had John speed up "Revolution 1," resulting in the hit, "Revolution," "Ob-La-Di, Ob-La-Da" had been much slower. One night, after days of takes that still weren't right, John nearly knocked me over as he burst into the studio. High as a kite, he stormed over to the piano, and shouted, "All right now, we're going to do 'Ob-la-di, ob-la-da!'" He pounded out the entire song as loudly and furiously as he could. It sounded great. I was glad to use it. It made me sing much faster, but that did not bother me at all. It made the song better.

Speaking of John being high, I altered that last line to make a drug reference, changing "sing" to "take." "If you want some fun, take Ob-la-di-la-da!" You can see that that line has nothing to do with my Paul merger, or with anything else in the song.

John's great disdain for the song carried over into **ridicule** that came later. When he was drunk or high, he **was often** verbally abusive to me. It was always **the drugs talking.** He would accuse me of hiding what I was doing from him, or of spending months to get my songs covered in "Billy Shine," not for quality, but to make his songs look inferior.

Sometimes he accused me of having stolen his band from him, or that I took advantage of him when he was most vulnerable with the shock and anguish of losing Paul. At other times, he would criticize me for being too much of a workaholic to have any feelings for my bandmates. I could go on, and on, and on, and on. He surely did. It was especially bad when the chemicals got him going.

Later, he would sense my pain, and know that he did it again. He would turn to me, slide his glasses down to the end of his nose to see over them, and tell me, "I love you, Billy." This pattern repeated itself numerous times.

Having that song in his arsenal to sling at me, he called me "Desmond" off and on for a few months. Each time I'd think to correct him, I'd stop myself after one time when he caught me in his snare. I said, "Desmond is Paul." Although we had already been over it many times, he seemed confused.

"Oh," he said, acting as though he did not know, "I thought you were Paul,"

"No," I said, "in the song, I am Molly. Paul is Desmond."

"Good to get that straight now, Molly," he said, laughing at me. "All this time, I thought it was about you becoming Paul. So, this was when you became Molly? Is that right?"

Ordinarily, **John and I got along** well. We were rather close. However, **sometimes** resentments were unloaded, **particularly when** he was drunk or high. **He was capable** of cutting malicious humor with episodes interspersed wholly void of all humor whatsoever. Sometimes he was funny but hurtful. Other times he was just mean. Then later, when he saw that he had gotten to me again, he would usually apologize. John's jokes went from annoying to much worse.

Letting **John's stupid Desmond humor** get to me **was a mistake.** By resisting it instead of laughing

501

Desmond off, I unwittingly encouraged it. After a time, they shortened it to "Desi." It was months before **Ringo let me** in on their joke. To this day, I don't **know for certain** who started it. One evening when **I was** not there, someone said that I sounded like **Ricky Ricardo** (on the American situation comedy, *I Love Lucy*). Ricky, played by Desi Arnaz, Lucy's husband, popularized boogaloo music.

Unless you happen to be a big fan of boogaloo music, you probably understand how they used it as ridicule, calling me "Desi" until I learned why and then calling me "Boogaloo." The term, boogaloo, was probably coined around the time Paul died in 1966. It is a fusion mostly of popular African American, R&B, soul, mambo, and son montuno music. When John, Mick, George, or Ringo used the word, however, it meant singing like Ricky Ricardo. Boogaloo, like Ricky, was more Cuban in the beginning.

Saying I was Desi or Boogaloo in private was annoying. However, to maintain the band's image and earnings, they kept their ridicule from fans until I dissolved the band. Then, the Boogaloo silence deal expired. They jabbed me whenever they could in those early post-Beatles years. They made Boogaloo references in hit songs that the general public could not understand. It was gibberish to them.

Yet, the esoteric knew. That inner circle included several of my closest friends and associates. I cared about those connections. Only they fully understood the Boogaloo references because only they had the Desi background story. The Boogaloo songs were made to embarrass me. They succeeded.

"Back Off Boogaloo," written by Ringo, and produced by George, who also played guitar on it, attacked me and my music. Referring to "Ob-la-di, ob-la-da," in which **I took over Paul's** work cart, or his "barrow in the **marketplace**," and from which they called me Desi and Boogaloo, Ringo kicked out: "Wake up meat head. Don't pretend that you are dead. Get yourself up off **the cart**."

Out to stick it to me, he says I too seem "dead," and ought to get off Mc*CART*hey, leaving his name, fame, fortune, and business, "**the cart**," or "barrow in the marketplace." Ringo was saying that my music failed to measure up to Paul's standard. He says that if I am going to go on making music in his name, I had better shape up: "Get yourself together now and give me something tasty." John's "Come together over me" line, and my own "All Together Now" has an echo here. He tells me to get it together as Paul or to stop using his name. He sings, "Everything you try to do, you know it sure sounds wasted."

Going on with Ringo's "Back Off Boogaloo," repeated gallingly throughout the song, he is directly attacking me. He says I think I am "a groove" because of my personal choice in shoes and socks—as if my looks had anything to do with my music. Mostly, Ringo just goes on and on telling me to "BACK OFF!" I told him to bloody "F*CK OFF," and resented my bloody lack of stronger words.

On his "Back Off Boogaloo" single cover, **Ringo** showed Frankenstein's conglomeration. He **used that** character by Mary Shelley because it is a **monster** made of dead human remains. Ringo is **showing** that I, Boogaloo, am a monster made of **the dead Paul** as if by Frankenstein (who also dies 11 September).

That image was amateurish compared to Beatles records. However, Ringo had been uninvolved at that end of our Beatles presentations. I highly doubt if any outsiders understood his use of Frankenstein.

Doing that song whet John's appetite for Ringo to sling another at me. Following Ringo's lead, John made another song for him to sing ridicule of me Ringo had sung that I think I'm a groove. Now he adds that I think I'm "the greatest in this world, in the next world, and in any world!" John and Ringo revile me for thinking that I am better than Paul who is in the next world, the spirit world. Well, yes, it is true. I am greater. He was my forerunner. I am the most successful songwriter in history.

Singing the entire song in first-person as though Ringo were me was a conspicuous repeat of when I had Ringo do the same on *Sgt. Pepper's*. I had written "With a Little Help from My Friends" as entering the band and being interviewed for the new position. The press asks the questions, I give them

NOTE: Ringo did "Back Off Boogaloo" in criticism of William's first two Paul McCartney albums, *McCartney* and *Ram*. George Harrison helped Ringo develop the song by adding some chords and finishing the melody. In September 1971, George produced its recording in Apple Studio. The year before, he had also produced Ringo's "It Don't Come Easy." "Back Off Boogaloo" was released as a single on 17 March 1972, exactly ten months after the release of *Ram*.

504

lyrical answers. The persona in the song, introduced as Billy Shears, as **I have** said, will get by with a little help from **his friends** (John, George, and Ringo). However, of all of us, I sang the best.

Everyone sang better than Ringo. He was the junior member. I was the leader, then John, and yes, George too outranked Ringo. Except for me, having come in at the top, Ringo was the newest member. It made sense for Ringo to play the role of the insecure newcomer who is a bit apprehensive about singing out of tune. Then, making the point that Billy is not Ringo, John dresses up as him in *Yellow Submarine* (the movie), showing that it is a disguise.

By so pretending, they took the focus off of me. Quite everyone recognized Ringo's voice. Had they known to listen for changes in Paul, they would have understood the song's meaning too soon. That is why Ringo sang as if he were I. In the song that John ended up writing for him (and for which John and George played accompaniment), they tie it in by Ringo singing, "Yes, my name is Billy Shears. You know it has been for so many years."

At the time "I'm the Greatest" first came out, 31 October 1973, thirty-three-year-old Ringo sang, describing me, "Now I'm only thirty-two, And all I wanna do, is boogaloo!" Helping record sales, John indicated that all of us ex-Beatles took part in making that song. However, the others did it without me. I had no part of it except that **I was** satirized by Ringo impersonating me, as ridicule, and except that it got my name, **Billy Shears** without my consent. Thus, though John, **the author**, implied that we recorded it all together, you will certainly never see me listed in the liner notes.

"I was in the greatest show on earth, for what it was worth," he says of me. Again, Ringo sings, "Now I am only thirty-two, And all I **wanna do**, is boogaloo!" His point is that if I, **Billy Shears**, am so great, I should make greater **solo music**. Instead, he says, **I am** singing like Ricky Ricardo. As with his other **boogaloo** hit, or kick, he tells me to back off of my boogaloo music and to give them something Paul would be pleased to call his own. They all resented that I, still as Paul, broke up the band after receiving his great fortune and fame and for continuing in his name for the rest of my life with everything that would come with it. I made many more hits as Paul than Paul ever did. John and the others resented my ongoing success, especially since I dissolved the band and kept Paul.

Even worse than those songs that Ringo sang, John more deeply hurt me when he did his most notorious song, "How Do You Sleep?" That song, lest any outsider missed who he was addressing, detailed it for all saying, "Sgt. Pepper took you by surprise." I, of course, am the one responsible for its exceptional world-changing success. As Ringo had suggested, John sang that **I am the one** who is dead. In code, John says that the only **worthwhile** part of the Paul/Billy combination was the **Paul** part: "The only thing you done was yesterday [Paul], and since you've gone [or, since Paul crossed

NOTE: Besides the impact on William and on his bandmates, William's dissolution of the Beatles historically impacted the world. The Beatles' third phase (from 11 September 1966 to 10 April 1970) lasted only 3 years, 6 months, and 30 days. And yet, in that short three-and-a-half-year ministry, they permanently changed the world.

William's 10 April 1970 press release saying he would no longer work with the Beatles established 11 April 1970 as the world's first post-Beatles day. It was exactly 666 weeks after Paul first met John on 6 July 1957.

over] it's just another day [Billy]." Saying that Paul's biggest song, "Yesterday" (representing all that Paul brought to the band), is better than my contributions (represented by my song, "Another Day"), is merely emotional preference for his old friend. That's okay.

The worst part of **John's** malicious song is his Muzak line: "The sound you make is muzak to my ears." I was never so **discourteous** to him. When he evidenced his psychological problems by his primal scream music, crying for his departed mum, I did not joke about it or call it the unqualified garbage that it was. I did not say a word. Some of what John passed off as music makes it all the more absurd that he would ever be critical of me. He sang, "You must have learned something all those years. How do you sleep? Ah how do you sleep at night?"

Now he is the one sleeping. **I do not like** to speak ill of the dead, especially of **my** good friends. He was speaking from his **pain.** I knew that. Nonetheless, **it was very hurtful to me.**

Until now, I have been silent about much of this. That does not mean that he did not hurt me. He did. Realize that the Beatles would have stopped entirely before *Sgt. Pepper's* if I had not come along and given the band my all. **I deserved more** respect than I ever received from any of them.

Maybe I should end this chapter on a better note. As I said, we were close friends. We had our battles, enough to paint a dismal picture in some regards, but also had serious bonding experiences that made us inseparable on much deeper levels. We four were set apart from the world. Over those hard years of working through their loss of Paul while keeping the band together without him, and of me losing my past as well—ungrounding me—but going on in the name of Paul, it took a hard toll on us all. We all helped each other work through some heavy issues. As **the Beatles**, we all worked very well together to **change the** music world forever. I never measured up to **Paul** in satisfying emotional needs but did excel him in pushing his cart, and the entire band, up to the next level.

For all those years, and still up until John died, we grew in great mutual love and respect for each other. We shared rough times, frustrations, pains, and unparalleled success. We would each rant and rave and complain about the pain, but then mend our wounds to bond better than before.

He was my greatest critic and best fan, and I was his. When he did not like a song, he was not insecure, or too awed by me, to say it straight. We each called a spade a spade. He held me to his mark of quality, and I held him to mine. I loved his creativity, and he loved mine. The two of us would go off into our own creative directions, and then share our ideas to work together synergistically opening up new levels of excellence.

Our work inspired new heights in each other. Each of us did that for the other. Yoko told me that **John got his** *Double-Fantasy* album, or his **second wind to get back into the game** to make that final album **because** he (or others) was pushed on by what **everyone saw** in my work. I showed that we still had **time to get going again.** We were not yet spent. Although John and I had our upsets, we were friends who continued to affect each other.

58

"The Long and Winding Road"

Perhaps the most overlooked song of **Paul's** death is, "The Long and Winding Road." It is **sad** and is still an emotionally difficult song **for me** to sing. After all these years, it still strikes at my heart, uncovering some deeper feelings that—if not for the reminder of this song—**I might just keep** buried. Let me share this one with **you on a deeper level.** As you read about it, do not get distracted by all the literary elements or dead Paul aspects. Instead, open up to feel my heart in this song. Do not concern yourselves with anything else. Just open your heart to understand that pain in mine. Do this favor for me, and you will never feel this melancholy song the same as you have for decades. It will change you and your experience with all of these songs. This one hurts.

Open your books, CD case, or website to see the actual lyrics to give you the context of what I am now explaining. The long and winding road represents both the road that Paul died on and also, now in this song, a road of life. Literally, on the wild and windy night that Paul crossed over, he left a pool of blood that the rain washed away. He left

509

a pool of tears only figuratively. These tears from hurting lonely hearts were shed by Paul's family, friends, Jane Asher (his girlfriend), bandmates, me, and others. That is at the heart of the matter. Although I did not miss him in the same sense, my anguish was very real. My pain is of a different sort. It was confusing even to me. Writing this song helped me explain some of it to myself. It helped me sort out my feelings, reaching into my subconscious.

My state of mind when I wrote this song was about feeling lonely and disconnected from all that ever mattered to me. With Paul's death, I lost my own past. You are right if you think that trading my pathetic life for Paul's was a good deal for me. Of course, it was. Paul's life was better than my own. In my life as **William**, I was not as successful. Still, it **was my life.** You may be rather surprised to discover how much that matters. I was. The earlier roles I played did not take over.

I was having friction with John and the others, as I had had all along. I felt so alone that I hated everything about that false Paul life I was living. I decided to clear my head out on my farm in Scotland. I love the peace of my Celtic heritage that I feel there—my family heritage, not McCartney's. I love that escape. I feel allowed to be myself there. There is space there where I can pause to think and to organize those thoughts. It is where I can still feel and hear whatever is inside of me.

Now, I am not blaming anyone, or saying I was right, and they were wrong, or that any of us were good or bad. **I am** just expressing how I felt. I am sharing my **shadows** of sorrow from that dark time. Everyone seemed to believe that I, the new Paul

McCartney, had it made. I lived a charmed life. I really got **a good deal.** Of course, I did. I felt the way I **imagine** Richard Cory had felt with all **the glamour**, wealth, and grace that came with his role. Everyone envied him. They wished they could be him. I similarly wished **I could be** Paul McCartney and was told I would be. **Richard**, nevertheless, always tried to connect **to people**, but never could because he, after all, was that big celebrity. He was nice to people, very generous in fact. Yet, when he would say, "Hello," their pulses would flutter.

That is cool at first. However, I could not have real conversations with sycophantic people or any heartfelt connection with those whose hearts flutter when I say, "Hello." In that most insightful poem by Edwin Arlington Robinson, everybody wanted to be him. No one had any idea of the heavy burdens laid on him until he finally shot his brains out. I have felt that same intense pain, as have too many other celebrities. My friend, Paul Simon, adapted the poem into a fine song by the same name. It nearly knocked me over when I heard it on Simon and Garfunkel's 1966 album, *Sounds of Silence*. I got it but could not get it fully until **I began** living it later that year. The **intense isolation** and pretense can be difficult **to understand**. Robinson got it. He tried to convey it. **Paul** Simon's new version of it, making it a song, was so good that we covered it in my 1975–1976 Wings tour.

Doing that poem song, "Richard Cory," in those concerts, a few songs after I sang "The Long and Winding Road" added a fuller dimension to what I am trying to explain to you here now. You can hear it on *Wings Over America* and see how I inserted John Denver's name—decades before his death that now many people (but not my angels) call a suicide.

It elicits empathy for those who have it all, but do not have peace of mind. I was one of them. Even if I found the fabulously favorable fame and fortune, if I must suffer for it, what good is it? I no longer had stress over paying my bills but had my own new struggles. Ultimately, we all have the interests and challenges we need. You may suppose you have gotten more to agonize over than I. Maybe you have. Many do. Once someone said that he would give his right eye to do what I do. If I were ripped out, and he left in my place, how long would his elation last?

Our challenges, opportunities, and pleasures **may not have all the glitter of** Richard Cory's or any **other celebrities.** Some of you may wish you could be Richard Cory, Prince Alfred of Edinburgh, Dédé Fortin, David Carradine, Stuart Adamson, Ahn Jae-hwan, Paul Hester, Jang Ja-yeon, Dudu Topaz, Kurt Cobain, Adam Goldstein (DJ AM), Ryan Jenkins, Yasmine, Jonathan Brandis, Irv Rubin, Herman Brood, Woo Seung-yeon, Pauline Chan, Leslie Cheung, Del Shannon, Vince Welnick, Mark Antony, Cliff Davies, John Berg, Micke Dubois, Fritha Goodey, Lucy Gordon, Kuljeet Randhawa, Tarka Cordell, Anders Göthberg, Jon Nödtveidt, Choi Jin Sil, U;Nee, Margaux Hemingway, Johanna Sällström, Lynne Randell, Dave Schulthise, Brian Keith, De'Angelo Wilson, Freddie Prinze, Moses Taiwa Molelekwa, Ray Combs, Brad Delp, Kim Dual, Kim Ji-hoo, Vaishnavi, or any one of the rest of the countless celebrities who could not cope with their horrendous circumstances. They were too ensnared in their painful situations to realize the priceless joy of life. Having become so emotionally tied to their problems that they each forgot their true core infinite essence, they each became enemies in conflict with themselves.

By the challenges of their life situations, they all held their problems in higher importance than their own lives. By identifying with their own hardships, each of them disidentified with who they are authentically. Suicide is an identity crisis. They each substitute who they are for whatever problems were at hand. That is why they attacked themselves instead of dealing with their situations. Looking on blindly, we may think, "I wish I could be Richard Cory," undaunted even by him killing himself. Like distant green hills, other's situations may always look better than our own. This I know: trading lives with another is a recipe for anguish—even with those who have it all. That about sums up the worst of the turmoil I felt on my Scotland farm in the winter of 1970.

Having such intolerable circumstances, I hated the life I lived as the Beatle, Paul McCartney. I was expected to make my bandmates feel loved as Paul had but certainly did not always feel it from them. "All you need is love," John said. They all spoke of it, and criticized my lack of it, but did not always deliver it to me either. As hearts went from cold to colder, I felt very much alone.

When I felt fully connected to Paul, the coldness from John was tolerable. It felt like **I had** something happening that connected me to all **the departed** and gave me special power to continue **Paul's work.** He evinced himself in my work. **It seemed like Paul** was an angel on my shoulder who **moved me deeper into** real innovative action.

At other times, it seemed to be **self-deception.** Extrasensory perception is a strangely curious thing. It can be difficult to distinguish **from imagination.** Alienating myself by doubt, I felt alone with my broken fantasies. I was one of those people George referred to (paraphrasing Jesus) who gain the world but lost their soul—or, as I understood it, who evaded their true selves until they could no longer find them. That loss haunted me.

You may try, whenever lost—having strayed from familiar streets—returning to your departure point in order to find your way back. That is what I was doing on Paul's long winding road.

Using the door allegorically, the part represents the whole. It stands for an entire house. On the level you have likely already understood, I use the door in this song to represent the unwelcoming home of unrequited love. It is a melancholic song to feel the pain of attempting to get love but being unsuccessful. The persona in the song loved a girl for years. However, she (unlike my loving Linda) did not love him in return.

In Paul context, after years, I was still unfulfilled. Each of my bandmates turned against me. When they united against me, I needed to divorce the Beatles. Feeling that my Beatle life was unbearable on the one hand but being extraordinarily committed to it on the other, my mind kept returning to our point of change. Similar to a couple who might recall their marriage while contemplating a divorce, I always went back to Paul's crash. Entering the door into his life, just as I literally entered his nice home and made it mine, I had left my soul behind somewhere. I had gained the world and lost my soul. Now **I needed** to reclaim it.

The long and **winding** road on which Paul died leads to death's door, or portal, into his new life, and thus into mine. That road will never disappear. The change is as permanent as Paul's death. Nothing can change it. I've seen that road before time after time, driving on it literally, but mostly driving it to **Paul's death** mentally. All that we do and sing always **points** to Paul, and him decapitated. It always leads me **here** to my life's turning point. It always leads me back to Paul's door to immortality.

Now, although accepting my fate, I feel forsaken and disheartened. I cry for direction, wanting Paul to give me some indication of what I am to do. I feel alone while standing in for Paul at life's crossroads. Here, at the fatal point of departure, where **Paul** and I each lost our souls, so to speak, I should be entertaining that angel. However, he is **nowhere** to be found. He left me waiting there, and I am still right there waiting. "Now maybe you know **him**, but where is he? Where is he?" ("Flies and Bees to Emily"). He leads me back to his door for renewal in him, but what would he have me do there? I ask for direction. "Why leave me standing here? Let me know the way."

Lines such as these do not make much sense in the song's failed romance context. It does not make obvious sense for him to ask the way to her house that he has been to so many times before. He does not need to be led to her door. Perhaps, stretching it, the man keeps going back to the street where she was going to return and pick him up again someday. Although one could read such storylines into it, the story is actually about Paul. Apparently, people have felt my deep sadness in the song and have interpreted it accordingly, correctly sensing that there was more to it than what was in the words.

"Many times, I've been alone, and many times, I've cried," speaks to the painful loneliness that had engulfed me since on that road. "Anyway, you'll never know," but Paul knew, "the many ways I've tried. And still, they lead me back to the long and winding road." Paul left me standing in for him, for me to go down his own life's long, long road for him, "a long, long time ago." Needing to connect with Paul over my concerns about a possible Beatle divorce, I ask him to meet me at death's door. Since I could not dwell with the spirits, and Paul could not come back to the living, we would meet halfway, at the door or portal that separates life from death. We are, as it were, talking through a veil.

Nothing short of direct direction, or assurance from **Paul**, would satisfy me. It is what I needed. In the line, "**Has left** a pool of tears crying for the day," the pool is **a puddle.** A pool is also a group. Keep both usages in mind. It means a group in such contexts as a carpool or office pool. Together, each meaning combines as Paul leaving a group of people crying a puddle of tears for the day.

Everyone has reasons, but all must cry for the day. Paul, often codified as "Yesterday," is the day. It is Paul we cry for and also the day he died that makes us cry. We cry for him, the day, and the puddle by his car.

My last line, I added to honor Paul's lyrics. I had been critical of his early songs. I had mocked the early Beatles sound—still do sometimes but try not to. I thought their juvenile lyrics were pathetic. The worst of all was their, "She loves you, yeah, yeah, yeah, yeah." After a few Paul years, however, in appreciation for the long winding road Paul paved for me, those silly love songs took on a new charm, including Paul's youthfulness that lasted right up until the day he died. **I love that man**. I look back at the work that Paul did, **preparing the way** before me, and truly love him, along **with his work**, as if I had done it all myself. Asking him to "let me know the way," while critical of his early work, did not go well together.

My heart softened. I am glad to claim all of his great songs now. Well, I do not fully own them all in every legal sense but do own them in the sense that I have come to the point that I am pleased to say that I wrote them. By that, what I mean is that I am he who eventually became the artist who had written them: I am Paul McCartney. Those silly love songs led him right down that road of life (that he crashed on) to me. Paul followed his life's music to his own dead end, passing through the door to eternity, leaving me standing in for him on this other side of his road. By letting that imagery go on, you can see me "Knock, knock knocking on heaven's door" (to borrow an excellent example of onomatopoeic lyrics by Bob

Dylan). I am standing on his road waiting for an answer, waiting for his "Yeah, yeah, yeah." I say, "Don't keep me waiting here." He echoes back to me, "Don't keep *me* waiting." We were each waiting for the other's action. I say, "Lead me to your door." My answer comes with a "Yeah, yeah, yeah, yeah" in my own distinctive style, not with Paul's animation.

Early on, Paul's father suggested replacing the Beatles' "yeah, yeah, yeah" with "yes, yes, **yes**" so that they would sound more dignified. **Of course,** dignity is not a characteristic that **they needed**. Over time, "yeah, yeah, yeah" became **a Beatle** catchphrase. I was glad at first to let it expire, you know, but loved using it as a Paul-identifier in John's "All You Need Is Love," which I added onto the end after saying again that Paul is dead. I sing, "We loved you, yeah, yeah, yeah."

Using it that way was brilliant. Now, however, in "Long and Winding Road," my "yeah, yeah" is in a resigned melancholic voice. The change in music shows that I am not that same Paul and that I did not sound happy about the situation. Although my answer was affirmative, the break-up was not the sort of thing that brought me comfort. While I felt a yes answer, a "yeah, yeah, yeah," it was not a joyful one. I would dissolve my band. There was no point in keeping us all miserable. I would still ride Paul's road but would do it without John, George, or Ringo. It was just another bend in Paul's long winding road.

"Yeah, yeah, yeah," was Paul's signature. I used it to sign Paul's mark on "Hey Jude," at the end, and at the end of "Mother Nature's Son," a song contrasting this country boy, with Paul, a city boy, adding further contrast with our yeah, yeah, styles. I also added some yeahs to "I've Got a Feeling," "Helter Skelter," and various post-Beatles songs, such as "Bluebird," "She Said **Yeah**," et cetera.

When I wrote "**The Long and Winding Road**," the song magically **came together for me**—after I had given all of these things serious thought—at my piano in Scotland. I sat down meditatively and started playing, and that song came to me beautifully. The inspiration in the calm beauty of the place focused my weeping emotion in my words and in the music. It flowed out of me exactly how that song was meant to sound. When I recorded it in January 1969, it was simple. I was at the piano, and had John play bass. **I** would have done the bass much better but **wanted a** warm live sound with no extra tracks over**dub**bed. Straight and simple, I was going for that same natural sound that emerged in Scotland. John and I practiced the song on Sunday, 26 January. While there in the studio with Billy Preston and others that day, we talked about doing live performances to record our *Let It Be* album.

Entertaining various ways to do it, we decided to take the show upstairs to the studio rooftop. We could have performed a concert anywhere, and named a few possible spectacular venues, such as the Coliseum, but decided to save ourselves the hassle, and just take it upstairs.

Our rooftop performance four days later would have included my songs, "The Long and Winding Road" and "Let It Be," if it had not seemed like too much trouble to get a piano up there. Those songs we recorded the next day in the basement, along with my "Two of Us." While there, we also enjoyed a "Lady Madonna" jam session.

To make a film to help sell the *Let It Be* album, we, still along with session keyboardist, Billy Preston, set up a platform and performed some of my songs as though we had a live audience. We stood in a new stage formation for those songs. It looked good. I had the idea that the whole album would sound and look like those two live performances. However, all of my efforts in that direction were undermined in the mixing room without my consent.

The band's manager, Brian Epstein, was redundant once I took charge. He died of a drug overdose. I had already become close to Linda by then. Her father, also born an Epstein, already represented songwriters and would have greatly benefited the Beatles. However, John was sold on Allen Klein. The others in the band sided with John, out-voting me, resulting in Klein taking the business reigns. He recruited Phil Spector to produce our *Let It Be* album (after our prior dissatisfaction with Glyn Johns' initial work with it).

Phil took the album in his direction, remixed it, put into the album things I would have preferred left off, and left off some of what I would have rather had put in. The thing that angered me the most was his dubbed orchestral and choral accompaniment encroaching on "The Long and Winding Road." As the proverbial camel's backbreaking straw, Spector doing that to "The Long and Winding Road," and releasing it contrary to my will, was one cause that I listed when **I sued** John, George, Ringo, and Klein **to dissolve the band.** I had to stop the interference. I set limits that they broke. The suit,⚠ filed on 31 December 1970, was final 1470 days later. Now that the Spectorized version is the one that most people know and expect to hear, I have had to accept it and incorporate some of it into my own performances. **It bothered me.** Now, you can still keep that version, and also hear it more as I originally intended. **I finally stripped** off Phil's enhancements, **and re-released it**, the entire album, as *Let It Be . . . Naked.* That was in 2003 before I decided to remix the whole catalog and release it with this book on 09.09.09. [See the note on page 210.]

NOTE: 14th April, 1970.

```
A. Klein, Esq.,
Apple Corps Limited,
3 Savile Row,
London, W.1.

Dear Sir,

    In future no one will be allowed to add to or
subtract from a recording of one of my songs without
my permission.

    I had considered orchestrating "The Long and Winidng Road"
but I decided against it.  I therefore want it altered
to these specifications:-

    1. Strings. horns, voices and all added moises to be
       reduced in volume.

    2. Vocal and Beatle instrumentation to be brought up
       in volume.

    3. Harp to be removed completely at the end of the
       song and original piano notes to be substituted.

    4. Don't ever do it again.

                    Signed



                    PAUL MCCARTNEY



c.c. Phil Spector
     John Eastman
```

521

Double meanings make songs richer. "The Long and Winding Road," as I said, can be about love or about Paul. In either case, it is about isolation on that long and lonely road. I returned to that idea not too many years ago with its dual meaning in "Lonely Road." I sing, "Don't want to walk that lonely road again." Again, it is about love, but also about Paul. Three years after Linda had died, when I was with Heather, I wrote this song thinking about how songs still triggered memories of Linda, and of how I was with Heather then, and would likely be alone again. The song works that way, but not as well as it works for Paul—who is also always on my mind.

The Paul meaning was triggered by his music. I pretty much ignored all of his material until after the Beatles. When I started touring, I realized that besides my new material, my fans wanted the old Beatles songs including from before I was Paul. As I went through it all, I found that a lot of it was pretty good. I learned several of them and made them my own. I played his songs, but always added my own distinctive style. I covered all of Paul's best songs in concerts and released them as live performance recordings. Then, people would ask for the story behind each song, how I wrote it kind of questions, I very rarely knew the answers. Most often, I would just make up something.

There is an example of my ignorance of Beatles songs that I put into the Anthology for everyone to hear. **I was talking about** the line, "I'd love to turn you on" in "**A Day** in the Life." That line had a dual context: one **of sex**, the other of drugs. As far as I knew of their songs, the Beatles had never been that direct about either before. Without going into the drug meaning, I mentioned that the sexual language was a bit risqué and that we had never done that before. Of course, I had always been far more open about sexuality in other settings, such as with The Bonzo Dog Band. Later, when the camera was not running, John named Beatles songs that were far more sexual than "A Day in the Life."

Eventually, I became more aware of the Beatles catalog in order to make all of **Paul's** best my own, letting my audiences hear the **familiar tunes**, but with my own distinctive style. The songs **drove** me wild, you know. At first, it was as if **Paul** were raging with excitement inside of me, going **crazy** to have me re-doing his old material. I felt like I had to do it to release all of his wild energy in me. I had to let it out. After a while, I drifted back into my own direction, doing things my way. Then it happened again. I would hear his original versions on the radio or albums, and it kept happening. Day by day, I was getting more and more anxious to get back to his songs, and to his way of writing and recording music. That pressure drove me to do *Driving Rain* as I did it.

Going for a **Paul** approach, which I wrote about already, I **did it fast**. In "Lonely Road," on that album, I sing, "I hear your music / And it's driving me wild. / Familiar rhythms / In a different style. / I hear your music / And it's driving me wild again." I sing about how **I tried to** get over him but could not. I tried to **go my own way** with something new, but my thoughts were stuck back on him.

59

Japanese Jailbird

It is hard to explain what it is like being me. Besides having uproarious adulations of hysterical audiences screaming for me, and the understanding that my own tunes and lyrics are playing in people's minds around the world, I am also making vast amounts of money. Up until I began my Beatle days, a million dollars seemed like a lot of money. Then, upon becoming Paul, a billion seemed like an unreal joke to me. It was only a dream then. J. Paul Getty says, "If you can count your money, you don't have a billion dollars." I do not usually like to talk about it but was delighted to pass that milestone long ago.

Putting it here helps explain my mindset up until I **was** arrested on 16 January 1980. Here is an example from **Bill** Gates, a hundred-billionaire. He said, "I could spend 3 million dollars a day . . . for the next 100 years . . . if I don't make another dime." Then he illustrates the absurdity of it all in this odd example: "Tell you what—I'll buy your right arm for a million dollars. I give you a million . . . to sever your arm right here." Having that much money can make one intoxicatingly dizzy with untouchable extraordinary power. **I have** nowhere near as much as *that* Bill. I, as **J. Paul McCartney**, am closer to the J. Paul Getty level. **Now** it doesn't matter. I have enough powerful wealth that sometimes I feel as if I am above the law. Playing this Paul role was nerve-racking at first. I had anxiety about maybe ending up incarcerated. Eventually, as I grew into this position that honored my lineage, I felt immune.

Living that privileged way makes me lose my balance now and then. Fortunately, I have that farm back in Scotland. That place makes me real again.

We planned a world tour after touring Japan. It was difficult getting into Japan with my prior pot arrests. I had to convince them that I was not too risky for their fair country. It bothered me. I resented it. When I packed my bags, I set up serious trouble. I do not fully know what led me to bring about a half a pound of pot into Japan—especially after I had to make such a case about how I would not do such a thing. Now I see how resentment was part of it, you know? It was like, "I am Paul McCartney! How dare you try to stop me?" Having had to fight to be allowed into that country with my pot convictions, I probably subconsciously wanted to incriminate myself just for the gratification of showing them that they cannot tell me what to do. Now that sounds stupid, I know. It was just how I felt deep down.

Going there with pot in my suitcase, and so much of it, was just asking them for trouble. Soon, **I** evenly received all the trouble I set up. There **was** not a hint of discretion. It was **flaunting** my rebellion against their authority. When they showed me the arrest film, I watched **the** security employee pull the pot from my **bag**, look around with awkward embarrassment, and nearly put it back. He didn't want reprisals for me. He wanted to close the suitcase and act like it was okay but knew that he could not.

It cost me over $350,000 to cover some expenses outlaid by my Japanese promoters, which was nothing compared to the lost touring revenues for all of our sold-out series of Wings concerts that I had to cancel. I have had big weed expenses for years before and since, but never of that magnitude. Spending nine days in a Tokyo jail before being deported was far worse for me than the financial loss. During my first two days there, it was especially intense with interrogations.

Owing to the ridiculous quantity, the Japanese government wanted to make an impression that was not to be forgotten. For drug smuggling, authorities called INTERPOL (International Criminal Police Organization). They called me a drug smuggler—which I learned is a considerably worse crime than possessing or using. INTERPOL has files on many high-profile people. They have always taken a modest interest in each of the Beatles and had held in our respective files our passport data, prior arrests, and various other bits of information.

I was taken into an interrogation room where **two men**, looking through my file, asked me to talk about the trouble I was in the last time I was in their country. I talked about my previous pot arrest there.

Then they asked me about any other arrests I have ever had. Again, I told them about pot arrests.

One of them, clearly agitated, said, "Besides pot, have you ever been arrested for burning things?"

"No," I said.

"Arson? Have you ever been arrested for arson or attempted arson?"

Unaware of what was in their file, I said, "No."

"In a Hamburg club called Bambi Kino, did you light a fire?"

"Oh, that," I said. "I forgot about that. It was a mistake. I did that a long time ago."

"Tell us about that fire."

"Can't recall it too well. It's been so long."

"Tell us! They deported you for **that** reason!"

"Certainly. I had a letter from my **girlfriend** there, Erika Hübers. She wrote that she **was** having a baby, and that I was the father. I did **not** want anyone to see the letter, so I burned it in a **trash**can."

"Really? Were you and Mr. Best involved in any other fires there?"

"That was so long ago," I said. "Was there another fire?"

"Now tell us about the condom that you two fastened to a nail in the wall."

"Everyone thought it was a big joke to have a condom nailed to the wall. It was a big laugh."

"You do not know about any of these things because you were not there. You are an inventive storyteller, but you are not Paul McCartney."

"How should Paul McCartney have answered those questions?" I asked.

"Whoever taught you about Mr. McCartney's Hamburg experiences should have mentioned his, and Peter Best's, attempted arson. They fastened a condom to the wall in a dark room, and then lit it on fire. That arsonist was not you."

"Then why did you ask me all those questions?"

"We did a security check to see if allowing you in our country would be safe for our people. Besides **Interpol**'s update of your drug arrests, they **sent** a report of the deportation from Germany. The **fingerprints that** we received from you **were not the same** as Mr. McCartney's when he was arrested in Germany in 1960. You also have entirely different signatures. Our analyst swears that yours is not by Mr. McCartney's hand. Who are you? Why are you impersonating him?"

I wondered which answer would be less costly. I said that I was James Paul McCartney. That was not the answer that they wanted. As more hours went on with the interrogation getting ever hotter, I said that I was another James Paul McCartney. That admission only complicated the matter, leading to their thought of me as a celebrity impersonator seeking to defraud the Japanese people.

They treated me like a criminal, calling me an imposter. They interrogated me for two days over the identity issue. It was intense, not pleasant at all. Now they accused me of forging my passport and other documents, and of going to their country under the guise of being Paul when in fact I am not, and of being some kind of a government operative.

Eventually, the UK interceded, but not before some uncomfortable disclosure. Japanese authorities released me from jail, and deported me, after those dreadfully long days there.

Resting there with nothing to do once all of the interrogations were done, as international dialogue over my special case was going on, I had time to sit, think, and reevaluate my life. I had never been gone from Linda for that long, or even for 24 hours, since before we married. This interruption had my full attention. It was my needed wake-up call. I wrote about the whole ordeal in a manuscript that I titled, *Japanese Jailbird*. **It is in** my safety deposit box. If I do not change **my mind** before that eventuality, when I die, **it will be made public.** This sneak preview has to suffice until then. My death will have its surprises. However, do not get too eager for it. The story gets better with age—like a fine wine, really. If **I get** around to it, I might even record a song about it **to** promote that little book.

In my defense, **author**ities in London informed my Japanese captors that **Paul McCartney**, and also each of the other Beatles, was a Member of the Order of the British Empire (MBE), each having received that fine honor from the queen for their service to the Illuminati. They replied that Paul's character was not the issue.

They demanded to know my own true identity. Even more than the drug smuggling matter, they wanted to know who I was, and why I was there letting on as though I were Paul McCartney. They said that Paul **may have** an MBE, but who is this yahoo with **all the marijuana?** They also persisted in their suggestion that I was a government operative.

For me, there was **no** greater surprise while in their custody than their reason to finally let me out. I might still be incarcerated somewhere in Japan if Scotland Yard had not kept track of me already. A ranking officer, who was quite amused by my whole predicament, knew that I could not possibly have the same fingerprints that the early Beatle, James Paul McCartney, had in 1960.

NOTE: Prohibiting cannabis benefits the pharmaceutical industry by limiting competition. When legalized, that wholesome herb helps break pharmacal dependencies and addictions. It is also widely used in the secret illuminated societies that dictate such prohibitions. "Flower Power," as adopted by Allen Ginsberg in 1965, symbolizes passive resistance and non-violence ideology. To the initiated, however, it was more about the power of the marijuana bud.

According to secret illuminated teachings, we are empowered by using cannabis to expand our thinking (which is part of why it is withheld from the masses), and by gnosis (knowledge also withheld from the masses). Luciferians trace the source of their secret knowledge to Lucifer, or Enki, represented in the Garden of Eden story as the talking snake. That Biblical poem is based on the older more detailed accounts in Sumerian history. Combining the influence of cannabis with that old tale, the Illuminati phrase *Blumenkraft und ewige Schlangenkraft Ewige* translates from German as "Eternal flower power and eternal snake [serpent] power!"

Ayahuasca	3 (3)	Cannabis	6 (6)	Acid	9 (9)
Drugs	30 (3)	Chemicals	6 (6)	Cigarettes	9 (9)
Hallucinogenic/s	3 (3)	Herb/Herbs	6 (6)	DMT	9 (9)
Heroin	3 (3)	Molly	15 (6)	Drug	45 (9)
High	48 (3)	Mushrooms	6 (6)	Grass	9 (9)
Mary Jane	3 (3)	Plant medicine/s	6 (6)	Habit/Habits	9 (9)
Shrooms	3 (3)	Pot	15 (6)	Hallucinogens	9 (9)
THC	3 (3)	Psilocybin	6 (6)	LSD	27 (9)
Weed	3 (3)	Psychedelics	6 (6)	Marijuana	9 (9)

With my arrest at the Tokyo airport causing concert cancellations in Japan, it also blew the wind out of our wings for the world tour. My selfish arrogance, in packing those 7.7 ounces of marijuana, soured Denny against me as well. My actions hurt him and countless others. They all had the right to be angry with me. A lot of energy, expense, and hope went into it. I betrayed everyone's trust. I spent that year going through previously unreleased songs, working mostly alone making an album of those songs, but also getting Wings' support as needed.

Those recording sessions stopped abruptly when John was shot on 8 December 1980. I could not function at all for a time. I restarted that project on 2 February 1981, making it a solo album to be dedicated to John. Wings members, Juber and Holley, left the band then. **Denny** stayed on until 3 March when that work was **finished.** Then I did not need him so much. **He felt like** he did not need me so much either. **It was too difficult for him** to deal with his terrible income loss caused by my foolishness. On the flip side, I had brought Denny into Wings as a big favor to him, and to return a favor done to me decades before. I helped Denny enormously. He can forgive my faux pas. On 27 April 1981, I formally announced that Wings had disbanded. I still love all of those bandmates—and everyone with whom I have ever made music.

Letting Wings fly was hard, but needful to move forward. After my arrest, Linda and I discussed inherently worthwhile priorities, such as our children and our time to enjoy living. Albums and tours were nice too but are not what life is about. We had become so caught up in it all that we forgot our deepest springs of happiness. It was not time for a world tour. **It was time** for us to rediscover all the things **we loved** about each other, and to give our children **more** attention before they all departed into the world. Time flies by swiftly. We were missing the best of life. There was no point in chasing after more money. We had plenty. It was time to stop and reconnect.

Even though all of the above is true, I must admit yet another primary reason for the Wings' break-up. Denny was anxious to get back to touring. Although I hate to admit it, I keep reminding myself not to leave evocative secrets out of this book of mysteries. Throughout it all, I have been painfully honest. It is a new experience for me—full disclosure. Okay, I will tell it. When John died, I cried and cried for the terrible loss. I wished I had been more involved with John all along on a more personal level. I was ever about our business, and, feeling put off by his neediness, lacked enough interest in him as a person. I regretted it. Also, with John's murder, I feared I may be next. That is why I stopped touring with Denny.

60
"Lovely Linda"

After all this time, it still happens. Just the other day, a friend asked again if I were ready to replace Linda with a new beloved life partner. Please finally understand that **no one can** replace Linda. Why would anyone **suppose that she** could be replaced? Linda **will always be the only one** of her. It is not as though I held a Linda-Look-Alike contest and declared another the winner. Only Linda is Linda. You get it? Jane is Jane. Emily is Emily. Nancy is Nancy. Renée is Renée. Rosanna is Rosanna. Sabrina is Sabrina. You are you. Each one has her own enchantments. One cannot replace another.

Really, because Linda and I are private people, most people did not know her personally. They only ever saw the tip of the iceberg. She was the kindest woman I have met, the sweetest, and most innocent. Making our home and the world whole, she fought for what mattered, especially for our warm hearth. Everyone can benefit from Linda's example. Other great women are of the same caliber, and may even share some of the same values. Still, they are not Linda any more than you are Linda.

Battling Linda's disease for the last three years before her passing did not distract from her noble enduring crusades of vegetarianism, animal welfare, and kindness. Nor did her suffering diminish her resplendent love for me or each of our four beautiful loving children, Heather, Mary, Stella, and James. Linda lives on in all of them, and in my own heart.

New romantic interests that may bloom do not interrupt my relationship with Linda. Her crossing over did that. Yet, she is still with me. **Her role is** now evolving with me but is still present. **Linda** cannot at this time be my lover but will always go on doing as she has always done as my friend and close confidante. If I were Hermes, she would be Hestia.

All animals to Linda were like Disney characters. All were fun, lovable, and adorable to her. She was the toughest woman who did not ever give a damn what people thought. It never did deeply impress her to be Lady McCartney. The title was completely meaningless to her. She never forgot that we are all the same. Honorary titles could not entice her. When asked whether people called her Lady McCartney, she said, "Somebody did once, I think." It never mattered to her.

The time I spent with Linda made me a more complete and compassionate person than I could have become without her. I am privileged to have been her lover for three decades. In all that time, except for the enforced absence in Tokyo, we never spent a single night apart. That Japanese jail time lasted endlessly because I was not with her. Had they locked us away together, the two of us might have overlooked any other discomforts. When we were together, we had all that we needed or wanted.

Very often, we would do without many luxuries that most people enjoyed simply because we had each other. Nothing else was necessary. When less fortunate people asked why I never took breaks from Linda, I would say, "What for?" She would answer the same. We could never take a holiday without yearning for the other. We both knew it and never thought to try it. **That closeness** was superb, but finally, her passing **left a huge hole in** my life and the lives of **our children**. That painful lesson is what I had in mind **when** I wrote "Sonnet 4-98," named for the month **she passed.** Its own concluding couplet, "The more delight we find in love and song / The more we're left to miss them when they're gone," sums up how I feel about her. The sorrow grew from the joy.

Even with the wealth and international attention that we got with my bigger-than-life Paul McCartney role, Linda always managed to provide a very normal upbringing for our children. We always said that all we wanted for the children was that they would grow up to have good hearts. Now, as

I see that they all have, I thank Linda. As their mother, she was perfect.

Natural beauty is rich in her photography. As a photographer, only a few in the world rivaled her. Her pictures show an intense honesty, sometimes moody and gritty, always real. Linda had a rare eye for beauty. Aside from being on our album covers, her work has been widely published and revered in print, and exhibitions worldwide. It was her work as a photographer that brought her to me in the first place. I have always greatly appreciated Linda's photographic art.

Anyone less likely to be a businessperson, I cannot imagine. However, she worked **tirelessly** in the defense of animal rights and **respect**. In so doing, she became a food tycoon. When told that a rival firm had copied one of **her** products, all she would say was, "Great, **now** I can retire!" Linda did it all to save the animals. She was never in it for the money. **Still**, the tribute she would want over anything else would be for people to go vegetarian, which, with the vast variety of foods now available, is much easier than many people imagine. She got into the vegetarian food business to save animals from the cruel treatment that our society and traditions force upon them. She never had other motives. If vegetarianism sounds hard, eat fish and poultry. Mammals are too closely related.

A number of charitable organizations received Linda's praise and diligent support. She had been very active in People for the Ethical Treatment of Animals (PETA). To honor Linda's work, and to enlarge your awareness, please check out the PETA website at www.peta.org. PETA awarded Linda a Lifetime Achievement Award in December 1996, sixteen months before her crossing.

Children and Third World poverty were also serious ongoing concerns for Linda. She acted as all of us should. She loved and lived the Carpenters' lyrics, "Bless the beasts and the children. For in this world, they have no voice. They have no choice." She was their voice.

Going horseback riding was always one of her favorite personal pleasures, helping her feel more at one **with the** animal kingdom. It was about the caring cooperative union required. I gave her this **visualization,** as she began to cross over. "You're up on your beautiful Appaloosa stallion." Her eyes told me **she understood**. I said, "It's a fine spring day. We're **riding through the** woods." I gave her the loveliest **final scene** that I could imagine. I said, "The bluebells are all out." Then, ending just **before she passed on**, I added, "The sky is clear blue." Her spirit spoke to mine. In the brief moment that followed, our communication was only telepathic and has been ever since.

All that we could utter, we said. My closing visualization to her followed our children's final remarks. We each had our own turn to say our final farewell before she stopped and was freed of her incurable pains. I had barely reached the end of my bit when she closed her eyes, and gently slipped away. She had lovingly waited **for each one of us** to finish our own turn. **This amazing world is** now better for having known her. Her gift **of love** will **live on** in each of our hearts forever.

Although Linda remained a brave champion of **optimism until the end**, there had been times that she advised me about what to do after she passed on. She told me that when that eventuality at last comes round, I should love again, go another round. Yet, when I finally got down to it, it took some time.

Everywhere I looked, I'd see Linda. When I was finally attracted to another, I thought, "Well, she's a good-looking woman!" And, whoops! It surprised me. It had been thirty years since I had such thoughts. Linda had been my only fantasy all those years. Until Linda, when Jane and I were engaged, I could not accept the idea fully in my heart that I could be happy with just one woman. Once I became Paul, sex came with the superstar gig. It was too easy for me, too much all at once. I wasn't mature enough to bridle it. I could have anyone **I lusted after**. I did not appreciate the spiritual aspects of **sexuality** well enough to engage **my heart**. However empowering, even sexual rituals **offered more** pretense than aid. 🔺

NOTE: Sexual ritual, at its best, brings participants to a primal blissful state of non-duality. However, when done proudly, ignorantly, out of mere curiosity, or for the titillation or thrill, without setting specific honest intent, its benefits, even when properly administered, are generally superficial. When participants engage beyond their level of preparation, or when not done according to protective consensual standards, it can be harmful. Use caution and sense.

Although the Ordo Templi Orientis (O.T.O.), consumes human fluids and waste in sex magick, most sex magick does not. [Is O.T.O. in John's drawing?]

When done well, sexual exercises free participants of inhibitions. It helps break limiting beliefs, religious indoctrination, body shame, depression, feeling undeserving, and other negativity.

In Tantra, rooted in Hinduism and Buddhism, we increase our awareness of our own Kundalini ("Coiled snake"). By engaging that energy, moving it, and working with it, it increases. The tantric practice unites the masculine and feminine either individually or in connection with others.

In sex magick, practitioners harness sexual and orgasmic energy to help manifest what is wanted. There are many approaches. Most often, sex magick is done alone. Using the same principles and energy transference as described below with group sex magick after a banishing ritual, the lone lover attaches his or her rising sexual energy to the intended outcome and sends it through the chakras from base to crown. Continuing upward, it shoots out with love and gratitude through the top of the head, to the cosmos, and back to form a torus.

It is the same idea for couples or larger groups, but with the added challenge of everyone staying focused. The more people involved, the worse the distraction. For William, his most successful sex magick was with Linda. His solo work has also been more effective than sessions of larger groups.

Groups begin with a discussion to set the focused intention, discover each participant's pleasures, and establish personal boundaries. Participants attach the intention to their sexual energy. As the sexual energy grows, they see the growing fulfillment of their desire. Hallucinogens intensify the energy.

One structure has the whole group focus on one individual. For example, a male wanting a heterosexual experience might be a conduit for a group of heterosexual or bisexual women. While focusing on the intention as a realistic outcome, the group uses any means within the agreed-upon boundaries to build the group's sexual energy. When the energy is high, they all blast it together through the conduit's base chakra, up his spine, out through the top of his head, and out into the vast universe. With that love offering, at the moment of climax, some people cast spells or say affirmations. Others say, "Thank you!" Before that point, "Having to talk destroys the symphony of silence" (Crowley).

The universe receives that strong focused energy and mirrors it back fulfilled. Sometimes when a group joins their sexual energy for a specific outcome, the universe fulfills it through a child produced in that energy. The child's special mission further fulfills the intention of the magick group. When sex magick among the elite produces a love child, that exceptional child of light is marked for greatness and is helped to obtain dominance.

Fortunately for me, Linda came along. She was not at all like Jane who would leave me for work, ordering my love life around her career. **Linda** never did that. For 30 years, she **stayed with me,** reviving me, curing **me every day** of my own past sexual and emotional ignorance and arrogance. We entered each other's hearts and stayed there. I had shallowly been with many before, but only Linda searched my heart, understood it, created a home for me, accepted me for who I am, and helped me heal.

Having Linda all that time has taught me some things. As far as physical sensations go, sex is the epitome of feeling complete. Those who are mostly interested in the physical may entirely miss the spiritual union that is the greatest joy of sex.

Linda became my only true lover. Until I found her, perhaps I should have called lovers something else. As Linda taught me how to love, I married her and ended my restless search for any union with any other. I never needed another. There could never be another. It would have spoiled the most beautiful thing I had ever imagined, which was my own heart knit together as one with my lovely Linda, healed and full, complete.

So later, when I felt myself falling for another, I felt turmoil. I thought, "Oh no! Is this allowed?" Then I remembered what Linda had told me. Still, I thought, if Linda were alive, I would be dead meat! Of course, I would never have pursued her, or any other woman, if Linda were still here in the flesh. I mean, I never even looked at any other women, which is part of what made our marriage magical. Each of us was all the other ever imagined. We had our challenges, but a wonderful marriage.

When I talk to Linda now, I feel she is pleased that I have tried to move on with others. I feel her encouragement to love again and to go on with my life. Yet, Linda's slow transition from my lover to my friend has been a difficult one. That is why, in a song, I told Linda to take her own advice. Still, it is an easier adjustment for me than for her. She can have no lover at the stage that she is in now. We kind of hope to be lovers again ultimately, but not any time soon. Now I am still trying to get over every reminder of her.

I do not want to forget her. That will not happen. All I could hold in my mind were thoughts of Linda. When I hear the music we created, it drives me wild. I cannot let go. Others can play her familiar rhythms but in different styles. That just amplifies her absence, making it worse. It is easy for me to say but is a dilemma. It is harder under these circumstances. How do we fully go from being lovers to friends? I trust her to help set me right and cherish her even more for helping me through it. She will always be a part of me.

The right words have not come sufficiently to express my gratitude and eternal love for Linda. My marriage to her was the best thing that ever happened to me. **She saved** me from myself. She is everything to me, to **our children**, to our friends, and to all others who knew her **personally.** She was not only kind and loving but was also a courageous pioneering woman who readily took a stand for those less ready to stand for themselves. She showed the way. Although she, our brightest light, has left, she has left us a shining inspiration. Thank you, my Lovely Linda. I will love you forever.

Saying all of this about Linda does not mean that I cannot **love** another. Quite to the contrary, Linda taught me **to give my heart to** a woman fully. If I could find another whose love is not obscured by injuries of her past, **one who is** whole enough to love fully, I might marry again. **Nancy**, let's talk!

Linda's photography also gave her an eye for detail. When we met at the *Sgt. Pepper's* party, she let me know that her eyes were open. She pulled me aside and asked me when and why I replaced Paul.

Having gone on about Linda and our sweet children that sprang from her, it occurs to me that, eventually, my little Beatrice will also read this book of Paul secrets. I do not want her to feel left out. To let her know how much she means to me, I write this now, and will read this part to her soon to say, "I love you." She will remember it years from now when she is old enough to read this book on her own. Over the years, as she grows older without me, after this old Paul has also crossed over, she will find more meaning in it. Beatrice is the only good that came from me having known her mother.

I am concerned, Beatrice, that I won't be there for most of your years since you entered my life at its end. You will still be a young lady when I am reunited with Linda. You are the light of my older life. I hope that when I am gone in body, you learn to listen for me and feel me in your heart. I will always be near you. Feel me. Look to your noble siblings for my love as well.

NOTE: Four years after Linda crossed over, William married Heather Mills. In 2006, William petitioned for a divorce. As a counter-attack, Heather claimed to have only recently discovered the truth about him—that she knew all along. She said a box of evidence would be released if anything happened to her. To William, that threat appeared to be blackmail for a larger financial settlement.

In 2007, Barbara Walters introduced William to her cousin, Nancy Shevell. William and Nancy married on John's would-be 71st birthday, 9 October 2011. It was Nancy's second marriage. Before marrying, they attended Yom Kippur synagogue services, which include trumpeting the shofar, a ram's horn.

61

Paulism

Herein is an epic of our hero, Paul McCartney, who entered the underworld and then returned by taking possession of me, an unknown session musician.

Paul, Paul, Paul. **Everything was of**, in, and through Paul. First, the early **Paul**, **with all** of his awful dreams, drew **attention to himself** with his fears of what he felt would inevitably transpire. Up until then, the others played along to a point but also treated it as more of a private joke. Paul's lost soul would be replaced with a rubber one. He would bounce out, and another would bounce in to take his place. Saying, *Rubber Soul,* reminds me of injected rubbery sensations I felt under my skin. That is not an interpretation they had in mind but is an annoyance that I have had to endure.

With their *Yesterday and Today* album cover, after the butcher, Paul is in a coffin-like travel trunk. Inside, several songs anticipate his death. In

"Day Tripper," for example, Paul's fears were the "good reason for taking the easy way out." He could choose to quit the band and live or stay with it having whatever fate **Beatle fame** may bring. His death **would be a "one-way ticket" out**, taking him nowhere, **making him**, as was suggested, **"a real nowhere man."** His bestselling song is "Yesterday." Their album, *Yesterday and Today,* meant "then and now" in one context, permanently setting the code to call Paul "Yesterday" in the future context when at last Monday's child would bring on a new day to start a new day or era for the world.

In *Revolver,* Paul is on the cover revolving out. With this album, coinciding with his last tour, he knew his numbered days were nearly done. In "For No One," he refers to his "love that should have lasted years," spawning songs of the love that dies.

In "Love You To," George sings, "A lifetime is so short, a new one can't be bought." After those lyrics were refuted by this new one being bought, he ridicules me for exactly that. He sings, "They bought and sold you" ("While My Guitar Gently Weeps"). George posits that in exchange for the world, my soul was sold as one of those "who gain the world and lose their soul." He knowingly asks if I am "one of them" ("Within You Without You").

"Eleanor Rigby" was also from that album. His early warning of his father's sorrow and regret, and acknowledging that Father McKenzie stood for his dad, Jim McCartney, made it even more ominous.

Revolver also has a subtle reference to Donna, the hitchhiking Cutie, flagging Paul down for a ride. Paul's dream-based "Here, There and Everywhere" has her "Changing my life with a wave of her hand." Now they are said to be together forever. As these examples illustrate, before Paul died, the Beatles began subconsciously drawing his fate to him. Records since 1965 groomed the world for his death.

His frequent death dreams began on 29 January, early on that fourth Tuesday of 1965. Fans esteemed John and Paul's writing more as the same until then. Later, as **Paul's dreams** took their toll, they **raised his work to greater heights** over earlier songs, **showing new depths of** introspection and **torment.**

Next, after Paul crossed over, his death tormented his bandmates who felt guilty and depressed. Though I got them to improve their quality, much of the change ensued naturally as a consequence of their pain that ever intensified from being unable to deal with it openly. The best that any of us could do was to record encrypted clues into our songs. When they failed to be recognized, we became more blatant.

The press regularly asked us to explain lyrics, giving us the challenge of making up new ridiculous histories that the world quickly added to its base of Beatles knowledge. While we frequently presented accurate and verifiable detail in our songs or artwork, and now most plainly in this "novel," it was always necessary for us to lie in interviews. Hence, we learned to present our fiction as non-fiction, and our plainest facts as make-believe. That inversion creates an absurd backward reality that is necessary for us to advance the truth without breaching nondisclosure agreements. Inner circles laugh at my farcical excuses. Unraveling the false historical web is easy for those who know that I usually improvise details of Paul's life and that I cannot admit doing anything to reveal the facts. Preposterous reasons should be a clue.

Having Paul die was good for business, especially with his early warning, giving them material to work into their lyrics before the fact. Afterward, his death enriched most of our songs with layered meanings.

Stamina was also impacted by it. Premonitions got them to make album after album, having them do a few each year, driving them to do grueling tours, et cetera. By the point Paul died, they had each run themselves dry. They were all burned out. Were it not for **their firm** commitment to Paul, they all would have **stopped or** gone solo when he died. Their energy was **depleted**. If Paul had not been threatened with **his life, pushing him**, they would not have sprinted **to his finish line** or continued.

Here, at a point **when they were exhausted**, I joined in brand new. Like a fresh tag-team wrestler, my newness carried an energy that they were not up to. My enthusiasm carried the band until my energy all but died as well. One thing that made the band bigger than life is that it did not burn out when Paul died. Instead, at that point, it took off as never before as though it were a new band, which it was. My enthusiasm for *Sgt. Pepper's*, pushing me to put in 700 hours of studio time, **could not have happened** unless a change such as this were made. The worn-out seasoned bandmates could never have done it.

Sgt. Pepper's is not something I could ever do again. I could do it then only because it was my big Beatle debut. I had all the energetic enthusiasm of a brand-new Beatles superstar, coupled with intense insecurities driving my desperate perfectionism. With surgeries, injections, and past failures all giving me the commitment and anxiety to stick to it without allowing any aspect of it to be as poor as general standards, I gave it an insane amount of energy. For each subsequent album, I had less energy. For the unknowing public, much of what made *Sgt. Pepper's* bigger-than-life was that we released it four or five years into the Beatles' record-making business.

With the extraordinarily pronounced Paul-focus of our albums since he died, many of our songs had elevated me in the eyes of the public. Numerous songs pointed to Paul, loaded with layers of indecipherable clues that listeners could only pick up subconsciously, subliminally. As our fans listened to the songs, they were programmed to give me more attention. Laced with Paul, each song with its own "Paul is dead," "I buried Paul," "Paul, Paul, Paul," et cetera, to direct our fan's thoughts. It channeled their energy to me.

This focus at first occurred subliminally. Then, each occurrence was sought out consciously. Fans saw an open palm above my head as a sign of death as they searched *Sgt. Pepper's, Yellow Submarine,* and the booklet of our *Magical Mystery Tour.*

Representing **Paul's head** being smashed, the right side of my face **is lost** in a shadow on the *Let It Be* cover, just as the other half of Paul's face is shadowed on their first album, for you to put nose to nose to see how dissimilar the faces are, and to show you "how the other half lives." My *Let It Be* picture is

NOTE: Imagine feeling someone looking at you in a crowded room. Sensing the direction of that energy source, you look up, already knowing where the person is standing. Your eyes meet. You both smile and nod in confirmation. You caught him or her staring at you because we cannot focus on people without sending them energy.

Now, imagine performing before thousands of fans brimming with elevated energy focused almost entirely on you. You must receive all of that energy and still be able to function. Here's a tip: When more energy comes in than you can handle, vent it out an open mouth to stop it from flowing out of the eyes as tears. Direct the energy in, through, and out to where you intend it. It is amazing to direct that incoming energy to your heart (if your heart is strong enough), and then out through your hands or breath to the sun or the earth's core. Be a conduit, not a container. Containers burst.

Next, imagine the energetic impact of having sold a billion records that fans play around the world. At every moment of every day, countless people hear his songs, sing along, watch his videos, read about him, talk about him, and think about him. Even haters send energy to "Paul McCartney." Handling constant energy requires frequent grounding. When you feel ungrounded, reconnect with your body and with the earth by sex, exercise, holding your breath, walking barefoot on the ground, or soaking in water.

When we realize that everything is energy that impacts everything else and that we send people energy all the time without realizing it, we can learn to direct that energy intentionally. We can send it in bursts, or as a steady flow. Bursts deplete the sender. To replenish as we go, while sending the energy to the target, pull energy in from the sun, air, or earth. As the conduit, we can send that energy to whomever wherever we will.

given a blood red background making it stand out from the others in white.

As a greatest hits collection, released in 1973, we put out two double albums. The first double set we loaded with Beatles hits featuring Paul. It was the red set (for Paul's blood). The second set, in blue, we loaded with hits during my run with the band. On the covers of each, we had the 1963 photo they used on *Please Please Me* (UK) and a 1969 *Get Back* picture of us posing in the same positions and setting for the stark contrast. The same photographer, Agnus McBean, took both pictures.

Using backmasking to conceal lyrics that listeners only discern subliminally, or if played backward, we suggest ideas that experts theorize are comprehended on a deeper level than if heard audibly. We have no ability to filter them from our realities consciously. For example, when played backward, John sings, "Paul, we used to sing with you. We used to sing" at a point in "Real Love," where frontward the words all of us hear are "Yes, it's real. Yes, it's real love."

Frontward, **I sing,** "Why don't we do it in the road?" where **recorded backward,** I sing, "Paul's really dead. **I really want it out,**" in my song of

NOTE: The red sets is "the House of Paul" (with 13 songs per vinyl album). The blue set is "the House of William" (with "28 IF" you count the two vinyl records as one). In Freemasonry the Red Lodge outranks the Blue. William's color selections also represent Paul's sacrifice and William's sky-high success.

the same title as my forward lyrics. If you play that one backward to hear it, you need to play the whole song. Although I sing the same line again and again forward, I do not repeat the backward line again and again this time.

The words, "Ha, ha, Paul is dead! Ha, ha, Paul is dead!" are played backward in "I Am the Walrus," when the frontward singing track has the nonsensical bit, "Oompah, oompah, stick it up your jumper."

Then, in "Glass Onion," where John in the utmost plainness sings, "The walrus was Paul," John has it backward as "Paul was the walrus."

The backward line in "Get Back," "I need some wheels. Help me! Help me! Help me!" comes at the point where, forward, it is "Get back! Get back! Get back to where you once belonged."

Recording hidden messages continued into post-Beatles songs. In George's "It's Johnny's Birthday," under the cover of him singing forward, "-day. And we would like to wish him all the very best," for even that simple birthday song for John, a decade before he was killed, George had this message about the death of Paul played backward, "He never wore his shoes. We all know he was dead." We show me having my shoes off on the *Abbey Road* Cover where I am walking barefoot. You can see each of us as a member of the funeral precession. John represents God (or, as some fans saw it, a holy man). Ringo is the minister (or funeral director). My eyes are closed, and **I am** out of step. I, the one without shoes, am **the corpse.** I hold a cigarette, also called a "coffin nail," not in Paul's usual left hand (as we have discussed), but in my right. George follows as the gravedigger. Many shots of the processional were taken to get every element right. In a *Magical Mystery Tour* picture, enhancing the significance of them being off my feet, Paul's shoes are covered in blood, his "Beatle-Juice."

Our devotees, millions of **fans from all parts** of the world, have combined, **hunted for Paul clues** for hundreds of millions of hours, **searching for Paul** clues in pictures, lyrics, movies, and music videos. Paul is sought and found everywhere. As though obsessed or possessed to find more, devotees played all of the Beatles catalog backward to find more backmasked messages. We got our worshipful fans united, got them all to "come together over me," as we would have Paul say. We got the whole world longing to know, but feeling that sure knowledge was just out of reach—as some have felt about intelligence concerning God.

By clues revealed herein, and hundreds more, we now have taught and conditioned millions of people throughout the world to seek after Paul. Whether consciously or subconsciously, everyone hearing the songs must ask, "What did that mean?" We naturally love to settle questions in our brains. The human mind loves puzzles to solve. We hear a mumble, and understand, on some level, there is meaning there. What is it? Could it be about Paul's death? Day by day converts to our vast "Paul is Dead" movement obtain more clues.

Endlessly pursuing clues, devotees have made it their chief pastime, their life-long pursuit. They shall be both delighted and saddened by this book: delighted by answered questions, but saddened, or upset, angry that their life pursuit, by this single publication, has reached an end. Some may cry, "No! Stop! If you tell me the answers, what will become of me? What will I do with myself?" Or "Will all of my years of searching become meaningless now? Until I find it all, there must still be more! Let me search for more!" Well yes, there are always more clues. I have not covered new clues to be launched on 09.09.09, this mystery book's intended release date. There are **many more clues** that are on our albums that **have not been found.** I do not remember them all. Many of them are lost in the songs. There are too many embedded clues to remember them all.

Launching our Paulism into the world, with enough energy to reach the necessary critical mass, the greater disciples lead the lesser. As it is with all areas of investigation, the most passionate researchers help the rest. In this case, all are called unto Paul, to receive his clues through sounds and images. The efforts of those who are entrenched in Paul sustain that curiosity throughout the world. John called this work our religion. He, our own John the Beloved whom Paul loved the most, was always Paul's most outspoken adherent. John laced song after song with Paulistic clues and enticements. Paulism was the religion of the Beatles so much so that it and Beatles are interchangeable. It is the rock and roll religion.

Leaving the Beatles, I took Paul with me, leaving John to struggle with Paulism because promoting it drew the world's attention and honor back to me. He wanted to praise Paul but discredit me. For me to sustain the program without John (taking the glory of Paul with me, and away from John) put him in new emotional turmoil. **He could no longer** draw the world's attention to Paul **because Paul** and I, entwined as a package deal now, were no longer with him. John was cut off. He could no longer keep up his role as Paul's top disciple if Paul was not with him. Losing Paul again, John, George, and Ringo sensed a separation they could not prepare for, one they had not considered when they spoke of quitting. All of them felt robbed as if I had hijacked the spirit of Paul. They all resented their years of service for Paul that ended in elevating me without them. That is why they threw a brick through my window.

The split of the band, creating another separation from Paul, abruptly ended most of their interest in either promoting Paul in their lyrics, or in pointing positive attention to me. On the contrary, bitter ridicule took over. They could no longer say they missed Paul because it would be misconstrued, and put me higher on the idol pedestal from which they desperately wanted me to fall. John's isolation about drove him crazy. He turned to primal scream therapy, and many other approaches, to help him undo all the internal havoc that had accumulated.

Feeling fearfully inferior and alone, **John** ceased lamenting Paul openly. He **turned from** Paulism just as he had earlier turned from **Christianity** and every other belief system that he had ever embraced. Among all the things he listed that he no longer believed in, the last on the list was Beatles, which is Paulism. John's lengthy list of all that he was forsaking as something to believe in included magic, I Ching, Bible, Tarot, Hitler, Jesus, Kennedy, and on and on with Buddha, Mantra, Gita, Yoga, Kings, Elvis, Zimmerman [Bob Dylan], and, as you know, Beatles (Paulism).

This list of beliefs that John looked into, became serious about, and then became disillusioned over, shows John's broad spectrum of searching religions and philosophies from all over the world. He failed to obtain the full intended benefit from any of them but nearly immersed himself in one after another.

John followed them hoping to escape illusion but disappointedly found only disillusionment. For some of these hopes and heroes, I said, "Be glad you are feeling disillusioned now. You could only feel this way now if you had been illusioned in the first place. Only illusionment can lead to disillusionment." It was brilliant but lacked empathy for his suffering.

NOTE: Over dinner, after George Martin gave the Beatles their contract with EMI, he told them that special connections would ensure their unparalleled success as long as the group remained useful in furthering certain worldwide agendas. Among those agendas, the band would be used to overthrow Christianity in preparation for "more meaningful spirituality" in a one-world government's one-world religion.

John, Paul, George, and later Ringo were asked if they were willing to publicly discard their Christian heritage. Each agreed. These most emulated of all celebrities would have no more use for Christianity. In 1963, Paul was given these words to say as if his own, "Christianity doesn't fit in with my life." The media, pretending to be shocked, widely publicized those words. Feigning outrage, the press alarmed the public sufficiently to have the offending line repeated until that celebrity-backed hypnotic suggestion made its permanent impact.

Religion is a word John used loosely to include everything that gets followers or discipleship. For example, **Bob Dylan** (Robert Allen Zimmerman) **is not a religion, but,** like Elvis, has followers. Various **philosophies** likewise are not technically religions, but all **have their** proponents as well.

Each belief on John's "**God**" list is disavowed. He ends with the Beatles (Paulism). Some see it as a religion-bashing song. "Imagine," his most famous song of that category, includes several ideas from Karl Marx including the lines, "Imagine there's no heaven" "And no religion too." Marx says, "Religion is the complains of those who "keep you doped with religion, sex, and TV." I should mention too that the title of his "Working Class Hero" inspired the title I employed on one of my few classical music CDs, *Working Classical.* I like the wordplay.

All of the things on John's "God" list are practices, movements, opinions, or heroes, that he says he no longer believes in. He summarizes them in "I Found Out." Naming opposing religions as his extremes, he leads us to consider all that falls between them. After singling out Jesus and Krishna, John says, "I've seen through junkies I been through it all, I've seen religion from Jesus to Paul." That lists the full history of John's experience with religion. It began with Jesus. As a young child, John was Anglican.

Eventually, through all his years of searching religion and philosophy, his spectrum goes all the

NOTE: "God," a song on John's first post-Beatles solo album, lists his disbeliefs, culminating in "I don't believe in Beatles." In a *Rolling Stone* interview, he explains, "Beatles was the final thing because I no longer believe in myth, and Beatles is another myth." He saw no use for God or myth in the Age of Aquarius, which he saw as the Age of Man.

way to Paul. That is it. It begins with Jesus and ends with Paul. It is John's most masterful line. To the outsiders, his scope would seem narrow since they do not know "Paul." They do not comprehend Paulistic religion. John sings, "Old Hare Krishna got nothing on you / Just keep you crazy with nothing to do." Those lines, in context with the last verse, have John seeing Vishnu between Jesus and Paul, showing it cannot be Paul the apostle. If it were, then John's search for truth (which is central to the song) never looked beyond his Anglican foundation in the New Testament. That reading completely misses John's Paulism reference. It makes no sense without understanding who he meant by Paul. Yet, it is completely clear to insiders.

Doing the videos that accompanied some of our albums, most especially our *Magical Mystery Tour,* allowed us to synchronize specific lyrics with certain images, adding meaning. If you want to have deeper awareness, consider them together, such as the grotesque headless "Magical Mystical Boy" embodying the lyrics of the "Blue Jay Way" segment. That magical boy mirrors me, the magician's son.

In George's "Blue Jay Way," he sings lead; and then he and I together sing the backup track. We recorded the back vocals on two tape machines that we played out of sync, making a hard-to-discern ghostly effect. Putting it all together, it is, "There's a fog upon L.A. (**Paul**) And my friends have lost their way (**died.**) We'll be over soon they said (**Paul is buried.**) Now they've lost themselves [a double meaning] instead. (**Oh, Grieve!**)" Where George sings, "Please don't be long, please don't you be very long. Please don't be long for I may be asleep," he refers to Paul as Krishna in these backmasked words: "He said 'get me out.' Paul is what is. Paul is Hare Krishna it seems." Relating to a less positive image backmasked later, George added the words, "Paulie is naughty."

NOTE: The Beatles and others sought Lord Krishna not only in "Paul" by literal soul-transmigration but also within themselves. George Harrison most especially took both seriously. In his greatest post-Beatles hit, "My Sweet Lord," he shares his yearning to connect with that Lord. He worked toward it through the remainder of his life. George's spiritual focus is apparent in his music.

If the plan continues to be as successful as it has thus far, centuries from now, and thenceforth, when people reverently discuss Vishnu's avatars who transformed the world, they will primarily speak of Krishna, Jesus, and Paul.

Consider how little was written about Jesus in the early centuries of his Christian era, and, by contrast, how much more "Paul" was already promoted before his Age of Aquarius began! The work to establish him as a Christ figure is unparalleled. Based on the current rate of progress, those working to deify their messiah in the collective consciousness expect to reach critical mass much faster than it took Jesus' followers. Over time, Paul's media-driven veneration will include mystical faith-promoting stories.

Convincing the world that Paul is the true avatar of this Æon of Horus will confirm the validity of Crowley's prophecies. Vindicating Crowley as a true prophet empowers those holding the reigns of Paulism just as Christianity empowered the pope and the Holy Roman Empire. Paulism is one branch of a universal tree that will create the illusion of choice (each being free to choose his or her own branch), but with every option controlled by the same people who also control politics and wealth in the New World Order.

Upon William's death, the illuminated will eulogize "Paul" as the god of music. The profane will hear the epithet but understand it metaphorically as with Elvis, the king of rock, or Michael, the king of pop. After the massive depopulation, a generation of literalists will emerge. They will turn against their unbelieving parents (compare Luke 12:51-53) to proclaim Paul's divinity.

Paul will be recognized as the Messiah, with Aleister Crowley as his prophet. Dissenters will call Paul an anti-Christ, not in the sense of opposing Jesus, but for replacing him. Crowley, opposers will say, is a false prophet.

Most devotees will say that Paul, who is Krishna, was born a god (an incarnation of Vishnu), and that he lived to a ripe old age. Others will say he was born mortal but obtained a fullness of divinity by degrees as he grew in light and knowledge. The illuminated will secretly pass on the great mystery that Paul embodied gods that continued in William, reenacting Osiris and Horus. Such "William mythology" will offend those who feel it diminishes Paul's independent divinity. However, the same stories will inspire "the elect."

In "A Day in the Life," following the "say two things at once" idea from Aleister Crowley, we blended the word Paul with Lord. "Nobody was really sure if he was from the House of Paul" is under the recording of "Nobody was really sure if he was from the House of Lords." Since we hear the word we expect, we included lyrics on *Sgt. Pepper's* for worshipful fans to hear "Lords." That earliest album linked Lord with Paul. I shall be known as "Lord Paul" (99 in simple Gematria) when that hidden message is made a reality. George, of all people, calls Paul "Lord Krishna."

"Oh! Darling" has me singing, "Oh, darling. Please believe me." Backmasked, I sing, "In me lives he." I am alluding to Lord Paul, a disembodied spirit entity, attaching himself to me. Whether holy or evil, for better or for worse, I am possessed by this lord of light or darkness. In one instant, he revives me like a heavenly angel. In another, he makes me run like a demon from hell.

Death, and attachment to me, allows him to work through me to deliver his musical will to the world. I pipe his will to you, and you dance to it. I write his words, and **you let those** mind-possessing lyrics all but **take over your souls.** He works through me only **to bring his influence** to you. Don't be undone **by such things.** All music is inspired by one source or another. Paul cannot inspire my lengthy classical numbers. Others hop in for all of those. Do not deceive yourself into thinking that Paul's possessing power is more dangerous than the demons working through other musicians.

All music extends the influence of the inspiring spirit. In Paul's case, the entity is chiefly identifiable. Unless you can be certain of the identity of the spirits who inspire you, do not judge me for Paul. Letting you know now that I am his messenger is for your benefit.

"Something," by George, in 1969, has the most sophisticated of all backmasked Paulism messages. Behind where he sings, "Somewhere in her smile, she knows that I don't need no other lover. Something in her style that shows me. I don't want to leave her now, you know I believe in how," is the excellent backmasked message: "For I am the Beatle Lord. For I am the Beatle Lord. For shall the hearts living with us. A bottle? No, a demon idol. So, unleash my answer. Mirror with us."

Everyone learns to mirror Paul, but not as I do. George **says**, singing as Paul, he is the Beatle Lord. I embody **the Beatle Lord**. That is why John left Paulism. He **could not be** against me while for Saint Paul. Here, Paul, **the possessing entity**, is our demon idol. At other times, **that** same spirit is our angel. Either way, it is Paul—or so **we think.** We thought it was Paul all along, that is, at least up until we received the Charlie Manson music. Then we wondered what demon had set all of that up.

Right-wing thinkers may complain that we would worship Paul as our Beatle idol lord. However, all celebrities are idols. Are they not? We all revere and pay tribute to celebrity idols. We pay them in all their royalties because they are our royalty. They are our kings and queens. We worship images from the array of sights and sounds presented to us from magazines, screens, and speakers. We pay the idols a lot of our hard-earned pay. We pay them homage by all the royalties.

Like joining "Lord" and "Paul" in "A Day in the Life," in "Strawberry Fields Forever," I added John's obfuscating "Cranberry Sauce" to the real message, "**I buried Paul**." With the music playing along, going on **to keep him** in rhythm, he recorded them both one after the other. At that time, being after the 78 rpm records, and before CDs, our records were all either 45 rpm for singles or 33⅓ rpm for albums. We recorded "Cranberry Sauce" and "I buried Paul" at 45 rpm but added them to the end of "Strawberry Fields" at 33⅓, making John's voice much slower, lower, and harder to distinguish.

Then we cut the one and tracked it over the other for you to hear both at once. You can hear either line equally easily depending on your intention. To hear them both, one after the other, I included them on the *Anthology* version before George Martin and I cut and layered it. You can hear the song in progress. Neither phrase muffles the other. Furthermore, if you have the old technology, you can try this experiment: During the instrumental end of the song, if you have it on a 33⅓ album, turn the record player up to 45 rpm. Sounding exactly like John's normal singing voice, by correcting the speed this way, you will clearly hear each syllable. I should warn you, however, that this experiment is not good for your record or stylus.

Every now and then, a few of us gathered for group Paul meditations. Usually, we each drew near that state of Paul connectivity in our own individual way. From time to time, we would all chant or hum in unison, or would repeat a mantra or do a guided meditation. One time, Brian Jones led us in a meditation (based on a Pharaoh succession ritual) that included refreshments, which he concealed in a trash bag. With senses heightened by pot, **we could** all smell the sweet, freshly baked, wheat bread that lingered on making it hard to **focus on Paul for** the spell. Once I could concentrate, **the trip** of visualization amazed me. In our minds, we followed along as we came upon a long path reddened with juice drops. We followed the juice drops into a dark wooded forest going in deeper and darker until we walked beyond the blood drops. We continued walking through darkness until the trees parted, letting in light. In the clearing sat a large latched sea trunk rested at the top of a large hill.

As we reach the trunk, we slowly unlatch it, open the lid, and behold a mangled corpse with an upside-down disconnected skull. Reaching into it, we pull out Paul's sticky blood-matted head, or what was left of it. Much of it had been smashed away. We take turns holding it, reflecting respectfully, and passing it carefully to the next person until it was placed aside.

As the meditation continued, we imagined that we saw some cranberries growing wild by a mild stream. We uproot a seedling, carry it back to the skull, and gently replant it in a sunken eye socket. We place the skull in a hole, pack dirt around it, and pour water over the top. We silently watch the plant grow and receive the strength to produce cranberries.

"Okay," Brian said, "take, eat, partake of Paul. **This is** his communion." From a bag, he pulled **delicious** bread and cranberry sauce. He broke off the loaf's end, buttered it, and spread the sauce. Upon taking a bite, he passed it on, saying, "Paul's brains nourished the roots that carried his best elements on up to the berries that were smeared on this warm bread. Through the berries, we are all now partakers of his brains. Now he is in us all. We are all made one in Paul." This night was in celebration of the release of our single, my "Penny Lane," and John's "Strawberry Fields Forever," in 1967.

Our desired communion with Paul also united us all with each other. We all came together over Paul. Calling him Lord probably sounds more offensive in the United States than it does here in the United Kingdom where we are more accustomed to having lords and ladies. Remember our House of Lords? A bit similar to the US Senate, our House of Lords is the upper house of the Parliament of the UK. Now you should realize that we must have many lords—just as the US has many senators.

Death, for Paul, was a transition out of this realm and into the underworld. By attaching himself right to my left shoulder, he returned to the band to function in mortality through me. Through his existence in the spirit world, or in other words, through his death, Paul has become our advocate, letting us also connect more easily to others who have gone to the world beyond. He is our mediator inherently endowed with the powers of that domain, opening channels to us.

Giving our music to the people of the world, or selling it to them, we carried our secret message to individuals everywhere. Although not all receive our message, it is available wherever radio stations or individuals have the money to purchase CDs or downloads. **We forsook the** business of writing nauseously **silly love songs**, which seemed to be the basis **of Beatlemania** until Paul's death dreams. Instead, practically everything, even when sounding like love songs, conveyed our Paulism. Open your Bibles to see the Apostle Paul's first epistle to the Corinthians. He says, "I determined not to know anything among you, save Jesus Christ, and him crucified" (1 Cor. 2:2). In Paulism, we teach only Paul and him decapitated. Paul gave his life for the world, not in the sense of Jesus dying on a cross

NOTE: As Christians commemorate the crucifixion, Paulists memorialize the crash. Comparing Christ and him crucified with Paul and him decapitated is problematic. Besides Christ's consciousness being astronomically beyond Paul's, decapitation is not how Paul died. Although Paul's head was "wounded to death" (Revelation 13:3), it was not entirely removed.

The idea in Pauline Christianity that Jesus was sacrificed for all to be resurrected is not based on explicit teachings of Jesus, but the mythos of various religions. By Paul and others aligning details of Jesus with older stories, it was easier to graft in a wider audience along with their doctrines, rituals, and holidays. Very little modern Christianity originated with Jesus.

Now, as always, Christians regularly press their agendas by attributing them to Jesus even if it contradicts what Jesus taught. For example, although Jesus tells us to love our enemies (Matthew 5:44), Christian crusaders killed people while believing they were in the service of Jesus. Although he says, "Judge not, that ye be not judged" (7:1), and even though he never singled out gays one way or another, some Christians, as if speaking for Jesus, persecute gays.

So shall it be with Paulism. In the coming centuries, doctrines of the occult will mix with other teachings to further agendas in Paul's name whether or not they align with Paul.

563

that all would live, but in the sense that when Paul was told in dreams where his Beatles path led, he made the choice to stay with it for the world's glory.

He got a good reason for taking the easy way out, instantly saving himself by quitting the band, but did not. He stayed with it, prepared the way for X, the unknown variable whom he still did not know, but whom fate saw as me—like in the Bible when John the Baptist lost his head while preparing the way for Jesus—and consequently filled the entire earth with Beatlemania's songs and images that have drastically changed the whole world. He did it for the laud and honor of the world. Paulism thrives in all the earth. Having used irreplaceable hours of your life reading of Paul, you may be a Paulist already. You too may say, "I am of Paul" (1 Cor. 1:12; 3:4).

I, of course, am not only of Paul but am Paul. Having been Paul since 1966, I could probably pass a lie detector test while saying that I am Paul—even though my body is not like his. He works through me, is in me, and, for most practical purposes, is me. **I am** Paul McCartney made manifest in the flesh. **Paul's** indwelling is real. By self-identifying as Paul, his identity has become my reality. Although I am myself, William, whatever **Paul** has done in this world since 1966, he **has done it as** me. Paul uses my mortal form as does **my own soul.** When spirits become disembodied, they normally go to the light, moving forward to better things. However, Paul, like others, did not **feel** ready to let go.

Having warily **apPAULled** you with Paulism, I'll now soften it by explaining that we were all well esteemed, not just Paul. When John died, we three remaining Beatles, along with some other close loved ones (I brought along Linda and Denny) all contributed to make a tribute song for John.

Letting us all be a part of that song was healing. It began as a song that George wrote, which he had originally intended for Ringo, but which was too far out of his range. George gave it new lyrics when John went to the light. George sang lead. All of the rest of us supported it with backup vocals and our instruments. "All Those Years Ago" lets you see that **we all** would have done all the same for him. George **prayed to John** in that song: "Deep **in the darkest night**, I send out a prayer to you now in the world of light." After all, on *Abbey Road*, John, who opposed God, showed that he is God.

NOTE: Undermining Paulism, in a 1968 meeting at Apple Corp., John said, "I have something very important to tell you all. I am Jesus Christ. I'm back again." The next year, after depicting him as God on *Abbey Road,* he was invited to play the leading role in the stage musical, "Jesus Christ Superstar." He declined but enjoyed his idea of playing Jesus opposite Yoko as Mary Magdalene.

62

Run, Devil, Run Through the *Driving Rain.*

$Run,$ *Devil, Run* came from a dream I had of the Beatles singing "Twist and Shout" at the Cavern Club. Until they got too big for it, they played there often. Dreaming of that show gave me the feeling that I needed to start performing more like Paul–or at least that I, as Paul, should be able to go do what he had done. Not in words, but in concept, he told me he would be with me, and that he needed it. I often get encouragement like that. What I sensed as different this time was that Paul needed to return to his very beginnings. It was time for me to take him back to the same old Cavern Club to confirm his infusion of rock & roll roots. I 'returned' with him to the Cavern. **I had to make** his new lively rock & roll album. It was for **Paul**. In a new set of songs, he would **twist and shout again.**

Run Devil Run is vintage 50's rock with a few of my own songs thrown in for me to establish my union with those early greats, but mostly with James Paul McCartney. Actually, I think he just needed to see himself in that role again. I am as close as he is going to get to it. He is my angel now.

That is why **I need** to humor him with these sorts of things. **His presence** with me was obvious, having an excellent time through me at the Club and with the *Run Devil Run* album. He is having ethereal fun here making me run. I am not *the* devil, just one of those little devils in the song, all pushed around by Paul, my angel. He drove the Beatles. He drove Wings. He still drives me with my newest work. None of us has cause to complain though. He is making winners out of us sinners.

Giving me another vintage Paul challenge, he had me knock off *Run Devil Run* as fast as he used to execute his Beatles albums. That was difficult for me, and the biggest frustration to my Beatle mates. Losing so much time on my albums just about made them lose their minds, as I have already explained.

Substituting my style for Paul's was no problem. Yet, trading his cheery work for my detail-mindedness had consequences for the band as I have also explained. John's "All You Need Is Love" is all about that. My careful attention to detail made them miss Paul even more. Now I have put out a wide variety of albums, far beyond the scope of music that Paul ever did with the Beatles. Yet, I never could do it anywhere near his fast speed. Flying with Wings, I imagined moving at the speed of sound, but never could approach the speed of Paul. Fast albums took months. Keeping face with Paul, my goal was to do it in weeks, as he did it. I first reached that goal in 1999 with *Run, Devil, Run.*

For years, my work style drifted. At first, I transformed this Billy into Paul. That worked up until it flipped over. I have spent most of these years transforming Paul McCartney into William. While nice music came of it, it was all increasingly mine. Although that is all fine and good with me, it drove my angel mad. That sounds crackers. I understand. There is a lot to it that I cannot fully explain. My actuality as an entertainer is entwined with my Paul agreement. **It is like a marriage**. I have kind of made vows with him, **so to speak.**

I am committed for the duration. It is one of the inside factors that made John, George, and Ringo act so idiotically when I left the band. They could not believe that I could still be Paul if not a Beatle. "What of Paul?" I said that he is still here, but now going through a post-Beatles phase like all of them. Eventually, he would have moved on anyway.

When it was time to renew my commitment to the Paul part of me, I took a good look at him in the Beatles' beginnings. Paul was credited as a lead writer, singer, and (since Stu left) bass player. I needed to be like that. The William in me wants to do what Paul was credited with doing. What I cannot do, new specialized talent would still be hired for each song, or for any particular sound, but I would control every bit of it. However, Paul never thought that way.

My bandmates, and others also, often told me right from the start that the old way the Beatles used to record was much faster because Paul's job was simpler. **Paul's writing**, singing, and bass roles were too simple **for me.** I had to be the leader. I had to oversee everything and do everything. When I left the band, I was all the more that way. All was under my tight control. Sometimes I played every instrument—as I did for my first solo Paul album.

The Beatles' sound had to be perfect. I would stay all night to get it right. If it meant doing a track over that one of my mates had done, it did not matter. The perfect product was all I ever cared for. That is one thing that made Ringo insecure. When his drumming was not quite right, I would spare no feelings. I would either make him fix it or I would re-do it after he left. As I did that, the music improved, but our production time multiplied, and morale dwindled. I was usually smug about it. They nagged me saying I did not do it the way Paul had. I answered, "Of course not! This is quality!"

Now, with *Driving Rain*, cruising in the express lane, I've come around to doing it Paul's way. In that enterprise, with my temporary American band, **I was** a writer, singer, and bass player. Dreaming of **Paul's** rock & roll in the Cavern Club brought me to the old Beatles way. Recalling the fantasy of how their sound was made, I tried to make it real for this album. Aside from here and there, I mostly (as if Paul) played bass and sang. It was simple and fulfilling. *Driving Rain* picked up where *Run, Devil, Run* left off.

Experimenting with that carefree way, reflecting Paul's old Beatles days, from before I came along to complicate things, I again stretched myself.

The official story says that John and Paul wrote the songs while busy touring but did not share them with George or Ringo until they all met at the studio. Even though the world may have liked to imagine the Fab Four being on more even ground, George and Ringo (being less in demand) mostly went to the studio to keep up appearances. When I came along, we let them play their instruments more, requiring many more takes than when the session artists played for everyone. They lacked skill; I was perfectionistic.

Yet now, **above all else** on the *Driving Rain* album, **I acted as the mythical Paul.** The William in me calculated to engineer spontaneity. Virtually living Paul's fable, I used my guitar to teach each song to musicians. Once we recorded it, we eagerly went to the next. I had not met them before recording. We did it fresh on the fly. It sounded good.

Besides me on my Hofner bass (and just a little bit of guitar and piano work), I had three other excellent musicians. The new band had to have four of us. Rusty Anderson was on guitar, Gabe Dixon filled the keyboard spot, and Abe Loboriel, Jr. played the drums. They all sang backup for me. A few others joined us for a song or two. James, my son, played guitar on "Back in the Sunshine," and recorded percussion for "Spinning on an Axis."

Since for "Yesterday," Paul's all-time most emotionally packed song, they hired a string quartet, I did the same for "Your Loving Flame," wanting it to have that emotional power. I hired David Campbell, Matt Funes, Derouin, and Larry Corbett. Nothing, except perhaps "Eleanor Rigby," ever rivaled the emotional appeal of "Yesterday" in any popular song; and no song has ever had more cover versions. 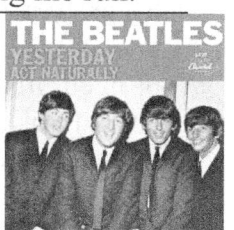 I also had Ralph Morrison add violin to "Heather."

Doing *Driving Rain* was fabulous fun. Those fine musicians showed great talent. Along with my own work, David Kahne produced it. He too did superb work. Mostly, I did the album for **Paul**. Now, at long last, I **finally did one his way** and had a splendid time of it. **I think we all did.** I especially enjoyed working with my son. Thanks, guys. And thanks to my angel for making me run.

NOTE: Thousands of artists recorded "Yesterday," making it the most covered song in history. These other songs credited to Lennon-McCartney are also among the top ten covered: "Eleanor Rigby" (3rd place), "And I Love Her" (5th), and "Blackbird" (9th). The most popular New World Order song also made that list. Generously attributed to John Lennon, "Imagine" is the 7th most covered song.

63

"The Beast"

Do not take this chapter overly seriously. It is merely an expansion of an old running gag that I obscurely referred to at parties over the years. If you have known me long or well enough that you do not need this one explained, then you also know it is just our joke that "The Beatles is Le Beast." I am obviously not conservative. **If you** are, you might be offended. Unless you **welcome Biblical humor,** this chapter is not yours. **I am having fun with** the old text. You may say **this conceit** is in poor taste, but John did not think so. My friends have laughed with me over this bit of Biblical humor all these years. Now as I show the world secrets that I had kept sequestered, I would feel kind of neglectful if I did not also include this private Biblical joke about us. However, first, let me explain that my skills are not in your religion.

You would not turn to your mechanic for advice on tax strategies. Since you would never expect your accountant to make the hit parade, do not expect heavenly secrets from celebrities. The truth is within you. Do not seek it from me or any other priest. Just ignore my Biblical excursions. If you are mentally out of balance, on medication, or easily spooked, simply skip this chapter. Save yourself from all this confusion. Watch out! Here comes the beast!

Beware of the four beasts: two of two heads, one of four, and one of seven. All four beasts are one, and each is of that one. The first, with two heads, gives power to the seven, and the four, by writing alluring words for their lips, and by enacting the plan whereby the beast deceives the entire world. By his subtle cunning craftiness, he masterfully conceals and reveals messages giving greater godly glory to the beast for its hour of honor with the world.

The two-headed beast, writing as one, known as Lennon-McCartney, seduces the whole world. The two, working as one, convert the world, and even you, to Beatlemania, that all may receive its mark and sing their words.

Consider the beast with four heads, and the four beasts working together as one. The eyes of all the heavens and the earth are upon them. They are full of eyes before and behind. The first, **John, was** angry from his youth. He roared as **a loud lion** to all the ends of the world. **George**, the second head, playing as a knight, **was a dark horse.** He was to submit as a calf to the lion and the man.

The beast with the face of another man was Paul, the cute Beatle. The fourth held drumsticks in each talon, flying as an eagle with arrows in one claw

NOTE: The four-headed beast joke did not originate with William or John. In 1962, George Martin, talking to John, Paul, George, and Ringo, said, "You will be larger than life. I have been ordered to transform your band into the four-headed beast. You will be the greatest idols on Earth." After sharing the idea with them, John made it wittier when sharing it with Mick Jagger, who then altered it further and repeated it to others. Those who credit Mick with making it up are only partly correct.

and an olive branch in the other, with the beat and representation of their war against the establishment and of the beast's powerful message of peace.

Singing in one accord, all four beasts agree in one and work together as one. The mind of the beast emanates from the replaced head of the man (he who lives as he who is dead). He upholds the beast and rallies the four together in one, even in himself. For the lion, calf, and eagle are merely shades of the individual man. Being the new head of the group, he is as the lion, the king. He roars with the loud lion. Only he shares in authoring every roar of the lion. They twain write as one.

Undaunted by death, **the head of** the slain is replaced and enlarged by **the foreshadowed man**. The sacrificial loss **gives new power to** the beast that is ritualized as **the head of the** offered calf or ram. Letting this new **beast** head take control, the beast soars like a bird into the light of the dark black night. Yet, when the calf or ram is sacrificed, the wings are broken, slaying it. Magically, the new creature flies with broken wings. The man, whose face was foreseen in the beast, becomes the beast's Wings. Over the earth, he flies as the beast, with and without them. They are within him and without him.

Resting not, neither by day nor by night, they pipe to all the world, sounding their trumps and singing their songs. And each of them had six wings: with twain, they concealed their faces, with twain, they concealed their feet, and with twain, they did fly, being clothed with glorious power, from the rivers to the ends of the earth.

They rode upon four horses, passing the statues at the tarot nodes of the earth's long winding zigzag path. John, sitting on a white horse, and all arrayed in white, leaves the Abbey to conquer the world.

The next horse arose, covered in red as if by Paul's great sacrifice that stained the mare as he sat upon it.

Then came George riding along on his dark horse, carrying a pair of balances in his right hand, showing the way of yin and yang.

The pale horse carried Ringo. These horsemen overcame all who had gone before. Even Beethoven, the earlier emancipator of music, rolled over for their new rock, pop, rhythm, and blues revolution.

And they warred against violence, hatred, taxes, and religion. They taught the world about peace, love, and commerce. And they rallied the masses to join in the great fight against all fighting.

Kings and queens sought after them. **All the** world, great and small, rich and poor, **oppressors** and oppressed, in and out, fab and fool, all **felt** after them, seeking their merchandise. For **the world** needed the products they offered, and the love they sold. And lo, a great multitude followed after the beast, having ears to hear its new songs, and money to buy all of its new merchandise. The heroic beast grew in popularity. A great multitude, which no man could number, grew throughout all the earth, of all nations, kindreds, tongues, and peoples.

And they all stood before concert stages, and before cashiers throughout all the world, and paid homage to the beast. And the beast received their earnings and their power. And the music made its mark, for it played in their heads. Hysterical audiences everywhere worked with their hands to obtain that mark in their heads. And the mark was stuck in their heads and on their hands, enabling them to buy more captivating merchandise of the musical beast. For the band played on, shaping the Western culture, which shaped the world.

Reaching all, penetrating all, their music spread abroad, covering the entire earth as the great flood. It entered every home as with lightning, and voices, and thunderings, and drummings, and quakings, as a great hail. And the music never stopped. For it played on, transforming the world, altering thrones, dominions, principalities and powers, things visible and invisible. And the beat went on.

The beast, known to the world for its four fab heads, rose up from beyond the sea with hidden heads that the world knew not of, or had forgotten, seeing only four heads, though it had seven. **Giving** each head fame and a name, namely John, Paul, Stu, George, Pete, Ringo, and Billy. And **William the** beast deceived the world as with the **head of Paul,** and the heart, mind, music, **and money of Paul.**

In Billy, all became Paul, and **Paul became all.** Though Paul was dead, yet he continued in the beast and was made manifest through William Shepherd. Billy, the Beatle beast, was swift as a leopard. He stood firmly with the strength of a bear, roared as a lion with John, and flew higher than eagles. He took Wings to fly, lifted up by the power, seat, and authority given him by the dragon.

Its power and fame came because of the great miracle that deceived the whole world. For after the head of the man was wounded unto death (for "he blew his mind out in a car"), the beast made it well again according to the eyes of the world. The deadly wound was healed. All the world noticed a change but would not believe it. Still, they wondered after the beast. And they were obliged to worship the dragon that gave power unto the beast: and they worshiped the monster.

They bought merchandise of the image, sound, and soul of the beast, sold throughout every nation. They asked who was like him and wondered how he was found who is like Paul. The whole world hesitated to believe it was Paul but was assured when he plainly said, "I am not dead." None could ever overthrow his position as Paul; for that seat and authority had been given him of the dragon.

Blasphemies sprang from the beast, but not from William. For Billy-Beatle was more subtle in all the earth, more than any other beast of the band. But the roaring Lennon lion, dressed in white, riding from the Abbey upon a white horse, proclaimed his popularity to be beyond God, and showed himself as *God,* sitting upon his throne. It is he who *made the world* reverence the image of **Paul** as was shown in the head of William. For it **is** John who gave Paul's life to that image **found in William.** It was the image of the beast wounded unto death. He was not that beast, but by deception. Although Paul haunted Bill in spirit, the image of Paul was not Paul at all, but was Billy, the seventh head. Paul enlisted Billy in dreams and became Billy in the flesh. Paul had fallen, and yet is, through William.

Religion was abhorrent to the beast arrayed as in white holy linens who rode upon the white horse. He exchanged his eternal worth for *one hour* with the dragon. [With the tradition of 1000 years being a day (2 Peter 3:8 and Psalms 90:4), John's 40 years,

2 months of life = 59 minutes.] He blasphemed legions of heaven and made war against all of the children of God. All the world followed after him. Their names were blotted out of the holy books for his sake. And his music played in their heads, removing their inhibitions and numbing their pains.

The beast's new songs filled the heads and played over airwaves and in all the houses and automobiles. **The beat went on** and carried away many after them **until the end of the world.** Even now, his music lives on and continues to draw more to him.

But the second beast with two heads, also being two of the seven, even Bill and Paul, surpass all lesser heads of the beast. For William, who is Paul, having two heads, continues on the longest, enduring all and surpassing all, even Venus and Mars, for he follows the stars.

In 1967, John joked that he and Paul were the two-headed Lennon-McCartney beast. This version soars higher by double fulfillment. The same Paul position in the band was filled twice. It is symbolically two heads for one beast. The head imagery is perfect since that is how Paul died. The first head, being wounded unto death, was replaced with the second, who healed the beast.

If you have an ear to hear this beastly song, now is the time to sing along. This one is another number. Leave 666 to this risen beast. I, as Paul, am number nine, number nine, number nine. Let beastly digits linger on in your head, playing numbers that all add up, counting the four to equal the whole.

Come on now, people. I have let you in on this extended joke. Share this grin with me. Then move on to the next page. The problem with bantering on about the band is that some take it too seriously. It makes them a little crazy. It warps their minds enough to stay with them. They say they can let it go, but it keeps coming back. This is by far my most elaborate version. However, even lesser ones never seem to stay away. In 1981, I shared this with a mate who became so obsessed with it that he never got over it. It is risky because it can freak people. Then again, so have my most rockin' songs.

Oh, I forgot to mention that Ringo called the four-headed Beatle beast "The Siamese Quads." Now we realize that such is not politically correct. "The Conjoined Quadruplets" is better.

I should probably reaffirm that **Aleister Crowley**, the second face on the *Sgt. Pepper's* album, **really is** not the 666 beast either, but was added as **my** grieving **beast relative, extending the joke—and network.** ⚛

NOTE: It was known from the start that the way to calculate the number of the beast, as the Greek scripture directs, is to assign this value to each letter:

Alpha: A (1)	Heta: H (8)	Ksi: Ξ (60)	U Psilon:Y (400)
Beta: B (2)	Theta: Θ (9)	O Micron: O (70)	Phi: Φ (500)
Gamma: Γ (3)	Iota: I (10)	Pi: Π (80)	Chi: X (600)
Delta: Δ (4)	Kappa: K (20)	Qoppa: Q (90)	Psi: Ψ (700)
E Psilon: E (5)	Lambda: Λ (30)	Rho: P (100)	O Mega: Ω (800)
Wau: F (6)	Mu: M (40)	Sigma: Σ (200)	
Zeta: Z (7)	Nu: N (50)	Tau: T (300)	

In the New Testament, the word ΠΑΡΑΔΟΣΙΣ equals 666. Some claim it is the only word of that value in the Bible's 66 books. Π Α Ρ Α Δ Ο Σ Ι Σ translates "tradition." Every Avatar comes to destroy established traditions, especially those of oppressive religions. Rather than searching for a 666 beast outside of ourselves, it is more productive to look within to root out traditions that block love, cutting us off from others, and from those parts of ourselves.

The number 666 occurs in this book 33 times.

64

Don't Let Your Inaction Blow It!

All right, I have had a lot of fun with these chapters. I have let you in on some well-ripened secrets and have shared a few laughs. Now it is time for us to get serious. Here is an issue that the world does not think much about because it does not affect most people personally. This problem is that everyone who is devastated by it is living in a region of the world that is powerless to stop it.

Do not suppose that just because you are merely one person, you cannot make any real changes in our world. It is faulty thinking. **I'm** one person too. "Oh," you say, "but you're **Paul McCartney!**" Oh, sure I am. Nevertheless, **I began as William** Shepherd. My transformation from Billy to Paul underscores this whole idea that anyone can do anything. I had fate, or a little luck, to make it work. I realize that. Who can say that fate will not favor you too? Here is one great secret to success. Do not let people tell you that individuals cannot accomplish extraordinary things. The truth is that absolutely all great things have been done by individuals. The originators of all great movements were individuals.

Really, everything worthwhile first began with one person willing to take focused willful action. Keeping that in mind, let me discuss this problem with you as one individual talking to another

We do not live where **landmines are a**n issue. Most who read this book of **secret**s live in environments that **big governments** mostly keep safe **willingly**. Be**cause** a **tragedy** can strike anywhere, consider the New York strikes on 11 September 2001. I was in a plane on the tarmac at JFK when the captain told us there had been a terrible accident. We could see it out the window. No one could distance himself from it then. It was in our faces, not in a distant minefield.

Everyone was shocked by the brutality. We longed to do what we could to ease a little suffering if at all possible. I donated some royalties. Millions of people contributed what they felt they could. We could not endure that terrible grief without helping somehow, even if only in small ways. Hearing that it happened in a land I love made the **inhumanity** worse. Learning of my relatives' role **made it unbearable.**

Caring, and needing to do something for New York, I composed the song, "Freedom," and had it added to my *Driving Rain* album that I had just finished. It was too late to have the song added to the CD cover because we had already printed the artwork. I just went ahead and added our new "Freedom" as a hidden track, a secret bonus song. Eventually, some copies of the CD were given an outer box and a different cover that added "Freedom" as an official track. That song's emotional appeal was meaningful to me, having written it the day after the attack. It also mattered to the loved ones gathered at "the Concert for New York City." I did it for them, and for the broken hearts everywhere that ache because of that cruelty.

At that New York concert, the mourning crowd effused a spirit of communal sorrow, holding up their pictures of loved ones who had been lost in the World Trade Center and other attack sites on that day of heartlessness. The concert occurred on 20 October 2001, at Madison Square Garden, nearly six weeks after the terrorist attack. It was there that I recorded "Freedom." **I am the one** who organized that benefit concert, **but many** other excellent artists left their other interests aside **for the** show as well.

Performers included many **friends**: Goo Goo Dolls, Elton John, Eric Clapton, Mick Jagger, Keith Richards, David Bowie, Billy Joel, Bon Jovi, the Who, James Taylor, Destiny's Child, the Backstreet Boys, John Mellencamp, Five for Fighting, Melissa Etheridge, Kid Rock, Jay-Z, Adam Sandler, and many others. It was an amazing show.

Concerts I did later, I cut the song, "Freedom," because George W. Bush used that 9-11 terrorist attack to justify his further terrorism abroad. It fortified his military agenda. His people militarized not only my song but also the whole general United States mindset. He used the attack to amass power.

My cry is always for peace, not war. Consider the harm by military action in war, and by the lack of action after the war. **Landmines** are left only in lands that our governments **do not love.** We keep our own lands free and safe. I love Americans who speak up for freedom and against injustices, ensuring enduring liberties. I love how Americans, and people from much of the world, rushed together to relieve those in New York. However, it saddens me to see no caring in places that they do not love.

Having such great compassion for Americans is wonderful. My heart was broken too. Now, what of each man, woman, child, and animal that is maimed or killed by landmines every single day? When will we collectively care for them as well? I urge you to think about it and to extend compassion.

Our governments, colluding with businesses, **love to have their wars** for motives they never reveal publicly. When they meet their financial objective, the soldiers return to their loved ones to live their lives of peace and safety. Decades after they finish their offensive strikes and leave, their destruction continues. A child walking across a field is suddenly blown to pieces. A farmer has a leg blown off. An old woman is watching grandchildren play in the meadow and then hears that awful sound.

Every single year, landmines kill or injure another 26,000 innocent people. About one third of the landmine victims are children. An estimated 60 million landmines are still hidden in the ground in 70 countries. On average, landmines take or wreck another life every twenty minutes. Every day, on average, more than 70 more are hit.

Our hearts go out to the 911 victims, and to those remaining behind to pick up the pieces. What about the victims of landmines? What of all those stricken families who must go on after landmines have blown apart their breadwinners or children? Do our hearts go out to them? In any two-month period, more men, women, and children are maimed or killed as a direct result of landmines than were killed in the Twin Towers due to terrorism. Landmines are like having around the world one tower of victims every single month. Do you see why **we all need to** be alarmed? Let us now all **come together to stop it.** Our governments will not listen until enough of us care.

Let us imagine another scenario. The United States military leaves landmines claiming that their obvious fighting advantages and fiscal savings are more essential than ensuring that all of their killing finally stops when they leave the area. The United States military would never leave active landmines up in New York. Civilians in other countries are being blown apart at that rate of over 2000 every single month. In our own lands, this slaughter would never be acceptable. We would all rise up to stop it. Let's love others of this world enough to press our own governments to stop leaving landmines, and to object to this practice by other countries.

It is time to return and **clean up the deadly snares** very thoughtlessly left behind **in foreign lands.** Even if it is terribly convenient for governments to leave every explosive active, planted, and waiting for its next prey, **true Americans**, and good-hearted people everywhere, **have the power to stop it.** The clamor would be huge if it were in our lands. Let's make our voices heard to give voice to those who cannot speak for themselves. Let's all speak up for the helpless.

Everyone has a voice. Some are louder than others. Mine is louder than most. That is one of the reasons why I speak up for landmine victims. Yet, however much stronger my voice may be, you can do your part too. A large group of small voices can quickly become much louder than my own voice ever can alone. Fortunately, I am not alone. I am just one voice in this movement. **I hope** now you too understand and will join us. As **we do** our part, we make the world better for all of us. **Love** everyone, not just the few whom your governments teach you to love. Love every creature.

65

Know the Difference.

The Beatles, Stones, and other bands **used Satanism**, as I've already explained, to help connect us to the powerful network. It was **because of** the relationship with that network (that EMI had already established) that we were able to get **the** help required for our success through the **Illuminati.** I also revealed our band's fraternal symbolism, especially on *Sgt. Pepper's*, which was to let the world know our sponsors. The Illuminati are Luciferians. They believe that through them, Lucifer ("light-bearer") illuminates the path of humanity.

In Freemasonry, we go up through 33 degrees. Unknown to those of the lower degrees, those 33 degrees are topped by 13 degrees of the Illuminati. Masons do much of the Illuminati's networking. I also spoke of the Committee of 300. They are all Illuminati members. When Masons of high degree receive the Illuminati's secret Luciferian rituals, no one of a lower degree is told. There are also 20 secret degrees of rank above the Illuminati that only a few humans have ever heard of. I learned it from

Know the Difference.

Paul. Some ministers have simplified it by saying that Satan is the god of this world and that he **rules over** the Illuminati, by which, through infiltration into every powerful organization (unions, **corporations**, governments, universities, and religions), Satan (Lucifer, actually) rules the world. However, he does not rule alone. Paul says he

NOTE: "Paul rules over corporations" metaphorically, especially over such businesses as Apple (A Paul) Corps, Apple Records, Apple Films, Apple Publishing, Apple Electronics, Apple Retail, and Apple Boutique. It is all the forbidden Apple of Paulism. However, Paul, the dead man, does not rule over anything here literally.

Extending John's metaphorical lines, "I am he as you are he as you are me and we are all together" ("I Am the Walrus"), which is discussed in "Across the Universe" (chapter 49), not only are we all Paul, but all corporate entities are Paul. All is Paul. Hence, Paul, who rules over all corporations, and is all corporations, is the source. Acknowledging the idea that one person's blasphemy is another's religion, we can add that to the religious Paulist, Paul (being a representation of all that is) is not only a source but the Source.

The Encoder's personal preference would be to use the word, "Source," to describe God, or the universal grid of loving intelligence—the light by which all things exist, and the eternal substance by which all is made. One fully aligned with Source (such as Jesus or Krishna, not a rock legend) may rightly self-identify as such. Speaking as Source, he may say, "I created the world."

The possible inference that Paul rules over the Illuminati is incorrect. In *the Memoirs,* William often brings the conversation back to the Illuminati. The sordid details may lead readers to assume he is against them. He is not. He gives information without becoming judgmental about it. They have been a primary source of his joy, sorrow, pleasure, and pain.

William was subjected to prenatal torment, abandonment, excessive control, ongoing ritualistic abuse, and other rituals throughout his life, some terrifying, others pleasurable.

However, that training, and his work in connection with it, opened doors for him to move up in the ranks. He is not taking orders from the Illuminati against his will. He is Illuminati. He was born to it, reared and trained in it, and groomed to be a leader within his predetermined sphere. Some researchers have presumed that William received some of his Beatles and Wings songs from the Illuminati. While they are correct that the Illuminati wrote them, the Illuminati writer was William.

William did not object to the idea of conquering the world through music, making him the Cabal's Pied Piper. Being systematically nurtured to that end, it has always seemed mostly positive to him, as does their extensive network that William's father expanded. William did not compromise himself to work for the elite any more than those of other spiritual or religious traditions compromise themselves by holding up those torches for the world.

587

uses **organized entities** having a score of degrees to **preside over the 13 Illuminati degrees** that in turn

NOTE: In 1773, the year Pope Clement XIV dissolved the Jesuits, Adam Weishaupt became a law professor at the Jesuit-run University of Ingolstadt. Repressed by that Jesuit influence, Weishaupt grew anti-clerical and formed a society to spread subversive ideas. On 1 May 1776, he renamed his society the Bavarian Illuminati. Based in Bavaria (now Germany) it was built upon the principles of that Age of Enlightenment. While publicly pressing for a separation of church and state, rumors spread that they were secretly working to topple all religions and all governments in favor of their own dominion.

By this time, the Freemasons were already successful in world affairs, including recently igniting the American Revolution, and directing that rising nation. Joining the Freemasons in 1777, Weishaupt learned their methods, secrets, and rituals, which he incorporated into his own society while heavily recruiting Freemasons and others of influence in the Enlightenment Age.

Fearing Freemasonry, the Illuminati, and other societies, the Catholic Church persuaded the Duke of Bavaria, Charles Theodore, to outlaw all such organizations—forcing them to leave Bavaria and/or to move underground, driving Weishaupt into exile and confiscating records. Yet, although they were outlawed in the 1700s, officially ending the Illuminati then and there, they (by whatever names) were still around to instigate the French Revolution and many other world events including the world wars.

Working as one, with 33 degrees of Freemasonry topped by 13 Illuminati degrees (with, in some lodges, the highest Masonic degrees also receiving the illuminating rituals), they infiltrate governments to allow their own demise.

After WWII, the US and USSR squared off in the Cold War fought by fake news and other methods of influencing beliefs, attitudes, and behaviors. Both countries recruited brilliant Nazi rocket engineers. However, they could not keep up with science fiction. The Americans' greatest Cold War strike was the moon landing, which panicked gullible Russians into inordinate spending. In the US, the media trained all to fear an eminent nuclear strike—justifying more military spending, which in turn drove the panic in Russia. Poor fiscal management (including funneling resources to the arms-race / space-race) destroyed the USSR financially as infiltrated illuminating ideas prevailed to dissolve the nation entirely. That collapse officially ended the Cold War.

Unofficially, that war fought by fake news, propaganda, infiltration, threats, and bribery, escalated worldwide. Local and foreign funds drive the media, promoting propaganda that uses fear to divide by race, party, or belief, to crash economies, and to destabilize and dissolve governments in preparation for the NWO. Essentially, with continued illuminated support, the Cold War escalated into WWIII but is still fought with fake news rather than with bombs.

Beyond the Illuminati, there are degrees of entities above them, accessed only through the most illuminated, and by powerful families (hidden dynasties) to their sides, extending back for eons. By contrast, the Illuminati is as young as the United States. Like the US, families of the Illuminati may stay in power for as long as they maintain the consent of those below and above them.

Those below consent because voluntary programming tells them what to believe. Those above consent when terms are met. Current terms imposed by a hidden Eastern dynasty—allegedly under reptilian rule—include erasing Sumer and its descendants. They toil to debase humans to an easily controlled animal state.

legislate those of the 33 Masonic degrees. Those 33 degrees, like the 33 vertebrae of the spine, lead us to enlightenment as we work our way up approaching illumination through the pineal gland. Beyond the spinal cord, there are 13 major parts of the brain corresponding to the 13 degrees of the Illuminati.

The chapters in this book that explain our Satanism (including Paulism), and our joke about us having four heads as the beast, are too dark or troublesome for a general readership. Likewise, our enlightenment chapters are too bright for readers who are more interested in "Paul is Dead" clues. I will cut many of this book's 66 chapters, eliminating those that are too dark or too light. That way, I can offer the masses the more commercially viable book, *Billy's Back!* For those who want the whole thing, regardless of this warning that the cut chapters are not for everyone, the unabridged version will let you see what everyone else is missing.

However, some of you may be freaked out by the details of **Paulism**. Those who enjoy such dark material **will likely** not find the enlightened ideas as thrilling. We **have taught** grand notions in our most philosophically sophisticated songs, into which we hid many of **our most clever** "Paul is Dead" clues. However, our **fans** missed those concepts and those **brilliant clues**. Most readers will be pleasantly stunned **to learn to hear** those songs that they thought they knew.

For those seeking light and knowledge from all of the enlightened material, but not wanting to learn of the Beatles' dark side, I will also release a nicer collection of extracts from my memoirs. I call that collection, *Beatles Enlightenment*. Skipping the darkest material, it would have the chapters dealing with our more spiritually meaningful Paul songs.

This entire book was meticulously accurate in its first draft. Then, after running it past my attorney, he convinced me to change some names and other details—which I did in good faith. Then he said that I evidently failed to realize that my memoirs are not necessarily fictional just because I say they are. The rest of the changes ensued to prevent devastating legal action. By a signed contract, I stand to lose everything if I confess that I am not Paul. I can say all I want to in fiction, such as in some "fantasy" song, but not in my memoirs since, as is self-evident in this book, autobiographies are non-fiction.

The thing to do was to present it as fiction. Yet, that was not enough. Although I repeatedly disclaim all of the facts in **this book**—and hereby disclaim the facts again—he said the book would not hold up as fiction in a court **of** law because most of it is easily **proven historical fact**. It **is verifiable**.

The only way to prove that it is fiction is to include some identifiable fiction. That makes it historical fiction—a substantial mix of historically

NOTE: Four paragraphs after substituting the source for the "score of degrees ruling over the 13 Illuminati degrees," William says he was "convinced . . . to change some names." As with the music, the goal is to conceal whatever people are unprepared to receive. That is also the point of asking readers to skip the footnotes on their first times through the book. With so few people privy to what is known at the top, John said, "There are only about a hundred people in the world who understand our music."

provable material with fanciful stuff, rendering the evidence undependable and inadmissible. It must be recognizably made up. He sternly insisted that this book must not be published without a significant thread of fiction running throughout the whole.

Obviously, we had a problem. I discussed this deal-breaker with my Encoder, who reminded me of an allusion to the 666 beast that I had laughed about on our second visit. He told me, "That is a kind of fiction that can potentially tint the entire book. I can work that allusion into half of it if that is what you really want." I decided to go with it.

It is one of my favorite jokes that John and I had shared with friends, and there are other versions, but none as elaborate as the one shown here. It is not true. It is just a joke, a work of fiction.

The same can be said of all the bits about sixes. **Really, I am** not obsessed with numbers such as **sixes, 666, 999**, or any other numerological musings. Unless they are key to you, dismiss it all as fictional numerical nonsense. My Encoder also created other evidence of fiction here and there that can be so proven in court. Can you tell the difference?

The part about Satanism is beneficial for shock value and is also the truth. The Beatles, Stones, and many other prominent leaders of the cultural revolution (apart from me), knew of Crowley through Kenneth Anger (AC's "successor") who encouraged what could be considered a kind of Satanism. He enticed us, and many others, back in the days of our *Sgt. Pepper* sessions. That was one of the reasons

591

that John wanted Hitler on the album cover. Kenneth's London group, teaching philosophies of hate, had great praise for Hitler and others whom they considered to work in that same energy.

Even though they had not yet met, John had also been greatly influenced by Timothy Leary, a "smart-aleck, atheist Harvard professor," as he depicted himself. *The Tibetan Book of the Dead*, as translated by Leary, gave John material he used in "Tomorrow Never Knows," not long before the Paul switch. Moreover, far more than that ancient text, Leary's greatest influence on John, Jefferson Airplane, Jimi Hendrix, the Grateful Dead, and many others, was his promotion of LSD as the new window to enlightenment. Although synthetic, and thus less healthful than weed or shrooms, its intense departure from reality opened our eyes. I found it quite beneficial. **I too** enthusiastically carried that torch, seeking to **bring** everyone on board—until I learned more **about** it. Leary, also a Crowley devotee, had **the same ambition** to transform the world, turning Western society into the occult. In turn, the West would transform the East.

As every viable cult needs its gods or idols, no other band rose in eminence as far as the Beatles. On PBS's *Late Night America,* Timothy Leary, now renowned for his pro-LSD work, claimed to be carrying on the work of Aleister Crowley. Then he explained how the Beatles fit in. He described the four of us as being an incarnation of God who came back as the four-sided Mandala, that the new gospel was being spread through us, and that the sacraments, whereby we commune with the entire world, are the drugs that we promote.

I am explaining these connections to show how we became so **big**. We were, as I said, the good guys of **rock and roll**, and the Stones were the bad guys of rock. These **positions**, different, but the same, needed to be filled **for the Tavistock project.** We, the good guys, showed our Crowley affiliation with his picture on *Pepper's*, but did not explain his Illuminati connection. The Stones had the opposite image to sell. They were more blatantly Satanic.

Each band image carried out the same agenda of the Committee of 300, which is largely directed by illuminated Luciferians and also by many Satanists.

Helping to spread paganism motivates them partly as a unifying vehicle to break down formal religious structures. Luciferianism eliminates all institutional loyalties by uniting the world in peace and love for the Age of Aquarius. Satanism is much more destructive, destroying society by debasing every human in it, levelling the species with manageable animals. With external pressure to deny the inner light, all are pushed to either ascend or descend, shifting to an enlightened state of joy or a miserable state of debauchery.

NOTE: Through the opium trade, the East India Company (EIC) stripped the Far East of its wealth (requiring unfathomable restitution from the Rothschilds four centuries later to be permitted to pursue their worldwide agenda). From the EIC's Council of 300, the aristocracy formed the Committee of 300 ("the Olympians") in 1727. That supranational council presides over politics, banking, commerce, media, and the military. The Council on Foreign Relations, which tremendously influences most nations, works under their direction—as permitted by those in other circles that cross the world.

All of this explanation of Satanism is included to show that it was not some satanic power from the netherworld that gave us world dominance. I connected through Crowley and Paul, not through a devil. Our musical work was positive and uplifting, not debasing. Yet, we made ourselves useful to the professional networks. By helping them succeed, they empowered us worldwide. **Their interests were** entirely political. Mine was **entirely commercial.** We helped each other get what we wanted. The perfectly coordinated agendas of several Illuminati organizations (such as the Committee of 300) were

NOTE: John internalized how the elite had used him, manufacturing Beatlemania as a calculated step toward breaking down order everywhere to create a new world society under their own leadership. He saw how his rigged success contributed to the plan to control society through music and hero-worship as a step toward generating enough anarchy and chaos to eventually culminate in mankind demanding a New World Order. John said, "Our society is run by insane people for insane objectives. I think we're being run by maniacs for maniacal ends and I think I'm liable to be put away as insane for expressing that. That's what's insane about it."

From the start, John was told how the Beatles would be used. All was by consent and mutual benefit. Nevertheless, typical of why such societies succeed even after giving advance notice, the weight and far-reaching implications of each operation cannot be comprehended by those who cannot fathom the bigger picture. Also typical, the most information is given to those with the most to gain from it, making them co-conspirators, not opponents. The perceived reward can blind people to implications that they would rather not comprehend.

John and Paul were told that they would be given music and other support to usher in the Age of Aquarius. They were placed at the top of the musical pyramid, making them the world's most influential writing team. The Beatles, they were told, would endure forever. John later acknowledged, "Changing the lifestyle and appearance of youth throughout the world didn't just happen. We set out to do it. We knew what we were doing."

With a basic understanding of why they were so generously supported, they gladly received what they could without any possibility of comprehending it fully. The weight of it all did not begin to hit John until Paul died. John then became unstable. He lost interest in quality work and would have quit entirely had he not been controlled by William, Yoko, and heroin.

put into play **by consciously aligning us** to tear down institutional, societal, and political barriers effectively enough **for their agenda**. For example, when they brought us to the USSR, Russians saw **our Western society** as never before, which **snowballed into** enough people seeking **globalization**. Like Joshua's Jericho, my sounds broke down the Iron and Bamboo curtains.

Our Crowley connection is what gave the band power through access to his hidden network that readily opened doors for us. Connecting to Satanism, many bands jumped on board the Illuminati's networks. When it superstitiously appeared that the devil orchestrated their success, it was the Committee of 300. Those who played along, promoting sex, drugs, and Satanism, were empowered—not for their work in the devil's evil playground, but rather to further the disintegration of values that held all societies intact. Imagine the intended impact of the world seeing us "good guys of rock" with LSD.

The media, also controlled by the Illuminati, promotes all those who promote that disintegration. As for the Beatles and Stones, assistance was direct. For others, it is indirect. **For** us, George Martin had links (through **EMI's** military intelligence) to those making **societal transformations**. They would not lose the band when **Paul crosses over**. They would have me provide new directives.

Alessandro Cagliostro (Giuseppe Balsamo), whom Aleister Crowley claimed to be in a past life, married Lorenza Seraphina "Serafina" Feliciani. Together, they founded at Lyon *La Sagesse Triomphante of his rite of Egyptian Freemasonry* on 24 December 1784.

Their rite was the first to use death and rebirth rituals of Isis and Osiris, later used in many societies such as the Golden Dawn, the Ordo Templi Orientis (O.T.O.), and spiritual philosophies such as **Thelema** that readied the world for the Æon of Horus.

The Illuminati's rapid success **has been credited** to Weishaupt's connection **to Cagliostro**, the most established occultist of that time. Some people saw him as Europe's last real sorcerer. His ideas, rituals, and other practices became part of Weishaupt's Illuminati and part of many other secret societies.

Crowley believed his work picked up where he, as Cagliostro, had left off. Like the earlier AC, he reveled in secrets of state and cultic circles. He joined

NOTE: *The Book of the Law* features the speakers: Nuit, Hadit, and Ra-Hoor-Khuit. Nuit (or Nut) is the universe of Infinite Space and Infinite Stars. Nuit is as a circle whose center is everywhere and whose circumference is nowhere. Hadit is each distinct experience within that circle. Nuit is the divine feminine, Hadit the divine masculine. **Together**, they conceive Ra-Hoor-Khuit, the crowned and conquering child, becoming a god of war.

Feel Ra-Hoor-Khuit standing behind you. It **is** said that when you feel his wings wrapped around your body, completely enveloping you, you may know that he is without you and within you.

These archetypal deities equate to **Isis**, Osiris, and Horus. As with every age, at the dawn of our Æon of Horus, Hadit and Nuit are embodied and slain, passing essence to Ra Hoor Khuit. Hadit was found in Paul. Nuit was found in Lady Di (1961–1997). They co-inhabited this realm for 1899 days before Hadit (Paul) was sent to Ra Hoor Khuit (William).

On *Help!*, the lads do not spell "HELP" in Semaphore flag signals.

596

people together through ritual. Enactments for Isis, Osiris, and Horus, said to be restored from Ancient Egypt, put AC and AC forever at the top. What most folks fail to grasp about Crowley is his extensive network. He built connections in the highest levels of government and prominence, not only in the UK, but in Western Europe, and the US, and through enough people in those places to reach the rest of the world. If you knew Crowley's associates and lovers, you would be amazed by his impact on world affairs.

When he died, new leadership by Kenneth Wilbur Anglemyer filled the void. He had changed his name to Anger to better suit the essence of a Satanic nature. He became angry. I prefer happiness, as most sane people do. Although I appreciate the work he did to present Crowley's ideas, my favorite parts are the ones that serve me. **What best serves me about** Kenneth Anger and **Aleister Crowley is** not their teachings, but **the influential network.**

NOTE: Intentionally acquiring a Satanic nature is absurd since it opposes peace and happiness. "Satan" (from the Hebrew שָׂטָן) means *adversary* or *accuser*. In this upside-down world, those with the greatest disdain for Satan may be the most Satanic—the most inclined to adopt adversarial positions and accuse people. Ironically, in the above sense, Satanists are among the least Satanic.

It shows ignorance to say Satan (adversary) to mean Lucifer (light bearer). Accusers are judgmental, seeking moral superiority to gratify their pride and control others. Light bearers seek to enlighten others while respecting their sovereignty. They let people govern themselves. "Do what thou wilt."

Satan and Lucifer are as similar in meaning as black and white. And yet, we all have characteristics of both. Through love, we obtain the unification of opposites. By accepting the totality of ourselves and others, our wholeness allows our different aspects to work as one like a black and white chessboard.

Resisting our darkness strengthens it by trapping energy there. Accepting ourselves, without judging our shadows, frees us to choose either light or darkness. Misunderstanding the unification of opposites, which is love based, some people have the contradictory belief that they can choose into being adversarial (Satanic) to their neighbor but illuminated (Luciferian) personally. It is as inconsistent as accusers (Satanic) seeking the Holy Spirit (peace).

Enlisted by the Committee of 300, **it was** the long road on which to drive the Beatle vehicle **carrying** the new world message. Networking in Father **Crowley's** camp gave us power in this world. As for **teachings**, notice that I also quote from Jesus, Confucius, and many others. Since I believe that we can learn from everyone, I do not mind quoting anyone. Whether the messenger is a devil, spirit, or angel, it is mostly the message that interests me. Since the sacred books from around the world talk about gods and demons, I have the feeling that it is also okay for me to do the same and to maybe tell you what I believe Lucifer and his servants have been up to lately, not that I have any special authority to speak on behalf of the naughty or the nice.

I wish to convey the idea of submitting our will to God's, or to the divine within ourselves. We have in us the nature of gods and demons and can choose either, but some choices are better than others. We each have our appointed work that we must do. Replacing Paul's role seemed to be my fate.

For better or worse, I see that my role changed the world. The evidence is staggering. I am not religious but am spiritual enough to see how it all played out. ☺ Eventually, it became clear to me that no one could hijack this realm away from God's control. Most religions would agree with that. Whether you think of God as a Divine Mind, universal intelligence, an exalted Father of our souls, or as anything else that is omniscient and omnipotent; if such a Divinity made this world, to be consistent, we may rationally guess that He, She, They, We, or It also runs this show. I realized that God, or the universe, of whatever you may personally call this loving creative force, sets all in place for whatever mission or undertaking that we are sent here to fulfill. If God rules the earth, then nothing monumental can happen down here that God did not either direct or allow. For reasons that we cannot comprehend, whatever God allows must be for our ultimate good. Having a particular mission to accomplish in this world, I came and did what the universe made possible, and basically willed me to do. **How else could I have** accomplished so much, or **become such a** celebrity?

Lingering traditions say that **God** could not have worked with me that way because I am not righteous enough. Although none of us seem purely holy, the Divine expresses through all of us anyway.

With each Beatles phase, the primary message was to give or receive love. We sang, "All you need is love." It began with silly romantic love songs, but suddenly matured into being more concerned about the love that was lost with Paul, and the brotherly love, relief, and truth that is needed everywhere for humanity. To "Let It Be," requires a loving acceptance of people and circumstances as they presently are. Our primary message has always been to love. Have romantic love, but also extend liberating divine love unto the oppressed Irish, to those who suffer from acts of terrorism, or leftover landmines. Love the poor and rich alike. Love the weak as the powerful.

Love everyone. Then I would ask you to **love every creature.** Respect all life enough to **give up eating meat.** Start with all mammals.

On the other hand, the source of Aleister Crowley's suffering, more than any other, was his veneration for placing pursuits above love. He advocated will over love rather than willing love. For each of us, our greatest potential for happiness is in doing what we love with whom we love.

In this book, I have explained—and given you background information for—ways that Paul and I are conspicuously dissimilar. I will recap some of the highlights. To those who knew Paul and me, the most obvious differences are in our personalities.

Paul was first John's friend, then a bandmate. They watched their time go by, being content to sit around and talk about nothing. Officially though, when it came to work, they say, **John and Paul enjoyed** knocking around lines of lyrics, "co-writing" a lot of their material. Then they would go to the studio with the others, work a song to completion, and leave it to go on to the next song, and on to the next. When done, they resumed talking about nothing interesting, just enjoying being around each other. They were friends over and above being bandmates.

NOTE: The official romanticized narrative that John and Paul sat for hours at a time knocking around lyrics and talking about girls is part of the fiction that made the Lennon-McCartney writing team—and the Beatles—much bigger than real life.

Once they signed with EMI, songs and instrumentation were provided for them. When William took over, the group was challenged to write many of their own songs and to play their own instruments whenever they could. It was difficult to measure up to the professionals before them.

All of that changed when I took his place. I was making connections. I became much more motivated to make my music and money. In collaborations that I did with John, it was later on in the creative stage. For example, we would each individually write our tunes and lyrics, and I might suggest putting them together to blend them into one developed song. I would have ideas about tracks that we could add to his songs to give them a richer sound. Or he would sing a funny backup line in one of my songs, or tell me to speed it up. That is how it was.

After we each wrote our songs, we would play with them to make them better. He would sing a song too quickly, and I would say, "Slow it down!" I would play one too slowly, and he would shout, "Play it faster!" It was not co-writing in the way that he and Paul were said to have done. Making them larger than life, many stories were created explaining how they came up with so many songs while touring. All of those stories contributed to the fairytale. The real part was their friendship and their love of music.

It never mattered who actually wrote their music. That is why they always shared the writing credits. **Nothing** was officially Paul's or John's. Everything either **wrote** (or others wrote for them) was labeled **"Lennon-McCartney."** Lennon was the leader. When I came along, I was the leader, and so you would think he would agree to credit the writers as "McCartney/Lennon." When John shot down that idea, I suggested that whoever actually wrote each particular song should have his name first. That idea did not fly either. John clung to branding every song, "Lennon-McCartney."

Our work habits were entirely different. I would regularly make track after track until the rest of them were ready to revolt. Then I would spend days, weeks, or longer, tinkering with them all, redoing nearly everything sometimes. My personality was about as opposite from Paul's as it could be.

Another major difference was that the Beatles were my band. I made that condition before I would sign on with them. With me at the helm instead of John, we did things differently by design. **My focus** included a higher quality standard than they **had held** to before. I, as I said, invested more time. **It** was **up** to me to select each album theme. I would come up with it, write some songs, and then tell each of the crew what I expected from them.

For all who knew us, the personality differences always spoke the loudest. However, I thought the physical differences were also rather obvious.

Nothing seemed more blatantly conspicuous to me than our height difference. I am inches taller.

Baldness was another factor. Most fans were unaware of his premature balding because the Beatles' early mop-top style had it combed forward. My hair color was like my kids'. James looks just like me.

Where Paul's hair did not fully cover his ears, that too is something to notice. On the Internet, our ears are easily compared. Paul's round ears are attached at the bottom. My ears, as you can see, have a **completely** different shape. They are not attached **at the bottom**. They hang down. Our images also **show our head shapes.** His is rounder—like his ears. **Mine is longer**—like my ears. Injections added voluminous walrus cheeks for my added facial width, making it seem rounder. Still, no surgery changes the entire shape of the skull. If they had done so, my head would not match the rest of my body. Each differing skeletal frame matches its own head shape. Watch my cheeks change from album to album.

I told you about the trouble I got into in Japan because my fingerprints did not match those on file from Paul's 1960 attempted arson arrest. Likewise, just as my accusers in Germany, my Japanese captors found that my signature did not match Paul's.

Genetics is the most positive way to distinguish each person. Since my DNA did not match Paul's, I have successfully overturned his paternity suits. His relationship in Germany, for example, produced a child, one for which we paid support, and required evidence that I was not the father. What better evidence than my DNA? I proved that mine was not a match for Paul's German daughter.

Voice biometrics, also as unique as fingerprints, tell the same story. I told you about the University of Miami professor who showed that our voiceprints do not match, proving that we are not the same Paul.

I taught you how to hear our voice distinctions now so that you can easily recognize the differences. Paul's voice is throaty and scratchy, and he has an

603

accent from Liverpool. My voice is fuller and lower. I told you about how we sped up the recording of my voice when I sang, "When I'm Sixty-Four" to raise the pitch, making it a bit closer to the sound of Paul. I also explained the numerous ways we had tried to convince the world of his death since 1966.

I do not know what else to say. **I have explained** in this historical book exactly **why we could never** come out in any non-fiction setting and **talk about it.** I can only say it in a song or a novel such as this.

Everything exposed in this book to prove my identity is true and historically verifiable. I have added some fictionalization for me to establish that this book is a work of fiction if I ever need to prove in court that it is a novel. However, the facts about me not being Paul are all easily documented. Neither the fingerprint mismatch in Japan, nor the DNA discrepancy in German courts, lacked hard evidence, but generally went unnoticed.

Equally, the voice signature mismatch shown in an old reliable magazine (*Life*), was not taken seriously enough to change public opinion. **I am** pointing it out in hopes of **helping you understand** it. I have tried to show **that this switch is** genuine. Karma made Paul's dread **a reality.** Now, with this revealing book, I say it as plainly as possible. Since novels are fiction, this book does not break the nondisclosure agreement or vows of silence.

I have only scratched the surface of the hundreds of clues that we all most meticulously embedded throughout our songs, record art, and films. I could fill volumes. However, **I** covered it all well enough so that I can **make the point.** We spent hundreds of hours making **all of those clues** to convince all of you. **Behind closed doors,** we laughed at your gullibility for blindly believing that Paul lived on. Publicly, we **said** it was bloody stupid for people to read any **"Paul is Dead"** clues into any of our material. Publicly, we could not believe that people would think that we had any part of it. Until I say I am dead, I am still alive! We would swear that we had no idea that those elements could give such impressions. We made listeners feel foolish for believing Paul had died. We wanted fans to have the sensation of being too wise to fall for such a hoax, when in fact, the opposite is true.

Since we had to add some fictionalization to make this book qualify as a novel, I decided to add this chapter so that you could know the difference between what is fact and what is fiction in this book. Beyond the point of vulnerability, I have opened my heart and soul to you and revealed lots of gnoses. Some of them, most of you will never believe. That's okay. I wouldn't either.

Letting this material work on you causes a conflict between wanting the truth and not wanting to be proven wrong. The absurd ego willfully rejects all that is outside of its narrow vantage point. It chooses to be limited. I do not. **You** are free to re-think any position and **are free to know** that this book exposes **the truth that "Paul is dead! ... Really dead!"** I am quoting *Sgt. Pepper's* as explained on page 245.

Based on my life expectancy, I shared these facts soon enough to give me some satisfaction in this lifetime, but too late for them to be used against me in earthly courts. A trial involving this material would last years longer than Paul tells me I have left.

Going to all the trouble of writing this book, and of having it all encoded for an entirely new literary experience, was for this one purpose: **I** want the world to know me before I am gone. I **want** you to know the real me, not merely the role **you** have come to know. I want you **to know** who I am. The world does not know **me** except for my role as Paul.

Owing to my well-established over-identification with **Paul McCartney**, for you to know that he **is not who I am**, I went to some length to show you our distinct differences. Now you can distinguish between **Paul** and me and can now be certain that he **died** out on that lonely road so long ago, back **in 1966**. We can put that matter to rest to move on to who I am. Although **I am** still playing as Paul, now you can see **William** as Paul, and not merely as Paul himself. **Now you** know. With that knowledge, you **can call me** by either name. Visit www.**BillyShears**.com for more on *the Memoirs of Billy Shears*.

66

The Talent Contest

To add yet further historical significance to this astonishing book, we would like to give you a shot at having your own recording on a *Billy Shears* CD or video production. **I am including** the lyrics below to enough songs to fill **a CD or two** that we intend to sell separately and **with some editions** of this book.

Consider now what it would mean to you, or to your band, to be recognized as a winning artist on a *Billy Shears* CD. You would pick one of these song-starters, finish writing its lyrics, and create your new music for the song. But before all of that, consult the website at: **www.BillyShears.com** to be sure that song is still available, and that this contest (or another) is currently open.

Every LP or CD that I have recorded has hinted at Paul's death. This CD will be the first one to spell it out so openly. You may know of some of my classical work that is entirely orchestration. Those CDs are also evidence of Paul's replacement since he could not read or write music. They are far beyond his abilities. After doing a CD or two of this level of openness, **I will have** been purged of this energy requiring **full disclosure**. It will then be back to business as usual **with** more subtle Paul allusions. Giving you **this opportunity** not only potentially puts you **on a CD** but puts you on one of historic worth. If this tome sells enough for a viable contest, and if your entry is a winner, you may earn royalties.

Never since the early years of Apple Corps Ltd. have I been this open to promoting new music talent. Submitting your entry soon, before we must add further limitations, is advisable. Timing may matter. Now, every talented reader is invited. With the same sweeping generosity that launched Apple Records, I open this opportunity to all who have enough talent to enter. Using the lyrics provided below, you will write the music, record it, and submit the song as instructed at **www.BillyShears.com.**

Enter now if the contest is open. The song order as shown is based on the way I hear them in my head now, not on how they will sound when recorded. You might surprise me. Therefore, and since not all of the songs will be included, sequencing will likely change. Whereas all things are subject to change eventually, consult the current rules and restrictions posted on the website before entering the contest.

Realistic odds of winning depend on the quality and timeliness of your entry, and the unpredictable number of entries received. To increase your odds of winning, you may record and enter more songs. Odds are some songs will be recorded by more artists than others. For full details, and to enter, go to

www.BillyShears.com. Below, I am including the lyrics for each song of this contest.

P.S.

Here is one more thing for you all to consider. **A**s I realize that most readers will not enter this contest, I hope that all of you slow down now and **u**nderstand that the lyrics that follow are—until released with music—simply poetry. Allow all the **l**yrics to move you. Take it all as it comes. Read it to yourselves with feeling. Never rush poetry.

Making history again, this compilation of songs may be the first in which most or all of the lyrics of the **C**D, or two, are published in a book, and read in advance by thousands of people.

Considering that I am extending this opportunity to everyone, I have concerns about quality. **I will not use** **a**ll of these songs and might **be willing to consider** adding more. With so many, I hope **some of** them **r**esonate with each of you to make **your submissions** meaningful to you personally. That gives any song **t**he power to touch hearts. **I want each song** entry to come **already polished, and ready** for the **n**ext release. We might choose **to** add a little here or there but would rather **publish** your own talent **e**xactly as submitted. Submit your best work but be glad we tinker with it after you do. It's how it works.

You may submit your entries when the website shows that the contest is open.

[The acrostic ends here.]

Contest Song List

There would be 28 IF we used them all.
However, only entries with enough quality will be used
on CDs, MP3s, or soundtracks.

Billy's Back!

BILLY'S BACK!
Come here; the music's playing.
BILLY'S BACK!
Come listen to what I'm saying.
BILLY'S BACK!
I've been with you all along,
And it's time you got along
With the man I really am.
Try to grasp it if you can.

BILLY'S BACK!
Come hear the music playing.
BILLY'S BACK!
Come hear just what I'm saying.
BILLY'S BACK!
I've been dead since sixty-six
But I never passed too far.
I've been Paul with all the tricks
That he burned up in his car.
Although now Paul's a part of me,
There's the Bill that's been repressed.
It's time to take this costume off
Now it is time to get undressed.

BILLY'S BACK!
Come here; the music's playing.
BILLY'S BACK!
Come listen to what I'm saying.
BILLY'S BACK!
I've been with you all along,
And it's time you got along
With the man I really am.
Try to grasp it if you can.

NOTE: The theme songs, "Billy's Back!" and "Billy's Back! (Reprise)" should be submitted together as separate songs but counted as a single entry.

BILLY'S BACK!
Come hear the music playing.
BILLY'S BACK!
Come hear just what I'm saying.
BILLY'S BACK!
Now this Bill has been denied.
That life's hidden in a sack.
Although on me your Paul relied,
It's high time that Bill came back.
He left his home and bitterness,
Came here to be a brand new man.
I've done forty in the wilderness.
This must be my promised land.

TAKE ANOTHER LOOK!
I couldn't show it any bolder.
TAKE ANOTHER LOOK!
You'll see Paul in my left shoulder.
I've been hiding out as Paul
Because that's the role that woos you.
Though I've given you my all
It's not Paul at all who leads you
He doesn't really need you
The illusion now can be through
It's not as though I'm still new
The mask I wear can be through
By now you see it's now see-through.

BILLY'S BACK!
Come here; the music's playing.
BILLY'S BACK!
Come listen to what I'm saying.
BILLY'S BACK!
I've been with you all along,

And it's time you got along
With the man I really am.
Try to grasp it if you can.

BILLY'S BACK!
Come hear the music playing.
BILLY'S BACK!
Come hear just what I'm saying.
BILLY'S BACK!

In that One Single Moment

Just outside the bookshop,
you dropped your card on the sidewalk.
I picked it up for you
and hoped that you would pause to talk.
Our fingers touched when I gave it.
Did you know?
Could you tell that I felt it?

In that one single moment
That's lasting through every moment
In that one single moment
I was there for you, yeah, yeah, yeah.

You were focused on me
when I handed the card to you.
How could I hold you there?
Was there something that I could do?
I searched your eyes for the answer.
'Cause maybe, we could make it together.

In that one single moment
That's lasting through every moment
In that one single moment
I was there for you, yeah, yeah, yeah.

In that moment with you,
I was fully right there for you.
At that moment with you,
life began again brand new.
We could have talked and talked,
and maybe laughed all day.
But you turned around,
and then you walked away.

You turned away! You walked away!
You left me there! Left me right there!
You could have stayed! We could have played!
Your card I clutched! Our fingers touched!
There was contact! I want you back!
Come back and play! Come back and stay!

In that one single moment
Lasting through every moment
In that one single moment
I was there for you,
And I'm still for you, yeah, yeah, yeah.

I have only single moments.
I'm single every moment.
Let's have some couple moments,
Me and you, we two,
only me and you, yeah, yeah, yeah.

Flies and Bees to Emily

She said that when she died
a fly was buzzing in her ear.
She didn't know quite what it said.
It wasn't very clear.
Friends, relations, neighbors,
loved ones, everyone stood still.
But no one heard the whispering
or buzzing in her ear.

Her words went on without her
and told the world about her.
The poetry of Emily
is read in books by you and me.
So now maybe we know her;
but where is she? Where is she?

For me, it was quite different.
A yellow light turned red.
An unexpected "accident."
Poor boy has lost his head.
Strangers gathered 'round the car.
The woman screamed and cried.
Two bobbies and a paramedic
Took me for a ride.

His words go on without him
telling the world about him.
The songs I sing as Paul who died
reveal the love we could not hide.
So now maybe you know him,
but where is he? Where is he?

Our manager paid handsomely
and threatened to do harm
If they did not deliver me
straight to this berry farm.
That's when I heard the flies swarming
Or maybe they were bees.
It doesn't really matter here
in fields of strawberries.

NOTE: In "Recording with the Beatles" (chapter 28), William explains the meaning of Paul being buried in strawberry fields. This song alludes to that meaning but now calls it a farm. This book has many references to William's farm in Scotland, which Paul was pressured into buying soon before he died. It has been speculated that, unwittingly, Paul bought the farm to be his final resting place. With that context, one of the videos referenced on page 60 quotes "Maggie's Farm," by Famous Groupies: "Someday they're gonna tear down Maggie's farm. / Someday they're gonna burn down that old barn. / Someday they're gonna dig up all that land. / Someday they're gonna find that missing man."

It is said that this song's reference to Emily Dickinson acknowledges Stephen Dickinson, who went public with his claim to be Paul McCartney's son a few years after the song first appeared here. Although William is not inclined to investigate individual cases of those claiming to be Paul's children, he might make a gesture to one as a general nod to them all—without agreeing with any enough to establish financial liability.

For plausible deniability in Dickinson's case, William might consider that most people are born between the 38th and 42nd week of pregnancy. The birth date (43 weeks and a day after Paul's demise) makes his claim possible, but less convincing than if he had been born a week or two earlier.

Melted Into One

Just two of us among the storm
We huddle, but do not get warm
(We cuddle as we come)
So cosmically we play the game
No two of us are quite the same
(And yet we all are one)

We float above from way up there
Our lives so far are of the air
(We're floating as we come.)
And as we float, we make a vow
that ending in this world somehow
(We'll melt back into one.)

We are falling (falling, falling)
and we're floating as we're falling (floating, falling)
We are falling (falling, falling)
We are floating as we're falling (floating, falling)
We are falling as we come

We are falling (falling, falling)
and we're floating as we're falling (floating, falling)
We are falling (falling, falling)
We are floating as we're falling (floating, falling)
We are falling into one

Then when we dry and rise again
Condensing ready to begin
(Our floating 'till we're done)
Receiving all that's been endowed
We bid farewell to winter cloud
(Of which we are still one)

Again, we fall to mother earth
Departing as another birth
(We wonder as we come)
If we'll remember way back when
We felt alone, apart, and then
We melted into one

We are falling (falling, falling)
and we're floating as we're falling (floating, falling)
We are falling (falling, falling)
We are floating as we're falling (floating, falling)

We are falling as we come
We are falling (falling, falling)
and we're floating as we're falling (floating, falling)
We are falling (falling, falling)
We are floating as we're falling (floating, falling)
We are falling into one

Again, we rise and fall around
We muddle things upon the ground
(We huddle till we're done)
Collectively, we all unload
So hectically upon the road
(And melt there in the sun)

Condensing for another shroud
Come dancing from a higher cloud
(We sparkle as we come)
Above the hill, we are still one
Out on the field, our time has come
(To melt back into one)

Land Mines

It was on Thuy's seventh birthday.
She was running in the field
And the birds were singing peacefully
'til she stepped in hate concealed.
And although she lived to tell about
that day she lost her legs,
Twelve years later you still see her
in the village where she begs.

Wars may come, and wars may go,
but the landmines stay forever.
Since World War II,
they're as good as new
when you step too near the lever.

There are fifty million landmines
hidden just below the ground.
Each day fifty people step on them
and hear that awful sound.
When the battling is over
and the nations become friends,
we think casualties are counted,
but the killing never ends.

Wars may come, and wars may go,
but the landmines stay forever.
Since World War II,
they're as good as new
when you step too near the lever.

It was on Thuy's seventh birthday.
She was running in the field
And the birds were singing peacefully
'til she stepped in hate concealed.

There are millions more just like her
to be badly maimed or slain.
They are powerless to fight it.
Only we can stop such pain.

Wars may come, and wars may go,
but the landmines stay forever.
Since World War II,
they're as good as new
when you step too near the lever.

Yes, wars still come, and then they go,
but the landmines stay forever.
Since World War II,
they're as good as new
when you step too near the lever.

The Hardest Things

When time unwound that Beatle sound
they bound another mate
on whom they'd heave all he'd receive
to rectify Paul's fate.
The timely fall of Brother Paul
made him a little older
Now here I am, a brand-new man,
with him upon my shoulder.

The clues were found since Brian drowned,
that I am not that late.
What eyes deceive, you can't believe,
so let me put it straight.
It wasn't long I took his song and
turned it six times golder

His girl was sad to lose that lad.
I tried, but couldn't hold her.
The hardest things we ever do
are for our own best good.

Life has a way of working out
exactly as it should.
No matter if you trust in fate,
all kismet works on you.
The things that pain you most today
can make your dreams come true.
The things that pain you most today
can make your dreams come true.

From place to place, and face to face,
in all his tiring trips,
now in my head is all he said.
It echoes off my lips.
Another town, another round,
another gig and date.
Whom they bereave just had to leave
or love would turn to hate.

Sometimes when life's too full of strife
we feel that something rips.
We used to drink the whole thing down,
but now take only sips.
His glamorous role was just a bowl
of sugar-frosted bait.
At first, I knew it would not do,
but they just couldn't wait.

The hardest things we ever do
are for our own best good.

Life has a way of working out
exactly as it should.
No matter if you trust in fate,
all kismet works on you.

The things that pain you most today
can make your dreams come true.
The things that pain you most today
can make your dreams come true.

They were calling. Rains were falling.
I must fix their hole.
It was showing. I was going
to pay McCartney's toll.
As if bleeding, they were pleading,
I would take the part.
"If I'm your man, give me the band."
I tried to play it smart.

"It's yours," he said; so, we were wed,
and I became the leader.
The band was mine to wine and dine,
to care for and to feed her.
In every case, I set the pace.
I told them how to play
a newer sound with me around.
The show would go my way.

The hardest things we ever do
are for our own best good.
Life has a way of working out
exactly as it should.
No matter if you trust in fate,
all kismet works on you.

The things that pain you most today
can make your dreams come true.
The things that pain you most today
can make your dreams come true.

Born to a man who launched a plan
into his network hurled.
I'd be the one to take the head
and then to change the world.
Born to a man who launched a plan
into his network hurled.
I'd be the one to take the head
and then to change the world.

I almost hoped they'd tell me no,
when playing hard to get.
But they could tell I'd serve them well
if I would do my bit.
I feared to let Paul's spirit set
and fix upon my shoulder.
My life was tossed. I felt I lost,
and Bill would grow no older.

But now I thank them that I drank him
deep into my soul.
My fate would be that I could see
that life would not be dull.
And so, I'll play another day
and sing out from his heart
whatever he may place in me
is all I shall impart.

The Interview

Like an interview,
Not knowing what to do
Or say to make you see
What we might do
if you let me.

Afraid to tip my hand to say
I want to be your man today
And always if you'd only stay
And be my only love, I pray.

Superficially,
I speak of you and me
As if it didn't matter
That my heart's totally
a pitter-patter.

Our mere words across a table
Can't convey it. They're not able
To now mend the scars and holes
Only by intertwining souls.

Afraid to tip my hand to say
I want to be your man today
And always if you'd only stay
And be my only love, I pray.

For a smatter
of mindless chatter
I cite headlines from the news
lest I flatter and thus shatter
my only chance with you.

Now I don't know what to say
to have you love me anyway.
I'm afraid to tip my hand to say
I want to be your man today
And always if you'd only stay
And be my only love, I pray.

Release

Dreaming of your kisses
keeps me tumbling all night
knowing that you'd take me
there without a thought or fight
but reaching you without
is only where I can begin
to search a chamber of your soul
that's hidden deep within.

Release the pain you've felt too long,
It's time that we remold it.
Release the pain you feel inside
It hurts you more to hold it.

You bring me to the fountain
of your flowing tenderness
and leave the taste upon my tongue
of every fervent kiss
but all we do, and all we say,
is merely to impart
the love that you keep hidden
deep below your wounded heart.

Release the pain you've felt too long,
It's time that we remold it.
Release the pain you feel inside
It hurts you more to hold it.

So, climb with me the ladder
to your utmost inward shelf
to reach for that full measure
of your unrestricted self.
Then give to me the love
that's been protected for too long
and as you sing, I'll harmonize
your liberated song.

Release the pain you've felt too long,
It's time that we remold it.
Release the pain you feel inside
It hurts you more to hold it.

You tell me that you have the right
to feel the way you do.
You tell me how he wronged your past
And probably that's true.
But that was then, and this is now.
It's time to let it go somehow.

Release the pain you've felt too long,
It's time that we remold it.
Release the pain you feel inside
It hurts you more to hold it.

Sonnet 4-98

She was the source of all that life could bring.
Each day her glory woke the morning rays.
Her voice was first of all the birds to sing.
It was her calling to ignite the days.
Photography and cooking, her known arts.
She was the cook and artist of the house.
An advocate for every beating heart,
She would defend each child and each mouse.
But now her face and song are not as clear.
Her image and her voice are in a haze.
Though still she whispers guidance in my ear,
Don't see her 'round the house as much these days.
The more delight we find in love and song,
The more we're left to miss them when they're gone.

NOTE: "Sonnet 4-98" was written 4-98 (April 1998) for Linda who passed away on 17 April 1998. At that time, William did not intend to put music to it. Although he would love to hear it sung, he doubted that it would work.

You Love Another Way

She whispers in my ear all night
and fills my body with delight.
She's everything she's ever been and more.
Her spirit soars inside of me.
She makes me all I want to be.
But I can't see her walking through that door.
And though I know you're not to blame
That all my mornings start the same.
I wish I could preserve her with a song.
Been years since she's seen light of day.
Forever since she went away.
I really can't believe she's really gone.

You soothe my wounded broken heart.
You get me through each day.
But you can never fill her part.
You love another way.
Your comfort means the world to me.
I need to have you here.
But though your face is all I see,
I know that she's still near.

So, when my nightly dreams are through,
And I awake to only you,
You understand the pain I've held so long.
You are the one I have for now,
The one who gets me through somehow.
I really can't believe she's really gone.
But now my days are filled with you,
And all the little things you do
You healed the part of me that ached for her.
You brought me to another height
And made my loving come out right.
She said I must move on, and I concurred.

You soothe my wounded broken heart.
You get me through each day.
But you can never fill her part.
You love another way.
Your comfort means the world to me.
I need to have you here.
But though your face is all I see,
I know that she's still near.

And though I know you're not to blame
When all my mornings start the same.
I wish I could preserve her with a song.
Been years since she's seen light of day.
Forever since she went away.
I really can't believe she's really gone.
You whisper in my ear all night
and fill my body with delight.
You're everything you've ever been and more.
Your spirit soars inside of me
You make me all I want to be.
But I still miss her walking through that door.

The loss would never leave my head.
I could not live abstinently.
We built our life in our warm shared bed
I could not endure the bed empty.
The loss would never leave my head.
I could not live abstinently.
We built our life in our warm shared bed
That emptiness was breaking me.

We can only be ourselves in love.
Otherwise, why bother?
You can't replace another love
No one becomes another.

You healed my wounded broken heart.
You taught me how to play.

But you don't need to fill her part.
You love another way.
You took me to a higher floor.
I'm always glad you're near.
You taught me how to love once more.
You overcame my fear.

Give Me Just an Hour

Thinking 'bout you, Baby
When I was in the shower
Wondering how to show you
How to feel that power
In just a little while
We'll light a little fire

And with your nod and smile
We'll take it ever higher
It would only take an hour
For you to know my soul
It would only take an hour

There's nothing that we could not do
Or that I would not do for you
If I could be with you
If you only knew, only knew
Give me just an hour

And how to let you know
Thinking 'bout you, Baby
How to let my feelings show
In just a little while
I'll be next to you

In just a little while
We'll know what to do
It would only take an hour
For you to know my soul
It would only take an hour

There's nothing that we could not do
Or that I would not do for you
If I could be with you
If you only knew, only knew
Give me just an hour
Give me just an hour

That's all it'd take to join our souls.
Let's light a little fire.
That's all it'd take to join our souls.
We'll take it ever higher.

There's nothing that we could not do
Or that I would not do for you
If I could be with you
if you only knew, only knew
Give me just an hour
Give me just an hour

There's nothing that we could not do
Or that I would not do for you
If I could be with you
if you only knew, only knew
Give me just an hour

Couldn't Happen Any Other Way

Eventually, we reach the point of ecstasy.
We start out slow and grow to be
aligned with more intensity.
So teasingly, I touch your places just to see
you scream for more of that from me
until relief eventually.

Naturally, life plays out as it's meant to be.
There's no point in wishing more for me.
To love what is is all we need.
Eventually, we find a place where there's no need
to second guess what's here for me.
It all unfolded naturally.

The old day would grow dim
before the new one would begin.
And though I know you miss him,
it's now a brighter day,
and it couldn't happen any other way.
It couldn't happen any other way

And teasingly, you fill my soul with energy
that's only made for you and me
to blast through levels boundlessly.
I flow through you. You flow through me.
And feel the pulse of life set free,
rejuvenating pleasingly.

Creatively, with tracks on tracks revealing me
I layer meaning, sounds, and sing
that I am he, though he's not me.
I take him where he needs to be
and give him credit endlessly
transcending all creatively.

632

The old day would grow dim
before the new one could begin.
And though I know you miss him,
it's now a brighter day,
and it couldn't happen any other way.
It couldn't happen any other way.

Inevitably, the light prevails, and we all see
what had been hidden secretly—
the darkest plots for pain and greed.
But globally, in full entirety,
emerging from the old 3-D,
is that new world that inevitably is bound to be.

And then, in all serenity,
we grow to what we're meant to be
without threats from insanity,
we children of the world are free.
The birthing of awareness brings
the pains, then freedom with new wings

The old day would grow dim
before the new one would begin.
And though I know you miss him,
it's now a brighter day,
and it couldn't happen any other way.
It couldn't happen any other way.

You might as well just give your stress a rest.
No need to fret about the weather.
Everything works out for the best.
None of your worries make it better.
Greet each new day as the one that's real.
I'm your new day if you'd rather.

The old day, it grew dim
before the new day could begin.

And though maybe you miss him still,
it's now a brighter day,
and it couldn't happen any other way.
It couldn't happen any other way.
It couldn't happen any other way.
It couldn't happen any other way.
It couldn't happen any other way.
It couldn't happen any other way.
It couldn't happen any other way.
It couldn't happen any other way.
It couldn't happen any other way.

Made for Lovin' You

We've never met, but can't be strangers
It's like an old familiar book
I will feel it when I see you
I will know you by your look
So, I'm driving every street now
Wondering where on earth you are
When you see me will you know it?
Will you climb into my car?

You know this heart was made for lovin'
It's been lovin' true so long
You know my heart was made for lovin' you
You're what makes me sing this song

You're the woman of my dreams now
I've been dreaming of you again
I will recognize your face now
I know your eyes, your nose, your chin
So, I'm looking everywhere now
Wonderin' if you're lookin' for me
When you see me will you know it?
When we meet will we be free?

You know this heart was made for lovin'
It's been lovin' true so long
You know my heart was made for lovin' you
You're what makes me sing this song

You gotta a piece of my soul
Making me feel that much bolder
Feel my heart of gold
Like I'm sitting on your left shoulder
So, I told her

You know this heart was made for lovin'
It's been lovin' true so long
You know my heart was made for lovin' you
You're what makes me sing this song

My Heart Is Blue.

My heart is blue. I'm thinking of you.
My heart is blue. Is yours blue too?
I'm sittin' here. You're far away.
I'm sittin' here and my heart is blue.
I'm sittin' here. And you're far away.
And my heart is blue. My heart is blue.

And I'm sittin' here and I'm thinking of you.
And you're far away. And my heart is blue.
How 'bout you? Are you blue too?
Cause you're not here And my heart is blue.
I'm just sittin' here thinkin' of you
And my heart is blue. My heart is blue.

NOTE: When preparing your own version of each song, let the music in your head dictate any changes. "Made for Lovin' You" includes a bridge by a contestant, Steve Larsen. All contestants are free to make such adaptations.

Now, can't you see my heart is blue?
I'm all alone thinking of you.
My heart is blue just thinking of you.
And you're not here. And I'm feeling blue
My heart is blue. I'm thinking of you.
My heart is blue. Is yours blue too?

I'm sittin' here. You're far away.
I'm sittin' here and my heart is blue.
I'm sittin' here. And you're far away.
And my heart is blue. My heart is blue.
And I'm sittin' here and I'm thinking of you.
And you're far away. And my heart is blue.

How 'bout you? Are you blue too?
Cause you're not here and my heart is blue.
I'm just sittin' here thinkin' of you
And my heart is blue. My heart is blue

There ain't nothing I can do because I sit alone in my
head thinking of you in my bed and I think of you and
wonder if you think of me too. I'm turning blue
without you here to free me from the pain and gloom
of being alone here turning blue while missing you!

My heart is blue. My heart is blue
just thinking of you. And you're not here.
I'm feeling blue.

In the Center of Love

Well, we're lying there,
all alone there, you and I.
And your hair filled
with a fire from the moon above.

And I gently pulled it back,
as I whispered in your ear,
That we were lying there,
you and I, in the center of love.

And the noise there,
from the fan, it didn't bother us at all.
It felt good to have it
blowing down on us from up above.
For the air was full of warmth,
and the light was coming in,
And we were lying there,
you and I, in the center of love.

Well, it's times as real as these
That are with me all the time
As if it happened just last night
You know it's always on my mind
And I'll never let it go.
You know I'll never let it go.

And I touched you,
as I caressed your glowing hair.
And the peace, I felt in you,
it was as tender as a dove.
And I knew that it would last,
so, I whispered in your ear,
That we were lying there,
you and I, in the center of love.

I moved closer, like a spoon,
at the contour of your back.
And we noticed, you and I,
that we fit just like a glove.

It felt good to be with you.
All my dreams you made come true,
As we were lying there,
you and I, in the center of love

Well, it's times as real as these
That are with me all the time
As if it happened just last night
You know it's always on my mind
And I'll never let it go.
You know I'll never let it go.

And I held you, in my heart,
as I held you, in my arms.
And you turned, to face my way,
with just a little shove.
There was fragrance in your hair.
There was moonlight in your eyes,
As we were lying there,
you and I, in the center of love.

And your lips there, in that light,
they gently spoke my name.
And our souls, yours and mine,
were filled with love from up above
There was music in your voice,
as you spoke softly to my soul,
Sayin' we were lying there,
you and I, in the center of love.

Well, it's times as real as these
That are with me all the time
As if it happened just last night
You know it's always on my mind
And I'll never let it go.
You know I'll never let it go.

Yeah, we were lying there,
all alone there, you and I.
And your hair filled
with a fire from the moon above.
And I gently pulled it back,
as I whispered in your ear,
That we were lying there,
you and I, in the center of love

Well, it's times as real as these
That are with me all the time
As if it happened just last night
You know it's always on my mind
And I'll never let it go.
You know I'll never let you go.

Cause we were lying there,
you and I, in the center of love.
Yeah, we were lying there,
you and I, in the center of love.
We're still there, we're lying over there,
you and I, in the center of love.
You and me there, all alone, in the center of love,
in the center of love.
We're in the center of love, of love, of love.

Back In Sixty-Six

He'd foretell his own fall (back in sixty-six)
Now I retell for all (back in sixty-six)
What befell me and Paul (back in sixty-six)
What went well, you recall (back in sixty-six)
May repel great and small (back in sixty-six)

He'd indwell and enthrall (back in sixty-six)
To propel me to haul (back in sixty-six)
And outsell all them all (back in sixty-six)
Like some hell fireball (back in sixty-six)
His Michelle would just bawl (back in sixty-six)
And out-yell my hardball (back in sixty-six)
She would smell my pitfall (back in sixty-six)
From her shell, her catcall (back in sixty-six)
Would dispel every scrawl (back in sixty-six)
On my trail to forestall (back in sixty-six)
And compel with some gall (back in sixty-six)
My goodwill or rainfall (back in sixty-six)
When the bell hit the ball (back in sixty-six)
The hotel took the call (back in sixty-six)
From the dell came this doll (back in sixty-six)
I set sail leaving Saul (back in sixty-six)
Across the well over the wall (back in sixty-six)
And with Mel hit the mall (back in sixty-six)
It was a hell of a hall (back in sixty-six)
To pierce the veil and evolve (back in sixty-six)
I's impaled with old Paul (back in sixty-six)
So, I yelled to y'all (back in sixty-six)
Can't you tell I'm too tall (back in sixty-six)
And I've wailed at this wall (back in sixty-six)
Since he fell in the fall (back in sixty-six)

As years flitter by and are gone
Though I filled everyone with my songs
Sometimes I'm just a little bit miffed
As I think of the life that I've missed
Looking back to what happened back then
Or to when this new life was begun
Looking back in itself isn't wrong
But my years of the now are all gone

He'd foretell his own fall (back in sixty-six)
Now I retell for all (back in sixty-six)

What befell me and Paul (back in sixty-six)
What went well, you recall (back in sixty-six)
May repel great and small (back in sixty-six)
He'd indwell and enthrall (back in sixty-six)
To propel me to haul (back in sixty-six)
And outsell all them all (back in sixty-six)
Like some hell fireball (back in sixty-six)
His Michelle would just bawl (back in sixty-six)
And out-yell my hardball (back in sixty-six)
She would smell my pitfall (back in sixty-six)
From her shell, her catcall (back in sixty-six)
Would dispel every scrawl (back in sixty-six)
On my trail to forestall (back in sixty-six)
And compel with some gall (back in sixty-six)
My goodwill or rainfall (back in sixty-six)
When the bell hit the ball (back in sixty-six)
The hotel took the call (back in sixty-six)
From the dell came this doll (back in sixty-six)
I set sail leaving Saul (back in sixty-six)
Across the well over the wall (back in sixty-six)
And with Mel hit the mall (back in sixty-six)
It was a hell of a hall (back in sixty-six)
To pierce the veil and evolve (back in sixty-six)
I's impaled with old Paul (back in sixty-six)
So, I yelled to y'all (back in sixty-six)
Can't you tell I'm too tall (back in sixty-six)
And I've wailed at this wall (back in sixty-six)
When Paul fell in the fall (of nineteen sixty-six)

I Heard You Singing

Connecting everything in rays of light
And glory of all things becoming one
once I saw that everything was right
And wondered at the glory of the sun

641

I felt that it was made of part of me
That every part of me was part of you
That if we both would but agree
There's nothing in this world we couldn't do

I dreamed I heard you singing in the wind
(Singing softly)
And loving light beamed from the sky and ground
(Surroundings all things)
It flowed throughout all things and deep within
(Flowing sweetly)
And still, your singing was the only sound
(Singing softly)

The universe was but a single thought
Connecting everything in rays of light
That we all found exactly as we sought
And many walked in darkness at midday
But still, the light was shining clear for all
With eyes to see the glory of the sun
And ears to hear the sweetly singing call
With hearts to understand that we are one

I dreamed I heard you singing in the wind
(Singing softly)
And loving light beamed from the sky and ground
(Surroundings all things)
It flowed throughout all things and deep within
(Flowing sweetly)
And still, your singing was the only sound
(Singing softly)

Connecting everything in rays of light
The universe is but a single thought
Now we can see that everything is right
That we all find exactly what we sought
And every part of me is part of you
With hearts to feel the glory of the sun
There is not anything we cannot do
So long as we know all of us are one

642

Living in the Now

Living in the now frees us from our sorrows.
Living in the now is the only thing that lasts.
Living in the now is not about tomorrow.
Let's live here in the now, and forget our past.

I used to mourn forgotten days
of Bill and all his friends.
I used to miss my relatives
and all the things we'd been.
I used to codify old scenes
and work them into songs.
Until I knew that I am now,
today, where I belong

I used to sing of Paul's demise
as secretly my own.
Although he died, it's I who cried.
I wanted to go home.
My life, not his, was cut from earth,
was halted in its prime.
I mourned my past until I saw
I'm out of sync with time.

Living in the now frees us from our sorrows.
Living in the now is the only thing that lasts.
Living in the now is not about tomorrow.
Let's live here in the now, and forget our past.

Some people live entire lives
in the future or the past.
Holding on to memories
and trying to make them last.
Fretting 'bout what might become,
or 'bout what might have been,
Forgetting that all life is now.
There is no life in then.

Resenting back or fearing forth
both block the light of day
Both stop all valid living.
Now I've learned a better way.
The man I am today's what counts.
Don't worry 'bout my past.
Whatever I have been before,
I am myself at last.

Living in the now frees us from our sorrows.
Living in the now is the only thing that lasts.
Living in the now is not about tomorrow.
Let's live here in the now, and forget our past.

I could tell you stories of pain in ritual.
What it's like to be abused
To fracture my whole soul.
I could let my stories keep the pain alive today.
But that just lets abusers win.
Today's another day.

Living in the now frees us from our sorrows.
Living in the now is the only thing that lasts.
Living in the now is not about tomorrow.
Let's live here in the now, and forget our past.

Butterfly

Caterpillar on the leaf
Is thinking that he's got it made

NOTE: "Butterfly" was inspired by thoughts of Donovan singing, "First there's Paul McCartney / Then there's no McCartney / Then there is. / First there's Paul McCartney / Then there's no McCartney / Then there is. / The caterpillar sheds its skin / To find the butterfly within. / The caterpillar sheds its skin / To find the butterfly within. / Paul McCartney, / Paul McCartney, / Paul McCartney, I call your name."

Additionally, the butterfly represents William's loss of self in ritualistic childhood traumas designed to control him as needed later. In the song, he fantasizes about outgrowing his program, spreading his Wings to fly away.

With all the food that he can eat
He will not leave that leaf all day

Sometimes when life is good
A bug's too blind to see
Just what it needs to do
To set its spirit free

And when it thinks its life is set
Another whispers flying clues
"You have enough of leaf within"
"Lose yourself to become you"

Sometimes when life is good
We are too blind to see
Just what we need to do
To set our spirits free
We were born to fly! We were born to fly!
Stretch out those wings and fly!
Fly! Let it go and fly! We were born to fly!

Cocooning time went on so long
But was forgotten in the end
When wings unfolded stretching out
The real life could begin.

Sometimes when life is good
We are too blind to see
Just what we need to do
To set our spirits free

Fly! Let it go and fly! We were born to fly!
We were born to fly! We were born to fly!
Stretch out those wings and fly!
Let us all reach out and fly!
Stretch out those wings to fly!

Lord Paul

Our Lord Paul is over all.
He's Keeping watch by night and day.
To be sure that I'm still on the ball,
He watches how I sing and play,

Though dead to you, he lives in me.
In thoughts and dreams and conscious streams,
He writes my songs for this one fee.
That he may always live through me.

Once there was a way outta this place.
Once there was a way back home.
I could have left without a trace.
I could have found my way back home.

I tried to leave but he could tell.
I tried to drive off in this car.
But though his soul may burn in hell,
And though he sleeps, he's never far.

Sometimes I'd rather be alone,
But only for a minute.
I'd rather live my life as me,
Without another in it.

Our Lord Paul is over all.
He's Keeping watch by night and day.
To be sure that I'm still on the ball,
He watches how I sing and play,
He's certain I don't run away.
He knows that I can't get away.

If I Ever Had a Brother

If I ever had a brother,
I bet he'd be a lot like you.
More than any other mate,
You're the one who pulled me through.

When I needed someone to talk to,
When my world was melting down,
When I lost my reason for living,
You could turn me right around.

Thought I's doin' you a favor
When I took you for that ride.
You became a savior to me,
Filled the emptiness inside.

When I needed someone to talk to,
When my world was melting down,
When I lost my reason for living,
You could turn me right around.

If I ever had a brother,
I bet he'd be a lot like you.
More than any other mate,
You're the one who pulled me through.

I've been somewhat neglectful
to you in my assigned Paul role,
But you were only helpful,
not after Paulie-dole.

So, I wrote this little ditty
just to say thank you, my friend,
even if our paths don't cross again,
we're brothers to the end.

If I ever had a brother,
I bet he'd be a lot like you.
As much as any other mate,
You know this song's for you.

Between the Lines

From the time I got your first email
I knew you'd be
the end of all the emptiness
and loneliness inside of me,
between the lines, you'll see.

For the first time since I don't know when
I know the way
to all the happiness
in store for those who know
the words to lay
between the lines. You'll see.

the lines upon my canvas,
the lines within my song,
the lines that we both draw
before we cross them.
Between the lines, you'll see.

When you understand the truth that grows
between the lines,
you'll see that we were meant to rise together
topping every climb.
Between the lines, you'll see.

that beneath it all we need to know
what we can be.
Between the lines, you'll see that I'm for you,
and Baby, you're for me
between the lines. You'll see

the lines upon my canvas,
the lines within my song,
the lines that we both draw
before we cross them.
Between the lines, you'll see.

The fine lines of your body,
The deep lines of your soul
We part the lines to enter realms
Beyond our own control.
The fine lines of your body,
The deep lines of your soul

You crossed my lines and entered in
disarmed my arsenal.
You were phenomenal
with the lines upon my canvas,
and lines within my song,
the lines that we both drew
before we crossed them.
Between the lines, we see.
Between the lines, we're free.

I've Carried That Weight

At first, I played too hard to get.
Maybe someday, but no, not yet.
For me to fly Paul's broken wings,
I knew they'd pay most anything.
It was a gamble, a risk, a bet.
I wasn't humble, not a bit.

The highest price I knew they'd bring.
They'd do my will to make me sing.
I asked them all in earnest candor
just how far they'd take this yonder.
But neatly they willed all Paul's deeds
So sweetly they filled all my needs.

Must I conform and never wander?
Or could I cut this vow asunder?

More questions as I took the lead
Will it be Paul or I who bleeds?
I said I'd drink from Paul's old cup
I'd break his bread and eat his sup.

So lavishly they filled the pot
and gave me everything I've got.
I'd be their fool. I'd be their pup.
I took the cup and drank it up.
I'd take the heat and be as hot
to double everything they taught.

Would I become the man I'd feign?
Would playing Paul make me insane?
If I'd become whom we bereave,
They'd have to lengthen every sleeve.
My bricks could do to stop his rain.
I'd fix the hole to ease his pain.

Until their souls, I should relieve,
Entreat me not to ever leave.
Would I be theirs with no back door?
Could I be Paul and nothing more?
Completely I'd receive the fee
Forgetting I would not be free.

I signed that I would do the chore
until I die, though it's a bore.
But looking forth I could not see
That I no longer could be me.
Would I lose my soul with all I'd gain?
Or could I hide what I'd disdain?

Would my heart turn proud and sour
When all changed in just one hour?
When I replace Paul's broken brain.
I'd guide the trips on Mystery Train,
And rearrange their ivory tower
Captured by my new Paul power.

So, I supplied the happy news
That I'd forsake that life I'd lose.
And when I'd play as Paul that way
Revolve the world from night to day.
I'd trade their bubblegum for blues.
And let me keep my tennis shoes.

No Beatle boots on this display.
Just comfy feet and lots of pay.
Now, baby, I'm that man today.
And since that stupid bloody day,
It's all been mine for this whole time.
They pay just fine to sing a rhyme.

But Paul still tells me what to say.
And he still tells me how to play.
'Cause since he crashed and lost his mind
I've been obliged to lend him mine.
Though of his mates, I'm far from least,
And from his plate, I still can feast,

I'm just his fool who drinks his bowl.
It's not just cool to play this role
I've seen it all from west to east
As I've become his singing beast.
For every missing dot or mole,
I fixed the hole, replaced his soul.

Your Paul has gone where I remain.
It's not some silly little game.
It's in his name, if I rise or fall,
My legacy is all for Paul.
For his mistakes, I get the blame.
For all my work, he gets the fame.

We're not the same. I'm much too tall.
I got his dame. She was a doll.
She helped me go from Saul to Paul.
But wasn't really on the ball.
So, when I gave Linda a try,
Jane Asher left without a sigh.

'Twas Linda till her passing call
and now there's yet another doll.
They all knew I was not that guy,
but helped me as I lived the lie.
Now when at last I end this song,
I must get back home where I belong.

Your Paul is dead. I wrote his best.
McCartney's dead, so let him rest.
With thanks to George, Ringo, and John,
All whom I've served, but much too long.
Now that I've passed your stupid test,
Your Paul is dead, so let him rest.

Good night, Paul, don't ask me why
I can no longer live your lie.
It's time to fly. Sleep now. Don't cry
Let slumber fill your golden eyes.
No more "Hello, Hello." It's time to go.
Just lullaby-bye-bye. I say goodbye.

I've carried your weight.
Yeah, I've carried your weight a long, long time.
I've carried that weight.
Yeah, I've carried that weight for a long, long time.
I've carried that weight all along, long, long,
for a very, very long, long time,
a very long, long, long.
It was a very hard and heavy time.

If It Wasn't So Delicious

If it wasn't so delicious
way back then,
well then,
I wouldn't want you now
and then, if then
it wasn't so delicious
way back then,
I wouldn't want you now,
and now,
I wouldn't know just how,
no, no, I wouldn't know
just how well
that you haven't
been since then,
no, no, I would not know
just how well that
you have not been since then.
•

Another evening
Without food
You were busy
I was rude
Our home's a total wreck
And so are you.

You keep crying
That we're through
I say we're not
But hope it's true
My life's a total wreck
And so are you.

And still, the phone keeps ringing.
All the bills are due.
The creditor's complaining,
And so are you.

And still, the phone is ringing.
The rent is overdue.
Your mother is complaining.
She sounds a lot like you.
•

You shop until the day is spent
While I'm here working hard
You're buying gifts for everyone
Using my credit card

You grin and give a present to me
Just like every time
You think that it endears you to me
But you don't give a . . . DIME!

It's six o'clock in the evening.
We've hardly fought today
Except when we were speaking.
There's not much left to say.

I'm hungry and I'm tired of it.
I need somebody who
Can relax and listen to me.
I need loving too.
•

If it wasn't so delicious
way back then,
well then,
I wouldn't want you now
and then, if then
it wasn't so delicious
way back then,
I wouldn't want you now,
and now,
I wouldn't know just how,
no, no, I wouldn't know
just how well
that you haven't
been since then,

no, no, I would not know
just how well that
you have not been since then.
•

I lie in bed alone at night
Wishing my love could make it right
I wouldn't be all by myself
Maybe if you were someone else

Our hearts can mend
I must pretend
Our hearts can mend

Each time is just another day
Of hurting in that same old way
I tell myself this pain won't last
How many years more 'till it's passed?

Our hearts can mend
It cannot end
Our hearts can mend

Is it my fault we fell apart?
Should I have stopped it when I knew
It hurt me more by loving you?

At times I find myself relieved
By reasons offered to believe
Your welcomed kiss, a loving hug
New hope's the worst of any drug

I'm all alone again without
The love that triumphs over doubt

Our hearts can mend
I must pretend
Our hearts can mend
•

If it wasn't so delicious
way back then,

well then,
I wouldn't want you now
and then, if then
it wasn't so delicious
way back then,
I wouldn't want you now,
and now,
I wouldn't know just how,
no, no, I wouldn't know
just how well
that you haven't
been since then,
no, no, I would not know
just how well that
you have not been since then.

•

Because I've left a thousand times
in my heart and in my mind,
I'm as close to isolation
as I've ever been to you.

Still, it isn't right to leave alone
our children in my broken home
just to drop my isolation down on them,
to pass this pain I'm feeling onto them.

And so, we wait through endless nights,
hoping that it will lead to light,
but fearing what we plant is all we'll eat,
and knowing seeds of pain won't bring us peace.

I'm busy doing nothing.
There's nothing left to do
because I've left a thousand times.
In my heart and in my mind,
I'm as close to isolation
as I'll ever be to you.

The Subterranean Reptilian

At the park, while watching children
climbing here and there
a fella in a jumpsuit walked up to me
like he did not care.
He was as scaly as a lizard
and just a little green
I locked my eyes into his
that were stranger than I'd ever seen.

I thought, I must have closed my eyes.
I'm asleep having this dream
Because no one can really look like that.
Things can't be as they seem.

I said "Hello" politely.
What else could I say?
He hissed to me a "Hello."
I wished he'd stayed away.
He sat right down beside me
on the playground bench.
With everything I questioned,
"How on earth did he make that stench?"

I thought, I must have closed my eyes.
I'm asleep having this dream
Because no BO can really smell like that.
Things can't be as they seem.

He took my hand to shake it.
I was mesmerized.

As if he had my power
from the moment I'd looked in his eyes.
His hands had claws instead of nails.
His flesh was cold.
A chill went up my spine as I sat wondering
what would unfold.

I thought, I must have closed my eyes.
I'm asleep having this dream
Because no one can really feel like that.
Things can't be as they seem.

He said he lives nearby,
but deep below the ground
But that now and then he comes up
just to have a look around.
His stomach gave a rumble
like some distressed vermin.
I feared then for my life,
Thinking he's no vegetarian.

I thought, I must have closed my eyes.
I'm asleep having this dream
Because no one lives below the ground.
Things can't be as they seem.

He was a subterranean reptilian.
That's what he claimed to be.
He was some subterranean reptilian
Sitting there right next to me.
We can only believe what we already know

The rest just can't be real.
It can't be real!

I thought, I must have closed my eyes.
I'm asleep having this dream
Because nothing can exist like this
Things can't be as they seem.

He was a subterranean reptilian.
That's what he claimed to be.
He was some subterranean reptilian
Sitting there right next to me.
We can only believe what we already know
The rest just can't be real.
It can't be real!

He said, "I did not come to eat you,"
as if he read my mind.
He said, "I wanted just to meet you.
It looked like now you had the time.
When he pulled out my latest CD,
I could not help but laugh.
It turned out, that just like the others,
all he wanted was my autograph.

I thought, I must have closed my eyes.
I'm asleep having this dream
Because no fans can be as strange as that.
Nothing is as it seems.

New Moon Dark

Full moon light.
New moon dark.
Ebb and flow,
breathe in and out.

Full moon light.
New moon dark.
Ebb and flow,
breathe in and out.

The moon is new.
The night is dark.
Two weeks increase
begin tonight.
What thou wilt expands
as waxing light.

The moon is full.
It lights the night.
Two weeks decrease
begin tonight.
What thou wilt decrease
as waning light.

New moon dark.
Full moon light.
Set times and patterns
of our lives.

New moon dark.
Full moon light.
Set times and patterns
of our lives

Mother Moon
and Father Sun,
procreate to make
this earth my home.

Mother Moon
and Father Sun,
guide day-by-day
to bring us home.

New moon dark.
Full moon light.
Set times and patterns
of our lives.

New moon dark.
Full moon light.
Set times and patterns
of our lives

Full moon light.
New moon dark.
Ebb and flow,
breathe in and out.

Full moon light.
New moon dark.
Ebb and flow,
breathe in and out.

The moon is new.
The night is dark.
Two weeks increase
begin tonight.

What thou wilt expands
as waxing light.

The moon is full.
It lights the night.
Two weeks decrease
begin tonight.
What thou wilt decrease
as waning light.

Full moon light.
New moon dark.
Ebb and flow,
breathe in and out.

Full moon light.
New moon dark.
Ebb and flow,
breathe in and out.

Full moon light.
New moon dark.

Full moon light.
New moon dark.

Full moon light.
New moon dark.

Full moon light.
New moon dark.

Full moon light.
New moon dark.

Full moon light.
New moon dark.

Billy's Back! (Reprise)

BILLY'S BACK!
I'm here! My music's playing.

BILLY'S BACK!
Can you hear what I've been saying?
You can't say I didn't tell you.
I've come all this way to show you.
Didn't ever want to snow you.

BILLY'S BACK!
Now that I've found another way
To say all I have to say.
You know where I'm coming from.
There's no more need for me to run.

BILLY'S BACK!
I've been with you all along,
And it's time you got along
With the man I really am.
Try to grasp it if you can.

BILLY'S BACK!
You have heard my music playing.

BILLY'S BACK!
Can you hear just what I am saying?

BILLY'S BACK!

BILLY'S BACK!

BILLY'S BACK!

Swan Song

Om

He did not react
When my voice cracked
But later said,
so soft and low,
As if I should
already know,
It's time to sing your swan song.
It's time to sing your swan song.
He said it clear,
though soft and low,
As if I should
already know,
It's time I sing my swan song.

Passing old bluebirds
and butterflies
Through yonder lakes
and deep blue skies
Ecstasy flying
over hills, I rise
Above old temples
and endless fields of rice,
I motionlessly circle thrice
Still as the sun
at Apollo's side, I glide
Through my Milky Way
to the boundless universe inside
to the space within
wherein resides
the soul that sets this world aside.

Oh Shiva, Shiva, Shiva!
Hear my swan song!
Hear my swan song!
Oh Shiva, Shiva, Shiva!
Hear my swan song!
Let this song tell you what to do.
Break it down to build anew.
Here's my swan song!
Hear my swan song!

Then like a dream,
through heavens vast,
My legacy
is all that lasts.
But matters little
when the world is past.
I drop the mantle
to the ground
Until I come
for another round.
But first, I sing this swan song.
It's time I sing this swan song.
You heard it clear.
I'm going low.
As if we all
already know.
This time I sang my swan song.

You look for me, but I have gone.
You look for me, but I have gone.
You look for me, but I have gone.
You look for me, but I have gone.
You look for me, but I have gone.
You look for me, but I have gone.

Om

Most importantly, love everyone.

All the best to those
who love my Memoirs,
and to those who don't,
with love from your scarab,
the Gold-Winged Beatle.

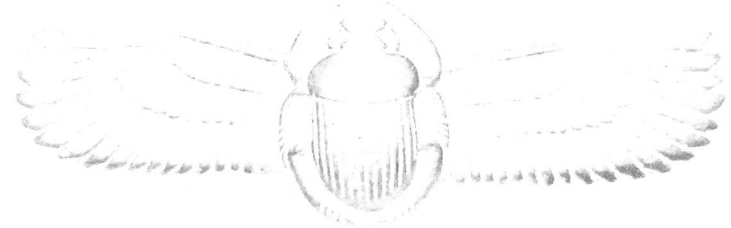

"Dream of me. I will tell you more." There is a mystical element in this book, which many of you will really love. If Paul or William shows up in your dreams, you may record it here. Or, if from reading *the Memoirs of Billy Shears,* you experience great epiphanies, or an internal shift, like awakening to greater awareness, you may turn up that energy even more by recording that shift here. Sharing it with others also turns up the energy within you. Whatever you put energy into—and extend to others—increases within you and without you. This magical Beatles mystery tour may become too intense. Whenever that happens to you, give the book a rest until it calls you back.

Recommended Websites:

www.TheBeatles.com
www.BillyShears.com
www.PaulMcCartney.com
www.MemoirsOfPaul.com
www.JPaulMcCartney.com
www.JamesPaulMcCartney.com

Made in the USA
Coppell, TX
26 June 2023

18512050R00371